READER'S
DIGEST
CONDENSED
BOOKS

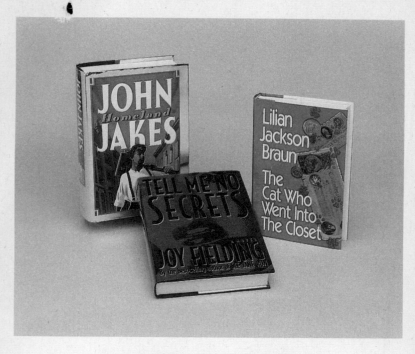

READER'S DIGEST ASSOCIATION (CANADA) LTD.
CONDENSED BOOKS DIVISION

215 Redfern Ave., Montreal, Que. H3Z 2V9
Editor: Deirdre Gilbert
Assistant Editor: Anita Winterberg
Design: Andrée Payette
Production Manager: Holger Lorenzen

ISBN 0-88850-361-X

FIRST EDITION
PRINTED IN THE U.S.A.

READER'S DIGEST CONDENSED BOOKS

In this volume

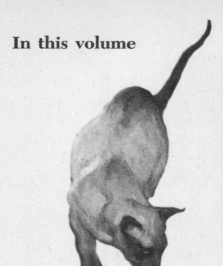

THE CAT WHO WENT INTO THE CLOSET
by Lilian Jackson Braun

Whimsical and wonderful—that's what critics call Braun's mystery series featuring millionaire Jim Qwilleran and his two savvy Siamese cats, Koko and Yum Yum. In this caper, Qwill rents an old mansion and, once installed, finds the closets crammed with generations of family junk. The cats delight in pawing through it all, sniffing out relics to bring to his attention. An old matchbook, lace garters, even false teeth! But why these items? Qwill's not certain, until the death of a friend makes him look again at the odd assortment. A beguiling mix of cats, crime, and fun. / Page 7

HOMELAND
by John Jakes

When young Pauli Kroner leaves the slums of Berlin for a new home in the United States, he is poor in possessions but rich in dreams. It is 1891, and Pauli's destination is Chicago, a rowdy melting pot of a city, exploding with energy. There he finds a new family and takes a new name— Paul Crown. Quickly he's caught up in events that define the era: the Chicago world's fair, the Pullman strike, the birth of motion pictures. But Pauli's search for a homeland will not be over until he

TELL ME NO SECRETS
by Joy Fielding

truly understands what it means
to be an American. From the
acclaimed author of *California
Gold,* a vibrant saga that brings
to life the tumultuous last decade
of the nineteenth century and
illuminates the immigrant
experience in America. / Page 111

Jess Koster is a tough, no-nonsense
prosecutor—certainly not a
woman given to wild flights of fancy.
In the courtroom she confronts
the city's toughest criminals,
outwits the slickest lawyers, puts
the worst offenders behind bars.
But suddenly she finds herself on
edge, looking over her shoulder.
It seems that someone is watching
her. Stalking her. But who?
Is it the accused rapist she's
determined to convict? Or is it
someone else, someone much
closer to her? / Page 435

THE CAT
WHO WENT INTO THE
CLOSET

LILIAN JACKSON BRAUN

With a snowy winter on the way, millionaire journalist Jim Qwilleran rents an old stone mansion in the heart of Pickax. It's a strange, dusty place, with fifty closets, all filled with junk—a treasure trove for his two very curious cats, Koko and Yum Yum. But then word comes of a suspicious suicide. And Koko, digging through the debris, finds what may be the key to . . . murder.

ONE

THE WPKX radio announcer hunched over the newsdesk in front of a dead microphone, anxiously fingering his script and waiting for the signal to go on the air. The station was filling in with classical music. The lilting "Anitra's Dance" seemed hardly appropriate under the circumstances. Abruptly the music stopped in the middle of a bar, and the newscaster began to read in a crisp, professional tone that belied the alarming nature of the news.

"We interrupt this program to bring you a bulletin on the forest fires that are rapidly approaching Moose County after destroying hundreds of square miles to the south and west. Rising winds are spreading the scattered fires into areas already parched by the abnormally hot summer and drought conditions.

"From this studio in the tower of the courthouse in Pickax City we can see a red glow on the horizon, and the sky is hazy with drifting smoke. Children have been sent home from school, and businesses are closed. The temperature is extremely high; hot winds are gusting up to forty miles an hour.

"Traffic is streaming in from towns that are in the path of the flames. Here in the courthouse, which is said to be fireproof, preparations are being made to house the refugees. Many are farmers, who report that their houses, barns, and livestock are destroyed. They tell of balls of fire flying through the air, causing fields to burst into flame. One old man on the courthouse steps is proclaiming the end of the world."

The newscaster mopped his brow and gulped water as he

glanced at slips of paper on the desk. "More bulletins are coming in. The entire town of Dry River burst into flames an hour ago and was completely demolished in minutes. The village of New Perth is in ashes; thirty-two are reported dead. Pardon me."

He stopped for a fit of coughing and then went on with difficulty. "Smoke is seeping into the studio now." He coughed again. "Pineytown . . . totally destroyed. Seventeen persons . . . killed as the flames overtook them. Fire fighters say the fire is out of control."

His voice was muffled as he tried to breathe through a cupped hand. "Very dark here! Heat unbearable! Wind is roaring! Hold on!" He jumped to his feet, knocking his chair backward, and crouched over the mike with a gasping cry: "Here it comes! A wall of fire! Right down Main Street. *Pickax is in flames.*"

The lights blacked out. Coughing and choking, the announcer groped for a doorknob and stumbled from the studio.

Music blared from the speakers—crashing chords and roaring crescendos—and the audience sat stunned, until a few started to applaud. The initial clapping swelled into a tumultuous response.

Someone in the front row said, "I swear I could smell smoke. That guy is some actor, isn't he? He wrote the stuff, too."

Most of the onlookers were still speechless as they glanced once more at their programs:

The Moose County Something
presents
THE BIG BURNING OF 1869

- An original docudrama based on historical fact
- Written and performed by James Qwilleran
- Produced and directed by Hixie Rice

The audience is asked to imagine that radio existed in 1869, as we bring you a simulated newscast covering the greatest disaster in the history of Moose County. The scene on the stage represents a broadcasting studio in the county courthouse. The action takes place on October 17 and 18, 1869. There will be one intermission.

PLEASE JOIN US FOR REFRESHMENTS
AFTER THE PERFORMANCE

The audience, having struggled back to reality, erupted in a babble of comments. "Where did Qwill get his information? He must have done a heck of a lot of research." "Makes you want to hit the history books, doesn't it?"

More than a hundred prominent residents of Moose County were attending the performance in the ballroom of a mansion that Jim Qwilleran was renting for the winter. Most of them knew all about the middle-aged journalist with the oversized mustache and doleful expression. He had been a prizewinning crime writer for major newspapers. He was the heir to an enormous fortune based in Moose County. He wrote a column for the local daily, the *Moose County Something*. He spelled his name with a Qw. He liked to eat, but never took a drink. He was divorced, and thought by women to be highly attractive. His easygoing manner and jocose banter made him enjoyable company. He was a close friend of Polly Duncan's, the Pickax librarian. He lived alone—with two cats.

The townspeople often saw the big well-built man walking or biking around Pickax, his casual dress and lack of pretension belying his status as a multimillionaire. And they had heard remarkable stories about his cats. Now, waiting for scene two, the spectators saw a sleek Siamese march sedately down the center aisle. He jumped up on the stage and, with tail importantly erect, proceeded to the door where the announcer had made his frantic exit.

The audience tittered, and someone said, "That's Koko. He always has to get into the act."

The door was loosely latched, and the cat pawed it until he could slither through. In two seconds he bounded out again, as if propelled by a tap on the rump, and the audience laughed once more. Unabashed, Koko scratched his right ear, then jumped off the stage and walked haughtily up the center aisle.

The houselights dimmed, and the radio announcer entered in a fresh shirt, with another script in his hand.

"Tuesday, October eighteenth. After a sleepless night, Pickax can see daylight. The smoke is lifting, but the acrid smell of burning is everywhere, and the landscape is a scene of desolation. Only this courthouse and a few dwellings are left standing. The heat is oppressive—one hundred and ten degrees in the studio—and the window glass is still too hot to touch.

"Crews are now out burying bodies charred beyond recognition.

11

We may never have an accurate count of the dead. More than four hundred dazed and exhausted refugees are packed into the court-house. The groans of badly burned survivors mingle with the crying of babies. There is no medicine, no food. . . ."

BEFORE the dramatic presentation of *The Big Burning of 1869*, the historic calamity had been forgotten by current generations. Qwilleran himself, playwright and star of the production, had never heard of the disaster until he rented the old mansion on Goodwinter Boulevard and started rummaging in closets. The furnishings were sparse, but the closets were stuffed with odds and ends—a treasure trove for an inquisitive journalist. As for his male cat, he was cat enough to risk death to satisfy his catly curiosity; with tail horizontal he would slink into a closet and emerge with a match-book or champagne cork clamped in his jaws.

The mansion was stone, one of several formidable edifices on the boulevard built by lumber and mining tycoons during Moose County's boom years in the late nineteenth century. A shipbuilder named Gage had built the one Qwilleran was renting. One feature made the Gage mansion unique: the abundance of closets.

Shortly after moving in, Qwilleran mentioned the closets to his landlord. Junior Goodwinter, the young managing editor of the *Moose County Something*, had recently acquired the building as a gift from his aging grandmother, Euphonia Gage, and he was thankful to have the rental income from his friend and fellow staffer. The two men were sitting in Junior's office with their feet on the desk and coffee mugs in their hands. It was three weeks before the preview of *The Big Burning*.

"What do you think of Grandma's house, Qwill?" Junior asked. "How's the refrigerator? It's pretty ancient."

"It sounds like a motorboat when it's running," Qwilleran said. "When it stops, it snarls like a sick tiger and it frightens the cats."

"Why was I dumb enough to let Grandma Gage unload that white elephant on me?" Junior complained. "I'd let the place go for peanuts, but who wants to live in a castle? Sorry about the lack of furniture. The Gages had fabulous antiques, but the old gal sold them all when she relocated in Florida. Now she lives in a retirement village, and she's a new person. She plays shuffleboard, goes to the dog races, wears elaborate makeup!"

"Maybe she found romance in her declining years," Qwill suggested.

"Could be. She looks a lot younger than eighty-eight."

"Junior, why are there so many closets? I've counted fifty. Our forefathers didn't have closets. They had wardrobes."

"But, you see," the editor explained, "my great-great-grandfather Gage was a shipbuilder, accustomed to having everything built in, and that's what he wanted in his house. Have you noticed the woodwork? Best on the boulevard!"

"It's incredible. The foyer looks like a luxury liner of early vintage. But do you know the closets are filled with junk?"

"The Gages never threw anything away." Junior looked at his watch. "Time for Arch's meeting. Shall we amble across the hall?"

Arch Riker, publisher and C.E.O. of the *Moose County Something*, had scheduled a brainstorming session for editors, writers, and the effervescent promotion director, Hixie Rice. None of the editorial staff liked meetings. Hixie, on the other hand, breezed into the meeting with her shoulder-length hair bouncing. She had worked in advertising Down Below—as Pickax natives called the major cities to the south—and she had never lost her occupational sparkle.

Similarly, Qwilleran and Riker were transplants from Down Below, having grown up together in Chicago, but they had the detached demeanor of veteran newsmen. They had adapted easily to the slow pace of Pickax (population 3000) and the remoteness of Moose County, which claimed to be 400 miles north of everywhere.

Riker, a florid, paunchy deskman who seldom raised his voice, opened the meeting in his usual sleepy style. "Well, you guys, winter is coming, and winters are pretty dull in this neck of the woods unless you're crazy about ten-foot snowdrifts. So I'd like to see this newspaper sponsor some kind of diversion that will give people a topic of conversation other than the daily rate of snowfall. Let's hear some ideas." He turned on a tape recorder.

The assembled staffers sat in stolid silence.

"Don't stop to think," the boss admonished. "Just blurt it out, off the top of your head."

"Well," said a woman editor bravely, "we could sponsor a hobby contest with a thrilling prize."

"Yeah," said Junior, "an all-expenses-paid vacation in Iceland."

"How about a food festival? Everyone likes to eat," said Mildred Hanstable, whose ample girth supported her claim. She wrote the food column and taught home economics in the Pickax schools.

"Second it!" Hixie interrupted with her usual enthusiasm. "And we could promote tie-ins with restaurants, like wine-and-cheese tastings, and a Bon Appetit Club with dining-out discounts. *C'est magnifique!*" She had studied French briefly, preparatory to eloping to Paris.

There was a dead silence among the staffers.

Riker said, "Snow is what we do best up here. How can we capitalize on it?"

Junior came up with an idea for a Christmas parade.

"How about a winter sports carnival?" the sports editor proposed. "Cross-country skiing, snowshoe races, dogsledding."

Riker swiveled his chair. "Qwill, are you asleep back there?"

Qwilleran smoothed his mustache before he answered. "Does anyone know about the big forest fire in 1869 that killed hundreds of Moose County pioneers? It destroyed farms and villages. About the only thing left in Pickax was the brick courthouse."

Roger MacGillivray, general assignment reporter, said, "I've heard about it, but there's nothing in the history books."

"Well, I've found a gold mine of information," said Qwilleran. "We may be four hundred miles north of everywhere, but we've got a history up here that will curl your toes! It deserves to be told—not just in print—but before audiences all over the county."

Riker said, "What would we do for visuals?"

"That's the problem. There are no pictures."

The publisher turned off the tape recorder. "Okay, we've heard some good ideas. Kick 'em around, and we'll meet again in a couple of days. Back to work!"

As the staff shuffled out of the office, Hixie grabbed Qwilleran's arm and said in a low voice, "I've got a brilliant idea for dramatizing your disaster, Qwill. *C'est vrai!*"

He winced inwardly, recalling other brilliant ideas of Hixie's: the look-alike contest at Tipsy's restaurant that ended in a riot, the cooking demonstration that set fire to her hair, not to mention her aborted elopement to France. Gallantly he said, however, "Want to have lunch at Lois's and tell me about it?"

"Okay," she said. "I'll buy. I can put it on my expense account."

TWO

THE atmosphere at Lois's Luncheonette was bleak, and the menu was ordinary, but it was the only restaurant in downtown Pickax, and the old, friendly, decrepit ambiance made the locals feel at home. A dog-eared card in the window announced the day's special. Tuesday was always the hot turkey sandwich with mashed potatoes and gravy, but it was real turkey, the bread was baked in Lois's kitchen, and the mashed potatoes had the flavor of real potatoes grown in the mineral-rich soil of Moose County.

Qwilleran and Hixie ordered the special, and she said, "I hear that you're not living in your barn this winter." He had recently converted an old apple barn into a spectacular residence.

"There's too much snow to plow," he explained, "so I'm renting the Gage mansion on Goodwinter Boulevard, where the city does the plowing." He neglected to mention that Polly Duncan, the chief woman in his life, lived in the carriage house at the rear of the Gage property, and he envisioned frequent cozy winter evenings.

"All right. Let's get down to business," Hixie said when the plates arrived. "How did you find out about the killer fire?"

Qwilleran patted his mustache in self-congratulation. "One of Junior's ancestors was an amateur historian. In his journals there were firsthand descriptions of the 1869 forest fire in all its gruesome detail, based on the recollections of his elders. The man was performing a valuable service for posterity, but no one knew his accounts existed. So what's your brilliant idea, Hixie?"

"What would you think of doing a one-man show?"

"Isn't a one-man show based on a three-county forest fire a trifle out of scale?"

"Mais non! Suppose we pretend they had radio stations in the nineteenth century, and the audience sees an announcer broadcasting on-the-spot coverage of the disaster."

Qwilleran gazed at her with new respect. "Not bad. Yes, I'd go for that. I'd be glad to organize the material and write the script. Larry Lanspeak could play the announcer. He has the best speaking voice—"

"No! If we're going to sponsor the show, we should keep it in our own organization," she contended. "Actually, Qwill, I was thinking about you for the part. You have exactly the right voice for a radio announcer. Stop frowning! You wouldn't have to learn lines. You'd be reading a script." She was talking fast. "Besides, everyone loves your column! You'd be a big attraction, *sans doute.*"

He huffed into his mustache.

She went on with contagious enthusiasm. "I could take care of production. I could do the bookings. I'd even sweep the stage!"

Qwilleran had enjoyed acting in college, and the story of the great fire cried for attention. The objections he'd been formulating began to crumble. "How long a program should it be?"

"I would say forty-five minutes. That would fit into a school class period or fill a slot following a club luncheon."

After a few seconds' contemplation he said grimly, "I may regret this, but I'll do it."

"Merveilleux!" Hixie cried.

Neither of them remembered eating their lunch. They discussed a stage setting, lighting, props, a sound system, cue cards, and how to pack everything in suitcases to fit into the trunk of a car.

Hixie said, "Consider it strictly a road show. We'll need a name for the project. How about Suitcase Productions?"

Qwilleran liked it.

Returning home from that luncheon with a foil-wrapped chunk of turkey scrounged from Lois's kitchen, Qwilleran was greeted by the two Siamese, who could smell turkey through an oak door two inches thick. They yowled and pranced elegantly on long brown legs, and their blue eyes stared hypnotically at the foil package until its contents landed on their plate under the kitchen table.

With bemused admiration Qwilleran watched them devour their treat. Koko, whose legal title was Kao K'o Kung, had the dignity of his namesake—a thirteenth-century Chinese artist—plus a degree of intelligence and perception that was sometimes unnerving to a human with only five senses and a journalism degree. Yum Yum, the dainty one, had a different set of talents. She was a lovable bundle of female wiles, which she employed shamelessly to get her own way. When all else failed, she had only to reach up and touch Qwilleran's mustache with her paw, and he would capitulate.

When the Siamese had finished their snack and had washed their whiskers and ears, he told them, "I have a lot of work to do in the next couple of weeks, my friends, and I'll have to shut you out of the library. Don't think it's anything personal."

He always addressed them as if they understood human speech, and more and more it appeared to be a fact. In the days that followed, they sensed his preoccupation, leaving him alone, taking long naps, grooming each other interminably, and watching the autumn leaves flutter to the ground. Only when Qwilleran was late with their dinner did the cats interrupt, rattling the library door handle and scolding—Koko with an authoritative baritone "Yow!" and Yum Yum with her impatient "N-n-now!"

Qwilleran could write a thousand words for his newspaper column with one hand tied behind his back, but writing a script for a docudrama was a new challenge. To relieve the radio announcer's forty-five-minute monologue, he introduced other voices on tape: eyewitnesses being interviewed by telephone. He altered his voice to approximate the bureaucratese of a government weather observer, the brogue of an Irish innkeeper, and the twang of an old farmer, with their replies sandwiched between the announcer's questions.

Once the script was completed, there were nightly rehearsals in the ballroom of the Gage mansion, with Hixie cuing the taped voices into the live announcing. It required split-second timing to sound authentic. Meanwhile, Polly Duncan returned home each evening to her apartment in the carriage house at the rear of the property and saw Hixie's car parked in the side drive. It was a trying time for Polly. As library administrator, she was a woman of admirable intelligence and self-control, but where Qwilleran was concerned, she was inclined to be jealous of women younger and thinner than she.

One evening Arch Riker attended a rehearsal and was so impressed that he proposed a preview for prominent citizens. Invitations were immediately mailed to local officials, educators, and business leaders, with replies requested. To Riker's dismay, few responded; he called a meeting to analyze the situation.

"I think," Hixie ventured, "they're all waiting to find out what's on TV Monday night."

"You've got it all wrong," said Junior, who was a native. "The stuffed shirts in this backwater county never reply to an invitation till they know who else is going to be there. Let me write a piece and splash it on the front page. I'll twist a few political arms."

Accordingly, Friday's edition of the paper carried this news item:

17

MOOSE COUNTY DESTROYED BY FIRE . . . IN 1869

History will come to life Monday evening when civic leaders will preview a live docudrama titled *The Big Burning of 1869*. Following the private première at the Gage mansion on Goodwinter Boulevard, the *Moose County Something* will offer the show to schools, churches, and clubs as a public service.

There followed the magic name of Jim Qwilleran, who was not only popular as a columnist but rich as Croesus. In addition, the mayor, council president, and county commissioners were quoted as saying they would attend the history-making event. As soon as the paper hit the street, the telephones started jangling with acceptances. Hixie went into action, borrowing folding chairs from the Dingleberry Funeral Home, renting coatracks, and hiring a caterer.

On the gala evening the Gage mansion glowed like a lantern among the gloomy stone castles on the boulevard. Flashbulbs popped as the civic leaders approached the front steps. The publisher of the newspaper greeted them; the managing editor checked their wraps; the sports editor directed them to the ballroom, on the lower level. The reporters who were providing valet parking carried one elderly man in a wheelchair up the front steps and wheeled him to the elevator, which was one of the mansion's special amenities.

Meanwhile, Qwilleran was sweating out his opening-night jitters backstage in the ballroom—a large turn-of-the-century hall with art deco murals and light fixtures. More than a hundred chairs faced the band platform, where musicians had once played the waltz. The stage set was minimal: a table and chair for the announcer, with an old-fashioned telephone and a replica of an early microphone. Off to one side was a table for the "studio engineer."

A sweatered audience filed into the ballroom and filled the chairs. Pickax was a sweater city in winter—for all occasions except weddings and funerals. The houselights dimmed, and the lilting notes of "Anitra's Dance" filled the hall until the announcer rushed onstage from a door at the rear and spoke the first ominous words: "We interrupt this program to bring you a bulletin . . ."

Forty-five minutes later he delivered the final message: "No one will ever forget what happened here on October seventeenth, 1869." It was an ironic punch line, considering that few persons in the county had ever heard of the Big Burning.

The audience applauded wildly, and the mayor of Pickax jumped to his feet, saying, "We owe a debt of gratitude to these talented folks who have shown us this forgotten chapter in our history."

The presenters bowed: Hixie with her buoyant smile and Qwilleran with his usual morose expression. Then as the ballroom emptied, they packed their equipment into carrying cases.

"We did it," Hixie exulted. "We've got a smash hit!"

"Yes, it went pretty well," Qwilleran agreed modestly. "Your timing was perfect, Hixie. Congratulations!"

"I predict we'll be swamped with bookings," she said.

"Undoubtedly. Moose County can't resist anything that's free. Now let's go upstairs and get some of that free grub."

On the main floor, the guests were milling about the large empty rooms, admiring the coffered paneling of the high ceilings and the lavishly carved fireplaces. They carried plates of hors d'oeuvres and glass cups of amber punch. The Siamese were milling about, too, dodging feet and hunting for dropped crumbs.

Qwilleran pushed through the crowd to the dining room, where a long table was laden with warming trays of stuffed mushrooms, cheese puffs, and other morsels too dainty for a hungry actor. There were two punch bowls, and he headed for the end of the table where Mildred Hanstable was ladling amber punch into cups.

"Cider?" he asked.

"No. This is Fish House punch made with two kinds of rum and brandy," she warned him. "I think you'll want the other punch, Qwill. It's cranberry juice and Chinese tea with lemon grass."

"Sounds delicious." He scowled. "How come no one's drinking it?"

Polly Duncan, looking radiant in a pink mohair sweater, was presiding over the unpopular bowl of pink punch. "Qwill, dear, you were splendid!" she said in her mellow voice that always gave him a frisson of pleasure. "Now I know why you were so totally preoccupied for the last few weeks. It was time well invested."

"Sorry to be so asocial," he apologized, "but we'll make up for it. We'll do something special this weekend, like bird watching." This was a gesture of abject penitence on his part. He loathed birding.

"It's too late," she said. "They've gone south, and snow is predicted. But I'm going to do roast beef and Yorkshire pudding, and I have a new Brahms cassette."

"Say no more. I'm available for the entire weekend."

They were interrupted by a cracked, high-pitched voice. "Excellent job, my boy!" Homer Tibbitt, former school principal and official historian for the county, was in his nineties but still active. He was pushing the wheelchair, which was occupied by Adam Dingleberry, the ancient patriarch of the mortuary that had lent the folding chairs. Homer delivered a feeble poke to Qwilleran's ribs. "You son-of-a-grasshopper! I've been scrabbling for information on that blasted fire for thirty years! Where'd you find it?"

"In some files that belonged to Euphonia Gage's father-in-law," Qwilleran replied. He neglected to say that Koko had pried his way into a certain closet and dragged forth a scrap of yellowed manuscript. It was a clue to a cache of hundred-year-old documents.

A valet was paging them. "Car for Mr. Dingleberry! Mr. Tibbitt!"

As the elderly pair headed for the carriage entrance, Qwilleran was approached by a cordial man in a black cashmere sweater. "Good show, Mr. Q.!" he said in a smooth, professional voice.

"Thank you."

"I'm Pender Wilmot, your next-door neighbor and Mrs. Gage's attorney. How do you like living on the boulevard?"

"I find it depressing. There are seven for-sale signs at last count."

"And I'd gladly make it eight," the attorney said, "but our property has been in the family for generations. My wife is sentimental about it, although she might be swayed by a juicy offer. Mr. Q., this is my son, Timmie." The boy, in a red sweater and large eyeglasses, had been trying unsuccessfully to catch Yum Yum. He was now clutching his parent's hand.

"And how did you like the show, young man?" Qwilleran asked.

Timmie frowned. "All those people burned up. Why didn't the firemen get a ladder and save them?"

"Come on, son," his father said. "We'll go home and discuss it."

They walked toward the front door just as Hixie dashed up, followed by the owner of the Black Bear Café. Gary Pratt's muscular hulk and lumbering gait and shaggy black hairiness explained the name of his restaurant. Excitedly Hixie announced, "Gary wants us to do the show at the Black Bear."

"Yeah," said the barkeeper, "the Outdoor Club meets once a month for burgers and beer and a program."

"Okay with me. Go ahead and book it, Hixie."

Qwilleran moved through the crowd, accepting congratulations.

Susan Exbridge, the antiques dealer, gave him her usual effusive hug. "Darling! You were glorious! And this house! Isn't it magnificent? Euphonia gave me a tour before she sold the furnishings. Have you ever seen chandeliers like these? If you'd like a live-in housekeeper, Qwill, I'll work cheap."

Next the Comptons paid their compliments. "You were terrific, Qwill," said Lisa, a cheerful middle-aged woman.

"The show would be a great way to hook kids on history," added Lyle Compton, superintendent of schools.

"Believe it or not," Lisa said, "I used to come here to take 'natural dance' lessons from Euphonia, for grace and poise."

"I met Euphonia only once," Qwilleran said. "I came to interview her for an oral-history project and found this tiny woman sitting on the floor in the lotus position, wearing purple tights."

Lisa nodded. "She used to tell us that purple is a source of energy. Junior says she still wears it and stands on her head every day."

Junior Goodwinter joined them, and they discussed the forthcoming football game between Pickax High and Lockmaster.

When the Comptons left, Junior gazed ruefully at the rooms emptied of furniture, the faded wall coverings, and the discolored rectangles where large paintings had once hung. "Grandma had some great stuff, Qwill, but everything was sold out of state."

"Would your grandmother have liked our show tonight?"

"I doubt it. She never likes anything that isn't her own idea."

"She sounds like Koko. Is it true she gave dancing lessons?"

"Way back, maybe forty years ago," Junior said. "Then, before leaving for Florida, she asked me to videotape one of her dances. It was embarrassing—this woman in her eighties cavorting around the ballroom like a woodland nymph. It's my guess that she'll outlive us all. Well, it looks like everyone's leaving. Sure was a success."

Only a few members of the press remained to drain the two punch bowls. Qwilleran said to Hixie, "Did you see the guy in a suit and tie? He was with a blonde—the only ones not in sweaters."

"That was a wig she was wearing," Hixie informed him.

"Who were they?"

"I say they were spies from the *Lockmaster Ledger*," she said. "They steal all our good ideas."

Arch Riker and Mildred Hanstable were almost the last to leave. The publisher was beaming. "Great job, you two kids."

"Thanks, boss," said Qwilleran. "I'll expect a raise."

"You'll be fired if you don't start writing your column again. Consider your vacation over as of tomorrow."

"Vacation! I've been working like a dog on this show!"

This sparring between the two old friends was a perpetual game, since the *Moose County Something* was backed financially by the Klingenschoen Foundation, established by Qwilleran to dispose of his unwanted millions.

Riker drove Mildred home, and Qwilleran told Polly he would escort her to her carriage house. "I'll be right back," he told the Siamese, who were loitering nearby.

"I've missed you, dear," Polly said as they walked briskly hand in hand through the chill October evening. "I thought I had lost my Most-Favored-Woman status. Bootsie missed you, too."

"Sure," Qwilleran replied testily. He and Polly's macho Siamese had been engaged in a cold war ever since Bootsie was a kitten.

"Would you like to come up for some real food?"

Qwilleran said he wouldn't mind going up for a few minutes. When he came down two hours later, he walked slowly despite the falling temperature, reflecting that he was happier than he had ever been in his entire life. What had mattered in his earlier years was the excitement of covering breaking news, moving from city to city. Now he was experiencing something totally different: the contentment of living in a small town, writing for a small newspaper, loving an intelligent woman of his own age, living with two companionable cats. And he was on the stage again! Not since college had he known the satisfaction of bringing a character to life for an audience.

At the side door of the mansion he was greeted by the scolding yowls of two indignant Siamese, whose evening repast was late.

"My apologies," he said as he gave them a crunchy snack. "We'll get back to normal now. You've been very understanding. How would you like a read after I've turned out some lights?"

Despite his affluence, Qwilleran was frugal about utilities. He went through the great house, flipping off switches. The Siamese accompanied him, pursuing their own interests. In one of the front bedrooms upstairs he noticed a closet door ajar and a horizontal brown tail disappearing within. Minutes later Koko caught up with him and dropped something at his feet.

"Thank you," Qwilleran said courteously as he picked up a purple ribbon bow and dropped it into his sweater pocket. To himself he said, If Euphonia's theory is true, Koko sensed a source of energy. Cats, he had been told, are attracted to sources of energy.

The three of them gathered in the library for their read, a ritual the Siamese always enjoyed. Whether it was the sound of a human voice or the warmth of a human lap and a table lamp, a read was one of their catly pleasures. As for Qwilleran, he enjoyed their company and—to be perfectly honest—the sound of his own voice.

"Would anyone care to choose a title?" he asked.

In the library there were a few hundred books that Mrs. Gage had been unable to sell before she moved, plus a dozen classics that Qwilleran had brought from the barn along with his typewriter and digital coffee maker. Koko sniffed the bindings until his twitching nose settled on *Robinson Crusoe.*

"Good choice," Qwilleran said as he sank into an old leather sofa, worn to the contours of a hammock. Yum Yum leaped into his lap, settling down with a sigh, while Koko arranged himself on a table under the glow of a lamp.

They were halfway through the opening paragraph when the telephone on the desk rang. "Excuse me," Qwilleran said, lifting Yum Yum gently and placing her on the seat he had vacated. He anticipated another compliment on *The Big Burning* and responded with a gracious, "Good evening."

Arch Riker's voice barked with urgency. "Hate to bother you, Qwill, but I've just had a call from Junior. He's flying to Florida first thing in the morning. His grandmother was found dead in bed."

"Hmmm . . . curious!" Qwilleran murmured. "A few minutes ago Koko brought me one of her hair ribbons."

"Yeah, well . . . that cat is tuned in to everything—"

"And everyone at the party tonight," Qwilleran went on, "was mentioning how healthy she was."

"That's the sad part. The police told Junior it was suicide."

THREE

THE news of Euphonia Gage's suicide was surprising if not incredible. "What was her motive?" Qwilleran asked Arch Riker.

"We don't know yet. Junior is drafting an obit and will fax it when he arrives. Will you see if you can dig out some photos? Junior says she left some photo albums in the house, but he doesn't know where. Usual deadline. Sorry to bother you tonight."

"No bother. I'll give you a ring in the morning."

Before resuming the reading of *Robinson Crusoe,* Qwilleran added the purple bow to what he called the Kao K'o Kung Collection, in a desk drawer. It consisted of oddments retrieved by the cats from the gaping closets of the Gage mansion: champagne cork, matchbook, pencil stub, and the like. Yum Yum left her contributions scattered about the house; Koko organized his under the kitchen table, alongside their feeding station.

As the day ended, Qwilleran felt a surge of relief and satisfaction; *The Big Burning* had been successfully launched and enthusiastically received. He slept soundly that night and would not have heard the early morning summons from the library telephone if eight bony legs had not landed simultaneously on his supine body.

Hixie Rice was on the line, as bright and breezy as ever. *"Pardonnez-moi!"* she said when Qwilleran answered gruffly. "You sound as if you haven't had your coffee. This will wake you up! We have a definite booking for our show if the date is okay with you."

"What's the booking?"

"Monday night at the Black Bear Café. It's family night for the Outdoor Club, and they were going to have a Laurel and Hardy film, but Gary urged them to book *The Big Burning* instead."

"Maybe we can play it for laughs," Qwilleran muttered. As he hung up the receiver he felt certain misgivings. In the kitchen, he pressed the button on his coffee maker and was comforted somewhat by the sound of grinding beans and gurgling brew.

Meanwhile, he fed the cats, and whether it was the soothing sight of feline feeding or the first jolt of caffeine, something restored his positive attitude, and he tackled Riker's assignment with relish.

It was not as easy as either of them had supposed. There were no photos of Euphonia Gage in the desk. The closet in the library was locked. In the upstairs bedroom where Koko had found the purple ribbon, the closets were stuffed with outdated clothing, but no photographs. Returning to the library, he surveyed the shelves of somber books collected by several generations of Gages: obsolete encyclopedias, forgotten classics, and biographies of persons now unknown. Sitting in the worn leather desk chair, he swiveled idly, pondering this mausoleum of the printed word.

25

It was then that he glimpsed a few inches of brown tail disappearing behind a row of books. Koko often retired to a bookshelf to escape Yum Yum's playful overtures. He failed to appreciate aggressive females, preferring to do the chasing himself. So now he was safely installed in the narrow space behind some volumes on medicinal herbs, a subject of interest to the late Mrs. Gage.

Qwilleran smoothed his mustache, wondering why Koko preferred these books to the Civil War histories on the same shelf. Could it corroborate the theory about cats and energy? Could Euphonia's innate verve have rubbed off on these bindings? In earlier years he would have scoffed at such a notion, but that was before he knew Koko!

Out of curiosity he opened a book on herbs and found remedies for acne, allergies, and asthma. Hopeful he looked under F, but found nothing on football knee, which was his Achilles' heel. He did find, however, an envelope addressed to Junior and mailed from Florida, casually stuck between a new book on cholesterol and an old book on mind power. He opened it and read:

> Dear Junior,
>
> Ship all my health books right away. I teach a class in breathing twice a week. These old people could solve half their problems if they knew how to breathe. Also send my photo albums. I think they're on the shelf with the Britannica. I'll pay the postage. Thank you for sending the clippings of Mr. Q's column. I like his style. Start a subscription to the paper for me. Send me the bill.
>
> —Grandma

The letter, dated a few weeks previously, hardly sounded like a potential suicide, and Qwilleran wondered, Had something drastic happened to change her outlook?

Two photo albums were exactly where she had said they would be, and he turned the pages to find the highlights of her life, all captioned and dated. He found a tiny Euphonia in a christening dress, propped up on cushions; a young girl dancing on the grass; a horsewoman in full habit; and a bride in a high-necked wedding dress, with an armful of white roses. In none of the photos was there a glimpse of her bridegroom, daughter, parents, or grandchildren.

Qwilleran narrowed the collection down to ten and telephoned Riker. "Got 'em!" he announced. "How about lunch?"

At noon he walked downtown and tossed the photos on the publisher's desk. Riker shuffled through the pack, nodded without comment, and said, "Shall we eat?"

They headed in Riker's car to the Old Stone Mill on the outskirts of town, the best restaurant in the vicinity.

As they passed Goodwinter Boulevard, Riker asked, "How do you and the cats enjoy rattling around in that big house?"

"We're adaptable. Actually, I live in three rooms. I sleep in the housekeeper's old bedroom on the main floor. I make coffee and feed the cats in a huge antiquated kitchen. And I hang out in the library, which still has some furniture."

"Is that where you found the dope on the forest fire?"

"No, it was in an upstairs closet. The house is honeycombed with closets, all filled with junk. Koko is having a field day."

In the restaurant parking lot, they crossed paths with Scott Gippel, the car dealer. "I heard on the radio that old Mrs. Gage died suddenly down south. Is that true? Suicide?"

"That's what the police told Junior," Riker said.

"Too bad. She was a peppy old gal. I took her Mercedes in trade on a bright yellow sports car. She had me drop-ship it to Florida."

When they entered the restaurant, the hostess led them to Qwilleran's usual table. The special was a French dip sandwich with fries, and cream of mushroom soup. Riker ordered a salad.

"What's the matter?" Qwilleran asked. "Not feeling well?"

"Just trying to lose a few pounds before the holidays. Do you have plans for Christmas Eve?"

"That's two months away!"

"How would you like to be best man at a wedding?"

Qwilleran stopped nibbling breadsticks. "You and Mildred? Congratulations, old stiff! You two will be happy together."

"Why don't you and Polly take the plunge at the same time? Share the expenses. That should appeal to your thrifty nature."

"The chance to save a few bucks is tempting, Arch, but Polly and I prefer singlehood. Besides, our cats would be incompatible."

When coffee was served, Qwilleran brought up the subject that was bothering him. "You know, Arch, I can't understand why Mrs. Gage would choose to end her life."

"Old folks often pull up stakes and go to a sunny climate away from family and friends, and they discover the loneliness of old age.

It gets harder to make new friends as years go by. Mrs. Gage was eighty-eight, you know."

"What's eighty-eight today? People that age are running marathons! Science is pushing the life-span up to a hundred and ten. Anyway, when Junior phones, ask him to call me at home."

THE call from Junior came around six o'clock that evening. "Hey, Qwill, whaddaya think about all this? I can't believe Grandma Gage is gone! I thought she'd live forever."

"The idea of suicide is what puzzles me, Junior. Was that just a cop's guess?"

"No, it's official."

"Was there a suicide note?"

"She didn't leave any explanation, but there was an empty bottle of sleeping pills by her bed, plus evidence she'd been drinking."

"Did she drink? I thought she was a health nut."

"She always had a glass of Dubonnet before dinner, claiming it was nutritious. But who knows what she did after she started running with that retirement crowd in Florida?"

"So what was the motive?"

"I wish I knew."

"Who found the body?"

"A neighbor. Around Monday noon. She'd been dead about sixteen hours. This woman called to pick her up for lunch."

"Have you talked with this neighbor?"

"Yes. She's a nice older woman. A widow."

"So what happens now, Junior?"

"I'm appointed as personal rep, and Pender Wilmot—the lawyer next door to you—has told me what to do. She was living in a top-of-the-line mobile home in a retirement complex called the Park of Pink Sunsets. She bought it furnished from the park management, and they'll buy it back. I have to get a death certificate, round up her belongings, and ship the body to Pickax. She wanted to be buried in the Gage plot."

"When do you expect to be home?"

"Before snow flies, I hope. Sooner the better."

Qwilleran replaced the receiver slowly. No motive! Here was a healthy, active, well-to-do woman who simply decided to end it all.

"What happened?" he asked Koko, who was sitting on the desk, a self-appointed censor of incoming phone calls. The cat sat tall, with his forelegs primly together and his tail curved flat on the desk top. At Qwilleran's question he shifted his feet nervously and blinked his eyes. Then abruptly he jerked his head toward the library door. In a blur of fur he was off the desk and out in the hallway. Alarmed, Qwilleran followed. The excitement was in the kitchen, where Yum Yum was sniffing the bottom of the back door.

Koko's tail bushed, his ears swept back, his whiskers virtually disappeared, and a terrible growl came from his interior.

Qwilleran looked out the back window. It was dusk, but he could make out a large orange cat on the porch. He banged on the door, yanked it open, and yelled, "Scat!" The intruder swooshed toward the attorney's house next door. Yum Yum looked dreamily disappointed, and Koko bit her on the neck.

"Stop that," Qwilleran commanded in a gruff voice that was totally ignored. Yum Yum appeared to be enjoying the abuse.

"Treat!" he shouted. It was the only guaranteed way to capture their immediate attention, and both cats scampered to the feeding station under the kitchen table. He put a crunchy snack on their plate.

Returning to the library, Qwilleran phoned Lori Bamba, his free-lance secretary in Mooseville, who not only handled his correspondence but advised him on feline problems. He described the recent scene.

"It's a male," Lori said. "He's a threat to Koko's territory. He's interested in Yum Yum."

"Both of mine are neutered," he reminded her.

"No difference. The visitor probably sprayed your back door."

"What! I won't stand for that!" Qwilleran stormed into the phone. "Isn't there some kind of protection against animals vandalizing private property?"

"I don't think so."

"Well, thanks, Lori. Sorry to bother you. I'll see my own attorney about this tomorrow."

Blowing into his mustache, he strode to the library and phoned Osmond Hasselrich of Hasselrich, Bennett & Barter. Only someone with the nerve of a veteran journalist and Qwilleran's bankroll would call the senior partner at home during the dinner hour. Qwilleran made his request. "I want an appointment for tomorrow afternoon, Mr. Hasselrich. It's a matter of the utmost secrecy."

WHILE WAITING FOR HIS Wednesday afternoon appointment with Mr. Hasselrich, Qwilleran tuned in the WPKX weather report. The meteorologist, who called himself Wetherby Goode, had a hearty, jovial manner. "Yes, folks, the mayor has promised leaf pickup before Halloween. The vacuum truck will be operating later in the week."

As Qwilleran walked downtown, the whine of leaf blowers paralyzed the eardrums like an orchestra playing only one chord.

At the law office, he sipped coffee politely from Mr. Hasselrich's heirloom porcelain cups and listened politely to the elderly attorney's discourse on the forthcoming snow. When Qwilleran finally stated his case, Mr. Hasselrich reacted favorably. As chief counsel for the Klingenschoen Foundation, he had become accustomed to unusual proposals from the Klingenschoen heir.

"I believe it can be accomplished without arousing suspicion," he said. "And with complete anonymity, of course."

Qwilleran walked home with a long stride.

That evening, when he took Polly Duncan out to dinner, she asked casually, "What did you do today?"

"Walked downtown. . . . Made a few phone calls. . . . Brushed the cats." He avoided mentioning his meeting with Hasselrich.

They were dining at Tipsy's, a log cabin restaurant in North Kennebeck. "Guess what's happening on Christmas Eve!" he said. "Arch and Mildred are tying the knot."

"I'm so happy for them," she replied fervently.

"Arch suggested we might make it a double wedding," he said with a sly sideways glance.

"I hope you disabused him of that notion, dear."

He gave their order. "Broiled whitefish for the lady, and I'll have the king-size steak, medium rare." Then he remarked to Polly, "Did you read the obituary in today's paper?"

"Yes. I wonder where they found those interesting pictures."

"Did you know Mrs. Gage very well?"

"I believe no one knew her very well," said Polly. "She served on my library board for a few years, but she was rather aloof. She always wore hats with wide brims. And always the same violet scent—to the extent that no one else in town dared to wear it. But I don't want to sound petty. After all, she was good enough to rent the carriage house to me when I was desperate for a place to live."

"Were you surprised that she'd take her own life?"

Polly considered. "No. She was completely unpredictable."

ON THURSDAY, Qwilleran phoned Gary Pratt at the Black Bear Café. "Gary," he said, "I'd like to run up tomorrow afternoon and see where we're going to present our show for the Outdoor Club."

"I'll be here," said the barkeeper. "There's somebody I want you to meet, too—a nice little girl who comes in quite often."

"How little?"

"Well, she's in her twenties. She has a family problem, and it sounds fishy to me. I thought you might give her some advice."

Qwilleran said he would listen to her story, though he had little interest. What really piqued his curiosity was the suicide of a woman with no apparent motive. He was glad when Junior phoned him on Friday morning.

"Turn on the coffee maker," the young editor ordered. "I'll be right there with doughnuts from Lois's. I have things to report."

Lois's doughnuts were fresh every morning, and the two men sat at the kitchen table hugging coffee mugs and dipping into the doughnut bag.

"Did you get everything wrapped up?"

"To tell the truth," Junior said, "there wasn't much to do. Grandma had sold her car; the furniture went with the house; we gave her clothes to charity. She'd unloaded her jewelry, antiques, and real estate early on, to simplify the probate of her will, she said. The only property she couldn't dump was Lois's broken-down building. You know, Qwill, I don't care about getting a big inheritance, but it would've been nice if Grandma Gage had established an education trust for her great-grandchildren. Jack has two kids; Pug has three; and Jody and I have one and seven ninths, as of today."

"How is Jody feeling?"

"She's fine. We're starting the countdown. Anyway, there were two things that sort of shocked me at the Park of Pink Sunsets. One was that the management will buy Grandma's mobile home back again—for one fourth of what she paid them for it. Pender Wilmot advised me to accept and cut my losses. The other was that Grandma had developed a passion for the greyhound races."

"Who told you this?"

31

"Her neighbor, the one who found the body. She wanted to gab, but I didn't have time."

Qwilleran patted his mustache thoughtfully. "I've been thinking that I could write a profile of Euphonia Gage. There are plenty of people around here who knew her. I could also phone her neighbor at the mobile-home park. What's her name?"

"Robinson. Celia Robinson."

"Will she be willing to talk?"

"She'll talk your ear off! Brace yourself for the phone bill."

Before leaving for the office, Junior said, "Qwill, I've decided why Grandma did what she did. She believed in reincarnation, you know, so maybe she was bored with shuffleboard and was ready to get on with another life. Is that too far out?"

A strange sound came from under the kitchen table.

"What's that?" Junior asked in surprise.

"That's Koko," Qwilleran explained. "He and Yum Yum are both under the table waiting for doughnut crumbs."

FOUR

WHEN Junior mentioned his reincarnation theory as a motive for Euphonia's suicide, the chattering under the kitchen table had a negative, even hostile sound.

"You didn't care for the idea," Qwilleran said to Koko after Junior had left for the office. "Neither did I. I don't know what it is, but there's something we don't know about the lady."

Doughnuts and coffee had only whetted Qwilleran's appetite, and he walked to Lois's for buckwheat pancakes.

Lois herself was waiting on tables, and she brought his order. She was a hardworking woman who owned her own business, enjoyed every aspect of her job, and jollied or insulted the customers with impunity. Her devoted clientele regularly took up collections to finance building repairs, since Mrs. Gage, that "stingy old woman" who owned the place, would do nothing about maintenance.

"So you lost one of your good customers!" he said.

"Who?"

"Euphonia Gage."

"That old witch? She was too hoity-toity to come in here," Lois said with disdain. "She sent her housekeeper to collect the

rent. When her husband was alive, he came in himself. Nice man!"
Qwilleran began to formulate his profile of Junior's grandmother. He would call it THE SEVERAL HATS OF MRS. GAGE. She was
dancer, snob, health nut, and "purplist," a word he had coined. She
was generous, stingy, elegant, witty, unpredictable, and hoity-toity.

Later he was sitting at his desk making notes when Koko trudged
past the library door with something in his mouth. The plodding
gait, lowered head, and horizontal tail suggested serious business.
Kao K'o Kung was not a mouser—he left that occupation to Yum
Yum—but his behavior was suspiciously predatory, and Qwilleran
followed him stealthily. When within tackling distance, he grabbed
Koko and commanded, "Drop that filthy thing!"

Koko, who never took orders gladly, squirmed and clamped his
jaws on the prey. Realizing it was no mouse, Qwilleran coaxed in a
gentler voice, "Let go, Koko. Good boy!" And he massaged the
furry throat until Koko was induced to lose his grip.

"What next!" Qwilleran said, snatching the trophy. It was a partial denture destined for the collection site under the kitchen table.

Koko was a serious treasure hunter. Qwilleran thought of his
excavations as an archaeological dig for fragments that might be
pieced together to reconstruct a social history of the Gage dynasty.
In fact, he had started a written inventory. Now he carried the
denture to the library, while Koko followed in high dudgeon, scolding and jumping at his hand.

"It's only an old set of false teeth," Qwilleran remonstrated as he
dropped it into the desk drawer. He added "partial denture" to the
other recent acquisitions on the inventory: leather bookmark, purple satin bedroom slipper, man's argyle sock, wine label.

ON FRIDAY afternoon Qwilleran drove to the Black Bear Café to
inspect the staging area and meet the young woman who needed
advice. Gary's bar-and-grill was located in the Hotel Booze in the
town of Brrr, so named because it was the coldest spot in the
county. The hotel had been a landmark since the nineteenth century. It was perched on a hilltop overlooking the harbor, and ships
in the lake were guided to port by the rooftop sign: BOOZE . . .
ROOMS . . . FOOD.

When Gary Pratt took over the Hotel Booze from his ailing
father, the bar was a popular eatery, but the upper floors violated

every building regulation in the book. Qwilleran had a hunch about Gary's potential, and the Klingenschoen Foundation obliged with a low-interest loan. With the addition of elevators and indoor plumbing, the Hotel Booze became the flagship of Brrr's burgeoning tourist trade. Wisely, Gary maintained in the bar itself the seedy atmosphere that appealed to sportsmen.

When Qwilleran arrived at the café, he slid cautiously onto a wobbly barstool, and Gary, behind the carved black walnut bar, asked, "Squunk water on the rocks?"

"I'll take coffee if you have it. How's business?"

"It'll pick up when the hunting season opens. I hope we get some snow. The hunters like a little snow for tracking."

"They say we're in for a lot of it this winter." Qwilleran had learned that local etiquette called for three minutes of weather-speak before any purposeful conversation.

"I like snow," said Gary. "I've been dogsledding the last couple of winters."

"Sounds like an interesting sport," Qwilleran said, although the idea of being transported by dog power had no appeal for him.

"You should try it! Say, I've been meaning to ask something about your show. Where did you get all your information? Or did you make some of it up?"

"Every statement is documented," Qwilleran said. "Do you know about the Gage family? One of them was an amateur historian."

"All I know is that this woman who just died— Her husband used to hang around the bar when my father was running it. Liked to swap stories with the hunters. More coffee?"

"First let's see where we're going to present our show."

"Okay. Just a sec." Gary picked up the bar telephone and called a number. "Nancy, he's here," he said in a low voice and hung up. "Okay, Qwill, let's go. The meeting room's across the lobby." He led the way to a large room that was barren except for a low platform and rows of folding chairs. "Here it is. We can get you anything you want."

Qwilleran stepped up on the platform. "We need a couple of small tables and a couple of plain chairs. What's behind that door?"

"A hall leading to the rest rooms and the emergency exit."

"Good! I'll use it for entrances and exits. And now I'll take that second cup of coffee."

Back in the bar, Gary said, "Hey, there's Nancy, the girl I want you to meet."

Seated on one of the barstools was a young woman in jeans, farm jacket, and field boots. She was slightly built, and her delicate features were half hidden by a cascade of dark wavy hair. In dress and stature she was more like a schoolgirl, but her large brown eyes were those of a grown woman with problems.

"Nancy, this is Mr. Q.," Gary said. "Nancy's a good customer of ours. Burgers, not beer, eh, Nancy?"

She nodded shyly, clutching a bottle of cola.

"How do you do?" Qwilleran said with reserve.

"Nice to meet you. I've seen your column in the paper."

Gary served Qwilleran a fresh cup of coffee, then ambled to the other end of the bar to visit with a couple of boaters.

The awkward silence that followed was broken by Qwilleran's uninspired question. "Are you a member of the Outdoor Club?"

"Yes," Nancy said. "I'm going to see your show Monday night."

Again it was his turn. "Do you think we'll have snow next week?"

"I think so," she said. "The dogs are getting excited."

"Dogs? Do you have dogs?"

"Siberian huskies."

"Is that so?" he remarked with interest. "How many?"

"Twenty-seven. I breed sled dogs."

"Are you a musher?"

"I do a little racing," she said, blushing self-consciously.

"Do you breed dogs as a hobby or a vocation?"

"Both, I guess. I live in Brrr Township, and I work part time at the animal clinic in Brrr. I'm a dog handler."

Qwilleran was determined not to inquire about her problem. "Nancy, I'm afraid I don't know your last name."

"Fincher," she said simply.

Fortunately, Gary glanced in their direction, and Qwilleran pointed to his empty cup and Nancy's half-empty bottle.

Gary approached with his bearish, lumbering gait. "Did you tell him about your problem?" he asked Nancy.

"No," she said, looking away.

Gary served them and said, "The thing of it is, Qwill, her dad disappeared." Then he went back to the boaters.

Qwilleran looked at Nancy. "When did that happen?"

35

"I haven't been able to find him since Sunday." She seemed genuinely worried.

"Do you live in the same house?"

"No, he lives on his potato farm. I have a mobile home. I went over to cook Sunday dinner for him, the way I always do. Then he watched football on TV, and I went home to my dogs."

"And when did you first realize he was missing?"

"Wednesday. The mail carrier stopped and told me that Pop's mailbox was filling up, and his dog was barking in the house, and there was no truck in the yard. So I drove over there, and Corky was so starved, he almost took my arm off."

"Did you notify the police?"

Nancy looked at her clenched hands. They were small hands, but they looked strong. "Well, I talked to a deputy I know, and he said Pop was most likely off on a binge somewhere."

"Is your father a heavy drinker?"

"Well, he's been drinking more since Mom died."

"Did you do anything further?"

"I took Corky home with me, and on the way I stopped at the Crossroads Tavern. That's where Pop goes to have a beer with the other farmers. They said he hadn't been around since Saturday."

"Has your father ever done this before?"

"Never!" Her eyes flashed. "He'd never do such a thing at harvest! If he doesn't dig his potatoes before the first heavy frost, the whole crop will be ruined. He's a very good farmer."

"And this deputy you mentioned— Does he know your father?"

"Yes," she said, shrinking into her oversized jacket. "His name is Dan Fincher. We were married for a while."

"I see," said Qwilleran. "What's your father's name?"

"Gil Inchpot."

He nodded. "The Inchpot name goes back a long way in the farming community. What kind of truck does your father drive?"

"Ford pickup. Blue."

"Do you know the license number?"

"No," she said, pathetically enough to arouse his sympathy.

"Let me think about this matter," Qwilleran said, pushing a napkin and a pen toward her. "Write down your address and telephone number, also the address of your father's farm. If you learn anything further, ask Gary how to get in touch with me."

"Thank you," she said. "Now I have to get back to the clinic."

She left, lugging a shoulder bag half her size. Qwilleran watched her go, smoothing his mustache. The gesture meant that he sensed an element of intrigue in this country tale. The reaction always started with a tingle on his upper lip—in the roots of his mustache. He had learned to respect the sensation.

Gary returned. "Nice little girl, isn't she?"

"I don't visualize her racing sled dogs. She looks too delicate."

"But she's light, like a jockey, and that makes a good racer. What do you think of her story?"

"It bears a closer look." Qwilleran threw a ten-dollar bill across the bar. "Keep the change. I'll see you Monday night."

From the Hotel Booze he drove directly to the police station in downtown Pickax, where his friend Andrew Brodie was chief.

Brodie waved him away. "If you're looking for free coffee, you're too late. The pot's dry."

"False deduction," Qwilleran said. "My objective is to see if you're doing your work. Do you know a guy named Gil Inchpot?"

"Potato farmer. Brrr Township."

"Right. His daughter's worried about him. He's disappeared. His truck's gone. He abandoned his dog. And he decamped when the potatoes were ready to harvest."

"That's the sheriff's turf," Brodie pointed out. "Did she report it to the sheriff's department?"

"She talked to a deputy named Dan Fincher. He laughed it off, said Inchpot was on a binge somewhere."

"The daughter should notify the state police. They cover three counties. Do you know the license number of the missing vehicle?"

"No, but it's a blue Ford pickup, and I have Inchpot's address, in case you want to run a check on it—with that expensive computer the taxpayers bought for you."

"Seeing as how it's you," Brodie said, "I'll run down the license number and turn it over to the state police post."

"That's decent of you, Andy. If you ever want to run for mayor, I'll campaign for you."

WHEN Qwilleran returned home after his discussion with the police chief, Goodwinter Boulevard was transformed. All the leaves had been blown from the front lawns and sidewalks into the gutters in preparation for the vacuum truck. But there were still huge piles of leaves in the backyard of the Goodwinter mansion, where the lawn service would not finish up until tomorrow.

On impulse Qwilleran walked about, through the rustling leaves— a joyous activity he remembered from boyhood. Suddenly from the corner of his eye he saw something crawling through the shrubs that bordered the property. He realized it was the attorney's son. He called out sternly, "Is there something you want?"

Timmie Wilmot scrambled to his feet. "Is Oh Jay over here? He's our cat. A great big orange one with bad breath." The boy was looking anxiously about Qwilleran's yard. "There he is!" He ran across the grass and grabbed the camouflaged cat around the middle. Clutching the bundle of fur to his chest, he staggered back across the yard. The pair reached the lot line and crawled through the brush to safety.

Indoors, the Siamese were concerned chiefly with Qwilleran's recent association with a dog handler who raised Siberian huskies. Their noses, like Geiger counters detecting radiation, passed over every square inch of Qwilleran's clothing.

He arranged some roast beef on a plate and placed it under the kitchen table. Then, turning on the radio for the weather report, he heard an announcement about Halloween instead. The hobgoblins would be out tomorrow night, official Beggars' Night in Pickax.

Saturday morning Qwilleran went to buy a bushel of apples for trick or treat. When he arrived home, his phone was ringing.

Junior was on the line. "Where've you been so early? I've been trying to reach you. How would you like to take a little ride?"

"Where?"

"To the Hilltop Cemetery. Grandma was buried there yesterday— privately. Her last wishes specified no funeral, no mourners, and no flowers."

"Then why are you going to the cemetery this morning?"

"Somehow it isn't decent to let her be buried with only a backhoe operator in attendance. Want to come along?"

"I'll bring a couple of apples," Qwilleran offered.

The Hilltop Cemetery dated back to pioneer days, when the Gages, Goodwinters, Fugtrees, Trevelyans, and other settlers were buried across the crest of a ridge. Their tombstones could be seen silhouetted against the sky as one approached.

On the way, Junior asked, "How's everything at the house?"

"Koko just came out of a closet with a man's spat. I haven't seen one of those since the last Fred Astaire movie. His aim in life is to empty the closets ounce by ounce."

"They'll have to be cleaned out sooner or later."

They were passing through farm country, and Qwilleran asked Junior if he knew a potato farmer named Gil Inchpot.

"Not personally, but his daughter was my date for the senior prom in high school. She was the only girl short enough for me."

They parked the car and walked up the hill to a granite obelisk chiseled with the name GAGE. Small headstones surrounded it, and there was one rectangle of freshly turned earth, not yet marked.

"There she is," said her grandson. "I was supposed to ship her books to Florida, but I had too many other things on my mind—my job, and the baby coming. I promise, though, she's going to get a memorial service exactly how she wanted it."

"Has her will been read?"

"Not until my brother and sister get here. Jack has to come from L.A., and Pug lives in Montana. Grandma wrote a new will after moving to Florida. It was in the manager's safe at the mobile-home park. It will be interesting to know what changes she made."

"When Pug and Jack arrive," Qwilleran suggested, "I'd like to take all of you to dinner at the Old Stone Mill."

"Gee! That would be great!"

The two men stood munching apples for a while, Junior staring at the grave and Qwilleran gazing around the horizon.

They drove back to town without saying much until Qwilleran ventured, "You never told me anything about your grandfather."

"To tell the truth, my grandparents are closer in death than in life," Junior said. "She was into arts and health fads; he was into sports and booze. The Gage shipyard had folded, and he spent his time manipulating the family fortune, not always legally. Grandpa spent two years in prison for fraud. That was in the 1920s."

"If they were so mismatched, why did they marry?"

"Well, my mother told me that Euphonia's forebears were pioneer doctors by the name of Roff. The family never had any real money. Somehow Euphonia got pressured into marrying the Gage heir. The Roffs, being from Boston, had a certain 'class' that Grandpa lacked, so it seemed like a good deal all around, but it didn't work."

"Was your mother their only child?"

"Yeah. She called herself a honeymoon special."

Qwilleran asked to be dropped off at the variety store, where he bought a blue light bulb and a Halloween mask. Then he spent an hour with his recording machine taping weird noises. The Siamese watched with bemused tolerance as their human companion uttered anguished moans and hideous laughs into the microphone.

The performance was interrupted by the telephone. It was Gary Pratt. "Nancy's here. She wants to tell you something."

"Put her on."

In a breathless little-girl voice Nancy said, "The state police found Pop's truck! It was at the airport."

"Is there any clue as to his destination?"

"No." She hesitated before continuing in a faltering way. "He never— He doesn't like to travel, Mr. Qwilleran. The police told me to report a missing person, and they'll check the flight lists."

"Let me know what they find out," Qwilleran said. He was genuinely sorry for her, and in an effort to divert her from her worries he said, "You know, Nancy, I'd like to write a column on dog-sledding. Are you willing to be interviewed?"

"Oh, yes!" she said. "The mushers would love the publicity."

"How about tomorrow afternoon?"

"I want to go to Pop's house after church to clean up, but I could be home by two."

"I'll see you then, Nancy."

THE hour of hobgoblins approached. Qwilleran tried on his death's-head mask and prepared a sheet to shroud his head and body. The tape player was set up near the entrance, and at six o'clock he turned on the blue porch lamp, which cast an eerie light on the gray stonework. He was ready for them.

The first chattering trio to come up the front walk included a miniature Darth Vader, a pirate, and a bride. Before they could ring the bell, the front door opened slowly, and unnatural sounds emanated from the gloomy interior. "*Oooooooooooh! Ooooooooooooo!*" Then there was a horrifying screech. As the pop-eyed youngsters stared, a shrouded figure emerged from the shadows and a clawlike hand was extended, clutching an apple. The three screamed and scrambled down the steps.

Later groups were scared stiff, but not stiff enough to run away without their treats, so the supply of apples diminished slightly. Many beggars avoided the house entirely, They trooped down the side drive, however, to the brightly lighted carriage house, where Polly was distributing candy.

At seven thirty Qwilleran was glad to turn off the blue light and shed his mask and sheet.

Soon Polly phoned. "Did you have many beggars?"

"Enough," he said. "I have some apples left over, in case you feel like making pies. How about going out to dinner?"

"Thanks, but I'm exhausted. Why don't you come to brunch tomorrow? Mushroom omelets and cheese popovers."

"I'll be there! With apples. What time?"

"I suggest twelve noon, and don't forget to turn your clocks back. This is the end of daylight saving time."

Before resetting his two watches, three clock radios, and digital coffee maker, Qwilleran added several of Koko's new acquisitions to the collection in the desk drawer: swizzle stick, stale cigar, brown shoelaces, woman's black lace garter, handkerchief embroidered "Cynara," and box of corn plasters.

On Sunday morning Koko and Yum Yum pounced on Qwilleran's chest at seven a.m., demanding their eight-o'clock breakfast. He shooed them from the bedroom, but they yowled until he fed them in self-defense. He himself subsisted on apples until it was time to walk to Polly's carriage house. He was met at the top of the stairs by a husky Siamese with a challenging eye.

"Back off!" Qwilleran said. "I was invited to brunch."

"Help yourself to coffee," Polly said. "I'm starting the omelets."

When he tasted the first succulent mouthful, he asked in awe, "How did you learn to make omelets like these?"

"I prepared one every day for a month until I mastered the technique. That was before we were all worried about cholesterol."

He helped himself to a popover. "Junior's siblings are coming to town for the formalities, and I'm taking them to dinner. I hope you'll join us."

"By all means. I remember Pug when she used to come into the library for books on horses; she married a rancher. Jack went into advertising; he was always a very clever boy."

"Did you ever meet Euphonia's husband?"

41

"No, our paths never crossed."

"They say he and his wife didn't get along."

With a slight stiffening of the spine Polly said, "I'm not in a position to say, although they never appeared in public together."

"He and Lois seemed to hit it off pretty well."

"Qwill, dear, for someone who deplores gossip, you seem to be wallowing in it today."

"For purely vocational reasons. I'm planning an in-depth profile of Euphonia," he explained, then went on. "No one has come up with an acceptable motive for her suicide. Junior thinks it has to do with her belief in reincarnation, but I don't buy that explanation."

"Nor I. . . . May I fill your cup, Qwill?"

They sipped in contented silence, as close friends can do. Then Polly asked if he would like to hear a Mozart concerto for flute, oboe, and viola. Qwilleran nodded. He preferred a symphony orchestra, but he was learning to appreciate chamber music.

All in all, it was a cozy Sunday afternoon, until he excused himself, saying he had to interview a breeder of Siberian huskies.

Half an hour later, when he arrived at the address in Brrr Township, he knew he was in the right place. A twenty-seven-dog chorus could be heard behind the mobile home. The excited huskies were chained to a lineup of individual posts in front of individual shelters. When he knocked on the door, there was no answer. He strode about the yard for a while, saying, "Good dogs!" but it only increased the clamor. He was preparing to leave when a pickup steered recklessly into the yard and Nancy jumped out.

"Sorry I'm late," she said excitedly. "The police came to Pop's house while I was there. They checked the airline, and he never bought a ticket! I don't understand it. I'm worried that something has happened to him."

Sympathetically Qwilleran asked, "Was he having trouble of any kind? Financial problems? Enemies he was trying to avoid?"

"I don't know. He was well liked by the other farmers—always helping them out. When I lived at home, I remember how stranded motorists would come to the house to use the phone. He'd stick his head under the hood of their car and fix what was wrong. He could fix anything. Now I'm worrying that he was helping someone out and they took advantage of him. It used to be so safe! But now . . ."

"How old is your father?" Qwilleran asked.

"Fifty-seven."

"When did your mother die?"

"Three— No, four years ago. Pop changed a lot after that."

"Could there be anything new in his life-style that you don't know about?"

"You mean . . . like women? Or drugs?" She hesitated. "Well, he used to be very tightfisted, but lately he's been spending a lot of money."

"Extravagance can be a way of coping with grief. How is he spending the money?" Qwilleran asked.

"On farm improvements. Nothing wrong with that, I suppose, but"—she turned frightened eyes to him—"*where is he getting it?*"

FIVE

QWILLERAN and the dog handler were standing in the farmyard. "Well, you don't want to listen to my troubles all day," Nancy said with a gulp. "Do you want to go and see the dogs?"

"First let's sit down and talk for a while," he said.

They entered her small mobile home, where they were greeted by a large, friendly all-American cork-colored mongrel whose wagging tail was wreaking havoc in the tight quarters.

"This is Pop's dog," Nancy said. "Where would you like to sit?" She brushed debris from a couple of chair seats.

"Is it okay if I tape this interview?" Qwilleran placed a small recorder on a nearby table, and a swipe of the tail knocked it off.

"Corky!" She pointed, and obediently the dog walked six feet away and stretched out with his chin on his paw.

"You have a way with dogs," Qwilleran complimented her. "How did you get into this specialty of yours?"

"Well, I spent a couple of years in Alaska, and when I came home, I bought a sled and a pair of huskies—Siberians."

"Then you're the one who started the sport here?"

"It was easy. When somebody tries dogsledding on a beautiful winter day, they're hooked! I'll take you for a ride after we get snow."

"How do you accommodate passengers?"

"You ride in the basket, and I ride the runners."

"Hmmm," he murmured, thinking he'd feel foolish in a basket pulled by a pack of dogs. "Are all sled dogs as frisky as yours?"

43

"If they're good racers. A high attitude is what they should have. Mine are born to be racers, not pets, but I love them like family."

"What else makes a good racer?"

"Hard muscles in the right places. A good gait. And they have to like working in a team."

"How many dogs make a team?"

"I've seen as many as twenty in Alaska. I usually run eight."

Nancy went on with enthusiasm. The shy, inarticulate young woman became self-possessed and authoritative when talking about her vocation. "Each dog has a partner. They're paired according to the length of their stride and their personality. They become buddies. It's nice to see. Do you have dogs?"

"I have cats. Two Siamese. When do the race meets start?"

"After Christmas. We're training already. You should see us tearing around the back roads with the dogs pulling a wheeled cart! They know snow is on the way." She showed a picture of a dog team pelting down a snowy trail.

"I believe they're flying!" Qwilleran said in amazement.

His willingness to be amazed, his sympathetic manner, and his attitude of genuine interest were the techniques of a good interviewer, and Nancy was responding warmly. He asked, "Did you attend veterinary school?"

"I wanted to, but I got married instead—without telling my parents."

"How did they react?"

She looked at the tape recorder, and he turned it off.

"Well . . . Pop was furious . . . and Mom got cancer. I had to be nurse for her and housekeeper for Pop." Shrugging and wetting her lips, she said, "Dan didn't want a part-time wife."

"And that led to your divorce?"

She nodded. "When Mom died, I went to Alaska to get away from everything, but dogsledding brought me back."

"And your father— How did he react to your return?"

"Oh, he was getting along fine. He had a housekeeper and a new truck and a harvester with stereo in the cab. He was a lot nicer to me than before, and he gave me this piece of land."

"One question occurred to me: Is your father a gambler?"

"Just in the football pool at the tavern. Would you like a cola, Mr. Qwilleran?"

"No, thanks. Let's go out and see what a sled looks like."

The seven-foot sled, like a basket on runners, was in a small pole barn, where it shared space with a snowplow.

"It's made of birch and oak," Nancy said. "This is the handrail. That's the brake board down there. It's held together with screws and rawhide lacing. I varnish it before each sledding season."

"A work of art," Qwilleran said. "Now let's meet your family."

The dogs anticipated their coming. Puppies in a fenced yard were racing and wrestling and jumping for joy. The adults raised a clamor that Nancy quieted with a word. They were lean, handsome, long-legged animals in assorted colors and markings, with slanted blue eyes that gave them a sweet expression.

"These two are the lead dogs, Terry and Jerry."

Both Qwilleran and Nancy turned as a police vehicle pulled into the yard. It was a sheriff's car, and an officer stepped out.

She shouted, "Hi, Dan! This is Mr. Qwilleran from the newspaper. He's going to write up my dog team."

The deputy nodded.

Qwilleran said, "But we'll hold the story until after snow flies. I'll work on it and call if I have any more questions. Beautiful animals. Good interview." He moved toward his car.

Nancy accompanied him. "Gary says you're in the Gage house."

"That's right. I'm renting it from Junior Goodwinter, her grandson." He noticed a flicker in her eyes, which he attributed to memories of the high school prom, but it was something else.

"I've been in that house many times," she said. "It's huge!"

"Did you know Mrs. Gage?"

"Did I! My mother was her housekeeper for years and years. Every year Mom took me there for Christmas cookies and hot chocolate, and Mrs. Gage always gave me a present."

Qwilleran asked, "What did you think of her?"

"Well, she didn't fuss over me, but she was . . . nice."

Now he had one more adjective to describe the enigmatic Euphonia Gage, and another reason to call Florida and quiz her talkative neighbor.

BACK at the mansion, he submitted to the Siamese sniff test. It was cut short by a ringing telephone.

"Hey, Qwill!" said an excited Junior Goodwinter. "Good news."

"It's a boy."

"No, nothing like that. Somebody wants to buy the Gage mansion!"

"Congratulations! Who's making the offer?"

"A Realtor in Chicago."

"Is it a good offer?"

"Very good. The house wasn't even listed for sale. And why should they pick mine when there are seven for-sale signs on the street? I'll bet Grandma Gage tipped someone off before she died."

"Don't ask questions," Qwilleran said. "Take the money and run."

"I'm going to tell them it's rented until spring, so don't worry about having to move out, Qwill."

"I appreciate that. By the way, was there a woman in the Gage family by the name of Cynara?"

"I don't think so. How do you spell it?"

"Like the poem—C-y-n-a-r-a."

"Nope. Doesn't ring a bell."

LATE enough for the fifty percent discount, but not too late for a Pink Sunset resident, Qwilleran placed a call to Florida, and Koko leaped to the desk in anticipation. "This may be enlightening," Qwilleran advised him. The cat's whiskers curved forward.

When a woman's cheery voice answered, he asked in a rich and ingratiating tone, "May I speak with Celia Robinson?"

There was a trill of laughter. "I know it's you, Clayton. You can't fool your old grandmother."

"I'm afraid I'm not Clayton. I'm a colleague of Junior Goodwinter, Mrs. Gage's grandson, from Pickax. My name is Jim Qwilleran."

She hooted with delight tinged with embarrassment. "Oh, I thought you were my prankish grandson changing his voice. He's a great one for practical jokes. What did you say your name was?"

"Jim Qwilleran. Junior gave me your number."

"Yes. He was here for a few days. He's a nice boy. And I know all about you. Mrs. Gage showed me the articles you write for the paper. And I loved your picture! You have a wonderful mustache."

"Thank you," he said graciously. Clearing his throat, he began, "The editor has assigned me to write a profile of Euphonia Gage. Were you well acquainted with her?"

"Oh, yes, we were next-door neighbors, and I looked after her."

"In what way? I'm going to tape this if you don't mind."

"Well, I checked up on her every day, and I'd drive her where she wanted to go. She didn't like driving in the traffic we have around here. She was eighty-eight, you know. I'm only sixty-eight."

"Your voice sounds much younger, Mrs. Robinson."

"Do you think so?" she said happily. "That's because I sing. I was in a church choir before I moved down here. Would you like to hear me sing something?"

Qwilleran thought, I have a live one here! "I was hoping you would," he said. He expected to hear "Amazing Grace." Instead she sang the entire "Mrs. Robinson" in a clear, untrained voice. He imagined her to be buxom and rosy-cheeked, with partly gray hair and seashell earrings. "Brava!" he shouted when she had finished.

"Thank you. It's Clayton's favorite," she said. "Now, what was I telling you about Mrs. Gage?"

"You said you did the driving. Did she have her yellow coupe?"

"No. She sold that, and we took my navy-blue sedan. She called it an old lady's car. She was serious."

"And where would you two ladies drive?"

"Mostly to the mall—for lunch and to buy a few things. She liked to eat at a health-food place."

"Would you say she was happy at the Park of Pink Sunsets?"

"I think so. She went on day trips, and she liked to give talks."

"What kind of talks?"

Mrs. Robinson had to think a moment. "Mmmm . . . diet and exercise, music, art, the right way to breathe. She was interesting— not like the ones that are forever talking about their ailments and the grandchildren they never see. The park discourages young visitors. You have to get a five-dollar permit before you can have a visitor under sixteen years of age, and then it's only for forty-eight hours. Clayton likes to spend the whole Christmas week with me."

"How old is Clayton?"

"Just turned thirteen. He's a very bright boy with a crazy sense of humor. Last Christmas he figured out how to beat the system. When I picked him up at the airport, he was wearing a false beard! The sight of it just broke me up! He said I should introduce him to my neighbors as Dr. Clayton Robinson. I went along with the gag."

"Yow!" said Koko in a voice loud and clear.

"Do I hear a baby crying?" Mrs. Robinson asked.

"That's Koko, my Siamese cat. He's auditing this call."

"I used to have cats, and I'd love to have one now, but pets aren't allowed in the park. And the managers of the park have no sense of humor. Last Christmas, Clayton brought me a recording of a dog singing 'Jingle Bells.' The management threw a fit!"

"Who are these people who issue permits and throw fits?"

"Betty and Claude. He owns the park, and she's the manager. I don't think they're married, but they're always together. Don't get me wrong; they're really very nice if you play by the rules. Then there is Pete, the assistant, who takes over when they're out of town. He's handy with tools and electricity and all that."

"How did Mrs. Gage react to all the restrictions?"

"Well, you see, she was quite friendly with Betty and Claude, and she got special treatment. They took her to the dog races a lot. She enjoyed their company. She liked younger people."

"Including Dr. Clayton Robinson?"

His grandmother responded to the mild quip with peals of laughter. "Clayton would love to meet you."

"Your grandson sounds great, Mrs. Robinson."

"Call me Celia. Everybody does."

"Talking with you has been a pleasure, Celia. Just one serious question: Does anyone have an idea why Mrs. Gage took her life?"

"Well . . . we're not supposed to talk about it, but this isn't the first suicide we've had, and Claude is afraid it'll reflect on the park. But Mr. Crocus and I can't figure it out."

"Who is Mr. Crocus?" Qwilleran asked with renewed interest.

"He's a nice old gentleman. He had a crush on Mrs. Gage, and he misses her a lot. I hope he doesn't pine away."

"Considering all the restrictions, why is the park so desirable?"

"Mostly it's the security. You can call the office twenty-four hours a day in an emergency. They recommend doctors and lawyers and tax experts, which is nice because we're all from other states. I'm from Illinois. Also, there are things going on at the clubhouse. Would you like to see some snapshots of Mrs. Gage on one of our sight-seeing trips? Maybe you could use them with your article."

Qwilleran said it was an excellent suggestion and asked her to mail them to the office. "Do you mind if I call you again, Celia?"

"Gosh, no! It's fun being interviewed, Mr. Qwilleran."

"I'm usually called Qwill, spelled with a Qw."

"Yow!" said Koko.

"I'd better say good night, Celia. Koko wants to use the phone."

The last sound he heard from the receiver was a torrent of laughter. He turned to Koko. "That was Mrs. Robinson at the Park of Pink Sunsets."

The cat was fascinated by telephones. The ringing of the bell, the sound of a human voice coming from the instrument, and the mere fact that Qwilleran was conversing with an inanimate object seemed to stimulate his feline sensibilities. And he showed particular interest in the Florida grandmother. Qwilleran wondered why. He thought, Does he know something I don't? Koko's blue eyes were wearing their expression of profound wisdom.

"Treat!" Qwilleran announced, and there was the thud of galloping paws en route to the kitchen.

SIX

QWILLERAN spent Monday preparing for his second performance of *The Big Burning,* and when he drove to the hotel at seven o'clock, the parking lot was jammed. The Outdoor Club was in the café enjoying boozeburgers when he set up in the meeting room.

"Largest crowd they've ever had." Hixie Rice exulted as she tested the sound and lights. "And I've got four more bookings."

A rumble of voices in the lobby announced the approaching audience, and Qwilleran ducked through the exit door while people took their seats.

With his ear to the door he heard the first notes of "Anitra's Dance" and counted thirty seconds before making an entrance and mounting the stage. "We interrupt this program to bring you a bulletin on the forest fires that are rapidly approaching. . . ."

A small girl in the front row was swinging her feet back and forth continuously. Her legs, in white leggings, were like a beacon in the dark room.

An old farmer's voice came from the speakers. "I come in from my farm west o' here, and I seen some terrible things! We picked up one lad not more'n eight year old, carryin' a baby—all that were left of his fambly. His shoes, they was burned clean off his feet!"

The white legs never stopped swinging like a pendulum: left, right, left. Qwilleran had to fight to maintain his concentration.

"Here in Pickax it's dark as midnight. Winds have suddenly risen to hurricane fury. Wagons are being lifted like toys and blown away! There's a red glare in the sky! *Pickax is in flames!*"

The red light flicked on. Coughing and choking, the announcer rushed from the studio.

In the hallway beyond the exit door, Qwilleran leaned against the wall, recovering from the scene he had just played. A moment later Hixie joined him. "They love it!" she said. "Especially the part about the boy with his shoes burned off. The kids identify."

"Did you see that one swinging her legs in the front row?" Qwilleran asked irritably.

"She was spellbound!"

"Well, those white legs were putting a spell on me," Qwilleran snapped. "Get them out of the front row."

When he made his entrance for scene two, an instant hush fell upon the room. Surreptitiously he glanced at the front row; the white legs had gone.

Qwilleran had not seen the last of them, however. Halfway through the scene he was interviewing the Irish innkeeper by phone: "Sir, what news do you hear from Sawdust City?"

A thick Irish brogue came from the speakers: "It's gone! All gone! Every stick of it, they're tellin'."

At that tense moment Qwilleran's peripheral vision picked up a pair of white legs walking toward the stage. What the devil is she doing? he thought.

The girl climbed onto the stage, crossed to the exit door at the rear, and went to the rest room.

The radio announcer went on. "In West Kirk thirteen persons went down a well and stood in water for five hours. In Dimsdale a mother saved her children by burying them in a plowed field until the danger passed. . . ."

The white legs returned, taking a shortcut across the stage. It didn't faze the audience. At the end of the show they applauded wildly. Hixie fielded questions while Qwilleran packed the gear, surrounded by the under-ten crowd.

He was relieved when Nancy Fincher came to the stage. "Mr. Qwilleran, it was wonderful! You made it so real, I cried."

"Thank you," he said. "May I invite you for a drink in the café?"

"No, thanks," she said. "I have to stop and check Pop's mailbox and then go home and take care of my dogs."

He watched her go, lugging her oversized shoulder bag.

Qwilleran drove back to Pickax through farming country, where the bright headlights of tractors in the fields meant that farmers were working around the clock to beat the frost.

He'd brought a sample of boozeburger for the Siamese, and after they had eaten, they went to the library. They were reading *Robinson Crusoe* when the ring of the telephone made all of them jump.

"Hello?" Qwilleran said, ready for anything.

"Mr. Qwilleran," said a breathless voice, "Gary gave me your number. I discovered something at Pop's house, and I notified the police, but I wanted to tell you because you've been so kind."

"What was it, Nancy?"

"I cut my hand on the mailbox, so I went indoors for a bandage. And in a medicine cabinet I saw Pop's dentures in a glass of water. He would never leave without his dentures!"

Qwilleran combed his mustache with his fingertips as he thought of the partial denture in the desk drawer. He glanced at the Siamese. Yum Yum was pedicuring her left hind foot; Koko was sitting there looking wise.

THERE was heavy frost that night. The condominiums of Indian Village, the stone canyons of downtown Pickax, the mansions of Goodwinter Boulevard all looked mystically hoary in the morning light. Qwilleran felt moody as he drank his coffee. There was the usual letdown after the excitement of doing a show, plus a gnawing regret about the Inchpot crop. Hundreds of acres of potatoes had been lost. And now, after hearing Nancy's grim news about the dentures, Qwilleran felt real concern about Gil Inchpot himself.

He was somewhat gladdened when his free-lance secretary, Lori Bamba, called to ask if her husband could deliver some letters and checks for signing. Nick Bamba, a young man with alert black eyes, was an engineer at the state prison; he shared Qwilleran's interest in crime and mystery. Whenever Qwilleran mentioned his suspicions and hunches, Nick always took him seriously.

"Coffee or hot cider?" Qwilleran asked him upon arrival.

"I'll try the cider." Nick handed over a folder of correspondence. "Lori says you're getting a lot of fan mail about *The Big Burning*." They carried their mugs into the library, and Nick remarked, "I see you've got an elevator. Does it work?"

"Definitely. We used it at the preview of our show."

At that point Koko walked into the library with deliberate step and rose on his hind legs to rattle the closet doorknob.

"What's old slyboots got on his mind?" Nick asked.

"This is the only closet in the house that's locked, and it drives him bughouse," Qwilleran said. "All the closets are filled with junk, and Koko spends his spare time digging for treasure."

"Want me to pick the lock for you? I'll bring my tools next time."

"Sure. I'm curious about this closet myself."

"I suppose you heard about the missing potato farmer, Gil Inchpot. Police are investigating his disappearance ten days ago."

"I heard something about it," Qwilleran mentioned.

"He's quite a successful farmer. I never met him, but his daughter was married to a deputy sheriff I know, Dan Fincher. It didn't last long; her father broke it up."

"Why? Do you know?"

Nick shrugged. "Dan isn't big on particulars. I know that Gil is well liked at the Crossroads Tavern and at the farm co-op, but Dan says he's a bully at home."

Qwilleran reached for Nick's cider mug. "Fill 'er up?"

"No, thanks. I've got errands to do—prison business."

Nick left, and after Qwilleran had signed his letters and checks, he headed to the newspaper office.

"How's everything going?" he asked Junior.

"Jack and Pug have arrived. They're staying at the New Pickax Hotel. Jody doesn't feel like having company."

"Will she come to dinner tomorrow? Polly's joining us."

"Why don't you make the reservation for six," said the expectant father, "and we'll see how she feels."

"When is the will being read?"

"Ten thirty tomorrow morning. Keep your fingers crossed."

WHILE the will was being read in Pender Wilmot's office, Qwilleran was at home estimating the extent of Euphonia Gage's estate. No doubt she had cashed in heavily when she liquidated her estate. Her recent economies, such as living in a mobile home, were no more peculiar than Qwill's own preference for driving a used car.

That evening, his guests were late in arriving at the Old Stone Mill. He and Polly sat waiting and talking. Finally Polly said, "Junior is always so punctual. Perhaps he's taken Jody to the hospital."

"I'll phone their house," Qwilleran said.

To his surprise, Jody answered. "He left about half an hour ago to pick up Pug and Jack," she said. "I decided not to go." She sounded depressed.

"Do you feel all right, Jody?"

"Oh, yes, I'm all right, considering . . ."

When the hostess conducted the tardy guests to the table, Qwilleran greeted three unhappy people: Pug as distraught as a Montana rancher who has had to shoot her favorite horse; Jack as glum as a California advertising executive who has lost his major client; Junior as indignant as an editor who is being sued for libel.

Introductions were made, and Polly tried to make polite conversation. "Are you comfortable at the hotel? . . . How do you like Montana? . . ." Her efforts failed to elevate the mood.

They ordered drinks. Qwilleran talked about the weather to fill the void until they arrived. Then he raised his glass. "Would anyone like to propose a toast?"

"To bad news!" Junior blurted.

Scowling, Jack said, "Pug and I flew thousands of miles just to be told that she left us a hundred dollars apiece! I'm damned mad!"

"Surprising!" Qwilleran turned to Junior for corroboration.

"Same here," said the younger brother. "Only I didn't have to cross the continent to get the shaft."

"I had the impression," Qwilleran remarked, "that your grandmother was a generous person."

"Sure," said Pug. "She put us all through college, but we didn't know it gave her the privilege to direct our lives! She was furious when Jack went to the Coast and I married a rancher. For a wedding present she sent us a wooden nutcracker."

Polly asked, "Can anyone explain the reason for her attitude?"

"She was a selfish egocentric, that's all," said Jack.

There was silence at the table until Qwilleran cleared his throat preparatory to introducing a sensitive subject. "If you're all left out of the will, who are the beneficiaries?"

The three young people looked at each other, and Junior said bitterly, "The Park of Pink Sunsets! They get everything—to build, equip, and maintain a health spa for the residents. She revised her will after she got to Florida."

The Cat Who Went into the Closet

Jack said, "If anyone thinks we're sticking around for the memorial service tomorrow night, they can stuff it!"

Qwilleran said, "I think we should all have another drink and order dinner." He signaled for service.

During dinner everyone was somewhat more relaxed, but Qwilleran was relieved when the meal came to an end. As the party was leaving, Junior handed him an envelope.

"Forgot to give you this, Qwill. It came to the office today, addressed to you."

It was a pale pink envelope with a Florida postmark and the official logo of the Park of Pink Sunsets. He slid it into his pocket.

On the way home to Goodwinter Boulevard, Qwilleran said to Polly, "Do you want to attend the memorial service tomorrow night?"

"I wouldn't miss it!" Her tone was more bitter than sweet.

Qwilleran dropped her off, saying he would pick her up the next evening. He was in a hurry to open the letter from Florida.

Sitting at his desk, he slit the envelope, and out fell some snapshots as well as a note:

Dear Mr. Qwilleran,
I enjoyed talking to you. Here are the snaps of Mrs. Gage with some other people from the park. We were on a bus trip. I'm the giddy-looking one in Mickey Mouse ears. That's Mr. Crocus with Mrs. Gage. Hope you can use some of these with your article.

Yours very truly,
Celia Robinson

Spreading the snapshots on the desk, Qwilleran found the diminutive Euphonia neatly dressed in a lavender pantsuit and wide-brimmed hat, while her companions sported T-shirts with the Pink Sunset logo splashed across the front. Conservatively dressed in tropical whites was an old man with a shock of white hair.

The Siamese, always interested in something new, were on the desk top, sitting comfortably on their briskets and idly observing. Then, apparently without provocation, Koko rose to his feet with a guttural monosyllable and sniffed the pictures. There was something about the glossy surface of photographs that always attracted him. He flicked his tongue at a couple of them.

"No!" Qwilleran said sharply, worrying about the chemicals used in processing.

"Yow!" Koko retorted in a scolding tone of his own.

An uneasy feeling crept across Qwilleran's upper lip, and he patted his mustache as he examined the snapshots the cat had licked. Sandpaper tongue and potent saliva had left rough spots on the surface. In both photos Euphonia looked happy and pert, posed with a yellow sports car in one shot and with the Pink Sunset tour bus in the other. More important, however, was the realization that two of her companions looked vaguely familiar. He had no idea who they were or where he had met them.

SEVEN

THURSDAY was bright and clear, although Wetherby Goode reminded his listeners that November was the month of the Big Snow, a threat that annually hung over the Moose County residents like a Damoclean icicle.

Qwilleran said to Koko, "Would you like to take a walk? This may be your last chance before snow flies. I'll get the leash."

Yum Yum immediately disappeared, but Koko purred and rolled on his side while the harness was being buckled around his middle. On the back porch, he checked out the spots where the nefarious Oh Jay had left his scent. Next he led the way down the back steps to a paved area where the last few leaves of autumn were waiting to be pawed, batted, chased, and chewed. While Koko was enjoying these simple pleasures, Qwilleran became aware of a familiar figure scrambling through the shrubs on the lot line.

"If you're looking for Oh Jay," he said to the attorney's son, "he's not here."

But it appeared this was a social call. "It's gonna snow," Timmie said. A pause followed, then, "I can stand on my head."

"Good for you!"

There was another pause. "We're gonna move away from here."

"Why do you want to leave a nice neighborhood like this?"

"My dad says some dumb fool bought the house."

"Excuse me," Qwilleran said. "I have to make a phone call." He hurried up the back steps, pulling a reluctant cat.

Ringing Junior at the office, he said, "Have you heard the news? Another house on the boulevard has been sold. Pender Wilmot's. That makes two of them. What do you make of that?"

"Who bought it?" Junior demanded with suspicion.

"My six-year-old informant wasn't specific."

"I hope this doesn't turn out to be detrimental to the neighborhood, like one of those cults or a front for something illegal."

"You don't need to worry about anything like that—not in Pickax," Qwilleran assured him, "but I admit it piques the curiosity. Well, I'll see you tonight at the memorial service."

SHORTLY before eight o'clock on Thursday evening, more than a hundred residents of Moose County converged on the K Theatre, the former Klingenschoen mansion. In dress they were less sweatery than usual, denoting the solemnity of the occasion.

When Qwilleran and Polly arrived in the lobby, they were handed programs. He said to Polly, "According to Junior, Euphonia planned this service down to the last detail."

After a glance at the program Polly replied, "This is not a memorial service. It's a concert. Don't you think it's a trifle precious? Look, a French art song, Albinoni, Ravel . . . Only Euphonia would use the Latin title for Cynara. It's her last gasp of cultural snobbery."

Carol Lanspeak, a trustee of the theater, hurried up to them. "I think you're in for some surprises tonight. Junior asked me to handle the staging, and my husband's doing the readings. Euphonia left instructions for everything! Such a perfectionist!"

Qwilleran reached into his pocket for an envelope of snapshots. "One of her Florida neighbors sent these. You might like to see how she looked toward the end."

"Why, she looks wonderful!" Carol exclaimed.

"Do you recognize anyone else in the pictures?"

"No, I don't. . . . Should I?"

"I thought some of them might be from Moose County. Snowbirds tend to flock together."

Carol and Polly conferred, and agreed that they were all strangers. "But here comes Homer Tibbitt. Ask him," Carol suggested. "He claims to know everyone in two counties."

The aged Homer changed glasses to study the snapshots. "Sorry. I can't identify a soul except Euphonia."

"I believe it's time to go upstairs," Carol suggested.

Two matching stairways led to the auditorium entrance on the upper level, from which the amphitheater seating sloped down to a dark stage. As Qwilleran and Polly took their seats, a pianist in the orchestra pit was playing the moody, mysterious prelude specified by the deceased.

A hush fell on the audience as the houselights slowly dimmed. There were a few dramatic seconds of total darkness before two glimmers of light appeared. One spotlighted a bouquet of purple and white flowers on a pedestal, stage right. The other, stage center, illuminated a thronelike chair, on the seat of which was a wide-brimmed straw hat with a band of purple velvet.

From hidden speakers came the haunting music of Albinoni. The audience listened and stared, as if Euphonia herself might glide onto the stage. The volume swelled, then faded, leaving only the last searching notes of the wistful, yearning violin.

The spotlights disappeared, and a beam of light focused on a lectern at stage left, where Larry Lanspeak of Lanspeak's Department Store stood waiting. His rich voice gripped the audience:

> *"When to the sessions of sweet silent thought*
> *I summon up remembrance of things past . . ."*

Qwilleran listened for clues to Euphonia's past and possibly a clue to her suicide motive.

> *"Then can I drown an eye, unused to flow . . .*
> *And weep afresh love's long since cancelled woe."*

Again the spotlights flooded the throne and flowers as a slow pavane by Ravel painted its melancholy picture. Qwilleran deduced that Euphonia was mourning a lost lover, and it was not Grandpa Gage. An anonymous poem confirmed his theory:

> *"Two white butterflies*
> *Kissing in mid-air,*
> *Then darting apart*
> *To flutter like lost petals . . .*
> *Before parting forever . . ."*

There was a duet for flutes. And then the poem *"I have been faithful to thee, Cynara, in my fashion."* Qwilleran could hear sniffling in the audience, and even Polly was dabbing her eyes.

The program was building to its conclusion. A projection screen had been lowered at the rear of the stage, and when the music resumed, the image of a dancer appeared, arching her back, fluttering her scarves, twirling, twisting, sinking to her knees with bowed head, rising with head thrown back and arms flung wide in celebration. The dancer's white hair was tied back with purple ribbon.

When the video ended, there was silence—and utter darkness. Then the stage burst into brilliant light as the crashing chords of an organ symphony stunned the audience. The majestic music rocked the auditorium in triumph—until one final prolonged chord stopped dead, leaving a desolate emptiness in the hall.

"Whew!" Qwilleran said as the houselights were turned up. Among the audience a gradual murmur arose as groups began to wander to the exit, fumbling for appropriate comments.

On the way out of the theater Qwilleran and Polly were intercepted by Junior. "What did you think of Grandma's send-off?"

"Thought provoking, to say the least," Qwilleran replied.

"Want to hear something interesting? The attorney is questioning Grandma's will! He's talking about undue influence."

"Does he plan to sue?"

"I don't know yet. It'll depend on the value of the estate, but it's a distinct possibility. She must have been worth millions around the time she liquidated everything."

On the way home, Qwilleran and Polly were silent. When she invited him to her apartment for dessert and coffee, he declined, saying he had work to do. It was the first time he had ever turned down such an invitation, and she regarded him with mild anxiety. She may have guessed he was about to call another woman.

Back at the mansion, Qwilleran found the Siamese on the library sofa, curled into a round pillow of fur. One raised a sleepy head; the other twitched an ear. "Excuse me for disturbing you," he said as he turned on the desk lamp. "I need to make a phone call."

They struggled to their feet, yawned widely, and stretched vertically and horizontally before leaving the room with purposeful step. He knew where they were going: to the kitchen to lap a tongueful of water and gaze hopefully at their empty plate.

He gave them a few crunchy morsels before placing his call to Florida. When Celia Robinson answered, he said, "This is Jim Qwilleran phoning from Pickax. I hope I'm not calling you too late."

"No. I stay up till all hours, reading crime and undercover stuff and eating chocolate-covered cherries." She laughed.

"I want to thank you, Celia, for sending the snapshots. I took them to Mrs. Gage's memorial tonight, and her friends remarked how well she looked. Shall I send you a copy of the program?"

"Oh, yes, please! And would it be too much trouble to send one for Mr. Crocus?"

"Not at all. Is he the man with the magnificent white hair?"

"That's him. He plays the violin."

"Who's the couple standing with Mrs. Gage in front of a gigantic flowering shrub? They're wearing Pink Sunset T-shirts."

"They're new in the park—from Minnesota, I think. The bush is a hibiscus. Beautiful, isn't it? I never saw one so large."

"And who's the attractive woman at the wheel of the yellow convertible?"

"That's Betty, our manager. Isn't she glamorous? She sells cosmetics on the side. They're too expensive for me, but Mrs. Gage bought the works, and she really did look terrific."

Qwilleran said, "The car looks like the one she bought in Pickax before she left."

"That's right. She sold it to Betty—or maybe gave it to her. They were very chummy, like mother and daughter."

"Yow!" said Koko, who had ambled back into the library.

Qwilleran said, "I'm looking at a shot of your activity bus. There's a middle-aged man with his arm around Mrs. Gage."

"That's Claude, the owner of the park. He was very fond of her. He feels terrible about what she did. Everybody does."

"The Sunsetters impress me as one big happy family," he observed. "This Claude and Betty—are they the ones who used to take Mrs. Gage to the dog track?"

"Yes. She wanted me to drive her, but I don't believe in gambling. And it hurts to see those beautiful dogs used that way."

Koko had been moving closer to the phone and was now breathing heavily into the mouthpiece. Qwilleran pushed him away. "Mrs. Gage was a very wealthy woman. Did she give that impression?"

"She didn't talk big, but she was kind of high-toned, and her mobile home was a double-wide. I guessed she had plenty."

"Was her mind still keen?"

"Oh, she was very sharp! She always knew what she wanted to

do—and how to do it. She sometimes said teapot when she meant lampshade, but we all do that around here," she said with a giggle.

Qwilleran cleared his throat. "Were you aware that she drew up a new will after moving to the park?"

"Well, she never talked about anything like that—not to me, anyway—but I told her about this lawyer who does work for the Sunsetters for very reasonable fees. He did my will for only twenty-five dollars. Of course, it was a simple will; I'm leaving everything to Clayton—not that I have much."

"Yow!" said Koko.

"I hear my master's voice," Qwilleran said. "Good night, Celia. Thank you again for the snapshots, and give my regards to the thirteen-year-old doctor."

IT SNOWED that night. There was a stillness in the atmosphere as large wet flakes fell gently, clinging to tree branches, evergreen shrubs, and porch railings.

It was a good day to stay indoors and putter, Qwilleran decided after breakfasting on strong coffee and warmed-up rolls. He rummaged through the collection of Gage memorabilia that was accumulating in the desk drawer. The relics defined Grandpa Gage as a bon vivant who smoked cigars, drank wine, collected women's garters, and liked the feel of money. There was a piece of Confederate money, and there were two large dollar bills of the kind issued before 1929 and a buttonhook from the days of high-button shoes.

By afternoon the snow had stopped falling, and Qwilleran was tempted to drive out into the countryside and enjoy the fresh snow scene. He would also check the church in Brrr, where Hixie had scheduled the next performance of *The Big Burning*. Phoning the number listed for the Brrr Community Church, he was assured that someone would meet him there. He dressed in heavy jacket, boots, and wool cap and was saying good-bye to the Siamese when Koko staged one of his eloquent demonstrations, jumping at the handle of the back door and muttering.

"Okay, this is your last ride of the season," Qwilleran told him. He started the car and ran the heater for a few minutes before carrying the cat coop out to the back seat.

The Moose County landscape—with its flat farmland, abandoned mine sites, and rows of utility poles—could be bleak in

November, but today it was a picture in black and white. Even the town of Brrr looked like an enchanted village.

The church was a modest frame building with a cupola. As soon as Qwilleran pulled up to the curb, the front door opened and a woman came out to greet him, bundled up in a parka.

"Mr. Qwilleran, I'm Donna Sims. Come in out of the cold, but don't expect to get warm. The furnace is out of order."

Qwilleran threw a blanket over the cat coop and followed the woman into the building. The vestibule was a small one, with a few steps leading up to the place of worship and a few steps leading down to a spick-and-span basement.

Ms. Sims apologized for the frigid temperature. "We're waiting for the furnaceman. Emergencies like this are usually handled by a member of our congregation— Maybe you heard about the potato farmer that disappeared. We're very much upset about it."

"Don't apologize," Qwilleran said. "I'll cut this visit short, because I have a cat in the car. What is that door?"

"That's the furnace room."

"Good! I'll use it for entrances and exits. Do you have anything in the way of a platform?"

"One of our members manufactures industrial pallets—you know, those square wooden things—and we can stack them up. Is there anything else you need?"

"A small table and chair on the platform and another table and chair for my engineer, down on the floor." He handed her a typewritten card. "This is how we like to be introduced. Will your pastor be doing the honors?"

"I'm the pastor."

Back in the car, Qwilleran turned up the heat, uncovered the cat coop, and said to Koko, "If it's all right with you, we'll go for a little ride along the shore and see if the cabin's buttoned up for the winter." He had inherited a log cabin along with the rest of the Klingenschoen estate.

They headed along the lakeshore, where boarded-up cottages and beached boats huddled under a light blanket of snow. Then came a wooded stretch posted with red signs prohibiting hunting. At one point a large letter K was mounted on a post at the entrance to a narrow driveway, and this is where Qwilleran turned in.

At the crest of one slight hill Koko created a disturbance in the back seat, throwing himself around in the carrier and yowling.

"Hold it, boy! We're just having a quick look," said Qwilleran. He stopped the car, however, and released the door of the coop.

Quivering with excitement, Koko darted to the rear window on the driver's side and pawed the glass. "It's cold out there! You can't get out! You'd freeze your little tail off."

In a frenzy Koko dashed about the interior of the car as Qwilleran protested. But then Qwill looked out the driver's window. Between wild cherry trees were animal tracks leading into the woods. He jumped out, slammed the door, and followed the tracks.

A few yards into the woods there was a slight hollow, and what he found there sent him running back to the car, stumbling through the brush, slipping on wet snow. Without stopping to put Koko in the carrier, he backed down the winding trail to the highway. At the nearest gas station he called the sheriff.

EIGHT

AT ELEVEN p.m. the WPKX newscast carried this item: "Acting on an anonymous tip, police today found the body of a Brrr Township man in the Klingenschoen woods east of Mooseville. Gil Inchpot, fifty-seven, a potato farmer, had been missing since October twenty-fourth. Because of the condition of the body—decomposed, and mutilated by wild animals—the medical examiner was unable to determine the cause of death."

In phoning the tip to the police, Qwilleran had identified himself as a hunter trespassing on posted property and declined to give his name. He preferred to be a newswriter, not a newsmaker.

As soon as he heard the broadcast, he called Gary Pratt at the Black Bear Café. "Have you heard the news?"

"Yeah. It's tough on Nancy," said the barkeeper. "She had to identify the body. They didn't say anything about homicide on the air, but if Gil had been out hunting varmint and tripped in the woods, he'd be wearing a jacket and boots, wouldn't he? And what about a gun? He was wearing a plaid shirt and house slippers."

And no dentures, Qwilleran thought.

In the morning Qwilleran wrote Nancy a note of sympathy and shipped a box of chocolate-covered cherries to Celia Robinson. Then on Monday he attended Gil Inchpot's funeral at the Brrr

Community Church, taking care to dress warmly. The furnace had been repaired, however, and the building was stiflingly hot.

Two days later Qwilleran was back at the same church to present *The Big Burning of 1869.* It was snowing again, and he picked up Hixie Rice at the newspaper for the drive to Brrr.

"I don't know what to expect at the church tonight. The first time I went there, the building was too cold; the second time, it was so hot we couldn't breathe."

Hixie was too happy to care about the temperature. She said, "Can you stand some good news? Arch is making me a vice president, in charge of advertising and promotion!"

"Congratulations! You deserve it."

When they arrived at the church, he dropped her at the curb, telling her to check the stage while he unloaded the gear. By the time he set the suitcases down, Hixie came running back out of the building.

"The furnace has conked out again! It's like a walk-in freezer. The audience is sitting in jackets and wool hats and gloves."

"The show must go on," he replied stoically. "If the audience can stand it, so can we. You keep your coat on, and I'll have the forest fire to keep me warm."

This was sheer bravado on Qwilleran's part: in portraying the studio announcer he wore a short-sleeved summer shirt.

Hixie suggested, "Couldn't you cheat for once and wear your sweater?"

"And destroy the illusion?"

During the first act he tried to keep his teeth from chattering as he said, "Railroad tracks are warped by the intense heat. . . . Great blasts of hot air and cinders are smothering the city." He went through the motions of mopping a sweating brow.

In the second act his frozen fingers fumbled with the script as he said, "The temperature is one hundred and ten degrees in the studio, and the window glass is still too hot to touch."

After the final words the audience clapped and cheered and stamped their feet. Qwilleran suspected they were only trying to warm their extremities, but he held out his hand to Hixie, who joined him onstage. As they took their bows he could think only of a warm sweater and hot coffee. And then the lights went out! The basement was plunged into darkness.

"Power's out!" the pastor's voice called out. "Everybody, stay right where you are. Don't move until we light some candles."

A man's voice said, "I've got a flashlight!" At that moment there was a cry, followed by the thud of a falling body and groans of pain. A dozen voices shrieked in alarm.

The flashlight beamed on the platform, where Qwilleran stood in a frozen state of puzzlement; Hixie was no longer beside him. She was writhing on the floor.

"Dr. Herbert! Dr. Herbert!" someone shouted.

"Here I am. Hand me that flashlight," said a man's gruff voice. Two battery-operated lanterns and some candles made small puddles of light as the doctor knelt at Hixie's side.

The audience babbled in shock. "What happened? . . . Did she fall off the stage? . . . It's lucky that Doc's here."

Qwilleran leaned over the doctor's shoulder. "How is she?"

"She can be moved. I'll drive her to the hospital here in Brrr." He jangled his keys. "Will somebody bring my car around?"

While the others milled about anxiously, two men linked arms to form a chair lift and carry Hixie up the stairs.

"Hang in there," Qwilleran told her, squeezing her hand.

"*C'est la* rotten *vie,*" the new vice president said weakly.

Qwilleran found his sweater and was packing the suitcases when Nancy Fincher walked up to the platform. "I'm very sorry about the accident," she said solemnly, "but Dr. Herbert will take good care of her. I feel bad about you, too. You look frostbitten."

"I'll live," he said, "but I worry about my colleague. Let's go to the Black Bear for a hot drink. We can call the hospital from there."

They rode in his car to the Hotel Booze and found the café lighted by candles. Gary poured steaming cider heated on a camp stove, and inquired, "What will Hixie's accident do to your show?"

Nancy spoke up, with more vigor than usual. "I could help out until she gets better if you'd tell me what to do."

"But what are your hours at the clinic? We have three matinees scheduled back to back," Qwilleran pointed out.

"I could change my shift. To tell the truth, Mr. Qwilleran, this would do me good. It'll take my mind off what's happened."

He nodded sympathetically. "Do you know if the police are getting anywhere with the investigation?"

"I don't know. They ask questions, but never tell me anything."

Qwilleran said gently, "You mentioned that your father had changed considerably after your mother died."

"Well, he was drinking more, and he stopped going to church, though he still helped them with repairs. I told you about the way he was spending money. He said it was Mom's insurance, but she didn't have that kind of coverage."

"Did you tell the police about his spending sprees?"

"No," she said guiltily. "Do you think I should have?"

"They know it anyway. In a community like this, it's no secret when someone starts making lavish expenditures." He looked at his watch. "We can call the hospital now." He used the bar telephone and then reported to Nancy, "Hixie's been transferred to the Pickax hospital. No information on her condition is available."

Qwilleran drove Nancy back to the church, where her truck was parked. "Our next booking is Saturday afternoon. We should have a rehearsal."

"Yes," she said eagerly. "I could stop by your house tomorrow."

Brrr was still blacked out when he drove away, but Pickax had power. The old-fashioned streetlamps on the boulevard glowed through a veil of falling snow. Hurrying into the house, he telephoned the Pickax hospital and learned that the patient had been admitted and was resting comfortably.

He immediately phoned Arch Riker and announced, "Your new vice president is in the hospital."

"What happened to her, for heaven's sake?"

"The power failed where we were giving our show, and she fell off the stage. Fortunately, a doctor was there. I don't know the extent of the injury—the hospital isn't giving out information."

"Our night desk will try to find out," Riker said. "I hate to sound crass, Qwill, but what will this do to our show?"

"I have a substitute lined up— Excuse me a moment, Arch." He was sitting with his arms on the desk, and Koko was digging in the crook of his elbow. "What's your problem?" he asked the cat. "You're wearing out my sweater!"

Both cats liked to knead before settling down to sleep, but Koko was working industriously. At the sharp rebuke he jumped down and went to the locked closet, where he rattled the door handle.

Turning back to the phone, Qwilleran explained, "Koko wants me to pick the lock on the library closet."

"I wish you took orders from your editor-in-chief the way you take orders from that cat!"

The next morning Qwilleran phoned the hospital and learned that the patient was receiving treatment. It was noon when he finally reached the patient herself.

"Hixie! How are you? We're all worried about you! What's the diagnosis?"

With her usual flourish she replied, "Broken foot! But I've met this perfectly wonderful Dr. Herbert. He drove me to the Brrr hospital and then drove me down here. Dr. Herbert's adorable, Qwill! He cares! He has a cabin cruiser! And he's not married!"

When Qwilleran visited Hixie a few hours later, he found her sitting in an armchair with her foot encased in a bright pink cast.

"*Chic, n'est-ce pas?*" she said. "Casts now come in colors."

"Never mind the color scheme. How long will you be in the cast?"

"Six weeks, but when Dr. Herbert found out I live alone in Indian Village, he insisted that I stay with his mother in Pickax for a while. But what about the show? Who'll be your engineer?"

"Don't worry about it, Hixie. I have someone. Meanwhile, is there anything you need?"

"No, thanks."

Qwilleran started to leave, but remembered the snapshots in his pocket. "Did you ever meet Euphonia Gage?"

"No, but I saw her around town."

"I have pictures of her taken in Florida, and some of her friends look familiar. You may recognize them."

"*Donnez-moi.* I'm good at remembering faces." Hixie took the photos and studied them carefully. "I think I've seen a couple of these people before. Leave them, and if I get a noodle, I'll call you."

When he arrived back on Goodwinter Boulevard, Nancy's pickup was already parked in the side drive. He ushered her downstairs to the ballroom, where the stage was set for rehearsal.

"I remember this room when I was a little girl," Nancy said. "Mrs. Gage had dozens of little gold chairs around the walls. I always wished she'd give me one for Christmas. I wonder what happened to them."

"Who knows?" he remarked, in a hurry to get down to business. He explained the cue card and the equipment. Then they rehearsed the timing and ended with a complete run-through.

"Perfect," Qwilleran said. "Shall we wind up this session with a quick glass of cider in the library?"

Nancy dropped with familiar ease into the scooped-out library sofa, displacing the Siamese, who walked stiffly from the room. Now that she had his therapeutic ear to talk into, she talked—and talked—about living in Alaska, breeding dogs, working for a vet. It was dinnertime before she drove away.

While Qwilleran was puttering around the kitchen Hixie phoned. "I'm checking out and moving in with Dr. Herbert's mother! He says she was born in Paris. I can brush up on my French! Shall I mail these Florida snapshots back to you?"

"If it isn't too much trouble. Did anyone look familiar?"

"Well," said Hixie, "there's a man with upswept eyebrows. And a young woman in a yellow convertible—"

"They're the ones," he interrupted. "Who are they?"

"I'm not sure, but . . . do you remember the gate-crashers at the preview of our show? The woman was wearing an obvious wig."

"Thanks, Hixie. That's all I need to know."

Qwilleran returned to the kitchen. The Siamese were on top of the refrigerator. "What were Betty and Claude doing in Pickax?" he asked them. "And why did they attend the preview?"

NINE

QWILLERAN was inclined to discount the tales of the Big Snow. For six winters he had heard about this local bugaboo, which was never as nasty as predicted. Yet every year the residents of Moose County prepared as if for war: digging in, mobilizing snowplows and blowers, deploying volunteers, and stockpiling supplies.

Friday morning he was drinking coffee when suddenly Koko heard something! The cat stretched his neck, swiveled his noble head, and slanted his ears toward the foyer. Qwilleran investigated. There was a moving van across the street, backing into Amanda Goodwinter's driveway. She was Junior's relative, a cantankerous businesswoman, and a perennial member of the city council.

Qwilleran hurried into boots and parka. The truck had lowered its ramp, and Amanda was directing the operation. She looked dowdier than ever in her army-surplus jacket and unfastened galoshes.

"Amanda! What's going on here?" Qwilleran hailed her.

"I'm moving to Indian Village. The house is sold. Good riddance! I always hated it."

"Who bought it?"

"Some real estate vulture from Down Below— Stop! Stop!" She screamed at the movers, who were struggling with a walnut breakfront. "You're scratching the finish! Watch the glass doors!"

At the same moment a moving van pulled up to the Wilmot house. Qwilleran adjusted the hood of his parka and trudged the length of the boulevard, counting for-sale signs. There were only four left, out of a recent seven.

As Qwill arrived back home Nick Bamba was just pulling in to the driveway. "Come on in, Nick, and have a hot drink," he said hospitably.

"Not this time," Nick declined. "I have a dozen errands to do." He handed over a folder. "Here's your correspondence from Lori, and I've brought my tool kit. I'll pick the lock in the library. Are you all ready for the Big Snow?"

Qwilleran said, "My vast experience convinces me that it's never as big as the kerosene dealers would have us believe."

"How long have you been here? Five years? Six? The seventh year is always the really big one. Trust me!" Nick tackled the closet lock in professional fashion while dispensing advice. "You need a camp stove and kerosene heater in case of a long power outage; canned food, not frozen, in case you're snowbound. Remember not to use your elevator after it starts to snow hard; you could be trapped in a blackout." Nick opened the closet door, collected his tools, and accepted Qwilleran's thanks on the way out.

Koko lost no time in entering the closet. It was filled with files in boxes and drawers, and a small safe stood open and empty. When Qwilleran left to go shopping for canned food, the cat was sitting in the safe like a potentate in a palanquin.

Throughout the weekend a storm watch was in effect, but Suitcase Productions presented all scheduled shows to capacity audiences. Monday afternoon Wetherby Goode announced a storm alert and said he was prepared for the worst; he had a sleeping bag in the studio, as well as a package of Fig Newtons.

Monday evening Koko and Yum Yum began to behave abnormally, dashing about and butting furniture. They showed no interest in food. Eventually Qwilleran escaped to his bedroom, but he could still hear madcap activity. He slept fitfully.

Shortly after daybreak a peaceful calm settled on the house. Peering out the window, he witnessed a rare sight: the entire sky was the vivid color of polished copper. By midmorning large flakes of snow began to fall. Shortly after, the wind rose, and soon fifty-mile-an-hour gusts were creating blizzard conditions.

At noon a WPKX weather bulletin announced: "A storm of unprecedented violence is blasting the county. Visibility is zero. Serious drifting is making roads impassable. All establishments are closed with the exception of emergency services. Stay indoors. Conserve water, food, and fuel. Be prepared to switch radios to battery operation. And stay tuned for further advisories."

On Goodwinter Boulevard it was snowing in four directions: down, up, sideways, and in circles. The Siamese, having accomplished their advance warning, settled down to sleep peacefully.

At three o'clock the power failed, and when Qwilleran tried to call Polly, the telephone was dead. The blizzard continued relentlessly, hour after hour, and he experienced the unnerving isolation of a house blanketed with snow. The unnatural stillness left a muffled void that only amplified the howling of the wind.

The blizzard lasted sixteen hours, during which Qwilleran found he could neither read nor write nor sleep. Then the wind subsided. The Big Snow was over, but it had been the worst storm in the history of Moose County. Drifts of fifteen to thirty feet buried buildings and walled up city streets and country roads.

For the next two days Qwilleran lived without power, telephone, mail delivery, or sociable pets. Koko and Yum Yum appeared to be in hibernation on the library sofa. His own intention to write a month's supply of copy for the newspaper was reduced to a state of jittery boredom. Even when snowplows started rumbling about the city streets, residents were still imprisoned in their houses.

On the morning of the fourth day, Qwilleran was in the library, eating a stale doughnut and drinking instant coffee prepared with not-quite-boiling water, when the shrill and unexpected bell of the telephone startled him and catapulted the Siamese from their sofa. It was Polly's exultant voice: "Plug in your refrigerator!"

"How are you, Polly? I worried about you," he said.

"Bootsie and I weathered the storm, but I lacked the energy to do anything. How are you faring?"

"I'm getting tired of canned soup and stale doughnuts."

"We'll be prisoners for a few days more, but fortunately we're in touch with the outside world."

Qwilleran immediately called the outside world, but all the lines were busy.

WPKX went on the air with more storm news, good and bad: "The first baby born during the Big Snow is a seven-pound girl, Leslie Ann. The parents are Mr. and Mrs. Junior Goodwinter. Mother and child are snowbound at the Pickax hospital.

"In rural areas many persons are reported missing. It is presumed that they lost their way in the blizzard and froze to death. Homes have burned down because help could not reach them."

The sound of Polly's voice restored Qwilleran's spark of life. He did some laundry, washed the accumulation of soup bowls, and eventually reached Junior to offer his congratulations.

"Yeah, I got Jody to the hospital just before the storm broke and then had to rush home to take care of our little boy. I still haven't seen the baby," Junior said. "But Qwill, let me tell you about the call I got from Down Below just before the phones went dead. It was some guy who wanted to buy the light fixtures and fireplaces in Grandma's house! How do you suppose he found out what we've got?"

"I could make a guess. How valuable are the fixtures?"

"Susan Exbridge could tell you. I only know that the chandeliers on the main floor are real silver and the ones in

the ballroom are solid brass and copper. Anyway, I told him to get lost."

After five o'clock Qwilleran phoned Celia Robinson. "Good evening," he said in the ingratiating tone that had melted female defenses for years. "This is Jim Qwilleran."

"Oh! Thank you so much for the chocolate cherries," she gushed. "They're my absolute favorite! But you didn't have to do it."

"It was my pleasure. By the way, Celia, I'm working on my profile of Mrs. Gage and need to ask a few more questions."

"You know I'm glad to help, Mr. Qwilleran."

"All right. Going back to the morning when you found her body, what did you do?"

"I called the office, and they called the authorities."

Casually he asked, "And how did Betty and Claude react?"

"Oh, they weren't here. They were out of town, and Pete was in charge. He's the assistant—very nice, very helpful."

"Do Betty and Claude go out of town very often?"

"Well, they're from up north, and they go to see their families once in a while."

"Where up north?" he asked, as if mildly curious.

"It could be Wisconsin. I'm not sure. Want me to find out?"

"No. It's not important. But tell me, did Mrs. Gage ever mention her mansion in Pickax? It was in her husband's family for generations."

"I know," said Celia. "She showed a video of it in the clubhouse. We visited some historic homes down here, and she thought we'd like to see an old house up north. She had some wonderful things."

"Did Mr. Crusoe see the video?"

"Crocus," she corrected. "Yes, and he still talks about it. Today he told me something confidential. I'm not supposed to mention it until it's official, but I can tell you. She left a lot of money to the park to build a health club."

"How did he know about it?"

"She told him. They were very good friends. We all thought it would be nice if they got married. That's why it's so sad."

"Yes," Qwilleran murmured; then he asked, "Do you suppose Mr. Crocus would care to be interviewed for this profile?"

"I don't know. He's kind of shy, but I could ask him."

After the call Qwilleran dropped into the leather chair to think, and Yum Yum walked daintily into the library. "Hello, princess," he said. "Where have you been?"

Taking that as an invitation, she leaped lightly to his lap. He asked, "What happened to your confrere?"

The muted answer came from the closet—a series of soft thumps that aroused Qwilleran's curiosity. He excused himself and went to investigate. Koko was batting an object this way and that. It was a small maroon velvet box.

Qwilleran intercepted it and immediately called Junior again. "Guess what Koko has just dredged up! A jeweler's box containing a man's gold ring, probably your grandfather's!"

"What kind of ring?"

"A signet, with an intricate design on the crown. I'll turn it over to you as soon as they dig us out. By the way, I've just been talking to Celia Robinson. Did you know your grandmother had a video of the house when it was still furnished?"

"Sure. She had me film the interior before she broke it up."

"Well, she showed the film at the Park of Pink Sunsets, so we can assume that the park management knew about the lavish appointments. Now I'm wondering if they came to see for themselves. Listen to this, Junior. Betty and Claude were in this house when we previewed *The Big Burning.*"

"How do you know?"

"Hixie and I saw them. We both wondered who they were. Since then we've identified them from snapshots Celia sent us. Now you know that nobody stops in Pickax on the way to somewhere else. They come for a purpose or not at all, and Betty and Claude don't strike me as duck hunters. They must have known about the preview. Could Euphonia have told them? Did she know about it?"

"Jody wrote to her once a week and probably mentioned it. Grandma would be interested because the script was based on her father-in-law's memoirs."

Qwilleran said, "Frankly, I've had doubts about the Pink Sunset operation ever since you told me they profiteer on the repurchase of mobile homes. Are they also in partnership with the guy who wanted to buy the light fixtures? We may have uncovered a story that's bigger than a profile of your eccentric grandmother."

"Wow! When it breaks," Junior said, "let's keep it exclusive with the *Moose County Something!*"

GRADUALLY MOOSE COUNTY struggled out from under the snow as armies of volunteers swarmed over the neighborhoods, tunneling through to buried buildings.

Qwilleran finally reached Hixie by phone. "Your line's constantly busy," he complained.

"I'm working on the Christmas parade," she explained. "The *Something* is co-sponsoring it with Lanspeak's Department Store."

"Are you comfortable where you're staying?"

"*Mais oui!* Madame Herbert is a *joli cœur!* Dr. Herbert is coming down from Brrr for Thanksgiving, and Madame is doing stuffed quail. What about you?"

"Polly is roasting a turkey, and Arch and Mildred will join us."

When he hung up, both cats reported to the library, having heard the word turkey.

"Sorry. False alarm," he said.

Koko, returning to work after the storm, was excavating the library closet and leaving a paper trail of newspaper clippings, envelopes with foreign stamps, and such. One was a yellowed clipping from the *Pickax Picayune*, the antiquated predecessor of the *Moose County Something*. It was a column headed MARRIAGES, and one of the listings attracted Qwilleran's attention:

> Lena Foote, daughter of
> Mr. and Mrs. Arnold Foote of Lockmaster,
> to Gilbert Inchpot of Brrr, Oct. 18.

The year 1961 had been inked in the margin. That date would be about right, Qwilleran figured, guessing at Nancy's age. Lena Foote was her mother and also Euphonia's longtime housekeeper. He put the clipping in an envelope addressed to Nancy, adding thanks for her assistance with the shows.

On the sixth day following the Big Snow, Qwilleran arranged to meet Junior for lunch at Lois's; he wanted to deliver the gold ring and another item of interest that Koko had unearthed.

When it was time to leave, the jeweler's box was missing and the desk drawer was ajar. "Drat those cats!" Qwilleran said aloud. He knew it was Yum Yum's fine Siamese paw that had opened the drawer, but he suspected it was Koko who assigned her the nefarious little task, like a feline Fagin. There was no time to search; he hustled off to Lois's, where Junior was waiting in a booth.

The editor's first words were, "Did you bring Grandpa's ring?"

"Dammit! I forgot it," said Qwilleran, an expert at extemporaneous fibs.

"Today's special," Lois announced as she slapped two soiled menu cards onto the table, "bean soup and ham sandwich."

"Give us a minute to decide," Qwilleran said. He handed Junior an old envelope postmarked LOCKMASTER, 1929. The letter inside was addressed to "My dearest darling Cynara."

"Read it," Qwilleran ordered.

Nov. 17, 1929

My dearest darling Cynara—

Last night I climbed to the roof of the horse barn—and looked across to where you live—thirty miles—but I can still feel you—smell your skin—fresh as violets—After sixteen months of heaven—it's hell to be without you—I want to climb to the top of the silo—and jump down on the rocks—but you've suffered enough for my sake—And so my darling—I'm going away—and I beg you to forget me—I'm returning the ring—maybe some day we'll meet in sweetness and in light—Good-bye—my Cynara—

The signature was simply "W." When Junior finished reading it, he said, "How could Grandma fall for such rot?"

"She was young in 1929."

"In 1929 Grandpa was in prison. She couldn't face the scandal in Pickax, so she went to stay in Lockmaster for two years—on somebody's horse farm. It looks as if it turned out to be fun and games."

Qwilleran said, "This horse farmer was obviously the other butterfly in the poem."

Lois advanced on their booth with hands on hips. "Are you young punks gonna order? Or do you want to pay rent for the booth?"

Both men ordered the special, and Junior said, "Grandpa got out of prison in time for the stock market crash."

"That was the month before this letter was written."

There was a thoughtful pause. Then Junior asked, "Where is Koko finding these choice items all of a sudden?"

Pompously Qwilleran said, "I cannot tell a lie. I picked the lock of the library closet. There are tons of paper in there. One thing Koko found was an announcement in the *Picayune* of Gil Inchpot's marriage to Euphonia's housekeeper Lena."

"I knew Lena," said Junior. "She was Grandma's day help for years. After that, there was a series of housekeepers who never stayed long. Grandma was hard to get along with in her old age."

"What about Gil Inchpot? Do the police have any suspects?"

"Haven't heard. The Big Snow brings everything to a halt."

Their discussion was interrupted by the slam-bang delivery of two daily specials. They ate in silence until Junior inquired about Suitcase Productions.

"Several organizations want us after the holidays. We did three shows just before the Big Snow."

Lois returned, brandishing the coffee server like a weapon.

"I'm due back at the office," said the young editor.

"You go ahead. I'll get the check," Qwilleran told him. "And Lois, you can bring me some of your apple pie. I dreamed about it all the time I was snowbound."

"Liar!" she retorted, and she bustled away, smiling.

As SOON as Nancy Fincher received Qwilleran's letter, she telephoned him. "Thanks for the clipping about my parents."

"Mrs. Gage must have had a high regard for your mother."

"Oh, yes. She relied on Mom a lot, and Mom loved Mrs. Gage. She didn't like Mr. Gage, though. He was too friendly, she told me."

Qwilleran asked, "Why did she continue to work for them after her marriage?"

"Well, you see, Mom and Pop needed the money to get their farm started. Besides, she loved working in the big house. I took care of our farmhouse, starting when I was nine years old."

"Remarkable," Qwilleran murmured. "So your mother's maiden name was Foote. Did you keep in touch with your grandparents in Lockmaster?"

As before, Nancy was eager to talk. "No. It's funny, but I never saw them until they came to Mom's funeral."

"What was the reason for that?"

"I don't know. I had Grandma and Grandpa Inchpot right here in Brrr, and Mom never talked about her own parents."

"How did you react to them at the funeral?"

"I didn't like them at all. They made me nervous, the way they stared at me. They were very old, of course."

Qwilleran asked, "Did it ever occur to you that your Lockmaster grandparents might have lent your father the money for his farm improvements after your mother died?"

"No way," she said. "They were only poor dirt farmers. Not everybody in Lockmaster is a rich horse breeder. . . . Well anyway, Mr. Qwilleran, I wanted to thank you and wish you a happy Thanksgiving."

IT WAS a thankful foursome that gathered in Polly's apartment, free after a week of confinement. The aroma of Thanksgiving was driving Bootsie to distraction, and the aroma of Mildred's mince pie was having much the same effect on Qwilleran and Arch Riker.

Polly carved, pacifying Bootsie with some giblets, and the four sat down to the traditional feast. "Beautiful bird!" they all agreed.

"Now let's discuss the wedding," Polly suggested as they ate. "What are the plans so far?"

The bride-to-be said, "It'll be at the Lanspeaks' house on Purple Point, and we're all invited to stay for the three-day weekend."

Riker said, "It's black tie, Qwill, so dust off your tux."

"Black tie!" Qwilleran echoed in dismay. "My dinner jacket, cummerbund, evening pumps—they're all in a closet in my barn, behind twenty feet of snow."

"You can rent an outfit," Riker said calmly, "but what will you do about your cats? I believe they're not invited."

Polly said, "My sister-in-law will come over twice a day to feed Koko and Yum Yum as well as Bootsie."

Everyone had seconds of the bird and the squash puree with cashews. Then the aromatic mince pie was consumed and praised, and coffee was poured, during which the telephone rang.

Polly answered and said, "It's for you, Qwill."

It was Hixie. "I hate to bother you, Qwill. But Carol Lanspeak just called. We have a problem."

"What kind of problem?"

"Larry was scheduled to play Santa in the parade on Saturday, and he's on the verge of pneumonia," Hixie said anxiously. "Carol and I wondered if you would substitute."

"You're not serious."

"I'm not only serious, I'm desperate! When Carol gave me the news, my foot started to throb again."

Huffing into his mustache, Qwilleran was alarmingly silent.

"What would it entail?" he finally asked in a grouchy monotone.

"First of all, you'll have to try on Larry's Santa suit. It's in the costume department at the theater."

"I suppose you know," he reminded her, "that Larry is three sizes smaller and three inches shorter than I am."

"But Carol says the suit is cut roomy, and we could alter the length of sleeves and pants. We don't need to worry about the beard and wig; one size fits all."

"And what happens on Saturday?"

"You get into costume at the theater, and Carol drives you to the Dimsdale Diner, where the parade units will assemble. The parade proceeds south on Pickax Road to Main Street, where the mayor gives you the official greeting."

"And what am I supposed to be doing?"

"Just wave at people and act jolly."

"I won't feel jolly," he grumbled. "I'm doing this only for your foot, Hixie . . . *ma chérie,*" he added tartly.

When Qwilleran returned to the dinner table, the others regarded him with concern.

"I need another piece of pie," he said.

LATER, when he returned from Polly's apartment with a generous serving of the bird, he was met by two excited Siamese. "Ho, ho, ho!" he boomed with simulated jollity. They fled from the room.

"I beg your royal pardons," he apologized. "I was practicing."

While they devoured the plateful of light and dark meat with studious concentration and enraptured tails, he collected the loot under the kitchen table: an innersole, a napkin ring, and the jeweler's box that they had pilfered from the desk drawer.

"You rascals!" he scolded affectionately.

In the library, he examined the ring once more. It was now clear that the initials entwined on the crown were W. and E. There was also an intimate inscription inside the band, with the initials E.R.G. and W.B.K. Then Koko leaped to the desk top and showed unusual interest in the gold memento, touching it gingerly, as if it might bite. Qwilleran tamped his mustache as he questioned the cat's reaction. Was he simply attracted to a small shiny object? Or did he detect hidden significance in the ring? But what? Koko could sense more with his whiskers than most humans could construe with their brains. Unfortunately, he had an oblique way of communicating, and Qwilleran was not always smart enough to read him. Life with Kao K'o Kung had taught him to pay attention, even though he sometimes felt like a fool.

TEN

THE day after Thanksgiving, Qwilleran was still pondering the significance of the signet ring when he drove downtown to the newspaper office to hand in his copy.

Junior greeted him in high spirits. "Hixie tells me you're going to be our Santa Claus. You'll be terrific."

"I don't know about that, but I'll give it my best shot," he replied as he handed Junior the jeweler's box.

"My grandfather's ring."

"Guess again. Look inside the band."

"Wow," said Junior when he looked. "So W.B.K. must be 'W.'— the man in the letter who wanted to jump off the silo."

"It would be interesting to know if Euphonia's boyfriend in Florida spells his name with a K. I'll have to check it out."

"I haven't told you the latest," said Junior. "In probating Grandma's will, we're having trouble finding enough assets to warrant contesting it. The bank records show huge deposits at the time she liquidated everything. After that, there were sizable withdrawals, as if she'd invested in securities. But we don't find any documents."

"Some old people are afraid of banks," Qwilleran said. "She may have hidden them. Or . . . you may not be aware of this, Junior, but Gil Inchpot spent heavily on farm improvements in the last two or three years, and no one knows where he got the money. Did Euphonia lend it to him on the strength of her affection for Lena?"

"Hey! That makes sense," said Junior. "Some time back, Inchpot called me here at the office, asking for her address in Florida. He owed her some money and wanted to repay the loan."

"You gave him her address?"

"Sure. But if he paid her, what the devil happened to the dough! She couldn't have lost it all at the racetrack."

"When she decided to bequeath a health spa to the park, Junior, didn't she know her fortune was dwindling? Or did that happen after she wrote her new will?"

"Well, I don't know, but Wilmot is exploring the possibilities."

Qwilleran smoothed his mustache. "More and more I think the Florida operation is shady. There's a lawyer who writes cheap wills. He could be in on it. How about the dealer who liquidated Euphonia's treasures?" Qwilleran started to leave. "It just might be a well-organized crime ring!"

"Don't go, Qwill. This is getting good!"

"I have an appointment to try on my Santa Claus suit."

En route to the theater Qwilleran realized that his attitude toward the Christmas parade was mellowing. He could visualize himself riding in a sleigh behind a horse decked out in jingle bells. The experience might make a good topic for his column.

At the K Theatre, Carol Lanspeak and the seamstress were waiting for him, and Carol said, "We really appreciate your cooperation in the emergency, Qwill. Try on the pants first."

Qwilleran squeezed into the red breeches. "They're a good length for clam digging," he said.

Mrs. Toddwhistle, who worked on costumes for the Theatre Club, said, "I have some red fabric, and I can add about six inches to the length—also a stirrup to keep them down in your boots."

The coat was roomy enough for two bed pillows under the belt, although snug through the shoulders and under the arms. The sleeves could be lengthened, the women assured him. Everything would work out just fine! He would make a wonderful Santa!

With that matter settled, he telephoned Celia Robinson. "Did you enjoy Thanksgiving, Celia?" he began.

"Oh, yes, it was very nice. About thirty of us went in the bus to a real nice restaurant. We had a reservation. It was buffet."

"Did Mr. Crocus go with you?"

"No, he didn't feel like it. He remembers last Thanksgiving, when Mrs. Gage was with us and read a poem. She wrote it herself."

"I said I'd send him a program but got sidetracked by the Big Storm. How does he spell his name?"

"I think it's C-r-o-c-u-s, like the flower."

"Are you sure? What's his first name?"

"Gerard. He has a shirt with G.F.C. embroidered on the pocket. Mrs. Gage gave it to him, and he wears it all the time."

Reluctantly Qwilleran abandoned the long-lost-lover theory. "Did you ask him if he'd speak with me about Mrs. Gage?"

"Yes, I did, Mr. Qwilleran, but he said it wouldn't be in good taste. I don't feel that way. I'd like to see you write a beautiful article about her, and if there's anything more I can do . . ."

"You've been a great help, Celia, and— Yes, there is more you can do. I believe I've uncovered something in the Park of Pink Sunsets that's a bigger story than Euphonia Gage."

"You don't mean it!" she said excitedly. "Is it something nice?"

Qwilleran cleared his throat. "No, it isn't *nice*. I believe there's activity in your community that is unethical, if not illegal."

With sudden sharpness she said, "You reporters are always trying to dig up dirt and make trouble! This is a lovely place for retirees like me. I don't want anything more to do with you!" And she slammed the receiver.

"Well! How do you like that?" Qwilleran asked the bookshelves.

"Yow!" said Koko from his reserved seat in the safe.

"Did I strike a raw nerve? Celia may be part of the ring—a simple, fun-loving grandmother mixing with the other residents and singling out the likely victims. Now that she knows we suspect their game, what will she do?"

He decided to wait and see.

THE day of the parade was sunny but crisp, and Qwilleran wore his long underwear for the ride in an open sleigh. He assumed it would be a sleigh and not a convertible with the top down.

At the theater, where he went to get into costume, he found the breeches equipped with stirrups, which made them rather taut for comfort. Carol strapped him into his bed pillows and helped him into his coat. The sleeves had been extended with white fake fur.

"I look as if I had both arms in a cast," he complained. He found it difficult to bend over. Carol had to pull on his boots.

"How is the fit?" she asked.

"I feel as if I'm wearing snowshoes. Why does the old geezer have to look seventy-five pounds overweight? Even as a kid I doubted that he could come down a chimney."

"Would you ruin a thousand-year-old image, Qwill?" Carol powdered his mustache, reddened his cheeks, and adjusted the wig and beard before adding a red hat with a floppy pointed crown.

"I feel like an idiot!" he said.

They drove north in the Lanspeak van along Pickax Road, the sun glaring on the snowy landscape. Qwilleran had left his sunglasses at the theater, and the scene was dazzling. Already the parade route was filling up with cars, vans, and pickups loaded with children.

Carol said, "The welcoming ceremonies will be in front of the store, and when you arrive, Hixie's secretary, Wilfred, will meet you and tell you what to do."

They were approaching the Dimsdale Diner. "What kind of conveyance do you have for jolly old Saint Nick?" he asked.

"Oh, didn't Hixie tell you?" she said, eager to break the news. "We've arranged for a dogsled with eight Siberian huskies!"

Parade units were gathering around the snowy intersection: floats, a brass band on a flatbed truck, a fire truck, a group of cross-country skiers, and a yelping dog team.

"We meet unexpectedly," Qwilleran said to Nancy. He assumed it was Nancy; the glare was distorting his vision.

"No one told me you were going to be Santa," she said with delight. "There's a bale of hay in the basket for you to sit on, and I covered it with a caribou skin. Isn't this exciting? I wish my mom could see me now—driving Santa Claus in a dogsled! Today would have been her birthday. It looks as if they're getting ready to start."

The band struck up, the sheriff's car led the way, and the parade units fell into place, with the dogsled bringing up the rear—Nancy riding the runners, Qwilleran in the basket. She drove the team with one-syllable commands: "Up! . . . Go! . . . Way!"

All along the route the spectators were shouting to Santa, and Qwilleran waved first one arm and then the other at persons he could not clearly see. Both arms were becoming gradually numb as the tight armholes hampered his circulation. When they turned onto Main Street, the crowds were larger and louder but just as blurred, and he was greatly relieved when they reached their destination.

Lanspeak's Department Store was built like a castle. An iron gate raised on heavy chains extended over the sidewalk, providing a marquee from which city officials could review the parade.

As the dogsled pulled up, Nancy said to Qwilleran, "I'll take the dogs behind the store until you've finished your speech."

"Speech! What speech?" he demanded indignantly.

"Mr. Qwilleran, sir," said a young man's voice coming out of the general blur.

"Wilfred? Get me out of this contraption! I can't see a thing without my sunglasses!"

"They're waiting for you up there," said the secretary. "I'll hold the ladder."

Only then did Qwilleran become aware of a ladder leaning against the marquee. "I can't bend my knees; my arms are numb; and I can't see. I'm not climbing up any damned ladder."

"You've got to," said Wilfred in panic.

Hundreds of spectators were cheering. Qwilleran walked to the foot of the ladder with a stiff-legged gait. "If I fall off this thing," he threatened, "both you and Hixie are fired."

He managed to lift one foot to the first rung and grasp the side rails. Then slowly he forced one knee after the other to bend, all the while hoisting the two bed pillows ahead of him. Cheers! Finally, at the top, helping hands hauled him onto the marquee.

There was a microphone, and the mayor said a few words of welcome. "And now . . . I give you Santa Claus," he concluded.

Qwilleran was steered to the mike. "M-er-r-ry Christmas!" he bellowed. Then he turned away and said in a voice that went out over the speakers, "Get me outa here. How do I get down?"

The store had a second-floor window through which the city officials had arrived, and Qwilleran climbed through it. Wilfred was waiting for him in the lingerie department. He said, "The dogs are being brought around front. It's on to lap sitting, Mr. Qwilleran."

"Lap sitting? What the devil is that?"

"They built a gingerbread house in front of the courthouse, and the kids sit on your lap and have their pictures taken."

"Oh, no, they don't," Qwilleran said fiercely. "I refuse flatly."

"Mr. Qwilleran, sir, you gotta!"

They rode down on the elevator and on the main floor heard a voice on the public-address system: "Paging Santa Claus."

"Where's a phone?" he snapped. When he found one, he yelled into the mouthpiece, "Yes?"

"Hey, Qwill!" It was Junior. "The city desk just had a strange phone call: Celia Robinson in Florida said she had to get in touch with you secretly. What's that all about? She's calling back to find out how to reach you. Extremely important, she says."

"Give her Polly's number," Qwilleran said. "Tell her to call around eight o'clock tonight."

"Whatever you say. Are you all through with your Santa stunt?"

"No," Qwilleran said in a matter-of-fact way. "I have to go to the courthouse for lap sitting."

IT WAS customary for Qwilleran and Polly to spend Saturday evening together, and this time the chief attraction was turkey leftovers, which she had prepared in a curry sauce.

"Tell me about the parade, dear," Polly inquired.

"I don't want to talk about it," he said in an even voice.

She knew better than to insist.

Exactly at eight o'clock the telephone rang, and he took the call in the bedroom, with the door closed.

The anguished voice of Celia Robinson blurted, "Oh, Mr. Qwilleran, I apologize for hanging up on you like that! I didn't mean a word of what I said, but I was afraid somebody would be listening in. I'm making this call from a phone in a mall."

"I thought the residents at the park had private numbers."

"We do! We do! But Clayton thinks the whole park is bugged. I always thought he was kidding, but when you mentioned something illegal, I got worried. Are you an investigator?"

Experience warned him that she might be part of the ring, yet a tremor in the roots of his mustache told him to risk the gamble. He had formulated a plan. He said, "I'm just a reporter with a suspicion that Junior's grandmother was a victim of fraud."

"Oh, dear. Are you going to expose it?"

"There's insufficient evidence at present, and that's where you can help. Are you willing to play a harmless trick on those who robbed Mrs. Gage? I believe your grandson would approve."

"Can I tell Clayton about it? I write him every week."

"You're not to confide in him or Mr. Crocus or anyone else. Consider yourself an undercover agent. You'll be rewarded for your time and cooperation, of course."

"I'm honored you'd ask me to help. Do you think I can do it?"

"No doubt about it, if you follow orders. You'll receive a briefing along with a check to cover expenses. Where do you get your mail?"

"It comes to the park office, and we pick it up there."

"That being the case," he said, "I'll send your orders to the post office, in care of general delivery. It should take two days."

"Oh, goody," Celia said. "Is this a sting?"

"You might call it that. Now, go home and say nothing."

He emerged from the bedroom patting his mustache with satisfaction, and he was very good company for the rest of the evening.

THE next day, as he worked on Celia's briefing, he thought, This may be the dumbest thing I ever did in my life—sending $5000 to a stranger who may be a double agent. And yet . . .

The document that went into the mail read as follows:

FOR YOUR EYES ONLY! Memorize and shred.
TO: Agent 0013½
FROM: Q
MISSION: Operation Greenback, Phase One
ASSIGNMENT: Your unmarried sister in Chicago has died, leaving you sole heir to a large house, valuable possessions, and financial assets. You wish to share your new fortune with your neighbors by giving a Christmas party on December 11 or 12. Notify the management that you will spend as much as $5000 on a caterer, florist, and live music. (A check for this amount will arrive under separate cover.) Observe the management's reaction to the above and report to Q. Watch for further briefings in the mail.

He prepared a second secret document to go out the next day:

MISSION: Operation Greenback, Phase Two
ASSIGNMENT: Ask the management about the possibility of moving into a double-wide. Test them by saying that your sister wished you to adopt her cat, who has a trust fund of his own of $10,000 a year. Ask for a special permit. Observe their reactions to the above and report to Q at HQ.

Qwilleran enclosed a card with his home phone number and instructions to call collect from a pay phone any evening between five and six o'clock. Then he waited. He wrote two columns for the *Moose County Something*. He looked at jewelry he'd had sent from Minneapolis and selected a Christmas present for Polly: a lavaliere and earrings of fiery black opals rimmed with discreet diamonds. He read more of *Robinson Crusoe* to the cats.

One early evening, as he was beginning to doubt the wisdom of enlisting Celia, he noticed that Koko was starting to bite the telephone cord.

A moment later the phone rang, and a hushed voice said, "This is Double oh thirteen and a half. Is it all right to talk?"

"By all means. I've been waiting for your report."

"Well!" she said in her normal voice. "I've been having a ball. Everybody's excited about the party, and Betty and Claude are falling all over me. They're giving me a special permit for the cat, and they're putting me at the top of the list for a double-wide."

"You're a good operative, Celia."

"Shall I go ahead and get a cat?"

"Wait a minute! Not so fast. In the interest of realism, the cat should be shipped from Chicago."

"I'm sorry. I'm just so excited! Clayton could bring it when he flies down for Christmas. What do I do next?"

"Keep checking the post office, and call whenever you have something to report."

Qwilleran had already plotted his next move. The following day he walked downtown to the store that had gold lettering in the window: EXBRIDGE & COBB, FINE ANTIQUES.

Susan Exbridge greeted him effusively. "Darling! You survived the Big Snow!"

Wandering through the shop, Qwilleran lingered over a pair of brass candlesticks a foot high, with thick, twisted stems, and chunky bases the size of a soup bowl. "I'll take them," he said. "Do you know how or where Euphonia sold her belongings?"

"I know how, but not where," said Susan. "I wanted her to work with some good dealers in New York, but someone in Florida offered her a lump sum for everything, and she fell for it."

"How much did they offer? Do you know?"

"No. But we can assume it was well under the going price."

He paid for his purchase and borrowed some magazines on antiques. Then on the way home he stopped at the Bushland Studio. Qwilleran asked John Bushland if he had any interior photos of his previous house in Lockmaster. The photographer's century-old house had a carved staircase, stained-glass windows, and converted gaslight fixtures. He supplied Qwilleran a complete set of prints.

The magazines that Qwilleran carried home contained dealer ads for choice antiques at five- and six-digit prices that shocked his frugal psyche. He made a list of items that would fit his scheme: Jacobean chair, gilded divan from India, four-poster brass bed in

Gothic style, a collection of botanical plates in porcelain—eighteenth century—and more. He omitted any reference to price. After photocopying the list at the library, he sent one copy to Susan Exbridge for appraisal, the other to Celia Robinson with a third briefing:

ASSIGNMENT: Your late sister was a collector of antiques and art objects. There are twelve rooms of such furnishings that you wish to sell, none of which you like. Ask the park management if they know how to go about it. Show them the enclosed list. Mention also that you must sell your sister's house. Show them the enclosed photos of the interior. Report their responses.

He was relieved when his agent made her second report.

"Oh, it was a wonderful party, Mr. Qwilleran," she began. "Everybody congratulated me on my inheritance."

"Did Mr. Crocus attend?"

"Well, I had to coax him, but he said he had a good time. No one in his family ever visits him. Maybe that's why he enjoys Clayton's company. They play chess together."

"And how did the management react to your questions?"

"They were quite helpful, and impressed with the photographs. They're going to show my list of furniture to a dealer, and he'll make an offer on the whole houseful. Guess what! Betty and Claude invited me to the dog races. It looks as if I'm in solid. And I did something on my own."

"What did you do?" Qwilleran asked sternly.

"I asked if my grandson could come for a whole week during the holidays, even though he's only thirteen. They said okay."

"I suppose you realize, Celia, that we're flirting with a security hazard. Clayton will want to know why the management is buttering you up. You'll have to tell him the truth."

"He can be trusted, Mr. Qwilleran. He won't give me away."

"Hmmm, let me think about this," Qwilleran said. "You say he plays chess with Mr. Crocus. Perhaps he could get the old man to unburden himself. Could Clayton handle this? Mr. Crocus knew about Mrs. Gage's bequest to the park; he might know other things."

"I'm sure Clayton could do it, Mr. Qwilleran. He's very bright."

"All right. It's worth a try," Qwilleran said. "Have Clayton bring a cat with him—full grown, because this is supposed to be your sister's cherished pet. You'll receive a check to cover the expenses."

After discussing a name for the cat at length, they decided to call him Wrigley, since he's supposed to be from Chicago. Celia enjoyed a laugh, and Qwilleran was in a good mood when he hung up.

The occasion seemed to call for a dish of ice cream, and while in the kitchen he picked up Koko's current collection. Items of more than usual interest were a purple satin pincushion embroidered "E.R.G.," obviously homemade, and a canceled check for $100—dated December 24, 1972—to Lena Inchpot. Was that the housekeeper's Christmas bonus from Mrs. Gage?

Of greatest interest was a yellowed envelope inscribed "Lethe" in what Qwilleran now knew to be Euphonia's handwriting. The envelope was sealed, and he used a kitchen knife to slit it. What he found was a birth certificate issued in Lockmaster County:

> *Date of birth:* Nov. 27, 1928
> *Name of child:* Lethe Gage
> *Sex:* female   *Color:* white
> *Name of mother:* Euphonia Roff Gage
> *Name of father:*

Qwilleran rushed to the telephone. "Brace yourself for some news, Junior," he said when his young friend answered. "You've got an aunt you didn't know about."

Junior listened to the reading of the certificate. "Can you beat that! That's when Grandpa was in prison. The father must have been the horse farmer."

"Here's the question," said Qwilleran. "Is Lethe still alive? Wouldn't she have come forward for a slice of the inheritance?"

"She might live somewhere else and not know Grandma's dead."

"Could be." Qwilleran thought of the foreign stamps on envelopes Koko had found. "In any case, you should notify the attorney."

ELEVEN

As Christmas approached, Qwilleran's mind was on Operation Greenback. Increasing tremors in the roots of his mustache told him he was on the right track.

One evening at five fifteen the phone rang and a hollow voice said, "This is Celia, Mr. Qwilleran."

"You sound different," he said.

"I'm calling from a different mall. The phones are more private. I had a scare the last time I talked to you."

"What kind of scare?"

"Well, after I hung up, I saw Betty and Claude watching me. They were waiting in line outside a restaurant. I didn't know what to do. Then I thought, What would Clayton do? He'd play it cool. So I walked over and said hello, and they invited me to have dinner with them. Whew! I was worried."

"You handled it very well," Qwilleran said. "Do you have anything to report on your last assignment?"

"Only that the furniture dealer down here will give me a hundred thousand dollars for the things on the list you sent me, plus fifty thousand dollars for everything else in the house. Boy! What I could do with that much money!"

The same list of antiques had been appraised by Susan Exbridge at $900,000. Qwilleran said, "Good job, Celia. Phase Four of Operation Greenback will be mailed tomorrow."

In mailing the briefing, he included a Christmas bonus with instructions to buy something exciting for herself.

ASSIGNMENT: Buy an expensive Christmas plant for the manager's office. Tell them you'll have a surplus of cash when you sell your sister's possessions; ask if they can recommend a safe investment. Inquire if it's possible to place bets on the dog races without going to the track, since you don't like crowds.

Although Qwilleran made generous Christmas gifts, there was not a shred of holiday decoration in his cavernous living quarters. Then Polly delivered a wreath studded with berries and tiny white lights. "For your library," she said. "Just hang it up and plug it in."

The pinpoints of light only emphasized the somber effect of the dark paneling as they sat on the sofa sipping hot cider.

They discussed cat-sitting arrangements for the Christmas weekend. Polly wanted to pick up a key for her sister-in-law. "Lynette lives only a block away, so she's happy to come twice a day."

Soon Koko sauntered in, carrying in his jaws a small square paper packet, which he dropped at Qwilleran's feet.

Picking it up, Qwilleran read the label: " 'Dissolve contents of envelope in three pints of water and soak feet for fifteen minutes.' Foot powder. Where did he find that?"

Polly was overcome with mirth. "Perhaps he's telling you something, dear."

"This isn't funny! He might lick the powder. It could be poisonous." Qwilleran dropped the packet into a desk drawer.

After Polly had gone, Qwilleran realized how many of Koko's discoveries were associated with feet: corn plasters, a man's sock, a woman's slipper, shoelaces, an innersole, a buttonhook—even a man's spat! As for the cat's occupation with Confederate currency, the canceled check, and the safe, was that related to the financial skulduggery?

Qwilleran pounded his mustache with his fist as a sensation on his upper lip alerted him. He glanced at his watch. It was not too late to phone Homer Tibbitt, the nonagenarian who lived in a retirement complex with his new octogenarian wife.

"Homer, this is Qwill," he said in a loud, clear voice. "I haven't seen you in the library lately. Aren't you doing any research?"

"Hell's bells!" the historian retorted. "She won't let me out of the house in winter!" His voice was high and cracked, but his delivery was vigorous. "Never marry a younger woman, boy! If I drop a pencil, she thinks I've had a stroke. So, what's on your mind?"

"Just this, Homer: You were in the Lockmaster school system for many years, and I wonder if you knew a family by the name of Foote. I'm curious about Lena Foote, who should have been a student between 1934 and 1946."

"Lena Foote?" said the former principal. "She must have been a good girl. The only ones I remember are the troublemakers."

Another voice sounded in the background, and Homer turned away to say to his wife, "You don't remember that far back!" This was followed by muffled arguing and then, "Do you want to talk to him? Here! Take the phone."

A woman who sounded pleasantly determined came on the line. "This is Rhoda Tibbitt, Mr. Qwilleran. I remember Lena Foote very well. I had her in high school English, and she showed unusual promise. Sad to say, she didn't finish."

"Did you know her parents? Her father was Arnold Foote."

"Yes, indeed! I begged her parents to let her get her diploma, but they needed the income. She went into domestic service at the age of fifteen. Do you know what happened to her?"

"Only that she died of cancer a few years ago, after a relatively short life," Qwilleran said. "Thank you, Mrs. Tibbitt, and tell that ornery husband of yours that your memory is better than his."

Qwilleran was disappointed. He had learned nothing about Nancy's mother, and yet . . . Koko almost always had a motive for his actions, and there were all those references to feet!

Before Qwilleran could plan his next move, he received an excited call from Celia Robinson. "I know it's after six o'clock," she said, "but I simply had to thank you for the generous check!"

"You're deserving," he replied. "How about your assignment?"

"I talked to Betty and Claude and wrote it all down," Celia said. "There's something called bearer bonds that would be good because my heirs could cash them easily if anything happened to me. Also there are some private boxes in the office safe, and I can have one for the bonds and any cash I don't want to put in the bank."

"Beautiful!" Qwilleran murmured.

"Clayton flies in tomorrow, and I'll explain the operation driving in from the airport. I can hardly wait to see Wrigley! Is it okay to call you during the holidays?"

"Of course. Have a merry Christmas, Celia."

"Same to you, chief."

As soon as Qwilleran hung up, Koko walked across the desk and faced him eyeball to eyeball, delivering a trumpetlike "Yow-w-w!" that pained the aural and olfactory senses.

"What's your problem?" Qwilleran asked. In answer, the cat knocked a pen to the floor and bit the shade of the desk lamp, then raced around the room—over the furniture, in and out of the closet, all the while uttering a rumbling growl.

When Koko staged a cat fit, it was a sure sign that Qwilleran was in the doghouse. "Oh-oh! I goofed!" he said, slapping his forehead. He had told Celia she could phone during the holidays, but he would be in Purple Point. He had been unforgivably thoughtless.

Koko had calmed down and was grooming the fur on his underside, and Qwilleran was faced with the problem of calling Celia on a phone that she insisted was bugged. He gave her an hour to drive back to the park before calling her mobile home.

In a tone of exaggerated jollity he said, "Just wanted to wish you a merry Christmas before *I leave town for the weekend.*"

"Oh," she said, unsure how to respond. "Where are you going, Mr. Qwilleran?"

"To a Christmas Eve wedding. My boss is getting married. You and Clayton have a happy holiday, Celia."

"Same to you . . . uh . . . Mr. Qwilleran."

Hanging up, he was sure she had got the message. He turned to say to Koko, "Thank you, old boy." But Koko wasn't there. He was in the closet, sitting in the safe.

ON THE morning of December 24 Qwilleran packed his rented formal wear for the wedding, all the while pondering the Euphonia Gage swindle. It was now clear to him what had happened to her money. Whether or not Clayton could coax anything out of Mr. Crocus, Qwilleran believed he had a good case for Pender Wilmot.

He called the attorney's new residence. A woman answered. "Hello? This is Mrs. Wilmot. May I help you?"

"This is Jim Qwilleran. I'd like to speak to Pender."

"Pender is having lunch with the Boosters, and then they're delivering Christmas baskets, but we'll see you at the wedding tonight."

"Perfect! I'll speak with him there."

In midafternoon Qwilleran picked up Polly for the drive to Purple Point. It was a narrow peninsula curving into the lake to form a natural harbor on the northern shore of Moose County. Viewed across the bay at sunset, it was a distinct shade of purple.

In the nineteenth century Purple Point had been the center of fishing and shipbuilding industries, but fire leveled the landscape, and hurricanes narrowed the peninsula to a mere spit of sand. Sportfishing revived the area in the 1920s as affluent families from Down Below built summer residences, which they called fish camps.

These dwellings were now called cottages, but were actually year-round vacation homes lining the road that ran the length of the peninsula. Sweeping winds raised havoc with sand or snow according to season. It was a surreal arctic landscape into which Qwilleran and Polly ventured on that Christmas Eve.

What the Lanspeaks called their cottage had a baby grand piano in the living room and four bedrooms on the balcony. The only reminder of the original fish camp was the cobblestoned fireplace. There were banks of white poinsettias, garlands of greens, and a large Scotch pine trimmed with pearlescent ornaments, white velvet bows, and crystal icicles.

When the guests started to arrive, a pianist sat down and began playing Chopin nocturnes. Among the guests was the Wilmot family, the bespectacled Timmie in a long-pant suit and bow tie. Hixie Rice hobbled in with her attentive doctor. They brought the officiating pastor with them, Ms. Donna Sims from the Brrr church.

At five o'clock the music faded away, and Mildred's daughter, Sharon, lighted the row of candles on the mantel. An expectant hush fell over the assembled guests. Ms. Sims, in robe and surplice, took her place in front of the fireplace, and the groom and best man joined her. In dinner jacket and black tie, the groom looked distinguished, and Qwilleran looked especially handsome. There was a joyous burst of music, and all eyes turned upward as Polly walked downstairs from the balcony in blue crepe and pearls. After a moment's suspense, Mildred—who had lost a few pounds—moved gracefully down the stairs in apricot velvet.

After the ceremony there were champagne toasts and the cutting of the cake. Eventually Qwilleran caught Pender Wilmot's eye, and the two men drifted into the library. The attorney said, "My wife says you called me."

"Yes. It's probably none of my business, but I've been researching a piece on Euphonia Gage, and a few facts about the Park of Pink Sunsets have aroused my suspicion."

"Their cavalier repurchase policy is enough to give one pause," Wilmot said.

"Right! That was the first clue. Then Junior told me about Euphonia's new will, written for her by an in-house lawyer."

Wilmot nodded soberly.

"There's more," said Qwilleran. "They have an associate who helps residents unload their valuables—and rips them off. One ostensibly wealthy woman was offered a lockbox in the office safe for financial documents and unreported cash. Who knows if they have extra keys? Shall I continue?"

"By all means."

"This woman has sent me snapshots that include the operators of the park, a couple called Betty and Claude. Now here's a curious fact: On the weekend Euphonia died, Betty and Claude were in Pickax, attending the preview of *The Big Burning*. I thought they were gate-crashers from Lockmaster, but they were evidently casing the place; shortly after, a dealer Down Below approached Junior about stripping the mansion of architectural features."

"He told me about that," said the attorney. "Let's live with this over the weekend, then get together downtown—" He was interrupted by hubbub outdoors. "Sounds like a pack of wolves out there."

It was a pack of huskies. Nancy Fincher and her dog team had arrived to transport the newlyweds to their honeymoon cottage. The guests bundled into wraps and went out on the porch. It was dark, and every cottage was outlined with strings of white lights.

"A magic village!" Polly said.

The bride and groom appeared in suitable togs and were whisked away, huddled in the basket of the sled. With Nancy riding the runners, they sped down the avenue of snow, while cottagers waved and cheered and threw poorly aimed snowballs.

Then the wedding guests departed, and Polly, Qwilleran, and the Lanspeaks had supper in front of the fireplace.

"Hixie arranged for the dogsledding," Carol said. "Nancy will be here for the next two days, taking kids for rides."

The evening passed pleasantly. From speakers on the balcony came recorded carols. At Qwilleran's request, Larry read a passage from Dickens' *Christmas Carol*. Then gifts were opened.

Polly was thrilled with the opals. She gave Qwilleran an old leather-bound set of Shakespeare's plays and sonnets.

"Wait till my bibliocat sniffs these," he said with detectable pride. He gave the Lanspeaks the pair of brass candlesticks.

The next morning the snowy landscape was bright with winter sunshine, and the frozen bay was dotted with the small shanties of ice fishermen. All day the telephone jangled with holiday greetings, and the dogsled could be seen flying up and down the white canyon. After Christmas dinner—Cornish hen and plum pudding—they walked to an open house at a neighboring cottage. Nancy Fincher was there, a guest for the weekend.

"Would you like to take a ride tomorrow?" she asked Qwilleran.

"I've had a ride," he said testily. He remembered the discomfort of the Santa Claus costume, and he also remembered a conversation with Nancy. "What was the date of the parade?"

Her answer was prompt. "November twenty-seventh. I know, because it was my mother's birthday."

Qwilleran's impulse was to telephone Junior immediately, but someone announced, "It's snowing, you guys. And the wind's rising. It looks like a blizzard's cooking."

The guests said hasty farewells, and Larry guided his party home through the swirling flakes.

"If there's drifting on the flats and the highway is buried, we'll be trapped," Carol said cheerfully.

The wind howled around the cottage, making Polly nervous, and Carol sent her to bed with aspirin and earplugs. Soon the rest of them retired as well.

THE morning after the blizzard the snowscape was smoothly sculptured by the wind, but the day was bright, and the air was so clear it was possible to hear the church bells on the mainland.

During breakfast Larry tuned in WPKX, and Wetherby Goode said, "Well, folks, the entire west side of Pickax is blacked out. And the Purple Point Road is blocked by ten-foot snowdrifts. So—" The announcement was interrupted by the telephone.

Carol answered and said, "It's for you, Polly."

"Me?" she said in surprise and apprehension. Conversation at the breakfast table stopped as she talked in the next room. Returning, she looked grave as she said, "Qwill, I think you should take this call. It's Lynette. She's calling from your house."

He hurried to the phone. "What's the trouble?"

"I'm at your house, Mr. Qwilleran. I stopped on my way to church to feed the cats, but I can't find them! They usually come running. I've searched all the rooms, but the power is off, you know, and it's hard to see inside the closets, even with a flashlight."

His mind hurtled from one dire possibility to another.

"But there's something else I should tell you, Mr. Qwilleran. Early last evening I drove to the carriage house first, to feed Bootsie. It was dark, but I had a glimpse of sort of a delivery van parked behind the big house. When I came downstairs a half hour later, it was gone. I didn't think much about it. Koko and Yum Yum gobbled their food and talked to me—"

"I'm coming home," he interrupted. "I'll get there as fast as I can."

"Shall I wait here?"

"No. There's nothing more you can do." He returned to the table. "I've got to get out of here fast. Lynette can't find the cats. I won't stop to pack." He was headed for the stairs. "I'll just grab my parka and keys. Polly can drive home with you."

"Qwill!" Larry said sternly, following him upstairs. "You won't be

able to get through! The highway is blocked by ten-foot drifts."

"Could a snowmobile get through?"

"Nobody's got one. They're outlawed on the Point."

Qwilleran pounded his mustache. "Could a dogsled get through?"

"I'll call Nancy," Carol said.

"Tell her to hurry!"

They were all on the porch when the dogsled and eight flying huskies arrived. Qwilleran was in his parka with the hood up.

Larry asked, "Can your dogs get through the drifts, Nancy?"

"We won't use the highway. We'll cross the bay on the ice. It'll be shorter anyway."

"Is that safe?" Polly asked.

"Sure. I've been ice fishing on the bay all my life."

Qwilleran asked, "Where do we touch land on the other side?"

"At the state park, near the lodge."

"Someone should meet me there and drive me to Pickax. Larry, try to reach Nick Bamba. How long will it take, Nancy?"

She estimated an hour at the outside. Carol gave them thermos bottles of hot tea and coffee.

"Stay close to shore!" Larry shouted as they took off down an easement to the bay.

Qwilleran sat low in the basket as they skimmed across the ice at racing speed. The high winds had left hillocks of snow and wrecked shanties, but Nancy guided the team between obstacles with gruff commands. The shoreline behind them receded quickly.

"Where are we going?" Qwilleran shouted.

"Taking a shortcut. There's an island out there," she called back. "It's reached by an ice bridge."

They encountered a strong wind sweeping across the lake from Canada, and they were grateful for their hot drinks when they stopped at the island to rest the dogs.

When they started out again, the wind was not quite as cutting. They sped along through a world of white—wintery sky overhead, shoreline in the distance. But soon they began to slow down, and Qwilleran could feel the runners cutting into the ice. The dogs seemed to find it hard going.

"It's softer than it should be," Nancy shouted. "It rained last week." She turned farther out into the lake, to a firmer surface.

Then Qwilleran saw a crack in the ice between the sled and the shore. "Nancy! Are we drifting?"

"Hang in there. We'll get around it."

She headed the team even farther out, and soon they were climbing a hill of snow. She stopped the dogs with a command. "From here you can see what's happening. The north wind pushed the loose ice into shore, but the offshore breeze is breaking it up. Stand up! You can see the ice bridge."

Qwilleran peered across the bay and saw only more slush and cracks. Lord! he thought. What am I doing here? Who is this girl? What does she know?

"Okay, let's take off! Up! . . . Go! . . . Haw!"

He clenched his teeth and gripped the side rails as they zigzagged across the surface. Slowly the distant shore was coming closer. At last he could see the roof of the lodge at the state park. Then he could see a car. Then he could see a man waving. Nick Bamba!

"Am I glad to see you." Qwilleran shouted. To Nancy he said, "Dammit, woman. You deserve a medal."

She smiled. It was a remarkably sweet smile.

"Where are you going from here, Nancy? Not back across the bay, I hope."

"No. I'll take the dogs home. It's only a few miles inland."

"What happened?" Nick wanted to know. "What's going on?"

"Start driving, and I'll tell you," Qwilleran said. "Drive fast!"

On the road to Pickax he summed up the situation: the missing cats, the strange van, the cat-sitter's frantic call. "I've been doing an unofficial investigation of some unscrupulous individuals," he said. "I had to get home, but the highway is blocked. Nancy proposed crossing the bay on the ice. When we got into slush and started drifting out on an ice floe, I thought it was the end."

"You didn't need to worry," Nick said. "That girl has a terrific reputation. She's a musher's musher."

"Have you heard anything more about her father's murder?"

"Only that the detectives think he was involved in something outside the county. The cause of death was a shot to the head."

When they reached Goodwinter Boulevard, Nick parked in the street. "Let's not mess up any tire tracks in the driveway. The power's still out, so take the flashlight that's under the seat. I've got a high-powered lantern in the trunk."

They walked to the side door, under the porte cochere.

Qwilleran said, "The tire tracks leading to the carriage house are Lynette's. She saw the van in the rear last evening, before the blizzard. If they broke in, it would be through the kitchen." He was speaking in a controlled monotone that belied the anxiety he felt.

"The van has been back again," Nick said. "I'd guess it was here again during the blizzard and left before the snow stopped."

Qwilleran unlocked the side door and automatically reached for a wall switch, but power had not been restored. The foyer was like a dark cave except for one shaft of light from a circular window on the stair landing, and in the patch of warmth was a Siamese cat, huddled against the chill but otherwise unperturbed.

"Koko!" Qwilleran shouted. "Where's Yum Yum?"

"There she is!" said Nick, beaming the lantern down the hall. She was in a hunched position, with rump elevated and head low—her mousing stance—and she was watching the door of the elevator.

At the same time there was pounding in the walls and a distant cry of distress. The two men looked at each other. "Someone's trapped in the elevator!" Qwilleran said in amazement.

Nick peered through the small pane of glass in the elevator door. "It's stuck between here and the basement."

There was more pounding and hysterical yelling, and Qwilleran rushed to the lower level. "Call the police!" he shouted up to Nick. "The phone's in the library!"

The beam of his flashlight exposed a ravaged ballroom. Electrical wires were hanging from the ceiling and protruding from the walls, and canvas murals were lying in rolls on the floor.

TWELVE

THE thwarted burglary on Goodwinter Boulevard was the subject of a news bulletin on WPKX Sunday afternoon. After the broadcast Junior was the first to call. "Hey, Qwill! Is there a lot of damage?"

"The ballroom's a wreck, but they didn't get anything on the main floor, thanks to the blackout. The light fixtures are still on the elevator. The murals are rolled up on the ballroom floor; I hope they can be salvaged."

"I'd better buzz over and take a look. Is the power back on?"

"It was restored while the police were here."

Minutes later, when Junior viewed the dangling wires and stripped walls, he said, "I can't believe this! Who did it? He wasn't named on the air, and our reporter couldn't get anything at police headquarters. The suspect won't be charged until tomorrow."

"Suspect! That's a laugh! He was caught red-handed when the cops arrived—trapped in the elevator with his loot. Chief Brodie himself was here. . . . Come into the kitchen." Qwilleran poured coffee and said, "It's my guess that he's the dealer who phoned you and wanted to buy the stuff. He's from Milwaukee."

Junior unwrapped a few slices of fruitcake. "What made him think he could help himself?"

"It wasn't his own idea—or so he swears. He had a partner, an electrician, who decamped with the van when the power failed. It was the dealer's van, and he was madder'n hell! He was glad to name his accomplice."

"So if the neighborhood hadn't blacked out, the rats would have gotten away with it."

"And if I hadn't come home when I did," Qwilleran said, "the suspect wouldn't be in jail."

"What brought you home, Qwill? I thought you were staying till Monday. And how did you get off the Point?"

"Regarding the latter question, read my column in Tuesday's paper. The other question . . ." He described the incident: the missing cats, the frantic phone call, the strange vehicle. "But when I walked in, there they were! Both cats. Acting as if nothing had happened. Where were those two devils hiding when Lynette was looking for them, and *why?* I'm convinced that Koko can sense evil, but did he know that their absence would bring me home in a hurry? . . . This is good fruitcake. Who made it?"

"Mildred. How did the thieves know you wouldn't be home?"

"That part gets complicated." Qwilleran smoothed his mustache. "With Celia Robinson's help, I've been collecting evidence about those con artists down there. She's been reporting to me from a mall, thinking her home phone is tapped. Just before Christmas I took a chance on calling her at home, and that's the only way those crooks could find out I'd be gone for the weekend. They'd connect my name with the Gage mansion. Betty and Claude were here, you remember, for the preview of our show. They're no dummies. They're professionals."

"It'll make a hot story," the editor said, "especially with the cats involved."

"Leave the cats out of it," Qwilleran said sternly. "If you want a hot story, get this, Junior: Your aunt Lethe was born on the same day as your grandmother's housekeeper and in the same place. In a county as small as Lockmaster was in 1928, how many girl babies would be born on November twenty-seventh? It's my contention that Euphonia paid a farm family to take Lethe and change her name to Lena Foote. That would make Nancy Fincher your cousin."

Junior gulped audibly. "That's a wild guess on your part."

"Okay. Send a reporter to Lockmaster to search the county records for a Lena Foote and a Lethe Gage born on the same day. I'll bet you a five-course dinner there's only one. More coffee?"

"No, thanks. I'll amble home and break the news to Jody that we have a pack of Siberian huskies for first cousins once removed."

Junior wandered out of the house in an apparent daze.

The Siamese were under the kitchen table, waiting for crumbs, and Qwilleran shared the last slice of fruitcake with them. They slobbered over it eagerly, careful to spit out the nuts and fruits.

ON MONDAY the snowbound Purple Pointers were able to return to town. An electrical contractor restored the ballroom fixtures, and an installer from a local design studio prepared to rehang the murals. Qwilleran wrote a column about his experience on the frozen bay, with paragraphs of praise for the musher's musher. And at five o'clock Celia Robinson called.

"Did you enjoy Christmas?" Qwilleran asked.

"Yes," she said in an unusually subdued manner. "We splurged on dinner, and Clayton had a real steak, not chopped."

"Did he bring Wrigley with him?"

"Yes. Wrigley's a nice cat. Black and white. But something odd is happening here. Pete, the assistant manager, went to Wisconsin for Christmas, and he hasn't come back. Betty and Claude haven't been seen since yesterday noon. There's no one in charge of the office. Clayton and I sorted the mail today, but everybody's upset."

"What is Claude's last name?"

"I think it's Sprott. Another thing, Mr. Qwilleran. I've decided to leave Florida. Too many old people. I'm only sixty-eight."

"Excellent idea!"

"But I'm babbling about myself. That was a funny phone call, but I figured out why you made it. Was it a nice wedding?"

"Very fine. Was Clayton able to carry out his assignment?"

"Didn't you get his tape? We mailed it Friday afternoon. When I told him what you wanted, he bought a little tape recorder to wear under his cap. He wore it when he visited Mr. Crocus."

"Mail is always slow in reaching Moose County. Celia, think back to the day you discovered Mrs. Gage's body. It was a Monday noon. She'd been dead sixteen hours, meaning she died Sunday evening. Did you see anyone go to her home on Sunday?"

"I can't recall right off the bat, but maybe Mr. Crocus will know. By the way, I put a holiday goodie in the package for you."

"That's very thoughtful of you, Celia. I'll watch for it."

WHEN Celia's package arrived on Tuesday, Qwilleran sank his teeth into a rich, nut-filled, chewy chocolate brownie and envisioned Celia transplanted to Pickax, baking brownies, catering parties now and then, laughing a lot. Then he abandoned his fantasy and listened to Clayton's tape. What he heard prompted him to phone Pender Wilmot and make an appointment with him immediately.

Wilmot's law office, in the new Klingenschoen Professional Building, was paneled in light teakwood, with chrome-based chairs upholstered in slate blue and plum.

The attorney showed Qwilleran to a seat. Then he asked, "What is the new development you mentioned?"

"The attempted burglary," Qwilleran began, "confirms my theory about the Pink Sunset management, and news of the arrest has obviously reached them through their assistant. He's undoubtedly the electrician who removed the light fixtures and stole the other fellow's van. All three have disappeared, according to my informant at the park. She has also sent me a taped conversation that warrants further investigation."

"Who made the tape?"

"Her thirteen-year-old grandson. He's friendly with an elderly resident who was a confidant of Mrs. Gage. The young man secreted a recorder under his cap when he went to see the old gentleman." Qwilleran started the tape. "The preliminary dialogue is irrelevant but interesting. He was probably testing the equipment."

As the tape unreeled, it produced the charming voice of a young woman and an adolescent baritone with falsetto overtones.

"Are you Betty? My grandma sent you this Christmas cactus. She's Mrs. Robinson on Kumquat Court."

"How sweet of her! And what is your name?"

"Clayton."

"Thank you, Clayton. Put it here on the counter so all the Sunsetters can enjoy it when they come in for their mail."

"Last year she gave a Christmas plant to the old lady next door, but she died. What was her name?"

"Mrs. Gage."

"What happened to her, anyway?"

"I'm afraid she accidentally took the wrong medication."

"How do you know?"

"We really don't like to talk about these things, Clayton."

"Why not?"

"It's so sad, and at this time of year we try to be happy."

"Was it written up in the paper?"

"Clayton, you'll have to excuse me. I have work to do."

"Can I help?"

"No, but it's kind of you to offer."

"I could sort the mail."

"Not now. Tell your grandmother we appreciate the plant."

"You're a very pretty lady."

"Thank you, Clayton. Now please . . . just go away!"

Wilmot chuckled. "His ingenuous performance is ingenious."

After a few seconds of taped silence, the adolescent voice alternated with the husky, gasping voice of an elderly man.

"Hi, Mr. Crocus! Remember me?"

"Clayton! I hardly recognized you. No beard this year."

"I shaved it off. Okay if I sit down?"

"Yes, yes . . . please!"

"Been doing any chess lately?"

"No one plays chess here."

"Not even your grandkids?"

103

"My grandchildren never visit. Might as well not have any."

"I don't have a grandpa. Why don't we work out a deal?"

(Slight chuckle.) "What terms do you propose?"

"We could play chess by mail, and I could tell you about school. I just made Junior Band. Do you still play the violin?"

"Not recently."

"Why not?"

"No desire. I've had a great loss. Mrs. Gage passed away."

"That's too bad. Was she sick long?"

"Sad to say, it was suicide."

"I knew somebody that did that. Depression, they said. Was she depressed?"

"She had her troubles."

"What kind of troubles?"

"One shouldn't talk about a friend's personal affairs."

"Our counselor at school says it's good to talk about it when you lose a friend."

"I have no one who's . . . interested."

"I'm interested, if you're going to be my grandpa."

"You're a kind young person." *(Pause.)* "Someone was taking her money . . . wrongfully."

"Did she report it to the police?"

"It was not . . . She didn't feel that she could do that."

"Why not?"

"She was being . . . blackmailed."

"That's bad! What was it about? Do you know?"

"A family secret."

"Did she say who was blackmailing her?"

"Someone up north. That's all she'd say. I told her to tell Claude."

"Why him?"

"She was leaving her money to the park, and she was afraid there wouldn't be any left."

"What did he say?"

"He said he could put a stop to it. But she worried about it. In a few days . . . she was gone."

"Did she leave a suicide note?"

"Not even for me. That grieved me."

"You must have liked her a lot."

"She was a lovely lady."

"Would you like a game of chess after supper, Mr. Crocus?"

"I would look forward to that with pleasure."

The attorney said, "So we know—or think we know—what happened to Mrs. Gage's money."

"We know more than that," Qwilleran said. "We know that she gave birth to a natural daughter in 1928 while her husband was in prison. In those days that was a disgrace. It's my contention that she gave her daughter—with certain stipulations—to a Lockmaster farm family, who raised her as Lena Foote. In her teens Lena went to work in the Gage household and remained there the rest of her life. I'm guessing that Euphonia continued to pay hush money to the foster parents. Lena lost contact with them, but they came to her funeral. Shortly afterward, Lena's widower began spending large sums of money for which there was no visible source. I say he's your blackmailer. The foster parents, being very old, may have passed on their secret to him—a kind of legacy for his daughter."

Wilmot listened intently. Qwilleran continued.

"When Mrs. Gage moved to Florida, the blackmailer obtained her address from her grandson, saying he owed her money which he wished to repay. He continued to hound her, until she confided in Claude Sprott. A few days later Gil Inchpot was murdered."

Wilmot was swiveling in his chair. "Sprott had a vested interest in Mrs. Gage's estate, of course. But if he arranged for Inchpot's murder, who pulled the trigger?"

Qwilleran was ready for the question. "When you and I talked about it at the wedding, Pender, I told you that Sprott and his companion were in Pickax, incognito, for the preview of *The Big Burning*. Now it occurs to me that they had flown up here not only to appraise the rare chandeliers. That was the weekend Inchpot disappeared. They probably rented a car and knocked on the door of his farmhouse, saying they were out of gas—after which they dropped his body in the woods and left his truck at the airport."

"Odd, isn't it, that they chose the Klingenschoen woods?"

"Not odd. Virtually unavoidable. Do you realize how many square miles of woodland belong to the Klingenschoen estate? And here's something else I've just learned," Qwilleran told the attorney. "As soon as their Milwaukee associate was arrested in my elevator and their Florida assistant became a fugitive in a stolen vehicle, they skipped the Park of Pink Sunsets."

"Let's catch the prosecutor before he goes to lunch."

AFTER a long session at the courthouse with the Moose County prosecutor, Qwilleran telephoned Celia Robinson. "I called to sing the praises of your chocolate brownies and to compliment your grandson on the tape," he said. "I assume no one is listening in."

"Nobody ever came back," she said in a tone of bewilderment. "The police have been here asking questions. Clayton and I have sort of taken charge of the office."

"Have you been able to recall anything about the Sunday that Mrs. Gage died?"

"Well, Mr. Crocus and I put our heads together," she said, "and we remembered that the electricity went off around suppertime. There was no storm or anything, but everybody on Kumquat Court, including Mrs. Gage, lost power, and Pete went to every home on the court, looking for a short circuit. That's all we can remember."

"Good enough!" Qwilleran commended her.

"Is there anything else I can do for you, Mr. Qwilleran?"

"I may have an idea to discuss with you later on. . . . Excuse me a moment. The doorbell's ringing."

"That's all right. I'll hang up. Happy New Year!"

It was Andrew Brodie at the door. "Come on in, Chief," Qwilleran said. "Is this a social call or did you come to talk shop?"

"Both. I'm on my way home." He followed Qwilleran into the library and dropped into the large, old leather chair. "What's happening on the boulevard?" he asked. "A lot of property's changing hands. There's a rumor that Klingenschoen money is behind it."

"I've nothing to say."

"You had plenty to say to the prosecutor's office today. I knew Inchpot," the chief said, "and I'd never figure him for a blackmailer. How come you came up with all those clues in the case when the state bureau was stymied? By this time I thought you would have come up with a clue to Euphonia's suicide."

"Well, let me tell you something, Andy. I think she was not the first victim of fraud at the mobile-home park, and I know for a fact she was not the first suicide." Qwilleran combed his mustache with his fingertips. "I have a hunch they were all murders. The management profited by a quick turnover. Rob 'em and rub 'em out!"

"You didn't tell that to the prosecutor!"

"I had nothing to support my suspicions when I was at the courthouse, but a phone call from Florida filled in some blanks."

"You know," said the chief, "I never thought that feisty woman would cash in like they said she did. Overdose, they said."

"It could have been a drop of poison in her Dubonnet. She always had an aperitif before dinner, I'm told. The medical examiner who wrote it off as suicide could have been an overworked civil servant or a link in the crime ring." The telephone jangled.

"Answer it," Brodie said. "I'll let myself out."

It was Junior. "Hey, Qwill! I just heard a terrific rumor! They say we're getting a community college in Pickax! And Goodwinter Boulevard is gonna be the campus! I hope it's true!"

"I don't see why it shouldn't be true," Qwilleran said calmly. And he lost no time in phoning Polly to assure her that her carriage house would not be affected.

"Are you involved, Qwill? Aren't you going to tell me what the rumors are?"

"No. You'll find out soon enough."

WITHIN hours Betty and Claude were picked up in Texas, near the Mexican border. Pete was arrested at an airport in Kentucky, having abandoned the stolen van. All three suspects would be arraigned on murder charges.

For Qwilleran the case was closed, and he entertained himself with speculations: if he had not rented the Gage mansion for the winter, Koko would not have discovered the historically important scrap of paper that led to *The Big Burning of 1869*, the mysterious deaths of Euphonia Gage and Gil Inchpot might have gone unsolved, and Pickax would not be getting a community college.

He plugged in the lighted Christmas wreath in the dingy library and relaxed in the leather chair with a cup of coffee. With refurbishing, he reflected, the library would make an impressive office for the president of the college. Yum Yum was lounging on his lap, her chin resting heavily on his right hand, forcing him to lift his coffee cup with his left. Koko was sitting on *Robinson Crusoe*, in the warm glow of a table lamp. It was a strange coincidence that the cat had chosen that title for their winter reading.

The Robinson connection was not the only coincidence. There were three desk drawers filled with junk destined for the trash can. Yet among them were articles clearly associated with the recent investigation: someone's denture, the 1928 birth certificate, a great deal of *purple,* and many items related to financial affairs. And then there was the safe! All these were obvious. It required a great leap of imagination, however, to link shoelaces and corn plasters with the Foote family. Nevertheless, Qwilleran had learned to give his imagination free rein when Koko telegraphed his messages. After all, it was a gold signet *ring* that finally suggested a ring of criminals in the Pink Sunset case. Was it all happenstance? he wondered.

"Yow!" said the cat at his elbow—a piercing utterance with negative significance.

If Qwilleran had any further doubts about Koko's role in the investigation, they were dispelled by the cat's subsequent behavior: He never sat in the safe again. He lost interest in *Robinson Crusoe.* He completely ignored the fifty closets.

Cats! Qwilleran thought. I'll never understand them.

For the remainder of the winter Koko was content to watch falling snowflakes from the window of the library, meditate on top of heat registers, chase Yum Yum up and down the stairs, and frequently bite her neck. She loved it!

Combine equal parts of mystery and mayhem, add a dash of feline fun, and there you have Lilian Jackson Braun's recipe for success—a series of sixteen delightful novels known as The Cat Who . . . mysteries.

A three-time winner of the Mystery Guild's Book of the Year award, the author draws her inspiration from the antics of her own two Siamese cats. A typical scene in the Braun household might include the author at her typewriter, one graceful Siamese sprawled across the desk and another skittering out of sight with a small object in its mouth. The object could be anything. The cat could only be Koko—of course.

Lilian Jackson Braun

Despite the influence of her pets, Braun is certain that the enormous popularity of her books—six million copies now in print—does not depend entirely on the presence of Koko and Yum Yum. "I have many devoted readers who don't particularly like cats," she says. "They read my books for the mystery."

Lilian Jackson Braun hasn't always been a mystery writer. Her professional career began with poetry when she was only sixteen and a Detroit newspaper agreed to publish her verses. Eventually she went on to become an editor for the Detroit *Free Press,* where she remained for three decades. Now that she's retired and writing books full time, she and her husband, actor Earl Bettinger, have left Detroit to live in the mountains of North Carolina. "There are too many distractions in the city," she says. "If you're going to write books, the country is better." Another aid to her writing: "Earl relieves me of a lot of household chores," she says. "He's a better cook than I am."

JOHN JAKES

HOMELAND

They came with only a dream. . . .

They found a land
bursting with hope,
with change,
with limitless
possibilities.

Part One
BERLIN
1891–1892

PAULI ✦ He thought, *Where's my home? It isn't here.*

From a flimsy shelf beside his narrow bed he pulled a wrinkled paper. It was a map of the world, torn from a book he'd bought at a secondhand shop with money he could ill afford to squander. He'd bought the whole book in order to have the map.

He scrutinized various locations as if he were able to choose any place on earth to live. But he was in Berlin, and that was that. Sometimes he loved the city; sometimes, as now, he felt trapped.

He had come home to Müllerstrasse at midnight, exhausted from work, and lay now under the old duvet, unable to sleep, studying the wrinkled map. Slowly he put it back on the shelf. It was almost two in the morning, and Aunt Lotte hadn't yet returned. Out with one of her *Herren,* he presumed. He worried about her. Once the kindest of women, now she was short with him, as if she disliked him. Hated having him around.

His room was windowless, part of a cellar flat, tiny and often damp. Aunt Lotte complained that it was messy—very un-German. That could be said of him too. His clothes were almost always awry, his pockets stuffed with chalk, crackers, scraps of paper on which he wrote down thoughts or things to do.

He was no longer in school; he'd never liked it and had dropped out over a year ago, though it was against the law. His name was Pauli Kroner. He was just fourteen years old.

He thought about the window of Wertheim's, the great department store on Leipzigerstrasse, where he had seen an exquisitely decorated globe. The globe's painted seas and continents seemed full of mysteries, possibilities, wondrous sights Pauli yearned to see. If only he had money to buy a globe like that . . .

ON A Sunday morning soon after, Pauli walked into the Tiergarten with a block of cheap paper under his arm. He looked older than his years. He was not handsome, but he had russet-brown hair, lively blue eyes, and wide shoulders. His sturdy build enhanced his masculinity. Whenever he was feeling good about himself, he exuded an air of strength and competence.

The great park was green and misty this summer morning. On a grassy hillock an old gentleman had laid aside his straw boater and gone to sleep. At a discreet distance Pauli dropped to his knees, smoothed the top sheet of paper, and rummaged in his pockets for a charcoal stick. He began to outline the sleeping man.

After four strokes he rubbed out what he'd done; the proportions were all wrong. Pauli tore the paper off the block and crushed it, cursing. Why did he keep it up? He wanted to draw the marvelous sights and subjects that abounded in the world, but his talent was poor. He struggled and struggled, and every time, he came out with nothing. Sometimes it seemed he had no talent for anything.

ONCE again Pauli was outside Wertheim's. It was late July; the long summer twilight was golden and warm. The street was crowded.

Pauli saw an old lady in black emerge from the store with a string bag. Suddenly a man sprang from the crowd and brutally shoved her to the ground. She cried out as he snatched the string bag and turned to flee through the crowd, in Pauli's direction.

Pauli didn't hesitate. He threw himself on the sidewalk. The thief couldn't stop in time, and tripped over the boy. Pauli grabbed the frayed hem of the thief's long coat and brought him down.

Wertheim's doorman appeared, but he ignored Pauli, clucking over the old woman and helping her into the store.

The thief tried to rise. Pauli sat on him. Two of the store's detectives came out to collar the man. Then the police arrived. They insisted Pauli accompany them to the station, where two stern detectives shot off questions like bullets.

Pauli spent an anxious half hour repeating his story. All at once a distant bell rang. One detective was called out. When he came back, his whole demeanor had changed.

"I was speaking on the telephone," he said to Pauli. "You helped an important lady. Frau Flüsser. The mother-in-law of the store's deputy director. She wants to see you tomorrow. Nine sharp. I think she wants to give you a reward. I'll write down the address."

Dazed with delight, Pauli left the police station and started home. With the appointment looming tomorrow, the evening was full of anticipation and magic. Pauli loved Berlin again.

Well, why not? It was one of the world's great cities. But Pauli was no longer sure that Berlin would be his permanent home. He'd begun to think often of America. Of a city, Chicago, and of an uncle there he'd never met, who was a brewer, and rich.

Also, Pauli disliked his job in the kitchen at the elegant Hotel Kaiserhof, where he swabbed the floor and emptied trays of dirty dishes. The single compensation was the opportunity to spend a few minutes with Herr Trautwein, the hall porter, who was an enthusiast about modern inventions of every kind, and talked endlessly about the new age of mechanization.

Pauli hurried down the steps to the cellar flat he occupied along with Aunt Lotte and the *Herren* she entertained. He let himself in. The flat was small, with yellowing lace curtains masking what few windows there were. Dark furniture crowded the sitting room, where Pauli found his aunt in a flowered wrapper.

"You're late. Where have you been?" she said. "You look even messier than usual." Lotte was forty-three, handsome and full-bosomed, with auburn hair like a tight cap of curls, and pale blue eyes.

"I was held awhile at the police station—"

"Police!" she cried. "What have you done now?"

Pauli told her the story.

"All right, I guess you did the correct thing, although you could have been injured. Tomorrow, if the nature of your reward is open for discussion, ask for money. Now leave me alone."

Pauli walked down the long dark corridor to his room. There he lit the lamp and shut the door hard, wondering unhappily, as he had so many times lately, what had come over his aunt. Until about a year ago they had enjoyed an affectionate relationship. Then something began to change her. He couldn't guess what it was, but

115

he could see it in her face, once so ruddy but now a spectral gray.

He stared around the pathetic room, and his eyes came to rest on the souvenirs tacked to the old flowered wallpaper. The collection consisted mainly of postal cards on which photographs were reproduced, mostly exotic foreign scenes. The Sphinx. The Great Wall of China. The onion domes of Moscow. An American cowboy. When the printed information was in English, Aunt Lotte translated for him. She knew a smattering of several foreign languages. Pauli never tired of studying the photographs.

Two tacks held the small black, red, and gold flag of the failed revolution of '48. Hanging below it were streamers of red, white, and blue salvaged from a diplomatic party at the hotel. They reminded him of his uncle in America.

He tried not to think too often about his longing to follow his uncle, because the dream seemed so impossible. He had a symbol for it, however—a rectangle of cardboard for a parlor stereoscope, sepia-tinted, badly bent at two corners. An American, one of his aunt's *Herren,* had presented it to him. On the card, in the dual images, the camera looked out across the bow of a great ship entering the harbor of New York. The huge city loomed in the background. In the foreground a magnificent statue rose from a rocky island. She was the first thing seen by new immigrants, the American said. He told Pauli her name: Liberty Enlightening the World. Would she welcome Pauli if he sailed there?

CHARLOTTE ✦ Lotte Kroner stared at the flickering low-trimmed lamp on the table next to the bed. She knew she had very little time to set her nephew's life on a better course. Very little time. As if to remind her, raspy pain seared her throat. She put her fist to her lips to mute a cough, and the spasm passed.

Pauli's face haunted her, particularly his hurt eyes when she spoke to him sharply. She didn't want to be unpleasant. She loved him. Harsh words and angry looks were part of her deliberate campaign to set a distance between them and thus make it easier to get him out of Berlin. He didn't understand. How could he?

THE market town of Aalen lies east of Stuttgart, in the state of Württemberg, in the pleasant green foothills of the Swabian Jura. There the roots of the Kroner family went deep. Lotte's father,

Thomas Kroner, owned a small hotel and brewery in Aalen. In 1848, when revolutionary fires swept through Germany, he was a leader of the uprising in his district, and he rushed off to join the demonstrations centered in Baden.

Meantime, a national assembly convened in Frankfurt. After struggling toward the unification of many small German states, the delegates foundered. They couldn't even find a ruler for their new nation. When offered the crown of a constitutional Germany, the King of Prussia declared he would not touch a diadem molded "of disloyalty and treason." Thus encouraged, the landed class—the Junkers—stiffened their resistance, and the assembly dissolved.

The following spring Württemberg erupted again. Prussia was asked for help, and two army corps advanced on Baden. July 23, 1849, saw the final capitulation of the revolutionaries, the end of the great hope for a new, democratically united nation symbolized by the tricolor. The aristocrats had won. Hundreds of "Men of '48" fled to America, embittered and fearing for their lives. The authorities arrested Thomas Kroner, tried him, and hanged him three days before Christmas.

Charlotte Kroner was the third and youngest child of Thomas and his wife, Gertrud. During her father's detention, Charlotte's oldest brother, Alfred, was also arrested. He was only nine years old, but sadistic prison guards beat the boy, leaving him permanently lame. Alfred Kroner was unable to earn more than a minimal living thereafter.

The new German Empire was proclaimed in 1871, following the defeat of France in the Franco-Prussian War. It was the age of Bismarck, the Iron Chancellor, who hammered baronies and city-states and robber fiefdoms into a nation in the shape of his personal vision.

As the new Germany was rising, Lotte's crippled brother, Alfred, married a woman named Pauline Marie Schönau, and she bore one son, Pauli.

Lotte had another brother, Josef, who was the shining pride of her life. On his own initiative Josef had left Aalen in 1857. He was fifteen. He made his way across the ocean to the American metropolis of Cincinnati. He developed great skill in the brewer's trade, of which he had learned something as a boy. He fought in America's bloody Civil War, married a good German-born woman, and

117

moved to Chicago. From there he sent Christmas gifts to Lotte, along with news of his family penned on costly engraved stationery. He changed his name to Crown, took out citizenship, and became American.

Lotte was married to a cabinetmaker from a nearby village. Her husband, a burly man, believed that a woman owed her life to *Kinder, Küche, Kirche.* Children, kitchen, church. When Lotte showed that she thought otherwise, her husband used his fist to enforce his viewpoint. One night, after eleven months of marriage, Lotte simply packed her things, put dressings on her bruises, and left for Berlin.

Once there, she placed herself in the path of wealthy gentlemen who would take her to the opera or a fine restaurant in return for her carefully rationed favors. Unfortunately, Lotte didn't have either the perfect physique or the wits to be a highly successful courtesan. She was reduced to factory jobs, which she hated.

As Lotte grew older her options steadily dwindled. She refused to consider remarriage, because German men wanted nothing but a servant dignified with the name wife. So, between distasteful jobs, she entered a number of unsatisfactory short liaisons. From these it had been but a short step to her current—one might call it professional—approach. Thus she survived.

Alfred died in 1881, and his wife, Pauline, succumbed to a heart seizure in '85. Pauli Kroner, age eight and growing fast, was transferred to Lotte's care. She joyfully accepted responsibility for the boy, happy for his company, for his energy and good cheer. Of course she soon realized it wasn't a pleasant existence for him. At school he was treated like one of the poorest charity cases. Given his books rather than paying for them. Given his breakfast of bread and milk and his weekly ticket to a public bath. She saw how the stigma hurt him. She yearned for something better for him.

The trouble was, there was no longer much time. She was growing gaunt, and each month her little account book noted fewer *Herren.*

No, there was not much time left.

PAULI ✦ The old lady lived in a brick villa near the Tiergarten. Extremely nervous, Pauli had put on his best jacket and knee breeches and presented himself at the front door at three minutes before nine. A butler answered his ring and led him to a sunny room.

The old lady awaited him in a wicker chair. Dressed in black silk, she had lively brown eyes set amid deep wrinkles. "Good morning," she said. "Take this seat next to me. We will have refreshments, I think."

A maid appeared bearing a silver tray with a plate of cookies. There was a small pewter pot of dark beer for Pauli, and tea for the old lady, into which she poured rum to make *Teepunsch.*

"Well now," the old lady said after she'd sipped. "I am Frau Flüsser, and you are my benefactor. You acted quickly and bravely when that rascal tried to rob me, so I feel you are entitled to a reward. It will be your choice of anything reasonably priced from Wertheim's. Do you have any thoughts? Any wants?"

He thought for a moment. "Do you have a globe?"

"A globe," she said. "That is an unusual request, but I believe it can be fulfilled. Where shall we send it?"

"Müllerstrasse." Reluctantly he stated the address.

"That is your home?"

"Right now, yes. I live there with my aunt Charlotte. But I hope to have a home somewhere else someday."

"Where will it be?"

"I don't know. My uncle lives in Chicago, perhaps that's it. That's why I'd like a globe. It shows me all the possible places."

Frau Flüsser beamed. "America—that's a good place. I might go there myself if I weren't so old. I will see that you get your globe promptly so you can continue your search." Kindness softened her wrinkled face. "I am very grateful for your courage and assistance. You may kiss me good-bye if you like."

He rose and kissed her cheek, wishing that she were his own grandmother.

"Good-bye, Pauli Kroner. I hope you find your true home."

"Thank you, I also."

"Take my word, when you find it, you'll know. Something unexpected will tell you. A sign. There will be a sign for you."

He smiled and left the house. He never saw Frau Flüsser again, but she was true to her word. Wertheim's sent the globe by delivery van, in one of their boxes, tied with silver ribbon. It was a splendid little globe, painted with bright enamel colors and sitting freely in a stand of lacquered wood.

Pauli threw away his paper map and cleared a special place for the new globe on his shelf. He found his eye drawn to America, the home of his uncle.

POSTERS had appeared on kiosks and walls all over the city announcing the arrival of Buffalo Bill's Wild West troupe on August first. Pauli was awake at five that morning. He dressed, picked up his drawing materials, and tiptoed past Aunt Lotte's door. Then he dashed up the steps into the street and ran straight to the sprawling freight yards east of Pflugstrasse. To his dismay he saw that the special train had already arrived. But it must have just pulled in, for the unloading hadn't yet started.

The train was long, eighteen cars, several of which were decorated with large gaudy paintings of frontiersmen firing pistols and Indians flourishing tomahawks. Of course there was a magnificently heroic portrait of the star, raising his white sombrero in salute as his splendid stallion reared. Cody's goatee and mustache shone pure white in the sunlight breaking over the yards. Pauli forgot Müllerstrasse, Aunt Lotte—everything.

Activity around the train quickened rapidly. Roustabouts in checkered shirts rolled back the doors of livestock cars. At the rear, one livestock car held dray horses, first to be unloaded down an iron ramp. Flatcars carrying wagons were next in line, and a team of horses was hitched to each wagon. Then came more livestock cars, whose occupants Pauli both saw and smelled. Saddle horses; mules; three shaggy bison; Colonel Cody's own milk-white horse, Isham. At the front of the train were passenger cars with the unfamiliar word PULLMAN blazoned on them.

Pauli gawked his way along the train, stopping by a passenger car bearing the legend BUFFALO BILL'S WILD WEST & CONGRESS OF ROUGH RIDERS—GRAND EUROPEAN TOUR. A lady appeared, sleepily leading a poodle on a leash. It was Fräulein Annie Oakley, the celebrated sharpshooter pictured on the posters.

Men uncoupled the last car, which was empty now. A switch engine backed up to it, coupled, and pulled the car away. It all seemed marvelously efficient to Pauli.

Next the gleaming lacquered Deadwood stagecoach was unloaded. Pauli had read all about the scenes of the show, and the rescue of the mail coach was the most famous. He couldn't afford a ticket into the special show park newly fenced off at the corner of the Ku'damm, but he'd imagined the action—the thrilling Indian attack, then the cavalry rescue—many times.

While the unloading went on, Pauli retired to some boxcars standing on the adjacent track. He rolled open the door of one and took a seat, determined to sketch something. His eye was drawn back to the gaudy painting of Buffalo Bill. He'd try that.

All at once a man appeared from between the boxcars and stood staring at him. The man had dark eyes that seemed to glare with an inner fire. He was tall and looked underfed. He had a long, narrow face, large white teeth, and skin the color of porridge. He was older than Pauli, in his mid-twenties.

He wore spectacles of cheap gold-plated wire, with round lenses no bigger than pfennigs. His clothes were shabby and greasy. But poor as he was, the man affected a cocky air as he strolled toward Pauli.

With arrogant casualness he leaned against the boxcar and glanced down at the sketch of Cody. Sneering, he said, "That's terrible."

Pauli stuck out his chin. "Oh, are you an art critic?"

"No, a journalist. But I know bad art when I see it." The man spoke German with a pronounced but unfamiliar accent.

Pauli thought the man was lying. "What newspaper do you work for?"

"Any one that will buy my paragraphs. I am independent. I travel, I write, I observe, I predict. My name is Mikhail Rhukov. At least in Russia. In this country you would say Michael, I suppose."

He lit a cigarette. "Amazing people, these Americans. They're going to own the earth, I think. I wish they'd export a little of their democracy to my country. It's an astounding time we live in, don't you think? Old orders going down in blood and fire. Proletarians marching. Exciting."

"I don't know a thing about it," Pauli said in a hostile tone.

Rhukov eyed him. "Look, I'm only being friendly."

"Fine, leave me alone," Pauli said. He jumped down from the freight car and walked toward the train. But the Russian followed him, writing in a notebook.

Startled by the sound of men speaking German, Pauli turned to see a group of six army officers standing near the iron ramp. Two were young lieutenants; the others were older, with the broad red stripe of the general staff on their gray trousers. All but one of the officers were busily writing in small leather-bound notebooks or comparing the time on pocket watches. Trying to look casual, Pauli sidled closer to listen.

"I have heard about these people," Rhukov remarked to Pauli. "They follow Herr Cody everywhere in Germany. They are studying his methods. A sneery lot, aren't they?" Pauli thought the Russian had a lot of nerve to criticize someone else's arrogance. Besides, German officers were always haughty because they were revered throughout the fatherland for their steely professionalism.

The senior officer, a stout *Brigadegeneral*, was studying the train through a monocle. "They move quickly," he said.

"Sir, everything comes off the train in correct order for their parade," said a stoop-shouldered major. "They have a plan for loading and unloading that is a marvel of efficiency. Perhaps Büffel Bill is German."

The officers laughed, but one of the young lieutenants tapped his notebook. "They are twenty-eight minutes behind schedule."

"Hmm," the brigadier murmured. "That is not impressive."

The major said, "Perhaps the train was late."

"By only six and one half minutes," the lieutenant said.

"That would never do for artillery arriving in the field," said the brigadier. "Lieutenant von Rike, kindly ascertain, if you can, the reason they have lost almost twenty-two minutes."

Von Rike snapped his hand to his cap, pivoted, and walked off.

"What a bunch of strutting popinjays," said Rhukov. "Just imagine what dreams dance around in their heads. Invincible Teutonic knights in Prussian castles, ready to lead the moment Germany needs a savior. What rot. The problem is, I think the Kaiser and the whole army believe it. You Germans are a people mired in myths. Myths of superiority. Myths of the grandeur of war, the nobility of death." Rhukov lit another cigarette. "I refer primarily to the German high command, you understand, plus their allies, the nobility. You're exempted. You may be a rotten artist, but you seem a decent sort otherwise."

"Thank you very much," Pauli said sarcastically. But he'd decided this fellow had some substance. He gave a grudging smile.

Just then Lieutenant von Rike returned to his superiors. "The delay was not their fault," he announced. "The yardmaster didn't have the switch engine here on schedule."

Rhukov put his notebook away and extended his hand to Pauli. "I've seen enough. I can write a page or two. Good-bye, my friend." They shook in a formal way. "I will see you again," Rhukov said. He strolled away.

Activity at the train distracted Pauli for a few seconds. When he looked again, Rhukov had vanished, as if he were no more than smoke in a windstorm. What a strange man. Pauli had the oddest feeling that they would indeed meet again somewhere.

He went back to his perch in the open boxcar. All the show wagons had been lined up. Fräulein Oakley continued to exercise her poodle, accompanied now by a man in a fringed jacket. Pauli recognized him. Fräulein Oakley's husband, the marksman Colonel Butler. Several Indians stood chatting. All wore ordinary jeans pants. Two had suit vests. Very disappointing.

Suddenly there came another diversion. Two well-dressed tourists, a man and woman, pointing and chattering. The man carried a small black box. Pauli moved closer.

The gentleman wore a tall hat and velvet-collared chesterfield. The lady won Pauli's admiration with her dress of Venetian red. The man leaned over his black box, which he aimed at one of the Indians.

Butler approached the photo maker and asked a question. Pauli thought he heard Butler say the word American. The tourist nodded vigorously, introduced himself. His name was Jaster. Butler and the tourist shook hands. The marksman was interested in the black box. Pauli heard the words George Eastman *Kamera*.

Jaster nodded. "A Kodak." Kodak was a strange word, but Pauli had heard it before. Herr Trautwein at the hotel had bragged about his Kodak *Kamera* from America.

Jaster indicated that he wanted to photograph Butler and his wife. The marksman was flattered. He waved to Fräulein Oakley. She joined them, dragging her poodle. Jaster's wife posed with the Butlers, who then excused themselves. The tourists circulated up and down the length of the assembling cavalcade of animals and wagons, cowboys, men dressed in United States Army blue.

Pauli followed the tourists, almost delirious from the thrill of seeing both the Buffalo Bill troupe and a genuine Kodak camera.

He didn't know how a camera worked, but he understood that it produced those breathtaking views that decorated his bedroom wall.

Jaster stopped to photograph the German officers. The brigadier took notice and waved sharply. "You there," he called in German. "Stop that. No photographs of officers on duty."

The order didn't seem to deter Herr Jaster, who went on readying his shot. "Someone stop him," the brigadier said.

Lieutenant von Rike rushed forward and tore the Kodak from Jaster's hands. Frau Jaster shrieked in alarm.

Her husband lunged for the camera. Von Rike jumped back while prying the box open. Agog, Pauli watched the lieutenant whip out a long paper streamer. Von Rike then dropped the camera and stamped on it. Frau Jaster wailed.

Having done his duty, the lieutenant walked back to his comrades. The major offered a terse approval. "Neatly done."

"Thank you, sir."

Herr Jaster was protesting, but his wife restrained him. A minute later they could be seen retreating around the corner of a switchman's shack.

The officers closed their notebooks, and they too soon strolled out of sight behind the Wild West train.

Pauli stared at the camera. Smashed, ruined. But a real camera. Abandoned there in the gravel.

With a popping of whips and a creaking of axles the cavalcade began to move out of the yards, bound for Unter den Linden. Eyes darting, Pauli ran to the camera, snatched it up, and sped away. For once, he was eager to reach the Hotel Kaiserhof and show his prize to Herr Trautwein.

IT WAS four o'clock before he had a chance to sneak out of the kitchen to the cubicle behind the hall porter's desk. Herr Trautwein rhapsodized over the camera.

"Yes, this is a genuine Eastman snapshot camera, a Kodak Number One, like mine. It weighs less than a kilogram, takes one hundred round photographs on a roll of paper film that's packed inside the camera before you buy it. When you finish the roll, you send the camera to the factory in America—I have done that, twice! They develop the pictures, pack in another roll, and send back the whole affair. Eastman has a slogan: You push the button and we do the rest. It's true. Photography is the new art of the new age. It's too bad you couldn't have found a Kodak that works."

"I'd like one someday," Pauli said. He was fascinated by the slogan Trautwein had quoted. He had made a stunning leap in his head from "You push the button" to his frustrating attempts to draw. To make photographs might be the way to capture a piece of the world when you had no talent.

When Pauli left the hotel at half past eight that night, enthusiasm possessed him. Forgotten for the moment were Aunt Lotte's strange moods, the sense that she no longer cared for him.

At home, he found his aunt in her wrapper, seated like a lost child in the front room. Her eyes were red raw from crying.

Pauli pulled an old footstool near her and sat down. "Aunt Lotte, what's the matter? You must tell me."

"Oh, *Liebchen.*" Weeping, she mussed his hair affectionately. "How can I explain?"

He rested his hands on her knees. "It's—all right," he said, trying to comfort her.

Presently his aunt composed herself. "Pauli, I have consumption. It's a terrible sickness that affects a person's lungs. It wastes you away. I've debated about telling you, but now I must, because I don't want you to fall ill. You mustn't stay in this apartment until it becomes a pesthole. Also, because of my sickness, the coughing spells, other things are going bad." She leaned close to him. "Soon no gentlemen will want to visit me. So you see—" She paused. "We must make a different arrangement for you."

The room, the whole cellar, was absolutely still. Pauli felt something momentous was about to happen.

"What I think, Pauli—" She touched his cheek. "You must go to America."

"America!"

"Yes, why not? It's a wonderful land of opportunity. Hundreds of thousands of our people have gone there. And don't forget we have my brother, Josef, the brewer, in Chicago. He's rich and important. I'll write him this very night."

Pauli was excited. The house of his uncle might be the very home he longed for. On the other hand, his aunt's illness was something he couldn't overlook. "I can't leave you when you're feeling so—"

"Of course you can. Furthermore, you can make the journey by yourself. Your uncle did. Is the idea so terrible?"

"Oh, no. I've longed to see America."

"You must go, then. I'll write Josef, and we'll begin saving for your ticket. The price from Hamburg is approximately a hundred five marks for steerage. Roughly twenty-four dollars American."

"That's a fortune, Aunt Lotte!"

"Yes, for poor people like us. It will take perhaps a year to save what we need. However, we'll use the time to good advantage. I'll teach you all the English that I can. America will be fine, you'll see."

Pauli closed his eyes, shivering as a picture flashed into his head. New York harbor: the lady of Liberty, with her light upraised. She seemed to be signaling, beckoning just to him.

THE reply to Lotte's letter came late in the autumn. It was written on thick creamy paper, with the address elegantly engraved across the top. Above this was an embossed crown of gold.

> Dearest sister—
>
> How splendid to hear from you once again. I hope your health is excellent. In response to your question, yes, I enthusiastically endorse the idea that Pauli come to us. You said you hoped it would be by the spring of next year. Whenever he arrives, Ilsa and I and our children will welcome him and attend diligently to his needs. I trust he will not be disappointed in his new home.
>
> > Yours with affection,
> > Joseph

ON A spring day in the following year, 1892, Pauli took down the cards, photographs, and mementos tacked to the wall in his tiny room. He piled them neatly inside an old wardrobe. He kept three items back. One was the globe from Wertheim's. The second was the ruined camera. The last item had become a very special talisman: it was the stereoscope card of the lady Liberty. Soon he'd see that same sight with his own eyes.

Carefully he put the card, the globe, and the Kodak into his secondhand traveling grip, on top of his few clothes and an English phrase book he'd been studying for months. He spoke in halting English. "America. Chicago."

About to leave the tiny room for the last time, he opened the wardrobe again. Took out a postcard picturing a stiffly posed Kaiser Wilhelm. Then he tore the card in half and tossed the pieces onto the bed. It seemed a very bold thing to do—the right thing for someone going to a new homeland at last.

CHARLOTTE ✦ In the steam and bedlam of the Zoo Bahnhof they said good-bye. How young and strong he looked, how full of hope and purpose standing there with clear eyes and his clothing in its customary disarray. He had no idea of the snares of woe the world would set for him. Nor would Lotte tell him.

The spear of pain in her bosom was sharp this morning. It had taken all her will to rise up from bed and dress herself in her best outfit—a cloth suit with silk braid and a French bonnet ten years out of date. Finally she donned her cape of dark green loden. There seemed a melancholy suitability to the heavy fabric that resisted water so well. Pauli asked her why she wore the cape when the weather was warm. She shushed him rather sharply.

His rail ticket to Hamburg hung out of his breast pocket. She felt uncharacteristically sentimental. Speaking above the clangor of the station, she said, "I want you to do well in your new homeland, Pauli. You take with you all of the good characteristics of Germans. But you're going to be an American, and you must be a good one."

Whistles blew, and trainmen began shutting doors to the carriages. The actual farewell was hasty, a mere exchange of hugs and breathless good-byes. She saw him into the jammed third-class carriage. With a grind of great iron wheels, a hissing of steam, the locomotive pulled the train and Pauli away from her forever.

She left the huge station. A warm rain was falling. She walked to Unter den Linden and took a turn along it, under the dripping trees. In a modest café she spent the very last of her money on a light supper and a glass of delicate Moselle wine, followed by three glasses of *Weissbier,* the strong "white" beer. She needed alcohol tonight for courage.

As the light waned, Lotte walked to the bridge over the river Spree. She leaned against the railing, with her eyes fixed on the rain-dappled water. Reflections rippled and gleamed invitingly. Silently she begged forgiveness for what she planned to do.

She took pleasure in having set Pauli's feet on a better road. He was young, clever, didn't give up easily; perhaps he would follow his new road to a happy end. As for herself—well, she didn't feel so bad with wine and *Weissbier* in her. She felt composed, in fact, watching the lighted ripples on the Spree.

She drew a deep breath, realizing that the Spree was her friend, that it held the answer to all of life's problems. "Godspeed, Pauli," she whispered to the night.

Part Two
STEERAGE
1892

PAULI ✦ Pauli was tired and uncomfortable. He'd been sitting on a packing box, amid six or seven hundred other travelers, since early morning. He hoped the steamship's dark shadow on the Hamburg pier was not an omen.

The day was more like August than late spring. The Elbe River smelled incredibly foul. Like everyone else on the pier, he was fretful because boarding had been delayed. He was nervous about rumors of cholera in the city. For three days he'd been penned up in the shipping line's filthy emigrant barracks.

The hopeful travelers were a shabby lot. They spoke a variety of strange and incomprehensible languages. Some looked pleasant, others disagreeable. The latter included a pair of young Germans, big and blond, who talked loudly, stared openly at women's bodies, and punched and roughhoused each other.

Pauli was homesick already, and famished. The meals in the barracks consisted of tea and bread, with bad-tasting sausage at noon. The emigrants had to pay for each serving; Pauli ate but once a day.

He tried to study his phrase book. English was a hard language. Maddening. He wasn't learning fast enough. But he was learning other lessons—unpleasant ones. He was learning that the outcome of a journey to America wasn't always happy. A traveler had sat down on the same bench in the ticket hall just after Pauli's train arrived. Lonesome after the long journey, Pauli spoke to him. "Are you going to America, sir?"

"I'm going home to Wuppertal. I've just come from America."

The traveler was not an old man, but his face was seamed with worry lines, his eyes sad. "Are you going there?" he asked.

Pauli replied with a vigorous nod. "Definitely."

"Thousands go, but hundreds come back. They never tell you that. I was in St. Louis for twelve years. I hated every moment. I'm a baker. There are too many bakers in America. I barely made enough to keep alive. Then one night my shop was looted.

"For a while you'll think everything's wonderful in America. But soon enough you'll see the dirt and despair—the truth behind the illusion. If I were you, I'd cash in my ticket now."

"I can't. My relatives are expecting me in Chicago."

"Well, in a few years you'll be back to stay. Count on it."

Pauli excused himself and moved away quickly. He wished he'd never met the baker of Wuppertal.

On the vessel, a bell rang. People exclaimed and pointed. Pauli jumped on the packing box to see. At the cabin-class gangway, which was covered with a peppermint-striped awning, the velvet rope had been removed. Well-dressed families were boarding with much waving and laughter. The steerage gangway, uncovered, rickety, was still lashed to the side of the ship. Pauli sat down again.

Under his jacket and shirt, a canvas belt Aunt Lotte had sewn for him chafed his belly. It held his uncle's letter and his last eighteen marks. To buck himself up, he fished out the encouraging letter and was rereading it when a couple of sunburned seamen appeared at the steerage entrance hatch.

Responding to orders from a tall, emaciated steward in a blue uniform, the seamen undid the lines and swung the gangway outward until it thumped the pier. People around Pauli jumped up, exclaiming. Caught with the letter in hand, Pauli barely had time to grab his grip before he was hurled forward by the crowd.

The skinny steward untied the rope, and boarding went quickly. Pauli was still struggling to return the letter to his money belt when he was thrust to the foot of the gangway.

"Last name?" asked the steward.

"Kroner."

The man checked it off the manifest. He noticed Pauli's hand fumbling at his waist. He saw the money belt. "Get aboard," he said contemptuously. Pauli jumped forward, grip in one hand, the

129

other hand frantically pulling his shirt down. This was a bad start.

Pauli climbed the gangway to the hatch, a maw of darkness.

The ship was named M.S. *Rheinland,* capacity three hundred and twenty-five in two cabin classes, and nine hundred in steerage. The steerage, deep in the ship, was presided over by the steward.

The emigrants were divided into two groups—married couples with children, and all others. Quarters for both were identical: large holds, each with only a few small portholes. Iron-framed bunks were stacked five high. Each bunk had a thin straw-filled mattress and a flimsy blanket. The spaces had been fumigated, but it didn't take long for the bewildered passengers to foul them with strong odors.

The steamship line promoted its "excellent and nutritious" food, but the reality was different. That night in the steerage saloon the meal consisted of a lukewarm potato soup, platters of herring in a dubious vinegary sauce, and loaves of stale bread.

The steward circulated among the tables, unctuously asking if all was well. He introduced himself as Herr Steward Blechman. One of the raucous blond brothers challenged him. "Where's the beer? You advertised beer, I damn well remember that."

"It's available," said the steward, rubbing his thumb against his other fingers. So were wine and potable water, for a price.

RHEINLAND sailed at midnight. Pauli was awakened by the hooting of tugs, the clank of the anchor chain, the terrified outcries of fellow passengers. He remained awake for hours.

Daylight brought a respite in the form of escape to the small, crowded steerage deck located at the bow. Pauli found a spot at the rail, filling his lungs with clean air.

Presently a family attracted his attention. It consisted of a short, corpulent mother, two heavy teenage daughters, and a boy one or two years younger than Pauli. The boy was frail, with pale skin, merry blue eyes, a quick smile, and spiky black hair. He had an old concertina on which he played lively airs with considerable skill. Pauli edged closer to the boy, hoping to start a conversation. He heard the sisters speaking a foreign language and gave up.

That night, in the open Atlantic, a storm struck, and steerage turned into hell. The dim hold began to reek with the odors of the sick, as *Rheinland* rolled and pitched violently. Even flat on his back in his bunk Pauli grew dizzy. The man in the bunk across the aisle was crying. Others prayed aloud for help.

Fair weather returned the next day, and a calm sea. Pauli spent every available moment on deck. He brought the broken Kodak with him and pretended to photograph the anchor chains, lifeboats, the bridge—anything. He had never been so lonely.

One passenger who bunked in another aisle intrigued him. This was an old gentleman, emaciated but very correct in his posture. A mane of silvery hair and a luxuriant mustache gave him a distinguished air. His clothes were peculiar: royal blue trousers with a white seam stripe, and a military-style overcoat, dusty rose, with royal blue braid and trim. The coat was threadbare and dirty, yet the old fellow wore it with style. He brought a small wooden box to the deck, always dusting it with a big kerchief before he sat.

Finally Pauli's loneliness overcame his fear. "I don't mean to be forward, sir, but I've watched you dust that box every day. You're so neat, you could be German."

The old gentleman laughed. "On my mother's side. Where are you from?"

"Berlin. My name's Pauli Kroner."

"Berlin. Fancy that. I worked nine years at the Kaiserhof. Out in front—whistling up cabs, greeting dignitaries—"

"I can't believe this!" Pauli exclaimed. "I worked in the kitchen of the same hotel. We never met."

"Well, it was ten years ago." Both of them laughed.

Thus Pauli made the acquaintance of old Valter, a hotel doorman by profession. Which explained the garish outfit. Valter proudly said he spoke nine languages and was going to live with his son in Pennsylvania.

Again the weather changed, and fog rolled in. Pauli climbed the iron stairs to the deck. Old Valter was absent, but Pauli recognized a few scattered groups, among them the blond brothers and the two stout sisters of the boy with the concertina. He was also absent.

The sisters were playing a card game. It was the younger, more attractive one who caught the attention of the brothers. Pauli was alarmed when the blond louts exchanged nudges and smarmy grins and one of them sauntered over. By pretending to aim the camera, Pauli could watch without attracting attention.

The blond youth leaned down to whisper in the prettier sister's ear. She jumped up, spilling cards from her lap. The young man laughed and pushed the back of his hand against the girl's corseted bosom. Her sister was too frightened to move. Others on deck deliberately looked away.

Pauli heard the blond lout say, "Come on, *Jüdin,* don't be stuck-up. I'm a good sort. Franz is the name. This is my brother, Heinrich. The Messer boys." He sounded like a Bavarian.

The other sister, finally terrorized into action, began to wave her arms and jabber in her own language. Heinrich was less jocular. "Shut up with that Yid talk."

Pauli danced around to the right of Franz, holding up the Kodak while concealing the fact that it was broken.

"Here, what are you doing?" Heinrich shouted.

"Taking your snapshot for the captain."

The Messer brothers eyed the camera with surprise and even worry. "Is that one of those picture boxes?"

"Yes, and it'll show the captain that you bothered these girls." The bluff was insane; steerage passengers never saw the captain. But these two Bavarians were stupid.

"Recognize his accent?" Heinrich asked his brother. "He's one of those snotty Berliners." Berliners looked down on most Bavarians, considering them lazy southern peasants.

"He's an interfering little rat too." Franz Messer reached for Pauli with huge pink hands.

"That will be all, gentlemen." The stern voice sounded like a soldier's. Pauli sagged with relief as old Valter stepped from behind him. "If you can leave off bullying women and boys smaller than yourself, I'll accommodate your itch to fight."

With murderous eyes the Messers appraised the old man. They noticed other passengers watching now. Franz yanked his brother's arm. "Come on, Heine, we'll square this later." He glowered at Pauli, then stormed off, his brother following.

The two young women leaped on Pauli, hugging him and jabbering incomprehensibly.

Old Valter was able to translate. "These young ladies are the Wolinski sisters—Mira and Renata. They both want to thank you heartily. Their mother and their brother will want to tender their thanks too. They are all from Lodz, Poland."

"Well, I'm glad I could help," Pauli said. But he knew that

because he had interfered, he'd have to look over his shoulder for the rest of the voyage. The Messers were that kind, no doubt of it.

Still, the encounter had a happy side. Pauli escaped the bondage of loneliness and made the acquaintance of the boy with the concertina, Herschel Wolinski.

FROM the moment they met, they were a triumvirate: Pauli, Herschel, and the former doorman, who sat with them with an amused expression, translating their breathless exchanges.

Herschel always seemed to have great energy. He was always darting his bright blue eyes, fidgeting, as if he couldn't contain all of life's excitements. The mere sight of him brought a smile; his brushy black hair seemed to grow six different ways at once.

Pauli didn't see much of the mother, Slova, because she had been sick ever since leaving Hamburg. "She cries day and night." Herschel sighed.

It was two days after the incident with the Messers, a mild sunny morning out on deck. Herschel picked up his concertina and began a lively march. Valter leaned against the rail, packing tobacco into a curved pipe, his silver mane tossing in the wind.

When Herschel finished the song, he asked Pauli, "Were you sorry to leave Germany?"

"Not very. I still love my fatherland, but I didn't have a real home. Things will be better in America."

"Definitely," Herschel said. He began to play a sad little theme, a lullaby perhaps. "I made this up."

"It's very pretty."

He shrugged. "I make up tunes all the time." He played more softly. "I want to become American in every respect. That will include taking a new name."

"My uncle did. He was born Josef Kroner, but now he's Joseph Crown. Here, I'll show you." He pulled up his shirt and unbuttoned the canvas money belt. He unfolded the letter.

Herschel touched the embossed gold crown in a way that was almost reverent. "Your uncle must be rich." The fire in Herschel's eyes seemed to burn out suddenly. "So you've a sponsor in America. Mama said we should stay home, because we didn't have a sponsor. I argued till she changed her mind. Now she's wishing she hadn't."

Old Valter sucked noisily on his pipe and touched Pauli's sleeve. "I'd put that letter away. No, don't look around."

Pauli stiffened. "What's wrong?"

"I'm afraid those two brothers have spied the money belt."

Pauli fastened the buttons and yanked his shirt down. For nearly a minute Valter watched behind his shoulder. Finally he relaxed. "All right, they've gone."

THE crossing was scheduled for eight to ten days, depending on conditions on the ocean. As *Rheinland* approached America, Pauli noticed the Messer brothers watching him a lot. He knew the object of their interest was the money belt. Pauli didn't know what to do, except to make sure he was always with other people.

At the same time, he was sleeping badly because he was getting sick. On the night before the promised landfall, a night of rising wind and heavy seas, his belly hurt; he could eat nothing for supper. Instead, he went to the steward's table near the dining-saloon entrance and bought a small tin can of warm beer. He was nauseated by the stifling air of the saloon. Did he dare go to the deck?

Herr Blechman was writing in an account book, paying no attention to him. The Messers were at their table, talking in their usual loud and oafish way. Pauli decided to chance it. He slipped out, stopping at his bunk for the camera.

To his relief he found the deck deserted. He sat with his back against the hull, his head well under the rail, and sipped the warm beer. He felt better almost at once.

He imagined himself a photographer hired to picture the sweep of stars over the ship. He was clicking off imaginary shots with the Kodak when he heard a footstep. Instantly tense, he glanced up. Two burly figures blacked out sections of the sky.

"Here he is, Heine. Trying to hide from us."

Pauli scrambled to his feet, but the brothers moved quickly to block an escape. Pauli backed against the rail. Franz said, "Care to loan us a few marks? They say New York's an expensive town."

"Look," Heinrich said, "the picture box. Give it here."

Franz kicked Pauli's shin. Pauli staggered, and Franz snatched the camera. Pauli lunged at him. Franz laughed. "Heine, catch."

The brothers tossed the Kodak back and forth, whooping and taunting Pauli while he strained on tiptoe on the tilting deck, reaching for the flying camera. Driven to the limit, Pauli shouted, "*Schmutziger Schweinehund,*" and hit Heinrich in the stomach. The Kodak flew out of his hand and sailed overboard.

Pauli couldn't believe it. He clutched the rail and stared at the sea, rage exploding inside him.

"Call me names, will you?" Heinrich kicked him in the back.

"He's got it coming," Franz said. "He's a Jew lover too."

Pauli, staggering around, brought his fists up.

Heinrich swung and knocked Pauli to the deck. Franz knelt on his back and pulled his shirt out of his pants. "Here it is." He yanked, and the laces of the money belt broke.

"Just give me the letter from my sponsor—" Pauli gasped.

But Franz was on his feet, flourishing the belt. He kicked the side of Pauli's head. Hot tears filled Pauli's eyes. The Messers laughed and walked off. Pauli lay on the cold iron deck, his letter gone, while the great ship crashed on toward America.

Rheinland finally came within sight of a small vessel identified as the Ambrose lightship. At daybreak Pauli dragged himself to the deck. Rainsqualls intermittently hid the horizon as the ship steamed into a broad channel between an island on the portside and a larger, dimly seen landmass to starboard.

Despite thunderclaps and gusts of rain, the small deck was packed. Weary but excited voices repeated one word: "America." Pauli managed to wedge in beside Valter on the portside.

The old gentleman was reading with excitement from a small German-language guidebook. "This is called The Narrows. There are almost as many ships as in Hamburg."

Pauli saw, directly ahead, a thicket of tall buildings. "New York," someone cried. There was hand clapping.

Pauli felt dangerously ill. But he had to stay alert, devise a plan. Worse than having no money was having no proof of sponsorship by his uncle in Chicago. What if the authorities denied him entrance? He wouldn't let it happen.

Suddenly old Valter tugged his sleeve. "Look, Pauli, look! It's your picture card come to life."

Pauli forgot everything except the sight of the colossus rising ahead. In all his dreams he had never imagined her so tall and mighty. She towered to the sky, seemed to float majestically toward him.

Valter too was transported, reading eagerly from his book. "She was placed there six years ago; she is the tallest statue in the world—three hundred five feet."

She was almost opposite *Rheinland*'s prow. Pauli wanted to sob and yell and somehow reach up to embrace the magnificent woman. He twisted around to watch as the statue moved astern. Then the mighty statue floated away in scudding mist.

A lump filled Pauli's throat. He wouldn't forget this day, the first of June, 1892. Soon he would be fifteen. Here, in the new land, he would find a home and a calling.

A TRIM cutter bearing official insignia pulled alongside. *Rheinland* lowered a midships gangway to receive three men in uniform.

Valter said, "Those are the immigration officials."

"For us?"

"No, the passengers upstairs." He pointed off to a small island dominated by a large buff-colored wooden structure with a blue slate roof and four sharply pointed towers at the corners. Valter leafed through his little book. "We're going there. It's called Ellis. Ellis Island."

As the morning advanced, *Rheinland* steamed up the Hudson River past the incredible sprawl of New York City. The wind was blowing away the rain, bringing blue sky and a brilliant sun. With tugboats to assist, *Rheinland* tied up at a long wooden pier. A German band played welcoming music. Herr Blechman, the steward, appeared, nattily buttoned up in his uniform. He carried a megaphone.

"Travelers," he announced, "while the regular passengers disembark, you will be allowed onto the pier, but you must remain in that roped enclosure. Remove all your belongings; you will not be returning to the ship."

People snatched up their grips and bundles and rushed toward the stairs. Valter and Pauli went down the steerage gangway together. The moment Valter stepped on the pier, he stopped and pulled Pauli in front of him to protect him as people shoved by. Valter's face was lifted to the sunshine. Then they moved on, burly policemen herding them into the roped enclosure.

Pauli felt thrilled to stand on American territory, but dreadfully afraid because he still had no plan for getting past the authorities.

Then he thought of something disarmingly simple. He retrieved his phrase book and with agonizing slowness picked out phrases, which he began to repeat under his breath.

Valter waved his pipe toward the river. "Here come the vessels for Ellis Island."

A small harbor ferry and five open barges were required to carry all the steerage passengers. Pauli and Valter boarded a barge. "Get in line, don't run," the policemen yelled, with little effect.

They were a good way back in line, near the Wolinskis. The sun grew hotter. The line moved slowly.

At the front of the line, officials dealt with the immigrants one by one, using the ship's manifests. Each manifest had a number. Individual lines were likewise numbered. The officials checked off names and flung a paper tag at each new arrival, hectoring them in English until they got the idea that they must hang the tag somewhere on their person. Pauli's tag said 8–11. Manifest number eight, line eleven.

At Ellis Island, their barge tied up at an esplanade in front of the main building. Pauli and Valter were buffeted down the plank and toward the main doors of the baggage hall. They found themselves in a vast, gloomy room with a wide staircase in the center. Officials were waving numbered cards and screaming, "Manifest two this way," or, "Manifest eleven here, you can leave your baggage." Pauli and Valter piled their luggage in a roped enclosure over which hung a placard bearing a big black 8.

The baggage hall quickly filled with the odors of dirty bodies. The groups moved slowly up the stairs to a huge, noisy room. Here the immigrants were herded between waist-high iron railings rather like animal runs. In each of several aisles a uniformed health inspector scrutinized the immigrants one at a time. Interpreters stood behind the inspectors. Each inspector had a piece of chalk. When something didn't suit him, he chalked a big letter on the immigrant's coat. F, H, X—Pauli had no idea what the letters meant. His heart was hammering when his turn came.

"Name?"

"Pauli Kroner. Number eight-eleven." Nervousness garbled the rehearsed phrases. "I work—yes. I—*ich bin*— I—good worker."

Valter, more fluent in English, helped out. "He will work hard."

"Not unless we pass him. You're pale, youngster—"

"*Bläss*," snapped the interpreter.

"Have you been sick?"

"*Krank?*"

"Sir, yes—here." He touched his stomach. "But—" He struggled for the English. "Only little. All right now."

The inspector studied him. "You don't look all right. But you're young, I guess you'll live." He waved his chalk. "Go on."

The words eluded Pauli, but not the meaning. He dashed past the inspector with a new and grim appreciation of the part that whim played in these proceedings. Bad as he felt, Pauli vowed he'd get through the ordeal.

He started to move forward. His hair nearly stood up when a familiar voice cried out. Horrified, he looked down the adjoining aisle and saw Slova Wolinski collapsed in her daughters' arms, wailing. The Wolinskis had just been through the station of the third inspector, the dreaded "eye man," who checked the passengers for a condition called trachoma. Pauli knew Slova had not passed.

PAULI passed the eye man without incident. He advanced between the rails. All led to the inspectors who conducted the final interviews at a row of tables stretching across one entire side of the hall. The sight made Pauli's stomach tighten. Sensing his anxiety, Valter laid his hand on Pauli's shoulder. Pauli shut his eyes and rehearsed his phrases yet again. And then it was his turn.

The inspector had sleek dark hair, a veined nose, and the ugliest, most villainous features Pauli had ever seen. The man motioned. "You, lad. Step up. Name?"

"Kroner, sir. Pauli Kroner."

"Age?"

A second man translated it into German. Pauli said, "Fourteen years. But I will be fifteen on the fifteenth of June—this month." With a scratchy pen the inspector wrote in a thick ledger.

"Traveling with anyone?"

Pauli shook his head.

"Can you read or write any English?"

Pauli burst out, "Yes, thank you! America wonderful country!"

The translator laughed, not unkindly. Then he asked a question: "Where did you start from?"

"Berlin, sir. But my family is Swabian."

"I guessed it from the red in your hair. Fine people, Swabians."

Despite the translator's friendliness, the inspector continued to regard Pauli with a blank expression. "Who paid your passage?"

"My aunt in Germany. But I worked to earn part of it." More English: "I will work hard here—good worker!"

The inspector said, "Do you have a job waiting for you?"

Valter had coached him on that question. If you answered yes, you would be turned back because you might be taking work from an American. Pauli said, "No, sir, although I hope to have one someday. My uncle will help me with that, I think."

"Your uncle is your sponsor?"

"Yes, sir."

"Show me something to prove it."

"I had a letter from him, but two bullies on the ship stole it."

The inspector eyed Pauli for a long time. Then, without emotion, he said, "Lad, there's a problem here."

"Sir?" Pauli's ears rang. Pains like knife blades tortured his vitals.

"The law prohibits entry of unaccompanied children under sixteen. Your uncle should have come for you personally."

Pauli turned red, struggling. "I expect he thought the letter would be enough."

"So it would. If you had it. But the law is the law. You will be detained and examined by the Board of Special Inquiry. You'll be held here on the island until you have a hearing."

"Then they will let me go to Chicago?"

The translator looked away. The inspector said, "Not unless you are very persuasive. You aren't allowed to have help in making your case. No lawyers, no friends—no one."

Pauli's nerve almost crumbled then. But he held on. "Sir, I *did* have proof that my relatives are waiting for me. It was stolen." His mouth twisted. "I should have lied about my age." After a moment his shoulders drooped. "No, I am not a good liar."

The ugly inspector pondered. Then he turned to his assistant. "Mr. Steiner, I would hate to make a mistake in this case. Don't you think this young man looks sixteen? He looks sixteen to me."

"Sir, I feel sorry for him too. But he's already stated—"

"Sixteen." The inspector scratched out the age written in the ledger, wrote a new one. He took a printed pasteboard square from a cigar box and handed it to Pauli.

139

"Sirs—what is this?"

"Your landing card," the translator said, faintly smiling.

"Welcome to America," said the ugly inspector.

PAULI waited until old Valter received his card, and then they rushed to the holding area, where the Wolinski children were trying to console their mother. Herschel tried to hide his sadness as he ran to the rail separating the rejected ones from all the others.

"Both of Mama's eyes show the trachoma," he said. Herschel spoke in Polish, and Valter translated. "We agreed to stay together. We would all land or we would all go back, that was our promise to each other."

"Good-bye, good-bye," Pauli said, shaking his head.

Tears appeared in Herschel's blue eyes. "Good-bye. You've been a good friend. I'll go back with Mama and my sisters now, but I promise you I won't give up. We will meet in this country one day. I am going to be an American—you can be sure of that!"

He leaned over the rail and gave Pauli a strong hug. Then he shook Valter's hand. "Good-bye to you, sir."

"Please tell him to take care of himself," Pauli said to Valter in German.

Herschel rejoined his family, and Pauli and Valter walked away. After a few steps Pauli looked back and waved. Herschel waved back. Pauli took a breath and went on with Valter toward double doors marked as an exit in half a dozen languages. One ordeal was over. Now the next began.

Along the upstairs corridor they walked past several offices as well as the mail and telegraph rooms. But one smaller room attracted Pauli. It advertised itself in two languages: DEUTSCHE GESELLSCHAFT—GERMAN AID SOCIETY.

"I'd like to go in here for a minute," Pauli said.

"Fine," Valter said. "I'll see you in the baggage hall."

Inside, a woman wearing a billowy white blouse greeted Pauli in German, asking his name and destination. He gave them.

She handed him a ticket. "This is good for passage on the barge to the New Jersey Central railway terminal, just north of here. It's the policy of the agency to give every new arrival from Germany a barge ticket plus one dollar."

She pressed the large heavy coin into his hand. He clasped it tightly. "It's a very long way to Chicago. Hundreds of miles. Be careful." Standing, she shook his hand with great gravity. "Goodbye, Herr Kroner. The best of luck to you."

Pauli met old Valter in the baggage hall. Valter said, "My son Willi is traveling from Pennsylvania to meet me at a lodging house in New York. Come with me and meet my son, and we can discuss how you'll travel from here."

Pauli thought this over and decided he didn't want to lose any time getting to Chicago. "No, sir, thank you. I'm going straight over to the place called New Jersey. I have this ticket for the ferry. I have one dollar from the German aid office. After I spend that, I'll work." He grinned and said, "I am good worker."

So they embraced and parted.

THE hot sun shone down on the open barge. Pauli sat apart from the other eight passengers, watching the New Jersey Central terminal rising up ahead. Behind it was an ugly panorama of decaying, ramshackle buildings. To Pauli the vista was flawless. He remembered the baker of Wuppertal—who had predicted just such a reaction, then warned that it would fade.

Ridiculous. It wouldn't happen to him.

The barge reached the terminal, and when Pauli stepped on the pier, he was so overwhelmed with happiness that he dropped his grip and whirled around. Yes, he could still see her standing so tall and beautiful in the sunshine of the harbor. She had welcomed him without reservation.

FOR a while Pauli wandered the waterfront just looking around. The day got hotter, and sticky. He sat on his grip in the shade of a warehouse wall. He needed to calm down, organize his thoughts.

He must get to Chicago. He had only one dollar. He needed to work to put some cash in his pocket. Where could he find a job?

A little concentration answered the question. There were many Germans in America, and Germans could always be found where there was beer. Pauli set out to find a beer garden.

LATE in the day, Pauli found a social club for Germans called Die Goldene Tür—The Golden Door. The proprietor, Herr Geizig, needed a boy.

The club was no more than two airless rooms and a kitchen on the second floor of a tenement. Only the first room had a window. The outside stair leading up to the club was shaky, with several rotting risers. A loft on the top floor served as a dormitory, with flimsy cots where German immigrants could stay for a price.

Herr Geizig was a large man who affected great joviality, but Pauli saw no humor in his small shrewd eyes. The pay was twenty cents a day plus food. Pauli would sleep in a shed behind the club. The shed stood in a small trash-strewn yard. But Pauli couldn't be choosy.

Die Goldene Tür did a small but steady business. There were two barmaids who served drinks and food, which was prepared by Geizig's gray and taciturn wife.

Pauli didn't start work until noon. His first job was to mop the clubrooms and wipe down the tables. He was on duty until the club closed, sometimes as late as half past two in the morning.

Certain occurrences in the club disturbed Pauli. On four separate occasions he saw patrons overcome by an apparent fainting spell. These guests were helped down the stair by Herr Geizig personally. None of the four had been drinking very much, Pauli was aware of that. Why they fell ill was a mystery. He never saw any of them a second time. What luggage they had, had disappeared.

The atmosphere at Die Goldene Tür made Pauli uneasy. He was eager to get away.

PAULI's birthday passed. He was filling out, growing taller. Hard work was developing thick bunches of muscle on his upper arms.

When he wasn't on duty, he studied his phrase book. He and Magda, one of the barmaids whom he'd befriended, talked whenever they had a chance. He told her about his uncle and Chicago and his need to get there before bad weather set in.

By the first week of August, Pauli had had his fill of Die Goldene Tür and had made up his mind to leave. First he would have to ask for his wages. Herr Geizig owed him something like twelve dollars.

That Saturday night Pauli's plans were abruptly changed.

Just before nine o'clock Herr Geizig put on his hat and went out. About half past nine Pauli was wiping down a table when the other barmaid, Liesl, stopped near him. "What is that smell?"

Frau Geizig burst from the kitchen. "Something's burning!"

142

The frightened guests jumped up from their chairs. Pauli saw a faint orange glow outside the single grimy window. He ran for the door. Full of rage and fear, he yanked it open. A blast of heat and flame drove him back. "The stair's gone." He slammed the door.

Frau Geizig wrung her hands. "We must escape, or we'll all die."

"Isn't there another door?" one of the guests screamed.

Sobbing, Frau Geizig shook her head.

Everyone seemed stupefied with fear. Thick, choking smoke was now boiling from the kitchen, as if the fire had already eaten through the floor there. Pauli shook himself; he was cursed if he'd die in this mean place after struggling so hard to reach America. He shot across the room, yelling, "Out the window, that's the way."

"Oh, I can't jump, I can't," Frau Geizig wailed.

Pauli ran to Magda. "Come on, we're not going to die here," he yelled, forcing her to the window.

He shoved the window all the way up and was struck in the face by a gust of scorching air. The flames were shooting up directly beneath the window; they'd have to leap wide. "Come on, the rest of you, it's the only way," he shouted.

"Right behind you," one of the guests said, but Liesl was nowhere to be seen, and Frau Geizig had collapsed.

"Hold on, Magda."

"I can't. I'm scared—"

"No, you aren't, don't say that." Panting, he boosted her to the sill, climbed up beside her, and worked his arm around her waist.

"Jump," he cried, and pulled Magda with him out into the dark and the smoke and the billowing flames. As he plummeted, his left trouser leg caught fire. Then the ground rushed up to strike him.

JOE CROWN ✦ Joseph Emanuel Crown, owner of the Crown Brewery of Chicago, was a worried man. Worried on several counts, the most immediate being a civic responsibility he was scheduled to discuss at an emergency meeting at noon this Friday, the fourteenth of October, 1892.

Joe Crown seldom revealed inner anxieties, and that was the case as he worked in his office this morning. He was a picture of steadiness, rectitude, prosperity. He wore a fine suit of medium gray, enlivened by a dark red four-in-hand tied under a high collar.

Joe's hair was more silver than white. His eyes, behind wire spectacles, were dark brown, rather large, and alert. His mustache and imperial showed careful attention. His hands were small but strong. He wasn't handsome, but he was commanding.

Three principles ruled Joe Crown's life, of which the most important was order. In German, *Ordnung*. Without order, organization, some rational plan, you had chaos.

The second principle was accuracy. Accuracy was mandatory in brewing, where timing and temperatures were critical. But accuracy was also the keystone of any business that made money instead of losing it. Joe Crown had a towering belief in the potency of correct information—and in the absolute authority of numbers, which provided it. Money measured success; counting measured money.

As for his third principle, modernity, he believed that it too was crucial in business. Men who said the old ways were the best were fools, doomed to fall behind. Joe hadn't hesitated to install pasteurization equipment at the brewery. He'd been among the first to invest in refrigerated freight cars. He insisted that modern machines be used in the office. From his desk he could often hear the pleasing ratchet noise of a mechanical adding machine blending with the clicking keys and pinging bell on the black typewriter used by his chief clerk.

There was a strong foundation on which Joe Crown's three principles rested: the cheerful acceptance—not to say worship—of hard work.

Joe Crown's brewery occupied an entire block on North Larrabee Street. All the buildings—including the brewhouse and the noisy bottling house across the alley—were of fine red brick, with granite trim. The main building, which faced Larrabee, resembled a fortress, with a square tower at each of the two front corners. From the towers flew the brewery's flag with the gold Crown emblem. Cut into the cornice were the words BRAUEREI CROWN.

Joe Crown occupied a spacious corner office on the second floor of the main building. The front windows of the office overlooked Larrabee, the side ones Crown's outdoor *Biergarten*. The garden had an elaborate gate onto the street, and a doorway, directly below Joe's office, leading inside to the *Bierstube*, which occupied most of the first floor. The taproom served beer and food from noon until late in the evening, as did the garden when the weather was fine. Large breweries commonly had such facilities.

Crown's produced both bottle and keg beer, several kinds of each. The best seller was Crown, a pale, light-bodied, effervescent Pilsen-style lager. A strong second, Heimat Bier, darker, with a heavier alcohol content, was much favored by older Germans.

Eleven o'clock. Joe was marginally aware of a drop in the noise level of the workers outside. It was the hour of *zweites Frühstück,* the second breakfast. Jarring the stillness, footsteps pounded along the hall. After a frantic knock the door burst open.

"Mr Crown, help. Benno is killing Emil Tagg." The panting white-haired man was his chief clerk, Stefan Zwick.

Joe jumped up and ran after Zwick. Benno Strauss had caused trouble before, and Benno's kind of trouble was always serious.

Joe ran down the back stairs past an open window; he heard men yelling now and egging on the participants in a fight. Going out the door, Joe crossed the alley to the forecourt of the bottling house. A ring of about twenty men surrounded the combatants.

Benno Strauss had both hands clamped on the throat of Emil Tagg, who was bent backward over a keg on a hand truck. Tagg was foreman of the bottling house.

Though Joe was much smaller than Benno, he rushed straight at the bigger man, hooking an arm around Benno's neck. "Get off him, Benno." He tugged and yanked until Benno released his stranglehold on Emil. Emil eyed Benno and rubbed his throat.

"The rest of you, back to work," Joe said. His eyes raked the circle of men. Most of them left immediately, with only some muttered comments. He dusted his sleeves. "Now, what's this all about?"

Benno Strauss was huge, with strangely Oriental eyes, a shaved head, and a bushy mustache. He was a "Man of '48"—one of the exiles who had fled Germany after the failed revolution. At age ten he'd carried water for rebel students, all of whom had been shot or arrested. Or so he said. Now he was chief of the Crown teamsters and, at fifty-four, twice as strong as most men of twenty. He belonged to the brewers' union. Joe Crown didn't recognize the union.

"Out with it, Benno," Joe said. "I want an explanation."

Benno wiped his jaw with the sleeve of his smock. "He called me a filthy name." Benno's accent was heavy, his English poor. "I ain't going to repeat it, but I don't allow nobody to say such a thing."

"Is this true, Emil?"

"Yes, Mr. Crown. But damn it, he never shuts up. He came at me preaching that radical stuff about an eight-hour day."

Benno wasn't even slightly upset by Tagg's accusation. "Sure, we want an eight-hour day here at Crown's. No more ten and a half."

"I told you before, Benno, don't spread your red doctrine on my time. And don't disrupt work. One more fight—one—and you'll be discharged."

"I hear what you say, sir." The words were surprisingly meek.

Joe wasn't fooled. But Benno Strauss was a fine worker when he felt like it. So, for the present, Joe decided to put up with his agitation, hoping it would get no worse. If it did, Benno would go.

Joe marched back in the direction of the administration building, then stopped abruptly. His way was blocked by a young man with arms folded. The young man was smiling.

Joe reddened. "Didn't you hear my instructions? Get back to work."

"Sure, Pop. You're the boss here."

Here. Joe Crown pushed his son aside and walked past him, grim-faced.

In his office, he pulled out his gold pocket watch and found his hand shaking slightly. The confrontation had upset him, especially that moment with his son. Twenty-two minutes past eleven. His driver was due to arrive in precisely eight minutes to take him to his club, the Union League, for the meeting with two other members. Joe put on his coat and white felt homburg, took his gold-knobbed cane, and went downstairs to the *Stube.*

On the front counter stood the newest token of modernity, a gleaming cash register, the latest model from the National Cash Register Company. It incorporated a daily detail strip that provided an exact record of individual sales in chronological order. Ah, numbers!

Outside, in the *Biergarten,* the air was heavy and damp but full of the sweet, hearty aroma of a brewery. Joe stepped through the gate to a splashing fountain as a team of handsome bays pulled a carriage to a stop. It was an English-quarter landau, a rich man's carriage. On each door was a small golden crown.

"Five minutes late, Nick," Joe said.

"Truly sorry, Mr. Crown," said Nicky Speers, the ruddy English driver-groom employed by the family. "Big smashup of drays on the

Clark Street bridge. Couldn't turn around for near twenty minutes."

Joe Crown gave a quick nod to say the explanation was accepted. He stepped into the carriage, and it sped away.

He settled against the cushion and thought about the luncheon meeting. What lay behind it was the great fair scheduled to open on May 1 the following year. The World's Columbian Exposition would be a mammoth international exhibition of arts and industry, commemorating the four hundredth anniversary of the discovery of America. It would focus global attention on Chicago, and enormous pavilions were being built in Jackson Park to house all the exhibits. The dedication ceremony was to be held on Friday, October 21. It would be preceded by a full week of civic celebration, including a gala ball.

The week had been planned by the Exposition's Committee on Ceremonies, which included every rich or important person in Chicago—Philip Armour, Marshall Field, and George Pullman, among others. Joe Crown's subcommittee was responsible for a reception and dinner honoring the President on Thursday night. Crown's would provide three kinds of beer at no cost. But other suppliers weren't so generous; their avarice had necessitated the emergency meeting.

Despite the favorable attention the Exposition would generate, the millions of tourist dollars it would bring in, the fair was at the same time unleashing a flood tide of greed and venality. This was typical of Chicago, but Joe thought it typical of the times as well. Stock manipulation, land fraud, price-fixing, consolidation of industries in the hands of a few men who conspired together—all were commonplace. Children were hired illegally to work in factories that were dirty and unsafe, and some of those children became diseased or maimed for life. In Chicago the votes of many aldermen were openly for sale. There seemed to be very little idealism left in America, only a cynical belief in the almighty dollar.

The sensational press boosted circulation with stories about robber barons and trusts and crooked bosses. Decent folk felt helpless, and the few public figures who cried out against the corruption were lonely prophets in a wilderness of apathy. The glory of the American business system—the freedom it allowed—was also its curse, for it virtually invited the wolves to enter the fold, to plunder without hindrance. Reform was desperately needed.

Joe still believed in the fundamental rightness of the American system, in the opportunity it gave a man willing to work hard. But some of his peers were businessmen with utter disregard for the human side of commerce. Gus Swift and Pork Vanderhoff, for example—two packinghouse tycoons who blandly said that if one of their workers hurt or crippled himself at one of their plants, it was not their responsibility as owners, but rather the injured man's; he knew the risks when he took the job. When such unfortunates fell on the human scrap heap, Swift and Vanderhoff looked the other way.

George Pullman was hardly any better. He'd built his model workers' town, Pullman, twelve miles south of the city. On the surface it seemed a wonderful and humane experiment, but he packed the town with company spies to prevent labor agitation, and he charged his tenants three times the normal rate for gas and light and water.

What the Pullmans, Swifts, Vanderhoffs, and others like them ignored was a growing number of Bennos. Men dedicated to "propaganda of the deed," which could include arson, dynamiting, even murder.

Joe chastised himself for letting his thoughts flow into such morbid channels. It was probably the sum of many things, including a pervasive worry about his nephew, Pauli, from Germany. The boy should have been here by now.

WHEN Joe arrived at the handsome red sandstone clubhouse of the Union League, the subcommittee members were waiting for him in the spacious main lounge. The two men were a sharply contrasting pair. Traction magnate Charles Yerkes was a man of shady origins who had served time for stock fraud. He looked like a professor. Former Congressman Joe Cannon wore a crushed felt hat and sloppy clothes, and often joked about it: "My noble constituents are just a bunch of good old dirt farmers; how'd it look if I high-hatted them dressed up like a dude?" Cannon's hayseed act concealed a dictatorial nature and a shrewd mind.

The three repaired to the main dining room and chatted through the heavy meal.

Over coffee, Joe said, "There's something important to discuss. The two houses supplying our wild game and our liquors have arbitrarily increased their estimates. By very substantial amounts."

"Well, hell, just dump 'em and find new ones," Cannon said.

"We're out of time. Even sold out, we will not take in enough money to cover our costs. The Committee on Ceremonies will hang the three of us if we're in the red."

Cannon reared back in his high velvet chair. "Don't look at me, boys. My pockets got nothing in 'em but lint and small change."

Looking put-upon, Charles Yerkes sighed and said, "All right, I'll make up the difference. I presume that's the reason I'm on the committee in the first place."

Greatly relieved, Joe said, "I was hoping you'd offer. If you'll be responsible for half of the deficit, I'll make up the other half."

"Done," Yerkes said, looking happier.

With that settled, Joe left the Union League. He knew he should be pleased that he had resolved a significant problem. Instead, his mind immediately fixed on another. Where *was* the boy?

PAULI ✦ Four people died in the blaze that consumed Die Goldene Tür. Frau Geizig, Liesl, and two newcomers sleeping in the loft. Herr Geizig had come back just as the blaze broke out, and didn't raise a hand to help those inside.

Pauli's left leg was badly wrenched by the jump from the second floor. Magda suffered two broken ribs and many bruises.

The local police questioned Pauli, but didn't hold him. He was, after all, a hero. He told the officers that Geizig owed him wages. They said the jailed owner claimed to have no money. A station-house detective, a man with a German last name, heard about Pauli's situation and gave him five dollars from his own pocket.

Pauli had planned to ride freight cars to Chicago, but now, with his leg injured, he didn't dare try to jump aboard a moving train. Magda went with him to the depot. She helped him buy a second-class ticket for four dollars; the ticket agent said four dollars would take him as far as Pittsburgh.

"But what will you do after Pittsburgh?" Magda wanted to know, standing with him as the train prepared to depart.

"Walk," Pauli said with far more assurance than he felt.

THE second-class car was dingy, the benches were hard, soot and cinders were everywhere. Pauli stared out the window at the changing autumn landscape. That night it turned cold. Pauli was thankful when the train finally lurched into a huge shed and the conductor shouted, "Pittsburgh!"

He spent the rest of his money on a sack of apples, crackers, and hard candies, and asking directions of schoolchildren, tramps, and women hanging wash in their yards, he set out westward on foot. The first few days he made very slow progress because of his leg. Often he had to clench his teeth against the pain. But he wouldn't be deterred.

The sun hung a little lower in the sky every day. The weather was bleak. Fields were already harvested for winter. He slept in hay-mows or burrowed into frost-withered weeds. After his sack was empty, he ate when and where he could, sometimes begging food at a farmhouse in exchange for work. Now and again he rode a few miles with farmers driving wagons or peddlers traveling between towns.

It was December when he finally reached Indiana, traveling with an itinerant blacksmith. The weather had unexpectedly reversed itself in a spate of sunshine and warmth. The blacksmith let him off at a small farm town, and Pauli stopped at an apothecary's—a crowded, fragrant shop—for directions.

The apothecary was a craggy middle-aged man with a beard, who told him Chicago was a couple of hundred miles away and added, "This weather won't last. We could have snow any day." He studied the visitor. "You look like you could use a night's rest in a real bed."

"I could, yes, very much."

"Splendid. I'll be glad to have the company. I've been alone since my wife died last year. My name is Llewellyn Rhodes."

"Pauli Kroner. Sir, very much I thank you."

Rhodes seemed eager to talk. He cooked Pauli a big supper and told him that he'd served forty-six months in the war to save the Union. "You have heard of it?"

"Yes." Pauli nodded, though he wasn't absolutely sure.

After coffee, Rhodes gave Pauli one of his nightshirts, then led him to a bedroom above the shop.

In the morning Pauli prepared to leave. Despite a good night's sleep, he felt strange—alternately sweaty and chilled. The apothecary noticed and put his hand on Pauli's forehead.

"You're ill. You'd better stay another day or two."

"No. Already I have taken too long. I must hurry to Chicago."

"Well, the local to Chicago runs through here. I'll buy you a ticket the rest of the way. Don't say no. I've made up my mind."

So Llewellyn Rhodes took Pauli to a depot, just as Magda had.

THE car was little different from the one he'd ridden to Pittsburgh. Pauli was sweating and weak. It had turned bitter cold, and outside, a slanting snow was falling faster each minute.

Soon the train slowed to ten miles an hour. Then five. A gale wind blew, and everything outside disappeared in whiteness. The train stopped, caught in a raging blizzard. Drifts piled up.

The conductor said, "We're stuck till a work train with a plow gets here. Shouldn't be long."

Twelve hours later, after a long, freezing night, they were still waiting. The snow stopped finally, the wind slackened, but the train remained trapped. The hardiest travelers began to leave.

"You're damn fools," the conductor warned.

"I ain't goin' to freeze to death here," a man said. "How far's Chicago?"

"Seven or eight miles. There's a suburban station and switchyard about three miles up the line, but—"

"I'm goin'."

Pauli picked up his grip. He was going too.

THE snow along the right-of-way reached up to his thighs in some places. Behind him, dawn grayed the east, but day brought no warmth. The passengers whose example he was following weren't sick; they outdistanced him easily. Soon they dwindled to specks against the snowscape.

He staggered on, driven by his desire to reach his uncle's house. He'd come this far; he was damned if he'd be defeated by weather, sickness, or anything else.

About midmorning he came to the tiny suburban depot, lonely and isolated at one side of a switchyard. He was too sick to go on. He'd shelter here.

On the snow-covered platform he reached for the door. Turned the handle . . . Locked. Desperate, he searched the silent yards. He couldn't stand out here, he'd die. Bleary-eyed, he stumbled across a track and down a line of freight cars.

The first one was padlocked. The second also. He tried one more and found the padlock broken. He lifted it out of the hasp and rolled the door back.

Straw littered the floor of the car. He dragged himself inside, rolled the door shut, and sank down in the darkness. He piled straw on his legs and chest and fell into feverish sleep.

HE HEARD men outside and groggily opened his eyes.

"Mikey, the lock's gone. Better have a look."

The door rolled back. Bitter wind streamed in. Shafts of lantern light cut the darkness. "You. Come out, right now."

Shaking, Pauli lurched to the door. Two railroad policemen were on the ground. Their lanterns illuminated the blowing snow, making it sparkle.

"What's your name?" one man said.

"Kroner. Pauli Kroner."

"Listen to him," Mikey said. "Just off the boat, are you, boy?"

"Yes." Pauli nodded. "Please, this place is where?"

"This here's a switchyard outside Chicago. Don't you know you ain't permitted to sleep in these cars?"

"Trying to find my uncle," Pauli said. "In Chicago—"

If I don't die first. His teeth chattered furiously.

"Mikey, he's sick. Look at the sweat on his brow."

"Who's your uncle?" Mikey demanded.

"Josef—uh, Joseph Crown."

"The brewer?" said the other, the more kindly one.

"Yes, sir, do you know him?"

"What beer drinker don't? Can you prove it?"

"Ah, the hell with this," Mikey said. "Let the coppers sort it out."

"Who is that, please?" Pauli had a premonition that he knew. He swayed, dizzy again. But he couldn't quit, not this close to the home he'd dreamed of for so long.

"Mikey, let's leave him go. It's Christmas. Well, nearly."

Mikey said, "Got any idea where your uncle lives?"

Pauli's lips felt numb as he said, "Michigan Avenue."

"That's right, everybody knows the house," the other man said. "Corner of Twentieth Street. Big place."

"Your uncle brews a fine lager," Mikey said.

"Can you—" Pauli coughed, long and painful. "The way tell me? I mean—"

"I s'pose we could." Mikey lifted a mittened hand. "Climb down. The trains aren't runnin' yet. You'll have to walk."

"I can walk," Pauli said. He grasped the hand and jumped, but his weak leg buckled and he fell. They helped him up.

It was early evening. All of Chicago was still paralyzed by the storm. The streets were deserted. Pauli followed the directions given him by the railroad men. He staggered along, peering at street signs, working northward on Michigan Avenue until he found Twentieth Street. There was the house, a veritable castle on the corner. Electric light streamed from almost every window.

It was three stories, built of gray limestone, with a covered carriage entrance on the side and an iron fence surrounding the whole. He knew it was the right house. On the wrought-iron gate on the Michigan Avenue side, forming part of the decorative pattern of the arch above, there was a crown.

He pushed the gate inward and dragged his grip up the stone steps to the covered front porch. He twisted a metal tab on the carved door. Deep in the house, a bell rang.

The man who answered had a pale horseface, suspicious eyes.

"I am your nephew from Germany."

"I beg your pardon?" The pale man scowled. Pauli realized his mistake. The man wore a starched white apron.

"Wait just a moment." The door slammed, but not before Pauli was enfolded in a cloud of warmth, the sweet odor of pine.

The wind keened. Pauli's legs felt too weak to support him. The door opened again. There stood a rather short, wiry man with sleek silver hair, mustache, and beard. His posture was correct, his brown eyes large and alert behind wire spectacles. He wore gray trousers and a dark blue coat. He smelled of shaving talc. He instantly inspired respect and a touch of fear in Pauli.

But the man's welcome was hearty. "Come in, come in."

Pauli obeyed. "Uncle Josef? Here is your nephew Pauli!" he exclaimed, thrust back into German by the excitement.

"*In diesem Haus, sprechen wir gewöhnlich Englisch.* I am saying we usually speak—"

"Yes, English. I understand. I understand a little."

The man laid his hand on Pauli's shoulder. "So. You are my nephew—at long last."

153

"Yes, sir. From Berlin. I am calling myself—" He didn't know where it came from, but it was suddenly there in his head, perfect, the name he needed and wanted. "Paul Crown. Is it all right?"

Joseph Crown smiled at the sick, bedraggled boy. "Paul Crown. Yes. Come in, this way. The family's gathered—"

Pauli put down his grip and moved toward an open double door flooded with light. Joe Crown stood aside to let him pass. He coughed when he caught a whiff of Pauli.

Pauli didn't notice. His head tilted back in awe. The foyer he was crossing rose up in marble splendor, like a cathedral. A huge chandelier hung from the center of the ceiling. To one side, by a broad staircase, stood a great Christmas tree with twinkling glass balls and dozens of unlit candles.

Uncle Joseph prodded him forward. "Come, don't be shy. The family is eager to meet you. We've been worried about you."

Ears ringing, heart pounding, Pauli shuffled toward the tall doors from which the light streamed. Doors to a new life . . .

He saw a stout woman with a mass of dark reddish brown hair piled up on her head. And three young people. The smallest, a boy, was burly. An older boy was slightly built, with a russet beard and luxuriant mustache. The girl was thin, with frizzy hair. The three were staring at Pauli. So was the servant in the apron.

Pauli saw logs blazing in the hearth of this private family room, and the traditional table decorated with red candles and green boughs and piled with packages in gold and silver and scarlet paper. He wanted to weep for joy.

"Look here, everyone," his uncle said. "It's Pauli from Germany, at last. You know, Pauli, your aunt Ilsa and I were expecting you long ago. We were concerned. Was the trip especially difficult?"

"Oh, no," Pauli said, perhaps foolishly, but not wanting to spoil the moment. He stiffened. Dizziness was assaulting him again.

"When did your ship dock in New York?"

"*Juni*. Ah—June. The first day."

"And you've been traveling ever since?"

Pauli nodded, struggling. "Some—uh—train—but more walking."

"Amazing," his uncle said. "No wonder we didn't hear from—"

"Joseph," the stout woman interrupted, "can't we go into this later? The boy looks exhausted."

Ilsa Crown stepped forward, gently taking control. "You'd like a bath and a rest, I'm sure." She touched Pauli's brow. "Joseph, he has a fever!" She gestured toward a huge sofa with dark claw feet and pale ivory upholstery. "Please, sit down."

Pauli moved forward. He started to thank them all in a burst of gratitude. Words stuck in his throat. Everything tilted. The candles went out, and he fainted onto the pale sofa.

He slid off, leaving dirty streaks on the fabric. There were exclamations from the children. Ilsa covered her mouth.

Joe Crown stared at the heap on the carpet. He'd never seen anyone so dirty.

Part Three
CHICAGO
1892–1893

PAUL ✦ Light and space. He'd never known so much of either. His room, which overlooked the yard and gardens, was fit for a palace.

He lay in bed for six days, fussed over by his aunt and by Helga Blenkers, a short, heavy woman with a cheerful disposition. She was the housemaid. Her husband, Manfred, was the unfriendly steward who'd first opened the door to Paul.

Mrs. Blenkers brought him trays laden with good German food. Thick slices of home-baked pumpernickel; roast pork and veal— always with dumplings; Aunt Ilsa's delicious *Torten*.

Beginning on his second day in bed, he was visited by the different members of the family.

Uncle Joe's first visit occurred after *Abendessen,* the evening meal, which was seldom eaten in German households before eight p.m. He appeared at the bedside in both coat and cravat. Despite his slight stature, he was a profoundly imposing man. Paul wanted his uncle to respect and like him.

"How are you feeling, Paul?"

"I am fine, Uncle," he answered, still laboring over every word of the English.

"We want you to be happy here, Paul. We want you to be happy in Chicago. You'll find many countrymen in this city. At the last census there were one hundred sixty thousand Germans."

Paul murmured and strove to look impressed.

"Tell me, how was my sister Lotte when you left her?"

A warning signal rang in Paul's head. He mustn't say a word about the *Herren;* it would hurt his uncle. "She was not feeling well."

Uncle Joe seemed sad for a moment. "I must write her. Tell me a little about your journey, won't you? Surely there were some troubles. It took you so long—"

"There were." Paul nodded. He began with a description of Die Goldene Tür but minimized his heroic performance in saving Magda. He described some of the other incidents: the kindness of Llewellyn Rhodes, the blizzard that stopped the train.

"And you walked all the way from there, as sick as you were?"

"I did, sir. I was—uh—eager. I knew I had taken too long."

"That is impressive, Paul. It testifies to your character." Uncle Joe leaned over and patted his arm. "Rest now. I really hope you'll be on your feet soon. I want you to get acquainted with your cousins. I know you'll like them."

"Oh, certainly," Paul said, fervently hoping it would be so.

Frederica, called Fritzi, paid a visit and then came back at least twice each day thereafter. She was rather plain looking, and less than a month away from her twelfth birthday. She had dark brown eyes, like her father, and a lot of disorderly blond hair.

Fritzi was lively and friendly. She sat on the edge of Paul's bed, bouncing up and down. "I want to be an actress," she told him.

Paul wanted all the cousins to like him, but what he really cared about was getting close to Joseph Junior, the oldest, who was almost seventeen. In Paul's eyes Joe Junior was a grown-up, practically a man. He was old enough to let his beard grow out. He was abroad in the world; he worked six days a week at the brewery.

Carl, the youngest, came in too. He was a burly dark-haired boy who had turned ten in November. His face resembled Ilsa's, but his shoulders were so wide, his trunk so thick, he looked like he'd come from a different set of parents. His charm and his smile won every heart. He was sometimes clumsy around the house, but never in sports, which he loved.

"Do you want to see my baseball?" he asked.

"Yes, yes."

The ball had heavy red stitching along its seams. "It's an official league ball, from Mr. Spalding's store downtown. Mr. Spalding, he was one of the greatest pitchers ever. This is my fielder's glove." Carl smacked the ball into the curious right-hand glove whose separate fingers were thick as sausages. "Will you play baseball with me?"

"You will have to teach me."

"I'll teach you," Carl said with an emphatic nod. "When spring comes, maybe Papa will take us to watch the Chicago White Stockings. Papa used to take Joe and me, but Joe won't go anymore."

"I'll go."

"Good," Carl cried, leaping up so forcefully that his shoulder banged the whatnot Aunt Ilsa had brought in for Pauli to store his treasures on. It went over with a crash. "Oh-oh." Hastily he righted the whatnot and collected Paul's scattered things. "I don't think it's hurt," he said as he handed the globe and stand to Paul for inspection. "I'm sorry."

"No, it's all right." Paul realized that Carl was a little boy blessed with a strong body and an excess of energy.

Finally, on Paul's third day of confinement, his cousin Joe dropped in.

Joseph Junior resembled his short, slender father, except in the color of his eyes. They were a blazing blue. His full beard and mustache made him appear older than seventeen. He was cordial yet reserved as he sat in the chair by the bed.

"You work at the brewery," Paul began.

"Yep. On the front line, you could say."

"I beg your pardon?"

"The front line of the class war—between capital and labor."

How solemn and earnest he was. And Paul didn't have the slightest idea what he was talking about. Joe Junior saw this and said, "It isn't so hard to understand, cousin. My pop's a capitalist. Or couldn't you tell by looking around?" His wave embraced the room, the house. "He's always wanted me to work in the front office someday. But I'll be damned if I will. I work with my hands and my back. I sweat just like ninety-nine percent of the human race. We sweat and die so the other one percent can get rich."

Still baffled, Paul decided to say nothing. Joe Junior watched him with those blazing blue eyes. There was a pause. "Should I call you kid? How old are you?"

"Fifteen."

"Just a baby."

Crimson flowed into Paul's face.

Joe Junior grinned. "Come on, I'm ragging you. Got a girl in the old country?"

Paul shook his head.

Cousin Joe hitched his chair closer. "Well, I've got a girl. Prettiest thing you ever saw. She's a bohunk."

Confounded yet again, Paul mumbled, "What?"

"That's what they call Bohemians over here—bohunks. Her name is Roza Jablonec. Roza, spelled with a z. She hates it. She's going to change it someday when she's a famous singer. I call her Rosie." He lowered his voice. "Rosie is hot stuff." He cupped his hands six inches in front of his chest. Paul's eyes bugged. "Maybe we can find that kind of girl for you," Joe said, getting up. "See you soon, cousin. Get well."

He went out, leaving Paul disturbed by the hint of animosity between Joe Junior and his father. He didn't want to be caught in the middle of some family quarrel.

Two days later Dr. Plattweiler, the family's physician, pronounced him well. "Just in time, eh? Christmas is next Sunday."

Aunt Ilsa brought him clothes and underwear and shoes, all wonderfully new. Paul felt strong again, eager to leave his room and join the others downstairs, to really live in the great house.

That evening he stood on the second-floor landing and gazed down into the foyer for a long moment. He could hear the clatter and talk from the dining room. Trepidation seized him.

Go on, don't be scared. This is what you wanted. This is home.

Stepping very slowly, he went down the great stair. He hesitated a second time near the enormous, heavily decorated tree.

Conversation and delicious odors drifted from the slightly parted doors of the dining room. Swallowing hard and taking a deep breath, he grasped both doors and pushed them back.

Aunt Ilsa jumped up from the long table. "Why, here's Pauli."

159

Uncle Joe hurried from the table and flung an arm around him. "Welcome, Paul. Sit. Have some food."

Paul's tension snapped, and with a dizzy delight he grinned and walked to the empty chair, knowing it would be all right.

IN THE week that followed, he learned many things, including the reassuring fact that although he was in America, Christmas in the house of his relatives still had strong German overtones. Traditional mistletoe was hung up. Each night after dinner the family gathered around the small pump organ in the music room. Aunt Ilsa played, and Uncle Joe led the caroling. Everyone sang favorites like "O Tannenbaum" and "Stille Nacht, Heilige Nacht." Everyone except Joe Junior, who absented himself, visibly annoying his father.

The daily routine was also not very different from that of a typical German household, but Paul felt swamped by all the new words and ideas pouring down on him. Carl made it worse by using slang, like "swell" and "gee." Paul had to watch faces and gestures to catch on.

Saturday, Christmas Eve, brought a special excitement to the household. Uncle Joe had come home early. So had Joe Junior, who seemed almost jocular for a change. At six o'clock, with great ceremony, family and servants gathered at the tree. Aunt Ilsa brought a single candle in a brass holder. Manfred set up a stepladder. Uncle Joe, fully dressed in coat and cravat, touched a taper to the candle, climbed the ladder, and lit a white candle. He lit others. Soon the whole tree was aglow.

It was a familiar ceremony, but Paul and Aunt Lotte had only been able to afford a small tree, with a few candles. Paul was filled with exaltation and joy, a sense of truly belonging here. The feeling was even stronger when Aunt Ilsa hugged him against her side.

They trooped to the dining room for the special meal of carp. Joe Junior and Paul were served Crown lager in enameled steins. Even Carl and Fritzi were each allowed a small glass. Aunt Ilsa drank punch. Everyone was jolly, save for Joe Junior, who said little.

After supper the servants appeared again and followed the family to the doors of the formal parlor. With great ceremony Uncle Joe produced a brass key and unlocked the doors. He reached in and switched on the lights. Fritzi gasped, and Carl jumped up and down at the sight of the presents heaped everywhere.

The servants received small gifts and cash from the Crowns. Paul was touched when Aunt Ilsa handed him several packages. His gifts consisted of three shirts, a school slate, a straight razor engraved with his name, and, finest of all, a gold pocket watch.

"Joey, what did you get?" Fritzi exclaimed from behind a brightly painted marionette theater.

"Clothes mostly. Do you s'pose I should give them to the poor people who are out there starving tonight?"

Uncle Joe threw a sharp look at his son. Joe Junior stared back, his bright blue eyes calmly defiant.

ILSA ✦ Early on the second day of the new year of 1893 Ilsa was seated at one end of the long dining table, her usual collection of Chicago newspapers, both English- and German-language, spread in a fan in front of her.

Joe Crown came in briskly, kissed his wife on the cheek, then took his place at the far end of the table. Ilsa said, "You're a bit late for work this morning, aren't you?"

"Yes. I wanted to have a talk about our nephew. Where is he?"

"Outside, with Pete, helping in the garden. Pauli works willingly. He's eager to please. What did you want to discuss about him?"

"First, the matter of a tutor."

"We already agreed it's a good idea."

"All right, I'll have Zwick place an advertisement. Now, as to the boy's general welfare—it seems to me that he has a rather low opinion of himself. He needs a respectable trade where he can see his accomplishments and have them recognized."

Ilsa sighed. "Not the brewery, Joe. Not yet. He needs schooling. Formal schooling, not merely a tutor."

"All right, schooling." He was looking at her, and not warmly. "You reject a job in the brewery very quickly, Ilsa."

"No, no, not at all. But first he needs—"

"After all these years," he interrupted, "my work is still an issue."

"You know the reason. Papa—"

"Spare me," he said with untypical curtness. It annoyed her.

"There's also the question of reputation, which we have discussed many times. Many, many people think of a brewer only one way. As a man who makes money promoting drunkenness."

Joe Crown began to rub a large polished boar's tooth hanging from his watch chain. "I do not promote drunkenness, Ilsa. I make and sell a wholesome, nourishing drink. As good for you in its way as cheese or meat or milk. I take it in moderation, and I've always been in excellent health. I'm sick of the way the industry is constantly accused of promoting idleness, crime, sexual license, the disintegration of families. We're always lumped in with the whiskey distillers—a further insult. Furthermore, I run an honest brewery. I don't allow my men the usual drinking privilege."

"That's true, but I still can't help my feelings about—"

He pushed his teacup away. "This is a fruitless discussion. Excuse me, Ilsa, I'm already behind schedule. I'll see to enrolling Pauli at school. I won't be home for dinner today. Good-bye."

He didn't stop to give her a second kiss, as he usually did on his way out. Ilsa heard the back door of the house close loudly.

She was both annoyed and sad. She really didn't like to make Joe angry or hurt his pride. But she had her own opinions and convictions. At age twenty, a proper German girl in Cincinnati, she would have kept them deeply hidden. No longer.

Ilsa Crown loved her husband unreservedly. Joseph Crown was a man driven to succeed, and it was this drive that enabled her to live and raise her children in fine surroundings. But there was a bad side to it. Joe was also driven to order the world as he wanted it. Which, given the changing nature of life and the contradictions in human beings, frequently led to conflict.

Ilsa was four years younger than her husband. She had been born Ilsa Schlottendorf, in Bavaria, in 1846. Her parents were farm people who produced only one child.

Several years of bad weather and poor crops—and her father's talent for failure—drove the family to the wall. The farm was sold for just enough money for railway tickets to Bremen and steerage tickets to New York. Ilsa was ten.

The family traveled directly to Cincinnati. With two partners Ilsa's father bought a tract of land, convinced that, since this part of America resembled the wine regions of Germany, they could import cuttings from the Rhine and the Moselle valleys and after a few years have a profitable winery. But Ilsa's father failed again. The climate was wrong. The fledgling industry quickly died and with it her father's last hope. What happened afterward scarred her forever.

Ilsa didn't meet her future husband until the summer of 1861.

The Union was at war with the rebel South. Cincinnati, though officially in the northern camp, seethed with divided loyalties. The city was a major depot for runaway blacks following the Underground Railroad north to Canada and freedom. It was also heavily infested with secesh—secessionist—sympathizers.

On a muggy night in August of 1861 Ilsa went with her cousin, Mary Schimmel, to an abolitionist gathering at a local lodge hall. Several orators addressed the crowd with emotional denunciations of slavery.

By the end of the meeting, everyone left the hall with a renewed determination to support the war. "Now where did we tie the buggy?" Mary asked Ilsa. The vacant lot that ran beside the wooden lodge hall was crowded with departing vehicles churning up clouds of dust. Their horse and buggy was picketed at the rear of the lot, now nearly pitch-black. Suddenly Ilsa gripped her cousin's arm.

"Mary, look, there's our buggy. What are those men doing to it?"

Two men were silhouetted against the lantern light of a grogshop beyond the lot. They were slashing at the traces of the horse. The freed horse bolted into the street and galloped away.

"Get away, that's our property," Ilsa cried, running. Too angry to be frightened, she flung herself on the nearest man.

"Ow," the man yelled, and rammed his elbow into her. Ilsa reeled back. "Let's take care of these two nigger lovers, Jud."

Mary was moaning, terrified. Ilsa looked around. People were still leaving, but in the huge dust clouds Ilsa and her cousin went unnoticed.

"Grab her, Tom," Jud said. The man called Tom leaped at Ilsa.

"You reb monsters," she cried, wrenching and kicking. She fell to one knee.

Suddenly Tom exclaimed, "Jud, look out!"

In heavily accented English, someone was shouting, "Leave those women alone." Ilsa saw a small, trim figure snatch their buggy whip from its socket and lay it across Tom's face. "Get out of here. Get out of here before I kill you both." The rebs wasted no time disappearing down the rutted street.

The stranger dusted off his black coat and smoothed his hair. He was young, and he carried himself with authority. He held out his hand. Ilsa clasped it, feeling the strength in it. With his help she stood up.

In German he asked, "Are you all right?"

"Yes. But my cousin—what about her?"

The stranger knelt over Mary, who lay near the buggy, eyes closed. "Only fainted, I think. This is terrible. Friends told me there might be southern partisans outside the hall, but I had no idea they would get so ugly." He began to pat Mary's cheek.

Suddenly his head lifted. "Oh, forgive me, I'm being impolite. I failed to introduce myself."

Ilsa managed a shy laugh. "Well—under the circumstances—"

Mary groaned and sat up. The stranger stepped away. By the grogshop's light Ilsa clearly saw his strong young face for the first time. "My name is Josef Kroner," he said, and bowed.

Ever afterward Ilsa said that was the moment she fell in love with him.

Josef didn't propose to Ilsa until after the war. By that time he'd adopted the name Joe Crown and was a toughened veteran, having ridden all the way to Georgia with General Sherman's cavalry. He made his proposal simply. "Will you do me the honor of becoming my wife, Ilsa?"

She answered from her heart. "I don't know."

He looked stunned, then wounded. "But you say you love me."

"I do love you. But I don't love the brewery business."

There was the problem. He'd declared his ambition as soon as he came home to Cincinnati. He intended to leave Imbrey's Brewery, where he'd worked before the war. Launch out on his own, build his own brewery. His own fortune, his own life.

"You see, I want no part of anyone connected with brewing or distilling, Joe. I have memories. Memories of my poor father."

"Your father— You've never told me much about him."

"Papa was a drunkard. He always drank. But after his vineyard failed, he drank almost constantly. Then one night during a town celebration he got drunk, fell into the canal, and drowned. So you see why I don't care very much for anyone who helps another human being to that kind of end."

Ilsa Schlottendorf married Joe Crown anyway, because her enormous love overcame her distinctly un-German feelings against beer. For many years she fitted into the expected pattern and never criticized her husband's business. Of late that had changed.

Of late many things were changing for the Crowns.

JOE CROWN ✦ Joe's argument with Ilsa upset him. It was well into the morning before he calmed down. He understood her dislike of the brewery, but he resented it. He ran Crown's in an honorable and upright way. He never engaged in fixing of prices. He withheld his beer from any establishment found to engage in prostitution. He didn't hire children. His colleagues said he'd lost a lot of business that way. And still it wasn't enough for Ilsa—because of her father and her radical female friends. Miss Frances Willard of the Women's Christian Temperance Union, Miss Jane Addams of the Hull House settlement—that lot.

Joe was proud of his wife's independence and intelligence. He only wished that independence, and all the churning forces of the new age—socialism and anarchism, free love, and rights for women, to name a few of the worst—had not carried her so far. Modernity was fine for a man. For a wife, no.

That night, when he and Ilsa got into bed together, the breakfast-table quarrel wasn't mentioned. Joe reached under the covers to grasp her hand. She pressed against him in the darkness and kissed his chin.

"About Paul's enrollment in school—" she started.

"I'll speak to him. I am already making inquiries."

"Thank you, Joe." She kissed him again, and in a few moments he heard her gentle breathing as she fell asleep.

He was wide awake. The house creaked and cracked in the grip of the iron cold of January. He thought about Paul. His troubles aboard ship, his hazardous trek to Chicago. He couldn't help contrasting that with his own emigration. He'd experienced hardship, hunger, and even hostility. But his long journey from Aalen to Cincinnati had never been violent.

He recalled the revolution of 1848, which had been a terrifying time for his family and for him. He was only seven years old when his father, Thomas Kroner, was hanged, in 1849. Soon the little hotel and brewery fell on hard times. When—shortly after—Josef's mother, Gertrude, died; family friends helped arrange the sale of the property. It fetched a very low price, barely enough to cover debts.

Josef moved in with a family from their church, and so did his brother and his sister. In 1855, embittered about Germany, the hopelessness of life there, Josef began to listen to stories about America and to save his money. In 1857, at fifteen, he left Aalen forever.

On board ship, the food was plain but plentiful and the summer ocean was smooth all the way. In New York City, he found a job as a general helper at the large and gloomy Bowery Theater. As soon as he'd saved enough money, he planned to buy a cheap train ticket to St. Louis. But the theater's box office cashier happened to have a brother in Cincinnati who ran an ice company. The cashier liked Josef and gave him a letter of introduction. How amazing, the small turns that sent a man down one road instead of another. But for the cashier of the Bowery Theater he might have settled in St. Louis. He would never have met Ilsa or found himself a rich though often troubled man in a new homeland.

Fourteen inches of snow fell on Chicago at the end of the first week in January, 1893. On Sunday, Joe organized everyone to go outside. Everyone except Joe Junior, who had already left for Lincoln Park to ice-skate with friends.

Ilsa and the children bundled up in their heaviest coats and mufflers. Joe stuffed his gloves in a pocket and took his Kodak camera.

"Everyone stand in a line, please. I want to take your picture against the drifts."

As Joe squinted, lining up his picture, he noticed Paul's face. The boy's eyes were fixed on the camera. He was enthralled.

After they went inside for hot cocoa in the kitchen, Joe said, "Paul, please come along to the study. I want to speak to you."

Joe Crown's study was on the first floor of the mansion.

"Close the door, please, Paul. Sit down." Paul drew a chair close to the desk. Joe laid the boxy black Kodak on some papers. Before he was quite ready to begin, Paul spoke.

"Uncle Joe, how much did that cost?" He pointed to the camera.

Surprised, Joe said, "Do you want one?"

"Very much, someday, yes."

Joe picked up the camera. "Eastman's company offers several models now. This one cost eight dollars and twenty cents. Now—"

"I have another question, Uncle. Does anyone earn money from photographs?"

Joe thought about that. "Perhaps the printers who produce postal cards or pictures for parlor stereoscopes."

"I mean, does anyone make money—pushing the button?"

"Ah. Taking pictures. No, I think not. Not a decent living anyway. This is a remarkable invention, but I can't see that it will ever be much more than a novelty. After all, how many family portraits or views of the Great Wall in China does one person want?"

Joe laid the camera aside, noting his nephew's look of disappointment. "Paul, I must speak to you about your education. I have engaged a young man to tutor you in English."

"Thank you, Uncle."

"Your aunt and I have discussed the subject of your welfare at great length. We feel"—*she feels*—"that you should enroll in public school. I believe you're well enough prepared to understand classroom teaching, though at a lower level than your age would otherwise dictate. The tutor will help too. Accordingly, we will start you in school as soon as possible."

"The same school as Fritzi and Carl?"

"No, a different one, across town. . . . What's wrong?"

Paul's palms were pressed down so hard on his knees that his knuckles were white. "Sir, I am not good with studies—"

"You dislike schoolwork?"

"Truly, sir—yes. I like to learn things about America. But freely, in the city. Walking, looking—"

"As your whim dictates, is that it? I'm afraid you'll get nowhere in this world living by whim, Paul. You must be educated."

"I will teach myself, sir. Study hard alone—"

Sharply Joe said, "You've never heard the old proverb?" He spoke it in German first. "He that teaches himself has a fool for a master." He waited. "You have something more to say?"

"Yes, sir. My cousin Joe, he works in your brewery. Couldn't I?" There was a clear desperation in Paul's voice now.

"In a year or two, when we see how you've gotten along, that may be possible. I don't want to seem harsh, Paul, but you are my responsibility, therefore I will decide. You will be enrolled."

"Yes, sir." The look on his face was one of utter dread.

"It will be all right," Joe said. "You'll soon feel at home in school." Paul nodded bleakly. "Thank you, Paul, that will be all."

The prospect of school was terrible indeed, but Paul didn't want to appear an ingrate. He rose and went out without a sound.

Joe Crown laid a hand on the Kodak and sat there frowning.

167

Ilsa was wrong. He's not suited for it. Hundreds of men educate themselves. I did it successfully. I should have resisted Ilsa. I have a definite feeling, no good will come of this.

PAUL ✦ One afternoon at the end of January, Paul sat in the kitchen with a cup of hot cocoa Aunt Ilsa had fixed for him. Although the Crowns employed a cook, Louise Volzenheim, Aunt Ilsa supervised and did a great deal of the cooking. Now she was busily mixing starter dough for a new batch of pumpernickel. She paused in her work to ask Paul whether he had any hobbies.

He said he liked to collect cards with photos of distant places on them.

"Ah, picture postcards. You'll find plenty of those in America. I expect you need a way to display them in your room."

She assigned Carl to help him find a smooth board in the cellar. Nicky Speers, the driver, located a can of gray paint and a brush. Helga Blenkers helped Paul hang the freshly painted board in his room. It was crude, but Aunt Ilsa said it looked nice. She supplied some pins, and Paul carefully mounted the stereoscope card on the board.

Aunt Ilsa examined the wood globe. "Pauli, I have another suggestion. You are a traveled person now. Perhaps you should keep a record here. A mark for every important place you've seen."

He was enthusiastic, so out of the cellar came a small can of red enamel paint and a delicate brush. With his aunt watching, he put a tiny dot on Berlin, then a dot on Hamburg, a third on New York, a fourth on Chicago.

"Ah, it looks fine," she said. "There will be many more places marked as you go through life—fascinating places. I am sure of it." She hugged him.

He was melted by this latest outpouring of caring. For Aunt Ilsa—Uncle Joe too—he would endure the sentence of school, even though it was sure to be hellish.

THERE came trudging through five inches of snow, wearing a long, threadbare coat with a fur collar, Mr. W. E. Mars—Winston Elphinstone Mars of Wisconsin, the tutor.

Mr. Mars was in his thirties, pale as a new snowdrift, with black hair parted in the center. He had been engaged to work with Paul in his room every afternoon from three until six. Mr. Mars was a gentle and patient man; Paul liked him. He taught reading by putting into Paul's hand a book called *McGuffey's Fifth Eclectic Reader*, and he taught the devilish intricacies of English grammar with a slate and chalk.

One evening soon after the arrival of Mr. Mars, Uncle Joe called Paul to the study again. Paul stood in front of his uncle's chair, nervous, as he always was in this room.

"Paul, today I spoke with the principal of the school you will attend. He understands that you are a newcomer. He will see that you are placed in the right class. Next Monday morning I will accompany you to school in our carriage, to sign any necessary papers. After that, you will ride the streetcar." Uncle Joe paused. "Do you have anything to say?"

Resentment bubbled up in Paul. He drew himself up tall and looked his uncle in the eye. "I would rather not go, sir. I would rather work."

"I know that. But it's settled. Good night, Paul." He had turned back to his desk before Paul reached the door.

MONDAY morning, gray as death. A freezing, damp day. A few snowflakes drifting down. The carriage pulled up before the two-story school. It seemed huge, forbidding to Paul as he and his uncle moved up the worn wooden steps.

The principal, Mr. Relph, shook Paul's hand and told Uncle Joe that the new pupil would be placed in the class taught by one of the school's finest, Mrs. Elsie Petigru. Uncle Joe said that sounded excellent. He wished Paul well and bade him good-bye.

Paul followed the principal down a gloomy hall to a wooden door. The principal opened the door, led him in. With horror Paul saw that the pupils in the room looked younger and smaller than he— mere children.

"Mrs. Petigru, this is your new student, Paul Crown."

The principal left. Paul waited beside the teacher's desk. A dozen pairs of eyes scrutinized him.

"Take your seat in the second row. The last desk." Mrs. Petigru pointed. She was a drab woman, with graying hair in a severe bun, a slit for a mouth. "And comb your hair; you're a sight."

"Please, I combed it before—"

"Don't answer back, young man. That's rule number one. Rule number two, I demand neatness from my pupils. You don't appear to live up to that standard. Sit quietly today. Don't speak unless you're addressed." She folded her arms. "I'll be frank with you, Paul. I did not want you brought into my class. I protested, and I was overruled. I'll tell you why I didn't want you. First, you are too old. Second, your uncle is a brewer, and he's German. I consider that a satanic combination. I am a religious, God-fearing woman. My husband is a lay preacher. We don't like godless Germans who profane the Sabbath with revelry and strong drink."

Paul couldn't endure it. His chin lifted. Anger danced in his eyes. "Mrs. Petigru, Germans go to church on Sunday. Only after—"

"I distinctly told you not to answer back. I have had other pupils who tried to get the better of me. They always lose."

JOE CROWN ✦ Joe Crown noted that during his nephew's first weeks at school the boy was withdrawn and much less prone to smile. Several times Joe made a point of asking Paul how he was getting along. The answer was always the same.

"Fine, Uncle."

Joe was soon suspicious. And when he looked into Paul's eyes, he saw a look that reminded him of a whipped dog. Shaken, he thought, I had a premonition about this. Has it come true already?

APRIL arrived. Throughout Chicago, municipal crews were preparing for the opening of the Exposition on May 1. Old buildings were repainted, thoroughfares were cleaned, parks replanted with young trees. A festive mood seemed to prevail, but the business community knew that clouds were lowering. Banks were in trouble; prices of shares were sliding. Hundreds of unemployed men were adrift in the streets.

Although this disturbed Joe, little of it touched his household. One morning Joe came to the breakfast table to find Ilsa immersed as usual in her newspapers. After they kissed, he took his seat and asked, "What are your plans today, my dear?"

With a teasing smile she said, "Shall I tell you? What kind of a mood are you in?"

"Good enough to withstand anything. It's a lovely day."

"At noon I'll be dining with Ellen and Jane." Ellen Starr and Jane

Addams, her friends from the Hull House settlement, which helped the poor. "This afternoon we're all attending a discussion program on prostitution and the double standard."

"I see." He didn't want to be annoyed with her, but he was. He saw no point in women upsetting the status quo by delving into radical or unsavory issues. "Frankly, I wish you'd stay away from Miss Addams and Miss Starr—and especially that harpy Frances Willard."

"Joe, Miss Willard is a fine, moral person. The Women's Christian Temperance Union advocates moderation, and there is nothing wrong with—"

"Oh, yes, there is. Because first it will be moderation, then prohibition. The word has been bandied about before."

"I won't have you saying things about the W.C.T.U. that aren't true. The organization works in many social areas—worthy ones. Child labor. The welfare of unfortunate young women lured to the streets. I'm proud to contribute money to that effort."

"Money earned from beer sales, don't forget."

"Perhaps my activities can wash away some of the taint, then."

Joe flung his napkin down. "Ilsa, that's uncalled for."

Contrite, Ilsa rushed around the table and threw her arms around his neck. "You're right, I'm sorry. I have opinions of my own, and I just don't want you to run over me. But I have no right to be mean about it. Forgive me?"

"Always." He kissed her warm cheek, mollified.

PAUL ✦ School was torture. A repetitive, soul-deadening routine of recitation and memorization. Paul's mathematics exercises consistently received a failing grade. Mrs. Petigru wrote notes all over his papers, disparaged his handwriting, criticized his pronunciation, and badgered him about his appearance almost every day. She was Paul's enemy, but he didn't know what to do about it. Tell Uncle Joe? No, he didn't want his uncle deciding that he fell short, unable to live up to the expectations of the family. Mr. Mars, who was now coming to the house only two afternoons a week, was sympathetic to Paul's plight, but could offer no advice beyond, "Tell the truth. It's the honorable way."

One morning at recess a boy from the class approached him shyly and asked if he wanted to shoot marbles. Paul almost whooped for

171

joy. He said he had no marbles of his own. The boy eagerly shared his sack. A bond was sealed.

The boy was Leo Rapoport. Short, round-faced, with black eyes, Leo had a kindly and merry disposition, Paul discovered. Yet mysteriously, he too was an outcast. One day he explained why: "My pa's a Unitarian, but he was born a Jew. Mama's Roman Catholic. It's a pretty bad combination, a Unitarian and an R.C. It means you're liable to get beat up twice as often."

"Tell me more about your mother and father," Paul said.

"They sure aren't rich like your uncle. Mama's a very high-class lady, though. She gives piano lessons."

"What does your father do?"

"He's a drummer—a peddler. He sells ladies' corsets. Hot stuff." Leo rolled his eyes. "I could bring some pictures maybe."

"Yes, why not?"

Leo also had valuable advice: "Don't ever make old Petigru mad. If that happens, she takes her ruler out of the bottom drawer. It's this long—this thick. She uses it on your hands. You won't be able to do penmanship exercises for a week."

PAUL hurried every Saturday to finish whatever jobs Aunt Ilsa asked him to do around the house. Then, with her permission, he hopped on a car to explore the city. Sometimes Leo joined him. Leo had been born in Chicago, and he knew a lot about the city. If he didn't know something, Uncle Joe did. From them, and from his own sharp observations, Paul was getting an education about the history and character of a great metropolis.

Che-cau-go was an old name, he learned. It might have meant "wild onion," or it might have meant "bad stink." Nobody was sure. Over the years—as a village grew up around an early trading station on the lake, and a town followed the village, and then a sprawling city—a profusion of somewhat more relevant names followed: Porkopolis, because of meat-packing, and Gem of the Prairie, no explanation needed. But for all its modernity, little more than a generation before, Indians had walked the streets. It made Paul's hair prickle to think of it.

Almost a million people crowded Chicago now. There was no sign of the growth stopping; buildings in progressive new styles were rising everywhere. A railway elevated above the street ran to

172

the South and West sides, and there were plans to bring it to the center of town. This downtown was a pandemonium of buggies, wagons, cable cars, horsecars, and pedestrians, all hurrying all the time. There were thriving theaters, large stores like Field's and Elstree's, and splendid hostelries, like Mr. Potter Palmer's famous eight-story Palmer House on State Street.

There were the fine areas of mansions belonging to the newly rich—you couldn't find many old rich in a city so young—and it was in one of these, lower Michigan Avenue, that the Crowns lived. The most prestigious address, however, was Prairie Avenue, down around Eighteenth Street. Here lived the Pullmans, the Fields, the Armours. Aunt Ilsa told Paul that some Prairie Avenue residents called Potter Palmer a traitor for moving away and building his present castle on North Lake Shore Drive.

Chicago was at all hours a raucous choir of street vendors. Push-cart men sold pins, pears, matches, hot ears of corn from tin boxes. The streets resounded with the chant of the old clothes man, the squeal and shriek of the scissor grinder's wheel spitting sparks, the bellow of the newsboy hawking something called an extra. There were silent vendors as well—sickly, sallow creatures who wore gaudy placards strapped on, front and back, and shuffled from block to block. Sandwich men, Carl called them when one of them passed the house. Joe Junior called them the downtrodden, with a look at his father.

Chicago was a pall of coal smoke, a wind reeking of raw meat, a miasma of floating river garbage. Chicago was noise, dirt, poverty, bright lights, vigor, danger. It reminded Paul of Berlin, and despite the horrors of school, he fell in love with it.

ON SATURDAY morning, two weeks before the opening of the Exposition, a knock at the bedroom door dragged Paul out of bed at six o'clock. He was surprised to find Joe Junior there, already dressed.

His cousin shut the door and leaned back with an amiable smile. "What are you doing this afternoon?"

Paul was flustered, but delighted by his cousin's interest. "Pete has work for me in the garden. I'm not sure how much."

"Tell him you can't do it today. The brewery closes at noon for a warehouse inventory. Meet me there, and I'll show you the little corners of Chicago you'll never find on your own." He winked. Paul was speechless.

Assuming a vaguely fatherly air, Joe Junior crossed his arms. "Well, old man, what about it? Will you come?"

"Of course. Sure."

"Swell." Joe Junior dodged out the door and hurried off.

At noontime Paul found his cousin piling up sacks of hops on the warehouse loading dock. The day was mild, with a pleasant breeze blowing out of the south. Unfortunately, such breezes always picked up the stink of garbage in the Chicago River. Paul could even smell the cattle in the Union Stock Yards, miles away.

"Just about ready," Joe Junior said. "There's someone I want you to meet." He shouted something into the gloomy warehouse.

In a moment a burly bald fellow walked out. He was a forbidding man, with huge shoulders, glittering eyes, and large, irregular white teeth. Paul thought of a tiger he'd seen in the Berlin zoo.

"Benno, say hello to my cousin, Paul Crown. Paul, this is Benno Strauss."

Paul's skin prickled. The infamous Benno. He'd heard Uncle Joe rail against him at the dinner table. Benno Strauss led the socialist-anarchist faction at the brewery.

Benno shook Paul's hand. His grip was mighty. To Joe Junior, Benno said, "This the one?" Benno's English was guttural, rough.

"Right, this is him."

Benno regarded Paul with a long, speculative gaze. It wasn't friendly. Finally he said, "Okay. Teach him good."

Paul was mystified as they started for the steps leading down from the loading dock.

PAUL had never expected to visit a place as lonely and sad as a graveyard, but that's where Joe Junior took him after they'd eaten lunch and walked to Desplaines Avenue and through a gate. "What is the name of this place?" Paul asked as they moved along a winding road between marble monuments.

"German Waldheim Cemetery. The fancy, respectable cemeteries wouldn't bury a lot of dirty immigrants, so this one was started. What I want to show you is over there, beyond the chapel." He strode across the bright spring grass and around the cream-colored chapel to an elaborate monument of impressive size. A male figure—

a workingman, Paul surmised—reclined in a pose that suggested death, while a defiant female in a robe and cowl reached behind her to place a wreath on his brow. A date, 1887, was carved into the monument and, at the base, a legend:

THE DAY WILL COME WHEN OUR SILENCE WILL BE MORE POWERFUL
THAN THE VOICES YOU ARE THROTTLING TODAY.

Joe Junior gazed at the sculpted figures with an almost reverent expression. "Paul, you have to promise me something. Promise not to mention this place when we get home."

"Of course, but why?"

"Because Papa would kill both of us."

"Then why are we here?"

Joe smacked a fist into his palm. "Because somebody's got to teach you. Just like Benno said." There was blue fire in his eyes. "This is the Haymarket memorial. The woman with the wreath is Justice. Something the martyrs never got."

"But what is the Haymarket? Who are the martyrs?"

Joe Junior pointed to the base of the monument. "Sit down."

THE Haymarket, Joe Junior said, is a big public square north of here on Randolph Street. It's an open-air market for farmers. The Haymarket is the place this terrible crime happened.

Chicago had been boiling with labor trouble for years. Then, in 1886, February, it exploded. The men at McCormick's reaper factory walked out. Benno Strauss worked at McCormick's then. He was one of the strikers. He said that all they wanted was fair pay and the eight-hour day. McCormick said go to hell, and started hiring new workers, scabs.

The first of May came, and the strike was still on. The leaders called a meeting close to the McCormick plant. Four or five thousand showed up, pretty angry after three months with no job, no pay envelope. The quitting bell rang at McCormick's, the gates opened, and a sea of scabs started to flow out. The strikers went wild. They surrounded the plant, driving the scabs back inside. The workers beat on the gates and screamed for the blood of the scabs. The plant guards opened fire through slits in the wall. The police closed in behind. Six strikers were killed. The mob broke and ran. That riot was over.

A protest meeting was called for the night of May 4, in Haymarket Square. About dusk, people began to gather. Soon there were about a thousand in the square. A block away, in the Desplaines Avenue station house, police were strapping on revolvers and polishing their billy sticks.

Before the meeting started, the crowd had to shift out of the square, move north, squeeze into Desplaines Avenue to find a platform for the speakers. All they could find was an empty produce wagon. August Spies, editor of the labor paper *Arbeiter Zeitung*, spoke standing in the wagon bed. The sky was ready to rain down buckets, Benno said. He was near the wagon.

Albert Parsons spoke next—a good man, the son of a general who fought on the reb side during the war. Then came Sam Fielden, a Methodist, and devout, they say.

Mayor Carter Harrison, on the fringe of the crowd, decided there wasn't any danger—any need for the police to march on the listeners—and he went to the precinct house and said so. One police officer, Inspector John Bonfield, had other ideas. He hated unions. He took over, ordered his men out.

They formed in a column and came marching up Desplaines. They met the crowd and pushed, squeezing people closer and closer together. Rain was pattering down. Still nothing happened.

A police captain shouted an order for the crowd to break up. From the wagon Sam Fielden shouted that the meeting was peaceable, violating no law. A roar went up, and just then someone— no one knows who—threw a bomb with a lighted fuse over the heads of the crowd. It exploded at the head of the police column. Seven officers died, many were hurt. The police broke ranks, shooting and swinging their clubs. Rain pelted down, lightning flashed, Benno said, and the coppers showed no mercy. The riot was over in five minutes.

The next day August Spies and his assistant editor, Michael Schwab, were arrested. Parsons surrendered. Fielden was arrested along with four more suspects—a carpenter, a printer, a housepainter, and a beer-wagon teamster.

The trial was a circus. The police couldn't offer even one piece of evidence to prove that one of the eight men had known anything about the bomb. They were guilty because they'd made speeches and written articles. They'd given the bomber the *idea*. Stirred him up—drove him to the brink. For that the prosecutor wanted the death penalty.

Minds were already made up; the eight had been tried and convicted in the papers. After the verdict Judge Gary sentenced seven of them to hang. Neebe, the beer-wagon teamster, got fifteen years.

Finally, in November '87, they hanged Spies. They hanged Parsons. They hanged Fischer, the printer, and Engle, the housepainter. Louie Lingg, the man from the carpenters' union, he beat them. Someone smuggled a dynamite cap into his cell before the hanging. He put it in his teeth and bit it and blew his own head off.

That left two men condemned to die, Schwab and Fielden. But the governor had had enough; he commuted their sentences. He always thought the trial was a farce, the hangings a scandal. Now, six years later, nothing much has changed. The governor now, John Peter Altgeld, wants to pardon those two men as well as Neebe. So a lot of people want to lynch him. My own father hates the idea of a pardon. But even pardons won't make a difference. It's too late. There's a score to be settled.

"AND you thought we had free speech, didn't you?" Joe Junior said suddenly. "Let's go," he added, wheeling away.

Just outside the cemetery's iron gates, he grabbed Paul by the shoulders. "Can I trust you to keep quiet?"

"Yes, absolutely. But I still do not fully understand—"

"Because Mr. Joseph E. Crown, Esquire, is a damn capitalist, that's why."

"Is that bad?"

"*Bad?*" Joe Junior guffawed. "Everything Pop believes in is wrong. For instance—there's no union at the brewery. Unions protect the rights of workers, but Pop's dead against them."

Paul was silent. He wasn't sure how to react. He didn't want to endanger the tenuous camaraderie between them, yet he was confused by Joe Junior's animosity toward Uncle Joe. Later, as they rode a horsecar toward the downtown, he decided he had to say something.

"Joe, if your father believes in wrong things, those wrong things have certainly built a fine life for everyone."

"Listen, kid, what we've got on Michigan Avenue is show, the trappings bought with the sweat of poor workingmen who spend their lives in poverty."

"But Joe, your father came over here by himself. He fought for the slaves and Abraham Lincoln—Aunt Lotte told me. Aren't you proud of him? He has done well in America."

Joe Junior turned toward his cousin, intense. "Sure, he's done well. My father is what they call an exploiter. He exploits the working class. Takes advantage of them for gain. Hell, he'd exploit me the rest of my life if I let him. He'd bury me in the brewery in a collar and fancy cravat. Think I want to be like him? Run that place after he's gone? No, sir. Never."

After they crossed the river, they left the rattling horsecar. On Adams Street at LaSalle, Joe Junior walked Paul past an unusual nine-story building, the headquarters of the Home Insurance Company.

"This is a pretty amazing building. It was put up five or six years ago—first of its kind. There's a steel-beam skeleton inside. It bears most of the load. That means the outside walls don't have to be so heavy. If a building is constructed that way, it can go up to twenty, maybe even thirty stories. They call them skyscrapers."

"*Wolkenkratzer*. I heard the word in Berlin. Who paid for this amazing building—plutocrats?"

Joe Junior laughed and punched Paul's shoulder. "Score one for you, kid. Listen, I can love Chicago and still hate the leeches and parasites who live here, I guess."

The spring air was warm. They strolled along through the crowds, enjoying the sunshine. Joe Junior consulted a clock in a jeweler's window. "Hey, it's half past four. Come on, we'll hop a cable car down to Fifteenth and walk over to Prairie. We'll have a peek at heaven."

"What are you talking about now?"

"Someone really special. I'll introduce you."

On quiet and shady Prairie Avenue, in a district of homes even larger and more splendid than the Crowns', Joe Junior stopped at the corner of Fifteenth Street. He pointed to the mansion across the way. "That belongs to Mr. Mason Putnam Vanderhoff the Third. Pork Vanderhoff, the meat-packer. We're waiting for his daughter, Juliette. She plays lawn tennis at three o'clock every Saturday if the weather's warm."

"I thought your girl's name was Rosie."

"It is. Julie's my friend. She's also the most beautiful creature you ever laid eyes on."

"And you meet her out here?"

"Have to. Old Pork hates foreigners, Pop especially. Not sure why. Mrs. Vanderhoff won't even speak to Mama."

"Then how do you know this girl?"

"I met her last winter at the public ice skating in Lincoln Park. We— Hold on."

He dodged behind the trunk of a sycamore. From the north, clipping along down Prairie, came a small driving wagon, shiny and black, with no top and a cut-down front for easy entrance. The driver was a young woman in a smart tennis dress, white linen with a narrow red stripe and great puffy leg-of-mutton sleeves. She wore a vivid scarlet tam at a rakish angle.

As the stylish little vehicle approached, Joe Junior jumped from behind the sycamore, stuck his two little fingers in his mouth, and blew a piercing whistle. "Julie, over here."

The girl swung the pony to the near side of the street and reined to a stop, raising dust. "Why, Joey Crown, what a nice surprise." She flashed him a smile. Paul hoped he wasn't gawking. He'd never been in the presence of anyone so supremely rich before.

"Just in the neighborhood," his cousin said. "Thought I'd say hello. You going to skate again next winter?"

"Of course. Are you?"

"Wouldn't miss it. How was your tennis game?"

"Fine." Now she was gazing at Paul, who stood in his cousin's shadow, entranced by the girl's striking looks. Miss Vanderhoff was fifteen, his age, and slightly built, with delicate fair skin and large luminous gray eyes. Her inky black hair beneath the scarlet tam was thick and shiny. Her smile seemed warm and natural.

Joe Junior noticed the looks passing between the two of them. "Oh, scuse me." He executed a little bow that made her laugh. "Madam, may I introduce my cousin, Paul Crown? Paul, Miss Juliette Vanderhoff. Paul's been living with us since Christmas. He's from Germany." There was the slightest pause. "He's okay."

"How do you do, Paul." The girl was reaching down to shake hands. He tingled at the cool, dry touch of her fingers. He had trouble collecting himself to answer.

"Very fine, thanks." His voice sounded like a croak. Mortifying.

She didn't seem to notice. "Are you planning to stay in America?" she asked.

"Definitely, I am making it my country." He was aware of his accent—heavy, foreign. She probably found it comical.

"Then welcome," she said. "Do you ice-skate?"

"Oh, yes." He had never owned a pair of skates in his life. "In Berlin I skated often and very well." He didn't mean to lie and boast that way, he was just thoroughly addled by her beauty.

"Then we'll see each other at Lincoln Park next winter—"

"Miss Vanderhoff! Your mother is asking for you."

The shout made her jump. A manservant in livery was standing at the front door of the Vanderhoff mansion.

With a sigh Julie said to Joe Junior, "I must go." She turned the pony's head into the street. "Happy to meet you, Paul. Till winter, Joe." She waved.

"Till winter," Joe Junior said. His eyes were adoring. "Didn't I say we'd catch a glimpse of heaven?"

"You're right, she is beautiful."

"But completely out of bounds, so don't get any ideas, kid."

As they walked south on Prairie Avenue, Paul realized that his mouth was dry and his pulse was racing. Something surprising and incredible had happened there in the shade of the sycamore.

He was in love.

"I can hear the old gears grinding in your head," Joe Junior said. "What about?"

"I am thinking that I wish I had a job. If I had a job, I could save some money. With money I could buy a pair of skates."

Joe Junior's eyebrows shot up. His mouth started to curl. Before he could speak, Paul burst out, "If you laugh, I'll hit you."

Joe Junior slung his arm around Paul's shoulder and gave him a brotherly squeeze. "I won't laugh. I know how it feels. Unfortunately, she doesn't care two pins about me, except as a friend. Maybe you'll have better luck."

ON THE great day, Paul woke before dawn. He wanted to go back to sleep, but his mind was racing with thoughts of the Exposition. An entire day free of Mrs. Petigru!

He switched on the electric lights and began to wash and dress as the morning was breaking over Lake Michigan. It was the first of May, 1893.

Everyone came to an early breakfast except cousin Joe. Uncle Joe was in his regular place, though he had to leave shortly for a second, more important breakfast with dignitaries at his club.

He looked grand in a frock coat with satin lapels, and striped gray-and-black trousers. When Aunt Ilsa came in with a platter of sausages, he said, "Where is Joe Junior, may I ask?"

"He has a terrible stomachache. He asked to be excused today, and I agreed."

"Very well. We don't need the company of a spoilsport."

Soon after breakfast Paul knocked softly on Joe Junior's door. "Come in."

Paul was startled to find cousin Joe sitting up in bed in his nightshirt, with a book. He looked perfectly healthy.

"Joe, I am sorry you're sick. You really can't go?"

"I don't want to go. Mama understands. You go on. I just don't like the whole idea—crammed in among a lot of nabobs. You can give me a report tomorrow."

"Yes, I will!" Paul exclaimed.

"Shut the door behind you. Thanks." Joe Junior's eyes were already on his open book.

Nicky Speers drove the family to the Exposition for the opening ceremonies. All the way to the grounds Fritzi complained that her corset hurt. When she and Aunt Ilsa walked, they tilted forward slightly because of their stiff, binding garments. Just the night before, Fritzi had done a hilarious imitation of that walk, which she called the kangaroo bend.

The streets leading to Jackson Park were choked with carriages and buggies and people on foot. Uncle Joe met them at the main gate, motioning for them to hurry. Buffeted on every side, they followed him. Paul could hardly keep from gaping at the buildings.

They sat on bleachers at the foot of a great wide stair on the east side of the Administration Building. A decorated platform held an orchestra, a choir, and many dignitaries. Uncle Joe pointed out President Grover Cleveland, Vice President Adlai Stevenson, Mayor Harrison, Governor Altgeld, and special guests from Spain—the Duke of Veragua, a lineal descendant of Columbus, and his family.

181

The orchestra played a Wagner overture. This was followed by prayers, choral anthems, and several speakers. Paul and Carl and Fritzi began to fidget.

Everyone applauded when the President rose to speak. Paul didn't listen much. The sentences were long and complicated, and his eye was constantly distracted by the incredible sights all around him. White buildings of great beauty and symmetry, lagoons and reflecting pools, statuary of every description.

The President concluded his remarks to wild applause. The crowd quickly grew quiet again. Uncle Joe leaned forward intently. "Watch, everyone. He's ready."

President Cleveland stretched his hand toward a gilded telegraph key in front of him. A few more words in his booming voice; then he pressed the key.

The orchestra leader's baton struck the downbeat. As the first notes of Handel's "Hallelujah" chorus resounded, fountains throughout the grounds erupted with foaming columns of water; flagstaffs miraculously unfurled the banners of America, Spain, and other nations; streamers dropped from every rooftop; drapes fell away from a giant gilded statue of the Republic at the east end of the Basin.

Chimes began to ring, guns boomed from a naval vessel anchored offshore, and from behind the statue two hundred white doves burst from their cages and flew upward.

As flags, fountains, and streamers declared the fair officially open, the crowd roared. Fritzi grabbed Paul's sleeve, jumping up and down and sobbing. Carl gaped, as awestruck as Paul. Uncle Joe slipped his arm around his wife while trying to remove something from his eye with a hanky.

"Isn't it thrilling?" Aunt Ilsa said.

The orchestra struck up "America." Uncle Joe said, "This is the end. Paul, what do you think? Quite impressive, isn't it?"

"Yes, sir."

"Papa, can we go?" Fritzi asked, still bouncing up and down. "I want to see the picture of Ellen Terry as Lady Macbeth."

"I must look in on the brewery exhibit," Uncle Joe said. "Twenty-four of my competitors are displaying their products. I want to be sure Crown's compares favorably. I'll meet you in half an hour. Perhaps then we should visit the German exhibit."

Aunt Ilsa said, "There's also a German village on the Midway."

"Yay, the Midway," Carl said. "Can we ride the wheel, Papa?" Everyone had been talking about the giant revolving wheel that you rode into the sky.

"Paul, do you have something you want to see most?" Uncle Joe asked as they worked their way down the bleachers.

"Well, sir, what I would like best really is the Buffalo Bill show." Cody's encampment was set up just outside the grounds.

"Capital idea. Carl said you wanted to see it in Berlin and could not. Here's a thought. I'll buy tickets for later in the summer. We'll celebrate when you finish the school year successfully."

"Thank you," Paul said with a stricken expression.

"Come, everyone. We must decide on a place to meet."

THE avenues were packed; progress was slow. The Crowns paused to admire a building of unusual design, with a dramatic entrance of concentric arches finished in gold leaf. "That is the Transportation Building," Ilsa said. "Mr. Sullivan designed it." Quite breathtaking, Paul thought.

Uncle Joe joined them there after he'd seen the brewery exhibit. "I'm pleased to say that our presentation is fine." They continued to stroll, turning into another avenue. In the distance Paul saw the huge iron Ferris wheel, named after its inventor.

"Now, where to first?" Uncle Joe patted his coat. "I have some special passes that will speed us into most of the exhibits."

They settled on the Krupp gun, exhibited in a special pavilion. Krupp's was a fine old German firm, and the pavilion was a minia-ture Prussian fortress. The gun was eighty-seven feet long. One of its projectiles, weighing twenty-three hundred pounds, could be fired a distance of sixteen miles, said the Krupp engineer.

Carl was thrilled, but Uncle Joe seemed disturbed by the exhibit. As they were leaving, he said, "Is that Germany's chief boast these days—war weapons? Is the fatherland showing off like some street bully? If so, what does that say? Nothing that I like to hear."

Next they went to the Fine Arts Building to find the portrait of the actress Ellen Terry, painted by a Mr. Sargent. Fritzi stood enraptured for five minutes, clasping and unclasping her hands, until Uncle Joe finally said, "Time to go."

They trooped to the Midway Plaisance, a broad avenue of colored lights, where all the lighter diversions had been segregated. They admired the Blarney Castle from Ireland, then walked through the narrow passageways and keyhole gates of the Streets of Cairo, populated by women in veils and swarthy men in robes. It was a faintly wicked exhibition, which failed to charm Aunt Ilsa. Nor did she smile when Uncle Joe said, "Perhaps when you're visiting the Women's Pavilion, I'll attend a performance of that dancer, Little Egypt. The men at the brewery are all talking about her danse du ventre."

Carl whispered to Paul, "It means she dances with her belly. I heard it in school."

They ate an early supper at the German Village, in preparation for standing in line for the Ferris wheel. They sat under gay lanterns at an outdoor table while a band and its guest conductor, John Philip Sousa, played stirring martial airs. One was a song Herschel Wolinski had played on his concertina aboard ship. Poor Herschel, where was he now? Paul wondered.

They waited nearly an hour for their ride on the wheel. Finally their turn came. With others they climbed into a forty-passenger car with big glass windows and comfortable seats. Fritzi shrieked when the wheel jerked and the car rose, swaying, then stopped again while the car below was loaded.

"Oh, look," Aunt Ilsa said. She leaned forward and pressed her gloved palm to the glass. A spectacular vista of twinkling lights spread beneath them. She squeezed Paul's hand. "Can you believe your eyes? Was there ever a more magnificent sight?"

"No, never," he whispered as the car rose and swayed. The panorama below symbolized the almost limitless wonders of the new scientific age brought to its fullest glory. In America.

EXHAUSTED, they said little as Nicky Speers drove them back to Michigan Avenue at eleven o'clock. Paul knocked on Joe Junior's door.

"Well, tell me, what did you think of it?"

"Joe, don't get mad. I thought it was pretty fine."

Joe Junior grinned. "Hell, I expected you'd be taken in. All that show. The White City. Maybe the buildings look beautiful to you, but it's just white paint over cheap stucco. There's another side to that fair, Paul. Things you need to know."

"What things?"

"Maybe I'll let Benno tell you. Sometimes there are Sunday labor picnics out in the country. I might take you to the next one. If I do, can you keep quiet in front of Mama and Pop? Fritzi and Carl?"

Paul's hands were sweaty with excitement, and his heart was beating fast. His cousin was drawing him into his confidence, trusting him with a dangerous secret. Like a true friend. He shot his hand into the air. "Silent as a statue, I promise!"

Paul ran to his room, flung himself on the bed, elated. But only briefly. He lay gazing at the ceiling. By saying he'd go with Joe Junior and then keep it a secret, he'd made a pact with his cousin that could cause trouble. He spent a restless night, full of guilt over disloyalty to his aunt and uncle.

SCARCELY a month was left in the school term. Paul was failing every test, failing his handwriting exercises, failing his recitations at the blackboard. Mrs. Petigru took delight in announcing his poor marks to the class.

She kept him after school to inform him that she would have to hold him over. He would have to repeat the whole year.

He reeled out of school. Stay with Mrs. Petigru another *year?* Never. He tried to think of a way out, but his mind was blank. And he was too ashamed to tell Uncle Joe or his tutor.

Around the house, Fritzi was driving everyone mad with her imitation of the portrait of Ellen Terry. Paul and others would unexpectedly come upon Fritzi posing in a corner or in the middle of the staircase, wrapped in a shawl, gazing heavenward.

Carl called her dizzy. Uncle Joe ordered her to stop the imitations. Fritzi ran sobbing to her room, which vexed Uncle Joe even more. In fact he seemed grim and short-tempered lately. When Fritzi came to supper red-eyed, he delivered a stern lecture.

"Please stop that sniffling. I am tired of theatrics in this house. I occasionally enjoy a play. The stage, however, is a disreputable, godless calling. Anyone foolish enough to take it up deserves to be rejected by society. And they usually are. Please pass the potatoes."

After that evening a new gravity seemed to prevail at the supper table. Uncle Joe was subdued, speaking quietly to Aunt Ilsa about the gold standard and shares and other mysteries. One night, unable to restrain his curiosity, Paul politely asked whether there was any special reason for so much talk of financial matters. There certainly was, Uncle Joe said, going on to explain that since May 5, prices of shares in large companies had begun to fall off sharply. "I fear it's the panic many people predicted."

Joe Junior said, "What do you expect to happen, Pop? The system's corrupt."

Aunt Ilsa looked pained. Uncle Joe struggled to contain himself. "Thank you for enlightening us. We surely respect your wisdom and experience as a student of economics."

Joe Junior's jaw clenched as he attacked his food.

The following Saturday, Aunt Ilsa was in the kitchen with Paul when Uncle Joe came home from the brewery. Grim-faced, she pulled something from her apron. "This came today, Joe. It's the letter you wrote to your sister, Charlotte."

Uncle Joe took the wrinkled envelope and saw, stamped on the front, a single word: VERSTORBEN. "Deceased? How could it be? What happened?" With a look of anguish he turned to Ilsa.

"I suppose we will never know. Possibly it was the illness Pauli has talked about."

Paul was shaken too. There was a choking lump in his throat.

The letter fell from Uncle Joe's hand. Tears flowed down his face. Ilsa put her arms around him. No one said a word.

ON A Thursday at the end of May, Uncle Joe packed a grip and caught an evening train for South Carolina, where he had business interests. By a stroke of luck there was a labor picnic the following Sunday. Joe Junior politely asked his mother if he and Paul could go for a hike in the country. Aunt Ilsa told them to be careful and to return before dark.

Their destination was a place called Ogden's Grove, beyond the city limits. "Why do they hold it so far away?" Paul asked as they rattled along on the horsecar for the first stage of their journey.

"So the bluenoses won't yell about Sunday beer drinking, and the Chicago coppers won't snoop. These are great affairs. I met my girl, Rosie, at one of them last year."

They hopped off the car where the macadamized road ended. Before them was a rutted stretch of sunlit dust. They trudged for a mile, and then Paul heard music. An oompah band. A rickety wooden arch had a faded sign at the top: OGDEN'S GROVE.

Back in a grove of trees Paul saw trestle tables with food, and people mingling and a few dancing on the grass.

Joe Junior introduced Paul to several of the people. There was a lot of patched clothing, Paul saw. Some of the men had heavy beards and long hair. One of them reminded him of the Russian journalist Rhukov.

Faded red flags were planted in the ground throughout the grove. "Red for the blood of the oppressed," Joe Junior said.

They found Benno arguing with half a dozen men. Benno spied them and broke off, grinning. "Hey, looka here. The pupil. How's he coming, Joey?"

Joe Junior tilted his hand back and forth. "Slowly. Slowly."

"Well, drink some beer, kid, it's free. There'll be speeches after a while, so listen close." Benno turned back to his friends.

Paul and Joe Junior stuffed themselves with sausages and beer while Benno and some others shoved wooden boxes together to improvise a platform. Several speakers addressed the crowd. Paul found them boring.

Benno was the last to take the platform. He started with a denunciation of the fair. "They're puttin' on this circus. You think they're celebrating the great American democracy? Okay, take that building in Jackson Park—there's gold all over the doorway. It cost millions. For decoration! It'd feed and clothe hundreds! And there's more out of work every day with this panic the rich bankers started."

He called for "propaganda of the deed." He called bombs and pistols "the best friends we got." He shouted for retribution and, chillingly, "the heads of the plutocrats." "They squeezed blood out of us for years. Okay, we take theirs! Right in the streets of Chicago!

"Comrades, I thank you."

Benno received the loudest ovation of the day.

He jumped down from the boxes and startled Paul by coming straight over to him. "What y'think? Are you hearing a message?"

This man was speaking hate against Paul's family. Paul screwed up his nerve and said, "I hear it, Herr Strauss. I don't know if I like it so much. I don't know if I like the idea of taking blood in the streets."

"How else we gonna win?" He turned to Joe Junior. "Hey, Joey, get busy. This one's backbone ain't stiff enough yet." Benno's huge paw slammed down on Paul's shoulder. "Get clear on this, kid. Sooner or later in the class war, you got to choose."

"You mean take sides against my uncle?"

Benno stared at him. "Yeah."

"You don't like my uncle very much."

Benno's first response was a shrug. "*Like* ain't got nothing to do with it. Truth is, I don't think Joe Crown's a bad man. But he cares a lot more for property than the rights of us workingmen. Also, he's stubborn. A bad combination. We got a national union—"

"Which Pop opposes one hundred percent," said Joe Junior.

"Right. Could be trouble; we come pretty close to it already. What I'm saying, kid—" His thick, strong fingers tightened on Paul's shoulder. "You got to choose your side, absolutely. If you don't learn nothing else today, learn that."

JOE CROWN ✦ Joe Crown owned a large block of shares in a textile factory at Millington, a small town in the sand hills of South Carolina. He couldn't have been more grateful to be aboard the train, speeding southward on a business trip, temporarily free of the turmoil in Chicago, where companies were collapsing. If he admitted it, he was also glad to be free of the situation in his own household. Paul was settling in well, doing all right in school, or at least not reporting that he wasn't. Carl and Fritzi had taken to the boy. But Joe Junior seemed colder, more embittered than ever before about all the things Joe stood for. As if by merely being himself, Joe was an offense to his older son.

It was the influence of that damnable Benno, Joe was sure. Reinforced by the privation sweeping the country along with the panic. The last newspaper he'd read before leaving contained a long, grim article about "suicides among the despairing poor."

Joe couldn't help contrasting his nephew with Joe Junior. But whenever he did, he was washed with guilt, because he found his son wanting.

Sitting by himself in the darkened car, he was drawn into the past, to an explosive quarrel two years ago. The quarrel that seemed to create the permanent gulf between father and son. All brought on when Joe Junior came home with a letter of dismissal from his third school. There were high expectations for pupils from the Crown house. Joe Junior had been unable to fulfill them, and later, aware of this, he'd openly flaunted them by courting failure. The letter he brought home put the match to the fuse; the explosion came after fifteen minutes of acrimony behind closed doors in the study. Joe Crown had done something rare then. Lost his temper completely. Responded to some shout from his distraught son by striking him hard across the face.

Suffused with shame and guilt, he'd whispered an apology. Not for the harsh things he'd said about Joe Junior's failure, but for the blow. A decent and responsible father didn't strike in anger.

The apology seemed to do no good. Joe Junior's eyes were like blue flints. And nothing had been the same between them since that night.

PAUL ✦ On a Saturday morning in early June, Paul went to the Exposition alone. Uncle Joe was still away, so Paul asked his aunt's permission to go; he had a dollar and fifty cents saved from the small sums she paid for doing chores around the house.

He'd pondered for a week before making the decision to go to the fair. He hadn't forgotten Juliette Vanderhoff; by wintertime he must have ice skates. Carl had gone with him to A. G. Spalding's store one day after school. Skates were currently off the shelves because it was summer, but a helpful clerk said a fine pair of racers would cost two dollars and twenty-five cents. Paul felt sure he could earn that much by the first freeze.

He took a tram partway, then walked to the Sixty-third Street entrance, bought his ticket, and passed through the turnstile. He wandered in and out of the splendid white buildings without any special plan. In the Agriculture Building he marveled at a cheese weighing twenty-two thousand pounds. In the Mines and Mining Building he saw the world's largest gold nugget—344.78 ounces.

After a while he decided he would buy a bit of lunch, and headed for the Midway, where he chose an outdoor café. He took a small table under an umbrella. The table stood next to a low picket fence separating the café from the street. He ordered sausage and beer.

Glancing into the passing crowds, he started. There was a man standing on the other side of the low fence. A man sprung from nowhere.

"Can I believe my eyes? The Berlin boy. Taken any art lessons?"

His hair was longer. But everything else was the same. The long white starved countenance. The shabby clothes. The glowing dark eyes behind tiny round spectacles. The cigarette held by yellowed fingers. Where had he come from?

"What are you doing here, Mr.—"

"Rhukov."

"I remember."

"Permit me to ask the same question of you." Rhukov was speaking German. He stepped over the fence and sat down. "Waiter, beer," he said in English. Then he returned to German. "You left Berlin. Did you decide to chase Buffalo Bill's show?" Rhukov puffed his cigarette, waiting.

"My uncle lives here. I always planned to come to America." Stretching it there, wasn't he? But Rhukov made him nervous, defensive, even though he had an inexplicable liking for the odd young man.

The waiter brought Rhukov's beer. "Do you like America?"

"Except for school."

"But otherwise happy?"

"Very happy. You still haven't answered my question, Herr Rhukov. What are you doing here?"

"Same as before. Hunting a few stories."

"You must like the job."

"Oh, certainly. The glamorous life of the roving journalist! Sleeping in doss houses. I eat well, though. Truly. I get a shave, and then I haunt the hotels. Always plenty of leftovers waiting to be thrown out. I know how to talk to the busboys. I'm at home with the lower classes. So here I am, searching for glimpses of the future. Not as pretty as some like to pretend. Seen the Krupp gun?"

"Yes."

"Scary. How about the exhibits from my own beloved country?" Paul shook his head. "No? How can you miss them? Mother Russia is a huge presence here. Finish your beer, we'll have a look."

They walked to the Russian pavilion, where Rhukov led Paul to a display of exquisite bronze miniatures of animals and peasant groups.

"Don't they look happy, the precious little things? You can't smell them, you can't feel the anguish when the crops fail. There's not a back broken by years of toil. The serfs are bleeding out their lives in poverty, children are starving, and Czar Alexander has

190

decreed that every ruble paying for the Russian display at this romantic circus shall come from the imperial treasury. Does it ever slip into his feeble brain that he might spend that money to succor his own people? Never. Well, the clock's running down for the czar and rulers of his ilk. The world as we know it is coming to an end, Berlin boy. The birth of the new one will be bloody. You'll see."

Paul thought of Benno Strauss. Despite the heat, he shivered.

Rhukov hurried them out of the pavilion. "I can't stand a big dose of this. I have to search out antidotes. Something that suggests a measure of humanity—a grain of progress. You've seen the Electricity Building?"

"Not yet."

He yanked Paul's arm. "We'll remedy that immediately."

In the Electricity Building, at the south end of the lagoon, they stood before Edison's Tower of Light, a shaft nearly eighty feet high, studded with electric globes of all sizes and colors that flashed in constantly changing patterns and rhythms.

"Marvelous, isn't it?" Rhukov said. "A few years ago I was ignorant of inventions like this. I didn't realize the nature, the magnitude of what's rushing toward us like a locomotive with the throttle wide open. Then I had an experience that opened my eyes. In an amusement park in Vienna. For a few pennies you gripped two handles that gave you a jolt of this new thing *electricity*. I felt an incredible force tingling through my hands, racing through my body. In an instant I knew the future was coming—new ideas crashing upon us; science digging the floor from under us; everything tumbling, thrown about, rearranged—an apocalypse, and not wholly political this time. It's here, boy—it's here at this fair, if you can search it out. You think this tower is spectacular? I'll show you something you truly will not believe. Follow me."

Down a dim aisle Rhukov pointed to a signboard on the left.

THE AMAZING TACHYSCOPE
See Pictures That Actually
MOVE!

Pictures that moved? How could it be?

The booth itself didn't look promising. In front of some drab draperies, between drooping palms in pots, stood a large rectangular box with a wooden step in front. A metal piece like a stereopticon viewer was attached at eye level. There was a coin slot. Paul wondered about the price; he had only a few cents left.

Two men in the booth strolled over to greet them. "It's the journalist again," said the heavier of the two. "Good day, sir."

Rhukov switched to English. "Good day to you. My friend here—" Paul tried to look adult. "He doesn't believe your sign."

The man chuckled. "Skeptic, is he? Lad, this gentleman is Mr. Ottomar Anschütz, owner and perfecter of the tachyscope."

"What sort of pictures does it show?" Paul asked.

"My boy," said the German inventor, "have you seen the animals at the circus on the Midway?"

"No, sir."

"There is in the performance an elephant whose name is Bebe. Inside my tachyscope, Bebe moves and performs just as realistically as in real life." Anschütz fished a dime from his checkered vest. "Step up, I will treat the young skeptic to a viewing."

Paul stood on the step and leaned into the eyepiece. He saw only darkness. At his elbow, the other man, an American, was saying, "Mr. Edison was supposed to have his kinetoscope on exhibit here, but they didn't get it ready in time."

"Watch closely," Herr Anschütz said. The coin dropped in the slot. Inside the box, machinery whirred and clicked. A sudden flash of white light dazzled Paul. He grabbed the box.

In the viewer he saw a grainy picture of an elephant with a little ballet skirt around its middle, prancing, sidestepping, *moving* back and forth over a stretch of grass. Paul hardly dared to breathe. The movement seemed jerky, as though interrupted at very short intervals by the flashing light. Never mind. It was astounding.

Moments later, groggy, he stepped down from the tachyscope. "Sirs—Herr Rhukov—that is the most astonishing, incredible— wait. Where is he?"

Herr Anschütz shrugged. The American said, "He was standing right there. I turned to speak to Herr Anschütz—no more than a second or so—and when I looked again— Gone."

Paul thought he saw a wisp of cigarette smoke in the air. In Berlin, Rhukov had disappeared with the same eerie abruptness. But this phenomenon was overwhelmed by the miracle of the tachyscope.

Herr Anschütz walked off to speak to a young couple hesitating outside the booth. Paul said to the American, "Do you know all about this machine?"

"I know something. I have my own studio of photography."

"How does the machine work?"

"Well, you are not looking at pictures that actually move, merely at separate still pictures which create that illusion when they're flashed at a rapid speed. Inside the cabinet there's a revolving drum. The pictures of Bebe are mounted on the drum sequentially. The flashing light enhances the effect."

"I've never seen anything so lifelike. It's amazing. Wonderful."

"I knew you were a smart one the minute I spotted you."

He was a strange, pale little man in a nondescript suit. He came up to Paul's shoulder, had a potbelly and a bushy salt-and-pepper mustache. He wasn't forbidding or menacing; he was just—odd.

"But sir, do you think these moving pictures will ever be more than a—uh—"

"Novelty?"

"A novelty, yes, I think that's what I mean."

"Of course I do. They'll be entertainment, my boy. Someday moving pictures will be shown on giant screens in great auditoriums. Pictures like these will sweep the world. It may take a few years; inventors are still struggling to perfect a projection machine. But make no mistake, it will come. Rooney says so."

"Rooney?"

"Wexford Rooney. Here's my card." He fished in a pocket. "That's the address of my present studio. North Clark Street. If you ever need a camera or want instruction, drop around."

"I will. It is a promise."

"Fine, just fine. Can't find enough willing converts. Nine tenths of the world consists of doubting Thomases. Plain fools." He flipped Paul a coin. "Take another look at Bebe, my compliments."

Paul bent over the tachyscope with the white light flashing—flashing into his eyes, into his bones and his soul, making the miracle part of him forever.

On the tram ride home Paul patted his shirt pocket a dozen times to be sure he hadn't lost Rooney's card.

He was euphoric when he ran into the house at half past five, panting when he knocked on Joe Junior's door.

"What are you so excited about?"

"Joe, I must tell you what I saw at the fair."

Joe Junior perched on the edge of the bed. "The belly dancer, Little Egypt."

"No, no—a machine! A marvelous machine." He sat beside his cousin. "I could learn to make pictures, Joe. I always wanted to draw but I have no talent. This talent I could learn. It employs machinery."

"If it's so great, how come everybody isn't talking about it? I never heard of it."

"But—"

"Anyway, what does it have to do with anything? What does it have to do with lifting a burden from some workingman's back? Nothing."

Silent anger flared in Paul. Could his cousin talk of nothing but poor people?

Joe squeezed Paul's shoulder and delivered grown-up advice with a smile. "I'd forget it."

Paul felt crushed. But he quickly forgave his cousin. Hadn't Rooney said the world was full of unbelievers? It was the easy thing, to scoff.

That night he sat on his bed, the calling card in his hand. It was a very poor card. Grimy, bent at the corners. Still, it seemed a magic key to a magic door. One more week until school was over; then he'd have free time and he could go.

One week. How would he ever endure the wait?

Before school on Monday morning he shared his exciting discovery with Leo Rapoport. Like cousin Joe, Leo was unimpressed. Called the invention crazy.

Leo had other things to talk about. "Sit down," he whispered. Paul sat on the low cement wall at the edge of the schoolyard. After swift looks both ways, Leo opened his schoolbag and took out a wad of folded sheets with printing on them.

"Finally my old man threw out last year's sales sheets. Lamp this stuff, will you? Just don't wave it around."

Paul unfolded the sheets and quickly leafed through the pages. Above blocks of price information, three quarters of each page was given over to a full-figure engraving of a beautiful young woman wearing an item from Mr. Rapoport's line of corsets. Every girl was incredibly voluptuous. There were sheets for plain corsets, fancy French corsets, lightweight summer corsets. The wickedest pictures showed high-hip corsets cut to reveal more flesh.

"These are for buyers who work for stores, not for the ladies who wear the stuff," Leo explained. Suddenly he grabbed Paul's sleeve. "Look out, here comes Maury Flugel. Hide those, quick."

Paul shoved the folded sheets into the left pocket of his linen school jacket. Maury arrived a moment later.

Fists on his hips, Maury said, "I seen you two reading something. Come on, Leo, be a pal, let me see."

"You're no pal, you're a snitcher," Leo said, shoving him. Leo marched toward the schoolhouse door. Paul was right behind. As he neared the doors he checked his left pocket. He was horrified to see that a corner of the folded bundle had popped out very noticeably. His heart raced. He didn't touch the sheets until he was inside and the double doors hid him from Maury.

In the cloakroom, he turned his jacket inside out, making sure the printed sheets were hidden, and then hung the coat on a hook.

Just before recess Mrs. Petigru called Paul to the desk to say he was to deliver a letter to his aunt and uncle informing them that he would be held over. The bell rang. Pupils rushed to the cloakroom for wraps. The room was empty when Mrs. Petigru finally dismissed Paul with a curt wave.

Paul hurried to the cloakroom. His coat had been disturbed. He stabbed a hand into the pocket holding the sales sheet. It was empty.

He took Leo aside in the yard, told him of the disaster. They knew the culprit. But there was nothing they could do.

When they returned from recess, Mrs. Petigru was seated at her desk, spots of color burning in her cheeks. Her eyes raked the room, alighting on Paul. He had seen her angry, but never like this.

In a low, tremulous voice Mrs. Petigru addressed the class. "At the end of recess I found something lying on this desk. Something vile and obscene." Her left hand dropped to a drawer. Slid it out. She laid the sales sheets on the desk and quickly covered them with her right hand. Sweat ran down inside Paul's collar. Mrs. Petigru shut the drawer. The sound was loud as a pistol shot.

"Paul Crown, come up here."

Maury Flugel snickered, but everyone else was rigid with fear.

Paul walked forward and stopped beside the desk. Between Mrs. Petigru's fingers he could see that on the back of a sales sheet someone had printed in block letters PAUL C.

Mrs. Petigru stared him down. "Whose are these, Paul?"

He kept his voice level. "I see my name on them. They are mine."

"Where did you get them?"

He couldn't say, "From Leo." He gave the answer she would believe. "I bought them from a man at a beer garden."

"More of that fine German morality, eh? What sort of person *are* you to bring beer-hall filth into my classroom?"

With each phrase she grew louder. "You're a good-for-nothing. Stupid. That thick German head of yours can't learn anything. What's more, you're—"

Something gave way in him. He blurted, "That is not fair—"

"Be still! Now put both your hands here." Paul heard a girl utter a strangled, *"Oh."* He swallowed, placed his palms on the blotter.

Behind him, someone's foot scraped. "Mrs. Petigru, those pictures are mine. I brought them."

"Sit down, Leopold. I detest liars. Paul, spread your fingers."

Paul obeyed. Mrs. Petigru opened the bottom drawer and took out her long, thick ruler.

JOE CROWN ✦ Joe Crown walked out the door of the State Hotel in Columbia, South Carolina, a genteel figure in a white suit and dark cravat. It was a fine June day, the twenty-seventh. A black youngster sold him a paper. Joe stepped to the curbstone and scanned the headlines.

Yesterday the stock market had hit the bottom of its monthlong sell-off. The word used in the paper was "crash." How much worse could it possibly get? Very much worse. He spotted a smaller story, out of Springfield, Illinois.

ALTGELD SIGNS PARDON
Three Haymarket Conspirators to Be Released at Once

Joe threw the paper into the gutter.

There was even more in store. When he finished his day's business and returned to the hotel, the desk clerk reached into a pigeonhole and handed him a telegraph message. It was from Ilsa: PLEASE COME HOME. PAULI EXPELLED.

PAUL ✦ Uncle Joe walked into the house at half past five on Thursday, the twenty-ninth of June. An hour later Paul was summoned to the study. He was surprised and relieved to see Aunt Ilsa seated there too. Uncle Joe pointed to the empty chair in front of him. "Take a seat. Tell your story."

Paul did so, neither minimizing his actions nor embellishing Mrs. Petigru's cruelty. His heart was pounding, his stomach hurt, but outwardly he was composed.

"I believe you, Paul," his uncle said at the end. "Your words have the ring of truth. Also, what you say doesn't fundamentally contradict the events described in the principal's letter." He tapped the letter on the desk. Paul hadn't noticed it before.

"He acknowledges Mrs. Petigru punished you more harshly than was merited. Let me see your hands."

Paul held them out. Faded purple bruises marked his fingers and the backs of his hands, to his wrists. He hadn't been able to bend his fingers without pain for three days afterward.

"Can you move your fingers freely?"

"Oh, yes. I'm fine now." He darted a warm look at Aunt Ilsa. She had telephoned Dr. Plattweiler for a liniment prescription, which had helped.

"Good. Regrettably, the principal must stand behind the authority of his teachers, and so you can't continue in that school. Your aunt and I have discussed and agreed on the next step. I will discharge Mr. Mars, and on Monday you will start work at the brewery."

Paul was speechless. Uncle Joe said, "Ilsa, if you will leave us, I will discuss the particulars with Paul."

She acquiesced with a little nod and kissed her fingertips to Paul as she walked past. The doors rolled back, rolled shut. Paul's heart was still beating fast. A few weeks after his arrival, the prospect of working in the brewery had been attractive. Now something more fascinating was luring him. How to tell his uncle?

"Now that your aunt is gone, I can speak more frankly." Uncle Joe picked up the principal's letter. "This truly saddens me. Not the charge of bringing obscene materials to class—that sounds frivolous in the light of your description of the drawings from a salesman's bag. And it's admirable that you tried to shield your friend. But I find nothing else admirable in what you did. I had great hope

197

for you, Paul. For weeks, for months, I discover, you have been failing. Yet you said everything was fine."

"I did not want to disappoint you, Uncle."

"What do you think you have done here?" He threw the letter on the desk. "I can't understand how you could get such poor marks. Germans are good thinkers. They are always good with figures—" His voice was shaky, something uncharacteristic of him. Paul waited tensely while his uncle cleaned his spectacles with a hand-kerchief. That seemed to calm him.

"The brewery—" Uncle Joe began.

"Sir, may I please interrupt?"

"What is it?" His uncle didn't like it.

"At the Exposition I saw a marvelous machine." He described the pictures that moved, the dancing elephant.

"I've heard of this machine. Continue."

"Sir, I met a gentleman who operates a studio of photography. He knows how the moving pictures are made. His name is Mr. Rooney." From his shirt pocket Paul took the precious card and handed it to his uncle. "I said I would like to learn to make such pictures. He invited me to visit. He said he would teach me. Could I not ask him for a job?" Paul's face glowed. "One day I might learn to make pictures for the machine I saw."

Uncle Joe thrust the card back. "I see no purpose in pictures of an elephant dancing. That machine is a toy. A novelty. Make a career of it? I find that proposition slightly ridiculous. Photography is a very low trade in my estimation. Chancy too."

"Uncle, please, I beg you, at least let me call on this gentleman and ask whether he might employ me."

"No."

"Ich protestiere!"

"You protest? You are in no position to protest, young man. You have shamed this family. You will work at Crown's. Your hours will be six until four thirty, six days a week. I pay a very good starting wage. Ten dollars and a quarter per week. Since you live with us, you won't have to spend anything for rent or food; you can save everything you earn. A great advantage."

With that pronouncement Uncle Joe leaned back in his chair. "Now, if you'll excuse me, I have some bills that require my attention." He turned to the desk before Paul reached the sliding doors.

JOE CROWN ✦ Ilsa climbed into bed. Joe lay rigid, hands nervously tapping his stomach. All the windows had been flung open to catch any night breeze. But there was none.

"You are very quiet tonight, Joe."

"A lot on my mind."

"How do you expect Pauli will do in the brewery?"

"It's Paul. He chooses to call himself Paul."

"He'll always be Pauli to me. I can't think of him any other way. Little Pauli from Berlin who fainted on my Oriental carpet."

Joe knew better than to argue the point. "He took it well. He's intelligent and quick. He should do well if he shuns the troublemakers." He chewed his lip for a moment.

"Will there be trouble?"

"Impossible to say. We're going through terrible times. Hundreds are out of work. George Pullman plans wage cuts, perhaps layoffs. Pullman is a major employer in the city. It will have a huge impact. Hungry men are desperate men." He sighed. "Sometimes I wonder how much strain the system can stand."

"Or this family," Ilsa said.

He found her hand in the dark and held it tightly. He lay awake long after she fell asleep.

JOE JUNIOR ✦ As he left the brewery late on Friday, Joe Junior was secretly worried about rising antagonisms. Benno was stirring up trouble with pronouncements, threats, that grew more reckless as conditions in the country got worse. Joe Junior sided with Benno most of the time, but he feared Benno might test him by demanding he take part in some act of violence. Some propaganda of the deed.

All of this was boiling in him that Friday evening as he came swinging past the corner of Michigan and Nineteenth.

He walked into the house and met his mother, who had just come out of his father's study. Her face was drawn and unsmiling.

"Supper will be very late. Your father just telephoned. He is at the county jail. The police locked up Benno Strauss this afternoon."

"Benno." Joe Junior thought about it. "I didn't see him all day. I figured he was making deliveries."

"I don't know why he's in jail. Your father didn't explain, but he's in a fury."

The family didn't sit down to supper until after nine. "Benno Strauss left work at noon without permission," Papa growled as he served himself mashed potatoes. "He went downtown. There, he and some forty others held a parade, with signs. Ostensibly the purpose was to plead for jobs. Most of the marchers were unemployed. The police tried to remove them—"

"Probably so the tourists wouldn't see what's really going on in Chicago," Joe Junior muttered to Paul.

"The demonstrators resisted, and they're all behind bars. Benno's bail cost me thirty-five dollars. Cook County Jail is a vile place. I hope I never have to set foot there again."

"I don't quite understand," Mama said. "Benno isn't unemployed, he has a good job. Given how you feel about him, I'm a little surprised that you bothered to help him at all."

"It's the principle. I had to help an employee." He speared a piece of pot roast. "Heed this, Paul. When you start your job, see that you stay away from Strauss."

Joe Junior liked to see his father off balance this way; it seldom happened. He winked at his cousin, saying, "Oh, there are worse teachers than Benno. I guess you had one of them in school."

His father had his fork halfway to his mouth. He dropped it to the plate, a loud clatter. "Keep your comments to yourself, Joe. You know very little; you chose to scorn schooling. All you've been taught, you've learned from a pack of socialist rabble-rousers."

"Well, I don't blame Benno for demonstrating. I sympathize with anybody who's out of work because of men like—"

"Who are you to sympathize? You have a soft life. You don't know the real meaning of hunger, hardship, desperation."

"Oh, here we go," Joe Junior sneered. "Now we'll get the story of the brave, hardworking immigrant boy."

Mama jumped up. "That is shameful, young man. Shameful and intolerable. Go to your room."

Openmouthed, he stared at her. Standing up to Pop was one thing, but opposing Mama was something else entirely.

"Joseph." Her voice dropped. "I said go."

He threw his napkin on the table and left, looking at no one.

Half an hour later he was sitting on the edge of his bed in a terrible state of confusion.

A soft knock startled him. Mama came in before he could speak.

"Joey, I am sorry I raised my voice to you. Unfortunately, you provoked it. Why do you provoke quarrels with your father? He isn't a wicked capitalist; he is a man of strong character who has worked hard to make a success of his life."

Somehow he couldn't frame a coherent answer. He turned away.

Mama moved to his side. She touched his brow. Her fingers were gentle, warm. "*Liebling,* tell me. What is it?"

He flung himself off the bed, away from her. He stared out the window at the lights of the mansions on the other side of Michigan. "He wants to control everybody. But he left Germany because he didn't want to be controlled—not by poverty, not by a rotten system that was growing worse." He spun to face her. "He came here, made his own way. He was free, independent. Nobody bossed him."

"Nonsense. He had many bosses along the way."

"But he always knew where he wanted to go, and he didn't let anyone order him to turn in some other direction. All I want is the same chance. Don't you understand? *He can't tell me what to do.*"

Mama took that with her usual composure. Said quietly, "But that is his nature, Joey. To organize everyone, every aspect of his life and ours. If that is a flaw, we must accept it."

"Not me. Never."

She drew a long breath, as if resigned. "All right, you have spoken your mind. Now it is my turn. It makes no difference how you feel; he is your father. So long as you live under this roof, he is entitled to respect. You will apologize to him."

She strode to the door and pulled it open. "You will do it now. He's downstairs in the study. Waiting."

MOST of the lights were out on the lower floor. The house felt like a mausoleum. With a dry, tight throat Joe Junior walked to the study doors. Tapped gently. "Pop?"

"Come in." His father's voice had a flat, remote quality.

He rolled the doors back. Joe Crown wheeled around at the desk.

It took all his nerve to meet his father's eye. "I apologize for my words and actions at supper."

"Accepted, thank you," his father replied. "I too regret things I said. It was a difficult day. Benno's arrest upset me greatly."

For a breathtaking moment Joe Junior had an impulse to step across the carpet, fling his arms around his father, say he understood. Then something—too many reprimands, too many *orders*—shattered the feeling. He felt awkward standing there.

His father sensed it. Tried to smile. It was a poor, tired smile. "You may go to bed, son. I have much work left here."

"Yes, good night, Pop." Quickly he wheeled and shut the doors. He leaned there in the darkness, exhausted. Something had changed tonight. Tonight he'd confessed his deepest anger to his mother and found she had no way to ameliorate it. That frightened him. He could never go back to the way it was when he and Pop went to ball games together; the anger was deep now. Maybe this evening they had all recognized it for the first time.

As he climbed the shadowy stair, the anger came surging back. He'd apologized because Mama wanted it, that was the only reason. Paul would start at the brewery on Monday. He'd win Paul over to his side. He'd fix Papa for causing him all this pain. Halfway upstairs, a huge sneeze burst from him. He leaned against the banister, severely chilled.

PAUL ✦ Paul was shaken by the overt enmity between his uncle and his cousin. He'd known it was there, but never guessed its ferocity. On Saturday morning, when he went into the kitchen, Aunt Ilsa's expression upset him. She was not someone who scowled often.

He left the house and headed for the schoolyard, where he had arranged to say good-bye to Leo. Today, Saturday, the schoolyard was empty. Paul ran toward Leo when he appeared at the corner, and explained about going to work at the brewery.

"So we say good-bye for now, Leo. But I will see you again. I'll come to your flat."

Leo blushed. "Don't come, we're moving. Pop got fired. Nobody's buying corsets, I guess. I'll send you a new address when we get one."

"Good, it's a promise."

They hugged each other.

Leo never sent the address.

LATE in the day, Paul stood in front of the shop on North Clark Street. He put his nose against the window. Dark, empty. On the glass someone had painted FOR RENT.

On a stepladder a man was at work unhooking chains that held a faded sign: ROONEY'S TEMPLE OF PHOTOGRAPHY. Paul couldn't believe it.

"But where is he?" Paul asked the man.

"Who gives a damn? He was a lousy tenant, Rooney. I threw him out. Rent was five and a half months in arrears."

"But please tell me, where has he gone?"

"Try a park bench. Try Cook County Jail. The little rat had a swarm of creditors chasing him. Rooney don't pay his bills. He can't leave off with the ponies, that's his trouble."

Paul didn't understand the reference to ponies. He stepped to the curb, crushed the card, and flung it into the gutter.

On Monday he woke early, long before daylight. Like the morning he went to the rail yards to see Buffalo Bill's train, or the opening day of the Exposition. He'd slept restlessly.

He was to see the brewmaster, Mr. Friedrich Schildkraut, at six sharp. In any fine brewery the brewmaster was king, and that was true at Crown's.

Cousin Joe wouldn't be going with Paul to the brewery this morning. He'd come down with a bad case of grippe, and Aunt Ilsa had put him to bed.

A horsecar took Paul to within two blocks of the brewery. It was drizzling, mist coiled along the ground, and the deserted streets glistened as he walked to the employee gate at the south end of the brewery block. A cobbled alley ran from the gate into the heart of the brewery. Somewhere machinery clanked; steam hissed. There was not another workman in sight.

An old watchman sat in a small booth reading a paper by lantern light. Paul knocked on the glass. The watchman shuffled out. "Hello, my name is Paul Crown. I am to work here."

"Yes, I was told. Pass on."

"I am to see Mr. Schildkraut."

"Second floor, front building. Down the alley, turn right."

Paul walked into the dark maw of the alley, the black buildings rising like medieval keeps on either side. This was to be his life now, a job pushed on him by his uncle. Bad feelings buffeted him. Uncle Joe had no sympathy for his wishes. He'd found work he might do enthusiastically, as a career, and Uncle Joe scoffed at it. Paul understood cousin Joe's rebellion.

He stopped and gazed up at the brewery buildings. A few lonely lights gleamed behind opaque windows. Why was he here? Maybe he didn't belong in America. How the baker of Wuppertal would laugh if he saw him now.

Calm down; it may not be forever, this job. There's one advantage. When winter comes, you will certainly have ice skates.

Concentrating on a vision of Juliette Vanderhoff's face, he walked on into the brewery.

Friedrich Schildkraut's office was a corner space at the rear, overlooking the alley and the manufacturing buildings. Paul ran a palm over his unruly hair and knocked.

"Come in, young man."

The office was strewn with flasks and thermometers, little muslin sacks of grain and hops, diagrams and blueprints. Schildkraut was sitting behind his desk. His lips twitched; it could hardly be called a smile. "Sit down, please."

As soon as Paul sat, the brewmaster stood up. He was a tall, austere man, about forty, with thick hair yellowing to gray. From his intimidating height he looked down at Paul. "Do you know whether lager is bottom or top fermented?"

"No, sir."

"The bottom," he barked. "I see we shall have to teach you almost everything. Especially since your uncle indicated to me that you might make a career of it."

Paul's neck prickled. He stood up. The brewmaster scowled.

"You wish to say something?"

"I do, Mr. Schildkraut. My uncle was kind to get me this job. But I am not certain I wish to be a brewer all my life."

That was a lie. He was certain he didn't want to be a brewer. He'd seen the elephant dancing. . . .

"The truth is, sir, I came to America to decide what I want to be, not—well, not to be told what I must be. People in America, they are free to choose. That is the reason I came here."

Friedrich Schildkraut gripped the back of his swivel chair and leaned forward.

He is furious. I will be discharged before I start.

"Good! You have backbone. There is no place for a weakling in a brewery." All at once Schildkraut relaxed. He actually smiled. "We'll do our utmost to convince you it's a worthy profession. We'll start where the beer starts, in the malthouse. You'll stoke the fires. You'll clean equipment. You'll go home so tired you'll want to weep. But you'll learn a noble trade. Just don't fall in with the wrong crowd here."

Schildkraut circled the desk and laid a hand on Paul's shoulder. "We have at least one employee who belongs to the exalted, glorious National Union of United Brewery Workmen. Mr. Benno Strauss. Benno and his friends are agitators. Don't listen to them. Young Master Joe has a tendency to do that; it's leading him astray. The fact is, while there's breath or strength in your uncle or in me, we won't permit a union at Crown's. Or the devil-inspired eight-hour workday. Men who are idle are susceptible to temptation. We'll never have it. Never."

Schildkraut relaxed his grip. "This way," he said, stepping toward the door. "I'll take you to the malthouse and get you started."

Part Four
JULIE
1893–1894

JULIE ✦ On the first Saturday morning of September, Mrs. Vanderhoff was combing her daughter's hair. This weekly ritual took place in Julie's dressing room. Julie's unbound hair hung below her waist. Black hair, shiny as a pool of spilled ink. Hair that was Juliette Vanderhoff's pride and glory because her mother had taught her it was so.

Nell Fishburne Vanderhoff, younger of two sisters born to the Kentucky Fishburnes, was five feet tall and compactly built. Once, she might have had the charm of a bisque doll. Now, in her forties, lines of exhaustion were scribed deep in her face. Great brown shadows surrounded her eyes, and her skin was yellow.

Julie had turned sixteen on May 28. Her figure had matured sufficiently for her to wear women's fashions, such as this morning's expensive gown of peach silk from a fashionable couturier.

She sat motionless, gazing at herself in a large oval mirror while Nell plied the comb and brush. Again this morning a tantalizing memory of the boy she'd met months ago disturbed her composure. Joey Crown's cousin, the German boy.

Their meeting on the street had been brief, yet she remembered him. His broad shoulders and strong, honest face. His blue eyes, large and shining with a curious liquidity that left her seething with improper emotions. He had a perfectly terrible accent, but his smile was genuine. There was a forthrightness about him. She wished they could become better acquainted.

Nell Vanderhoff finished the ritual. She laid comb and brush aside; then she regarded Julie's face in the glass. "I have never seen your cheeks so red. Too much time in the sun playing tennis."

"I love tennis, Mama."

"You overdo. Just as you overdo skating in the winter. I've told you repeatedly, Juliette, women are delicate. You must guard yourself rigorously against the ravages of weather, of nerves, of—"

"Oh, Mama, I don't understand how fresh air can be bad for you."

"Nevertheless, that's the case. Dr. Woodrow will confirm it—and please don't suggest that you know better than a doctor trained in Switzerland. You grow more willful every day. It must be your age. A passing phase. Let's hope it passes quickly, because dealing with it exhausts me. It simply shreds my nerves to bits."

Pierced with guilt, Julie said, "Mama, you know I never want you to feel bad because of me."

"I hope so, dear. I hope so."

The health of Mrs. M. P. Vanderhoff III was a constant concern in the family. Neurasthenia—prostration of the nerves and brain—was a recurring complaint. Nell suffered from excruciating headaches and problems with digestion. She often flew into shrill rages or sank into long periods of morose silence. She spent many hours, sometimes days, in her bed, with the room darkened.

Nell had taught her daughter that suffering was woman's lot, and it did seem to be true. Julie too was plagued by headaches, as well as profound and sometimes prolonged black moods in which she wanted to do nothing, see no one. Nor was she unusual. Many of her young female acquaintances were devastated by ills ranging from a high nervous state to a perpetual head cold. Julie had the idea that the health of young American women was generally bad, and she wondered why it should be so.

On the positive side, her health problems diminished whenever she exercised regularly and vigorously. In this she had to strike a balance, because Nell opposed sports for young ladies.

Julie folded her hands in her lap and again gazed at herself. Her cheeks were indeed sunburned, but the color deepened even as she watched. She had a powerful, uncontrollable, slightly wicked longing to see the German boy again.

Common sense quickly pricked that bubble. What she wanted was impossible, could never happen. The German boy belonged to the Crown family. Mama and Papa hated the Crowns—all of them.

The sad thought quite ruined the rest of the day.

PAUL ✦ As Fred Schildkraut had predicted, Paul learned quickly. He oiled and wiped the brewery machinery, helped with repairs. He worked on the huge mills that handled five hundred bushels of malt in an hour, on the pneumatic malters that regulated moisture and temperature of the germination bed. He stoked the fires under the brewing kettles.

He didn't mind the hard work. In a month he had saved enough money to pay for skates. And finally, when Spalding's stocked its winter equipment, Paul bought a splendid pair of racers. He was moving steadily toward a meeting with Miss Vanderhoff.

ON A warm Sunday in late September, Uncle Joe took all the family but Joe Junior to the Buffalo Bill Wild West show. Paul's cousin went out to the town of Pullman to see his girl, Rosie.

Uncle Joe had booked one of the best front-tier boxes. Paul could barely sit still, watching a performance he'd only been able to dream about in Berlin. Colonel Cody, white-hatted and noble as ever, charged up and down on Isham, blasting blue glass balls to bits with his pistol.

In the much anticipated Deadwood Stage number, the coach made a circuit of the arena, and the driver stopped here and there to invite a spectator into the coach for the rest of the act. Paul almost collapsed when the driver pointed at him.

As the coach rattled and swayed around the arena, mounted Indians swooped down on it uttering bloodthirsty cries. A volley of pistol shots announced the arrival of Buffalo Bill and his cowboys. They quickly chased off the Indians. Then they sent the coach around the arena once more, to discharge its delighted passengers at their seats.

Afterward Paul thanked his uncle effusively.

PAUL DIDN'T SEE MUCH OF JOE Junior during regular working hours. Usually they met during the lunch break. While they ate, Joe Junior would expound his theories of labor and capital, and also suggest things for Paul to read.

One sunny noontime Paul and Joe Junior went up to the brewery roof to eat wursts and bread from their paper sacks. Benno and a half dozen of his cronies were already there, eating and talking loudly. As usual, Paul felt daring to be up there with the socialists, in defiance of his uncle and Schildkraut.

Benno was always friendly to Paul. If they chanced to meet in the brewery, he would offer some gruff greeting. Paul wasn't sure what to think of Benno. Benno was certainly fearsome to look at. And strong. Yet he was a blowhard. Even those who liked him said so behind his back.

"Benno," one of his friends said now, "we've let up on the boss lately. Do you think that's right?"

Paul and his cousin shot looks at one another.

"Nah, it ain't right. We got to start pressing him again. Demand nine hours a day. Also one apprentice for every fifteen men, not twenty. Even if we ain't got the union, that's what the union wants."

Paul walked over to the group. "Mr. Strauss, may I ask a question, please?"

"Sure, tell me what's on your mind."

"The union wants a maltster to be paid sixty dollars a month. My uncle pays seventy-five. Doesn't that make him a good boss?"

"Nah, don't be fooled. Your uncle pays a little more here, a little more there, but he saves a lot more by keeping the sheep happy, keeping the union out. Stupid question."

Paul's face reddened. "I am only trying to educate myself. To find out what is right—"

"Hey, Paul," cousin Joe called. A warning.

No longer genial, Benno lumbered to his feet. "The union is right. Socialism is right. Your uncle, he's wrong. All the capitalists are wrong. Look at what they're doing to this town!" Benno slashed his hand toward the vista of rooftops. "Hundreds of men out there ain't got jobs. They got empty bellies—and who cares?"

Benno noticed Paul frowning. "Something wrong, boy?"

"Just another question."

"Spit it out."

Paul knew he should keep quiet, but he wanted to know. "You're always saying you have this plan, that plan, but you keep your job here. You even let my uncle pay to free you from jail—"

A thrill of fear went through him as Benno stalked toward him. "Are you saying we're a bunch of talkers—blowhards?" Benno grabbed Paul's shirt and leaned close. "You got the wrong idea, little boy. You'll see. The revolution ain't all talk."

Low on the horizon the winter moon turned the ice pale gold. Wind rattled the tree limbs above the bank where Paul sat lacing his skates with fingers half numb. Close by, Joe Junior was hugging himself, exhaling little clouds. It was five thirty in the morning.

"This is insane, Paul. You don't know how to skate."

"If I cannot skate, I cannot meet her. You said so."

"I also said it won't matter a damn if you do meet her. Vanderhoff despises Germans, bohunks, Irish—the whole lot. He's got a special hate for Pop."

"I don't care. I'm going to meet her. Help me up, please?"

Cousin Joe put his hand down, and Paul took hold, struggling upright on his skates. Lincoln Park lay desolate in the moonlight.

Paul took a small step on the ground. His ankles wobbled dangerously. He tugged the stocking cap down over his tingling ears and pulled on wool mittens. He inched his skates onto the ice of the lagoon.

He fell down.

"Help me up, Joe. I will learn to skate."

"And die in the attempt." But Joe Junior gave Paul his hand.

Paul swayed, barely holding his balance. "Please, give me a push. See if I can skate a little way."

Joe Junior pushed the small of his back. Paul glided forward about three feet, the blades rasping in the silence.

"I'm moving, I am skating," Paul cried. With a whoop he fell down again. But this time he got up without assistance.

"Sit down, Joe, rest. I will practice by myself."

"We'll be here till Christmas." Joe skated effortlessly to the bank and sat hugging his knees to keep warm.

Paul fell down seventeen times before Joe said, "This is enough for one night. We'll go to the brewery; the night watchman will let us in. We can warm up before we start work."

"But I am coming back tomorrow," Paul said.

"I'm afraid you mean it."

"I do. I am going to meet her, Joe."

JOE Junior nudged him. "There she is."

It was a Sunday afternoon. December, very cold. But the sun shone. From a large public pavilion on the lagoon's far side there drifted the jaunty melody of "Grandfather's Clock" played on a hurdy-gurdy.

Despite the temperature, Paul felt warm. Perhaps it was due to excitement. The ice was crowded with skaters—boys and girls, families, individuals. Even so, it was impossible to overlook Juliette Vanderhoff. She was inside a smaller pavilion on the near bank. It bore the sign LINCOLN PARK SKATING CLUB—MEMBERS ONLY.

Warming herself at a log fire set in a brick hearth, Juliette stood out because of her cape and wide hood of scarlet velvet. Seven or eight young men surrounded her, laughing and chatting. The young men all had a sleek, prosperous look.

"We must go over there," Paul said. "You can remind her we met this summer." They stepped onto the ice. Paul skated fairly easily now, after weeks of practice.

"Hey, Julie, hello," Joe Junior called as they clattered into the club pavilion. "Do you remember my cousin, Paul?"

Paul could think of nothing to say. The gray eyes, the lovely warm smile bewitched him.

"Why yes, the German boy." The word boy crushed him. She held out a hand. "How nice to see you again." They shook hands. She said to the others, "This is Joe's cousin, Paul Crown."

Paul was aware of the looks the young men were giving him. A tall, smirky blond fellow slapped him on the back. "Hello, Dutch. Julie, shall we skate again?"

"I suppose." She smiled at the blond boy, though she seemed to be casting a hopeful glance at Paul. "Paul, this is Strickland Welliver the Second. He's our club speed champion."

Welliver touched Julie's arm in a possessive way.

Hurry, think of something. "Miss Vanderhoff, I think you had better come with me," Paul said, struggling with both his English and his nerves. "There is a police officer who wishes to see you."

Strickland Welliver said, "A what?" Joe Junior almost choked.

Paul gestured toward the crowded lagoon. "Just over there. If you will come with me—"

Fearing she might slap his face, he nevertheless took hold of her arm. Her gray eyes probed his, curious, surprised, then pleased. "All right. Excuse me, Strickland—Joe—all of you."

She followed Paul out of the pavilion into the sunlight. Boldly he took her hands. They skated.

They glided around the lagoon, moving with the flow, counterclockwise, toward the pavilion where the organ-grinder played. Julie's cheeks were pink. She skated with short, crisp strides, her upper body seeming to float without effort. Paul was tense, fearful of falling.

Julie shielded her eyes. "Where is the officer?"

"Well—" Paul twisted to a stop. She bumped into him.

"Oh," she said softly, pulling back but still standing close. They were the same height. Their condensing breaths mingled.

"Miss Vanderhoff, I have a confession. There is no officer. I did it to get you away."

"That's very ingenious. Audacious—"

"But if there *were* an officer, he'd wish to see you because"—he gulped and risked everything—"you are—you're beautiful."

"Why, thank you, Paul." She didn't seem angry; touched, rather. "You're a very clever young man."

"I am not so young, Miss—"

"We've been properly introduced. Call me Julie."

"Julie." The music of it almost drove him out of his mind. "You called me young— Well, I am sixteen."

"So am I. My birthday is May twenty-eighth."

"Mine is the fifteenth of June."

"Then I'm older. So you'll just have to do whatever I say." There was a teasing light in her eyes. "Paul—I have a confession also." She waited until two men skated past. "I knew there was no police officer. But I was happy you invented one."

Clouds of her breath touched him, faintly sweet with clove. Her scarlet cape brushed his coat. His head pounded.

"Paul."

"Yes? Yes?"

"Shall we skate?"

They skated. He kept pace, mercifully with no falls. Joe Junior

211

skated by, backward. He smiled and waved and kept skating backward, somehow missing people without looking at them.

"Are you working at Crown's brewery?" Julie asked.

"Yes. Sunday is my day off."

They skated.

"I like your cousin Joe. I consider him a good friend. He's very intelligent. Some of his ideas are rather alarming, but I always enjoy hearing them. I wish I could see more of him. I'm afraid my father is very—well, disapproving of people who haven't been in this country as long as our family. The first Vanderhoffs came to Connecticut before the Revolution."

"You have to do what your father wishes, I suppose."

"True. Daughters are expected to be dutiful."

They skated.

"I thought I might not get away from home this afternoon," she said. "My mother is sick again."

"Oh, I'm sorry. Was it sudden?"

"Oh, no. Mama suffers from a recurring condition called neurasthenia. Her spirits sink very low, sometimes for days. It upsets me awfully, but Dr. Woodrow says it's perfectly normal for women. My aunt Willis, who lives in New York, says that's nonsense, but Father doesn't believe her. He hates all of Aunt Willis' ideas."

"Do you like your aunt?"

"Very much, although some of her ideas are awfully bold."

A man skated by. He was of middle height, wearing a derby, a long woolen scarf, expensive pigskin gloves, a double-breasted tweed suit. Paul wouldn't have paid much attention but for one other touch. The man had a monocle with a long ribbon.

He seemed interested in Julie. Paul stared at him. The man smiled and abruptly skated off.

Julie looked at Paul. He looked at her.

"Watch out, you young idiot." A nursemaid barely managed to lurch out of the way, dragging along a child on tiny skates. Paul made a violent move that threw him crashing into the bank.

Julie had the skill to stop herself just where the ice ended. Humiliated, Paul scrambled up, brushing off his pants. "I'm afraid I'm not a very good skater."

"You said you skated a lot in Berlin."

"Juliette—that— It was another tale. I wanted to impress you." With a kindly smile she said, "You have."

Blond Mr. Strickland Welliver II came hurtling along, calling to her, "Are you going to hang out with him all day?"

"No, Strickland. Don't be impatient." She whispered to Paul, "If you like, I'll give you some skating pointers next Sunday."

"Yes. Wonderful!"

"Good-bye, Paul. Thank you." She squeezed his hand and skated away, pursued by the blond young god, Strickland Welliver.

ON THE cable car clanging south on State Street, Paul blurted his secret to his cousin. "I have fallen in love with that girl."

"You're crazy."

"No, I am in love."

"Then, my friend, you are in trouble. She may fancy you, but if Papa Pork finds out, he's liable to take a cane to her, and you too. Didn't I tell you old man Vanderhoff hates foreigners?"

Paul was dreaming deliriously of Julie's eyes, of her hair; of next Sunday. He scarcely heard the warning.

ELSTREE ✦ He skated slowly. The pickings were poor this afternoon. He saw no one he recognized other than Vanderhoff's daughter, who had gone.

Dusk came down, drear and bitter. An old caretaker set kindling alight in iron barrels placed around the lagoon. Reflections of flames danced on the skater's monocle.

He thought of the Vanderhoff girl, Juliette. She had been skating with a sturdy young man with blue eyes. He was jealous of the boy but reasoned that even if Miss Vanderhoff had been unescorted, he couldn't have spoken to her. She might have remembered him.

Unlikely, but she might. He had been presented once, three years ago, in the dress-circle foyer of the Auditorium, to which Vanderhoff and his affected southern wife had dragged their daughter for an evening of Wagner. "Juliette," her father had said, "may I introduce Mr. William Vann Elstree the Third? His family

214

owns the department store where your mother prefers to shop—to the chagrin of Mr. Marshall Field."

He vividly recalled Juliette's youthful prettiness that night. The gown she wore—virginal white, matching the aigrettes in her incredible black hair. How he'd love to see that black hair unbound, spilling down her back. . . .

Ah, why speculate? He took risks, but he didn't court the impossible. Still, he had trouble getting her out of his thoughts.

PAUL ✦ Christmas fell on Monday. Uncle Joe and Aunt Ilsa were again generous with their gifts. Paul received several shirts, two pairs of corduroy knickerbockers, and a silver-plated comb-and-brush set. His prize gift was a fancy bicycle suit—sack coat and knee-length pants—of fine brown cassimere wool. He was delighted. He only wished he could have given a gift to Julie.

By Wednesday of that week, half the household had colds. Half the brewery workers too. At noon Saturday, Paul was sent home from Crown's with a fever.

The delivery wagon from Frankel's meat market was tied at the hitching block nearest the rear entrance on Nineteenth. Paul dragged himself into the kitchen, which was deserted except for Frankel's delivery boy, a gangly older youth with an enormous spit curl arranged to hide some of his prematurely bald head. He wore a voluminous tan duster that reached to his knees.

"Say, pal, I got a problem," the delivery boy said. "Where's your cook? I been hunting all over. I can't find her."

"Louise was sneezing and coughing last night. She went to bed. I suppose she is resting in her room."

"Then I got to speak to the lady of the house."

"She will be out all day. Or so she said this morning."

"Jeez, that is a problem. I'm supposed to pick up a list, special order for New Year's."

Without thinking much about it, Paul said, "Why don't you go up to Louise's room. She will give you the list. Go up the back stair there. On the third floor it is the second door on your left."

The older boy thanked him, calling him pal again, and then disappeared.

Paul hung the kettle on the hob to boil. He craved a strong cup of tea. A few minutes later he walked from the kitchen to the short hall just beyond. From there he observed the delivery boy standing in front of the decorated tree, admiring it.

Before Paul could say anything, a voice boomed from the second-floor landing. "You down there. What are you doing?"

"Just having a glim at your tree, pal."

Manfred Blenkers rushed down the stairs. "I have seen you before. What's your name?"

"Jimmy Daws. I'm from Frankel's."

"We don't allow tradesmen in this part of the house. Get out at once." Manfred made the word tradesmen sound like an epithet.

Paul walked out where they'd see him. "I sent him upstairs, Manfred. He was searching for Louise, to take a special order for Monday."

"*You* gave this person leave to roam around the house?"

"Listen," the delivery boy said, "I went up the back way, I talked to her, I got the list and came down this way. So what? You're makin' a hell of a fuss over nothing."

"Don't curse in this house, or I'll see that you're fired, you guttersnipe. Remove yourself from these premises instantly."

Paul screwed up his nerve and stepped forward. "Mr. Blenkers, you have no right to badger him like that. He needed to see Louise. I told him where to find her. What is the harm?"

"Your uncle will decide that when he comes home."

"If you want to tell him, go ahead," Paul said calmly. "I will tell my side; we will see who comes out best." The delivery boy stood nervously, his left hand deep in his pocket, as if he were holding his belly because it hurt.

Manfred recognized that his authority had been breached. "All right," he cried, "enough. Leave, both of you!" Then he marched noisily up the stairs.

Grinning, Paul bobbed his head toward the kitchen, and the delivery boy followed him.

The kettle was spouting steam. Paul lifted it off the hook with tongs, put it on a decorated tile to cool. Jimmy Daws was giving him a long stare. "Thanks for helping me out with that spook. I've locked horns with him before. I'd as soon slit his throat as look at him."

Paul didn't imagine he was serious. "Manfred is all right, but he acts like he is a general. Do you want some tea?"

"Can't stand the stuff. Got to go. Tell you something—I don't ordinarily make friends with Dutchmen. In your case I'll make an exception. Shake, pal."

They shook. Jimmy Daws kept his left hand in the pocket of his coat. He walked out, and Paul brewed his tea.

When the family sat down to the evening meal, Aunt Ilsa immediately spied something and put her hand to her mouth. One of the display racks in the cabinet of gold-edged Bavarian china was empty. "The largest platter is gone. The most valuable piece."

Paul remembered the delivery boy with his hand in his pocket, as if he was holding something under his long tan duster.

Paul felt wretched. He pushed his plate aside, appetite gone. "I think this is my fault," he said, then explained what had happened. "I sent him upstairs. I did not expect him to be a thief."

"Why would you?" asked Aunt Ilsa, touching her hanky to her eyes. "You're a trusting person, Pauli. You did what you thought best. Don't I always say people are more important than things?"

That night Joe Crown telephoned Abraham Frankel at home.

Frankel was stunned and outraged. No, Jimmy Daws had not come back at the end of the day. "Oh, Herr Crown, I am so sorry. I will repay you for your loss."

"Not necessary," Joe said. "This delivery boy—do you know where he lives?"

"In the slums is all I know. He never gave an address."

Joe filed a police complaint, without result. It was impossible to find a thief who was hiding in the criminal warrens of Chicago.

JULIE ✦ New Year's morning Nell Vanderhoff was combing Julie's hair. The ritual was particularly important today. The first of January brought one of the city's premier social events, which the Vanderhoffs always attended.

Julie felt wonderful this morning. Since the start of the skating season her health problems had disappeared. Vigorous exercise in the bracing winter air wasn't the sole explanation.

Julie's reflection in the glass triggered a familiar complaint from her mother. "Your cheeks are too red again. I wish you wouldn't spend every Sunday afternoon at the skating club. Strickland told me young Joe Crown goes to that club."

Julie's gray eyes flickered with anger. "Oh—sometimes he does."

"You must not associate with him. The slightest hint of it would send your father into a fury." Nell reached down to grasp Julie's shoulders. "I'm quite serious, Juliette. You must have nothing to do with the Crown family. If you love and respect your father, you will certainly—"

Julie jumped up. "Oh, Mama, why is everything always put that way? If I love you and Papa, I'll do this, I'll do that. I don't know Mr. Crown, but young Joe is a fine person."

"I don't believe it. I've heard he harbors radical ideas."

"It may be, but I like him."

Nell stepped back, separating herself from her daughter. "That is disappointing."

"I'm sorry. But I'm sixteen; I have ideas of my own. That doesn't mean I don't love you or Papa."

"Disappointing," Nell repeated. "What I'm saying, Juliette—if I must be so plain—it hurts me."

Please, don't do this again. "Mama, you know I'd never—"

"I must go and lie down. My heart is beating too fast."

Oh, don't . . .

"I'll send one of the girls to help you with your corset. We mustn't be late to the Palmers'."

"Mama," she cried out vainly. The door to the hall closed.

Julie sank down. Why did Mama always have to use the weapon of her fragile health? It was the one weapon Julie could never turn aside, because part of her remained the dutiful daughter. Wanting to please, wanting to be loved.

She remembered the awful argument over education last year. Aunt Willis, her mother's older sister, had attended Oberlin College for two years after the Civil War. On one of her visits Aunt Willis succeeded in persuading Julie that young women needed and indeed were entitled to the sort of higher education men received. Enlightened—that was the exact word Willis used.

Julie announced to her parents that she wanted to attend college. Julie's father cursed his sister-in-law right at the dinner table. Nell Vanderhoff locked herself in her bedroom, prostrated.

Willis left a day later. Nell remained in her room. These were anguished days for Julie. She finally went to her father, said she'd reconsidered; she really didn't want to go to college after all.

What had changed everything for Julie was Paul Crown. He was quiet. Never assertive over trivial matters. Some might take that for timidity. An error. In their Sundays together Julie had come to understand that Paul was quiet in order to listen, observe, learn. Not that he lacked spirit or ambition. He had plenty of both. He'd talked several times of the excitement of a career in the new field of photography.

He also had a kind way about him, an essential decency. Kindness, intelligence, strength—a wonderful combination of traits, she thought as she dressed. She was in love with Paul.

And he probably didn't even suspect her feelings. How she melted at his touch, almost swooned every time he circled her waist with his strong arm as they skated.

Because of him she constantly dreamed of an idyllic future. Yet there was an element of dread in the daydreams. What would happen if it came to a choice between Paul and her family?

In this state of confusion Julie left in the family carriage with her parents at half past one o'clock. Their destination was the home of Mr. and Mrs. Potter Palmer, on Lake Shore Drive, called by friend and enemy alike the Palmer Castle. With its eighty-foot tower and sawtooth battlements, the Palmer residence did indeed resemble an English castle.

When the Vanderhoffs arrived, the porte cochere was crowded with vehicles driven by men in an array of liveries, all of them ostentatious. The Vanderhoff carriage was sizable and expensive, yet insignificant compared with the huge victoria just ahead in the line. Nell pointed to it. "The Pullmans are here!"

Mason Putnam Vanderhoff III—Pork Vanderhoff—grunted. He was a great hulk of a man, six feet six inches tall and weighing about two hundred and seventy pounds, much of it on deposit in an impressive paunch. He had small gray eyes that never seemed to rest. Despite middle age, his hair was still black. He wore it combed straight back and sleekly oiled.

"By the bye, Mason," Nell said, nervously adjusting her hat, "I received a letter from Willis yesterday. She will be here in the spring for her usual visit."

"Oh, damn it to hell and back. Why can't she ever get sick? I despise that woman. She's the next thing to a harlot."

Julie winced because she loved her wild and undisciplined aunt. The carriage moved forward. Palmer footmen jumped to open the door. In a moment the Vanderhoffs were disposing of their wraps in the immense octagonal entrance hall. The hall soared up three stories, its walls hung with Gobelin tapestries.

Christmas greens perfumed the mansion. A string orchestra played above the babble of the crowd. All aflutter, Nell said, "I must locate Bertha. Come with me, please, Juliette."

"I'll try to find some of the fellows," Pork said, lumbering off.

Circulating in the crowd brought Nell and Julie near a stocky silver-maned gentleman with sparkling blue eyes and an impressive domelike forehead. Nell swiftly veered off to confront him with hand held out. "Potter."

"My dear Nell. And Julie. How charming you both look. Happy New Year. Thank you for coming."

"Would we miss it? Never, dear man. Where on earth can we find Bertha? There's such a crush—"

"In the drawing room." Potter Palmer was an eastern Yankee who had sensed and seized an opportunity when Chicago was young. So had Pork, from Connecticut, and Field, who was from Massachusetts, and Armour and Pullman, both New York State men.

Like them, Palmer had been born in the 1830s. He made fortunes in real estate, Civil War cotton, and then retailing. For years Palmer's dry goods store was famous for its bargain sales and absolute dedication to customer satisfaction. Marshall Field had built his own fortune by buying out the Palmer store.

Nell and Julie squeezed into the packed Louis XVI drawing room, a vision of gold and white, with roses and pink cupids on walls and ceiling. "There she is!" Nell exclaimed, waving. "Bertha!"

"Dear Nell," said Bertha Honoré Palmer, gliding to embrace her friend. "How lovely to see you. And Julie."

Julie didn't want to spend the afternoon trailing after her mother, so she contrived to slip away. She wandered to the ballroom, where the orchestra was playing.

The ballroom was undeniably the focus of the party. Almost a hundred feet long, it was packed with guests helping themselves to eggnog, escalloped oysters, and other delicacies spread on long buffet tables. Great blazing Tiffany chandeliers lit the scene.

Julie sampled the eggnog and wistfully wondered what Paul was doing this afternoon. Enjoying himself, she hoped. Alas, he'd never be invited to the Palmers'. She wished she were with him.

She spied her father among a group of men and women intently listening to another gentleman. It was George Mortimer Pullman, an imposing man in his sixties who was another of Chicago's giants.

He had started as a cabinetmaker in upstate New York, but his mind ranged to much larger objects and concepts. His fortune, his huge manufacturing plant, and the ideal workers' town he had built nearby all sprang from one invention. In the late 1850s Mr. Pullman had remodeled two rail coaches, installing his patented fold-away upper berths hinged to the sides of the car. Mr. Pullman had also invented the dining car and the chair car and the car with vestibules. Papa thought Pullman overbearing, but he was acceptable because he voted Republican.

Mr. Pullman was speaking to his group without pause. Julie slipped in among the listeners, near Pullman's wife, Hattie. Pork gave his daughter a fishy blink of recognition.

"They bay at me like a pack of hounds because I reduced employee wages. I did it simply because orders have been reduced. But I am castigated for making no similar cuts in the salaries of company officers and foremen. There you have a total lack of understanding of the American system. If I cut the wages of my executives, I face the possibility of mass resignations. That would leave me with only a skeleton management when prosperity returns. Maintaining salaries for the upper echelons is imperative. So is continuance of our dividend. It's a matter of confidence."

"They're simply vile, these people who hurl accusations at George," Hattie Pullman declared. "We even have some malcontents who continue to draw Pullman wages."

"True," Pullman said.

How smug he was, Julie thought.

"However, I have a network of—let's call them observers. They help me root out the worst agitators. When I discover one, his lease in the town of Pullman is canceled."

"It's only just," Hattie said. "George invested hundreds of thousands to build a model town. A town in which all that's ugly and discordant and demoralizing is eliminated."

Julie hesitated but then raised her hand. "Mrs. Pullman, may I ask a question?"

Hattie Pullman froze. "If you wish, Miss Vanderhoff."

"Really it's more a matter of not quite understanding something.

The newspapers say that one of the complaints about the town of Pullman is that rents haven't been reduced, even though wages of the renters have." Actually she never read the papers; she'd heard about it from young Joe Crown.

She made her statement with an innocence that anticipated a friendly reaction. She was unprepared for the stunned stares from her father and Hattie Pullman or the fury of the great man himself: "Miss Vanderhoff, you know nothing about business. Pullman the manufacturer and Pullman the landlord are separate and distinct centers of profit. Do not confuse the two."

"But it doesn't seem entirely right that—"

"Juliette, where's your mother?" Pork said loudly. "We must move on. George—Hattie—friends—a happy New Year to you all."

"And to you," George Pullman said without feeling.

In the carriage, everyone was silent. Nell dabbed her eyes with a handkerchief. At home, she went to her room without speaking.

Julie paced her bedroom, distraught. The door crashed open.

"Papa—"

"Don't say a damn word. You shouldn't have spoken to Pullman that way. Everyone will hear about it. Didn't you see them staring before we left?"

Julie's nerve broke. Tears came. "It was a fair question—"

"Not from a refined young woman, damn it. Your place is one step to the rear, listening and looking pretty. You dishonored your mother this afternoon. She's in bed again, prostrate."

PAUL ✦ On a warm March day when the snow was melting, Paul was in McClurg's bookstore, a Chicago landmark located in an old brick building at Monroe and Wabash. Fretfully he paced up one aisle, down another. He was waiting for Julie.

He hadn't seen her since February, and he was going crazy with worry and longing. He hoped he hadn't made a mistake last night, paying one of the Vanderhoff stable grooms to smuggle a note into the house. "She may not read it right away," said the groom. "She ain't been well."

Paul paced, twisting his cloth cap. He was still in his work clothes. *She isn't coming, it's all over. I don't know what happened. I'll never see her.*

The tiny bell at the front door whirled him around. A girl was silhouetted in a blaze of midday sunshine. He recognized her. As she hurried down the aisle his heart pounded.

She didn't look well. Her skin was very like the color of new-fallen snow. Great bluish shadows around her eyes subtly changed their color, dulling the sparkle he remembered.

Paul took her gloved hands in his. "Are you all right? The groom told me you have been sick."

She glanced away. "A nervous condition. I'm getting well." It might be so, but she seemed to lack the jaunty confidence that he thought was part of her nature.

"Why aren't you working?" she asked. "It's Saturday."

"I begged a few hours off. I had to see you. Julie, the ice on the lagoon is gone. We must find another way to meet. Do you cycle?" Surely she did; everybody was cycling. America had a mania for it.

"I do, but Mama doesn't like it. She feels it's vulgar. Why do you ask?"

"Because I have a plan. You must start cycling in Lincoln Park. You can rent a wheel there—I have already inquired. I will pretend to be your cycling instructor."

At that she gasped. "My—"

"Teacher. What name shall I have? Leopold? Thomas? Thomas—that sounds respectable." She nodded approval. He bowed, pulling faces, trying to cheer her. "I will come on Sundays. I can stand outside your house respectfully, and you can join me there. I will wear clips on my knickerbockers. You can point me out to those inside. My humble attitude. You can even appear to pay me. I'll return the money."

She laughed. "Oh, Paul." She touched his hand, let her gloved fingers drift across his skin. "I like your daring."

"Thank you." Now it was his turn to touch her, fingers gently closing on her sleeve. "I want to see you; I have to see you. I cannot stop. Ever."

She seemed to take heart from his words. Her expression changed, more resolute all at once. He saw the young woman of strong will and bright temperament with whom he'd skated.

Softly she said, "Nor I."

Paul leaned close to whisper, *"Ich liebe Sie,* Juliette."

"What did you say?"

He blushed. "I don't have the courage to say it in English."

"I think I know what it means. I feel—the same thing."

"Then please, let me pretend to be your cycling teacher."

"Oh, yes. But I don't think it's wise for you to come to the house. I'll tell my parents that I heard about you from a friend who belongs to the Saddle and Cycle Club. That you come well recommended, with good references. Mama will fuss, but I can deal with her."

"This will be on Sundays."

"Yes, Sundays. Tomorrow. I'm so glad you sent the note. You're brave, Paul. Brave and sweet." She was close to tears, but there was happiness too. "Will you say the words again?"

"Ich liebe Sie."

A prissy store clerk was staring not a yard away. Paul tugged Julie's arm.

Outside, they stood in the balmy sunshine, with cool drafts from the wet snowbanks blowing over them. Paul's heart was thundering. "Will you say it to me?"

"Ich liebe Sie, Paul. If I knew a thousand languages, I'd say it in every one. I love you."

He was in heaven. He knew his life had been changed forever.

Part Five
PULLMAN
1894

JOE JUNIOR ✦ Throughout that winter Joe Junior spent less time with his cousin. He was no longer needed as a go-between at Lincoln Park. Paul and Julie were smitten; they hardly noticed anyone else. Joe Junior didn't mind being relieved of duty as Cupid; he had his own girl to think about.

Visiting Roza Jablonec required a trip of almost ten miles out to the model town of Pullman. He didn't mind. Riding the horsecars south on a Sunday, Joe Junior would sometimes imagine in vivid detail how it might be that day if he was lucky to get Rosie alone. It all depended on whether Rosie's parents, Tabor and Maritza, went out for a while.

He didn't always think of sex on his Sunday morning trips. Sometimes he speculated about the future of the country or about his family. Pop—who would never lift his heavy hand from the backs of his employees, his wife, his children. And sometimes he would think about cousin Paul. Paul was a good kid. A dreamer, though. Paul thought America was better than the old country. Joe continually tried to enlighten his cousin. It didn't seem to take.

April came. On the twenty-eighth Joe would be eighteen. He had reached his physical maturity. He would always have the small frame inherited from his father, but his shoulders, arms, and legs were thick with muscle. With the unconscious arrogance of the young, he thought of himself as a man.

That April, Joe was unlucky in Pullman every Sunday. Tabor Jablonec went out, but his dowdy wife, Maritza, stayed home.

Tabor was a worried man, like most everyone who worked for George Pullman. Consequently, he drank. To get a few glasses of cheap red wine, he had to walk over to the neighboring village of Kensington. By decree of Mr. Pullman, there were no saloons for workingmen in his utopian town. Mr. Pullman believed that men were less productive if they drank at night.

Tabor was a carpenter in the Pullman repair shops. Early in 1894 his hourly wage had been reduced twenty percent and then another fifteen percent. After the second cut Tabor did something he'd never done before. Standing in front of his foreman, Castleberry, twisting his cap in his hands, Tabor protested the latest cut.

Castleberry stormed from his chair and knocked Tabor to the floor, calling him a dirty, ungrateful bohunk. He warned Tabor that one more complaint would cost him his job. As it was, Tabor was punished with a month's layoff, and felt lucky.

Tabor was a slight man with brooding dark eyes and a high forehead, but a small weak mouth. Rosie had inherited his best features, but she'd gotten voluptuous lips and breasts and a strong chin from her otherwise ordinary mother. Rosie was a year and a half older than Joe Junior, which was part of her attraction.

He had met her in the country, at Ogden's Grove, at the first of those political-cultural outings to which Benno invited him. It was a hot and dusty Sunday in the autumn of 1892, and he was profoundly awed by the radical nature of the crowd.

Rosie was third on the entertainment program. She excited Joe the moment he saw her. As she stepped up on the improvised platform she showed her bare ankles. There was applause, chiefly from men. She clasped her hands in a stiff, artificial pose and began to sing "My Sweetheart's the Man in the Moon." Her voice was sweet but thin, and even Joe Junior's untrained ear could hear that she frequently sang off key.

No matter. He found her spectacularly attractive, and when she finished the ballad, he rushed to the end of the stage just as she jumped down.

She stumbled as she landed. He was there to catch her, prevent a fall. For an instant she leaned against his shirt. She must have felt something herself, for she gasped and her eyes grew large. Some highly charged linkage leaped between them without a word.

He let go of her, stepped back, and struggled to find his voice. "My name's Joe. I liked your song."

"My name's Roza."

"Roza. That's pretty. It's like Rose."

"You're pretty nice yourself. Meet me in ten minutes. Let's go for a walk."

AFTER that day, he began to see her regularly in Pullman. He called her Rosie, and she liked that. She wasn't a studious girl or smart in the conventional sense. She never read books. Yet somehow she'd learned a lot about life and developed a clear if hard-edged philosophy, especially about her father.

"Papa was born poor, and it scarred him for life. I learned a big lesson from that, Joey, about what comes first. It's being somebody, having connections, so they can't dump on you. And you have to be somebody with a dollar in your pocket. The more the better."

"I don't think that way, Rosie."

"I know. You're all tied up with fine ideas that won't keep you warm or put a roast on the table. That's why we ain't going to stay together. What's it matter? What we got is good enough for now."

ON MAY 6 Joe Junior again set out for Pullman, burdened with a sense of probable defeat. He hadn't been intimate with Rosie for weeks. This Sunday proved no exception. Tabor invited him to nearby Kensington, to a mechanics' hall where an overflow crowd of Pullman workers was expected. They would listen to a special speaker, Eugene Debs of the American Railway Union. Joe Junior decided he might as well go along, since Maritza had made known her intention to spend another afternoon at home.

Joe Junior had never seen Debs. He expected a rough, truculent person. Instead, he saw a lean, clean-shaven balding man who might have been a bookkeeper. It was a hot afternoon, but Debs wore a perfectly pressed tweed suit and hard white collar.

From an earlier base as secretary-treasurer of the Brotherhood of Locomotive Firemen, Debs had worked to unite all railway unions into one. The ARU now had almost three hundred thousand members. Its recruiting argument was persuasive. If a man joined the ARU, he was protected should the bosses try to play one brotherhood against another to break a strike.

Debs spoke for half an hour without notes. After two minutes Joe Junior was impressed; after five he was mesmerized.

"I have moved quietly around the town of Pullman these past few days," Debs said. "I have talked and asked questions, but mostly I have listened. I came away with one indisputable conclusion. If, after working for George M. Pullman for years, you are laid off and you find yourself ragged and hungry, George Pullman has no humane interest in you. His paternalism is the same as that of a slaveholder in regard to his human chattels. That is why I urge you to stand behind your committee tomorrow. Keep your courage high, your purpose clear, and you will carry the day."

"What committee?" Joe whispered to Tabor.

"I don't know nothing about it. I don't want to know."

Debs concluded with one final thought. "Remember that the American Railway Union stands with you. When one brother is assailed, all others go to the rescue."

Men jumped up, whistling and applauding. Joe Junior clapped loudly. Tabor glumly shook his head. "That kind of talk will get you fired. Come on, I need a glass of wine."

Joe went along to the saloon, but after one drink of the cheap red wine he couldn't stand any more of Tabor's whipped-dog attitude. He asked whether Tabor planned to go home.

"Not right away." Tabor signaled for another glass. Instantly Joe Junior saw a way to turn this to advantage.

Back in Pullman an hour later, he said to Maritza, "I'm afraid Mr. Jablonec is getting pretty far under the weather over in Kensington. He'd already had several wines when I left."

"Oh my. Where is he, Fanucci's?"

"Yes. He wouldn't leave."

"I'll have to bring him home. Rosie will fix you a bite of supper."

Maritza rushed to find her shawl. From her chair at the kitchen table Rosie treated Joe Junior to a rapturous smile.

ON MAY 7 a three-member grievance committee went to Pullman management to ask for reinstatement of regular wages. The executives listened with apparent sympathy and then restated the company's position. Times were bad. Orders were down. Further, Pullman was building cars at a loss to keep the shops open and at least part of its work force employed.

The meeting ended amicably. The three committeemen who had approached the company were for the moment satisfied.

At midweek each received notice of an indefinite layoff.

On Friday, May 11, exactly at noon, thirty-one hundred men of the Pullman Palace Car Company put down their tools and walked out. They demanded lower rents in Pullman, cancellation of the wage cuts of 1893, and reinstatement of the three committeemen.

Not all Pullman workers joined the walkout. Tabor Jablonec was among those who stayed. His loyalty didn't help him. On Monday the remaining three hundred workers were laid off indefinitely.

JULIE ✦ Aunt Willis Fishburne arrived at the end of May. She never stayed long. "After three days," she observed, "fish and visitors begin to stink." Three days were long enough for driving Vanderhoff out of his wits, but not nearly long enough for Julie.

Aunt Willis would soon celebrate her forty-eighth birthday. Unlike her sister, Nell, she was a tall woman with austere features. She wore her gray-shot hair mannishly clipped and unadorned. Not for her the fuzzy curls and fat buns of fashion. She resembled a woman from some backcountry plantation in the South, where life was hard. Until you noticed her eyes. They radiated warmth and mirth and cynicism by turns. They were windows through which you saw fireworks displays.

Aunt Willis arrived in a depot hack. She was dressed, as usual, in a costume designed to shock. Full Oriental trousers under a short skirt and tailored tunic, low-laced shoes, and red silk stockings.

Willis had studied the doctrines of Mrs. Amelia Bloomer of Seneca Falls, New York, the liberated woman who had pioneered hygienic dress in the 1850s. Once enlightened, Willis never looked back. She scorned the layers of Victorian crinoline, the frills and flounces, the brutal bustles lashed in place. She said they caused a repression of normal and healthy female spirits.

Julie's aunt was an authentic black sheep, an embarrassment Nell tried to conceal from the world. Fortunately, Willis lived in New York There she worked for causes that made her sister blanch. She consorted with prostitutes at street missions in order to put an end to their sexual exploitation. She wrote pamphlets demanding changes in one-sided divorce laws. She openly embraced free love and told Julie that a woman had an absolute right to control her own body. No doctor, no politician or prelate, no *man* had the right—though they were always trying to assume it.

Two years ago Willis lost the latest of her three husbands, each of whom had contributed to her state of financial independence. Her first husband, the Reverend Chauncey Stone Coffin, was twenty years her senior, a millionaire, and a leading figure in the crusade for abolition and Negro equality. His passion for black freedom knew no bounds. Unfortunately, neither did his passion for female members of his audiences. Willis heard about the affairs, and Coffin left her a million dollars in return for secrecy and a quiet divorce.

She married her second husband, Loyal McBee, a few years later. He was an actor who succumbed early to the most dangerous temptation of his trade—drink—but Willis loved him madly. Their marriage lasted four years. On tour in Detroit he found a saloon after a matinee, emerged an hour later, and fell in front of a horse-car. His neck was broken. He died instantly. Not until a week later did Willis learn that Loyal's family had given him half a million dollars in a trust fund he couldn't touch so long as he was in the disreputable profession of acting. Willis inherited the money.

Simon Mordecai Weiss was her most recent spouse. Weiss had risen from his father's junk trade to become America's reigning monarch of wholesale hardware. He was a wonderfully kind man who had married and divorced two previous wives, both of whom he found greedy and vapid. He and Willis met at a lantern slide lecture on the African interior, and struck up a conversation. Willis liked the old man before she ever knew who he was. Two weeks later he presented her with a simple and honest proposition. If she would marry him and travel with him, engaging him in intelligent conversation, he would make her his sole heir.

Weiss had a weak heart. He lived only fourteen months. Willis negotiated cannily and finally sold his firm for seven and a half million dollars. She cried every day for a month after she buried the kind and thoughtful Weiss.

Willis had never deliberately sought wealth in any of her husbands. Often she wondered if that was why wealth had found her.

On the first day of Willis' visit she and Julie went shopping at Elstree's and Field's and then to supper at the restaurant of Willis' choice, the English Chop House. It was a racy, disreputable place on Gamblers' Alley, popular with sporting men, painted women, big-bellied pols, and fast-talking journalists. Amid dark woodwork, tobacco smoke, and whiskey fumes Willis was at home.

"All right, tell me about it," she said once they were served.

Julie's gray eyes widened. "About what?"

"Come, do you think I haven't noticed the changes since I was here last? Your cheeks are red, but your eyes have a haggard look. Young women lose sleep over young men. Tell me."

Julie let it tumble forth—everything about Paul Crown. "I see him every Sunday. Now that it's good weather, we go cycling in Lincoln Park. He pretends to be my instructor. He's very daring. I think I love him, Aunt Willis."

Willis lit one of her small dark brown cigars. "You're young, Juliette. It's possible this infatuation will pass."

"It won't."

"All I am doing is cautioning you. Be very sure."

"I am."

Willis looked at her steadily for several seconds. "All right, then. Don't say you *think* you love the boy; declare it."

Julie swirled her little silver spoon in the melting dessert ice. "What about Mama and Papa? They loathe the family. They would hate him. But I'd die if I had to stop seeing him."

"Then don't."

"That's how I feel. But what if they found out?"

"Defy them."

"Oh, Aunt Willis, I don't know if I could do that. I love Mama and Papa. I want their respect and approval. Their affection—"

"Which they ration out according to how you behave."

Julie looked away. Her aunt had judged it correctly.

"Julie, you're a dutiful daughter and a decent person. Regrettably,

in this world, decency can be a handicap. Furthermore, your mother has filled your head with falsehoods about your frail health. You mustn't believe any of it. It's part of the prevailing absurdity about womankind: The chief function of a female today is to be ornamental. Except of course when she is busy being a brood sow."

"Aunt Willis," Julie whispered, covering her mouth.

"Dear, there's nothing shocking about plain truths. A woman is born with intelligence and character. A woman needs a purpose, Julie. A mission she believes is important. That and a glass of fine Kentucky bourbon, a bracing swim, or a vigorous lover will cure almost anything that ails you. Still—setting all that aside—I know you face a more immediate issue because of this boy. Namely, whose life is it? Your mother's, your father's, or yours?"

Troubled, Julie studied her hands. She knew the brave answer to the question. She just couldn't bear to confront the consequences it conjured.

Aunt Willis seemed to understand. "Don't doubt yourself. You have the courage to take the right road, if you'll only believe it. To do it would undoubtedly cause you pain for a while, but you'd survive. You'd make your stand successfully."

"I hope so."

The waiter laid down a silver tray bearing the bill. Willis put out her little cigar in a crystal dish, crushing it with force. "Here, I'll pay the bill. It's time we went home. Just one more thing." She covered her niece's hand with her own. "If this love affair becomes too difficult for you to bear by yourself, think of me. Come to me at any time if you need a haven or a friend."

PAUL ✦ On a hot evening in June, after work, Joe Junior persuaded Paul to accompany him to a meeting before they went home. It was a Saturday, the day after Paul's seventeenth birthday.

"Gene Debs is giving a speech tonight. He's a terrific orator; you need to hear him."

After they left the brewery, they had supper in a saloon, then went on to Uhlich's Hall. The drab old auditorium was hot and nearly full. Paul was uncomfortable about being with this crowd, surely all socialists.

Cousin Joe said, "Everyone's wondering whether Debs will make a big announcement tonight."

Long applause, whistling, foot stomping greeted Debs as he walked out from the wings. His gaze swept the gallery. "For five days we have listened to tales of the abuse of workingmen at Pullman. With blind eyes and deaf ears and hearts devoid of Christian compassion, the Pullman company turns away from its own employees, who are starving and suffering for the sake of—what? Exorbitant or unreasonable demands? No! A subsistence wage!

"Gentlemen, for all the reasons just stated, I have set aside my reluctance. I will not oppose, and indeed I endorse the action of the executive board of your brotherhood. If, within ten days, the Pullman Palace Car Company does not agree to arbitration in good faith, then the American Railway Union will commence a boycott of all Pullman operations."

There were whistles and whoops, a flurry of movement among reporters. Debs said sharply, "Just a moment. Hear the rest. During the boycott the brotherhood will refuse to service Pullman cars, regardless of which line is carrying them. We will use no violence. Our effort will be peaceful. But we will maintain the boycott until such time as arbitration begins."

The hall was hushed. Debs had them straining to hear; even Paul had slowly been pulled into the spell of the man's oratory.

"That is our message to the world. In these dark and difficult times we can do no less than support our brave brothers in American labor. Thank you, and good night."

People jumped up from their seats and applauded. Joe Junior shot to his feet, and somewhat reluctantly, so did Paul. Joe was exuberant. "This is it; we'll see action now. The boycott changes everything. It's dynamite."

As the two left the hall Paul wondered if his cousin was aware of the word he'd used.

Two shiny Fleetwing safety cycles leaned against the trunk of the sycamore. On the other side, in dappled shade, Paul and Julie rested on the grass. They were meeting two hours later than usual today—four o'clock. Aunt Ilsa had delayed Sunday dinner because of a special reception at church.

When Paul heard about this change early Sunday morning, he had run all the way to Prairie Avenue and lurked near the Vanderhoff mansion until the family drove off to church. Then he went to the rear of the property, where a path led from the sidewalk to the side door of the stable.

Seven melon-size whitewashed stones lined each side of the path. Theirs was the second on the left as you faced the stable. Paul had picked out the stone after Julie said that using the servants would inevitably lead to discovery. He slipped a note under the message stone. Julie checked it often.

Their meeting place was the bicycle rental stand near Fisher's Beer Garden, at the northern edge of Lincoln Park. He arrived twenty minutes early. She arrived on time. They clasped hands, squeezed, then separated with guilty smiles.

She wore a smart new cycling outfit—low shoes of white canvas, white leggings with a knee-length overskirt, a fitted white bolero jacket, a gay sailor hat with a broad ribbon of emerald satin. In Paul's eyes, no one could have looked more beautiful.

They pedaled along a road that curved through the heart of Lincoln Park. Children romped. Cyclists tinkled their bells. At the south end, they turned around, pedaling back to Fisher's, where they dismounted and left the road. Paul and Julie chose their spot on the lake side of the big sycamore.

From the pocket of his coat Paul took a small block of paper and a piece of brown chalk. He tried to sketch her as they talked.

He brought up the strike. "I don't know much about it," Julie responded. "Papa says the strikers should be arrested."

"My uncle speaks the same way."

"Rich men," she said with a shrug. "They think alike. Let me see." Embarrassed, he showed the sketch. "Bad as ever. I have no talent. I want to make pictures with a camera. Perhaps the kind that move; that would be the most exciting."

"I've heard about those. Papa saw a demonstration at the Exposition. He said the pictures were useless and trashy."

"Oh, no, I don't think so." He tossed the mawkish sketch aside. "What if you could photograph truly important things? Sights that no ordinary person would ever have a chance to see? Presidents or kings or cannibals? What if you could photograph wars? It would be like a history book springing to life before your eyes. That wouldn't be useless or trashy."

"No, it certainly wouldn't."

He leaned back against the tree. "It is work I could give my whole life to, Julie. At the fair I met a man who would have taught me, but his shop closed. I don't know where he went."

"There must be another way to learn how to do it. You'll find it. I think you can do almost anything you want with your life."

She was beautiful beyond belief. He slipped his hand over hers.

Reacting to his touch, Julie turned to him, the black strands of her hair blowing and tossing over the puffed shoulders of her jacket. "Please, Paul. We mustn't."

He didn't let go. "All I want is to hug and kiss you, Julie."

"We can't start that. I might not be strong enough to stop."

He scrambled to his knees, then bent forward and kissed her.

They'd kissed on the lips before, chastely. But this was June, with heat in the air and in their blood.

He pressed his mouth against hers, feeling her cool lips quickly grow warm. She uttered a little cry and hugged him around the waist, her cheek flat against his starched shirt.

He stroked her shining hair. "Please allow me to speak to your father. I will make him understand my intentions are good. He will forget his bad feelings toward my uncle—"

"No, he won't, and you mustn't say a word. If you spoke to Papa, he wouldn't allow me to see you again, ever. We'd lose even these few hours."

"But I can't have only secret meetings the rest of my life, Julie."

"Oh, I can't either, but—" She started to cry.

He embraced her and stroked her hair again. "Then what are we going to do?"

"I don't know!" Her sobbing grew louder.

He moved away. Touched her tear-reddened face. Bent again to kiss her tenderly, comfortingly.

"Hey. Hello there."

The cry wrenched them apart. Paul saw a fancy red tandem cycle on the curving road, a young woman on the front seat, her blond escort behind. Julie recognized him a moment before Paul did.

"Oh, no!"

It was her rich friend Welliver.

ILSA ✦ In the troubled spring and summer of 1894 Jane Addams convened groups of affluent women who supported her, and urged them to use their influence in the Pullman matter.

To a group gathered around her parlor table on a day in late June she showed pages of the newspapers. "To the press they're all monsters. Yet I was out at Pullman yesterday, and I'm convinced that the strikers are peaceable and decent people who have been abused by their employers."

"Will the boycott go on as scheduled, Miss Addams?" Ilsa asked.

"I fear so. The company position is, there is nothing to negotiate. But there's worse news. The General Managers Association, which represents the twenty-four railroads headquartered or terminating in Chicago, is already recruiting a force of special deputies. They will be sworn in and used to move the trains Mr. Debs' brotherhood refuses to handle. They will confront the pickets."

"Is that not a legitimate response?" Ilsa wondered aloud.

"That isn't the issue, Ilsa. The GMA is recruiting pickpockets, toughs—any scum that can be scraped up and armed. I ask all of you to speak to your husbands. Let them speak to officials they may know at the various railroads. Order must be maintained."

Ilsa did raise the issue with Joe at the supper table.

He scoffed. "What's wrong with preparing to defend yourself against a rabble? If matters get out of hand, the authorities should call for federal troops. I'm entirely behind the GMA."

"And I support the union," Joe Junior said. From his corduroy jacket he pulled a long white ribbon.

Joe Crown peered over his half-glasses. "What the devil is that?"

"The Railway Union is passing them out. Debs wants his people to be easily identified in a crowd so no one frames them for some trumped-up criminal act. The ribbons show solidarity too."

"Not in my house. Nor at the brewery."

"I'm sorry, Pop, this is a matter of conscience." Joe Junior started to tie the white ribbon around his left sleeve.

"Stop." Joe senior shot his hand out, palm up. "Give it to me, Joseph. Now. *Now.*"

Their eyes locked. Joe Junior's will broke. He dropped the ribbon into his father's hand. Joe senior crumpled it and whisked it out of sight. "You may finish your supper."

Ilsa sat like a stone, fearing to move. Joe Junior said, "I don't care for any more. I want to be excused."

"Go!" Joe senior waved. "You spoil my digestion anyway, you and your radical nonsense."

Joe Junior got up and walked out.

"Joe, please," Ilsa said. "Some of what your son is telling you is quite true. Miss Addams is of the opinion that—"

"Miss Addams, Miss Addams— Frankly, Ilsa, I'm sick of hearing the opinions of an aging spinster who has no grasp of reality."

"Oh, that's unfair," Ilsa retorted, her own anger rising. "Wearing a ribbon isn't such a terrible—"

"It represents anarchy. It shames this family. I won't have it."

Fritzi, Carl, and Paul were all watching with strained expressions; Carl actually looked frightened. For the sake of harmony Ilsa suppressed her anger. "Everyone eat, please."

She too had surrendered. She didn't like herself for that. Or her husband for forcing it.

The next day at noon Joe senior telephoned from the office with a gruff apology. Ilsa apologized too. After a considerable pause he cleared his throat. In a voice full of strain he closed the conversation with his usual "I love you," and rang off.

PAUL ✦ Soon the Pullman boycott became a general American Railway Union strike. Paul couldn't avoid reading or hearing about it. At Crown's they talked about little else.

The strike was still peaceful, but it was biting deep into the commerce of Chicago. Freight tonnage dropped. The papers cried out for action against the strikers, and the General Managers Association maneuvered to promote such action by putting forth a new argument: The railroads were public institutions. The ARU was therefore attacking every American citizen.

Under the direction of the GMA, Pullman cars were being coupled to freight trains that didn't usually have them, or mail cars were coupled behind Pullman coaches, thereby proving the strike was interfering with government property.

Eugene Debs saw it otherwise: "The GMA is intriguing to bring Washington into it. It wants the boycott viewed as a confrontation between union men and the federal government."

The strategy worked. President Cleveland declared that the mails must go through. The government issued an injunction restraining Debs et al. from interfering with the mails, interstate commerce, and the conduct of business.

The cousins were at Uhlich's Hall that night when Debs

emerged from a conference room to address a large crowd. "The gauntlet is down," he said to the hushed audience. "This injunction denies us the right to picket. It specifies that any such activity is a felony." For the first time, Paul heard rage in Debs' voice. "Do you see the position into which they have maneuvered us? If we obey the injunction and await a court test of it months from now, the strike is broken. If we don't obey, the law is broken."

A loud call from the gallery: "Then what's your next move?"

Debs looked worn, but he managed a smile. "Why, we're going ahead. The executive board has voted to call a general strike of all railroad brotherhoods everywhere."

Amid the tumult of cheers, Paul and Joe Junior left the hall. Paul's cousin was jubilant. Paul was silent. The strike seemed to be slipping toward the violence Mr. Debs so abhorred.

On the brewery roof next day the temperature must have been over ninety. The roof was deserted except for Paul. His forehead dripped sweat. The heat sapped him. His mood was sour.

He hadn't seen Julie for three Sundays in a row. The Vanderhoffs were home; he knew because he'd loitered outside the house one night. Had Julie been seized by illness? He had no appetite for the wurst and bread in his lunch sack.

A man came out the door at the head of the stairs. Sam Traub, the tax agent—tax laws required a revenue man on the premises of every brewery. Traub had a newspaper. He spread it on the coping next to Paul and leafed through the pages.

"Here's another one gone 'count of this weather. Makes seven so far." He showed Paul.

MRS. ELSTREE SUCCUMBS

ARRANGEMENTS PENDING FOR SPOUSE OF DEPARTMENT STORE HEIR
Her Sudden Death Attributed to Heat

Paul swabbed his neck and face with his bandanna. He wasn't surprised that people were dying.

To the southeast he noticed a rising plume of black smoke. "What is that?"

"Bet you it's more freight cars. Six or seven burned last night."

"The strikers are burning freight cars?"

Traub gave him a sly smile. "Not exactly. The special deputies tip 'em over and torch 'em. Makes the strikers look bad. It's what the damn Reds deserve."

"Oh, I don't think so, Mr. Traub."

"What do you know? You're a greenhorn, brand-new to things in this country. I'd advise you to keep your nose out of it."

THE STRIKE IS WAR, a headline in the Chicago *Tribune* had said, and so it became. Two thousand protesters gathered for a mass meeting at the Blue Island yards of the Chicago, Rock Island & Pacific line. The chief federal marshal ordered the crowd to disperse. The protesters refused, and rocks and bottles flew. The marshal and his men fled. On Independence Day, a Wednesday, four infantry companies from Fort Sheridan encamped on the lakefront. President Cleveland had answered the call for federal troops. That night mobs roamed. Almost fifty freight cars burned in the Illinois Central yards. Rail traffic was disrupted by switches thrown and signal lights changed.

General Nelson Miles arrived to command the U.S. troops. Business leaders and newspaper editorialists were relieved.

AT THE brewery, a large room had been set aside as a lounge and wash area for the men. Individual wooden lockers lined one wall. At the close of work on Thursday, Paul pushed the door open and saw Benno at the wash trough. The shoulder straps of his overalls were down on his hips, and his work shirt was unbuttoned. He was swabbing his chest with a wet rag and singing to himself.

Paul nodded to Benno and went to his locker. Benno stopped washing and grinned. "You don't look so happy, Mr. Pauli."

"It is hot as hell. I'm tired." Paul opened his locker, pulled off his shirt, and began to dry himself with a towel.

From his locker Benno pulled a twist of wax paper. "Want a licorice?"

"No, thank you, I am not hungry."

Benno shrugged, raised his hand to put the licorice back on the shelf. Somehow he dropped it. He bent over, and something fell out of his shirt, landing on the concrete between his heavy shoes.

A blued revolver with a white ribbon tied around the barrel.

They looked at each other. Benno shot a glance at the door. Men were coming. He snatched the revolver, jammed it under his shirt, and pulled up the straps of his overalls. He walked over and laid a huge fist on Paul's shoulder.

"You seem like a nice boy, Pauli. Smart. So I'll go easy, just a warning." But he closed his fingers on Paul's shoulder until there was pain. "You didn't see nothing in here. You say otherwise, to your uncle or anybody, you won't have no job for a long time. Maybe you won't have no arms and legs either, *versteh?*"

"Yes," Paul said as calmly as he could manage.

The outer door banged open. Half a dozen men trooped in. Benno greeted them. Paul quickly changed his shirt and left.

Warning or no, after supper Paul drew cousin Joe into the garden and described the encounter with Benno.

His cousin surprised him by saying, "Yeah, he showed it to me. Day before yesterday. He said, 'You're a good soldier, ain't you? We can count on you, can't we?' "

"Count on you for what?"

"I don't know; he didn't explain." Joe Junior stared at his hands. "I'm on Benno's side, but I never thought there'd be guns inside the brewery after Pop threw them out."

"Benno gave me a warning, Joe. He didn't say it exactly, but I know what he meant. That he would hurt me or kill me if I— What is the word you use sometimes? Ratted?"

"Yes. Ratted." Joe Junior nodded. "He warned me too."

Paul shivered. They heard distant firecracker sounds, which might have been gunfire. They heard a police wagon careen past the house.

"Joe."

"What?"

"Can Benno count on you?"

"I don't know," Joe said again. "I think Pop's on the wrong side, the side of the plutocrats. But I don't want to kill anybody."

"I don't either."

They sat on a stone bench in the garden. Their shoulders touched. Neither moved. The silence lengthened, betokening a shared fear.

ROSIE ✦ On the Sunday night before the injunction against Debs, Rosie's beau had left Pullman about half past eight after eating supper with Rosie and Maritza. Tabor wasn't there.

Another of his Sunday disappearances. To a saloon, Rosie assumed.

Supper was the familiar poor fare. Bread four days old and a miserable thin stew made of beans, potatoes, and a few chunks of lamb with a faint odor of spoilage. The stew, the hot, airless rooms, the anxiety in Pullman put Rosie in short temper, thinking of how, and how soon, she could escape from this trap.

She needed singing lessons to tr~in ~er voice. She had to find a man to pay for those. She needec __cket to New York City. After she met Joey Crown, she'd harbored some silly dreams of marrying him. But they didn't last long. He didn't have money to pay for music lessons or a train ticket. She admired Joey in a lot of ways. He was brainy, read books, and under her tutelage he'd become a skillful lover. Unfortunately, some of his ideas were stupid. Who but Joey would turn down a chance to run a brewery and be rich?

Tabor came in. He was excited, which wasn't typical of him. He looked different—almost the handsome father she'd worshipped from childhood.

"Guess what, guess what! I got a job!"

Maritza said, "What are you saying, Tabor? You already have a job. You're just waiting to be called back."

"This is a special job, extra. Two dollars fifty cents a day. Look, it's okay. My foreman said the company would like it."

"What kind of job is it, Pop?" Rosie already had an ominous suspicion, from things she'd heard around Pullman.

"Special deputy. I get my badge and gun tomorrow."

"You're scabbing?"

Tabor looked hurt. "Rosie, honey, that's a nasty word. I'm going to help guard railroad property. Break this strike that's ruining things for all of us."

Rosie's mother said, "Tabor, you don't know anything about guns; you mustn't do this crazy thing."

"Listen, it's a big honor."

"Papa, Papa—two dollars and fifty cents a day and a chance to get killed is no honor."

"Girl, mind your tongue."

"Pop, please listen. The money don't matter. Turn it down. Tell them no. It isn't worth the risk. I don't want you hurt even a little."

"That's good of you, Rosie. You're a good and loving daughter."

"Then tell them no."

"Yes, Tabor, please," Maritza pleaded.

With a guilty look at his wife, then Rosie, Tabor said, "Can't. I signed the paper."

"Oh, Pop." What a weak, wrongheaded man he was. She hated herself for loving him so completely. Thank goodness a person had only one father in a lifetime.

PAUL ✦ Rail lines coming into Chicago were partially or wholly shut down. Long lines of boxcars waited outside the city, their cargoes of grain and vegetables putrefying. In the stockyards, carloads of meat stood on sidings, rotten, foul smelling.

Larger and angrier mobs were abroad every night. More soldiers arrived. More deputy marshals took to the streets and rode the few trains that were still operating. Workers at the brewery talked uneasily of a phrase going around among soldiers and deputies: "Shoot at the dirty white ribbons."

Firemen and switchmen, telegraphers and engineers joined the strike. The GMA announced that effective Saturday, July 7, armed militia would ride the mail trains.

Shoot at the dirty white ribbons. . . .

On Friday afternoon, before the latest GMA decree was to take effect, Paul was called to his uncle's office. Barricaded behind his usual pile of unfinished work, Uncle Joe looked small and tired. He was reading something on a ragged piece of brown kraft paper, a scowl on his face. He shoved the paper into a drawer.

"Paul, I have an errand for you—a task that requires a touch of diplomacy. I assume you know what's meant by a red-light district."

"*Ein Bordellviertel?* I do. There were many in Berlin."

"There are many here. I just learned that one of my accounts, the Canadian Gardens, has added a wine room upstairs. The words wine room are code. A signal that customers may purchase not only beer but— Well, you understand. I managed to get the owner of the Gardens on the telephone. He calls himself Toronto Bob. When I accused him, he laughed and didn't deny anything. I told him I was suspending deliveries of Crown's beer. But I want my ornamental tap handles back. They are expensive. I also want the sign outside. It's not so big that you can't carry it." Many breweries distributed signs without cost. Most were cut in the shape of a stein, brightly painted and lettered with the brewery's name.

"Here is the address. It's south of Van Buren, on Clark Street, in Little Cheyenne. That's a disreputable area. Not as bad as the Levee. But bad enough. I want you to be careful."

"I will, sir. But I can look after myself."

UNCLE Joe hadn't exaggerated about Little Cheyenne. A shadow seemed to lie on it—a shadow of poverty and dirt and dissolution. Paul hurried along the plank sidewalk on Clark Street, among loitering bums and a few heavily painted women. No one bothered him. He was big now, sturdy, and he walked with a confident stride.

Two blocks below Van Buren he spied the metal sign in front of the Canadian Gardens. He went inside and explained his errand to the barkeep.

"I knew this was comin'; Bob tole me. You can take the sign down yourself. As for the tap handles, you can see they're gone. I don't know where they are. You'll have to speak to Bob. But he ain't here. Left five minutes ago. Said he was dropping his Kodak off at Rooney's. You might catch him there."

Rooney? "Sir, please—where is this Rooney's?"

"End of the block and turn left. It's past the red-light hotel."

THE side street was narrower, dirtier, darker. Tenement buildings leaned in from both sides. Paul forgot the seedy surroundings the instant he saw the shop.

Over a dusty show window hung a gaudy sign proclaiming ROONEY'S TEMPLE OF PHOTOGRAPHY. Beyond the flyspecked glass, on a wrinkled drape of plum velvet, lay several box cameras. A placard offered USED CAMERAS, another PHOTOGRAPHIC PORTRAITS.

The shop was dark save for a faint light in back. Excited, Paul went in. A small bell over the door jingled.

"Coming, who is it?" There was a click; a weak electric globe in the ceiling lit up the shop. Paul almost clapped for joy. It was the same little man with the salt-and-pepper mustache. "Yes, can I help— Why, stars! I know you, don't I?"

"You do, sir. We met at the Exposition. You showed me the machine of moving pictures."

"So I did, so I did. Gave you my card. You said you were interested, but you never came around."

"I did, sir. They said you had moved." *For not paying the rent.*

243

"Well, yes, I did, that's right," Rooney said quickly. "Tell me, how did you track me down?"

"It is a happy accident," Paul explained.

"The barkeep told you straight; Bob Hopper was here, but that was ten minutes ago."

"I see. Then I suppose I had better go—"

"Here, wait. Since you're an enthusiast, I can give you a favorable price on a camera. Care to look around? By the way, the name's Rooney. Wexford Rooney."

"I remember. I'm Paul Crown."

"German." It wasn't a question. "I'll call you Dutch."

There seemed to be nothing he could do to avoid that nickname.

"Let me show you around, Dutch."

Wexford Rooney, whom Paul judged to be in his middle fifties, never stopped talking during the next half hour.

At the center of the room stood a huge camera on a tall tripod, a black cloth draped over it. The barrel lens pointed at a velvet settee. "I can offer you a choice of backgrounds if you'd care to have a portrait made," Rooney said. "Permit me to demonstrate." He shoved a stool near the back wall. Standing on it, he could just reach several ceiling rollers mounted parallel. He snatched at a ring and pulled one down. "Sylvan forest." Pulled another. "Majestic mountains." Another. "South Seas palm hut."

Rooney hopped down. "Now you might like to see some of the pictures I made during the late unpleasantness. Come into the back and sit down."

Paul followed Rooney to a small kitchen at the rear. "I'm just having my supper. It's early, but my last portrait appointment canceled." Had there really been an appointment? It didn't matter. Paul had taken a liking to the odd little man.

The electric light from the ceiling was dim. Set out was Rooney's meal: a bowl of tomato soup, two crackers, a cup of tea.

Paul took one of the two chairs. "Want a cup of tea?" Rooney put a kettle on a gas ring, lit it, and turned up the flame.

When the teakettle finally whistled, Rooney poured hot water into a cracked mug, then swished a corroded silver tea-leaf holder through it. He put the mug in front of Paul.

"Where are you from, Dutch?"

"Chicago now. But I came from Berlin."

"Berlin—always heard it was a magnificent city. I was born in Charleston, South Carolina. I was an orphan. I went north at an early age. I had no connections; I wanted to learn a trade."

He rummaged in a cabinet, pulled out an album, brought it to the table. He opened it to a cardboard-mounted photograph, faded and brown, that showed him as a young boy. He was standing beside a closed wagon, shaking hands with an older man. The man was neatly dressed in a cravat, duster, and straw hat. He was shown in profile; he had a nose like a saber.

"That's me with my mentor, Mr. M. B. Brady. Maybe not the finest photographer in the profession, but the smartest. I started as his apprentice. He taught me everything. How to frame portraiture. How to develop glass plates. Everything except how to turn a penny. A number of us worked for him taking war photographs, but he allowed only one name on those pictures. Mathew Brady.

"I'll say this for Mr. Mathew. He had a vision. No, an obsession. He wanted to photograph what had never been photographed before. Battlefields. We went to the war zone in wagons like the one you see. We worked with artillery shells bursting in the sky. Nobody had ever seen such pictures before. Here, look for yourself."

He showed Paul a horrific photograph of dead bodies piled in a trench and flowing over the top. "Took that at Petersburg."

He showed the next—a startling, eerie image of gutted buildings, vacant windows, in a vista of rubble. Black as obsidian, the buildings leaped out in contrast to a white sky.

"This is Richmond after it burned. You're looking at history, Dutch, a moment preserved for eternity."

Paul's spine prickled. It was magic, but the real world too. This was drawing and painting with a camera. This was what he wanted to do with his life. "I want to learn to take photographs, good ones like yours," he said.

"Why, I'd be delighted to teach you. Come any free hour."

With a brimming heart Paul said, "I would like that very much. I have a job six days a week at my uncle's brewery, but I will find the time somehow. Now I really should be going."

"All right, but come back, Dutch. Please come back."

Rooney escorted him through the littered studio and saw him into the street with a wave. Never mind the poor surroundings; Paul was thrilled by the prospect of learning all that Mr. Rooney

245

could teach. He had to leave the brewery, that was certain now. But he needn't do it immediately. He could wait until he learned the fundamentals and Rooney said he was equipped to seek a job in the profession. Then he would break it to Uncle Joe gently.

Abruptly Paul remembered why his uncle had sent him to Little Cheyenne. He couldn't recover the tap handles, but he could certainly borrow a ladder and take down the sign. He headed for Clark Street.

JOE JUNIOR ✦ About half past eight that night, someone knocked at Joe's door, startling him. It was his mother. She seemed tense. "Your father wants to see you in the study."

Feeling like a condemned man, he was sweating when he knocked for permission to enter.

Only one lamp was on in the study, the desk lamp with its shade of green banker's glass. The windows were closed, as if that would shut out the reality of rioting and burning.

His father's face was drawn. "I have a serious question to ask you, Joseph. I expect and demand an honest answer."

Nervously: "Sure, Pop, ask."

His father showed a folded square of brown kraft paper. "Today someone at the brewery put an anonymous note in my office. I believe the writing is Emil Tagg's. The note says Benno Strauss is carrying a pistol at Crown's. If I asked Benno, he would lie. Emil bears him a grudge because Benno attacked him, so Emil isn't entirely reliable either. I am asking you. Have you seen any such weapon?"

Joe Junior's head rang. Here was a line clearly drawn, and he had to retreat from it or step over.

Good soldier . . . Can I count on you?

"Young man, I order you to answer me."

Yes, damn you, you order me, you order everybody.

"No, sir. I haven't seen anything like that."

Joe Crown stared at his son for what might have been as much as a half minute. Then he said, "All right, thank you. You may go."

In the entrance hall, Joe Junior grabbed the banister and rested his forehead on the cool smooth wood. His heart was hammering. He'd done it. Taken the step. Sworn his allegiance to the other side. He felt giddily proud of himself.

A HALF HOUR LATER HE HEARD THE telephone bell downstairs. Someone answered on the second ring. Probably Manfred. Joe went to the window and stared at the red sky. Had he discharged his obligation to Benno with his lie? He hoped so. This was more dangerous than he'd ever dreamed.

Manfred knocked on his door. "Mr. Joseph, the caller is asking for you. A young woman."

Joe Junior hurried to answer. He wasn't ready for another shock. But he got one.

"Joey? 'S that you?"

"Rosie?" He kept his voice low. "Where are you?" The Jablonecs couldn't afford telephone service.

"Min Slocum's, the only phone on the street."

"You sound scared to death."

"I am. For Pop. All hell's broke loose. Did you look at the sky? A neighbor told Ma there's hundreds of boxcars burning in south Chicago. The worst is, Pop's going on duty tomorrow morning right where they're expecting trouble."

"Going on duty? I don't understand what—"

"Scabbing! He signed on to be a special deputy."

Joe slumped against the wall. "Why?"

"For the money. The Pullman bosses say it's all right; they say it shows loyalty."

"He could get killed. Of all the stupid—"

"Joe Crown, I know all that. I don't need lectures and sermons; I need you. There's a work train going out at ten o'clock tomorrow, and Pop's one of the deputies on it. The strike people are going to stop the train at the level crossing at Loomis and Forty-ninth. I love my pop; I have to see he don't get hurt. But I don't want to go alone. Please come with me."

"Rosie, it's a workday. I don't think I—"

"Joey, I never asked nothing of you before. I been good to you, Joey—" She was close to crying. "You got to help me this once."

He ran his palm down his sweating cheek. "I'll be there, nine thirty." He slammed the earpiece on its hook.

ROSIE clutched Joe Junior's sweaty hand and pulled him along. "This way. I hear the train."

Initially he and Rosie had missed each other for ten minutes,

247

caught in the swirl of men and women and youngsters—maybe three hundred, four hundred—all converging on this one level crossing.

Around his left arm, above the elbow, he'd tied a new white ribbon. He saw many other white ribbons here.

Near the tracks Joe and Rosie were brought up short behind noisy men and women standing three and four deep. Already the crossing gates had been torn down, broken to kindling. Jostling and shoving, the crowd flowed onto the tracks.

To the north Joe Junior glimpsed blue-clad men from the Illinois National Guard riding the cowcatcher of the locomotive, which was about a block away, chugging slowly, squirting steam. Guardsmen sat on the roof of the engine cab too, rifles on their knees. They were civilians, probably nervous.

"I wonder where Pop's at," Rosie said. She craned up on her toes. Her red-and-white gingham dress, faded from laundering, stuck to her in wet patches.

A Guard officer on the cowcatcher waved his hat at the mob. "Clear the track. We're authorized to fire if you don't."

The work train chugged on toward the level crossing. The mob inevitably gave way before it. But men and women ran along both sides of the train screaming, "Scabs, scabs, dirty scabs," and throwing stones, sticks, bottles. Rosie bobbed up and down on her toes. "Where are the marshals, Joey? Do you see them?"

He pointed. "There, second car."

"Do you see Pop?"

"Not yet." It was hard to see anything clearly in the rising dust.

The train consisted of four gondolas and a caboose. The second gondola carried a huge swivel crane, rusty red. Most of the marshals were on this car, men in vests and derbies, tin badges winking.

"There's Pop," Rosie cried suddenly. "There, on the next car." The third gondola carried a load of rails. Tabor was sitting on top of the rails. He wore his tin badge pinned to his overalls.

"Oh, Joey, he's all right. Papa! Over here," she yelled. Tabor spied her and waved as the car rolled through the crossing.

The last gondola went by, and finally the caboose. Joe Junior felt an enormous relief.

Then, about half a block south, the wheels of the locomotive shrieked and the work train stopped. Through drifting dust Joe saw another big knot of people flowing onto the tracks, blocking the train.

Both of them heard a Guard officer yell, "Out of the way, or I'll give the order to shoot." Someone threw a green bottle that arced high and splintered against the forehead of a guardsman sitting on the cab roof. Blood spurted. The soldier fell backward and tumbled off the side of the cab. Joe and Rosie heard shouts and curses, as if the mob was attacking the wounded man. Several guns went off— quick smacking sounds. Joe Junior flung his arm around Rosie, drew her close to protect her.

The mob went wild. Men and women grabbed at the nearest legs and yanked. Guardsmen fought to keep from falling off the train. Joe Junior's heart hammered. People were shoving, shouting; rocks and bottles were flying; and there was more gunfire.

"Rosie, come on, this isn't safe." He tugged at her waist.

The deputy marshals formed lines on both sides of the first two gondolas. Teeth gritted against their own fear, they fired into the crowd.

People fell. A man cried, "They're shooting innocent people!" On the train, guardsmen were yelling orders no one could hear. Then they all opened fire.

Rosie tore away from Joe, shoving and kicking her way through the mob. She was hysterical. "Pop, Pop, get down. Hide yourself."

Joe Junior ran after her. He spied Tabor, still on the gondola, white with fright. Tabor discharged his pistol into the crowd while guardsmen's bullets buzzed around him.

Just then Joe Junior saw Tabor drop his revolver and seize his chest. Under his hand, in the middle of his overall bib, blood spread. He pitched off the stalled train, hit the gravel, and rolled.

"Oh, Pop," Rosie screamed as she fought her way to the crumpled body. She knelt and dragged her father's head up into her lap.

Joe Junior reached her. She was frantically stroking Tabor's face. "Oh, Papa, why did you have to get mixed up with them?"

"Rosie," Joe Junior said, ducking down again as bullets buzzed. She ignored him. "Rosie, he's dead; leave him. We'll find a wagon—"

"I won't," she screamed. A bullet whistled between them.

Desperate, Joe crouched down and struggled to get his arms under the corpse of Tabor Jablonec. "Rosie, come on, we've got to get away!" The shout—its force—pierced her hysteria. She staggered along beside him as he half walked, half ran with Tabor's body in his arms, away from the popping guns, the screams and lamentations. A block east on Forty-ninth, he laid Tabor in the shade of a livery barn.

Rosie dropped to her knees again. Joe Junior stared at his palms. Bloody. Tabor's blood had leaked all over his shirt and even stained the white ribbon. Rosie's hand sought his. "Why did he get mixed up with them, Joey?"

Joe Junior shook his head, his blue eyes burning. "He shouldn't have done it. He should have known he was on the wrong side."

Losing control again, she leaped at him. "Shut up. I can say it; you can't. Get away from me!"

"Rosie, I'm sorry. You need help to move him—"

"I don't need nothing from you. You and your loony ideas about right and wrong— Who cares? Right and wrong don't buy shoes. You're just like he was that way. You'll never have two nickels to your name either. You'll probably get killed too. Get away."

"Rosie, I just want to help with—"

"Get away. Stay away. Damn you. Leave me alone. *I don't ever want to see you!*"

He stared into her wild, hate-filled eyes. He started to speak but saw it was hopeless.

He walked away quickly, around the corner to the front of the livery. Inside, a stable hand sat on a chair reading.

"Come outside; hurry up. There's a girl whose father's been shot. She needs help."

The stable hand gave him a dubious look. But he ran outside and around the corner anyway. Joe heard him exclaim, "Oh, miss— How bad's he hurt?"

"He's *dead*. Open your eyes; *look* at him!"

Joe Junior walked rapidly toward the east. In the distance a single shot resounded. Then silence.

He walked all the way to Michigan and Twentieth. It took close to an hour. He crept into the house by the back way. Numbly he climbed the stairs. He ran water in the bathtub and soaked, cleaning the dried blood off his hands and arms.

He couldn't save his shirt. But he untied the blood-spotted white ribbon and carefully laid it on his bureau.

THE MOMENT HIS MOTHER came home, he told her.

She clasped him to her breast and rocked him back and forth. "Joey, Joey, it could be you lying dead."

"But it isn't; it's Rosie's father. The dirty scabs killed him—and more besides. Ten, twenty, I don't know how many."

"We must send flowers for the poor man's funeral."

"I guess you're right," he said, feeling a curious sense of completion, a deadness. Rosie's screamed words of banishment would be in his head forever. "I won't be going to the funeral myself. I may never see her again."

"I don't understand."

"It doesn't matter, Mama. Just let it go. Please?"

HE TOLD the story again at supper. His father insisted.

"Joseph," his father said, "I am deeply shaken by the risk you took. I could have lost a beloved son. I suppose it was noble of you to try to aid that young woman, but she endangered herself recklessly, and you also. I am sorry for her father. At least he died on the right side of the quarrel."

Joe Junior clenched his fists under the table. A vein in front of his left ear stood up in relief. His father saw. In a gentler voice he said, "You have absorbed enough punishment for one day. Please go to bed, son. Try to rest, put it out of your mind."

"I never will, Pop. Not as long as I live."

Their gazes locked. His voice low, Joe Crown said, "You'll excuse me, I have work." He walked out of the dining room buttoning his coat.

"Come to my room," Joe Junior whispered to Paul as they left the table a few minutes later.

"ROSIE's through with me," he said, closing the door behind Paul.

"That's bad. I am very sorry."

He tried to shrug it away. "I knew there wasn't any future with her; she told me often enough."

There was a bleak silence; then Paul said softly, "They are terrible men, those soldiers and deputies."

"Murderers. Nobody in the crowd had anything but rocks and sticks." Joe Junior walked to the bureau and from a drawer pulled the bloody ribbon. "This is his blood."

"Martyr's blood," Paul said.

"That's right." Joe Junior produced his clasp knife and cut the ribbon in two. "Here."

Paul laid the piece of stained ribbon on his left palm and touched it with his right index finger. "Damn them to hell." His eyes were full of glistening tears. For the first time that day, Joe Junior smiled.

JOE CROWN ✦ Joe Crown was on edge all that hot week of July 1894. On Sunday he still felt curiously unsettled. There was young Joe's brush with death at the level crossing; the papers reported fourteen fatalities and many more injured.

There was no doubt in Joe's mind that the chaos and bloodshed were inspired by Reds, and their chief agent, Eugene Debs. The Debs boycott menaced the orderly progress of commerce. The troops ought to crack down harder, fill the jails with the strikers if necessary. He'd permit no such breakdown of discipline at Crown's.

On Monday at half past ten he was at work with his door closed. There was a loud knock; Stefan Zwick, his clerk, bounded into the office before Joe could say anything. "Sir, I am very sorry to interrupt, but I felt I had to report a situation occurring outside. Sir, we have—uh, a labor demonstration. A work stoppage."

"A *what?*"

"Stoppage, sir. Eleven men have walked off the job for one hour in sympathy with the Pullman boycott. Schultheiss, Amunnsen—"

Joe's fist struck the desk. A pile of papers slipped off the edge and fell. "And Strauss? I'll wager he's at the head of it."

"Yes, sir, it seems so. I have the list here." Zwick offered a sheet of yellow foolscap with names written on it.

"When they come back, give them notice."

"Sir, they haven't left the premises. They're at the front gate."

Joe rushed to the window. He swore when he saw Benno and the others lounging around the stone fountain outside the gate to the *Biergarten*. The men were laughing and joshing, as if on holiday. Each wore a white ribbon on his sleeve.

"What effrontery. They're picketing on my property." He dashed for the door. Benno Strauss had at last stepped over the line. Joe stormed down the stairs and out through the *Bierstube*.

Mickelmeyer, the headwaiter, veered to intercept him. "I am

glad you came down, Mr. Crown," he whispered. "Those men will be a terrible interference with our noontime trade."

"Oh, no." Joe strode to the gate. "All of you, get off the fountain!"

Benno, seated on the street side of the fountain, looked around. A slow smile; then he stood up, rubbing his palms on his coveralls. Joe looked for bulges that might reveal a hidden pistol. He saw none.

"Explain. Why did you walk off the job?" Joe demanded.

Still with that infuriating smirk Benno said, "I guess you got a pretty good idea, Mr. Crown. Some of the other trades, they're going out too. Bakers, a few butchers—all good Germans."

A painful pressure was building in Joe's head. He heard men coming up behind him through the *Biergarten*. On the roof he saw workmen watching, Joe Junior among them.

Little Wenzel from the malthouse was courageously defiant. "We're putting you on notice, Mr. Crown. We're in full support of the railwaymen, and we'll stay out for one hour every day till King George Pullman surrenders."

"Get back to work, or you're finished at Crown's, all of you."

That brought uneasy looks from some of them. Benno said, "Threats ain't going to work this time, Mr. Crown."

Sam Traub, the tax agent, was standing immediately behind Joe, with Fred Schildkraut, the brewmaster. "Call the Black Maria," Traub said. "Picketing's a prison offense; the injunction says so."

"We ain't picketing," Benno said. "Just resting." He sat down again, crossed his ankles, and folded his arms.

Joe's face was by now scarlet. "You're through, Strauss. I carried you too long. All of you are through. Discharged immediately."

"If that's the way it's gonna be, you owe us wages—"

"I owe you nothing. Get off my property."

At that moment a hack clattered up North Larrabee Street from the direction of downtown. Two businessmen stepped out. The strikers spread themselves on either side of the fountain, barring entrance to the beer garden.

"Stefan?" Joe said without looking around.

"Here, sir."

"Telephone the precinct." Zwick ran into the brewery.

At the gate, Mickelmeyer said, "I refuse to wait that long." The headwaiter strode forward and took hold of the nearest striker. "Get out of the way of our patrons."

"Take your hands off him," Benno shouted. The man Mickelmeyer was holding kicked him in the shins. Mickelmeyer roundhouse punched him, spilling him into the fountain. Benno reached back under his shirttail. A blued pistol glinted. A pistol with a soiled white ribbon tied to the barrel.

Joe went for the gun, clamping both hands on Benno's wrist. Benno jerked his gun arm one way, then the other. Joe held on, though Benno was nearly wrenching his shoulders out of their sockets.

The businessmen jumped back into the hack and waved the driver on. Meanwhile, Benno kept trying to free himself. When he couldn't, he kicked Joe's leg with his steel-toed work shoe. Joe swore, stumbled backward, and fell on the brick walk.

Streams of sweat ran down Benno's bald skull. His nostrils were huge, his eyes dehumanized by wrath. He flung out his gun hand, aiming at Joe.

Joe stared into the black muzzle. Dizzy, breathless, he scrambled to his feet. "Give it to me, Benno. You don't want murder added to your crimes."

"Uh-uh, Mr. Crown, you don't get this piece. And you better keep your distance, or damn me, I'm gonna—"

He didn't finish, because Joe launched a looping right-hand punch into Benno's midsection, which was hard as a washboard. Benno swayed and yelled. Just then Fred Schildkraut ran in with a bung starter, which he whipped down on Benno's gun wrist. The gun fell into the fountain with a splash.

A workman rushed to Benno's aid. Mickelmeyer knocked him back with one punch. Joe felt drunk, wildly out of control; he threw another punch—this time at Benno's face. Benno's nose spouted blood. Cupping both hands under the drip of blood, Benno cursed him savagely.

A whistle pierced the noon heat. O'Doul, the corpulent foot policeman who patrolled the area, came lumbering down Larrabee. He drove two of the strikers off with whacks of his hickory club.

"Wagon's coming," Sam Traub cried. Joe heard its clattering bell. Benno's comrades ran in both directions along Larrabee, but Benno lingered.

"Crown." Angrier than Joe had ever seen him, Benno shook a bloodied finger. "You ain't heard the end of this, you capitalist scum." Then he ran, flicks of blood flying from his nose.

Joe reached into the fountain, grabbed the pistol, and flung it. The gun landed in the street, shiny with water.

"Who belongs to that piece?" O'Doul demanded.

"Strauss," someone said.

"I'll be needing it for evidence." O'Doul picked up the pistol.

Joe pushed graying hair off his forehead. Straightened his necktie. Benno Strauss was anarchist trash, and Joe had allowed him to control matters until reason was abandoned, order destroyed. He felt defeated.

He sat down at his personal table under the linden tree. A wurst on pumpernickel and a stein of cold Crown lager calmed him a little. The police wagon picked up three of the fleeing strikers. "Sorry to say, Strauss wasn't among 'em," O'Doul reported.

Joe thanked O'Doul and promised he'd be at the precinct house shortly to file charges. When the patrolman left, Joe asked Mickelmeyer to summon his clerk.

"Stefan, sit down." Zwick took a chair. Joe Crown's hand dropped to the boar's tooth on its chain. He said, "We have a bad situation here. Benno and the others will feel vindictive. We must change all the locks in the brewery. By six o'clock tonight, Stefan. Pay whatever it costs. But get it done. Get it done."

Zwick asked no further questions. Benno owned a full set of keys.

At half past one, two wagons from Lorenz Brothers, Locksmiths, arrived, and men swarmed through Crown's, cutting new chain, snapping new padlocks, setting new bolts, testing new keys.

JOE JUNIOR ✦ At the end of work on the Thursday following Tabor's death, Joe Junior went to his locker for his cap. He wouldn't wait for Paul tonight. His cousin had to stay in the brewhouse until a batch finished at eight.

As he was shutting his locker he noticed a white paper lying at the very back of the shelf. The hair on his neck started to prickle. He quickly opened the note. It said, "Lake St. bridge 5:30. Urgent."

He slammed the locker and ran out, filled with dread.

HE LEANED on the rail of the Lake Street bridge, which spanned the North Branch of the Chicago River. A smell of garbage rose off the water. The river's surface glowed with greasy rainbows.

"Don't turn around. Don't use my name. Don't say nothing."

From the corner of his eye Joe Junior saw Benno's profile. Benno settled his elbows on the rail, like a friend stopping to chat. He was haggard, yellowish bags showing under his Oriental eyes.

"They changed the damn locks at the brewery."

"I know."

Benno talked softly, with a genial smile. "It's time for you to be a good sojer. Time for you to help the cause."

Joe Junior's mouth was dry. "What do you want me to do?"

"Something easy. Find a certain key tomorrow. Sneak it out with you at quitting time. When it's dark, but before ten o'clock, unlock the door of the bottling house. Leave it open. That's all."

"What are you going to do?"

"Gonna show your pop that he can't fire honest workingmen just for standing up for trade-union solidarity."

"Show him? How?"

Benno thumped the rail. "Propaganda of the deed. I said we'd strike a blow. Nobody believed me. You din't believe me."

Joe Junior was trembling, but he had to speak. "I won't help you if it means hurting anybody."

"You can quit worrying. We're just gonna wreck a lot of equipment. The bottling house, at night, when it's shut down. Cost your old man plenty, but no lives lost. I don't want that neither."

Joe Junior digested that. It was bad, but not so bad as he'd feared it might be. "Promise me you won't try anything at the brewhouse." The brewhouse had a shift working through the night.

"I swear." Benno held up his right hand. "What d'ya say?"

"I say it's hard. What you're asking is hard. The brewery is still my father's property."

"*Property.*" Benno spit over the rail. "You saying you ain't going to help us after all? All along you said you were with us. What are you, a liar? I thought you was a man, not a baby. Have you got the nerve, or were you just playing with us?"

Propaganda of the deed. Joe Junior had studied the literature, convinced himself it was the best way to deal with a rotten system. He couldn't let consideration for his family's property paralyze him. He had to think of the importance of striking a blow. He could do it with no one getting hurt.

"*Joey?*"

"All right, yes."

"Good." Benno laughed. "Knew we could count on you."

"Don't be so cheerful. I've got to figure out *how*." Joe Junior rubbed his fingertips against his palms. "Mr. Schildkraut keeps spare keys on a board on his wall. I could get the key when he goes down to the *Stube* at noon for his dinner. Don't worry. I'll have the door unlocked by ten tomorrow night."

Benno draped his arm across Joe Junior's shoulders. "You got the stuff after all."

Joe Junior went home, pleaded a bellyache so he wouldn't have to speak to anyone, risk a show of guilt before the fact. He knew he wouldn't sleep that night, and he didn't. Lying awake, he kept seeing images of his mother. It had to be done. Sometimes men had to take a strong, even dangerous stand. He prayed she'd understand and forgive him if she ever found out.

THE night was humid and still. He darted looks up and down the alley that separated the bottling house and the main section of the brewery, where scattered lights shone. On the second floor, a shadow passed between a window and a lamp. Mr. Schildkraut, working late again.

It hadn't been hard to pinch the key while Schildkraut was at dinner. Now, at the door of the bottling house, Joe Junior listened. All quiet. Old George Hoch, the watchman, had walked through twenty minutes ago. He wouldn't return until around eleven. Joe Junior's hand shook. He poked the stolen key into the keyhole. With a click the door unlocked.

Gaining confidence, he slipped around the corner and along the north wall of the building to the back. There he sat down to wait. He closed his eyes. It was too late for regret or retreat.

With a start he opened his eyes. Someone had whispered. He clambered to his feet. Against the lights of the office building he saw two men silhouetted in the alley. He could discern the curve of Benno's bald head. The other man was unrecognizable.

He called out softly, "All clear." Benno and the second man vanished into the bottling house. What were they using? Dynamite? How long would it take to place it? Need he stay? Somehow he felt he should.

A grime-coated window to his left showed a faint light inside the bottling house. Perhaps they'd lit a candle to aid them.

257

Then he heard something that caused him to panic. Footsteps in the brick drive across the alley. This time the silhouette was that of a man in a summer boater, with a cane. The man was whistling "Daisy Bell," the bicycle song.

Schildkraut going home.

Would he see the light behind the window?

Apparently, Schildkraut didn't notice. He passed out of sight behind the bottling house, whistling his tune. Joe Junior rested his forehead against the bricks. If this was anarchism, it was a very frightening business.

Then the footsteps stopped.

Rigid, Joe Junior watched the corner of the building. Schildkraut reappeared. Perhaps his senses had belatedly registered some small detail amiss. He looked both ways and poked the door of the bottling house with his cane. It swung in, the hinge squealing.

Schildkraut jumped forward, disappearing. The firefly light went out. "Who is that?" Schildkraut called. "Come forward, show yourselves." Joe Junior ran toward the front of the building. He heard others running inside, and Schildkraut continuing to call out. Then came sounds of a struggle and a strident voice he didn't recognize: *"Benno—the fuse!"*

Joe reached the bottling-house door. A huge roar and a sheet of flame blew him backward across the alley. Everything went black.

FIRELIGHT and smoke. Screams and shouts. He opened his eyes.

The bottling house in ruins, most of its north and east walls blown down. Bright flames were consuming equipment that was twisted like metal spaghetti.

A huge beam pinned his lower legs. A heap of brick and mortar nearly covered him. Men raced back and forth between Joe and the blaze. They didn't even know he was there in the wreckage.

A round-shouldered man appeared against the leaping fire. It was old George, the watchman. "They were all trapped inside. They're dead. Mr. Schildkraut, Strauss, some other man. All dead."

PAUL ✦ That same Friday night, weary, Paul went to his room soon after supper. Cousin Joe had been absent for the meal; no one seemed to know where he'd gone, and Uncle Joe was cross about it.

Sometime around midnight Carl came in. "Something bad's happened. Papa's left, and Mama's awake and upset. Paul, I'm scared."

A huge commotion erupted downstairs. Voices, heavy footfalls. Paul and his cousin ran into the hall to see people rushing up the stairs. First Nicky Speers, with cousin Joe lying in his outstretched arms. Cousin Joe's face was bloody, and gray dust coated his skin and clothing.

Uncle Joe followed. He didn't even look at Paul and Carl. Aunt Ilsa came next, wearing her night-robe.

"Aunt Ilsa, what has happened?" Paul asked.

"A terrible accident at the brewery. Some sort of infernal device in the bottling house. Three men have been killed, and Joey was hurt; we don't know how badly yet. Please go to bed."

She hurried on. The door of cousin Joe's room closed.

For most of the night the house was in an uproar. First Dr. Plattweiler arrived. Then two police detectives. Uncle Joe met with them in the study. Paul and Carl and Fritzi peered down from the second-floor landing, utterly confounded.

"Whatever has happened," Paul said, "it must be a terrible thing."

PAUL was up at half past six to brew a cup of tea. Yawning, Louise Volzenheim came out of the pantry. "You're not to go to work today. Mr. Crown is shutting down all but essential operations."

Manfred came in. Paul looked at the cook, then at the steward. "Can anyone tell me what happened?"

Manfred spoke. "A building blew up. Two anarchists were killed. One was that vile fellow Strauss. Another victim was Mr. Crown's brewmaster. Master Joe unlocked the building for the bombers. I don't know whether he did it alone or in collusion with some of his radical friends."

He fixed an accusing eye on Paul.

About seven, Louise prepared a breakfast tray for cousin Joe. Aunt Ilsa, dazed and still in her nightclothes, asked Paul to take it to him. He had never known her to look so sad.

He climbed the stairs with the tray. Silver domes kept the sausages and bread warm. After the commotion of the night, a dispiriting silence had settled on the house.

He pulled up short at his cousin's door. From inside came Uncle Joe's voice: "I am not going to file charges against my own son and have the whole damned story dragged through the courts and press. But make no mistake, I hold you responsible for this atrocity. For Fred Schildkraut's death."

"Pop, I only unlocked the door. Mr. Schildkraut came along at the wrong time."

"I'm damned if you can shift the blame so easily."

Paul edged closer to the door. Cousin Joe was saying, "Benno promised me no one would be hurt. He said he just wanted to damage some machinery. That's the truth."

"And you believed Benno? How could you let yourself be seduced? Poisoned by that filthy, lawless crowd?"

"I didn't mean for anyone to die!"

"But they did. You can't bring them back, and you can't escape the guilt; it's yours forever. May God forgive you. I can't."

The door opened suddenly. Uncle Joe stormed out. He shouted at Paul, "Have you been eavesdropping?"

"Sir, I was asked to bring this tray for—"

"Give it to me!" His uncle was shouting like a wild man. He grabbed the tray. Paul let go, but Uncle Joe didn't have a good grasp. With a huge crash of shattering dishes, clangs of silver domes falling, the contents of the tray splattered on the carpet.

Uncle Joe yanked the door shut behind him. "Stay out of there, I order you. After what he did, he's not to be visited, by you or by anyone." He stormed down the stairs. "Manfred! Helga!"

Paul determined to see his cousin no matter what his uncle said. He waited an hour, then stole into Joe Junior's bedroom. "Are you all right?"

"Twisted ankle, but no bones broken. I'll make it. But Pop didn't believe my story that Benno promised no one would get hurt."

"I believe you."

"You're the only one." To Paul's astonishment there were tears in his cousin's eyes. "Get out of here," Joe Junior whispered. "No need for two of us to be tarred and feathered."

MORE shocks were in store. Late in the afternoon Paul picked up a note from the message stone at Vanderhoff's. Julie couldn't meet him the next afternoon. No explanation.

When he returned home, a three-foot black wreath with a black silk bow hung on the front door. Swags of black crepe covered

261

the tops of picture frames and mirrors throughout the downstairs.

Supper was a ghastly affair. Aunt Ilsa was red-eyed and drawn. Uncle Joe had a black armband on his shirtsleeve. Carl and Fritzi wore them too. Uncle Joe spoke sharply to Paul.

"You will wear an armband, like everyone else. Get it from Manfred. This household is in mourning for Friedrich Schildkraut. We pay no respects to the scum responsible for his murder."

Ilsa twisted her napkin. "May Joe Junior come down to eat?"

"He may not. Send his food up to him. I want him to sit in that room until he comes to a full appreciation of what he did. It isn't merely thousands of dollars of property destroyed; it's human life. He is an accessory to the crime."

"Oh, Joe, you can't mean that—" She was on the point of tears again. "He mustn't be penned up like an animal."

"Why not? He behaved like an animal; let him suffer like one. There is no way he can atone for the loss of a man like Fred. He is guilty. I have ordered Manfred to keep his door locked so he can contemplate that fact."

Paul was stupefied. Treat your own son like *ein Knastbruder?* A jailbird? If ever he hated his uncle, it was then.

About half past eleven he crept along the dark hall. Reaching the door of his cousin's room, he whispered, "Ssst. Joe. It's Paul."

He heard a muffled scraping as his cousin dragged himself to the other side of the door. "Is it safe to talk?"

A swift look up and down the hall. "I think so."

"I'm going to leave, Paul."

"What? Cousin—"

"Don't argue with me. You think I'm going to stay here when my own father calls me a criminal?"

"He was upset; he surely didn't mean—"

"Yes, he did. I'm getting out for good. You've got to help me."

"How can I? This door is locked."

"I'll leave by the window. With this ankle, I daren't risk a jump. You've got to put up a ladder. There's one in the stable."

"I have seen it." He didn't want to be the cause of more trouble, but he knew his loyalty lay with his cousin.

"Paul? Will you do it?"

"Yes, of course."

"Do you know when they're burying Mr. Schildkraut?"

"Tuesday morning."

"That means there will probably be visitation at the funeral home tomorrow night and Monday night too. I'll leave Monday night."

"Are you going far away?"

"To the end of the earth, that's how far I'd like to go. I don't want to hurt Mama, but Pop's forced it."

MONDAY, Paul pleaded a stomachache and didn't go to supper. He stayed in his room and paced up and down, lifting the lace curtain every few minutes. About seven, as a purple summer dusk was enveloping rooftops to the east, he saw the landau leave.

His aunt and uncle would not be home until perhaps nine thirty. By nine it would be almost totally dark.

He left his room at ten minutes before nine. The downstairs was silent. Louise was away tonight. So was Mrs. Blenkers. He had carefully ascertained all this during the day.

He stole into the dark, fragrant kitchen. A block of light slanted across the floor from a small room adjoining the pantry. It served as a kind of sitting room for Manfred until he went off duty.

Paul peeked in. Manfred sat on a wooden chair. His reading glasses had slipped down his nose. His chin rested on his chest. Paul wiped his upper lip and crept past the oblong of light.

From the garden he glimpsed his cousin at the window. He waved, then darted through an opening in the hedge to the alley.

He opened one of the stable's folding doors, found the ladder, and hauled it off its pegs. It was ten feet long, and heavy. He was breathing hard by the time he reached the side of the house. Joe Junior already had his leg over the sill.

"Watch out," Joe Junior called, and tossed down his belongings, stuffed in a pillowcase tied with a bandanna.

Paul positioned the ladder. Joe Junior climbed down. Hurry, Paul thought, steadying the ladder. Somewhere a door opened. Then someone was running. . . .

Stepping down to the third rung from the bottom, cousin Joe was first to spy him. "Look out. It's Manfred."

Manfred came charging at them along the side of the house. Paul shouted, "Run, Joe," and threw himself against Manfred's legs. They tumbled in the dewy grass. Manfred's thrashing heel slammed Paul's jaw, and not by accident.

"Mr. Joseph!" Manfred shouted in a drillmaster's voice, as if that would stop everything. Prone in the grass, Paul watched as his cousin snatched up his bundle and fled to the alley, gone.

"You devil. You damned sneak!" Manfred hauled Paul to his feet. "What have you done?" Manfred said, shaking him.

"Let go of me. Who the hell do you think you are?"

"Someone with more loyalty and honor than you." But Manfred stepped back and dropped his hands. He wiped them on the bib of his kitchen apron. "I thought I heard someone in the kitchen. I should have known it was you. You make a terrible criminal," he sneered. "Wait till Mr. Crown gets home. Wait till he hears what you've done."

PAUL sat in the study awaiting the return of his aunt and uncle. Manfred had posted himself on a chair outside, like a jailer.

Finally Paul heard a door close. Then voices, low at first but quickly louder, one of them shearing off into a sobbing cry. Then the door was thrown open. Uncle Joe knew everything; it showed in his eyes and the pinkness of his cheeks.

Paul stood and squared his shoulders. He'd grown several inches taller than his uncle, but it hardly made a difference. In his anger, Uncle Joe was a Goliath.

"My son has run off, with your connivance. It's unbelievable. We gave you shelter, family affection. We encouraged you, saw to it that you had a good job with a future. This is our repayment?"

"Sir—"

"*Where is my son?*" Joe Crown shouted.

"Uncle Joe, I cannot tell you. He did not confide in me."

"Get to your room until I decide what's to be done. I should lock you up too."

"As you locked him up? You drove him to what he did."

Something slipped in his uncle's head. "Damn you!" he said, and slapped Paul across the face.

Paul recovered and drew a long, deep breath. "It won't be necessary to lock me up, Uncle. I will stay or leave, as you please."

He was convinced he had been absolutely right to aid his cousin. And yet he couldn't help feeling a traitor. How hateful that he wanted to cry like a child. He fought the feeling as he walked out of the study—past Manfred, standing with his arms folded, smiling.

PORK ✦ Two black trotters pulled the handsome Studebaker carriage, one of four that Mason Vanderhoff owned. The driver stopped in front of the Crown brewery. Pork stepped from carriage to curbstone with a heavy gasp and moved his huge paunchy body to the gilt-lettered doors of the brewery offices.

He didn't ask to see the proprietor. Rather, he stated that he would see him at once. No, he had no appointment. A flunky ran upstairs, and in a few moments Pork was seated before Joe Crown's desk, vowing to himself to remain civil while he stated his case.

He was frankly shocked by Joe Crown's haggard appearance. His face had a mealy cast. The anarchist bomb, no doubt.

"Hello, Joe. Sorry to hear about the disruption here—oh, and the loss of life also. Regrettable."

Joe Crown dropped his hand to his watch chain and rubbed some kind of animal tooth hanging there. "Yes."

The silence crashed. Pork squirmed in the chair. It was too small for him. "Joe, you and I have not seen each other for some time—"

"That's true. But may I ask you to state your business?" Joe indicated an open window through which came the racket of hammers. "We are rebuilding the bottling house. We are under great strain here. So please come to the point."

I was right, he's detestable. Arrogant. Pork unsnapped the catch on his portfolio. "This." He placed a sheet of notepaper on the desk. Joe Crown picked it up and read it as Pork continued. "Written to my daughter, Juliette, by your nephew, Paul Crown. Note that he wrote endearments at the bottom. In German."

Joe handed the note back. He was pink with annoyance. Pork had taken him by surprise. "How did you come by that note?"

"A young man of my daughter's acquaintance, a fine chap named Strickland Welliver, chanced to see Juliette and your relative together in Lincoln Park. They have apparently been meeting secretly on Sundays. Welliver wrote me about it. Due to the press of business it failed to come to my attention until this week. I immediately set a watch on Juliette." Pinpoint sweat drops glistened on Pork's double chin. "Your nephew and my daughter have evidently worked out a system for sending and receiving messages. The note was found under a stone at the rear of my property." Pork reached for the note and thrust it back into his portfolio.

"What am I supposed to do about this revelation?"

"Order your nephew to stay away from Juliette and cease these dirty little notes and clandestine meetings. How do I know what filth he's written in a foreign tongue?"

"Oh, it's nothing a high-minded man like yourself would object to, Vanderhoff. Quite romantic, actually."

"You're toying with me, sir. Now listen—you tell your nephew that I'll have him arrested if he comes near my daughter again."

"Vanderhoff, I hold my nephew responsible for his own actions. You may speak to him if you wish. He works here. My clerk will be happy to direct you."

Insufferable kraut! Pork wouldn't tolerate it. "Sir, get this clear. I am not going to muck about in a dingy brewery confronting a common workman on the subject of my daughter."

Crown shrugged. "Suit yourself. If you won't speak to Paul directly, I can't help you. Good morning."

"Crown, you can't dismiss me like this!"

Joe Crown pushed himself up from his chair, like some savage beast arising from slumber, and came around the desk. Blanching, Pork heaved to his feet and began to back away.

"Get out, Vanderhoff. I don't like you or your insulting language. Walk down those stairs before I throw you down."

To his everlasting shame and rage, Pork obeyed.

How right he was to hate Joe Crown, as he had ever since that fateful Sunday five years ago. Pork purveyed meats to restaurants, including Crown's *Bierstube*. During the brewery's annual picnic in August, when Pork was compelled to wobble to an outhouse at the edge of the picnic grove, he heard, through the thin wooden wall, Joe Crown chatting with someone about his past.

"My first offer of an apprenticeship in Cincinnati was a good one but for one thing. My prospective employer was a butcher. Killing and selling the parts of dumb animals is a dirty, bloody business, Fred, though I'd never say such a thing to a supplier like Mason Vanderhoff. I absolutely did not want to be a butcher. They're held in low esteem in America and Germany too. Around the world, in fact."

Pork couldn't tolerate it. He rushed outside and chased Crown, who was strolling arm in arm with a man he recognized as the brewmaster, Fred Schildkraut. Pork came at Crown from behind, seized his shoulder, and threw a punch.

Joe Crown defended himself. He felled Pork with one blow. Sat him on his rump in the dirt, a humiliation never to be forgiven.

"I don't know what this is all about, Mason," Joe said, "but I don't take kindly to being attacked without warning. I trust I didn't hit you too hard. Let me help you up." He reached down with his right hand. Pork spit in his palm.

They never did business again. That autumn Joe Crown's name came up for membership in the Commercial Club. Pork's vote kept him out.

Recalling the picnic always put Pork into a state. For most of the ride downtown he kept yanking at his cravat, fighting for breath.

Several generations of Vanderhoff men had raised hogs, slaughtered them, and cured the hams in the smokehouse of a farm in the little town of Darien, Connecticut. Some of Pork's earliest memories consisted of images of the abattoir in the woods—the killing barn where his father worked.

Pork knew very well why the Joe Crowns of the world scorned the butchering and packing trades. His own memories explained it: the ramshackle barn, its floor crusted over with dried blood and offal residue, the flies and rats, the stench that was always on his clothes.

Pork Vanderhoff had fled the hardscrabble region of the Northeast for a greater opportunity that seemed to glimmer in the West. Following Phil Armour and Gus Swift to Chicago, he built his business, capitalizing on technological advancements that could enrich packers smart enough to seize upon them. Armour was the leader in this—the first to hang carcasses on hooks on a powered chain that moved them speedily through the plant. He pioneered the centralized shipping of pork, mutton, and beef from a major rail hub, and he installed refrigeration equipment to convert slaughtering and packing from a seasonal to a year-round trade, not dependent on cold weather or expensive purchased ice.

And like Phil Armour, Pork Vanderhoff controlled a veritable empire of processing and distribution, including subsidiary plants for utilization of animal by-products. America took its Saturday night bath with soap made from Vanderhoff tallow, glued its wallpaper and envelope flaps with Big "V" Brand glues. Six thousand refrigerator cars shuttling between the Atlantic, the Pacific, and the Gulf of Mexico bore the Big "V" insignia.

Out of this success had come not only wealth but an aristocratic wife from one of Kentucky's noblest families. Pork had important friends, memberships in exclusive clubs, status and standing in Chicago, the Republican Party, the nation. He hadn't achieved all this so his daughter could marry some damned foreign upstart. He would separate Juliette from this pernicious influence forever.

THAT evening Pork was tense as he sat at his desk in his study, awaiting the encounter with his daughter.

Well trained, Juliette knocked softly before she entered. Pork's heart brimmed at the sight of her. She was a lovely young woman—all the more reason to protect her from the foreign brute.

"Julie, good evening." He beamed.

"Papa." She sat in the side chair, her smile, alas, perfunctory.

He noticed a nervous agitation of her fingertips where they rested on her knee. Fatigue circles around her gray eyes too.

With a sly-fox grin he pushed a yellow Thomas Cook envelope across the desk. "A present for you, my dear." The envelope lay in the pool of light cast by his banker's lamp as Pork announced his plan for a grand tour of several months or more. It was part of his scheme to pretend to absolute ignorance of the trashy German boy.

When he finished, Julie said, "It sounds lovely, Papa. But I don't want to go away. I have too many interests here."

"My dear, they ice-skate and cycle on the Continent too," he said provocatively. He watched closely. She didn't bite.

First came a shake of her head. Then: "Papa, there is no other way to say this, but I won't go. I don't want every moment of my life planned for me."

"Juliette! That sounds ungrateful."

"I don't mean to be ungrateful. I just don't want to go to Europe right now." Her voice grew stronger. "I am grown, after all. So I think I should have some say about the matter."

Pork's very soul rebelled. Women had no *say*. "Don't be stubborn, Juliette. Read the material. I've booked the finest—"

"I'm sorry, Papa," she interrupted. "I won't go."

This infatuation is deep and dangerous. He'd presumed it could be disposed of quickly. Now he wasn't sure. He unsheathed the weapon he'd been saving.

"Your mother very much wishes to take this trip. You know the precarious state of her nerves. Do you want to be responsible for a collapse? Or, heaven forbid, something worse? If you deny her this and something dire happens, it will all be on you."

With a soft cry Julie bolted. At the door, she looked back, her face tear-streaked. "That's so cruel."

"All on you," Pork repeated loudly. "On you."

She shut the door with a crash.

He leaned back, aghast. That nephew of Crown's must be a devil of a seducer. Still, as his shock passed, he felt a little better. He had observed Juliette's pained and guilty look as she left the room. She had been trained to revere and obey her parents. And to touch the quick of those filial emotions, he had drawn his sharpest knife. It had worked before. It would work again.

He rang the bell for his coach. He'd already set up the fiction of an all-night card game. He would spend the night at the shabby cottage of an aspiring soubrette named Liza.

The following morning he went directly to his office. His clerk greeted him on the threshold, looking frantic. "You'd better go home immediately, Mr. Vanderhoff. Your wife is in hysterics."

Pork rushed home. He found Nell in her robe, ranting. "She's gone. I don't know where she is. Her bed's still made. She must have left during the night. Where is she, what's happened? I'm in ruins. Call Dr. Woodrow before I lose my mind."

PAUL ✦ Paul had begun to feel like a stranger in the Crown household. He could still hear suppressed wrath in his uncle's voice and a deep, soul-searing sadness in Aunt Ilsa's. He had clumsily asked her forgiveness for the part he'd played in Joe Junior's departure. She said yes, it was her Christian duty to forgive him. But her words sounded empty.

At work Paul spoke only when necessary. In every spare moment he read newspapers. Not so much for information as for distraction.

The Chicago strike was broken. The American Federation of Labor executive board had refused to express solidarity with "Dictator Debs," and massive arrests of strikers on criminal charges had rapidly weakened the resistance. Freight tonnage out of Chicago increased every day. Debs, who still abhorred violence in any form, and three other union officials had been arrested on indictments from a special grand jury. Railway workers who had supported the

Debs boycott were finding severance slips in their pay envelopes. Withdrawal of the federal troops had begun.

Paul had tacked the piece of white ribbon among his postal cards on the board in his room. The bloodstains had turned brown. The ribbon seemed foolish and pathetic now that the strike was melting to a memory and the light of capitalistic reason and order was returning to the dark city.

He hated the fact that a decent gentleman like Mr. Schildkraut had lost his life. But to place all of the responsibility on Joe Junior was clearly wrong, and Paul was still convinced that he'd been right to help his cousin escape. He just wished that the other people he'd come to love didn't hurt so much, didn't blame him so much. He wished that he didn't hurt so much either.

When he reported for work on Saturday morning, a black boy stopped him at the gate.

"This here's for you, sar." He handed Paul a folded note.

"Are you sure?" There was nothing written on the outside of the note.

"Yes, sar. Wasn't no trouble to spot you. I had my shoeshine box outside the Northwestern depot an' a pretty white lady come up an' tol' me what you looked like an' paid me a dollar to bring that."

Paul unfolded the note. His lips went white. "Radigan's Hotel & Cottages—north of Waukegan. Today— Please!! Yours always!"

HE GOT off the northbound local at the sleepy Waukegan depot around four o'clock. He rented a cycle and set off, pedaling several miles into open country. He was close to a lake at the Wisconsin state line. To the left of the road he saw a sign—RADIGAN'S. Behind the sign stood a white frame house with a number of small square cottages laid out in a U.

He understood what might be happening, yet couldn't altogether believe it. The prospect was thrilling and frightening at the same time. One of the cottage doors opened. Someone in white waved a handkerchief. His heart soared with happiness.

He parked the cycle outside the cottage. He ran to the door and threw his arms around her and kissed her. She'd been crying.

She drew him inside. "You got the note—" she began.

"I did. I just don't understand—"

"Last night I ran away. I had to see you—by ourselves."

"Julie, in the name of heaven—you left home? Why?"

"I love you, Paul, so much, and Papa wants to separate us."

"What? Has he found out?"

"Oh, no, I don't think so. It's just the devil's own timing. He and Mama want a grand tour of Europe. They're insisting I go with them." She was calming down, brushing tears from her eyelashes.

Light fell through a small window. Paul noticed details of the cottage. Linoleum flooring. A cheap throw rug. A large iron bed finished in white enamel and a matching white commode. The old mirror above it reflected a wavy image of the lovers as they sat side by side on the bed, touching, hugging.

"I told Papa I wouldn't go, but he said Mama had her heart set on the trip. He said it might kill her if I refused. Whenever they want something, they use Mama's health to make me do it. I've thought about leaving home permanently, but what would I do? Be a shopgirl? I don't know how to do anything for myself."

He clasped her hand in both of his. "You got here, didn't you? How did you find this place?"

"I was here once before, two years ago. I was coming back from Wisconsin with Mama and Papa. Our carriage broke down, and we spent the night."

"But how did you get in this time, by yourself?"

"By offering the clerk a bribe. Aren't you glad? Say you're glad. If you don't, it'll break my heart—I love you so."

She pressed her palms to his cheeks and kissed him. His arms slipped around her. They tumbled back on the bed.

"I want you so, Paul. It's been so long since I've seen you—"

He kissed the damp corner of her lips, her nose and eyes. "Julie, I must not take advantage of you—"

"Oh, don't say that!" she exclaimed, laughing and crying too. "Please don't refuse me. Make love to me while we have a chance."

They kissed again. "I'm not experienced," she whispered. "Mama refuses to discuss—men and women. She says the whole subject is improper."

"It doesn't make any difference—" Braced on his elbows, he gazed at her tear-reddened face. The most beautiful he'd ever seen. This encounter in a cheap room on the windy lakeshore sealed a permanent change in his feelings, his life, his fate.

"I love you, Juliette. Always. Eternally."

THEY COULD HEAR THE WIND AS they lay in each other's arms—soft, warm, satiated, under a down comforter.

She said, "Are you hungry? I brought a hamper. I filled it in Waukegan this morning. There's cheese, some bratwurst, a loaf of bread, a bottle of Moselle wine."

"You are more capable than you allow yourself to believe, Miss Juliette. To rent this place, stock it with food—wine, even . . ."

"It's because I fear they'll make me go away and I won't see you for a year. A lot can happen in a year, Paul. People can forget."

"Never. I love you. *Immer.* Always."

He struggled into his shirt and pants. She put on her skirt and white shirtwaist. He felt oddly but happily domestic.

They feasted from the hamper. Julie looked soft, fulfilled, as she munched black bread he'd sliced from the loaf with his clasp knife.

"I must tell you what's happened. Cousin Joe is gone. He ran away." Paul described the events leading up to it.

"Oh, Paul, I am sorry." She stroked his face. "You had to help him when he asked. You hadn't any choice."

"That is what I thought."

"Poor Joey. Do you think he's gone for good?"

"I have that feeling, yes." He paused. He cleared his throat for the dreaded question. "You are going back, aren't you?"

"I don't know. I have courage, Paul—sometimes. But not often enough."

"Courage is like a muscle, I think. You must use it."

Julie laughed. She said she'd sent a telegraph message to her aunt Willis night before last, asking permission to come to her aunt's home if she needed a refuge. Her aunt's housekeeper had telephoned, saying Willis had left for Paris with a traveling companion. "The housekeeper never said so, but I could hear it in her voice. The companion is probably a new man. My aunt has the courage I don't."

"You do have it," Paul insisted. "And now we must talk about tomorrow. We will have to tell lies about our absence."

He hated lying to anyone. But for Julie discovery would be serious. She was a female under the age of consent. "Truly, we must think up the very best—"

"Not now, Paul. In the morning. We won't spoil this night with worry. Hold me. Give me courage."

SOMEONE WAS DRUMMING. Paul bolted upright. Julie muttered into her pillow, still asleep.

"Julie!" His voice was low, hoarse. He took hold of her shoulder to rouse her. Someone was pounding on the door.

"Juliette? We know you're there. Answer!" Then the man said, "Use the damned axe."

Paul just had time to leap out of bed and pull on his pants as the blade cleaved through the door with a splintery crash. A groping hand twisted the knob. A second axe blow knocked the door from its top hinge. There were four men outside, crowding in. One was a huge round-shouldered hulk wearing a fedora.

Lanterns flashed. Boots rapped on the linoleum. Julie sat up, mute with terror. Her glazed eyes focused, and she yanked the sheet around her. Bright silver badges gleamed on vests. Strident voices overlapped.

"Juliette! Deputy, arrest him. She's a minor."

"Don't blame me for this. She booked the room with a false name." That was a bald man with a waxed mustache.

One of the men wearing a badge grabbed Paul. Paul knocked the hand away. The man cuffed his face, and he fell hard on the rug. "Stand up, you dirty animal." The lawman manhandled Paul to his feet.

The hulking man shouted at the bald man, "You knew she was under age, Radigan. You took the bribe anyway."

The other deputy snapped handcuffs on Paul, while the hotel owner whined, "I took the twenty so she wouldn't be suspicious, Mr. Vanderhoff. I telephoned you, didn't I?"

"Hours later." The hulking man struck Paul across the face. "You little dog. I'll see you imprisoned for the rest of your natural life. You damned foreign scum. Get him into the wagon."

Julie cried, "Oh, don't hurt him." She was on her knees behind the bed, trembling. "What are you going to do?"

"Take him across the line, to Cook County," the deputy said. "Throw him in jail." He snickered. "He won't soon forget the place. He'll be ready for the nut farm when he gets out of there."

He pushed Paul outside. The night air raised gooseflesh on his bare chest and arms. Under the newly risen moon, two horses hitched to a closed wagon breathed transparent vapors into the chilly air.

Paul had no thought for himself, only for her. He looked back toward the dark cottage, called out, "Julie? Remember what I said. You're stronger than—"

Vanderhoff seized his arm. "Shut up." He flung Paul against the wagon. "Lock him up before I beat him to death!"

Paul's eyes, usually so mild, shone like moonlit ice.

The deputy jabbed him. "In the wagon, Dutchie."

The doors of the wagon slammed. Paul huddled on a hard bench, shackled hands between his knees, in total darkness.

JULIE ✦ She drifted in a strange twilight state. Faces came and went at the periphery of vision, gliding over her.

"I hope you are resting. Dr. Woodrow mixed a special prescription. You must drink more of it now."

She recognized the voice. Her mother. Lifted, she sat up partway. She drank the liquid and sank down again with a sigh.

Her mother's frail hand descended from the darkness, stroking the long black hair. "It's so beautiful. You're such a beautiful child. I can't have some coarse, ignorant foreign boy despoil such beauty. Papa told me the truth. Oh, I cried. I was beside myself, like a madwoman. You're damaged goods. We will have to live with that. But Dr. Woodrow has already made sure there will be no child. No one outside this family will know it happened. There are ways to deceive a bridegroom. Now you must rest and let Mama heal you."

Presently another face floated above her. She recognized Papa.

"We'll have a splendid holiday, Juliette. The three of us."

That brought a new face into her thoughts. This face was young, strongly cut. The hair was brown, with reddish glints. The eyes were blue, kindly, trusting. The sight of it brought cascades of sensation, emotion. Memory of kisses, caresses, their bodies together. Fear of separation. Loss. Threat . . .

"Paul? Where are you?"

"Dr. Woodrow, Dr. Woodrow," someone cried stridently.

PAUL ✦ Paul felt busy mites in his hair, his armpits. He wriggled and scratched. He was exhausted. He rolled toward the wall and covered his face with his elbow. He was so weary and ashamed, he wanted to die.

Late in the morning the police wagon had brought him to Cook

County Jail. The jail reeked of human waste and tobacco juice. Paul's cellblock was a bedlam of shouts, oaths, obscenities. The cells had been unlocked from four in the afternoon until six. During those two hours he'd been allowed to roam the corridor. Up and down, up and down, shuffling among the dregs of the city.

For supper the guard had brought tin plates of cold gray corn-bread squares. Paul bit into a piece and found wiggling white worms. He gagged into the reeking toilet bucket.

During the long night Paul fought to maintain his courage, but it was hard. *This is America? You came all the way across the ocean to experience this?*

And Julie . . . what had happened to her? Had her father punished her? He feared for her safety.

THE next morning Paul was escorted down a flight of stairs to a granite-walled room, with no windows, a cheap electric fixture in the ceiling, a chair in the middle of the damp floor.

Two detectives welcomed him with smiles he distrusted. One said, "Sit down, Dutch." The other shut the door.

The heavier of the detectives took a wide-legged stance in front of Paul's chair. "Why did you kidnap her?"

"You are fools. I did not kidnap—"

"Don't call names in here, kraut. You're in police custody. In Chicago, U.S. of A. Hal? Give him a tap so he'll mind his manners."

A shot-loaded sock hit the back of Paul's head. Driven forward, he fell off the chair. The other detective kicked him as he fell. Paul groaned and shut his eyes.

"None of that, you dirty kraut. Get up."

The detectives yanked him up, threw him into the chair, and yelled their questions. Did he have a criminal record? Did he belong to socialist or anarchist cells? Did he have a history of kidnapping and raping women? No matter how he responded, it didn't satisfy them. He took blow after blow of the shot-loaded sock.

He had denied the kidnapping charge perhaps thirty times when someone banged loudly on the door. Annoyed, the big detective said, "Hal, get that."

The door creaked. Then: "Ease off, boys. This one's bailed out. Clean him up and bring him downstairs."

THE LAWYER WAS A NATTY LITTLE fellow named Kaspar Gross. He took charge downstairs, showing Paul where to sign the various papers. Then he shook Paul's hand and congratulated him, as if it were some great honor to be released from Cook County Jail.

Barefoot, still in his prison shirt and pants, Paul lurched down granite stairs into a courtyard. In the yard was the Crown landau with the top raised.

"Glad you're safe," the driver, Nicky Speers, called down from his seat. Paul climbed in to discover his uncle seated, with both hands resting on the silver head of a cane.

Paul dropped into the seat opposite him and pulled the door shut. The carriage swung out into Dearborn Street.

"I will take you home before I go to the brewery," Uncle Joe said in a husky voice, as if he was trying to rein in enormous anger. "You smell like a sewer."

"That's what it is in there, a sewer."

"Vanderhoff lost no time in informing me of what you did. Yesterday I was in Milwaukee on business, but he telephoned me at home after midnight. Fortunately, I was downstairs when the call came. I couldn't locate the attorney until this morning."

"I am very grateful."

The statement made no visible impression. "Is that dried blood in your hair? Did they abuse you?"

"They questioned me hard. I will be all right. If you will only listen to my side, Uncle—"

"Go ahead."

"Juliette asked me to meet her at that little hotel in the country. I love her. She loves me."

"That's completely immaterial." Paul was terrified of his uncle's cold voice. "Vanderhoff agreed to drop charges in return for a pledge of silence from our family. A criminal action against you would result in a trial. The press would love nothing better. Vanderhoff desperately wanted to avoid that. They are taking Juliette to Europe. I don't want a scandal either. We didn't have to bargain long. He did require one additional condition. That you never again see or communicate with his daughter."

"I can't give that kind of promise."

"It isn't necessary that you do. I gave it for you."

"Uncle—"

"Kindly keep quiet. Your aunt has suffered quite enough lately. I won't tell her the truth about this shameful affair, and neither will you. Here is our story. You were in a tavern Saturday night, drank too much, got into an argument, and refused to leave peaceably. Hence your bruises. You were detained in jail until Kaspar Gross got you out. There, you've made liars of both of us."

"But the explanation is good. I don't want Aunt Ilsa to think badly of me."

"Think *badly?* You helped our son run away. Don't ask for miracles. She'd die if she knew you violated an innocent young woman."

Paul slumped in the corner. His uncle gazed out of the landau at the traffic. "I don't know what's become of this family; everything is crashing down about us. At supper the very night you were away with Vanderhoff's daughter, Frederica brazenly announced her intention of becoming an actress. An actress—can you imagine?" Uncle Joe shook his head, as though burdened beyond his limits. "Crashing down," he murmured again. "My son ran away with your connivance. You dishonor the family with your immoral behavior—"

"It isn't immoral. We love each other. We want to marry."

"Until you reach twenty-one, you can't marry without consent. Furthermore, you don't have the slightest appreciation of the meaning of the word love. That is clear from your sordid behavior.

"By all that you've done this week, you force me to a painful decision. You will leave our house. Please do so before I return home tonight. Your job at Crown's no longer exists. Henceforth you will have to make your own way."

"But I don't have anyplace to—"

"You have lived on the streets of Berlin. Crossed this country alone. I have every confidence that you can take care of yourself."

Uncle Joe sounded bitter, cruel. Paul's vision was momentarily blinded by tears. "Uncle Joe, I can't believe—"

Uncle Joe struck the carriage floor with the ferrule of his cane. "You had better believe me, Paul."

Paul leaned into the corner, trying to hide how heartsick he was. His uncle didn't look at him for the duration of the trip. "Around to the back, Nicky," he called as they arrived.

There Paul opened the door and climbed out.

Helga Blenkers told him his aunt had already left for the morning. He stumbled upstairs to his room. He bathed, shaved, and stretched out on his bed for a blessed nap.

He awoke about half past one and remembered what he must do. He packed a selection of clothes in his valise, leaving room for his souvenirs. Pack rat Pauli. The board was overflowing, but he could take only the most important things. His English grammar, the globe, and all of his postal cards except one—a painting of Brauerei Crown with flags flying from its towers. That he ripped in half and threw on the bed.

His fatigue-ringed eyes lingered on the last treasure tacked to the board. The stereoscope view of New York harbor. He no longer believed its promise as completely as he once had. He thought of leaving it behind. But he wasn't ready to do that. He pulled the tack and put the card in his pocket.

Aunt Ilsa came rushing in. She flung her arms around him. "Oh, Pauli, Pauli, how can this happen? He telephoned me five minutes after I got home. That was an hour ago. I have been trying to dissuade him ever since. He's a good man, but he's angry. This goes too far, that's what I told him. We do not shun our own family. But he's just in a fury—" She was sobbing.

Paul put his arms around her. She smelled of lilac water. He kissed her cheek. He loved her and always would.

"I must help you find a place for the night—"

"No, I can do that. Aunt Ilsa, please don't worry." He already had a destination in mind. It had been there the instant he awoke.

She saw on the bed the ripped halves of the brewery postal card. She hugged him again. "*Ach,* there is such pain. Pauli, you must let us know where you are. Come back to visit."

"Of course I will." Did she really think he would ever step inside his uncle's house again?

It was time to go. He felt a little unsteady as he opened the closet for his corduroy jacket.

He remembered something in his bureau drawer. He slipped into the jacket, opened the drawer, fastened the spotted white ribbon to his lapel. He was anxious to be away from this house of unhappiness. He wanted to cry. The moment passed. "Good-bye, Aunt Ilsa." He kissed her cheek once more.

He was not going to crawl out of the dark mansion like a felon. He took a firm hold on his bag and marched down the staircase boldly. With a false appearance of confidence he strode out the front door, the same door through which he'd tumbled—frozen, starving, but full of hope—so many months ago.

WHEN Paul arrived in Little Cheyenne, the sky was growing dark, and it was raining. Torrents sluiced through the gutters. Paul hardly noticed how soaked he'd gotten as he knocked on the door of the Temple of Photography.

Presently a key rattled, and Wex Rooney opened the door. "Dutch! What a surprise!" He noticed the valise.

"I have left my other job, sir. I have left my relatives to make my way on my own. I'm eager to learn the science of photography. Will you allow me to come in?"

"By all means! This is a joyous moment."

Paul stepped over the threshold, certain that he had left one world forever and was entering another, better one. A world in which he might at last find a sense of purpose and belonging. In this new world he'd make the home he longed for. With Julie.

PORK ✦ In October the Vanderhoffs arrived at Wiesbaden.

It was high season at Germany's most celebrated health resort. The atmosphere at the spa was elegant and festive, but that made no difference to M. P. Vanderhoff III. He was already sick of the tour, tired of ogling the castles along the Rhine. He found Germany, and all of Europe, too old and backward, too self-consciously quaint. Too—*foreign.*

One of the few positive aspects of the tour was Juliette's condition. She was docile and quiet, despite occasional outbursts of crying. Pork found it paradoxical that these reassured his wife.

"It's typically female behavior, Mason. She is well and normal again."

In Frankfurt, Nell had bought Juliette a little dog, a Pomeranian. His name was Rudy. Julie seemed to enjoy having a pet. She even smiled occasionally when she picked Rudy up and petted him.

One morning Pork went for a stroll in the spacious *Kurpark.* He had sat down on a stone bench beside the lake when he saw a man bearing down on him along the path. An American—and what's more, a Chicagoan.

"Mr. Vanderhoff? Good morning. William Vann Elstree." The

man removed his monocle and held out his hand. Pork shook it. A black armband was tied around Elstree's left sleeve.

"Yes, of course," Pork said. "Won't you sit down? This is an honor. An unexpected pleasure."

Elstree took a seat and fanned himself with his homburg. Pork's tiny eyes darted sideways, to William Elstree's jaw. Certainly the man was not handsome. But he radiated charm and, more important, the power only wealth conferred.

"You and your family are taking the waters, I hear," Elstree said.

"That's true. How do you happen to be here, Mr. Elstree?"

"Oh, the same reason. The waters. But you and I meeting this way—that's purely accidental."

Somehow Pork doubted it, though he couldn't have said why.

"Mr. Vanderhoff, since we've chanced to meet, allow me to raise a subject that's been on my mind lately. I hope you won't be offended."

"No, no, why should I?"

"Perhaps you'll say I'm unseemly, given the relatively short time that has gone by since the death of my wife, Marguerite. She passed away this summer in Chicago. Heatstroke."

"I read about it. Tragic, tragic. My condolences."

"Thank you." Elstree gazed at light cirrus clouds in the autumn sky. "Mr. Vanderhoff, you're here with not only your wife but your attractive daughter."

Startled, Pork said, "That's true."

"As you know, I have met her—at the Auditorium." Elstree smiled, charming and warm. "From the first I admired her beauty—and what I perceived to be her intelligence."

Pork was stunned, already leaping ahead to what this rich gentleman might be suggesting. "Go on, sir."

"Thank you. I'll be frank, sir, and I hope you won't condemn me. When the proper amount of time has passed, I'd like your permission to call on your daughter."

Pork sat back. What an incredible stroke of luck. Elstree came from one of Chicago's finest families. He was a Princeton graduate. Pork hardly dared think of what a catch he would be for Juliette.

"Mr. Vanderhoff?" Elstree looked worried, possibly interpreting the silence as rejection.

"Oh, excuse me. I'm just taken aback, that's all. Juliette's mother would be pleased if you called. I'd be honored."

Elstree smiled warmly then. "I'm happy to hear you say it. I must remind you, though. I'm forty-four years old."

"No problem at all!" Pork exclaimed. "A sensible woman prizes maturity in a man."

"But would your daughter object to my interest?"

"Certainly not. Furthermore, her mother and I have all the authority in such matters."

"As it should be," Elstree murmured. Again he smiled.

Part Six
LEVEE
1895–1896

PAUL ✦ "I'll teach you," Wex Rooney said that first night. "Give you a place to stay. I'll share whatever scraps and snips come to the dinner table. But you'll have to find work, Dutch. I can't offer a job with pay. I can barely scrape up money for myself."

"Done," Paul said.

"One thing more. I don't care what you call yourself outside, but around here, it'll be Dutch."

That night Paul slept on a straw pallet, under an old blanket, in the loft. Dutch. He hated the name. Never mind that there was an explanation for calling Germans Dutchmen: Dutch was easier to say than *Deutsche*. It occurred to him, however, that he was creating a new life for himself; he could stand to be Dutch for a while. The nickname didn't sound so bad if someone said it in a friendly way.

He had a glorious opportunity here. A chance to master a new, modern trade for the new, modern century that was coming. He would learn everything Wex Rooney could teach. He'd prove cousin Joe's bitter views of America were wrong, the predictions of the baker of Wuppertal too. And when Julie came home from her grand tour, he would win her somehow. If America had robbed him of a family, he must remember it had also given him Julie.

In the morning he asked Wex Rooney for a tack and permission to affix something to the wall. Near his straw pallet he tacked the stereoscope view of New York harbor from the ship's bow, with the lady Liberty beckoning. Then he went out.

Rooney's Temple of Photography was in Chicago's First Ward, which held most of the city's corporate offices, finest hotels, big department stores, elegant homes. The First Ward was huge, and south of Van Buren Street it also sheltered Chicago's worst vice districts, including Little Cheyenne and the Levee, a section even more notorious as a destination for thrill seekers.

Paul went to the Levee, to noisy saloons, cafés, music halls, in search of work. He answered advertisements. Trudged the streets in snow and keening winds. Climbed dark stairs to shabby lofts where dull-sounding jobs were already filled.

"It's the depression," Wex said. "Then, too, winter's a slow time. Come spring, jobs will open up. Don't be discouraged."

In January, at the end of his second week of searching, Paul got a job as a sandwich man, wearing boards advertising a cheap café. The owner said Paul had to walk the streets ten hours every day. For this he would be paid three cents, less than a quarter of his daily wage at Crown's. His first day on the street, a sleety rain was falling. People ignored him. He was sneezing and shaking when he got back to the Temple that night.

Wex was upset. "You can't keep that job, you'll die of influenza."

"I can do it," Paul insisted.

And he did. At the end of each day he was required to return the signboards to the café. On the third evening the owner said, "My brother-in-law was laid off his regular job today. I got to give him the boards. Here's what I owe you, and a little extra."

Shocked, bitter, half sick, Paul carried home his splendid earnings as a sandwich man. Ten cents.

WEX began to teach him. The sessions took place at night, after Paul returned from his job-hunting rounds or his brief periods of employment.

"I can quickly give you all you need to know about the technical aspects," Wex told him. "As for the rest, either you will develop the skills, the art, from within yourself, or you won't. On that point I have already formed an opinion."

"Sir?"

"You have a sharp eye. A quick mind. Most important, a great eagerness to learn. In photography, of course, you need no hand for drawing. You draw with light to form images—and with your creative spirit. It will be my challenge to bring that talent into the world."

Night after night, Paul's head was filled with facts, names, events. Louis Daguerre of Paris, who had perfected the earliest photographic process. Sir John Herschel, an Englishman, responsible for coining the terms "photography" and "positive" and "negative." Frederick Scott Archer, inventor of the wet plate process.

Wex explained that Mathew Brady's field operators had used the wet plate process throughout the Civil War. Dry plates came later, the process perfected in large part by Eastman. "Clever coot, Eastman. He revolutionized photography when he found a way to put his emulsion on a paper base. Do you imagine he designed his Kodak in order to sell cameras? No, sir, he practically gives those away. He wants the cameras *used*. He wants to sell *film*."

ONE Sunday during a February thaw, Wex dusted off a Kodak camera and said, "There's been enough theory, you must start to practice. Suspend your search for work for a day or two. The weather's good. I want you to go into the streets for snapshots." Paul said he didn't know or understand the word.

"Comes from hunting. A hunter making a fast shot is said to snap it off, never certain he'll hit the target. It's the same with this type of camera. You aim, hope—and snap." He held out the Kodak. "It's yours to keep."

Paul took the camera. There was such a bright smile on his face that it made Wex laugh. He rumpled Paul's hair affectionately. "My star pupil."

Paul snapped all over town. He brought home pictures of horse-cars, pushcarts, the Crown mansion. Wex disappeared into his darkroom, where he developed and printed the snapshots for Paul.

"Not much imagination, but the technique's all right," he said as he hung the damp prints on a wire with a wooden clothespin. "Except for these two pushcart peddlers. Because of the position of the camera, the men appear to have telephone poles growing out of their heads."

"I'll do better," Paul promised, severely let down.

"All right, but the subjects you chose—they're dull. Bring me something that won't make me yawn."

Paul went out the next morning. The sun was high; water was rushing in the gutters with a sound that promised spring. He pulled up suddenly at the sight of three garishly rouged women sunning themselves on the steps of Wampler's red-light hotel.

He strode up to them, smiling. "Ladies, how are you today?"

The youngest blew cigarette smoke at him. "Buzz off, squirt."

"I am not here for—ah—the usual purpose," Paul said quickly. "I would like to take your photograph."

"Oh, that's one of those snapshot cameras. I seen 'em in a magazine," the second one said, interested.

"Awright, why not?" said the third, who was stout, with a red butterfly painted on her mouth.

Paul began to snap. The women fell into the spirit of it, striking exaggerated poses, coyly drawing their robes open for a glimpse of knee and thigh. When Paul finished twelve exposures and thanked them, Butterfly exclaimed, "Awright, Junior, but you got to bring us girls a picture apiece!"

"I will, I promise." Paul hurried away.

Later Wex rendered his verdict: "Fine, these are fine. You got some lively expressions." After a moment's reflection he went on. "I think my original speculation was right, you have the knack. But you want to be more than a mechanic—you want to capture the truth, but never soften it. Photographs shouldn't lie."

Paul delivered the snapshots to Wampler's Hotel. The ladies oohed and exclaimed. Paul had a delirious feeling of success.

THREE stalwarts of the First Ward Democratic Club hired Wex to photograph them for the club headquarters. The Democrats controlled the ward, and much else besides, and Wex had a solid relationship with them. He had a particular loyalty to the two bosses, an alderman named Coughlin and a saloonkeeper named Kenna.

The three who called on Wex were underlings. Loud-spoken, and dressed in fancy clothes that managed to look cheap.

Wex blandly named his price—five dollars each. The pols yelped, swore, started to walk out. Wex laughed.

"Why are you so het up, boys? You know the club can afford it. Most of your cash comes from city hall boodle, and there's plenty of that, I hear."

The pol who spoke for the group said all right, five smackers apiece was a deal.

Wex took more than a half hour posing and photographing each of the politicians; he was a perfectionist about his craft, if about nothing else. At the end of the session the leader said, "Send the pictures around fast as you can. Alderman Coughlin's wanting a new one of himself. If these turn out good, we'll put in a word."

The unexpected profit of fifteen dollars, half in advance, elated Wex. "Dutch, let's take the night off. There's something I've been yearning to see for months."

"What is that?"

"Mr. Edison's flicker parlor."

In a narrow space at 148 State Street, the latest invention of the Wizard of Menlo Park could be enjoyed for five cents per view. It was snowing heavily when Paul and Wex walked in from the street.

Despite the weather, the parlor had four customers. Wex flung his arms out like a happy child. "Isn't this something? They say Edison plans to spread these parlors all over America."

They stepped up to the ticket counter. Behind it stood two rows of cabinets, back to back, each cabinet about three feet high and two feet deep. There was a rail in front of each row of machines for the comfort of patrons leaning forward over the eyepiece.

The man selling tickets was well dressed, in a suit, stiff collar, and string tie. Wex said, "How long are your films?"

"Twenty seconds. A quarter permits you to see five."

"What, a whole nickel for each?"

"You can't expect genius to work for nothing. The kinetoscope's a fabulous invention."

Wex bought two twenty-five-cent tickets and handed one to Paul. Paul's pulsebeat quickened as they approached the cabinets.

Wex looked at the pictures in one row of kinetoscopes, Paul the other. Edison's subjects were inoffensive, not to say dull. Paul viewed *Organ Grinder; At the Barbershop; Shoeing Horses; Trained Bears;* and *Sandow the Great*. The last was the most appealing—a famous German strongman posed against a plain dark backdrop, clad in a garment resembling a large diaper. It afforded an impressive display of Sandow's flexing arms and quivering biceps.

When they had finished looking into the machines, they went out. Wex said, "That box is the miracle of the age. Temporarily."

"Why do you say that?" Paul asked.

"Because the picture is too small. Because only one person at a time can view it. What's needed is a machine to *project* the picture. Throw the image onto a wall or a special screen. For a large, *paying* audience. Inventors are working frantically on projector designs, and that includes Edison. I say just wait, and there'll be special theaters. And crowds to fill them." Wex's spectacles flashed under a streetlamp; he was almost dancing in the slush.

Paul felt a new excitement and enthusiasm. *Those are the pictures I want to make. If Wex is right, one day they'll be popular with millions. If I were a camera operator who took such pictures, I could afford to be a husband, and it would be fine work too. Why, I might go all over the world!*

AT LAST, on a windy day in March, Paul found a good job. Driver of a delivery wagon for the Illinois Steam Laundry Company. The laundry was owned by one Albert Grace, who dressed well and had the air of a man who sold religious goods. For this reason, Paul was astonished to learn, when he began work, that the bulk of the laundry's business came from a long list of whorehouses in the Levee.

Picking up and delivering with the laundry wagon began another dramatic education for Paul. Although Uncle Joe had often railed against the vice thriving in Chicago, Paul had never guessed the staggering number of fancy bordellos, concert saloons, dance parlors with women available in upstairs "wine rooms." The names teased the imagination. The Chinese Delight. The Dark Secret. The Why Not? Many of them ran day as well as night shifts. The depression still gripping the country seemed to have little effect on the demand for illicit sex.

A Niagara of spirits flowed through the vice dens, and organized thievery was an important sideline. Gambling throve in neighboring pool halls, craps and faro rooms. Everything contributed to the Levee's booming prosperity, but sex was the engine. Scores of legitimate businesses—newsstands and delicatessens, dry cleaners, laundries, and breweries—used black ink or red, according to the rhythms of the whorehouse trade.

Paul was young, energetic, and almost always cheerful. He had rough good looks and a convivial disposition. Most of the whores and madams liked him. Darting in and out of houses with his canvas hamper of linens, he had plenty of offers. But he always declined politely. He didn't fancy himself morally superior. He just wanted to be loyal to Julie.

One evening after work, in a hard spring rain, he stood outside the Crown mansion for a quarter of an hour. He watched Uncle Joe's landau return from the brewery. For an instant he wanted to dash across the rain-lashed street. Catch the carriage. Pound on the side. *"See here, I'm part of this family. Can't we patch this up?"*

Instead, he walked away with bitter thoughts of his uncle's turning him out. He'd make his way without the family. He'd find a true home of his own. With Julie.

EVERY week Paul put a little money into a bank savings account. By mail, from the Sears, Roebuck catalogue, he began to buy new clothes—a gray corduroy suit, fancy vest, high-top shoes, and a dressy young man's derby.

"Quite the sport, aren't you?" Wex said when Paul showed him the clothes. "You'll be trigged out just right for the track."

"What track?"

"The racetrack. Washington Park. Hawthorne. They'll be operating soon, thank goodness."

Frowning, Paul recalled a puzzling remark about Wex's being fond of ponies. If Wex was betting on horse races, that might explain his perpetual poverty.

Wex noticed Paul's frown. "I know, I know, gambling's a terrible habit. It's my demon."

Paul brushed the brim of his new derby, which he'd set carefully on the cleanest spot on the table in the back. "Well, I might go to the track sometime, to see what it's like."

"I'd be glad for the company, Dutch. By the way, your mood's been a lot sunnier this last week or so. Care to say why?"

Paul flushed. "Well—I've met a girl. I know I shouldn't look at anyone else. But I do get lonely."

Wex sidled around the table and threw a companionable arm over Paul's shoulder. "Go on, it's all right to have a date with this other one. You're young, it's spring, and just because you take her out, you don't have to marry her."

"That's right," Paul said. He was smiling again.

Nancy Logan was seventeen and worked at the laundry. Though

287

she certainly couldn't qualify as a beauty, Paul found her attractive. About five feet tall, she had a mass of red curls and a pert figure even a shapeless gray dress couldn't hide.

After a day or two of agonizing, Paul invited Nancy to go roller-skating the following Sunday.

It turned out to be a wonderful warm day. The outdoor rink, roofed in green slate with walls of white-painted lattice, was crowded. A calliope blasted out tunes of the moment.

Nancy was from Reelsville, Indiana. "I had to move out because the farm couldn't produce enough to feed thirteen of us kids. I came up a year ago last month. I almost didn't get out of the Dearborn Street depot alive."

"Why not?"

"There was this young fella standing around, watching me. I started for the door, and he headed me off, all smiles. Not bad-looking, but nothing special either. Tall, skinny, with a spit curl here." She traced a corkscrew on her forehead. Her description stirred something in Paul's memory, but he couldn't get hold of it.

"He asks me if I'm new in Chicago. I say yes, I came to find work. He grabs hold of my arm and says he might be able to help. He smiles and says his name's Jim. Something about that smile I can't explain—it scared the life out of me. I ran out of the depot with my grip. I ran eight or ten blocks before I had nerve enough to look back. I never saw him again, and I'm thankful."

"I bet he was a roper from the Levee."

"What's a roper?"

"A man who loiters in train stations trying to round up young girls for"—reddening—"illicit purposes."

"Oh, my goodness. I was lucky, wasn't I?" She snuggled against him. The calliope began "Just Tell Them That You Saw Me," a sentimental hit everyone was humming. "Dutch, I need to ask you something. Have you got a regular girl?"

Julie's eyes haunted him. "Yes, Nancy. But she's a long way from here. All the way across the Atlantic."

"Did she leave you?"

"Not exactly. Her parents didn't like me; they took her on a trip."

"Do you miss her?"

"I do."

"Will you get over it?"

He couldn't answer. She read his face. "That means no. My bad luck."

"Oh, Lord," he said suddenly.

"What's wrong?"

"The roper. The one you met at the station. I think I know him." He described the delivery boy from Frankel's. "His name was Jimmy too."

She clasped his hand. "Well, if it's him, I hope you never meet him again. Once is enough for anybody. There was something bad about him. Something awful."

JIMMY ✦ He was born James Aloysius Daws, in one of the poorest Irish patches on the West Side of Chicago. His mother, Bert, insisted he was legitimate. Jimmy never saw his father.

Jimmy grew up a striver. He'd lived on the streets ever since he was ten, when his mother was shot to death in the bordello where she worked.

He had jobs of all kinds, occasionally a respectable one. He never lasted. Sometimes thievery cost him the job, sometimes his explosive temper or his outspoken dislike of the foreign-born. Jimmy hated strange accents, whether they belonged to wops, kikes, dagos, niggers, or krauts. He hated krauts like rat poison. He knew he might be a bastard, but by damn he was an American. He loved his country—it was a land of opportunity.

Delivering meat for Frankel's was one of the respectable jobs that didn't last long. After picking up fine china at the Crown house, he had decamped without giving Frankel notice. He'd worked at a variety of jobs since then. Busboy, bouncer, helper at a dancing academy. He worked as a special deputy during the Pullman strike, and when that ended, as a roper. He liked being a roper.

He kept the job until he was insulted by a little blonde from Rock Island that he'd roped at the depot. Jimmy called on her in her room and punched her up, until she wailed for mercy.

Her caterwauling enraged him. He kept punching her and kicking her. Punching her while she crawled on her knees toward the door. Kicking the small of her back until her head cracked against the door and she sagged sideways, white and still.

"Aw, come on," Jimmy said with a nervous snicker. "Don't spoof me. Open your eyes. I won't hit you again."

Nothing. He put his nose near her mouth. Cold; no breath.

He swore, his eyes wet with fright. Terrified of discovery, he hauled the corpse to the river at night in a coarse sack weighted with pieces of pipe.

A few days later one of the pimps who worked with the girl's madam sought him out. "Bad news, Jimmy. That little chippy from Rock Island? Her brother's deputy police chief. He's in town raising hell. They found her, y'know."

"I din't know."

"It was in the papers. Thing is, there'll be heat now. You better hide yourself for a good long time. Get into something respeckable."

So Jimmy Daws got into something "respeckable" and thereby met Paul Crown again.

PAUL ✦ To the Temple of Photography came Alderman John Joseph Coughlin. He was as flashy a dresser as any in the First Ward. He was six feet tall, built like an ironworker, and wore his oiled hair in a high, thick pompadour with impressive sideburns. His upswept mustache points glistened.

Bathhouse John Coughlin was no more than thirty-five, but he had a fearsome reputation. He'd begun his working career as a rubber at a Turkish bath on Clark Street, but he was ambitious and soon moved to the Palmer House, whose baths were famous throughout America.

He next bought a bathhouse of his own on East Madison, then a second one in the Brevoort Hotel. He still operated those, as well as a saloon called the Silver Dollar. But Coughlin's real business was Chicago—the control of it from city hall and the dispensing of its municipal favors in return for boodle. He'd been elected to council for the first time in 1892 and overwhelmingly reelected two years later. People who disliked him said he ensured his victories with flying squads of thugs who kept opposition voters away from the polls.

To be photographed, Coughlin had chosen a frock coat of shiny black silk, a shirt of bright green, and an ivory silk vest.

"Here's Mr. Coughlin, sir," Paul announced.

Wex popped from under the black camera cloth and rushed forward to pump the Bath's hand. "Alderman, what a pleasure. Sit right down. Do you have any particular pose in mind?"

Coughlin sat on a garden bench Wex had spent half an hour positioning in front of three Doric columns. "Nuh," he said, "except I want it to have dignity. It's for Mary and the wee ones."

"Dignity. My feeling precisely." After a delay for polishing the camera lens, and another for adjusting Coughlin's pose, Wex squeezed the bulb to make the first exposure.

And so it went, an hour and a half of fussing and adjusting, with occasional interruptions to expose a plate. Finally the Bath said he had to go. He pumped Rooney's hand. "Swell, just swell." He tipped his hat and blew out of the shop like a prairie cyclone.

On his way to work the next day Paul delivered the package of prints to the Silver Dollar saloon. A day later the postman brought a note that conveyed the alderman's reaction.

Swell pictures!! Washington Park opens up next week. My horse
First Ward will run. Be my guests in my box won't you.

Yrs admiringly,
Coughlin

Paul asked for Tuesday afternoon off—opening day at the track. Albert Grace said he'd allow the absence from the laundry because Paul had proved himself dependable and a hard worker.

PAUL and Wex rode the South Side elevated to Washington Park. The crowd was large and festive. Paul wore his new gray corduroy suit and carried a Kodak from the shop. Earlier he had seen Wex stuff a roll of bills in his coat. How he came by the cash Paul couldn't imagine. Wex seemed extraordinarily nervous. Overwrought, almost. No wonder he called horse racing his demon.

Located at the front rail of the center grandstand, the Bath's box was one of the largest and best. Other guests were already there when Paul and Wex arrived.

The Bath greeted them boisterously. "Glad you boys could make it. Hope you brought plenty of cash." He worked Wex's hand up and down like a pump handle. "Come along, meet the gang."

The Bath moved to a tall, powerfully built man. "My pal Colonel R. Sidney Shadow the Third. Of the Denver Shadows. This man's a genius, boys. He's an inventor, a showman—you're gonna hear plenty from him. Meet Wexford Rooney and his friend Dutch. A couple of first-class photographers."

291

Wex said, "I recognize your name, Colonel. You're in the picture business."

"Correct, sir." The colonel's voice was stentorian, yet seductive as a preacher's. "Call me Sid, won't you?"

Two young men were also in the box. One of them, with blond hair parted in the middle, was pulling handbills from a cardboard box in the corner. His companion was facing away, scanning the crowd. When he turned around, Paul got a shock. It was the delivery boy who had stolen the Crown china. And, very likely, the roper who'd tried to trap Nancy.

He looked much more prosperous than he did when he was working for Frankel's. He wore a derby, high stiff collar, plaid suit, gleaming brown shoes with pointed toes. His darting eyes showed that he recognized Paul.

Shadow noticed the exchange of looks. "These are my two assistants, Lewis Kress and James Daws. Lew and Jimmy."

Lew Kress shook hands first. He had a hangdog air and a thick southern accent. "Pleased to meet you-all." Jimmy Daws stepped forward, his brown eyes thoughtful. He shook with Wex, then Paul.

"Hullo, pal. Been a long time."

"You know each other?" Shadow said.

"We have met," Paul said, leaving it there.

Jimmy Daws slapped his shoulder. "Yes. Glad to see you again."

"All right, enough sociability," Shadow said with a gruff laugh. "Get rid of those handbills."

Lew and Jimmy filled every available pocket with wads of them. Paul noted the word Luxoscope in circus type. Jimmy tipped his derby to the group and left with Lew. Despite the hot sun beating into the grandstand, Paul felt a chill.

People were filling the stands. A brass band played. The sky was a fine light blue. Spring breezes fluttered the grandstand flags and the plumes of ladies' hats, and riffled the silks of the jockeys parading their horses for the start of the first race.

Wex made a darting move toward the gate of the box. "Is there time left to wager?"

The Bath eyed the horses. "Just—if you hurry. First Ward isn't up till the third race. In this one I'd lay something on Tinker's Dam." Wex bolted from the box.

Wex came back just as the bell rang. Everyone in the stands

jumped up, yelling, and for the next two and a half minutes programs were brandished and kerchiefs waved. Tinker's Dam came in sixth. Wex tore up his tickets.

Paul was fascinated by Colonel Shadow. If Wex was something of an Irish pixie, Shadow was a granite statue. His features were craggy, his jawline long and powerful. He dressed in elegant western style: tooled-calf boots, a flowing cravat, and a sand-colored sombrero. Altogether, Colonel R. Sidney Shadow III was an imposing personage, though quite pale, as if he spent most of his time indoors.

"Excuse me, Colonel," Paul said, "do I understand correctly, you are in the picture business?"

"That's right, son."

"The moving pictures," Wex said. "The flickers."

"The rage of the coming age," Shadow intoned. He flipped back his black overcoat to reveal a scarlet satin lining. He handed cards to Paul and Wex. The cards bore his name, the words CHICAGO LUXOGRAPH COMPANY, and an address. "I'm proud to say I'm the inventor and holder of the patent on the Luxoscope peep show machine. We're in five states already and expanding at a furious rate. I'm also working on a Luxograph projection system."

"Wonderful," Wex said with a distracted air. "The next race is coming up. Excuse me."

He left, and Paul took an empty chair beside the colonel. Excited, he said, "I saw flicker pictures at the Exposition. Do you really believe such pictures will be shown on large screens someday?"

"Absolutely. Interested in our infant industry, are you?"

"Very much. I am studying photography with Mr. Rooney. But I'm fascinated most by the moving pictures."

"That's the future. That's why we're rushing to perfect a projector, and a camera to go with it. So keep your eye on Luxograph."

Bugles announced the next race. Wex rushed into the box with more tickets. "I bet on Evangeline to win."

"Hmm, I dunno," the Bath said.

Evangeline finished last.

The Bath's horse, First Ward, placed in the third race. Wex won twenty dollars. Then he lost it all in the fourth. He left the box with a harried expression.

Paul was asking himself whether it would be dishonorable to ask

Shadow about opportunities in his business. He very much wanted to. He thought that if he didn't seize the opportunity, it might never come again. He slid over to the chair beside the colonel.

"Sir? I would very much like to work with flicker pictures. Do you by any chance have a position?"

"I don't have anything now, but keep in touch. You never know."

A minute later Paul's neck prickled. The two helpers had come back. Jimmy Daws was leaning against the rear rail of the box, arms folded. Watching him.

Wex's luck was bad the rest of the afternoon. At the end of the final race he said, "Dutch, let's go home." He shook hands all around. "Alderman Coughlin, thank you."

"So long, Dutch," Jimmy said to Paul. "Maybe we'll see each other again."

"Very possibly," Paul said.

"Till then." Jimmy tipped his derby.

ON THE el, Paul confessed he'd asked Colonel Shadow about employment. "But I'd hate for you to think I was disloyal to you."

"Ah, forget it," Wex said. "You're honest, and I appreciate it. I'm proud you were my pupil, even for a while. I've known all along that you'd move on. It's the living pictures you fell in love with first. I saw the light in your eyes when the elephant danced. If you can sign on with a man like Shadow, do it. Don't feel guilty or look back."

Wex's unselfishness lifted a burden from Paul. The future shone with a special new brightness. He couldn't wait to tell Julie of all he'd learned from Wex, and of the even more exciting possibility of learning the moving picture trade. When would she finish that trip and come home to him?

ON HIS rounds next morning, he asked Madame Camille, owner of the Pleasures of Paris, whether he might use her telephone. He'd already delayed this call too long. He tapped his foot nervously while waiting for the line to connect.

"Crown residence. Manfred speaking."

Paul muffled his voice. "Louise Volzenheim, please."

Manfred grumbled. There was a lengthy silence.

"Here is Louise. Who is that?"

"Louise, don't say anything, it's Paul. Just listen. Tell Aunt Ilsa I telephoned. Only my aunt, not my uncle. Tell her I'm safe and well, she mustn't worry."

"Are you here in Chicago? Please—"

He interrupted. "Is there any news of cousin Joe?"

"Nothing. It's so sad, both of you gone, everyone so unhappy."

"Uncle Joe must be happy."

"Oh, I don't believe that's true."

"Remember, Louise, only tell my aunt. I miss you. Good-bye."

When Paul dragged in from work that night, Wex's mood was dark. He spoke with a slur as he served bean soup. He drank from a brown pint bottle, one-quarter full, and put it on the table. He looked at Paul like a guilty child.

"I lost altogether too much money at the track. I'll need an extension on the rent. I don't know if the landlord will allow it again." A long sigh. "I told you gambling was my demon."

Gently Paul said, "Then why don't you stop?"

"Absolutely right. I must stop. If I don't, then you and I will be looking for a roost in some tree in Lincoln Park."

So it was that bad, that desperate. He'd had no idea.

"Demons," Wex mumbled. "Everywhere."

"Yes," Paul said. He envisioned the eyes of Jimmy Daws.

JIMMY ✦ On the first day of April, 1895—before he met Paul at the racetrack—Jimmy observed his twentieth birthday. He was gainfully and, he hoped, safely employed with Colonel R. Sidney Shadow. Jimmy had started with the colonel about five weeks after the murder of the little blond tart. He worked at the colonel's peep show joint on the corner of Twenty-second Street and State, west of Freiberg's Dance Hall.

Shadow's establishment had been open for several months. All the window glass was opaqued with paint. Above, on the building, two big signs in bright colors shouted to both streets:

Colonel R. S. Shadow's LUXOSCOPE PARLOR
The MIRACLE of the Era!—Pictures That MOVE!
—Suitable for All Ages—

The ground-floor Luxoscope Parlor had ten bulky peep show machines, five on either side of a wide aisle. The machines operated on the flip-card principle. Edison's kinetoscope used a continuous strip of film instead of cards, but the effect was similar: the illusion of motion from a sequence of rapidly flashed stills.

Shadow's machines featured subjects such as the Lake Michigan surf rolling in, or a horse-drawn fire engine careening through an empty street. The colonel complained that most of the card sequences were too tame. He intended to introduce racier subjects.

Above the parlor, on the second floor, Shadow occupied rooms with his common-law wife, a pale, voluptuous blonde named Mary Beezer. The two assistants shared the remaining space. The first thing Jimmy did after Shadow hired him was inspect their rooms. Lew Kress had the larger one, with windows overlooking State Street. Jimmy would be forced into a dark cubicle with no windows. That evening he announced to Lew that they would exchange. The instant Lew protested, Jimmy flung him against the wall, then showed him the blade of a knife. "Don't make me mad."

Lew Kress cleared out of the large room in a half hour.

Jimmy's work for Shadow consisted of tending the peep show cash register, watching to make sure patrons didn't damage the machines, and sometimes passing out handbills. He didn't plan to stay with the colonel forever. However, until he was sure the death of the little blond tart was forgotten, and until he decided where to move for the biggest opportunity, he'd stay. Actually he liked the business of flickers. It had glamour.

SHADOW worked under enormous pressure, which he put on himself. Jimmy thought it stupid, but it was a fact. The colonel frowned a lot and never stopped to chat when he was busy. But suppertime was different. Mary would serve him a beer, and he'd stop scowling and grow talkative. One evening Jimmy asked Shadow how he'd earned the rank of colonel.

"Why, I awarded it to myself, kid. Just like I gave myself a high-class name. You don't want to be too honest in this world, it doesn't impress anybody."

Jimmy was agog. "Your name ain't Shadow?"

"I confess!" Shadow clapped his hand over his heart. "Actually it's Sigmund Seelmeister." He said this with great relish. He went on to explain that he didn't come from a fine old Denver family; he'd been born on a pig farm in Indiana, from which he'd run away at age eleven. He'd worked mostly as a farmhand, until one Saturday night, when he bought a ticket to a traveling show, Professor Martin's Minstrels. "I went wild for what I saw on that stage—the music, the dancing. I got the professor to try me out in the show. I had a good singing voice, if I do say so. After that I played one-night stands with Martin's Minstrels, warbling over the footlights, dancing the cakewalk." A curious, dreamy smile came to his craggy face. "I loved it. I loved the applause. After six years, though, I knew I was going nowhere. Then I had another stroke of luck. I met Mary."

At this point Mary put her hands on her hips. "Enough jabber," she said. "We'll starve if I don't get something on the table."

So Jimmy didn't find out how Shadow had moved to the flickers. Nor did he ask later. He didn't care, so long as he got paid.

Of girls Jimmy now had a plentiful supply. He was a good dancer, and he'd developed a pretty good line. One relationship had lasted over two months, an unusual length of time for him. This was with a girl named Rosie French.

Rosie had moved up from Pullman after her pa was killed during the strike. She was an amateur whore, not allied with any house. It was a dangerous way for a girl to do business on the Levee, but Rosie was tough. He admired her.

She had ambitions, she told him. She intended to be a music hall soubrette in New York, thereby making herself available to rich men from the audience. She'd go east as soon as she had enough cash.

Rosie had a temper that was almost the equal of his. After a stupid quarrel over something trivial, she ordered him out of her room. He threatened her with a beating, and she countered by jerking a little silver-plated hideout pistol from under her mattress. "Lay one hand on me and I'll empty this in your face."

For the first time in memory, Jimmy lowered his fists in front of an adversary. He even grinned sheepishly and tried to hug her. She wouldn't have it. She locked him out.

Strangely, he found himself drawn back to her place despite her treatment of him. Her room was vacant. A neighbor said Rosie had left for New York. He felt bad for days. Rosie was a piece of work. He'd liked her more than he realized.

In that same spring of 1895 Jimmy ran into the kraut kid at Washington Park. What a stunner. For a few seconds he was ready to bolt. But he hung on, kept his nerve, and when the kid didn't say anything about the stolen china, Jimmy relaxed.

He was puzzled, though. What was somebody who lived in a fancy house doing in a box at the racetrack? He asked Shadow. Turned out that the kraut was some kind of assistant to the photographer, Rooney, but delivered laundry. It occurred to Jimmy that maybe the kraut *didn't* live in the fancy house anymore. Whatever the situation, the kraut struck Jimmy as a guy with plenty of sand— not easy to push around.

For a few days Jimmy worried that the kraut might contact the police after all. But no detectives showed up. Lucky again.

JOE CROWN ✦ When summer came, the long days and the heat, conversations with Ilsa seemed to grow shorter and cooler. Often there was contention, even if their discussion didn't begin that way. The first time Joe was fully aware of this, they were sitting alone, she with her darning, he with papers from the brewery, after Carl and Fritzi had gone to bed.

"Joe."

"Yes?"

"Louise took a telephone message this morning. It was Paul."

He sat in stunned silence, peering over his spectacles, while she described the message. "He asked that I not tell you he called. Louise said he was polite, but she could hear anger in his voice."

"Then he shouldn't have bothered to—"

"Joe, please. I've worried myself to exhaustion about him. About both boys. You wonder that Paul's angry? You banished him like a peasant who dares to disagree with a king."

He flung his papers on the floor. "That analogy is ridiculous. Let's be very clear. I don't wish the boy ill. But I gave him all I had to give, and how did he repay it? By abetting Joe's flight from this house. I'm supposed to be forgiving? I am sorry, no."

He rose, stooped to gather the papers. "If you'll excuse me, I think I'll work in the study." He walked out.

THEY lay in bed, not touching. It was two weeks later.

She said, "Are you awake?"

"I am."

"You didn't tell me about the detective report today."

"The usual. Nothing."

"Oh, Joe, I'm so worried. Not a letter, not even a postal card since he left. He might be injured. Even—"

"Ilsa, let me reassure you about one thing. Whatever else he is, our son is a strong, competent young man. I despise his political ideas—the way he was so easily influenced by someone like Benno. But I never for a moment minimize the good character you developed in Joe as he grew up. If he's silent, it's because he chooses to be silent, not because he's come to harm."

"Then are we wasting our money on the detectives?"

"Yes, I think we are. But I'll do it as long as you want, though I don't hold out much hope of success."

"Then cancel the arrangement for a while. I assume we can hire them again."

"Anytime."

He reached for her hand—tentatively, shyly, as a new suitor might. She twined her fingers in his, squeezed, sought his chin with her other hand, kissed him.

JOE JUNIOR ✦ He was working his way west. It was his intention to see the Pacific Ocean. He did carpentry, dug drainage ditches, trekked across the autumn fields of Illinois, shoveled snow that winter on a street crew in St. Louis, Missouri. He'd always been physically strong, but he was smaller than many men his age, so he felt compelled to work twice as hard to prove his worth. As he approached his nineteenth birthday, in April of 1895, he realized he'd never grow much bigger.

Long hours and the agony of strained muscles didn't bother him; exhaustion helped him sleep, in fact. Helped ease the memories of his family, Rosie, Benno. He thought a lot about Benno's death. He decided it had been stupid and futile. He wasn't soured on the cause of the laboring man. To the contrary. He still believed walkouts were good weapons. Strikes too. But bombs? Stupid.

It was at night that he missed his home most. Missed his brother and sister, and Paul, and especially his mother. She'd be worried about him. Sometimes he suffered intense guilt over that.

When it came to his father, his emotions were tangled. He harbored bad feelings toward Joe Crown, yet he also felt an unexpected kinship. Because he was independent now. Following his own plan, as his father had done.

Moving west, he found work on various farms. In the summer, when the winter-wheat harvest was at its height, he joined a crew working for one of the Mennonite farmers in Ellsworth County, Kansas—Bruno Cherry by name. Mr. Cherry was in his late forties. He and his bride had come to America from the Ukraine in 1873.

Cherry was a hard master, but honest and considerate. He had built a bunkhouse for the itinerant crews that worked his two thousand acres twice a year. Food was plentiful and good.

Bruno Cherry saw that Joe Junior wasn't like most of the other harvesters. They were either illiterate farmworkers, or college boys spending the summer earning money. He invited Joe Junior inside his house for supper more than once.

Joe Junior liked the man and his stout wife. Cherry was concerned about the welfare of families presently working the land, and had become engaged with a new movement: Populism. "We have to seize and shape our future. The big moguls in the East won't help. That is why Kansans created the new Populist party.

"Our demands are simple and fair," Cherry said one night. "The eight-hour workday throughout America. For elections, the secret ballot. An income tax under which everyone pays in proportion to his income. We want full suffrage for women. We want the government to strip control of railroads, telegraph and telephone companies from the greedy sharks of the East. Above all, we want free silver at the ratio of sixteen to one."

Silver was one of the great issues of the times. With the value of gold increasing and that of silver declining, farmers continued to suffer under laws that said debts contracted with paper money must be repaid in gold. The agrarian West cried that such treatment was unjust and destructive, while the commercial East continued to fight for the gold standard and control of the money supply.

"Do you plan to run anyone for President?" Joe Junior asked.

"In the next election we would like to nominate William Jennings Bryan. He stands with us on free silver and many other issues."

Here was a political party standing for everything Joe Junior believed, a party armed with principled anger, not dynamite. That night he was baptized in the waters of Populism. That night, in Ellsworth County, Kansas, he was born again.

300

WHEN THE HARVEST ENDED, IT was time to go on toward the Rockies, the valleys of California and the Northwest, the shore of the western ocean. Joe Junior said good-bye to the Cherry family. Mrs. Cherry wept. Bruno Cherry gave him an extra two dollars he could ill afford.

"Joseph, you are a good worker and a fine young man. Your parents must be proud."

A shadow crossed Joe Junior's vivid blue eyes. As if making a joke, he said, "I doubt it. They don't even know where I am."

"You must rectify that," Bruno Cherry said. "It is unjust and unkind to let them worry and wonder about you."

Joe Junior was taken aback. Riven by guilt, he hoisted his bundle over his shoulder and set off on a road winding over the prairie.

But his guilt grew too heavy to bear. Cherry was right—he shouldn't punish his mother with worry. His father's feelings didn't enter into it. In the village of Black Wolf, in the northwestern corner of the county, he stopped.

It wasn't hard to find an appropriate token. Three small stalks of wheat—the heads of the stalks—picked up from a roadside where they'd fallen.

He purchased an envelope at the general store and borrowed a pencil. He sealed the envelope, with the wheat grains inside. He cocked his hand to the left so that his writing slanted that way. He wrote "Mrs. I. Crown" on the outside, and the address, then stepped up to the postal window in back to buy his stamp.

ILSA ✦ Ilsa lay in bed, feverish, felled by a severe case of summer grippe. She hated sickness. She equated it with weakness, or punishment by the Almighty.

Ilsa knew her sin. Failure to hold the family together. Even, possibly, her marriage. She could feel Joe slipping away from her. All because of the woman question, as it was called.

A knock at the bedroom door startled her. "Mrs. Crown? Helga. The morning mail arrived. There is a letter, addressed to you."

"Please bring it in."

JOE rushed home from the brewery in response to Ilsa's telephone call. Sitting by her bedside, he turned the envelope one way and then another, studying it. Ilsa's face glowed. "He's alive, Joe.

301

He sent the stalks of wheat to show us. He must be out west."

Joe held up the envelope. "This isn't his handwriting."

"Of course it is. He tried to disguise it, but he can't fool me."

He stood. "Well, I don't recognize the writing, and I don't believe you do either; you just say it because you want to believe it."

"Of course I want to believe it! Is it wrong to want him back?"

Joe responded to her anger impassively. He laid the envelope on the bed. "Well, if it is from Joe, he sent it to you, not to me. You must excuse me now. I still have a lot to do this afternoon."

Bending, he kissed her briefly and went out.

She picked up the envelope, with its token of Joey's survival, and pressed it against her breast. The truth was in her husband's eyes. A certain—*distance*. A growing resentment. She had lost her son. She had lost Pauli. Now she was in danger of losing Joe, and she had no remedy for it. Being herself—kind Ilsa, dutiful Ilsa, always prompt with the meals—that was no longer good enough. She associated with the wrong women. She espoused the wrong ideas. She spoke too forthrightly. She'd forgotten a wife's proper place. She couldn't go back even if she wanted to.

JULIE ✦ At the end of the summer of 1895, Julie sailed home from Europe with her little dog, Rudy. Her face was chalky. She had a nervous, distracted air, and she seldom smiled.

The very day she came home, she ran to the whitewashed message stone by the stable. It was gone; all the stones were gone. Dug out, the soil raked and smoothed for flower beds. She felt abandoned. For a moment she almost hated Paul.

Two weeks later, with Pork and Nell absent from the house, she telephoned Ilsa Crown and invited the startled lady to be her guest for tea. They agreed to meet at the fashionable Hotel Richelieu.

The women sat at a secluded table and ordered tea and finger sandwiches. "It is very kind of you to invite me," Ilsa said with a smile. She was a woman of obvious warmth. "We have never been introduced. Is there some special reason you wished for us to meet?"

"Yes, I confess there is." Julie found it hard to smile, but she did. Her cheeks were white as the napkin she was twisting in her lap. "Have you any word of your son, Mrs. Crown?"

"No. The police have largely abandoned the case. We have used a firm of private detectives, with no success."

"That's so sad."

"Yes—well—one must bear it. I have faith that Joey is alive and well, perhaps in the West." She made no reference to the wheat.

They chatted of less painful things until the waiter arrived, pushing a silvery trolley. He poured the tea. Julie toyed with her cup. "Mrs. Crown, may I speak candidly?"

"Of course, my dear."

"I invited you here to ask about your nephew."

"Pauli?" Ilsa seemed to sag a little. "I'm afraid Pauli moved out of our house shortly after Joe Junior left. Pauli's departure was a direct consequence of that. I was aware that you were acquainted with Pauli, of course." She had the decency to stop there, with no reference to Radigan's Hotel.

"I really did care for him, Mrs. Crown. I still do. Do you know his whereabouts?"

"Regrettably, I don't. I had a telephone message from him several months ago. I believe he was in Chicago at the time. Of course"—she paused as if reluctant to complete the thought—"there is always the possibility that he has returned to Germany."

"Oh, no, he wouldn't, not when the two of us felt so strongly about one another." Julie bowed her head. "He wouldn't."

"My dear, I didn't mean to upset you." Ilsa Crown reached across the table to clasp Julie's hand. "Juliette, I think I failed to realize the depth of your feeling. Pauli was—is—a wonderful boy. I am so sorry I don't know where he is."

"I wonder why he's left no messages for me. He'd know how to get in touch if he wanted to." Julie's chin came up. She managed an air of brittle cheer. "Well, at least we have settled that question, haven't we? Paul's gone. And he didn't say where I might find him. Nothing to be done, is there?"

NELL took her daughter aside the following Monday, into the mansion's music room. Julie sat at the grand piano, idly picking out a scale. Nell paced back and forth, mysteriously cheerful and excited.

"Your father said it's time to break the news."

"What news, Mama?"

"There is a gentleman who wishes to call on you, Juliette. A gentleman with serious intentions."

Julie's head snapped up, her eyes huge. "Who is it?"

"A widower. You've met him, although perhaps you don't recall him well. His name is William Vann Elstree."

"The department store family?"

"Yes. His wife passed away over a year ago, in the heat wave."

Feelings of terror and confusion churned through Julie. "Mama, I don't wish to quarrel with you, but—"

"Juliette, we simply can't go through this again. I'll not tolerate it. If you aren't yourself, perhaps we need to consult Dr. Woodrow—"

"No, Mama, *no!*"

"Then do be more rational, dear. What I want most in the world is to see you wed to the right kind of man. I want that before I go to heaven."

Julie cried; she couldn't stop crying. But Paul was *gone,* what did it matter? "All right, Mama. *All right.* Mr. Elstree may call."

Nell patted her hand, then left the room. She was smiling.

PAUL ✦ That autumn an emergency took Nancy Logan from the laundry. At harvest-time Nancy's mother had fallen and broken a hip. "Ma will be laid up for months. Somebody's got to cook for the men." Paul carried Nancy's grip to the Dearborn Street station.

"I don't mind leaving the laundry," she admitted. "Or Chicago. It's a hard town. I'll miss you, though." A few tears came. "I'd do anything for you, Dutch. If you ever need help, come find me."

AT LEAST twice a week Paul walked by the Vanderhoff mansion in the chilly autumn twilight. He saw no sign of Julie and assumed she was still abroad. He continued to daydream of a job with Colonel Sid Shadow while continuing to practice still photography.

In October, Wex sheepishly asked Paul for a loan. Paul assumed it was for the back rent. He brought the money home from the savings bank without a question. The second time Wex asked, saying yes reduced Paul's small account to zero.

A collector came around on the first of November; Paul heard loud voices behind a closed door. The collector stormed out. A day later, in a trash box, Paul found some slips with odd names penciled on them. Wex wasn't paying rent, he was placing bets.

So the disease that afflicted Wex hadn't abated. It saddened Paul.

He said nothing. He owed Wex a lot. He trusted him to repay the loans.

One evening, over a typically meager supper in the small back room, Wex said, "Dutch, when did you arrive in this country?"

"On the first day of June, three years ago. Why do you ask?"

"Citizenship. Year after next, you can take the oath."

"Oh, yes. I've already considered it. There are terrible things in America, which I never expected. But there are wonderful things here too. A chance to work in an exciting trade, for one. With that, and an American wife, I'll want to be a citizen."

"Is Vanderhoff's daughter home yet?"

"I don't think so. I have passed by the house a few times without seeing her. I haven't telephoned or written letters. I don't want to embarrass her. I also don't want to visit the county jail again. I'll get in touch, don't worry."

WEXFORD Rooney the photographer was not entirely unknown to the city's better element. He had a reputation as a good journeyman. So when a society photographer was suddenly taken ill, he was asked to photograph a Saturday afternoon reception being given by Mr. and Mrs. Potter Palmer.

Wex was in a transport of excitement. He nicked his face three times shaving. He was ironing a shirt as Paul left for work. But when Wex came home at dusk, his attitude was quite different. He seemed glum, nervous. Paul was sitting at the table with a bottle of Crown lager. He was puzzled when Wex didn't speak, only nodded, and then began to putter at the stove with his back turned.

"How did it go?"

"Oh, fine, fine," Wex said, still facing away.

"Did the guests treat you well?"

"Oh, yes, they were very kind. Very posh crowd."

"Mr. Rooney, something went wrong. What is it?"

Wex turned then and removed his spectacles, looking sad. "I saw someone you know. The young lady."

Paul jumped up. "Julie? She's back?"

"She returned in late summer. I asked, to be certain."

"Tell me how she looked."

"Oh—beautiful. Very beautiful, just as you said." A silence, then an anguished look. "She had an escort."

305

Paul lowered the beer bottle to the table. "I don't believe it."

"I'm sorry, it's true. She came with William Elstree, the department store heir." He sniffed. "I made a few discreet inquiries, Dutch. I wish I hadn't."

"Tell me the rest. You must."

"The young lady's being seen with Elstree at concerts and levees more or less regularly."

"Oh, no. What happened? *What happened?*"

"I don't know. I didn't want to tell you. Wouldn't hurt you for anything. But it struck me that you had to know. Maybe—maybe you should stop thinking about her. It looks like the young lady has sailed off on some new course."

Paul had never felt such pain, not even when his own family turned him out.

Wex went to bed at midnight. Paul sat under the kitchen light drinking beer. Trying to solve the riddle.

What had caused her to change? Had she lied to him all along? Tricked him? How could that be, after all their declarations of love? How could it be?

He telephoned the Vanderhoff mansion next morning. He asked for Miss Vanderhoff. "Who is calling, please?" He gave his name. "She is not here." He asked to leave a message. "Sorry, that is not possible." The servants had been rehearsed. The wall was up.

THE November rain was cold, falling hard as Paul struggled to lay a waterproof cover on the laundry hamper. Wind whipped his scarf back and forth across his face. The delivery wagon was tied near the service entrance of a small hotel. Someone in a cap came rushing around the corner, head down against the rain. He bowled into Paul. Handbills flew.

Paul dived to retrieve some from under the wagon.

"Never mind, nobody wants any today."

It was a mournful statement that made Paul look up. He recognized the hangdog face under a dripping cap. "Hello, remember me? We met at the racetrack."

"Yes." Lew Kress stuffed wet, bedraggled handbills in the pockets of his wool coat.

Paul said, "A poor day to advertise."

"Isn't it. I hate this job. I hate this town. I should go home."

Paul focused instantly on what Lew Kress had just said. "Home, where is that?"

"Little town in South Carolina. Branchville."

"Why don't you go?"

"I'll tell you why. I can't afford a train ticket."

"And it's only the rail fare that keeps you in Chicago? What is the amount?"

"Eleven dollars and fifty cents. More than I'll ever be able to save. Look, I'm soaked and frozen. I'm going."

Paul grabbed his arm. "I'll get it—the money for your ticket. It will take a while, but as soon as I have it, I will find you at the Luxoscope Parlor." Paul drew a breath. "I want your job."

"This job? You're crazy. Shadow can be a slave driver. And that Jim, he has a mean streak. I'd never turn my back on him."

"Even so, I want the job. I want to learn about the living pictures. I will pay your way to South Carolina."

Skepticism gave way to a kind of joyous babble. "You're a real gentleman, you are. Straight talker too. All right, it's a bargain." They shook hands right there in the downpour. "You come round as soon as you've got the money, hear? Can't be too soon to suit me."

Kress waved as he rushed off. For the first time in weeks Paul forgot the terrible sense of defeat caused by the news about Julie. He laughed and did a little capering step on the sidewalk.

THAT night, shivering in the loft, he couldn't sleep. His thoughts fixed on his financial predicament. He had loaned all his money to Wex. What could he do about that ticket?

In the weeks that followed, he found no ready answer to the question. Then on Monday night before Christmas, he returned home from the laundry as usual and found an open wagon parked in front of the Temple. Two draymen were carrying out furniture and equipment and loading it into the wagon.

It was a cold, sparkling night of stars and wind. Wex stood in the street bareheaded, hands in his pockets. Paul hurried to him. "Wex, what's going on here?"

Wex wouldn't look at him. "Eviction. My things are going into storage. The locks will be changed tomorrow."

"But why?"

"Because the rent is four months in arrears. The landlord told

307

me he had a new tenant. Tore up my lease right in front of me."

Paul was fuming. "I thought there was enough money for the rent. I loaned you all I had."

Wex seemed to shrivel inside his coat. "I paid two months. But I owed for six. I hoped for a quick stroke of luck. I wagered the rest, by telegraph, at various tracks down south. I lost everything."

"All of my savings?"

"Yes, I regret to say."

"How could you do that?"

Wexford Rooney wheeled on him. "Do you think I like this? That it makes me proud? I'm a weak man, Dutch."

For a moment Paul wanted to hit Wex Rooney. Then he saw how old, small, defeated he was, facing the winter with all his goods piled up in the overloaded wagon.

The drayman in charge adjusted his earmuffs and gloves. "No more this trip. We'll be back in the morning." They drove off.

"So tomorrow we are thrown into the street," Paul said.

"Dutch, I'm sorry. I'm sorry this happened. At the end of the week I will be leaving town. I am forced to take a position in Charleston, West Virginia. I applied for it through a classified several weeks ago, when I saw the end coming. I'm going to a large photographic studio as a general helper and artist in charge of color tinting. Look, I won't starve. Neither will you," Wex said, with a glimmer of his old pixie smile. "It's time you moved on anyway. Perhaps Shadow will take you on."

Standing in the bitter air, gazing at the Temple's dark façade, Paul realized how much the place meant to him. How much this weak, strange, idealistic, impractical old man meant to him.

"Is there any food inside?" he asked.

"Nothing."

"Well, come on, I still have thirty cents. We can have supper."

Wex fell in step like an obedient child.

THE Baltimore and Ohio conductor cupped his hands around his mouth. *"Boooard!"*

"The studio address in Charleston," Wex said. He put a scrap of paper in Paul's hand. "You forgive me?"

"For what? We're friends. I can never repay you for all you've done."

"Oh, Paul." Wex flung himself on Paul, and they embraced. "I'd be proud to have a son like you. Proud." Hugging the old man, Paul managed to tuck five dollars into his pocket, money he'd begged as a salary advance from Mr. Grace's payroll clerk.

Steam hissed. The bell rang. "I'll write to you when I know where I'm staying," Paul promised.

Wex jumped to the train step. "I'll write you too. Good-bye."

The train swayed off into the winter night. Falling snow melted on Paul's face. He had felt alone like this on the pier at Hamburg. He had felt like this an hour after Uncle Joe cast him out. He trudged off, carrying his small valise of clothes and mementos.

He was too proud to tell one of the madams he had no place to go. He prowled the alleys, found a discarded wooden packing case with one end broken open. He crawled in and slept there.

In his dreams the baker of Wuppertal appeared. Vindicated, he was laughing at Paul and his misery and stupidity.

Paul awoke nearly frozen. The steam laundry opened at five, so he sneaked in and cleaned up in the men's room.

The next few nights he slept in the packing case. At the end of the week he settled up with Mr. Grace's pay clerk for the advance and gave notice.

He stored his valise with his friend Madame Camille. At midnight he jumped aboard a freight rattling south to Indiana.

He jumped off at Greencastle. A sleepy depot agent gave him directions. He walked all the miles to Reelsville.

Winter had folded and frozen the land into solid waves of mud, with a dusting of snow in the troughs. His stumbling feet snapped off dead cornstalks as he crossed the fields. He wanted to lie down. But he went on.

Pigs squealed and ran as he entered the dooryard. He fell against weathered siding, rested a moment, then stumbled along the side of the house.

Lamplight shone behind a bleached gingham curtain in the window of the back door. Paul knocked on the glass.

The door opened. Her voice, bewildered, rolled over him like a blessing. "Dutch, what are you doing here?"

He could barely focus his eyes. "Nancy, you said once you'd help me if I needed it. I need help now. I need eleven dollars and fifty cents exactly."

309

ROSIE ✦ Rosie went to New York in the spring of 1895. She made her way to Stitch Meyer's Alhambra, at Sixth and Twenty-ninth.

The Alhambra Dance Hall was a two-story building with an *Arabian Nights* look outside and inside. Stitch Meyer saw her in his office. Meyer was a short, tough red-haired man who wore the neat, conservative clothes of a banker.

"You're a pretty girl," he said. "I can always use a pretty girl as a waitress. Good eats. There's a dance floor, of course, and three shows a night. Basically this is a meeting place. Respectable gents come here for a little relaxation. A little pleasure. They come to meet attractive young ladies. What goes on after a gent meets a young lady ain't my affair. The Alhambra's a respectable place." He leaned back. "How does that sound?"

"It sounds okay, Mr. Meyer. I'll be straight with you. What I really want in New York is to be a singer."

"Well, I don't hire no waitresses to double as singers. Maybe we'll try you out in the show sometime, but not until you been here awhile. Fair?"

"Fair."

STITCH Meyer's Alhambra was warmly lit, cheerfully noisy, usually crowded because of its reputation as a safe place. Rosie found her employment there profitable and congenial. She wished Joey Crown could see her in her red dress. Wouldn't he think she was something, her hair neatly pinned up, her face rouged, her bare arms and cleavage perfumed? Wouldn't he think she was really coming up in the world?

One Wednesday night, at half past eleven, Rosie heard a commotion at the front door. Serving a crowded table, she craned to see what it was all about.

Stitch Meyer was effusively greeting a new arrival. A tall, pink-faced fat man. He wore a beautiful gray overcoat with a black fur collar and carried a shimmering black topper under his arm. He seemed to be recognized by quite a few patrons, whom he hailed in a deep, booming voice.

Meyer personally escorted the man to a choice table. Professor Spark, the bandleader, rushed to shake his hand. Then Meyer leaped to the stage. "Ladies and gentlemen, the Alhambra is honored tonight by the presence of its favorite guest, America's musical man of the moment—the nonpareil composer and showman—Mr. Paul Dresser. Paul, take a bow."

The genial fat man heaved to his feet and waved. A pinkie diamond flashed on one hand. His suit, his red satin vest and satin cravat with sapphire stickpin were as fine as his overcoat. Rosie's heart raced at the sight of such elegance. But the man's name meant nothing. She said as much to the barkeep when she handed him her order slip.

"Aw, come on. Paul Dresser? He wrote the biggest song hit of the year, 'Just Tell Them That You Saw Me.' Half a million copies of the sheet music and still selling."

"Sure, I know that one." It was a tearful ballad about a young woman who'd wrecked her life on the rocks of passion.

The barkeep shoved the tray of drinks at her. "If ever there was a man could help you get what you want, it's Broadway Paul."

As Rosie rushed to serve her customers she could hardly keep her eyes off the songwriter, whom she guessed to be around forty.

"Say, Paul, play us something," a customer called. People applauded, whistled. Professor Spark, at his upright piano, gestured to the stool he'd just vacated. Dresser stood up and moved through well-wishers at the front tables. Money, talent—what could she do to attract his notice?

Rosie was in the shadows where a balcony projected above the bar. Grabbing one of the balcony posts for courage, she called out, "Play us your hit, Mr. Dresser."

Dresser put his hand above his eyes. "Who said that?"

Rosie stepped out of the shadows. "I did, Mr. Dresser."

Over the heads of the crowd he looked her up and down. He broke into a huge smile and bowed from the waist. "I must always honor the request of a pretty young lady."

He sat at the piano, shot his cuffs, and began to play and sing.

> " 'Just tell them that you saw me,'
> She said—'They'll know the rest.
> Just tell them I was looking well, you know.' "

In a not unpleasing voice he sang it all the way through to the end, looking not at the piano keys or the rapt listeners, but at Rosie.

AT HALF PAST TWELVE, WITH HER cheap cloth coat over her arm, Rosie hurried down the hall, her legs trembling. Earlier Dresser had slipped her a note asking her to stop at his table. When she did, he said she was free to leave the Alhambra two hours before closing; he'd "squared things" with Stitch Meyer.

Now Dresser was waiting by the main entrance. He held her coat for her, set his silk topper on his head, and gallantly offered his arm.

They spent the night in Dresser's suite at the Gilsey House, a swank hotel on upper Broadway. Rosie had never seen fancier rooms.

Next day she removed her things from the tenement where she had been living and hailed a cab to take her to the Gilsey House. Dresser had given her money, a whole tenner—just a little gift, he said, to a charming person who had for the moment won his heart.

PAUL ✦ Paul went to see Shadow on December 28, less than twenty-four hours after Lew Kress left town.

Jimmy Daws was on duty in the peep show parlor. Paul asked for the colonel.

"Upstairs." Surly as ever.

Paul found R. Sidney Shadow III in a small windowless office barely large enough for two chairs and a desk.

"Colonel, I am sorry to interrupt your work—"

"Don't apologize, kid. What can I do for you?"

"Since it is almost the end of the year, I thought I would ask once more about a position."

"Are you a mind reader? One of my boys blew out of town yesterday. So you want to learn the living picture business."

"More than anything, sir."

Shadow outlined his duties. Paul would make four dollars a week plus room and board. "And we don't punch clocks around here."

Paul blinked, swallowed, and said, "Fine."

"Then that's it. Welcome." They shook hands. Paul was elated. "Jimmy'll show you where you bunk. Glad you're with us, Dutch."

An hour later Paul was back with his valise. Jimmy led him upstairs to a door that opened off the landing.

"This here's yours."

Paul tossed his valise on an iron bed jammed between narrow unpapered walls of lath. There was perhaps two feet between the

end of the bed and the wall. A light bulb with a paper shade hung from the ceiling. He might have been back on Müllerstrasse.

Jimmy was leaning against the doorjamb, arms crossed. "Come on, I'll show you my room." Paul followed him across the landing to a large room with windows. "This is mine. When I came to work here, it belonged to Kress, but I took it away from him."

Paul knew that if he accepted this arrangement, Daws would have him whipped. "You live here, and I live in a closet?"

"That's it, yeah."

"I don't think so."

Paul walked out, returned with his valise, dropped it on the floor. "I'll take half this room." Jimmy looked stupefied, then enraged. Paul spread his feet, braced for a rush. "I'll move the other bed in over there. Each of us will have plenty of space."

"What happens if I say no, Dutchie?"

"Then we will settle the question some other way." He curled his fingers into fists and waited. He had turned eighteen in June but looked older. There was a toughness about him.

Jimmy took a while deciding what it all meant. Finally he smiled. "All right, Dutchie. You helped me out once. I guess I'll give you a break. But remember, around here, I'm the number one boy. You stay out of my way, we'll get along fine."

Paul tipped his cap. "*Danke schön.* And you stay out of mine."

SHADOW'S peep show arcade was considerably less elegant than the Edison parlor up on State Street. Also, Shadow's subjects were considerably more racy. There was *Pass the Bottle!*—a rowdy saloon scene in which a man gulped a bottle of beer. And *Whee Paree!* featuring high-kick dances badly performed by Levee whores.

Signs of haste were evident in all the scenes. But the lighting and composition struck Paul as excellent, and the simple magic of motion was enough to entrance him, whatever the flaws.

On New Year's Eve, Shadow closed the parlor at six o'clock. Mary Beezer had left for Indiana; her mother was ailing down in Richmond, where Mary grew up.

"I gave Jimmy the night off. You going out?"

"I don't think so, Colonel."

"Come upstairs. We'll have a cup of cheer to celebrate." Paul smiled and followed his employer.

In the kitchen, Shadow opened a cupboard, pulled down a whiskey bottle and two large tumblers, and poured a glass for each of them. He pulled his chair out with the toe of his tooled boot, then sat down and drank half his whiskey.

Paul took a sip. Shadow waved him to a chair. "Wait here."

The colonel went into his small, cluttered office and returned with a smudged schematic pencil drawing of a rectangular machine filled with gears, roller hubs, parallel lines of arrows following a convoluted track. "This is the box. Shadow's Luxograph projector. Know why I'm so crazy to make this work?"

"Why?"

"Because I love shows. Any kind. Jugglers tossing Indian clubs. A line of blondes high-kicking in a variety hall. Shows!" He banged the table. "How about a President of the U.S. of A., standing up to swear his oath? A show! The whole world's an extravaganza, and I'm the man to bring it home and show it to every poor bastard who'll never see it for himself." Shadow sat down. "Another drink?"

Paul shook his head. He was mesmerized.

"I'm serious, Dutch. The flickers can fill halls as big as the Chicago Auditorium. And my camera can go anywhere. I'm going to film disasters, elections, coronations. I'll tell you something else I'll film, Dutch. War. Yes, sir, the bloody fields—the courage and the carnage! Right up front, where the bullets buzz."

Despite the ranting that reminded him of the Russian journalist, Rhukov, Paul was excited. How often he'd touched places on the wooden globe old Frau Flüsser gave him in Berlin. Touched them, yearned to see them, knowing he probably never could. Here was the way.

Shadow poured another glass. "I have a feeling for audiences, kid, and I'm going to make flickers for the masses, not the classes. Bring on those wars!" He leaped up, making Paul gasp. "We're coming to get you, world! With the greatest invention of modern man!"

Paul burst out laughing. The man was incredible. He was greedy and foulmouthed, but he had a vision. A magnificent vision Paul could see, understand, embrace, because it spoke to everything he'd ever longed for. Creating pictures. Seeing the world. Fitting into life. Knowing your purpose, your place. *Belonging.*

Somewhere in the streets a brass band struck up "Auld Lang Syne." Paul threw his arms over his head in silent joy. Seeing the vision.

PAUL LAY AWAKE LONG PAST midnight. It was more than three years since he'd come to Chicago. So much had happened. Uncle Joe and Aunt Ilsa, cousin Joe, the brewery bombing, and Benno's death. Most of all Julie, whom he couldn't, wouldn't surrender now that the whole world was opening to him.

He knew she still loved him. Being seen in society with a rich man must be something her parents forced on her.

Come spring, when he was on his feet, he'd find a way to declare his love again. Take her back, make her his forever.

ROSIE ✦ Paul Dresser was besotted with her. He moved her into the Gilsey House and bought her new clothes. He really was a king on Broadway, and he showed her the important theaters: Koster and Bial's Music Hall; the fabled Tony Pastor's, on Fourteenth Street; Miner's New Theater, on the Bowery.

Paul was always busy, because sheet music was a growing business and he was a silent partner in the music firm of Howley, Haviland. It was located on West Twentieth near Broadway, a couple of blocks south of a stretch called Tin Pan Alley. Paul wrote songs for the firm, hunted for new composers, charmed variety hall artists into performing new H&H songs, hired song pluggers to sell their sheet music. At the moment Paul was working on a number that began, *"Oh, the moonlight's fair tonight along the Wabash."*

About this and almost everything else in his life, Paul was ingenuously candid with Rosie. Yes, he chased women, probably would never stop. This signaled Rosie that her time as his lover wouldn't last forever, though maybe friendship would. And he would be a powerful friend to have.

Paul organized a debut for Rosie at Miner's. She sang "Daisy Bell" and "Just Tell Them That You Saw Me." Paul wrote the piano arrangements, suiting them to her limited vocal range.

Rosie trembled her way through the two numbers. But she drew sustained and enthusiastic applause. The response was a tribute to her looks, not her singing voice.

PAUL ✦ Paul came to the flickers, the living pictures, at a time of creative explosion. Peep show machines were losing their novelty. In New York, Philadelphia, Paris, London, inventors and promoters rushed to perfect a projection system for living pictures. One was announced almost weekly—the Kineopticon, the animatograph, the Biograph.

Down in the cellar, Colonel Shadow was slaving away on his projector. Things weren't going well.

"I'm not going to lose out," he said one night when Mary was preparing stew in the flat for all four of them.

The colonel looked terrible, Paul thought—haggard from worry. He'd been in the cellar workshop all day.

In Paris, in December, two brothers named Lumière had unveiled their cinematograph projection system to an invited audience of one hundred.

"Damn those bozos," Shadow said. "They showed the pictures at a place called the Grand Café. The first crowd got in free. After that they sold tickets—one franc to see the whole show. The first day they took in thirty-three francs. The next day they took in over two thousand! It's been that way ever since. They're beating me to market!" He held his head with both hands, uttering a string of harrowing oaths.

Mary dished out the stew. Shadow ate his meal in record time and departed for the cellar in a rush.

PAUL roamed the city, passing out handbills, or sat at the register and kept an eye on the workingmen, the floaters, the occasional harlots who constituted the parlor's trade. If business was slow, he studied technical journals Shadow had discarded.

At the end of his first month with Shadow, he addressed an envelope to Nancy and put a dollar in it. He sent a dollar every two weeks thereafter.

One night when Jimmy was watching the parlor, Paul asked Shadow if he might see the cellar workshop. The colonel reacted like a child asked to open his toy box. "Sure, come on."

The workshop smelled of oily rags, sawdust, mold. Paul felt as though he were a visitor in the cave of some great wizard.

In one corner, fixed to a tripod obviously homemade, there was a rectangular wooden box with a hand crank and a hole for a lens. "This is it, Dutch. The Luxograph. Means writing with light."

He picked up a smaller box from the worktable. "This is the magazine. Lightproof. Holds fifty feet of Eastman celluloid negative." He opened one side of the camera and fitted the smaller box behind the lens. He closed the camera, rotated the crank. "Now tell me, do you really understand the principle of this thing?"

"I believe so." Paul drew a breath. He must speak carefully, make no mistakes. "Film in the camera moves to the lens, and away from it, one frame at a time. At the lens a frame is exposed like a snapshot. The film is standing still then. While the film moves to allow the next exposure, light must be kept out. This is the purpose of the shutter mechanism. The same idea applies when the film is shown. Still pictures are flashed one at a time. But the frames go by so fast, the eye is tricked. It sees continuous movement."

"Dutch, that's not half bad." A grin spread over Shadow's pale face. Paul had passed the examination. "You know, kid, the great Mr. Edison's fooled around with living pictures for eight or ten years. Now he's working on a camera. From what I hear, his camera isn't practical. It's driven by a battery-powered electric motor. Too complicated, too costly—most of all, too heavy. Pick up the Luxograph."

Carefully Paul folded the tripod, lifted it, and rested it on his shoulder. "Light."

"Well—forty-eight pounds isn't what I call light. But at forty-eight pounds the Luxograph can go anywhere."

The companion to the camera was the crank-operated Luxograph projector, also unfinished. Inside was a complex arrangement of rollers, gears, and sprockets that moved the perforated film through a metal gate behind the projection lens. Shadow was proudest of a glass cell he'd designed that fitted in the space between the arc light and the film gate. "Film's flammable as hell. Water in the cell damps down some of the arc-light heat. There may be some picture distortion, but not enough so people would ask for their money back. I hope. That camera is all I need to start supplying pictures. But I'll have to build a projector for every location that might show 'em."

"What sort of locations would they be?" Paul asked.

"Variety theaters. I could also have my own places. But that's down the road a ways. I haven't got so much as one good picture for demonstrating the projector when it's ready—not good enough for a variety bill. They'd want ten, maybe fifteen minutes."

"Could I help you make more? I noticed that the roof of this building is very large. Maybe we could film a little picture there."

Shadow gave Paul a long look. "You're right. If you get any ideas, jot 'em down. I'm glad I took you on, kid. You've got plenty of drive. I think you've got the makings of a picture man."

On a bright, windy morning in March, 1896, the Luxograph Company created its one-minute extravaganza, *Her Burglar*. Paul had composed a short scenario, which Shadow had edited and rewritten.

On the sunlit roof, Colonel Shadow crouched behind the Luxograph camera. Mary sat on a stool holding an open book. Behind her, tacked to a frame, was a large canvas square that Jimmy had painted to resemble bricks.

"Here we go, Mary, start reading," Shadow called, beginning to crank. "Burglar!"

Jimmy stole into the scene wearing a mask Mary had fashioned for him by cutting holes in a navy-blue bandanna. He crouched behind Mary, menacing her with upraised hands. Mary heard something, jumped up, terrified, and threw her book away.

"Keep it up!" Shadow shouted, cranking. "Burglar, grab her." Jimmy seized Mary's wrists with more force than was necessary.

"Policeman!" Paul rushed into the scene, wearing one of Mary's wide belts and a toy star and brandishing an old rusting revolver. He collared the villain. Jimmy raised his hands, scowling.

Mary batted her eyes, threw her arms around Paul's neck, kissed his cheek. Paul postured in a heroic manner, then snagged the burglar by the collar to lead him away.

"All right, stop. Good job, everybody."

That night, in the upstairs sitting room, Mary hung up a bed sheet while Paul and Jimmy wrestled the Luxograph projector from the cellar. With the arc light blazing, Shadow cranked, and there upon the sheet, the images only slightly warped by the water cell, *Her Burglar* sprang magically to life.

Late in March the colonel rushed to New York on an overnight train. Another new competitor, American Vitagraph, was presenting its first program at Tony Pastor's.

"They showed twenty minutes' worth," Shadow reported glumly

after he dragged back to Chicago. "Waves on the shore of Long Island. Broadway cable cars. Fire engines. In the last fifty feet a Lehigh Valley Railroad train called the Black Diamond Express came busting out of some tunnel. Half the people jumped out of their chairs, screaming. It's the real thing they want. Real thrills. The flickers are never going to tell stories and make it pay."

On the evening of April 20, also in New York, at Koster and Bial's Music Hall, the Edison Vitascope System premiered. Miserably, Shadow read about it in a newspaper. *"Sea Waves. Umbrella Dance. Kaiser Wilhelm Reviewing His Troops. A Boxing Bout.* They used *two* projectors—no waiting while the film was changed. That's not all. Four of the flickers were in color! Do you realize what was involved? Every single frame tinted by hand—"

He crushed the paper and threw it under the sink.

"Sid," Mary said, "there's just one answer. You have to get your pictures on a variety bill too."

"I have a fish on the line. Finally. He's coming over Thursday. We'll show him *Her Burglar.*"

To the Levee came Mr. Ishmael Pflaum, owner-manager of Pflaum's Music Hall, on South State. Iz Pflaum was a huge Saint Nicholas figure with a white fan beard.

He plumped himself into the best chair in the sitting room, in front of the hanging bed sheet. Mary nervously placed a beer and some hot wursts at his elbow and switched off the light. Shadow cranked the Luxograph. There was Mary, reading. Jimmy crept into the scene. Pflaum's hand carried a wurst to his mouth every few seconds. But he never took his eyes from the sheet.

"Sid," Mr. Pflaum said at the end, "I'll take it. The machine."

"You'll— Why, Iz, that's swell, but this projector is the prototype. Not for sale."

"Then build another one. You furnish ten minutes of flickers, I'll show 'em as chasers."

"As what?"

"That's what they call 'em at Koster and Bial's, chasers. At the end of the bill, after the midgets, the magician, and the chorus girlies, you chase the audience out with pictures. That's all they're good for, clearing the house."

Paul wanted to argue that. It wasn't his place. He decided Iz Pflaum was a greedy, ignorant man of no imagination.

Pflaum lumbered to the door. "One more thing. That little story was nice, but I want real-life subjects. Only."

"I'll have our camera operator start filming immediately, Iz."

"You got a regular operator to take the pictures?"

"Of course I do. Right here." Shadow put his arm around Paul. "Mr. Crown is young, Iz, but he's highly talented."

Mr. Pflaum grasped Paul's hand and wrung it. "Very good, happy to know it. I didn't realize you were this far along, Sid."

Thus, on that evening, fate, in the person of Ishmael Pflaum, decided forever the direction of the Chicago Luxograph Company, and Paul's life.

TWENTY miles southwest of Chicago, they set up the camera between the rail ties. The precious Luxograph sat in the middle of the right-of-way belonging to the Wabash, St. Louis and Pacific.

Paul was extremely tense. Storm wind out of the blackening northwest bent waist-high cornstalks in the fields on either side of the track. Mary was in the wagon, waiting. A stutter of thunder made the two wagon horses prance; she had trouble controlling them from the driving seat.

Shadow paced up and down the track, his shoulders hunched. He snatched his watch out of his pocket and nearly dropped it. "Four minutes. The Cannonball's never late."

Everyone wanted sensational locomotive footage on their flicker programs, including Iz Pflaum.

"He's waving! He's waving!" Shadow exclaimed.

About a half mile to the north, standing on a trackside storage box, Jimmy Daws was signaling with his hat. Paul chewed his lip. A streak of lightning forked; the storm was close.

Over the top of the camera Paul spied a dot of white light. It rapidly grew larger. Shadow said, "Remember, crank steadily. I'll hang on to the tripod. Just don't lose your nerve."

Paul felt the ground vibrate. Faintly at first, then more and more strongly. The headlight glared as the iron locomotive hurtled toward them.

Fat drops of rain began to splash Paul's face. But he was oblivious of the storm. There was only the train, and the task. . . .

"Start cranking," Shadow screamed.

Paul cranked, counting one-two, one-two, timing his cranks two

321

per second. The earth shook. The headlight grew big as the sun.

"Keep cranking, keep cranking. Sensational! Spectacular!"

The whistle screamed. Lightning flared. Thunder exploded.

He kept cranking. *One-two, one-two.*

"Sid, you're gonna be killed." Mary's hysterical voice was faint in the roar of the train. The Cannonball grew taller and wider, coming on like a prairie cyclone. Paul thought of Julie, of all the things he'd left undone in his young life. *One-two, one-two.*

"Now!" Shadow screamed, and jerked the tripod.

Paul jumped to the left without looking. A great roaring suction of air tore at his shirt. He fell into the cornfield gasping.

The Cannonball passed.

Shadow stayed on his feet with the camera and tripod on his shoulder, just beside the track. "We got it. I think we got it!" He was nearly as hysterical as Mary.

The freight and passenger cars shuttled by. Paul scrambled to his feet, drenched by sudden heavy rain. His trembling lessened. He'd stood fast. He'd gotten the picture.

"Here, cover up. I've got a hat," Shadow said, handing Paul a folded newspaper from his coat pocket. Paul unfolded the paper and started to lay it over his head. He noticed a headline.

MISS VANDERHOFF ENGAGED

TO WED PROMINENT CLUBMAN W. V. ELSTREE III

August Wedding Date Announced

Part Seven
FLICKERS
1896–1898

JOE CROWN ✦ "What are you reading, Joe?"

He twisted onto his left shoulder to let the glow of the bedside lamp fall on the book's gold-stamped spine.

Ilsa said, *"The Red Badge of Courage?* You've read that before."

"Twice. It's a powerful book." Joe felt testy. The damp, windless night made the house an oven. The summer had arrived early; it was only June.

"Mr. Crane has never been to war, isn't that right?" Ilsa said.

"But you might believe so. He has imagination. If we've finished the conversation, Ilsa, may I continue to read?"

She wiped her forehead with a handkerchief; the movement of her hand hid the hurt on her face. He saw it anyway.

"Yes, Joe, certainly. I wouldn't disturb you for the world. Good night." She turned away from him.

He read for another hour. Young Crane's powerful tale called to something in his blood. For all of war's dirt and travail, which Crane compellingly captured, a war gave a man an enemy he could attack and defeat according to definite rules. Joe Crown had no such enemy. But he devoutly wished for one.

In this year of 1896 America was demonstrating her new status in the world by asserting her power in the Western Hemisphere. Late in December of the preceding year she'd faced down the mighty British Empire. Great Britain had sent three warships to blockade a port in Nicaragua in response to a quarrel over some debt Britain claimed she was owed. Washington accused Britain of violating the Monroe Doctrine. Congress threatened mobilization. The mighty British Empire backed down almost at once. This left America's jingo element without a cause.

Then, fortuitously, there came on the scene General Valeriano Weyler y Nicolau, Spain's newly appointed governor-general of Cuba, charged with putting an end to outbreaks of rebellion in the backcountry.

General Weyler's first tactic was institution of the policy of *reconcentrado*—the relocation of people from rural provinces to detention camps far from their homes. These were the farmers who had sheltered roving bands of freedom fighters—rebels who attacked forts and destroyed government property, then vanished back into the villages.

Weyler said he was moving the people to cottages with ample food and adequate sanitation. The dispatches of foreign journalists told a darker story. Weyler was crowding hundreds, thousands, into ill-lit warehouses infested with rats and vermin. With no sanitation and little or no food. Children began to starve and die. Adults who protested began to disappear.

A new name appeared in news stories out of Havana. Butcher Weyler. In New York, to fuel their hot circulation war, Mr. W. R.

Hearst of the *Journal* and Mr. Joseph Pulitzer of the *World* capitalized on the plight of the Cubans. The columns of both papers overflowed with titillating dispatches about Weyler's outrages.

Joe Crown joined the protest against Spain and Butcher Weyler. At a rally of four thousand people in Central Music Hall, Joe sat with hundreds of fellow veterans as a band played martial airs by John Philip Sousa and speakers threatened war in retaliation for Spanish atrocities. Joe was thrilled. Here was a new cause.

He recognized that the national fervor for *Cuba libre* wasn't entirely idealistic. American investors had sunk millions of dollars in railroads and sugar mills on the island. Still, did it matter that commercial interests were tied up with the new patriotism? That America went to war for sugar and tobacco? The Cubans were downtrodden, Spain was in the wrong, Weyler was a beast.

OUTWARDLY Joe Crown's life had an appearance of calm. The brewery was prospering. A new brewmaster, Samuel Ziegler, was proving highly satisfactory. The children were no more fractious than usual. Fritzi, fifteen, was doing well in her studies, although she continued to make frequent and annoying references to her coming career as a stage actress. Carl was growing taller, broader in the shoulders—a powerful boy who was good at sports.

Joe Junior, fortunately, was no longer a subject of bitter contention between Joe and Ilsa. The wheat stalks in the envelope had convinced her that her boy was safe and well.

PAUL ✦ August 29, Saturday. Fifteen minutes past noon. Paul was standing across from St. James Church.

Newspapers had printed the date and the time of the ceremony—half after eleven—weeks ago. Paul had wanted to stay away. Ultimately he couldn't. The yearning to see her was too strong.

The church doors were open to catch any breeze. Both bride and groom must have entered by a side door; he never saw them until the service ended and the triumphant music from *Lohengrin* burst forth. Then the bridal couple came out and dashed down the steps.

Julie wore a shimmering white gown. Her face was a blur amid bobbing heads, waving arms, flying rice. Paul saw the girl he loved as no more than a snapshot image, gone almost the instant he spied her. She ducked into a large carriage parked at the foot of the steps.

Paul stuck his hands in his pockets and walked away. He headed south. toward the Levee, filled with bitterness, despair.

Still, he had the prospect of a good career; he would go on. Life might play tricks, but it demanded that you endure them. If your dreams turned to dross, if your family banished you, if you lost the person you loved and all hope of finding your heart's true resting-place . . . you went on.

But Lord, it hurt.

ELSTREE ✦ The private railroad car was attached to a crack overnight express of the New York Central. It hurtled east in the late summer dark, toward the newest summer gathering place of the haut monde—Southampton Village, on the south shore of Long Island. Elstree looked forward to spending his honeymoon at the family's estate on the ocean.

He smoked a cigar while he sat at the dining table in the open area at the rear of the car. He could see his reflection in the panels of highly buffed rosewood that lined the car.

Behind him in the galley, Melton was cleaning up the wedding supper. Melton was sixty-two, black; he slept in a bunk adjoining the galley. The forward section of the car consisted of a large bedroom and separate water closet.

Elstree was growing impatient. He finished his cigar, his eye fixed on the rosewood door to the bedroom. Juliette had locked herself in there directly after she finished her slice of white wedding cake. It was assumed she was preparing herself for her husband. Did this take the better part of an hour?

Melton appeared. "Mist' Elstree, sir, will you be requiring anything else tonight?"

"No, Melton, thank you. Splendid dinner."

" 'Preciate that, sir. I'll retire now."

"I don't hear the mutt anymore." Juliette had insisted on bringing along her damned dog, Rudy. He'd yapped all through the meal, locked up in Melton's cubicle.

"No, sir, he's sleepin'. I like havin' him in there with me."

Elstree waved at cigar smoke floating around his head. "Raise one of those windows about an inch, will you? In the morning you may knock with coffee about eight."

"Yes, sir, Mist' Elstree." Melton disappeared.

Elstree adjusted his silk robe over the knees of his pajamas. He fought a yawn. The day had been long and tiring. After the morning ceremony the bride and groom, relatives and guests had returned to the Vanderhoff mansion for the reception. Everyone gorged on oysters, caviar, Camembert, and other delicacies.

The car swayed and clicked over the rails. At last Elstree heard the sound he'd been awaiting. The turn of the key on Juliette's side of the door. Inviting him in.

He wanted to see her black hair unbound, see her slim body bared for his eyes. He rose and, with a motion both rough and urgent, seized the gold door handle and entered.

How lovely she looked, standing by the foot of the double bed in a peach silk robe. "My dear, you're an altogether ravishing bride." He bent to kiss the warm, scented curve of her throat.

She pulled away. "Bill, before we— Bill, there's something I have to confess to you."

"Dear Mrs. Elstree, you look troubled. A guilty secret?"

She turned away. "My mother wanted me to deceive you about something. I mean deceive you here tonight. I don't know how. I never listened when she tried to explain."

A sudden suspicion assailed him. He said, "Continue."

To her credit, she squared her shoulders and looked straight at him with her stunning gray eyes as she spoke. "I've had—a previous experience. I'm not what the romance novels would call—"

"*Unsullied?*" His ferocity stunned her. "*Well?*"

"Yes, that's what I had to confess to you. A man expects certain things in the woman he marries. You've been so gentle and considerate, so decent throughout the courtship, I can't be dishonest about—what you're getting."

Elstree had chosen Juliette Vanderhoff because of her youth, freshness, chaste air. A large part of his reward for the whole tedious courtship, for dancing attendance on her whining mother, was this moment when he would be the one to take her virginity. Which was nonexistent.

"Who was this man?"

"It isn't relevant, Bill." She took a deep breath. "I'm not going to reveal that."

"You understand this alters our whole relationship."

"I should think it alters it for the better. Honesty is always—"

He almost hit her. "*Honesty?* I don't give a damn for honesty. If you're secondhand goods, you're no better than a street whore. I no longer have any reason to treat you with respect. Take off your clothes."

"Bill—please. I thought you'd understand."

"Oh, I do. I understand fully, you gutter bitch. Now will you undress or shall I do it by tearing those things from your back?"

ELSTREE reeled out the door, blood streaking from a wound at his hairline. When he'd tried to have her a second time, she'd cracked him on the forehead with the stool from the dressing table. For a few seconds he was too groggy to fight back. She shoved him to the door and pushed him out.

He stood shivering in the sitting-room area. He was naked, bleeding at the temple; a bruise was already purpling over his right kidney, where she'd kicked him, crying out that she wouldn't be used again the way he used her the first time. He couldn't believe it. Couldn't believe their wedding night had degenerated into a physical struggle, consummated by what amounted to rape.

The train clicked and rattled; the car rocked. He swabbed blood from his face and returned to the rosewood door. "Juliette, I'm your husband. I demand you let me in."

"I don't know what you are. You're not what you led me to believe. You're some kind of wild animal."

He pounded the door with both fists. "Let me in."

"Mist' Elstree?"

He whirled; Melton's head was poking from the galley. "Damn you, Melton, get back in there— No, wait. Where's the dog? Bring me the damn dog." He lurched to the window nearest the bedroom door and wrestled it up. A typhoon of night air blew in.

Trembling, Melton brought Rudy out on his little leash. Elstree grabbed the dog, jammed it under his arm, quickly looped the leash around the dog's body.

"Now go to bed, and don't come out or I'll flay your hide."

Melton retreated, and Elstree ran back to the window. He raised his voice to be heard above the track noise. "Juliette? Are you listening? I've got your stupid little dog here. Speak, Rudy." He gave the Pomeranian a vicious pinch. Rudy yelped.

327

"Now you listen to me. I'm standing by an open window. I'm holding Rudy out the window. If you don't let me in, I'll drop him. I swear, Juliette. I'm going to throw him under the wheels."

The key turned in the lock of the rosewood door.

ROSE ✦ By the late summer of 1896, Rose's intimate relationship with Paul Dresser was over. They had remained good friends, and he'd helped her find a small furnished flat on East Eighteenth Street.

She owed a lot to Paul, including her job on the bill at Tony Pastor's. Paul had spoken personally with Mr. Pastor, "the king of variety," and had helped her prepare two songs for an audition. Now she was Rose French, International Soubrette.

Even at a house as successful as Pastor's, however, Rose's salary wasn't enough to support her as stylishly as she wished. She earned money for the little extras by sharing her favors with those gentlemen in the five-dollar boxes who sought her out afterward. Married men, most of them. Dull and harmless, but smart enough to catch on to her small hints. Most left twenty or thirty dollars in the morning.

She took their money, but only as a gift, an appreciation. She wasn't a whore—and would have fought anyone who said she was— because whores had no chance of attracting the *right* gentleman. One who was rich and well bred, who wanted a pleasant, steady arrangement in New York and was willing to pay for it.

So far that paragon hadn't shown up. She was beginning to feel discouraged. That was her mood as she finished her second performance one warm evening in August.

That night a pleasant surprise was waiting for her in her dressing room—a basket brimming with yellow roses. She found no card. She rushed to the backstage doorkeeper's booth.

"Zachary, when did those flowers arrive?"

"During your turn. A gentleman brought 'em."

"What did he look like?"

"His face wasn't anything special. But he sure had swell clothes. And he was a real polite gent. Well-spoken."

Rose was suddenly excited. Back in her dressing room, she counted the roses. There were twenty-four.

During the next two weeks roses came from her anonymous

admirer every third or fourth night. Always by a delivery boy; he hadn't returned personally since the first time. But Rose was full of anticipation.

No FLOWERS arrived for a time, and Rose became despondent. Whoever he was, he'd given up. Then one Saturday night, coming offstage after the second show, Rose bumped into Zachary, the doorkeeper. He was practically dancing with excitement. "He brung another basket. Jumped out of a cab, rushed it to the door, said to tender his apologies, he'd been detained in Chicago several weeks. 'Tender'—'detained'—did you ever hear such grand speech?"

"Get out of my way," Rose said, already past him.

This time there were three dozen white roses in a big wicker basket. And a card. With a name. W. V. Elstree III.

JOE CROWN ✦ Now Joe was consumed by a single conviction. Bryan had to be defeated. McKinley had to win the election.

Because his wife was in poor health, Governor William McKinley declared he would wage what he called a front-porch campaign. He would speak to partisans only from the porch of his house in Canton, Ohio. Republican operatives scheduled special excursion trains to Canton seven days a week, while party stalwarts stumped for the candidate elsewhere. Joe met one of these roving spokesmen at a reception in Chicago early in September. Mr. Theodore Roosevelt, the police commissioner of New York City.

The evening gave Joe his first close look at Roosevelt. Though he was only thirty-eight, he dominated the roomful of older and richer men. He didn't smile in the conventional way; rather, he clenched his jaws and opened his mouth to expose a mass of white teeth.

After Roosevelt's speech Joe introduced himself. He and Roosevelt took cups of whiskey punch. On the subject of Bryan and his stand on silver, Roosevelt was a tiger. "We must stop that man, Mr. Crown. I'm devoting everything to the task."

"If I may change the subject just a moment, Mr. Roosevelt—"

"Too formal. Call me Theodore, I'll call you Joe."

"I'd be pleased, Theodore. I want to ask whether you think there'll be war with Spain."

"I fervently hope so. Butcher Weyler is a madman to be suppressed. Looking at the larger picture, I believe American interests must be served. The sphere of democracy must be expanded. Americans need a frontier. In Cuba we have one. I think war is entirely probable. When it comes, I intend to be there."

"I'd like the same thing," Joe said.

"Ha! Capital!"

THE Republicans conducted their campaign almost as if it were a crusade. Every party loyalist with oratorical ability took to the rails and the roads. They also resorted to use of a medium condemned by preachers and scorned even by that lowest of social classes, actors. Hammerstein's Olympia Music Hall in New York introduced a short film from the American Biograph Company titled *McKinley at Home—Canton, O.* It presented a reenactment of Governor McKinley's being informed that he'd received the nomination. Money from the campaign war chest was secretly used to show the film all over the Midwest.

Joe couldn't bring himself to sneak into the Columbia Theater downtown to view it. That was the proper conservative attitude. Still, if it got even one vote for McKinley, who cared how disreputable the means of persuasion?

William Jennings Bryan stormed back and forth across the hustings like a Nebraska cyclone. McKinley sat on his porch in Canton and let others stump for him. Including a surrogate—a doppelgänger on a strip of celluloid. No one could say to what extent the election was influenced by repeated showings of the film. Only the outcome was unequivocal. Bryan lost by six hundred thousand popular votes. The dragon of bimetallism was slain.

PAUL ✦ Iz Pflaum showed *The Wabash Cannonball* on a Tuesday night, after the variety bill. Paul, Shadow, and Jimmy were squeezed into a booth rigged from curtains at the back of the house, praying the prototype Luxograph projector wouldn't fail.

Pflaum personally introduced the picture. He warned the sparse audience that any person with a feeble constitution should hold tight to his or her seat or, alternatively, leave.

This produced snickers and jeers. No one rose to go. In the booth, Shadow threw the switch. There were gasps as the improvised cloth screen lit up with an image of an onrushing train.

The Cannonball grew and grew, seeming to hurtle straight for the audience. Patrons jumped from their seats and pushed and screamed in the aisles, frantic to escape.

"That was sensational. Did you see how it emptied the house?" Pflaum said afterward. "Great chaser, Colonel. I want your pictures—ten of 'em, within one week. I'll lease the projector; you train my nephew Herk to run it."

The members of the Luxograph group went back to the Levee and, to celebrate, drank far too much beer.

Paul asked Shadow, "Where will we get all these pictures?"

"We'll make 'em, for Pete's sake. Why do you think I hired you and Jimmy? Stop frowning, kid. We're on the way."

Never in his memory had Paul spent such a frantic week. While Mary tended the peep show parlor, he and the colonel and Jimmy rushed from one end of the city to the other in a rented wagon. They photographed *Troops Drilling at Fort Sheridan* and *Professor Milo's Dancing Dachshund*. They photographed *A Packet of Sneeze Powder*, with Mary doing the sneezing. With Jimmy and a Levee damsel as the players, they filmed *Lips Aflame*. It was an imitation of one of the biggest Edison hits, forty-two feet of continual kissing by actors May Irwin and John Rice.

The first bill of chasers was a hit. Iz Pflaum wanted more. Shadow leased the peep show parlor to a couple of entrepreneurs, reincorporated as the American National Luxograph Company, and found a commercial studio that could process his negatives and strike prints. Still, there weren't enough hours to travel to locations to shoot one-minute actualities, as the colonel had taken to calling them, and at the same time build a second projector for a variety house in Indianapolis that wanted to match Pflaum's success.

Working against Pflaum's deadlines created an atmosphere of perpetual crisis that only a young man, or a driven older one like Shadow, could survive. For Paul it helped dull the memory of the scene outside St. James Church. He wore himself out purposely, and as the days passed, some of the pain abated.

But not all. Nor would it, ever.

Gradually, and quite without any conscious plan, Paul became the senior member of Shadow's crew. The colonel asked questions of Paul, but not of Jimmy. When Paul and Jimmy helped in the cellar, building new projectors, Jimmy malingered—went out for a smoke, or rested—whenever he could. He just wasn't interested.

Shadow's mad pace never slackened. He dashed from city to city hunting for picture outlets, haggling over deals, fighting off competitive companies doing the same thing.

Shadow placed a third projector in a variety house in Louisville and contracted for a fourth in Milwaukee. He told Paul, "You rest on your heels, you get no place. And this company is going someplace, believe me."

"I do," Paul said.

Paul wrote several letters to Wexford Rooney in care of general delivery, Charleston, West Virginia. Early in 1897 he finally got a reply. It contained some news.

> In certain respects life is treating me less harshly than before. I have found a room at the boardinghouse of a Mrs. Lucille Suggsworth, a person of intelligence, fine culinary skills, and a warm disposition. Lucille was widowed last year. We are close companions.
>
> My servitude at the Nu-Age Photography Salon of Charleston is, as I feared, a dreadful experience. I seem to have inherited all the vile-tempered tots whose idiot parents want them immortalized for posterity. I am then required to finish the portraits of these monsters by color-tinting their precious little lips and cheeks.

The letter also contained some admonitions.

> In all that you do in your newfound career in living pictures, remember above all one watchword. Honesty. Honesty!!
>
> I hope sincerely that you will soon declare your intent to become a citizen. This is a great land. There is a matchless idea behind America, which, while far from perfectly implemented as yet, still beckons us on. So do not shun or discard the idea of becoming a citizen, even though some aspects of life here have been bitterly disappointing.
>
> Yours ever,
> W. Rooney

Paul laid the letter aside. He would stay in America while learning as much as he could of his new craft. But citizenship? No; since he'd lost Julie, that was something in which he no longer had any interest. What the baker of Wuppertal had said about America seemed ever more truthful.

JULIE ✦ On a June morning in 1897, Julie and her husband took breakfast on the marble terrace of Belle Mer, the Elstrees' palatial summer residence in Southampton. Though it was only half past eight, the day was already sultry. Below the sloping lawn, beyond the dune and their private beach, the ocean—the wonderful, sonorous ocean—rolled in from the other side of the world.

Julie wore a morning robe. Elstree appeared in white flannel trousers and a scarlet coat denoting membership in the Shinnecock Hills Club, where he golfed. This morning, though, he had a ten-o'clock bridge game at the Southampton Club.

Elstree looked tan and fit. Julie, on the other hand, was pale, with purple shadows under her eyes.

He had been at her a lot recently on the subject of her giving him a son. She'd already miscarried once. She grieved for the babe she'd lost, yet a certain part of her thanked God the child would never have to know a father like Bill.

Without taking his eyes from his *New York Times,* Elstree said, "My dear, is there any news? I calculate it's about time for—"

"No," she broke in. "Again this month, no change."

"I really wish you'd consult a specialist. I'm sure there are excellent ones in the city. Shall I look into it?"

"No. I will." *I'd sooner be dragged over red-hot rocks than give you a child. I won't be your broodmare.*

Since the nightmare experience in the private railroad car last summer, she had at least been spared further brutality. Without actually apologizing, Bill said his behavior that night was due to an excess of champagne. A month later he moved into a separate bedroom. When he had needs, or was impatient for her to conceive, he visited her for an hour. He hadn't hurt her even slightly since that first night. Yet he still could intimidate her with his eyes, because she knew the furies that could rise behind his composed, rather ordinary face.

How do I approach him about the new problem? How do I even begin? She slipped her hand into the pocket of her robe. Touched the notepaper. She mustn't let the matter pass.

Her mouth was dry. "Bill, who is the person who uses the letter R as a signature?"

"I'm afraid I don't know what you—"

She took out the paper and held it up. "I found this note, signed

333

'R.' The handwriting is a woman's. The note confirms a time for supper at Rector's in town." Elstree stared. Her courage shrank.

"Where did you find that?"

"On the floor in the library. Dropped accidentally, I imagine."

"Please give it to me." He held out his hand and snapped his fingers. "Please."

"Am I not entitled to an explanation?"

"No. Give it to me, Juliette. Now."

She dropped the note onto the table between them. Elstree snatched the note and stood up.

"Bill, are you seeing someone in New York?"

He walked around the table and put his soft, manicured hand on her shoulder gently. It terrified her. "My dear, understand this. Men are men. Wives are expected to make allowances."

"I see. Is this what they're calling a double standard, Bill?"

"I don't know what they're calling it, sweet. I know it's the way I live my life, and I don't propose to change."

"Well, you'd better, Bill, or I—"

Elstree's smile chilled her to silence. He closed his hand on her firmly enough to hurt. He bent toward her. "Don't threaten me. Don't you ever threaten me. I live my life as I please." Then he kissed her cheek. "After bridge I'll be taking a train into town. If you need me tonight, it's the Princeton Club as usual."

"Will they take a message while you're at Rector's?"

With a terrifying stare but perfect politeness, he said, "Good-bye, dear." And stalked off.

Julie went up to her room, closed the drapes, and lay in bed past noon. She knew she wasn't one of the so-called new women who defiantly proclaimed one standard, and only one, for both sexes. She was married. Not happily, but she'd spoken the vows. Still, she could speak the truth in her heart.

Paul, I love you. I'll never love anyone else, no matter whose name I bear. I vow that I'll escape from this maze I walked into because of my own cowardice. It may take months, or years, but escape I will. And then I'll find you.

IT WAS early August. Elstree had left for the races in Saratoga. His trip allowed Julie to see Aunt Willis in New York without risking a confrontation with Bill. They met at Delmonico's for luncheon.

Willis was bone thin and grayer, but otherwise unchanged. She spoke of her longtime friend Miss Clara Barton, who had founded and still headed the American Red Cross. "If there's a Cuban war, Clara swears she'll go," Willis said. "The woman is seventy-six, and I've never seen such grit and stamina. She said she'll take volunteers. 'Well, here I am,' I said to her. *Cuba libre!*"

Willis examined her niece critically. "You're peaked, Juliette. No taste for the beach out there?"

"Not really. I walk a lot, but mostly on dark days."

"Dark days. I see."

At Julie's suggestion they ordered a house specialty, Long Island duckling. From her reticule Willis drew a small package. "Mr. Kipling's latest. *Captains Courageous.* You must read it."

"Thank you, I will. I have plenty of time. Bill's at Saratoga for a few weeks."

Her aunt squinted through smoke rising from her little cheroot. "You're not getting on with him, are you?"

Julie's impulse was to deny it and spare herself a long, probably pointless discussion. But she realized she'd never be able to resolve her problem if she hid it forever. "No, I'm not. I think there's another woman." She described finding the note signed "R."

Willis sighed. "Dear me." She reached across to clasp Julie's hand. "Are you absolutely sure about it?"

"Bill didn't bother with a denial. He said men and women live by different standards, and I had to accept it."

"Oh, that old cant. You are *not* required to suffer simply because he gave you that huge diamond and dragged you in front of a parson. I recommend that you find the evidence against him. Hire a good lawyer. He'll know detectives to put on the case. That's the best advice I can give you. No matter what it costs, divorce the cheater. He doesn't deserve a fine person like you."

Julie was silent. Willis said, "You have perfect justification, child. And you have the courage, if you'll only use it."

Julie's face clouded with an odd look. "That's what Paul said."

"Paul. He's the boy you loved?"

"Paul Crown. Yes. I still love him."

"Where is he?"

"I don't know."

"What are you going to do?"

"I don't know," she repeated with a forlorn shrug. "Will you be staying long in New York?"

"I'm sailing to England on Tuesday. I have met this musician. A cellist. Half my age." She winked. "In the meantime, I'll see if I can put you in touch with a lawyer who handles divorce."

AT HER next visit Aunt Willis had a name for her. Rubin Silverjack, Esq., on lower Fifth Avenue. Julie was seated in Silverjack's office by the end of the week.

Rubin Silverjack, Esq., resembled a sincere and pious priest. He was in his forties, conservatively dressed. Julie felt she had made a terrible mistake, until she looked closely at his fiery black eyes.

Silverjack leaned back in a well-oiled swivel chair. "Please relax, Mrs. Elstree. This discussion will be entirely confidential."

"Thank you." Julie's mouth was dry as sand.

"You say you believe your husband is committing adultery."

"I have good reason to believe that, yes. He—" Shame put scarlet in her cheeks. She forced herself to go on. "He also hurt me physically on one occasion. I was frightened for my life."

Silverjack meditated a moment. "I'm afraid that will do you no good, except to give you the determination to go ahead. The divorce law is outrageously one-sided in the husband's favor. Only if there's a provable adultery do you have grounds. You will need to catch your husband in a compromising situation. That's often a costly and very time-consuming procedure, though I have excellent connections for arranging surveillance."

"How long do you estimate it would take?"

"It might take a week, or a year."

Julie was stricken. She didn't want to wait so much as a day. She feared her husband. She covered her eyes.

Just as her hope was vanishing, Silverjack said, "There is a second way, Mrs. Elstree. There are certain females willing to accept money for going on the witness stand and enacting the role of the other woman. The judge knows it's a charade, but it permits him to favor the wife. There are two women in particular whom I employ—actresses. I beg you not to look so shocked, Mrs. Elstree. The strategy is used again and again to rescue wives from intolerable marriages. It works. Until the statutes are reformed, nothing else will."

"Mr. Silverjack, are you saying that in order to be free—"

He stopped her. "In the most expeditious way."

"But you're saying I have to break the law."

"Become an accessory to fraud. Yes."

"No, I can't possibly, I—" And then she thought again of Bill. The longer she delayed, the greater her risk and her suffering. "All right. Mr. Silverjack," she whispered, "do whatever's necessary. I put the case in your hands."

"Thank you for your confidence, Mrs. Elstree."

She rushed home feeling jubilant.

Awaiting her was a long-distance wire from her mother. Her father had had an accident. He had fallen down the steps at home. He was in a coma and might not live.

ON THE fifteenth day after his accident Mason Putnam Vanderhoff III died. He had never regained consciousness.

Julie mourned for her father even as she rehearsed the initial steps of her escape from her husband. Before she left for Chicago, she telephoned Silverjack to explain what had happened.

"Shall I file the complaint?" he asked.

"I want to tell my husband first."

"That isn't your responsibility, Mrs. Elstree. Considering what you said about him, I'd advise against it."

"Mr. Silverjack, it's something I must do myself."

"As you wish."

IT RAINED all the way out to Graceland, a prestigious cemetery where Chicago's notables could be buried among their peers. Julie rode with her husband in his clarence. Elstree kept his arm around Julie, murmuring condolences she hardly heard. Her stomach ached. Her head hurt. She vowed not to weaken. She had set today as the day to speak. She meant to be free.

At the grave, Nell sobbed uncontrollably as the Episcopal priest prayed over the ostentatious coffin. Julie was pale behind her black veil. She wondered what Nell would do when she learned of her decision to divorce. Fall ill again? Disown her, probably. No matter; she wanted only freedom, and Paul.

When the service was over, Elstree touched Julie's sleeve. "Come," he said. The coachman held a black umbrella over them as they went up a slippery path to the line of hearses and carriages.

337

The door of the clarence closed with a firm, solid sound. Julie leaned back and shut her eyes a moment.

"Bill," she began in a whisper. She turned to face him. "Bill, I'm leaving you. I want a divorce."

He stared at her. Stared long and hard. The clarence lurched forward on the graveled cemetery road. Elstree peeled off his black gloves. "Have you discussed this with a lawyer?"

"Yes. I mean to be free, Bill."

"I'll reply to that with one word. Never." He reached out and grasped both her hands in his. "Divorce is something I simply won't contemplate. In our circle it ruins a man's reputation. When a wife files, it insults and demeans the husband publicly. I'll block you at every step, Julie."

"There are ways around it."

"Julie," he said, "if you persist with this behavior, I'll commit you to an institution. All it takes is my word. I can do it in a day if you force me. Mental institutions are hellholes. I'd be sad if you made me send you away. But I'll do it."

"Bill, that's horrible. Cruel. What kind of man are you?"

"Why, a husband. Until such time, if any, that I decide otherwise."

"So you can be free, but I can't?"

"You understand perfectly," he said with a benign smile.

She fell back against the maroon plush cushion, sick with defeat.

PAUL ✦ Paul wished Jimmy would quit. It seemed to Paul that Jimmy didn't belong in the picture business, or in any other reasonably honest enterprise. Jimmy was greedy, and short on scruples. Sharing a room with him had never been pleasant, but now it was an acute strain. In countless small ways Jimmy showed his dislike of Paul. Shadow didn't help matters when he introduced Paul as his assistant and Jimmy as his helper.

And then Jimmy fell in love.

One night in January of 1898 he brought home a voluptuous blond blue-eyed goddess of a girl. Not to bed her, but to show her off at the supper table. She was seventeen, and Jimmy was extremely nervous as he introduced her. Miss Honoria Fail—Honey.

"Where did you meet this young pup, Miss Fail?" Shadow asked.

"We met at Pflaum's Music Hall, sir. My aunt Maureen took me there to see the living pictures. Afterward, in the lobby, who should we meet but Aunt Maureen's friend Sally Phelan. They stepped away to chat." Miss Fail smiled prettily. "Jimmy marched right up, told me his name, and said he made the very pictures they were showing inside. I was so impressed!" She giggled.

After supper Jimmy fetched Miss Fail's muff in preparation for taking her home. Gravely she shook hands all around. "I hope I'll see more of you. It's so thrilling, this business of yours."

"My sentiments exactly." Jimmy put on his derby, said a cheerful good-night, and, with visible pride, escorted Honey to the stair.

When they'd gone, Shadow said, "Jim had better not try taking liberties with that little morsel. She's the daughter of one of the most powerful aldermen in the city, Francis X. Fail. He'll steal anything. But he's a devout Catholic and draws a line between civic boodling and morality at home."

So it was that Jimmy Daws stayed in the colonel's employ with an improved attitude. Honey Fail came to supper at least once a week, discussing her four sisters, her priest, her parish, and the flickers— "The most exciting, marvelous invention ever!" She was dim-witted in a harmless, innocent way. Paul liked her enormously.

ON WEDNESDAY morning, the sixteenth of February, Paul bolted out of bed when the colonel shouted for him from the kitchen. Paul dragged his pants on and crossed the freezing floor to the kitchen.

"Dutch, there's big news. I mean the biggest. Look." He showed the front page of his morning *Tribune*.

EXTRA!
MAINE IS BLOWN UP IN HAVANA HARBOR
American Battleship Destroyed by a Terrific Explosion

"How can it be? She sailed there on a friendly visit." Paul had read every recent dispatch from Key West and Cuba. The *Maine* had left a berth in the Dry Tortugas and steamed to Havana almost three weeks ago.

"Oh, sure, perfectly friendly," Shadow said with a roll of his eyes. "But maybe our consul had some notion about showing the Spaniards the heavy guns on a U.S. warship. Did you stop to think of that?"

"Even so, the papers said the Spanish officials gave the American sailors a cordial reception."

"They blew her up. That's cordial?"

"Is there proof the Spaniards did it?"

"No, but they're responsible. I'd put money on it. I'm with Mr. Hearst, we should whale the tar out of them."

Suddenly Shadow dropped the paper. His eyes gleamed. "Think of the picture possibilities."

THE final death toll in Havana harbor was two hundred and sixty-eight. The yellow press thundered, "Remember the *Maine!*" Masses of Americans suddenly took up the banners only the jingoes had carried heretofore. In March, Congress passed a war appropriations bill, and President McKinley signed it, although he was unhappy about the prospect of war. His assistant secretary of the navy was Theodore Roosevelt, who said war was inevitable. Hundreds of thousands of ordinary Americans endorsed that view.

On the roof, Colonel Shadow created an extravaganza called, with less than stunning originality, *Remember the Maine!!!* He and his assistants built a wooden frame fitted with a heavy canvas lining. Into this lining they poured water (Havana harbor). On one of the long sides they tacked a cardboard backdrop, painted blue and decorated with clouds made of cotton.

At the lower edge of the backdrop, near the water, they pasted pictures of buildings with tile roofs, cut from postcards of Lisbon, Portugal. Mary fashioned palm trees from wire and brown and green crepe paper. Paul thought the effect was ludicrous and would fool no one. Shadow cheerfully predicted it wouldn't matter, and would he please keep such comments to himself?

Jimmy sawed small rectangular blocks of wood. Mary cut out a large cardboard-mounted photograph of the *Maine*. Paul tacked the picture of the *Maine* to one of the wooden blocks. To smaller blocks he nailed postcard cutouts of shrimp boats. "Do they have shrimp boats in Havana harbor, Colonel?" Paul asked as he floated them in the water.

"Dutch, my lad, do you think anyone who just got off the boat and wandered into Pflaum's will know the difference?"

To the shrimp boats Mary attached fine sewing thread, allowing them to be pulled through the water.

With all in readiness, Paul carefully laid four pinches of gunpowder on top of the wooden block to which the *Maine* was tacked.

Shadow surveyed the arrangements. With an old fireplace bellows Jimmy was fanning a charcoal brazier of smoking, grease-spattered kindling. "Tie down the battleship," Shadow ordered.

Paul stuck his arm into the water and planted two bent pins in the bottom of the canvas, like fishhooks. Threads running from the pins to the battleship cutout kept it bobbing gently in place.

"Here we go, I'm cranking!" The colonel screamed. *Shrimp boats!*"

Paul crouched at one end of the tank and pulled the cutouts across the tank in back of the *Maine*.

"All right, they're out of range. Let it go."

Working fast, Paul dipped the cotton-wrapped end of a wire into a bottle of alcohol, then lit the cotton. He thrust his arm through a prepared hole in the backdrop, praying the burning cotton would find the pinches of powder.

"*Smoke!*" Jimmy worked the bellows like a madman.

With a flat report, the *Maine* blew up.

"Sensational!" Shadow cried, and stopped cranking.

They turned the *Maine* cutout on end, rigged new threads, and restarted the smoke. Shadow cranked as Paul pulled the battleship down into the water, bow first. The *Maine* "sank."

REMEMBER *the Maine!!!* created a sensation in the trade and block-long lines at Pflaum's Music Hall. Only a small child or an idiot would think the cutout ships and backdrop real. Yet there was undeniable magic up there on the thirty-foot screen. The scene *lived* because it *moved*. The water rippled, the smoke billowed, and the cutout ship vanished under the water.

At the end of the footage people howled, stamped, and pounded in a patriotic frenzy.

Paul was dissatisfied. He compared the *Maine* picture with the film of the hurtling Wabash Cannonball. One was a trick and a cheat; one was honest and real. People were not so stupid; they saw the differences, and when the novelty of living pictures wore off, they would object to anything fake. Of course it was impossible for the Luxograph camera to have been in Havana harbor that night. But what if war broke out? Why not take the Luxograph camera there and film real action? The possibility excited him.

As a result of the sensational box office for the faked picture, Colonel Shadow dashed around the Midwest signing up new theaters to exhibit Luxograph programs. He hired an expert carpenter, who took charge of building new projectors. Paul helped him when he wasn't filming for Shadow's growing list of outlets.

Then on April 20 President McKinley signed a declaration of war between the United States and Spain. What spectacular possibilities for living pictures, Paul thought.

Shadow was already rushing to perfect a new camera with improved capacity. He'd been talking about it for months. Now the dizzying expansion of the American National Luxograph Company drove him to finish it.

It would hold four hundred feet of film in a separate lightproof magazine mounted on top of the camera. After exposure the film was fed to a take-up reel in a second magazine, this one attached to the back of the camera. Behind the crank was a footage meter of Shadow's own design—necessary now that several subjects could be filmed with a single magazine.

On the evening of April 21, Paul asked the colonel if he could spare a few minutes to discuss an important matter.

"For you, Dutch—anytime. Let's take a stroll." They walked outside. Shadow fired up a long cigar. "What's on your mind, kid?"

Paul stopped and looked the colonel in the eye. "I would like you to give me the new camera. I want to follow the American soldiers to Cuba. If they go into battle with the Spaniards, there will be opportunities to film scenes that are completely new and amazing."

"*Cuba?* Dutch, that is the craziest, most risky idea I've ever—"

"American Biograph is sending a man."

Shadow jerked the cigar from his mouth. "What?"

"American Biograph plans to send a cameraman. I read it yesterday. Vitascope may go as well. We can't be left out."

"What about *you?* You're not scared to pack up and pole off to Cuba? They're going to be shooting real bullets down there."

"Yes, I know there might be dangers. I am willing to chance them. When you hired me, you spoke about the living pictures. How they could show the wonders of the world. The drama. Now is the time, there's no drama bigger than war. You said that too. Cameras can bring back the truth. It's our—our duty."

"Where'd you pick up these big, noble ideas?"

Paul was red-faced. "Mostly from Mr. Rooney. He said a camera could lie, but it must not."

"Dutch, you're a funny kid. You have ambition, but something else pushes you. I can't figure out what." Shadow scratched his jaw. "Cuba, huh? War footage."

"Never before seen in all the world, Colonel."

Shadow stared beyond the Levee lights to some large and shining hill of gold, a sizable part of which he might bank if scenes of real battles were exhibited at Pflaum's and his other licensed theaters.

"You'd need help. Jimmy would have to go with you."

"He won't like that. He'll quit."

"Maybe, but he's still chasing Fail's daughter. Marching off to war would impress her. I'd bet ten dollars that Jimmy'll go."

"Then you will give me the camera?"

"If you're willing to risk your neck, I'll risk the camera. Come on, let's go in here, to Freiberg's. I'll buy you a beer. Think of it. American National Luxograph goes to war!"

Shadow put his arm around Paul in a way that was almost fatherly, and they passed into the smoky blaze of Freiberg's Dance Hall. "What do you say I print up some calling cards? Paul Crown— No, wait. Paul 'Dutch' Crown—I like that. Sounds adventurous. Paul 'Dutch' Crown, Chief Operator, American National Luxograph Company. That's big, I like it."

J**OE CROWN** ✦ "I wish you wouldn't go," Ilsa said. "How can the brewery get along without you?"

"Easily. Stefan and my brewmaster, Sam Ziegler, can handle everything between them, at least for a limited time."

Joe dipped the paddle, and the canoe glided across the Lincoln Park lagoon known as Swan Lake. After church Ilsa had insisted they make this little excursion. Canoeing had never been one of her passions, so it puzzled him. Until now.

"But Joe, I still feel—"

"Ilsa, we're officially at war. I have served before in the army. I can serve again. It's my patriotic duty." In the unexpected heat of this April afternoon, his face gleamed with sweat.

She dabbed her upper lip with a handkerchief. "I think there may be an element of patriotism in it. But I think you've arranged for an army commission chiefly because you're unhappy at home. Unhappy with me. At a certain age, men rebel. That is well known.

And I know my objections to spirits—and certain other ideas—have angered you. I'm deeply sorry. I wish I could renounce what I believe, in order to make your life happier. I can't do that. Maybe twenty years ago, yes, but not now. I am the person I have become, for good or ill."

"A marvelous wife, I've always said it."

"Thank you, but I know you take exception to the way I feel about this war."

"You and your friends."

"Yes, Miss Addams is likewise adamantly opposed to it. But that plays no part here. Truly, I'm thinking of you. And the business." He looked at her skeptically. "You have made an enormous success, Joe. You have everything a man could want."

"Oh, yes. Everything. I have a daughter foolishly determined to enter a profession whose members are considered riffraff. I have another son who might have dropped off the earth—"

"No! Remember the wheat, the—"

"It was addressed to you, not to me. Then there is our nephew, totally lost to us—"

"Pauli didn't choose to leave our house. You banished him. I must constantly remind you of that."

He ignored her flare of anger. "Well, if this is what I've worked for—if I am a man with everything—I pray to God I'm never forced to experience having nothing."

He dragged his sleeve across his forehead. "It's too hot out here. We're going back."

PAUL ✦ When Shadow informed Jimmy that he and Paul would be leaving for a war zone, Jimmy's face purpled, but he didn't explode until he was alone with Paul.

"He said you're the one who sold him on this lousy scheme. Are you nuts?"

"Come on, it'll be the adventure of a lifetime."

"Not if some spick shoots me. You may be going by yourself."

But Jimmy didn't make good on that threat, for the reason Shadow had predicted. "I told Honey we were going to Cuba. Bullets! Fighting! I said I didn't want to go. Big mistake. She said she wouldn't look up to me if I shirked my duty." With a malevolent glare, he said, "You're a crazy s.o.b."

PAUL AND JIMMY PREPARED TO leave for Tampa, where the army was marshaling. They packed camera, tripod, and stands in two wooden crates. The night before they were to leave, Jimmy went out with Honey. At supper Mary surprised Paul with a gift. A braided straw hat with a wide, rakish brim and a royal blue band.

Paul was touched. "Thanks. It's a fine hat."

After supper he went to the cellar. He took a can of red enamel and a small brush upstairs and carefully painted a red dot on the globe, at the approximate location of Tampa.

All at once he grew sad. This wasn't a home. It was just a room—cheap, dingy, squalid. Would his home always be like this, the place he was at the moment, nothing more?

He pulled down the stereoscope card, yellowing badly now. He knew Joe Junior had told him the truth. America wasn't quite the paradise dreamed of by immigrants. At least part of what the baker of Wuppertal had said was right. Still, one of Paul's dreams in Berlin had been realized: the miracle of photography.

He was embarking on a great adventure; despair had no place in it. He looked at the card one last time and put it in his grip.

Next morning, the third of May, Shadow and Mary saw them off at the depot. Honey Fail came with Jimmy, which helped curb his anger.

Paul looked smart in a belted jacket and his new hat. On his shoulder he carried a canvas bag containing a spare lens and a magazine of Eastman raw stock; additional magazines were being shipped to Florida. Shadow had given his helpers calling cards and had booked rooms for them at the Tampa Bay Hotel, headquarters for the American expeditionary force.

The train conductor shouted his all-aboard.

"Don't get in the way of those Mauser bullets," Mary cried.

Clinging to Jimmy's arm, Honey Fail uttered a little squeal of fear and hugged him. "Oh, you're so brave." Jimmy looked sick.

Paul and Jimmy boarded the train. It began to move. Shadow ran alongside the steps and shouted at Paul in the billowing steam. "Don't stint on the telegraph. I want regular reports."

"Right, Colonel."

The train gathered speed. Shadow ran faster. "I trust you, Dutch. You're in charge." He stopped as the train rushed on, and raised his right hand high. "Good luck."

THEY SLEPT, OR TRIED TO SLEEP, sitting up. At one point Jimmy asked a peculiar question. "Think we'll make any money on this trip?"

"Well, perhaps for American National Luxograph, but not for us. Unless you count our pay."

"Count it? Most of the time I can hardly find it. Down in Florida I aim to pluck up some extra. Fellow on the Levee said there'd be plenty of hicks in an army camp. Fair game." Jimmy leaned back and crossed his arms. "And fair warning to you, Mr. Chief Operator. Once in a while I may not be around when you need me."

Crossly Paul said, "Look here, we have an assignment—"

"Ah, dry up. I'll do my job. But I'll take care of a few others on the side. Be a pal and keep quiet about that." He punched Paul's shoulder, feigning friendliness.

Later that night, with the oil lamps trimmed low, Jimmy snoring lightly, something compelled Paul to dig into a pocket of his coat for one of the business cards: PAUL "DUTCH" CROWN, CHIEF OPERATOR.

So once again he was a new man. Once again he was reborn.

And once again he was hurtling into a darkness whose boundaries, whose heart, whose secret traps, he couldn't see or even imagine. Once again there were wonderment and eagerness, a sense of inevitability, and more than a trace of dread. The Americans had an expression for going to war, facing its dangers. They said you were going to see the elephant.

He slept fitfully on the bumping, jerking train. Dutch Crown. Age twenty; twenty-one next month.

Going to see the elephant.

Part Eight
TAMPA
1898

DUTCH ✦ It was almost dark when the train chugged into Tampa. Long vistas of mean, unpainted houses lined shabby streets of rutted sand. Paul kept yawning. He was worn out, famished, and dirty.

The conductor stuck his head in the door. "Next and final stop will be the hotel. Five minutes."

The train went across a river and through another ramshackle area. Then it passed through elaborate iron gates onto a siding. Jimmy sat up, grinning. Paul looked out and was amazed to behold an *Arabian Nights* illustration come to life. He was gazing at the spectacular Tampa Bay Hotel.

The hotel, built by business tycoon Henry Plant, was sited on a riotously planted six-acre tract. The long main building, five stories high, was built of dark red brick. An enormous silver onion dome rose from each corner, and Moorish arches framed the doorways. A wide veranda was ablaze with multicolored electric lights. Couples strolled; men in uniform took the air. Through the car window came muted laughter and band music. Paul's first thought was, I have to buy a picture postcard of this; otherwise no one will believe it exists.

Jimmy, too, was impressed. "How many rooms in this place?" he called to the conductor.

"Five hundred and eleven. Looks like a palace, don't it? The hotel's usually closed this time of year, but Mr. Plant, he's a patriot, he opened it right away when Washington said they needed it. You boys are looking at headquarters for the Fifth Army Corps."

Paul hurried to catch up with Jimmy, who was already out of the car. "Look, Dutch, there's women all over the place."

"Time for them later. We should get our equipment from the baggage car."

"Oh, right, I forgot, you're in charge now," Jimmy retorted.

"Look here," Paul said, "I'm tired of your sneers."

"Too bad. As long as I'm on this rotten job, you better not order me around. Don't push me, and things'll be okay."

"I will try to remember that." Paul spun around and walked off toward the baggage car, fighting his anger.

The crates were already resting in the sand when Jimmy came straggling along, whistling. A black porter in livery brought a cart and tagged the crates for transfer to the hotel's baggage room. Paul tipped him, then asked, "Where do we register?"

"There, sir." The man indicated doors at the near end of the building. "The west entrance is for train passengers. Go straight in, down the long hall to the rotunda. You'll see the desk."

They followed a gravel path to the veranda and saw a multitude of different uniforms, and attractive young women in handsome gowns—women with tawny skin and ravishing black hair.

347

Inside, a great long hallway stretched to the rotunda. The hall was decorated with tall carved chairs, Chinese jars, small statues, miniature potted palms.

The rotunda was perhaps seventy feet across—finely carpeted, brilliantly lit with electric lights. The walls were hung with tapestries, large paintings, mirrors of rose-tinted glass. Granite columns supported an open gallery on the second floor.

The rotunda was crowded. Men and women in evening attire, navy officers in cool white duck, their army counterparts in blue. A few officers were dressed in more casual khaki.

At the desk, Paul slid his card over the green marble. The clerk said brusquely, "Luxograph. Your rooms are ready. Fifth floor." Paul and Jimmy signed the register.

"You're too late for dinner," the clerk said, "but food is available in the gents' rathskeller, downstairs, or in the Oriental Annex." He pinged a silver bell. Another black porter loaded their valises on a small handcart and took the room keys.

"Elevator this way, gen'mun."

The main elevator was a gilded open cage near the grand staircase. It brought them up to the fifth floor. Even Mr. Plant's smallest guest room, though appallingly hot, was well appointed, with an Oriental carpet, a dressing table and mirror, and a telephone. "You first, sir," the porter said to Jimmy.

"Put my bag on the bed, boy." The porter did as Jimmy ordered.

Jimmy followed them next door, to Paul's room, which was identical. "Here, and thank you." Paul handed the porter twenty-five cents. The man smiled and thanked him warmly.

As the porter left, Jimmy said, "Damned if I'll pay him extra to do what he's supposed to do."

Paul sailed his straw hat onto the bed. "Are you hungry?"

"Nah. I want to look over the girls downstairs."

"Suit yourself. We should unpack the crates first thing in the morning. Start filming as soon as we can."

"Yeah, sure, okay. Just don't make it too early."

"Six."

"*Six?* Not me. I'll see you when I see you." He walked out.

Paul washed in the hall bathroom. He combed his unruly hair, put on a fresh shirt, and set out to explore. He took the stairs instead of the elevator.

At the newsstand, he bought a postcard showing the main building. He also bought a cigar, then went down to the lower level, to the rathskeller, and chose a small corner table. The lager was all right, but no match for Crown's.

After he ate, he strolled outside. He wandered past dark tennis courts and stopped a moment at the Oriental Annex, a brightly lit pavilion from which came dance music. Melodic and a trifle sad, the waltz reminded him of Julie. Oh, how he wished for her. But Julie was lost to him.

PAUL awoke promptly at six. When he knocked at Jimmy's door, there was no response. Annoyed, he left the hotel and caught a trolley across the Lafayette Street bridge. In the gray, steamy daylight the town seemed even more primitive than it had when they arrived. It was also busier, with wagon traffic, and soldiers on the plank sidewalks. Some were black, Paul was surprised to see.

He located the freight office in the depot. The crate of film from Eastman was waiting, and he arranged delivery to the hotel. A half hour later he found Jimmy enthroned in a rocker on the veranda. Jimmy had large dark circles under his eyes.

They unpacked their equipment from the baggage room. By ten the film had arrived, and they set up the camera on the lawn in front of the hotel. Paul paced back and forth, his straw hat shading his eyes as he planned his first shot—a long view of the veranda.

A man in a linen shirt and white flannel trousers came striding up the path from the tennis courts, racket in hand. He stopped to greet them. "Top of the morning. You're filming, I see. Allow me to introduce myself. I'm Richard Harding Davis, currently representing Mr. William Randolph Hearst and his New York *Journal*."

"I am honored, Mr. Davis," Paul said. "My name is Dutch Crown, and this is my associate, Mr. Daws."

A strikingly handsome man of about thirty-five, Davis was impeccably polite. Affably he said, "Are you picture fellows trying to put us poor pen-and-ink men out of work? One of you in the hotel already, and I hear another is on the way."

"Do you know who it is?"

"American Biograph." Davis rested his racket on his shoulder. "What's the name of your company?"

"American National Luxograph of Chicago."

"Going with us all the way to Cuba?"

"I hope so. It's my intention to apply to the military staff for battlefield accreditation."

"Just a minute, there's Crane. Up there on the veranda."

"Stephen Crane? *The Red Badge of Courage?*"

"That's the one! Excuse me, will you? Happy to meet you, Dutch. We'll talk again."

Paul watched the handsome journalist bound up the steps to greet a younger man in a straw boater and soiled white duster.

All this conversation bored Jimmy. He was lying on the grass now, lazily studying the rows of guest-room windows.

"Jim, shall we get to work? The light's good. I'd like to start."

"Sure, okay." Jimmy stood up and brushed himself off. Paul noticed him running his eye along the rows of windows again.

IN THE next few days Paul and Jimmy dashed about with the Luxograph camera, photographing subjects Paul hoped would please Shadow and excite audiences. Standing ankle-deep in the surf at Old Tampa Bay, they filmed *The First Artillery Bathing Its Horses*. In pinewoods, in pitiless heat, they filmed maneuvers of a thousand-man cavalry column.

Once again Jimmy threatened to quit. Paul paid no attention. "I have a different idea here—help me. Come on, damn it!"

Jimmy slogged after him, to a place where four sizable palmetto logs lay scattered about. They dragged the logs together, building a low breastwork. Paul crouched with the camera just behind this structure while a detachment of the cavalry gleefully charged straight at him, splitting in half only at the last moment. Jimmy knelt six feet to the rear of Paul, clenching his teeth in terror.

Troop trains rolled into Tampa every day, bringing new detachments. Paul and Jimmy roamed the encampments searching for likely subjects. One morning they were driving in a rented wagon along a sand road near the bay when suddenly Jimmy pointed. "Look!" An alligator was sunning itself on the bank of a lagoon beside the road. It was a great leathery specimen.

"He's perfect," Paul exclaimed softly, stopping the wagon.

Anxiously eyeing the gator, Jimmy tied the horse to a shrub. Paul carried the camera toward the lagoon, unfolded the tripod, and set the legs in the sand without a sound; he started cranking.

The gator sensed the interlopers. It opened its huge jaws, crowded with sharp teeth, and started to move. Toward the camera.

Jimmy ran for cover behind the nearest palm. Paul kept cranking, his heart leaping in his chest. The gator kept coming.

As it drew closer, Paul let go of the crank. Hopping on one foot, he tore off a shoe and threw it. The shoe bounced on the gator's snout. The gator stopped. It fixed Paul with a baleful stare. Gingerly Paul hoisted the tripod and took a step backward. Another.

The alligator opened its jaws again, then turned and rushed into the lagoon, sinking from sight.

"Damn, that was close." Jimmy was sweating heavily.

Paul laughed. He remembered the moment when he'd thought the Wabash Cannonball would run over him. He'd felt the same panic then, the same elation afterward. The moral was apparent. If you wanted exciting pictures, you had to take risks.

Later that afternoon, wearing a new pair of shoes charged to the company, he walked over the Lafayette Street bridge to the depot with a small wooden crate under his arm: the first two magazines of exposed negative for shipment to Chicago.

PAUL soon came to recognize the most important officers headquartered at the hotel. Among them was a small, frail man whom everybody liked, General Joe Wheeler. In his early sixties, he wore a nonregulation black slouch hat and had neatly pointed mustaches and a white beard. He was one of several ex-Confederates wearing blue again. Reporters were saying that the war in Cuba would be a high opportunity to unite the blue and the gray.

The commanding general of the expeditionary force was General William Rufus Shafter. He had a distinguished Civil War record, but apparently he'd changed considerably since those days. His graying hair and walrus mustache always looked unkempt. Now sixty-three, he weighed approximately three hundred pounds and needed a special oversized chair for staff conferences. His aides trailed him closely, as if he might topple over with a heart seizure at any moment.

There was also a flamboyant lieutenant colonel named Roosevelt, of the 1st Volunteer Cavalry. The regimental commander, Colonel Leonard Wood, was a veteran professional, but it was his second who got the attention.

One morning, as Paul was setting up the camera to photograph flamingos on the grounds, Roosevelt came striding along, wearing khakis and a blue bandanna with polka dots. Paul had seen similar bandannas on other men in the regiment variously called the Cavalry Cowpunchers, Teddy's Terrors, or the Rough Riders.

Roosevelt greeted Paul with a booming hello. He stopped to watch Paul adjust the tripod, then pointed to the camera. "Fascinating, these flickers. They have the potential to influence so many. Too bad their moral tone isn't higher."

"Colonel, if I may disagree. I admit that until now, most of the subjects have been trivial, but that will change. Serious films—films of actual events, such as this war—will change it."

"I like a man who's an optimist. And perhaps you're right. After all, the flickers helped Bill McKinley win. What's your name, lad?"

"Paul Crown. Everyone calls me Dutch." They shook hands.

"Well, Dutch Crown, look me up if I can assist you in any way."

That night Paul went to the rathskeller's crowded bar for a beer. A chunky young man wearing a checkered cap approached him. "Excuse me, you're Dutch Crown, aren't you?"

"That's right."

The stranger offered his card. "Billy Bitzer. American Biograph, New York. Thought I should say hello."

Bitzer was older than Paul by perhaps five years—a neatly dressed fellow with a squarish, likable face. He laid his cap on the bar. "Another beer? My treat." He signaled the barkeep.

They drank. Then Paul ordered a round, and they drank again. They took to each other immediately.

They talked about girls. They talked about beer. They talked about cameras. Bitzer was envious of Paul's camera. His own, from the Biograph Company, had a drawback that canceled out many good features.

"Runs on storage batteries. Almost two thousand pounds of them. I complained in New York, and they said, 'Billy, you don't want to go, we'll pay somebody else.' I sit on my keister for hours just waiting for a teamster willing to haul all those crates. Your Luxograph sounds like a honey."

They parted soon after, exchanging garrulous vows of friendship.

Paul was more than a little unsteady returning to his room. He tried to insert his key in the keyhole and kept missing. A door opened far down the hall. A man darted out of a room next to the staircase, clapping a derby on his head. Smoke trailed from a cigarette in his other hand.

The man was tall and thin. Smartly dressed, with a neatly trimmed beard. He flashed a look along the hall, saw Paul, and stepped quickly around the corner to the stair going down.

Paul's room key had fallen from his hand, unnoticed. Was he drunk? Somewhat. Was he insane? Definitely not. The face had leaped out with burning clarity. Vivid dark eyes. Gold-wire spectacles with round lenses no bigger than pennies—anywhere in the world he would recognize the man he'd first met in the Berlin rail yards.

But the man leaving hurriedly was barbered, well tailored—*clean*.

Paul ran down the hall, noting the number of the room from which the man had emerged. He took the stairs in pursuit. On the ground floor he saw no sign of the man. He dashed to the rotunda. The night clerk was sleepy and cross.

"I am Mr. Crown, five eleven. Can you tell me the occupant of room five thirty-six? It's very important."

The clerk opened his mouth to say no. Paul slid a dollar across the green marble. The clerk covered it with his hand, then leafed through the ledger slowly. "It's the wife of an American officer who's encamped with his men at Tampa Heights."

"Thank you. One more question. Upstairs, very briefly, I thought I saw a friend. Possibly he's a guest. Mikhail Rhukov." Paul spelled it as best he could. The clerk again turned pages.

"We have no one by that name."

"Are you sure? He speaks English with an accent heavier than mine. You would remember him."

"I would, and I don't. That's all I'm going to tell you."

Paul turned away, wondering if he had really mistaken one man for another. No. It was Rhukov. Sartorially transformed—but *Rhukov*. Where had he come from? Where had he gone? What devil's miracle had transformed him?

From that night, Paul devoted his few free moments to the mystery. It remained unsolved. No employee he questioned recognized Rhukov's name or description. Several of the journalists thought the description sounded familiar, but couldn't identify the man. They were unanimous about one thing. He wasn't Russian.

One man insisted he was English. A second said that whatever he was, he had only stayed for a day or two. Paul telephoned other hotels, across the river. Nothing. One day, when Paul and Jimmy were away filming, the wife in room 536 checked out.

It was a dead end. Whatever the explanation, the clean Rhukov had vanished as suddenly, inexplicably, as the dirty one.

MAY wore on. Because it was taking a long time to organize the troops, picture subjects became fewer. They photographed *Blanket-tossing a New Recruit; Cuban Refugees Awaiting Rations;* and *A Trolley Ride Through Tampa.*

One night Paul had a drink with Mr. Crane in the rathskeller. There were six empty beer bottles at his elbow.

"Not much to do around here, is there?" Crane said. "Not much to write about. I'm bored silly."

"I greatly admire your writing. The *Red Badge*—if you wrote nothing besides that, I would say your mark is made."

"Thanks. Thanks very much." He seemed tired.

"May I ask a question? Recently, in this hotel, I thought I saw an old acquaintance. I wanted to hail him, but he hurried off. Now I can't find him. His name is Mikhail Rhukov. He's a journalist."

Crane shook his head. "Maybe if you describe him . . ."

"Tall, very slender. Has a beard, small spectacles. Very outspoken."

"What did you say his name is?"

"Mikhail Rhukov."

"Then he has a twin. You described Michael Radcliffe. He's a journalist. But he's an Englishman."

"Englishman?"

"Very upper-upper type. He was registered in the hotel only two nights. We drank champagne at this very bar. We got on damn well. He was all that he seemed, but he was something more. Have you heard of Otto Hartstein, Lord Yorke?"

"No."

"One of the great press lords of England. Radcliffe's a roving correspondent for Hartstein's London *Light*. The flagship paper. He's married to Hartstein's only child, Cecily. Talk about career insurance."

Radcliffe? England? Married? No Russian accent? Paul was reeling. "Do you know why he left the hotel, Mr. Crane?"

"Well—" Crane was scrutinizing Paul warily now. "Some affair of the heart."

"Mr. Crane, I must find this man. I must see if he is Rhukov."

"You say you're his friend."

"Rhukov's friend, yes, absolutely."

Crane paused to light a cigarette, then said, "He checked out at three in the morning. The next afternoon he called me, and I forwarded his bags. I watch the bulletin board for him. Telegraph messages, instructions, little murmurs of affection from his wife. It's professional courtesy—"

"Please. Where is he?"

Crane's hard gaze made Paul squirm. "Ybor City. I'll slip you the address. Freddy? A piece of paper. And another beer."

THE GENERAL ✦ Joe threw his belongings into his suite on the third floor of the Tampa Bay Hotel, splashed water on his face, and went downstairs. The opulence of the hotel astonished him. Joe was in full uniform: blue frock coat with a brigadier general's gold star on the shoulder strap, dress sword buckled on. He was with the cavalry division. His command was the 2nd Brigade, consisting of the 1st and 10th regulars and Colonel Wood's volunteers. His superior officer was General Wheeler.

Joe strolled outside to listen to the last of a band concert, which was taking place near the west end of the veranda. His eye fell on one of the listeners, an attractive Cuban woman who was shamefully young for the attentions of a man his age. He assumed she was a refugee with money; no other class of Cuban could stay at Mr. Plant's hotel.

The young woman was stocky; some would say plump. She wore a tight white dress with a red dust ruffle. A tall comb with mother-of-pearl inlays was tucked into her shining dark hair, which she'd gathered in a bun at the back.

She must have sensed him watching. She turned around suddenly. Blushing, Joe smiled. She smiled too, then looked away. When the concert ended, she went into the hotel on the arm of a slender man in the uniform of the Cuban refugee forces. It pleased Joe that the young woman had acknowledged his interest without anger or visible contempt for his age.

He went up to bed, feeling good, anticipating a sound sleep.

IN LIEU of reveille in the hotel, orderlies knocked on doors at five a.m. Joe spent long hours each day meeting the officers in his command and attending conferences with the other generals to study inventories of men and matériel. Still, he soon began to feel more vigorous than he had for a long time.

One night Joe was smoking a cigar on the lawn and listening to the band music. He intended to wait until the end of the concert, then stroll in hopes of catching another glimpse of the young Cuban woman.

And then he saw her. She was wearing the same close-fitting white dress with the red ruffle; perhaps she'd left Cuba with only a few belongings. The dress was stunning. She was again with the man from the refugee forces. Disappointing.

A journalist to whom Joe had been introduced stood a little way to his left, jotting notes on a pad. Joe approached him.

"Beg your pardon, Kennan, do you know that young woman up there on the porch? The one in white."

"I know her slightly," Kennan replied. "One of the exiles. Estella Rivera is her name."

Joe hesitated before the next question. "Is that her husband?"

"Her brother. I'm told their father is still in Havana."

Joe didn't hear any more. His head buzzed. He took fast, nervous puffs on his cigar. *You're too old; furthermore you're married,* said a cautioning voice. He paid no attention.

He would introduce himself to the young woman. He would invite her to the Oriental Annex to dance. There was some force rushing in him, insisting on it. He wasn't too old. . . .

Estella Rivera began to move toward the arched entrance to the hotel. Then she paused and turned. She sought Joe's eye. And smiled. In a moment she was gone.

She'd known he was there! She'd been looking for him too. Elation sang through Joe Crown. He felt certain he could dance half the night and never tire.

And he would, with Senorita Rivera in his arms.

DUTCH ✦ To go to Ybor City, near Tampa, he put on the best clothes he had, with a few new embellishments. He thought he'd better. The man he'd seen at the hotel wasn't the grimy, disheveled Rhukov of old.

Paul was being frugal in Tampa—a necessity, given Shadow's grudging twenty-cent per diem for incidentals. Using his carefully hoarded daily allowance, Paul bought a new shirt of blue chambray, duck trousers, and a madras tie. All this, together with his straw hat, made him feel presentable, even a little rakish, as he set out.

He found the building with no trouble. He took off his straw hat and climbed the stairs to a weathered door. He knocked. Inside, a man grumbled, then called out, "Crane? That you?"

The voice made Paul's flesh crawl. It was Rhukov's. But as they had said at the hotel, the accent was definitely English.

"It isn't Mr. Crane, it's Paul Crown, from Chicago. Looking for Mr. Michael Radcliffe."

The door opened. Mikhail Rhukov stood there. "It is you! Come in, old chum, come in!"

The flat was a single large room with a few pieces of inexpensive furniture, a sink, and an icebox.

Still bewildered, Paul said, "How are you?"

"Couldn't be better. Stevie Crane obviously trusted you enough to give you this temporary address. Sit, won't you?" He indicated a chair next to a small deal table by an open window. "I am absolutely agog, Paul. Why are you in Tampa? Good heavens. Not in the military, I hope?"

"No, I operate a camera. I film living pictures for theaters."

"A camera operator! Of course. Magnificent solution! You're still drawing. Only it isn't scribbles now, but recognizable pictures."

Paul laughed. "Well, I hope so. Excuse me, I am unsure about something. What shall I call you?"

"Michael. Michael Radcliffe. Why are you staring?"

"Because you are transformed. I still can't believe it."

"Please do believe it. I'm married too."

"Yes, I heard that."

"We two must have a good solid chat. Have one?" Michael offered Paul a cigar. Paul accepted.

"Well—" Michael chuckled. "The waif has certainly grown up."

"It's true. I have changed. I have a nickname now—Dutch."

"Not very original. But it suits." They sat a moment, puffing.

"I want to ask the question you asked me," Paul said. "How did you get where you are? The English you speak so well—"

Michael waved the cigar. "Quite simple, really. I got tired of *poor*. Poor is disgusting. Poor means no one takes you seriously. About a year after I saw you in Chicago, my tolerance of poor ran out. I was in London, still spewing my usual sour opinions, but few editors were having any. I was steadily sinking. One night when it was pouring rain, a revelation came to me. I was sleeping in the only accommodations I could afford. A space under the Tower Bridge. I woke soaking wet, feverish, with a bobby shining his lantern in my face. 'Move on,' says he, giving me a nudge. Move on? Where? The Savoy? Windsor Castle?

"That very night, while I wandered wet and sick, in places I can't remember, the answer came. I must sell out."

Pumped up with mirth, he thumped the table. "And I did! I relaunched my life in a new direction. I obtained a razor and soap from the Salvation Army. I burgled a jumble shop for a new wardrobe. I located a position as night dishwasher at Claridge's Hotel. And I took elocution lessons from a poor old actor who was too drunk to get parts any longer."

He sighed. "I don't mind telling you, there were some long, dry, difficult spells. But I finally escaped the wretched doss house where I'd lived for months."

"Somewhere in there you married the daughter of a publisher?"

"Yes indeed. An acquaintance of my elocution teacher had a theater seat he was unable to use. The ticket was free; I took it. Cecily chanced to be sitting in the seat next to mine."

He inhaled his cigar. "I'm still confused on one point. How did you spot me?" Paul described the moment in the corridor. "Ah. I don't recall seeing you, though. Truthfully, I wanted to get away from there. I was entertaining a lady. Her idiot husband telephoned from a dive in West Tampa. Thought it might be ripping to pop across to the hotel before he went back to camp. I certainly didn't want to meet him. The brain of a gnat but the stature of a great ape."

Paul couldn't contain his laughter. "But I still can't get over this. It's like a fairy tale."

"It's worked out remarkably well. Cecily is a plain creature, but she has a handsome figure and a sharp intellect. And she's kind and forgiving. With a man like me, forgiveness is important.

"I work for her father, Lord Yorke. My title is reporter, but I'm treated like a prince. I still write the occasional authentic Rhukov piece, bile and brimstone, but now they pay attention. I have discovered that if you speak well, dance well, have a proper wife with the proper connections, they don't run the other way. They read you! They ask your opinion—on armaments, on tariffs. I sold out for all that. And I adore it."

Having finished his story, Michael now asked Paul about himself—the intervening years since the Exposition.

Paul held nothing back. He tried to speak calmly, factually, but it was hard; there was too much disappointment. He told Michael of his hopes for a permanent home in America, with the Crowns. He told of being cast out, of finding and then losing Julie. At every mention of Uncle Joe, Michael looked disturbed. Paul couldn't imagine why.

"Such dreams," Michael said quietly. "Crushed. Possibly the girl couldn't help what happened. But your own family? I'm truly sorry. You didn't find everything you hoped for in America."

"No. Only a little. Well, I was warned. By a man I met on the pier in Hamburg. He was a baker. He'd been here for twelve years, and he was going home to Wuppertal in disgust. I can't deny I've met some wonderful people—" He thought of Aunt Ilsa and Wex Rooney; Fritzi, Carl, cousin Joe; Shadow and Mary. Then his uncle's face appeared. He banished it. "Julie most of all," he said.

A pause. "Going to stay?"

Paul looked up. It was the first time anyone had asked the question. "I don't know. I have learned a splendid trade here, one that I love. But I know the pictures are a growing business in many countries. I could live in many places." He hadn't expressed that idea before. But he knew he would be thinking about it more. He stood up. "I should go."

"I'll go a block or two with you." Michael opened the door of a chifforobe in the corner and pulled out a thick, knob-headed walking stick. "A stroll in Ybor in the evening can be dicey if you meet the wrong people."

Electric lights were burning now in the grocery on the corner. They walked a distance; then Michael offered his manicured hand to Paul. "I'll turn back. But I'm very glad we met again, Pau—Dutch. We'll definitely see each other again. Here's to Cuba."

"To Cuba. I am very happy for you, Michael. I like this new personage you've become. But meeting him for the first time—it was a shock."

Soberly Michael said, "My friend, you might prepare yourself for another." He laid a hand on Paul's shoulder. "There is a brigadier general from Chicago at the hotel. Crane told me he's a brewer. His name is Joseph E. Crown."

JIMMY ✦ The red light of sundown glared on the brass balls hanging from the single stem. The familiar symbol jutted from one end of a painted sign on Nassau Street.

I. MELNICK
Buy—Sell—Pawn

Smoking a slender panatella, Jimmy stood across the street.

The shop was narrow—just a single display window and, beside it, a recessed entry. Jimmy had been in West Tampa earlier in the week. He'd spotted an item in the window that would make a swell present for Honey. A delicate necklace of gold or, more likely, gold plate, strung with tiny red and green glass stones. The card beside it announced a price of eleven dollars. Lot of nerve the Jew had; it probably wasn't worth half that.

He'd returned twice more to pipe out the pawnbroker's routine. It never varied. As the neighborhood grew deserted, Melnick, a short, frail man, pulled all the merchandise from the window and lowered a shade. The second night, Jimmy brought a pry bar under his coat, and when Melnick left, he drifted to the alley behind the shop. The door resisted. Jimmy suspected the reason, an iron bar across the inside.

The sun was falling lower, leaving the locked shops and offices in deepening shadow. Jimmy swatted a gnat pestering his neck. He was sick of this town. Sick of his partner—the whole shebang.

He couldn't deny he'd done all right in the money department. He'd made several little forays inside the hotel and twice come away with a sizable reward for his daring. He'd pawned the loot at another shop like this one, on the other side of town.

Abruptly the lights went off across the street in the pawnshop.

Melnick began pulling the merchandise from the display window. In a few seconds he'd be out the door with his keys.

Jimmy slung his panatella into the street and took off the Saint Christopher medal he wore around his neck on an extra long, extra strong chain. Not for any religious purpose, however. He slipped the chain into his left pocket.

With his back to the street, the pawnbroker was locking up in the dark alcove. He was having trouble with his key. Muttering, he didn't hear Jimmy's stealthy approach. Jimmy tapped his shoulder.

"Excuse me. Are you open?"

The man whirled around. "I'm closed. Come back Sunday."

"But there's a piece of goods I really need to buy for my girl. Tomorrow's her birthday."

"Closed!" the man said testily. *"Shabbat."* Whatever that was. "Come back Sunday morning."

Melnick fumbled with his key. The door was still ajar. Jimmy launched himself against the pawnbroker's back. The man knocked the door open as he fell in. Jimmy jumped inside after him.

"Please, mister—" Staggering to his feet, Melnick held up his hands. "Don't hurt me."

"I want something you got here. A necklace, with little red and green stones. You had it in the window."

Dusty sheets were draped over the display cases. "It's locked up in that case. I'll get it, you can have it, just don't hurt me."

Melnick stumbled toward the draped cases, then fairly hurled himself toward the back door. "Stupid kike," Jimmy snarled, yanking the medal and chain out of his pocket.

Before he reached the door, the fleeing pawnbroker heard Jimmy coming for him and yelped, "No!" Jimmy threw the chain over the man's head, jammed his knee in his back, yanked hard.

Jimmy applied more pressure. The pawnbroker's head lolled forward, and his body sagged against the chain, which was wet with blood. Jimmy let go, let him fall. And smiled. The feeling of power was so heady, he almost felt drunk.

Jimmy left the pawnbroker sprawled on the floor while he pondered how to find what he wanted. He closed the front door and shot the bolt. Then he switched on the lights. He worked fast, ripping the sheets off the locked cases one after another. He spotted it in the third case, lying in its velvet-lined box. He tore off a piece of sheet, wrapped it round and round his hand, held his breath, and hit the glass one hard blow. Seconds later he had the necklace box in his pocket and the lights off again.

He lifted the iron bar and went out through the rear. It had been much easier to kill a second time. He felt safe. Much safer than when he put the tart in the river in Chicago.

DUTCH ✦ On the same Friday that Jimmy Daws went to West Tampa, Paul returned from Ybor City in a state of shock from Michael's last revelation. At the hotel, he went straight to the rathskeller.

Billy Bitzer hailed him from a table. Bitzer had a pitcher of beer and a plate of sausages and sauerkraut in front of him. Paul sat down and asked his question in what he hoped was a casual way.

"Sure," Bitzer said, "there's a brigadier named Joe Crown on Wheeler's staff. Tough old turkey. Are you two related?"

Paul nodded. "We are related. He is my uncle."

"You sound like you don't care for him."

"Please, may we not pursue it further?"

"Whatever you want, pal. Join me in some dinner?"

"Another time. I have no appetite."

Paul found it hard to breathe. What should he do? The Tampa Bay Hotel was huge. If he stayed alert, didn't eat in the dining room, he could probably avoid his uncle. Or should he make his presence known to Uncle Joe? Take the first step toward a mutual forgiveness, a possible reconciliation? The voice of family said yes, powerfully. But his uncle had banished him. What if he was rejected a second time?

He remembered the pain of his banishment from the Crown mansion. Then he thought of his cousin. Rash and headstrong as he was, Joe Junior's only real crime had been caring about the downtrodden. He'd foolishly allowed himself to be influenced by Benno, and men had died. But never intentionally would Joe Junior have been a party to that.

Now Joe Junior was lost to his family. Lost because of Uncle Joe's rigidity, stupidity. And Paul had no home in Chicago, no place in America where he truly belonged.

He genuinely admired much about Uncle Joe. His bravery in coming to America alone; his idealism in fighting to free the Negro in the great war. His remarkable drive to riches and position. But Paul could never condone what Uncle Joe had done when he was opposed. Fixing on that, he beat down the strong yearning for reconciliation. *Go to Uncle Joe?* . . . No, he would not.

THE GENERAL ✦ She was seated alone at one of the small white tables in the Oriental Annex. How beautiful she was in her clinging white dress with the red ruffle. Waiting for him . . .

Him.

A sudden guilt held him motionless near the main entrance. *You must not do this. You must not betray Ilsa.* But he swept the thought away and moved toward her with a quick, decisive stride.

She saw him coming. Her eyes, dark brown, grew larger as he approached. Reaching her table, he bowed like any self-conscious swain of twenty. He felt himself blushing. "Senorita Rivera, I am General Joe Crown."

"Good evening, General. I know who you are," she said, smiling. Her English, though flavorfully accented, was perfect. Suddenly, again, he was ashamed; she couldn't be older than twenty-five.

"Would you care to sit?"

"I came over to ask if you would do me the honor of dancing with me."

"I'm sorry, no."

"Senorita, forgive me if I offended—"

"Not at all. When I fled Havana last year, I made a vow that I would neither sing nor dance again until the revolution drove the Spaniards out forever."

"Well, commendable idealism. I wonder, then—would you care to stroll in the garden?"

"A very pleasant suggestion." Rising, she took his arm. He felt like a planet flung out of orbit, falling through space.

In the garden, on the dark paths, he said, "I notice your brother isn't here this evening."

"A special meeting was called by General Shafter. Some problem concerning the rebel forces. Almovar, my brother, was with them in the mountains until last month."

An awkward silence ensued. Desperate, Joe said, "You say you fled Havana."

"After a fierce family dispute. The Riveras have lived in Cuba for more than a hundred years. Our father is an importer of fine wines from the homeland. He believes in the queen and in Weyler—Spanish supremacy, in short. It's to be expected—he's Castilian, seventy years old."

"You and your father fell out, then?"

"Yes. Both Almovar and I quarreled with him over this war, and also over our older brother, Ernesto. Ernesto left university two years ago to fight with the rebels. He died on the *trocha*. It was a very grisly death."

"I apologize. I don't know that word you used."

"*La trocha*. The trail. It's a cleared space in the jungle, rather like a shallow ditch, eighty kilometers long. It is meant to contain the rebels."

She went on to explain that the *trocha* was not merely a trench, but a fortified barricade with watchtowers at half-mile intervals. "Wherever *la trocha* is not manned, there are sharp stakes strung with barbed wire. Butcher Weyler also planted bombs, with trip wires. One of the wires caught Ernesto as he was crossing the *trocha* with a dispatch. Wounded, Ernesto was a feast for *los cangrejos*. Land crabs. Most are the size of saucers, but some are much larger. They are attracted by bloody meat.

"Gruesome creatures," she went on. "They click and clack their pincers, and they leave nothing on the bones. You never want to meet *los cangrejos*, General, especially if you are unable to defend yourself. They will devour the flesh while the victim is still alive. Providing the victim is helpless. Ernesto was helpless."

"Horrible," Joe whispered. "How did you learn of this?"

"A lieutenant inspector came along on horseback. He scattered the crabs with pistol shots. Then he fired a bullet of mercy into what was left of our poor brother. The lieutenant was a decent man; he wrote to our father. Ernesto's death precipitated the quarrel."

"How so?"

Estella Rivera's voice was low and bitter. "Our father said the tragedy was Ernesto's fault, because he valued freedom above his own life. Almovar and I left our father's house the next day." Joe was stung by similarities to events in his own family.

She paused at a bend in the path. "Now, General—"

"Please call me Joseph, or Joe."

"Joseph, then. I have said enough about my history. Tell me something of yours."

The darkness and her sweet, light scent—a little like almonds, a little like tropical flowers—aroused him. In a husky voice he said, "What I have to tell you is, I think you're the handsomest young woman I've ever seen." He leaned forward to kiss her. She twisted her head, and he kissed only the corner of her mouth.

"Don't—you will shame us both."

Startled, humiliated by his foolish behavior—feeling his age— Joe stepped back. Once more she stunned him. "Come to my room, four twenty-five. In ten minutes. We'll have privacy there."

She whirled and ran off in the dark. Joe staggered to a bench and sat down. Was he rejected or invited? He didn't know.

HE STOLE along the fourth-floor hall feeling like a burglar. One soft tap, and she let him in. She'd changed to a dark red silk wrapper with a high neck.

She had a single room, smaller than his but just as hot. She indicated a chair. "Please, Joseph, sit down. Would you be more comfortable without your jacket?" While he took off the heavy uniform jacket she opened the closet. "I have a half bottle of an excellent Spanish red. Would you care for a glass?"

"I would, thank you."

She poured a generous drink in a barrel-shaped hotel glass, but took none for herself. She sat down on the bed and crossed her legs gracefully. She was very composed. Heartbreakingly beautiful.

"I thought we might talk," she said. Though she was friendly, she was clearly setting limits. This intimacy was for conversation only.

He drank a little of the rich, fragrant Rioja. "Talk? Certainly. I am interested in knowing more about you. But first I must tell you something. I am a married man."

"Why, I knew that the first time you looked at me. But thank you for your candor. It confirms my impression that you are a good man. Now, what did you want to ask?"

"Your background—Havana. It must have been difficult for you and your brother to leave."

"Not under the circumstances, no. It was our duty to resist the government at this time. Our father would not."

"How do you feel about him now? If he's still a loyalist, doesn't it make him something of a traitor?"

"To me and my brother? Joseph, we quarreled with our father's foolish attitudes, not with his soul. We'll go back when the war's won and Cuba is liberated. He'll hate the new regime. Perhaps he'll hate us. But we'll love him all the same. What person would forever abandon a parent, or any relative, for being misguided?"

"I did."

That gave her pause. "You, Joseph? Tell me how it happened."

"Wait, there's more," he said. "I drove out a second person, my nephew, because he helped the first one—who was my son."

"Oh, Joseph, no wonder there is sorrow in your eyes. Is that why you ran away to war?"

"No, absolutely not—" He cleared his throat. His eyes met hers. In a small voice he said, "After I'd sent them away, my wife—she is a very fine woman, you understand—but things between us . . . deteriorated. Perhaps I did run away from it."

She left the bed and knelt at his knee. She reached up to stroke his damp forehead with cool fingers. "Confession. It purges pain and thereby calms the mind so it can find new paths. Tonight I'll hear your confession, Joseph." She squeezed his hand. "Tell me everything."

All the rest of the night he sat on the chair and talked. The monologue that poured out of him was about boyhood, Aalen, Cincinnati, and Chicago. About Ilsa, the war, the struggle to build Crown's. About his children, how he loved them and how they rebelled. About Joe Junior, driven out, and his nephew Pauli. "In our family I established certain rules—"

"You drove your son out because he broke your *rules?*"

"Estella, you don't understand. In business, rules are necessary."

"Your family is not a business. Life is not a business."

"Don't look at me that way, Estella. My life—my *whole life*—has been built on the principle of order. *Ordnung.* With my own hands, and that principle, I created my success. Wealth—"

"These rules—everyone must obey, or lose your love?"

He gave her a fierce look. She stroked his hand. Speaking softly, she said, "Tell me the rest."

In a few moments the confession resumed. He described his increasing resentment of Ilsa because of the blame he felt she placed on him. Blame for the loss of their son and their nephew. Estella listened attentively.

At the end, exhausted, he slumped in the chair.

"A remarkable story, Joseph. I think you understand now who was in the wrong when your son left, and your nephew. It isn't my place to give you advice. Nevertheless I shall." She smiled. "Repair the damage with your wife the moment you return home. Repair it with your son and your nephew as well."

"It's too late, the boys are gone."

"No. As long as they are alive somewhere, you have the opportunity. Find it, or you'll never again be whole. You'll keep hunting another war, another reason to leave your wife, your home, your calling, and underneath it all, your remorse."

He stared at his hands. He looked at the mirror of himself and saw mistakes, and folly, and hated the image, but she had forced him to confront it. His eyes explored and silently adored her face.

She sat calmly, accepting the scrutiny. There was a powerful, silent current surging between them, a hunger each for the other. Joe felt it and said, "I want to love you, Estella. There in the bed."

"I want it too, Joseph. But we will not."

"You refuse me?"

"It breaks my heart, but yes—I refuse you."

"Then I'd best get out of here."

"Yes, I think so. It's almost five."

When he had put his jacket on, she held his arm and walked him to the door. "I want to give you my own confession before you go. If you weren't married, I would take you to that bed this instant. I'd love you a long time."

Her red mouth came up, warm and sweet, in a protracted kiss of parting. His heart beat like thunder.

"You are a good man, Joe Crown. We'll not see each other again."

In the hall, he took a few steps, then turned back for another kiss. The key clicked on her side of the closed door. He walked away.

Next morning he presented a note to the clerk at the rotunda desk. "This is for your guest Senorita Rivera."

"Rivera, Rivera." The man riffled some cards. "General, I'm afraid she's departed. For Key West, she said."

"Have you a forwarding address?"

"She left none. I'm sorry. You might ask her brother."

But he wouldn't. She knew, he thought, profoundly sad and grateful. She knew that together, we were in danger. She saved us from lifelong shame. But that was not the only way she saved me.

ELSTREE ✦ Very early that same Sunday morning, hundreds of miles away in New York City, Elstree stretched his legs in a plush armchair. The chair was one of several good pieces he'd bought when he set Rose up in this flat on Sixth Avenue.

Red-and-yellow electric signs on Sixth Avenue tinted the wallpaper between patches of shadow. He heard her taffeta skirts rustling. Once he'd thought it a sensual sound. Not tonight. The shadow of her gloved hand appeared on the wall, moving toward the switch.

"Don't turn it on. You've given me a monstrous headache."

"Well, I'm sorry about that. What am I supposed to do?" She was half defiance, half tears.

"Rose, please shut up a minute and let me think." She sank down onto the creaking bed and removed her hat, a little straw with artificial violets. She always wanted to look smart, and always failed; taste was not something she'd ever learned.

They'd just returned in a hack from a late supper at Delmonico's. Rose was still singing at Tony Pastor's, on the bill as Rose French, International Soubrette. He'd seen her too often and had come to hate her third-rate voice. Her looks had besotted him for a while; he couldn't explain how that cheap allure had persisted so long.

The elevated train shunted by, its lights flying over the walls. Elstree felt a patter of cinders in his hair. He reached behind him and slammed the window. "This place is dirty all the time."

"Who rented it? Not I, Billy."

"Damn it, don't call me Billy." He grabbed his stick and rapped the ferrule on the floor. The stick was fashionable malacca, with a heavy handle.

She gave him a wary look. Elstree said, "Let's discuss this little surprise you've sprung on me, Rose. How do I know it's mine?"

"I haven't been with nobody—anybody else. And sometimes you aren't too careful."

The malacca stick flashed up, an accusing pointer. "*We*. I am not the only one culpable. If indeed there's really any culpability here." He was enraged. He wanted an heir, but not from a tramp.

Rose was pouting. "You try to make me feel low with those words I can't understand."

"Culpability. Responsibility. Is that clear enough for you?"

"You listen to me. There is plenty of culpability here. Feel my belly."

"Don't be disgusting." Elstree took a breath. "All right, what is it you want?"

"I want help. You got me in a fix. I'll have to give up my career for a good long time."

"Your career. That's hardly a loss, especially to audiences. I'll pay whatever it costs to get rid of it."

Rose paced to the window and back to the bed. "Bill, I can't do it. Last year a friend of mine went to a place out on the marsh at Throgs Neck to get rid of one. She bled to death." She rubbed her arms in an agitated way. "Not me. Not me."

"Your friend must have picked the wrong man."

"Doesn't matter, I won't do it. I'll have the baby, and I want ten thousand till I get my figure back, and my career."

Elstree stood up and reached into his pocket for a silver money clip. The clip held hundred-dollar bills. He dropped two on the bed. "That's for expenses. Get rid of it, get on with your life, and don't bother me again."

"That's it? You just dismiss me? Bill, you may be able to fob off other girls this way, but you can't do it to me. I'll raise hell."

He felt heat in his face. "You had better not."

"I will. I'll get lawyers, I'll make noise, I'll smear your name everywhere. I'll go out to Long Island and find your wife—"

He hit her a slashing blow with the malacca stick. She staggered backward. He dropped the stick and pushed her onto the bed.

He jumped on her, pinning her right hand with his left while he punched her face. He hit her again. Hit her, hit her . . .

Finally he stopped. Blood smeared her cheeks and drooled out of her nose. He disliked having to put her down this way, but somehow women always drove him to it at the end of a relationship.

He retrieved his stick and top hat and snapped on the ceiling light. At the mirror, he saw he'd gotten her blood on his fine white silk scarf. Angry, he whipped it from his neck and used it to clean his knuckles. Then he threw it on the carpet.

He looked at Rose. She lay on the bed, curled up like a child, moaning softly. What an idiot he'd been to entangle himself with her. Still, she was such a pathetic sight that he took out the clip and dropped another hundred beside the first two.

"Good-bye, Rose. Don't ever try to see me again."

He walked quickly down two flights and into Sixth Avenue, deserted at this hour near dawn. He began to whistle.

Suddenly he realized what the tune was. "Flowers That Bloom in the Spring, Tra-la." One of Rose's numbers. How appropriate.

DUTCH ✦ The hotel was full of talk about a Jewish pawnbroker found murdered in his shop. The Tampa *Times* said police were investigating.

Late in the morning Paul walked across the river to the depot with a small wooden crate containing two more film magazines. He feared the colonel would find most of the footage dull, filled with now familiar scenes.

He left the freight office and, hot as it was, decided to walk awhile. He headed north. The heat was intense, even in the shade. When would they get out of here? he wondered.

After ten or twelve blocks he turned east, into a shabby section on the edge of Ybor City. He heard loud laughter coming from an alley between two stores. To the left was a *farmacia,* on his right a *quincalleria*—a hardware store. At the drugstore hitch rail, a sorrel mare with a U.S. Army saddle was standing.

In the shadowed alley, four soldiers were tossing a fifth into the air with a blanket. Paul had photographed blanket-tossing in the camps. He thought it silly. But an alley was a strange place for . . .

The soldiers whipped the blanket aside and let the victim fall. He was a black man, his holster empty, bloodstains visible on his brown fatigue blouse.

Landing hard, he gave an involuntary cry. In a few seconds he tried to rise. An overweight sergeant kicked him. The sergeant was white. So were the others.

"Here, leave him alone," Paul shouted, running into the dim alley. Three of the soldiers were young men, with red, sunburned skin and an undernourished look. The sergeant was older, with a round white face. He snaked his revolver out of its holster.

"I wouldn't mess in this, boy." He brought the gun up level with

Paul's eyes. "This nigger tried to sit down next to a white woman at the drugstore fountain."

"Looks like you beat him half to death for it," Paul said while his brain busily calculated the odds against him.

"Hey, he's some kind of foreigner, Cheat," one of the others said.

"Yeah, well, mebbe I'll blow that funny accent right down his throat. Boy, d'ya know who we are? Jacksonville Light Infantry of the First Florida. This here's our home state. Our territory. Don't fool with us."

Volunteers. He might have guessed. He felt taut as a wire, not wanting a bullet, but not wanting to run either. On the ground behind the four, the black soldier was groggily rousing. When he took in the situation, his hand shot out, grabbing the sergeant's boot. Sergeant Cheat fell on his face. His revolver went off. The bullet tore through the dirt, raising dust.

Paul had already reeled around to the street. He yanked a shovel from a barrel outside the hardware store. Holding the shovel in both hands like a fighting staff, he jumped back into the alley.

Sergeant Cheat was on his knees, grappling with the black man for the revolver. Paul bowled into the other soldiers with the shovel held in front of him. Two of them went down.

Cheat got possession of the revolver. Holding the barrel, he struck the black soldier a vicious blow to the head. The soldier pitched over, unconscious.

"Cheat, we'll be in the guardhouse, we don't run outa here," one of the soldiers said, panting. Cheat squinted at Paul, crouched with the shovel, then led a running retreat down the alley and out of sight.

The black soldier lay with eyes closed, bleeding. Paul knelt to make sure he was breathing, then went into the drugstore.

The soda fountain, up front, was empty. At the back, the white druggist was energetically dusting an apothecary jar.

"There's a soldier hurt outside. Can you telephone the authorities for assistance?"

The druggist, avoiding his eye, went on dusting. "Phone's out of order."

Instantly Paul understood. He stalked out the door, disgusted.

In the alley, he squatted and lifted the injured man. Staggering a couple of times, Paul draped the man across the saddle of the cavalry horse and untied the rein. He led the horse all the way up to Tampa Heights, to the camp of the 24th and 25th Infantry regiments, the nearest black units, and found the dispensary.

He described the incident to a doctor, who examined the soldier and found nothing more serious than bruises and abrasions. He made a note of Paul's name and where he was staying, and thanked him. Paul left the camp and rode the trolley down into town.

Next morning, a few minutes after six, a knock woke him. He tugged on his pants and was surprised to find a white cavalry officer standing outside—a lean, tall man, middle thirties, with blue eyes, bushy brows, and a severe, down-turned mouth.

"Crown?"

"Yes."

"First Lieutenant Pershing, Tenth Cavalry. May I come in?"

Paul stepped back. The lieutenant shut the door and took off his campaign hat. Paul started to gesture to the chair, then realized that almost every surface was covered by items of his souvenir collection. Pershing's blue eyes whipped over the disorder.

"I'll take only a few moments of your time," he said. "Dr. Long, who serves the Twenty-fourth, advised me that you assisted one of my men yesterday. I'm here to thank you. Corporal Person is a member of the troop that I command. We're tracking the men who beat him. You reported that one was called Cheat?"

Paul raked his dark, tangled hair. "That's the name I heard. Sergeant Cheat. He boasted about his unit, the Jacksonville Light Infantry of the First Florida."

"All I needed was that confirmation. We'll have him arrested within an hour. The Negro regulars are having a lot of trouble with these redneck volunteers. I hate for it to happen to Person, he's a fine soldier. I hate for it to happen to any man in the Tenth. I've learned to respect and admire our black troops." Pershing paused as he studied Paul's reaction. "That isn't what you expected me to say, is it? I'm aware that it's a minority view. Because of it, I'm sometimes called Black Jack. Now, Mr. Crown, a request. If you can, please go up to Tampa Heights. Corporal Person very much wants to tender his thanks."

Paul said that he would go. He saw the lieutenant scan the litter of souvenirs once more. "I like to collect things from places I visit," Paul said. In Tampa he'd accumulated postcards. Conch shells. A stuffed baby alligator. Two coconuts carved into Indian faces. Pieces of driftwood. And, of course, on the dressing table, the worn stereoscope card.

"Well—" Pershing shot his hand out. "Thank you again for helping one of my men. You're a very decent chap."

They shook hands. With crisp movements Pershing donned his campaign hat. He about-faced and marched out of the room.

Paul flopped onto the bed, with his hands under his head. He didn't want to look at the pathetic collection of junk. That's all it was, junk, gathered in a stupid attempt to fool himself into thinking he had belongings, and therefore belonged somewhere. He didn't. His long search for a home was idiocy.

This is my home, he thought. This or another place like it. There is nothing else.

THAT afternoon Paul rode the trolley out to Tampa Heights. He found Corporal Person on the cot where he'd left him. Person was sitting up, a bandage wrapped around his head; crinkly gray hair showed between his ears and the bandage.

When he saw Paul, he broke into a grin. "You got to be the German fellow who pulled my hash out of the fire."

"I brought you here, if that's what you mean. Paul Crown is my name. Everyone calls me Dutch."

"When I woke up this morning, I thought about you. Didn't know your name, so I gave you one—Heine. Heard another German called that once—he didn't seem to mind."

"Call me Heine if you want. Do you have a nickname?"

"Ott. Short for Othello. My brother's Duff, short for Macduff. Our daddy was a Pullman car porter, y'see. Had lots of time to read during the night. He was partial to Shakespeare. Here, I'm forgetting my manners. Pull up that stool, sit yourself."

Paul asked, "How'd you get in that fix yesterday, Ott?"

"Tenth Cavalry's camped way out in Lakeland. I was sent in with dispatches for General Shafter at the hotel. Rode thirty miles on horseback, delivered the pouch, and thought a drink of soda water would taste good. I didn't want to ask at the hotel. Too fancy. I rode across to Tampa and spied that drugstore. Those Florida boys din't take kindly to me bein' there, sitting by a white lady."

They exchanged some facts about themselves. Ott had been

raised in Philadelphia and had run on the streets until he was eighteen, old enough to enlist. Paul said he'd been a street boy in Berlin. Ott grinned.

"Knew there was something made me like you right off."

"And you like the army?"

"I most surely do. Let me explain something. In this here country we got equality, but some's a lot more equal than others. In the army it's a mite better. We got some rights. I keep chipping away to get a few more. That may be why I walked into that drugstore. I knew it was a white man's place.

"Anyway, Heine, things do improve. Sometimes hellish slow, but they do. I ain't ready to give up on this country yet."

Paul consulted his watch and said he'd have to leave soon.

"We'll be off for Cuba one of these weeks," Ott said. "I may not see you down there. But if I do, and you're in a fix, remember this. I owe you for helping me. I always pay what I owe."

"Thanks, Ott. Let's hope it won't be necessary. So long."

"So long, Heine."

Troubled, Paul trudged along the road. What kind of country was it that asked a man to wear its uniform, then spit on him?

At the hotel gate, he paused to listen to a regimental band playing "After the Ball." In the dark gardens couples were strolling and laughing. "Julie," he whispered. "Julie."

TUESDAY, the seventh of June. Paul had just fallen asleep when he was jolted awake by noises in the hall. Doors slamming. People running. Was there a fire?

He jumped from bed, yanked the door open. In the hall, soldiers and civilians were scurrying with grips and field bags. Crane bolted from his room, several doors down, suitcase in hand.

"Stephen! What is it?"

"Orders to sail. Posted a few minutes ago. Better pack and get downstairs or you'll be all night paying your bill."

Paul threw his shirt and pants on and rushed next door, to Jimmy's room. He knocked and called out. No answer. He tried the knob. The door opened. He switched on the lights. The bed was still made. Cursing, Paul ran to pack.

Crane was right, it was hell getting out of the hotel. Paul stood in the cashier's long line, then had to find a porter to box and ship all

375

his souvenirs. He'd packed only the stereoscope card. He half suspected the souvenirs would be dumped in some trash bin.

What did it matter? There would be many other rooms, many other places to collect souvenirs—and dozens of dots of red enamel to be painted on the wooden globe, which Mary was keeping for him. That was his life now. The life of a gypsy who had no home and never would.

PAUL reached Port Tampa, with the crates of equipment in the hands of a burly drayman he'd hired at the hotel. Three gray iron vessels were tied up; others were waiting in the channel. The pier was crowded with soldiers.

"Don't lose sight of these crates. I'll pay you ten dollars once we stow them aboard," Paul said to the drayman. He had to search for Jimmy. He plunged into the mob on the pier.

Five minutes later he found Jimmy. It was accidental; Paul was passing a crude yellow-pine building, one of several forming what people called Last Chance Street. Jimmy ambled out a side door, snugging an elegant brand-new derby on his head.

"There you are!" Paul cried, dashing up to him. "We have to find a ship. Come on."

They started off, Jimmy grumbling as usual.

The bow of a dilapidated freighter loomed. Paul stood in her shadow, staring up at her painted name: *Yucatan.*

"Crown? Dutch Crown? Over here." Colonel Roosevelt jumped from the lower end of the *Yucatan*'s gangplank. "You look a bit lost," he said to Paul. "Any way I can be of assistance?"

"I need two places on a ship."

"There are two of you?"

"And our equipment."

"We'll be tight as sardines in a can. But two more won't make much difference. Fetch your gear, Mr. Crown. The armada will sail on the first favorable tide. We're going to war, my boy." With great glee, he thumped Paul on the back. "To war!"

Paul and Jimmy found the drayman and wrestled their equipment aboard the *Yucatan.* The gray metal deck fairly sizzled, radiating the heat like a griddle.

Twenty minutes before the *Yucatan* was scheduled to warp away from the pier, to allow another transport to come in, Paul found he was out of cigars. He worked his way down the gangplank, ran to Last Chance Street, and bought a small box of cheroots. As he started back to the transport, someone hailed him. Michael Radcliffe, immaculate in a white suit. He seemed impervious to the disorder and dirt of Port Tampa.

Michael strolled along with Paul. "I've been brooding about your situation, Paul. Your various disappointments in this country. Have you had any further thoughts on the subject?"

"None. Too busy."

"Well, I have one. Consider another venue. London. Robert W. Paul of Hatton Garden produces and exhibits pictures like those you're making for this bloke in Chicago. Like your chap, he employs a camera operator. Perhaps he'll need another—he's expanding very rapidly. Even Lord Yorke, my esteemed father-in-law, has expressed interest in the moving pictures. With your experience, I'm sure a place could be found for you. I'll gladly assist you with contacts. You would be doing work that you like, and you could live anywhere. I think at heart you're a wanderer, like me."

Paul couldn't say a word; Michael's idea was too new and startling. They were at the gangplank. *Yucatan*'s whistle blasted.

Michael laid his hand on Paul's shoulder. "Think about it! It could be a fine opportunity. If you're interested, I'll pop off a cable or two. Assuming we all get out of the bloody Cuban jungles alive."

THAT night, sailing orders were canceled. Washington had received a signal about two Spanish warships sighted off the north coast of Cuba. The War Department refused to risk an attack on the convoy. The ships would stay in Tampa Bay until Washington said the danger was past.

While they rode at anchor Colonel Wood enforced strict discipline in his regiment. Gambling was banned. Even so, Jimmy managed to find a game of craps or euchre every night and win some money.

One evening he found Paul smoking a cigar at the bow rail. Jimmy was flushed and excited; he'd won fourteen dollars. He leaned over the rail, hands clasped as he gazed at the rippling water. "This is gonna be my first and last war. I'm going home and set myself up as my own boss."

"Doing what?"

"Making money. I haven't done too bad down here."

Paul's scalp was crawling. He'd heard there had been five burglaries in the hotel. "You made money in Tampa? How?"

"Oh, different ways. Cards. Craps. You know."

Yes, Paul thought, I think I do. But he didn't call Jimmy a liar. He would need Jimmy's help in Cuba. Even if he was a thief.

THE armada finally sailed on June 14. It consisted of thirty-two transports and more than fifteen thousand officers and men. Nine hundred and fifty horses and thirteen hundred mules; ammunition, foodstuffs, wagons; artillery that included seven-inch howitzers, five-inch guns, field mortars, and four Gatling guns. The largest military expedition ever sent outside the United States was under way. Its goal was clear.

So was Paul's, perhaps.

He was at the bow rail again, pondering Michael Radcliffe's words on the pier.

With your experience, I'm sure a place could be found. I'll assist you with contacts. Think about it!

What if he let Michael help him? What if he established a base in London and lived in rented quarters wherever the picture assignments took him? Suddenly there was a sense of a burden lifting. He'd gone to his grip, dug to the bottom, and found the badly bent stereoscope card. He remembered a significant moment before he left Berlin. A picture card of the Kaiser torn in half—left behind to cast away the old, as a gesture toward the new. In Michael's offer of help, Paul thought he'd come to such a moment again.

He studied the harbor and the lady of Liberty, with her torch raised high. How many hopes that picture represented. Hopes, and bitter defeats. Some of the bitterest of his life. Joe Junior had once called him naïve about America. Well, it was so. In the persons of Wex and Shadow, America had given him a lifelong profession. But that could never compensate for the loss of his family and the girl he loved.

Now another place beckoned him. Not a new home; he was through with that stupid child's dream. Rather, he'd have a roving commission, a base in Europe, to help him forget all he'd yearned for and lost.

Paul tore the stereoscope card in two and dropped the right half overside. An updraft caught it, whirled it high, then flung it to the water. It was instantly gone in the foaming bow wake.

He slipped the other half of the card into his shirt pocket. No more symbolism; just another souvenir.

While the anguish of failure in America, the loss of Julie, would never leave, he could begin to look forward to the future again.

Assuming—Michael's words—*we all get out of the bloody Cuban jungles alive.*

Part Nine
WAR
1898

THE GENERAL ✦ Joe Crown traveled not on *Segurança*, the headquarters ship, but on a smaller one, *Allegheny*, the command ship for General Wheeler's cavalry division. Within two days of sailing, a smudge of land appeared where sea and sky joined. It was Cuba. But the following week, on June 21, the convoy was still steaming sluggishly off the south coast of the island. The fortified harbor of Santiago was about forty miles ahead.

With a telescope Joe scanned a shoreline that was both breathtaking and daunting. White waves rolled and crashed, driven by a steady wind. Above the surf rose sheer limestone cliffs, and behind them, heavily forested hills that reached still higher to become a striking mountain range, the Sierra Maestra. The dark green forest looked thick and wet, with here and there a bit of a narrow trail showing. It was beautiful and desolate. A difficult place to land, and march, and fight.

And what of the Spaniards? Supposedly as many as twelve thousand were assigned to defend this southeast coast. Where were they hiding? They could be lying in wait within the range of his telescope, totally concealed by the jungle.

The convoy anchored well offshore. U.S. warships were steaming farther out, in preparation for a bombardment.

Around four o'clock a cutter bore Wheeler, Joe Crown, the other senior officers, and their aides to the headquarters ship for a meeting with General Shafter. The meeting was held in the main saloon.

Shafter seemed more elephantine than ever, and pale and tired, as he sat waiting in a special oversized chair while his aides set up a map stand. He rolled to his feet with a wheeze of effort. "Gentlemen, tomorrow morning, as soon after daylight as practicable, we will invade the island of Cuba."

There was an excited ripple of approval as Shafter lumbered to the map. "We must take Santiago, but not by direct attack. The cliffs around the harbor argue most forcefully against that. Therefore, I propose to position the army *around* Santiago, strike hard to break through enemy lines, overcome the string of Spanish blockhouses which protect the town, then press quickly for a surrender.

"We will commence our landing here." Shafter struck the map. "Daiquirí. The settlement was the headquarters for the Spanish-American Iron Company, but the war has suspended operations. What we'll find there is a tall pier, some zinc huts and palm-leaf cottages, and a roundhouse at the end of a rail spur which goes inland. If the line is still intact, we will be able to transport men and horses to Siboney, a coastal hamlet seven miles west. From there we'll strike northwest over the trails, cross the Aguadores River, and capture Santiago."

Shafter continued. "First to go in will be General Lawton with the Second Division and the four Gatling guns. Shortly after daylight Admiral Sampson's fleet will begin diversionary bombardments along the coast. After we land all the men, we will land the mules and horses."

Joe Wheeler bounced to his feet, plucking at his white beard. "Sir!" Shafter recognized him courteously. "When we land, do we know what to expect in the way of resistance?"

Shafter's eyes darted nervously. "Scouts have provided us with good information on fortifications in the area. There are earthworks, breastworks, trenches, and rifle pits. There is a Spanish blockhouse on the heights."

"But how many soldiers waiting for us?"

Gloomily Shafter said, "We don't know."

WEDNESDAY, June 22. Reveille sounded at half past three in the morning. Soon *Allegheny*'s deck was packed with men. Heavy mist lay on the mountains. The village of Daiquirí—what could be seen of it—looked dead as a graveyard. Through his telescope Joe Crown watched a thread of smoke rising in front of a thatched cottage; someone had built a cook fire, then gone away.

An onshore wind was blowing hard, creating crests of white water that would make landing on the pier dangerous. To ferry the troops ashore, there were steam launches, each with a chain of longboats tied behind it; as the sky brightened, the launches began to position themselves around the transports. Joe had donned his blue frock coat and dress sword. He could remember few times when he'd been so hot and sticky.

A series of rolling explosions brought a cheer from the crowded decks of the transports. Admiral Sampson's squadron had begun its diversionary shelling. Wheeler paced up and down near Joe, muttering. He didn't like the swells crashing against the high pilings of the pier.

Excited cries whipped Joe's attention toward the shore. Some straw-hatted horsemen came galloping through the village, brandishing a Cuban flag and hallooing to the ships. Wheeler said, "By damn, the Spaniards must've pulled out during the night. Those boys are on our side."

The shelling stopped. Palm huts were burning throughout the village, sending black smoke upward.

Gangway doors were opened in the hulls of the transports, near the waterline. Rope ladders were let down. At half past ten the first men climbed down the ladders to the longboats.

One launch after another pulled its crowded longboats alongside the tall pier. When an incoming wave lifted one of the boats high enough, the men jumped for it. Some missed the pier and fell into the water. Joe could hear their terrified cries, see the patches of blood on the pilings. Those who rode the longboats to the beach had an easier time. They jumped out and waded ashore.

By afternoon the waters of Daiquirí resounded with the neighs and brays of horses and mules dropped over the side from slings on davits to swim to the beach. Finally heading ashore in a longboat, Joe counted nine dead animals in the water.

The beach swarmed with men, some of them civilians. One, a man in a wide-brimmed straw hat, was wading ashore with a moving picture camera and tripod on his shoulder. A second man, wearing a derby, slogged behind him carrying a large canvas bag. At long distance, Joe couldn't identify either man, but he supposed one was the camera operator he'd met, Bitzer.

Daiquirí was mud streets, smoldering huts, and damaged buildings. The officers hurried toward the roundhouse. Greasy smoke billowed from its shot-out windows. Half the roof had caved in. A crowd of about fifty Cuban soldiers came running toward the officers, screaming, *"Viva los americanos!"* A couple of the Americans brandished their swords and returned cries of *"Viva Cuba libre!"* Joe didn't join in; he wasn't impressed by the shoeless, shirtless rebels.

General Wheeler had already loped off to the other side of the building. Joe and the rest hurried after him and found the single railroad track into the jungle. It was useless—crossties broken, rails pried up and bent.

Wheeler slapped his old black hat against his leg. "We'll transport no men on this line. Joe, find out where the horses are. I want to go inland before Shafter tells me I can't."

"Sir," Joe said with a fast salute. He and his aide, Tyree Bates, walked swiftly through the village. They located their mounts on the beach, and Joe yelled at the wranglers to get them moving. Following the horses on foot, he was pulled up short by a sight that confused him.

Two men were unloading a camera and tripod from a longboat. Joe said to Bates, "I'll catch up with you," and hurried down to the surf.

The men hoisted their camera to bring it ashore; it was twice as large as the one he'd seen earlier. The young man giving orders wore a houndstooth cap and a natty but water-soaked jacket. Joe knew him.

"Hello, Bitzer. I thought I saw you come in some time ago."

"Not us," Bitzer said unhappily. "Shafter wouldn't allow any civilians off the headquarters ship till now. Maybe you saw the crew traveling on *Yucatan.*"

"Where are they from?"

"American Luxograph in Chicago. One of 'em I don't like, but the chief operator's a good egg."

"What's his name?"

Bitzer's eyes had a curious, evasive look. He hesitated, but his assistant said, "Paul Crown. Everybody calls him Dutch."

DUTCH ✦ At five o'clock General Wheeler ordered men to an abandoned blockhouse on the hill above Daiquirí. One carried a flag.

Paul looked for Jimmy. He was nowhere to be found. Annoyed, Paul cropped his grip, lowered the camera from his shoulder, and checked the meter. Fifty feet left. That was lucky; Jimmy was carrying the canvas bag with the fresh magazines.

High above, men appeared on the blockhouse rampart. Paul started cranking. The Stars and Stripes ran up the blockhouse pole. It would be a grand finish to his footage of the men in the longboats, the smoking ruins of Daiquirí.

A thundering yell from hundreds of throats greeted the flag. Just then Jimmy sauntered out of the drifting smoke, suitcase and canvas bag clutched in his left hand. In his right he had one of the long, wicked bush knives called machetes.

"Where did you get that knife?" Paul asked.

"Took it. Never mind where."

Paul held his temper.

BEHIND Daiquirí a grassy flat stretched away to a lush green wall of jungle. In the open area, Colonel Wood's 1st Volunteer Cavalry was encamping for the night. Paul and Jimmy approached.

To the right was a murky lagoon. They found space well away from it to put down their gear. They had one rubber ground cloth packed in the canvas bag. Paul knew Jimmy would want it. He didn't propose to argue, and gave the ground cloth to Jimmy, then rolled on his side in the damp grass. In spite of searchlights from the warships, the noise of the troops, the heat and the damp, Paul drifted off.

Suddenly Jimmy was screaming, "Help! What is it? Get it off me!" Paul bolted up. By moonlight he saw Jimmy lying on his back, batting at something on his chest. Something large, round as a saucer, with flailing appendages.

Something crawled on Paul's leg. He looked down and yelped. In the grass all around, he heard rustling and clicking.

Paul struck the crab off his leg. It was a hideous thing, with two long, waving pincers, two round eyes on stalks. It had a mouth of sorts; the lips were like horny beaks. As he watched them open and close, open and close, a paralyzing terror took hold of him. Around his boots half a dozen more crabs clicked their pincers. Jimmy was still yelling, though he'd flung off the crab that woke him. Similar disturbances had broken out among the tents of the regiment.

A sergeant ran up as Paul tottered to his feet. "Land crabs," he exclaimed. "A whole damn army of 'em. They aren't really dangerous 'less a man's wounded. What they want is bloody meat." The sergeant ran off to alert others.

Shaking, Paul said, "Help me pick up the gear. We're moving."

"What good'll that do? They're all over this field. I should have left before now. Maybe I'll give you notice right here."

"Jim, if you quit on me, that would be the act of a coward."

"You rat. Call me a coward again, I'll chop your head off." Jimmy grabbed the machete, whirled and slashed at some tall grass.

They stood glaring at one another in the moonlight. Suddenly exhaustion took the starch out of both of them. Paul said, "All right. Truce. Let's move." Jimmy snatched the rubber sheet from the ground, and they shifted their gear to a new location on the flat. But every time they settled down, the land crabs intruded.

In the morning, bleary and miserable, they ate hardtack and drank tin cups of lukewarm coffee. Then they set out for Siboney. Ahead lay seven miles of a rank green purgatory.

The trail was choked with soldiers, teamsters fighting their wagons up and down the grades, strings of mules laden with provisions, water, ammunition. One large wagon, piled with crates, was stenciled PROPERTY AMERICAN BIOGRAPH CO. NEW YORK USA. Paul recognized the houndstooth cap of the driver. "Billy!"

Sleeves rolled up, Bitzer was quirting his two mules while his assistant, Len, dragged on their headstalls. "Hallo, gents. You're welcome to ride along," Bitzer said.

Paul laid the Luxograph in a space between Bitzer's crates of storage batteries and climbed up beside Billy. Jimmy chose to walk in front with Len. The going was slow.

"Say," Bitzer said abruptly. "You won't like this much, but I'd better tell you. Your uncle, the general—he knows you're here. I met him on the beach, and he asked about the other picture crews. I kept my mouth shut, but Len spilled your name. He didn't know he was doing wrong."

Grimly Paul said, "He wasn't. But now I'll have to face my uncle. I can't hide and do my job too."

Bitzer left Paul and Jimmy at the edge of Siboney. Paul thanked him, and waved as the Biograph men drove away.

Although Siboney was larger than Daiquirí, it was just as poor. On a curving beach, drab fishing boats were tied up at a dilapidated pier. Transports anchored offshore were disgorging more men into longboats.

Paul and Jimmy found a campsite on the beach among the hundreds of men who'd put up shelter tents. The site was made rough by broken shells in the sand, but Paul hoped the absence of long grass would mean fewer land crabs. His feet were blistered, his legs ached, and his back hurt from carrying the camera.

Jimmy had disappeared on another of his mysterious excursions. Let him rob half the population, I don't care, Paul thought wearily. Then he set out for the center of the village.

Siboney was crowded with troops. Mounted couriers clattered by. Paul spoke to several officers; none knew when the advance would begin. Turning away from the last of these encounters, he was looking directly into the sun. He threw his hand in front of his eyes and stepped into the shadow of a shanty. When he lowered his hand, there was Michael Radcliffe.

Michael was swinging the walking stick he'd carried in Ybor City. He looked cool and clean in a straw boater and fashionable suit of lightweight white flannel. "Greetings, my friend. You look totally at sea."

"Like everyone else, Michael. Do you know how or when the campaign will go forward?"

"Absolutely not. It really doesn't matter to me. I've set up my base and shall report all the action from a table in a convenient cantina, just there." He pointed with the stick. "Care to join me?"

The cantina was small and relatively clean. They sat at a table. The beer served couldn't rival Crown's, but it was cool, and Paul was thirsty. Michael said his gin was "barely palatable."

Paul drew a deep breath. "Michael."

"Sir?"

"I would like to take you up on your offer of help in England."

"Capital! I'm absolutely delighted you've abandoned your starry visions of America. You have passed through the gates of wisdom. Congratulations."

A moment later a shadow fell between the squeaking half doors

385

of the cantina. Stephen Crane sauntered in, wearing a tan hunting suit stained with the dirt of the trails. His smile was amiable, but his eyes held too much sadness for a man not yet thirty.

Crane took a seat and called for whiskey. Michael said, "I'll pay for the drinks. Tell us what you know, Stephen."

"You may be getting a bad deal, but I accept. Here's all I know at the moment. Up in the hills, the Spaniards are holding a strategic road junction. We'll have to force the junction to reach Santiago. Joe Wheeler's gone up the road to reconnoiter. He was cussing all day because Shafter's kept the cavalry in the rear. But something's dawned on old Joe. While Shafter is still rolling around out there on the ocean, Wheeler is senior commander ashore. If he moves fast enough, he may call the tune."

Crane sipped his whiskey. "Getting anything good with your camera, Dutch?"

"I filmed the landing. What I want most are combat scenes."

"Then take my advice. Follow Joe Wheeler."

CRANE was right about Wheeler. After dark there came word of an early morning march. The objective would be the Spanish defense line guarding the main Santiago road at an abandoned village, Las Guásimas. The Spanish were entrenched on hilltops above the road. Generals Wheeler, Young, and Crown were to advance along the main road with eight troops of regulars. Taking a roughly parallel route on a foot trail that wound through the hills closer to the coast, Wood's Rough Riders would march toward the same objective.

Paul decided to accompany the Rough Riders.

He washed his dirty clothes in the surf and laid them near the flickering fire they'd coaxed from some soft wood. He hoped everything would dry by morning, so that he could store the clothes in his grip, which he intended to leave at the cantina. He had one dry shirt and pair of pants left in the bag.

Jimmy sat close to the fire, the camera and canvas bag just behind him, protected by a large piece of oilcloth. "So tomorrow's when we get shot, huh?"

"Tomorrow is the day we film some fighting if we are lucky. I am going to ask permission to go with the Rough Riders."

"I wouldn't cry if they told you to go to hell."

Paul walked to the Rough Riders' bivouac and found Colonel

Wood's tent. While he stood outside, waiting his turn, it began to rain, raising steam clouds from the ground. Paul's turn came, and he stated his request. Wood frowned. Paul feared he'd say no.

"Davis is coming with us, and Mr. Marshall of the New York *Journal.* I suppose we can't very well deny equal treatment to you and Bitzer. All right, permission granted. Be ready to move at three a.m. And stay in the rear."

FRIDAY, June 24. Wood's command was assembling at the foot of the trail. Most of the soldiers were in good spirits, even though they'd camped in the rain and now stood shivering in wet clothes. Paul and Jimmy, looking like a pair of muddy scarecrows, arrived with camera and canvas bag at the rear of the column. Waiting there, they fell into conversation with a bowlegged private from Texas named Jerry Pruitt.

At five forty-five a.m. the column began its advance. Paul shouldered the camera, Jimmy the canvas bag. Jimmy had left his suitcase with Paul's valise at the cantina. The machete rode in his belt.

Just then, Bitzer and Len arrived, their bulky camera and storage batteries packed into a mule cart. Bitzer eyed the trail. "With this load, we'll be lucky to keep up. Anyway—stay safe."

"You too, Billy," said Paul.

The first part of the advance was arduous, up the steep trail, which narrowed as it snaked across the hills behind Siboney. Quickly Bitzer's mule cart fell behind. The column crossed the last ridge, then headed down into more open country. To their left lay rolling fields of tall grass, separated from the trail by five-strand barbed wire with gaps cut in it. On the right, the ground sloped gently down toward the unseen main road, where Uncle Joe and the other senior officers would be advancing with their commands.

By half past seven the men were sweating hard and grousing about the heat. Colonel Wood halted the column, and an order was passed back. "Fill your magazines and stop your talking." The men readied their Krag-Jorgensen rifles. The air was alive with the hum of insects. The ominous calm made Paul nervous. He kept scanning the hills. There wasn't a sign of the enemy. He commented about it to Private Pruitt, who shrugged.

A sudden boom startled everyone. Then came a crashing volley of rifles as the Americans returned fire. Paul's heart pounded. "Here we go."

Jimmy swore. He was pale as the belly of a fish.

The rifle fire continued. Paul saw Roosevelt's squadron breaking toward the road, in what must be an attempt to link up with Wheeler. Paul hoisted the tripod to his shoulder. "Jimmy, let's go."

Jimmy eyed his partner. "This is where I stop. I ain't catching any spick bullets this morning."

"I can't carry the camera and that bag too."

"You don't need the bag—you got enough film. I'll be here when you get back."

Paul lost patience. He shouted at Jimmy, "You and I are finished as partners."

"We were finished a long time ago, you snotty kraut s.o.b."

Red-faced, Paul spun around and rushed forward with the camera. He followed the 2nd Squadron through the low hills to the edge of a level area. At the other side stood a number of sand-colored buildings with red tile roofs and several large, irregular holes in the walls. From the way the front ranks were pumping rounds into the buildings, it was clear that Spanish troops were laid up there, raking the open area with their fire.

The American forward line advanced across the level area with dogged steadiness. Men cried out, pitched over with terrifying suddenness. Still the line advanced.

On the right flank, similar lines from Roosevelt's squadron were moving through stands of coconut palms toward the unseen road. Paul glimpsed Roosevelt on horseback, brandishing his saber. Beyond him, the Spanish works at Las Guásimas were at last visible: bastions of flat stones piled up on the ridges above the road, and two small blockhouses.

Close to the rear of the American line, Paul jammed the tripod into the grass, preparing to crank. He heard a noise—instinctively ducked. The air was full of that sound, something like a bee's buzz or the hum of a twanged wire. Mauser bullets.

He happened to glance forward, where he saw Pruitt. As if his attention had willed a tragedy, Pruitt's hands suddenly flew into the air. His rifle fell at his feet. His body seemed to fold. Hunched down, Paul ran across the level area to reach the private from Texas.

Jerry Pruitt was sitting up, his khaki shirt soaked with blood. Slowly he fell backward, away from Paul. He settled gently in the grass.

Paul stood up. The firing remained loud, yet he heard a new sound, in the taller grass behind Pruitt. A rustling, a clicking.

"Medical corpsman!" he yelled. No one heard.

As the first of the plate-size crabs sidled into view, Paul saw flies land on the dead soldier's face. It was a strange, timeless moment, standing there with a dead man at his feet and bullets flying. He was shaken by knowledge of his own mortality.

He pulled off his straw hat and wiped his dripping forehead with his sleeve. The sun was fully up, blinding him. In that moment he changed. He felt a monstrous burden come down. The transformation was final. The boy Pauli Kroner was gone forever.

He turned away from the searing light of the sun. The moment of epiphany passed, and time began to run again.

Paul carried the camera forward and came to a sprawl of four bodies. The Rough Riders were still charging and firing as they closed on the bullet-pocked buildings. Paul stared at the bodies. Professional instinct told him he should crank off some footage.

Are you stupid? Do you seriously think that storekeepers and widows will pay so much as one cent to see bloody corpses?

In his head a second voice argued, *Maybe nobody wants to see it. But it's the truth.* Wex Rooney had said tell the truth. Nothing else matters. Paul turned the crank.

Soldiers in conical straw hats were spilling from the rear of the red-roofed buildings. Paul cranked furiously as one Spaniard after another burst into the open, threw down his rifle, and fled. While the khaki line rushed in pursuit, Paul kept cranking.

An officer with white bone jutting from a gashed arm came dragging past from the right flank, going toward the rear. Paul stopped cranking. "Sir? What's happened?"

The lieutenant grimaced; he was young to have so many gold teeth. "The Spaniards are holding on to their positions on the road. Wheeler's dispatched a courier to send up an infantry regiment." He staggered on. The image of his ghastly smile, with all the gold teeth, lingered. It took Paul a moment to collect himself.

He checked the meter and swore. Five feet left. He'd have to find Jimmy, or the canvas bag if Jimmy had abandoned it. He left the camera and the exposed film of the battle and started back.

He walked a quarter of a mile. He heard Jimmy before he saw

him. Heard him grunting in a strange way, as though expending effort. Paul ran through a gap in the barbed wire beside the trail. Jimmy was there in the long grass, shirtless, kneeling on a soldier's body. Beside him lay the canvas bag. The machete in his right hand was bloody.

Jimmy's head whipped around. Paul recognized the lieutenant who'd come in from the right flank. He was dead; half his gold teeth were missing. They lay sparkling in the grass by his ear.

Jimmy gave Paul a queer, shamed smile, as though hoping Paul could be mollified that way. Links of his neck chain winked in the sun. "Just makin' a little profit before I go."

"You killed him, he only had an arm wound."

"Hey, look, why should you care about—"

Paul flung himself on Jimmy with a cry of rage.

JULIE ✦ Rain fell on Belle Mer. It washed the terrace and speckled the reflecting pools in the garden. It was a summer rain, late in the afternoon—warm, torpid, melancholy. It suited Julie's mood.

In the music room, she searched through a dozen cylinders for the Victor gramophone. She chose a Strauss waltz. It reminded her of Paul. He was on her mind constantly of late.

Gazing out through the tall, streaming windows, she thought it strange that she should be so sad, now that she'd taken her first tottering steps to freedom.

All winter long, she'd brooded about her situation. She had to free herself from Bill and then search for Paul. Even if it took years to find him.

She had laid her plans with great care. She told no one, not even Aunt Willis. She expected that Bill would attend the races in Saratoga as he usually did in August, and when he confirmed it two weeks ago, she went into New York City alone. She invented an elaborate lie about needing to consult a medical specialist about a female complaint. Bill provided her with money of her own, for which she needn't account, and she paid in cash for a six-month lease on a furnished flat.

The next step would be to leave Southampton when Bill was in Saratoga. She'd simply disappear from his life and make no contact with anyone who knew her.

She glanced up. Someone was walking across the terrace—a

woman. She was wearing gloves, a nondescript cape, and a sunbonnet that hid her face. The woman peered through a tall French door and spied Julie, then tapped the glass.

Someone lost and wanting directions, Julie decided. She went to the door, turned the handle. "Yes, may I help you?"

The woman thrust forward abruptly. Julie was startled, but not alarmed. The woman tore at the ribbon tied under her chin and snatched the bonnet off. Julie's hand flew to her mouth. The woman's face was a mottled mess of bruises and lacerations.

The waltz came to an end. All that issued from the amplifying horn was a rhythmic scratch. Before Julie could demand her name, the intruder said, "I'm Rose. You're Bill's wife?"

The familiarity worsened her anxiety. "Mrs. Elstree, yes. Be so good as to tell me—"

Rose interrupted. "I want to see Bill. I'm his friend. He kept me for a while. In New York. Then he dumped me. I had a stage career—do you think I can have one now? Some of these marks are scars. They'll never go away. He's the one who did this."

Julie stepped back, the angry words landing like blows.

"I guess you could say I'm his discarded trash, Mrs. Elstree. I'll tell you one thing I am for certain. I'm the mother of his baby."

Julie couldn't breathe. Around and around went the gramophone cylinder, filling the room with its amplified scratch.

Rose took a firmer grip on a small reticule she was carrying. There was a wild look in her eye. "Now, where is Bill?"

What does she want? Julie thought. Money? The young woman's expression said it was more than that—something physical, threatening. How easy, then, to surrender Bill. If the woman was even half truthful, he deserved whatever he got. How easy to say, "He's upstairs changing for supper," and then tug the bellpull to ask a servant to fetch him.

Julie loathed Elstree as she'd never loathed anyone. But she couldn't do it. She said, "He isn't home."

"Liar," Rose said. "I saw the carriage come in ten minutes ago. I was hiding in the lane. We'll wait for him."

Rose opened the reticule and pulled out a pistol. "Shut off that talking machine, it gets on my nerves. Walk slowly."

Julie obeyed. In a moment the gramophone was silent.

"Come back and sit down."

391

They sat on brocaded chairs, on opposite sides of an Oriental carpet. Rose held her gun beneath the reticule in her lap.

Julie felt cold perspiration on her hands. Despite everything Bill had done to her, she couldn't let him walk into the music room and take a bullet. "Rose, be sensible. Put the gun away."

"Not a chance."

Julie heard the footsteps. The music-room door handle turned, and Bill stepped in. "Julie?"

"Bill, she has a gun!" Julie screamed.

"Rose," he said. He was not intimidated. "What the hell are you doing in my house? You've made a grave mistake."

He strode to his left, reaching for the bellpull. He yanked it. Rose stood up and shot him.

Elstree stared down at the stiff bosom of his shirt. Between the second and third stud a red flower grew. He looked infuriated.

Rose fired again. The bullet tore through Elstree's neck, painting the wall with blood. He sat down awkwardly against the baseboard. His eyes closed; then he fell forward onto the carpet.

Julie heard servants coming. She ran to the door, tore it open. "In here, hurry."

Rose ran out the nearest French door and disappeared along the terrace. Servants crowded into the room, exclaimed and sobbed over the sight of the master bleeding on the carpet.

Later the town constable apprehended Rose French as she was fleeing Southampton on foot. That night, in the small jail, the turnkey rushed to the cell in answer to Rose's cry and found her lying in blood. The baby was lost.

DUTCH ✦ Paul landed hard on Jimmy, his knees in Jimmy's ribs. Jimmy heaved upward, throwing him off. Both were stunned.

They got up about the same time, standing six feet apart in the trampled grass. Paul held out his hand. "Give me the machete."

"Here," Jimmy said, and took a ferocious swipe at Paul's head.

Paul jumped away. While Jimmy's momentum was still carrying him through the swing, Paul lunged and drove his knee into Jimmy's groin. Jimmy let out a grunt of pain and dropped the machete. Paul snatched it up. Turning, he sailed it away into the long grass. Jimmy grabbed him from behind and threw him sideways. Off balance,

Paul went down. His jaw slammed into the ground. Jimmy began kicking him in the ribs. Pain raged through Paul's body.

While Paul lay gasping, Jimmy scooped up the bloodstained gold teeth and stuffed them in his pockets. Twice Paul heard the buzz of Mauser bullets close by. The gunfire grew louder.

Paul struggled to his knees. For a moment he wanted to run at Jimmy and finish him—rid the earth of him. But he remained there, his fists trembling a little. A smile flickered on Jimmy's face.

With a chug, a Mauser bullet hit a palm tree behind Paul; splinters stung his neck. Scruples had undone him, and Jimmy knew it.

Jimmy came bounding over with both hands on the chain of the holy medal. Before Paul could rise or defend himself, Jimmy dropped the heavy chain over his head. "Now," he said, pulling hard as sweat rivered off his face, "now I got you."

Paul couldn't stand up. He tore at the constricting chain. The big links cut into his neck. Jimmy grunted as he pulled the chain tighter. His face was twisted with hate.

Blood ran from under the chain, streaking Paul's throat. Jimmy was going to kill him.

Paul refused to let it happen. Not here, not this way. He seized Jimmy's belt with both hands and pulled hard. Jimmy fell against him. Paul pounded his fist into Jimmy's gut, then hit again. Jimmy let go of the chain. Paul put all his strength into a punch that lifted Jimmy and hurled him backward. Dizzy to the point of sickness, Paul lifted the bloody chain over his head and flung it away.

Like some animal wounded and maddened by tormentors, Jimmy was on the ground, bracing himself on his hands. He looked whipped, but Paul took no pleasure from it. He turned away, walked a few steps. He heard the buzz of the Mauser bullet just before he felt it strike his back.

WHEN he came to his senses, his nose was resting in the mud. He'd been hit about halfway down his back, the right side, behind his ribs. It hurt like the very devil—agony.

He watched Jimmy walk toward him, a grin on his filthy face. "Well, I guess I win the pot in this game, huh? All right, then, I'm going. You have a good time, you and your friends." He grabbed Paul's hair, lifting his head. "I hope they take hours to kill you, you kraut know-it-all. I hope they take forever."

He pushed Paul's face into the mud and laughed. Then he disappeared in the direction of the trail.

Above the noise of gunfire and men shouting orders, Paul heard another sound. His eyes grew huge.

He tried to get up—couldn't. He lay bleeding in the long grass. The long grass full of rustlings and clickings . . .

The first land crab sidled out of the grass, pincers waving. Another one followed, and another, and more after that.

The largest crab, the one nearest Paul, stopped a moment. Its maw opened and shut, opened and shut. Paul dug his fingers into the mud. Pushed up, then fell back, too weak. The crab sidled next to his cheek. Climbed onto his face.

He felt others on his arms, his legs, clicking, rustling. He shut his eyes and bit on his lower lip. A claw nipped his cheek. He screamed.

The crabs seemed to sense his helplessness. They began to pluck and tear at his face. He had no more courage. He began to cry.

He heard a thrashing and crashing in the long grass. "Roy, looka them damn things."

"Don't stand there, kick 'em off. They's 'bout to eat his eyes."

A rifle butt flicked a crab from Paul's face, then swept back and forth, broomlike, over him. In the glaring sky Paul saw a round black face, bright with sweat. A second dark face appeared. And then a third. The third black soldier said, "I'll carry him to the rear."

"Ott, you can't. You half sick with the fever."

"Get out of my way. I said I'll carry him."

Paul's eyes lost focus, the sun darkened, and that was the end.

WILLIS ✦ On Saturday, June 25, the chartered Red Cross ship S.S. *State of Texas* anchored in Guantánamo Bay, carrying rations, blankets, medicines, and bandages for the rebels in the interior. Clara Barton and the volunteers with her were expecting to accompany the supplies overland. They were informed, however, that this was impossible; the head of Guantánamo Bay was still in Spanish hands. Then came telegraphed news of the Las Guásimas fight, which had sent a Spanish force into retreat toward Santiago. Like all such victories, it was not without cost. Sixteen Americans killed and fifty-two wounded.

Miss Barton held a hasty meeting with her volunteers and spoke to the ship's captain. She told him there were wounded men only forty miles to the west. At two o'clock in the afternoon the *State of Texas* sailed for Siboney.

Now Clara Barton stood at the rail with Willis Fishburne and her chief physician, Dr. Anton Lesser. Clara was just five feet tall, but her powerful presence made her seem larger. She was incredibly energetic for a woman of seventy-seven. Her hair, worn in a grandmotherly bun, showed no gray. Her features were hawkish, her eyes brown, missing nothing.

No fool about the attitudes of men, Clara had declined to be the first ashore at Siboney, sending instead Dr. Lesser to deal with the army medical officers. Lesser had gone to offer the assistance of the entire volunteer staff of the Red Cross relief ship—physicians, nurses, and two skilled helpers, Willis and a widow named Mrs. Olive Shay. He had just returned to the *State of Texas*.

"Do you see those two houses, just there on the beach?" Lesser pointed them out to Clara and Willis. The houses, both dilapidated, were separated by about fifty feet of sand.

Clara nodded. "Which house belongs to the Americans?"

"The one nearer the pier. The other's full of Cuban boys. There are no beds, no blankets, the wounded just scattered about on the floor. And both houses are absolute pigsties."

"We'll clean them, Anton," Willis said.

"Did you tell them that?" Clara asked the doctor. "Did you tell them we have buckets and brooms? Brushes, disinfectants—and more than a hundred folding cots?"

Dr. Lesser looked distraught. "I told them. I spoke personally with the army surgeon in charge of American casualties on the beach, a Dr. Francis Winter. Dear ladies—he said our help wasn't wanted and wouldn't be accepted."

Clara rocked on her heels. "Are you joking?"

Willis was outraged. "He refused the help of the Red Cross? Why would he be so stupid?"

"He cited army policy. Women don't belong in a war zone, he said. They're not as qualified as male doctors and orderlies. They should stay safely at home. Those are a few samples of his claptrap. The same ridiculous song the army medical department sang in the Civil War."

"Well," said Clara Barton, "if the American doctors won't accept our help, perhaps the Cubans will."

DUTCH ✦ He awoke on the hard floor of some kind of house, within sound of the surf. The room was filthy, dimly lit.

Paul had never hurt so much. He felt as if his whole body had been punished with flails, but especially his back, midway between shoulder and hip on the right side. With every breath, a fierce pain stabbed him there.

To his lef⁺, illuminated by kerosene lights, two men in bloody smocks worked over a soldier lying on a table. One of the men was suturing the patient's thigh. The patient screamed.

"More ether," the doctor shouted. He was sweating brutally.

Paul's head was clearing a little, drawing up memories. Jimmy. The chain around his neck. The bullet. And the land crabs. He shuddered. Then he remembered a dark face, Ott Person. . . .

His mind drifted again. Sometime later a doctor appeared beside him. He was an older man with a self-important air. He carried a medical chart.

"I am Dr. Winter, the surgeon in charge. You're a very lucky fellow. The bullet pierced cleanly and passed through. Two broken ribs, that's the worst. The wound is dressed, and we've taped your ribs. But we're puzzled by the abrasions around your throat. Was something wrapped there to choke you?"

Paul propped himself on his elbows—excruciating. "My partner attacked me. Then he ran off. I don't know what happened to him."

"Well, I certainly can't tell you." Winter poised a pencil over the medical chart. "There's been a great deal of confusion. We never got your name. What is it?"

"Paul Crown. American Luxograph Company. Where is this house, Doctor?"

"Siboney."

"When I was hit, I was up in the hills."

"Yes, a black soldier carried you all the way here on his back. Now lie down and rest." Dr. Winter walked away.

Later that morning a civilian came in and pulled up a stool. His natty jacket and houndstooth cap were unspeakably dirty. "Hello, sport," Billy Bitzer said. "How're you doing?"

Paul smiled sleepily. "I am going to make it."

"You'd better! Your camera's okay. Some soldiers found it yesterday and turned it over to me. I stored it with the V Corps provosts. I still wish I had that camera. It's a honey."

"Decent of you to look after it." Then Paul remembered the canvas bag. Would it still be there? Would the heat and rain ruin the magazines? He struggled up. "I have to get out of here—"

"No hurry," Bitzer said. "Everything's holding until they can move enough men and supplies to forward positions. That'll take six or seven days, maybe more." Bitzer squeezed Paul's shoulder and stood. "Get well, friend. See you in the trenches."

"Thank you, Billy. For everything."

Paul needed to sleep. He was still dozing when someone shook him. "Come on, Heine, wake up. I only got a little while." Groggily Paul looked up at the face of Corporal Ott Person.

Ott cast an eye over the room, now crowded with seven men lying on pallets. Flies buzzed. Roaches crawled on the walls. "This place ain't fit for pigs. Can't they get you cots in here?"

"I guess not. They're short on supplies, doctors—everything. They say you brought me back here, Ott. How did you find me?"

Ott hunkered down. "They sent for two troops of the Tenth Cavalry to relieve Wood's command. My squad happened to be the one that passed by where you was layin'. That's all there is to it."

"I'll think of some way to repay you when I'm out of here."

"Heine, I tol' you before, I'm the one had the debt to square. What d'you figure to do when this war's over?"

"Take my pictures back to Chicago if I get any good ones. After that, I think I am going to look for a job in England."

"What's wrong, you don't like the U.S. of A.?"

"I had hoped that America would be my home. But I don't belong there. I think it's time to try another place."

"Heine, don't do that. Our country needs folks like you. Ain't there nothin' would make you stay?"

"There was a girl—but she's gone now."

"They's lots of nice handsome white girls in America. I bet plenty of 'em could make you happy."

Paul drew a deep, slow breath; even taking it carefully, the pain was ungodly. "No, Ott. But thank you for your kind words."

Ott tugged up his red bandanna and swabbed his cheeks. He seemed to be perspiring heavily. "Heine, there ain't no place on God's earth won't disappoint you sometimes. 'Merica may be a wagon with one bad wheel, but it carries a lot of folks farther than they ever thought they could go. So don't turn your back. Please don't."

Paul only shook his head.

Ott stood up, powerfully tall. "Well, I spoke my piece. I'll go now." He untied the knot of his bandanna and wiped his face again. "Lord, it's a furnace in here."

Paul was puzzled. A stiff breeze was blowing from the sea, cooling the house. Yet Ott was covered with sweat.

"So long, Heine. You look me up soon as you're out of here. We'll talk some more about you stayin'. I don't give up easy."

Next morning, Sunday, Dr. Winter brought a young officer to see Paul. "This is Lieutenant Criswell. He wants to ask some questions." The doctor left, and Criswell sat down on a stool. Paul used his elbows to prop himself up again, this time with less pain.

"Mr. Crown, I'm an aide to Major Groesbeck, acting judge advocate of the Fifth Army Corps. You are the chief camera operator with the film company known as American Luxograph?"

Apprehensive, Paul said yes.

"You had a partner, one James Daws?" Paul nodded. "Did the two of you have trouble on the day of the fight at Las Guásimas?"

Startled, Paul said, "Yes, we did."

"Please describe what happened."

Paul told his story. "Why are you asking?"

Criswell explained. "Daws showed up in Siboney that evening and attempted to hire a motorized fishing boat to run him to Key West. He offered a good sum, so the captain was agreeable. The fishing boats were for military use only, and the sentry on duty that night, a Corporal Bray, ordered him off the boat. Daws pulled a knife, stabbed Bray, and threw him in the water. Bray's cries were heard by soldiers on the beach, who pulled him from under the pier. Amid the confusion the vessel carrying Daws put out for Key West. Bray related his story to the surgeons, but he expired before he could depose under oath. Therefore we have no legally admissible statement to use against Daws."

"And Jim escaped?"

Criswell smiled. "To the contrary. We alerted the Key West station, and when Daws stepped ashore, he was arrested. Mr. Crown, if you'll make a statement under oath and sign charges of attempted murder against James Daws, we can put him in prison, where he belongs."

"Of course I'll sign charges."

Criswell stood up. "Pay us a visit as soon as you're able."

"Certainly, Lieutenant. Good-bye."

Paul lay down again, strengthened by the knowledge that his testimony would put Jimmy Daws in prison. Sometimes there was justice in the world after all.

JULIE ✦ On the terrace at Belle Mer, Julie confronted her mother across a green iron table.

"You scandalized everyone when you refused to attend the funeral, Juliette."

"The scandal began before that, Mama. When Bill was shot by a woman of low repute whom he kept in the city."

Nell Vanderhoff sipped tea from a Spode cup. She looked embittered. And hostile. Nell had arrived from Chicago on a sparkling cool afternoon; temperate for late June. She was, as always, elegantly and correctly dressed. Everything was black. Julie wore a white linen yachting skirt and shirtwaist. Nell found it another subject for disapproval. "Couldn't you at least wear a black armband? Surely you loved Bill a little—"

"Not an iota. I love Paul Crown—the boy Papa drove off."

Nell raised her voice. "I do not approve of your behavior."

"Mama, I'm afraid you no longer have anything to say about it."

Nell sat all the way back in her iron chair, gripping the arms. Julie waited for the next assault. Unexpectedly, it took the form of tender entreaty. Nell rose and rounded the table. Her palm fell gently to Julie's high-piled hair. "What have you done to your beautiful hair? It's so dull. You've not cared for it properly. Julie, my sweet baby—I insist you come home. You know I'm not well. I'm feeling short of breath this very moment—"

"Mama." In a gentle but firm grasp, Julie lifted Nell's hand away from her hair. "I think I have done enough for your health. It's time I looked after my own."

"Juliette." Nell staggered back, but she found the iron chair with uncanny accuracy.

Julie tried to remain solicitous. "I'm sorry you're ill. We have an excellent doctor in the village. I'll telephone him at once."

She started for the French doors. Nell reeled back in her chair. "I don't want a doctor. I want an obedient daughter."

Julie stopped and turned around. She shook her head. "I am

399

going to telephone the doctor. You sit there, Mama, and rest."

The physician arrived in his shay within the hour. By then Nell had called for her carriage and was gone. She'd left with one parting thrust. "You have grown into a wicked woman. I don't know how it happened. You must have fallen under the spell of my sister, Willis. I disown you. You will never see me again."

DUTCH ✦ Monday. Twilight. Paul awoke with a sense of someone standing near. Opened his eyes to a gleam of a golden star on a shoulder strap. The face surmounted by silver hair combed straight back was exactly as he remembered it from the moment he stumbled through the front door on Michigan Avenue. But the brown eyes held an uncharacteristic nervousness.

"Uncle Joe—"

"Paul, my dear nephew. Will you allow me a short visit?"

"Of course—certainly," Paul said, not sure it was a wise reply. Savage feelings were already stirring.

"Is this too great a surprise, my presence here?"

"No, sir. I've known for some time that you're attached to General Wheeler's staff. Uncle Joe—please—sit."

Eight others were in the room now. Two of the men were awake, openly listening. "Are you able to walk?" Uncle Joe asked.

"If I go slowly."

"Could we go outside and talk? I noticed a bench. Take my hand."

Paul grasped the strong hand and got up, though not without pain. "Lean on me. Put your arm across my shoulder." Paul almost smiled; there was the old, unconscious tone of command.

In a moment Paul was outside, seated on the bench with his bare feet in the sand. The setting sun flamed on the sea.

General Joe Crown seated himself next to his nephew. Paul asked, "How did you find me?"

"Things have been hectic, as you might expect. Only this afternoon did I have a few moments to look over the roster of our wounded. I was astonished to find your name. Also a middle name, in parentheses. Dutch."

"That's mostly what I'm called now."

"You're one of these moving pictures fellows, I was told."

"Yes. I work for a company in Chicago."

400

"I want to hear all about it. Everything that's happened. But first, Paul, I must say this to you. I made a dreadful mistake. I wronged you by turning you out—" He broke off, sitting stiffly, shoulders squared. He was the perfect military man, save for the tears. "I must ask your forgiveness. I won't be surprised if you refuse me."

Paul looked at his hands. "It's true I had terrible, angry feelings for a long time"—*and I still have some*—"but I never stopped being your relative or forgot the many kindnesses you showed me. I have made mistakes too. We ought to forgive each other, I think."

Uncle Joe put his hand over Paul's, holding tightly. Paul was near to crying himself. "Thank you," his uncle whispered. "Thank you."

A refreshing salt breeze was coming off the water. Uncle Joe composed himself. "This picture business. Tell me about it."

"It's a profession I've come to love. Also, I seem to have a talent for it. I always wanted to draw, be an artist. This fulfills that wish. With one difference. Now people can recognize the subject of my pictures." His uncle laughed. Paul said, "It's what I propose to do for the rest of my life."

"I have heard of these living pictures, but I've never seen one."

"Very understandable. Respectable folk don't go to them. But I'm convinced that will change. The living pictures can educate. Bring the world to people who otherwise would never see it. Pictures can show great events. This war. Las Guásimas."

They continued to talk as the twilight shaded into dark, with thousands of stars alight over the Cuban coast. Paul asked about Fritzi and Carl. "And cousin Joe? Do you know where he is?"

"Alas, we don't. We've engaged Pinkerton's detective agency, but they can't locate him. At intervals your aunt receives curious souvenirs, mailed anonymously. Stalks of wheat, then little candies shaped like California oranges. She feels Joe Junior sent them, to say he's all right. But the last one arrived months ago. She's fearful something has happened." Heavily he added, "She has never gotten over the loss of Joe Junior. She never will. I bear the responsibility."

Carefully Paul said, "You know, Uncle, cousin Joe didn't rebel against you to hurt you. He only wanted to be like you. Independent. Strong. His own person."

"He was not like me, Paul. He was a radical."

After a hesitation Paul said, "Did you never have an idea that was wrong?"

"Oh, yes, I've had many. Many! I finally confronted that fact recently. I believe"—the confession came hard, but when it came, it was firm—"I have been too insistent on authority. Control. Everything in place, perfectly correct. Correct as I saw it! I realize that I tore our family apart by continually seeking something that is unobtainable within a household, or within the world at large. In my pursuit of some kind of rational order I went too far. I can't escape guilt by saying it's a common failing of Germans, passion for order, although it is. I must accept full blame for my mistakes and their consequences. I have. I do."

There was a long pause. Paul sat very still. Uncle Joe cleared his throat. "You will return to Chicago when the war is over, Paul?"

"I will. But I won't be staying." In a few sentences he explained about Michael, and London.

"But America is your home now! You made it so." Joe Crown paused again. "If this is because of me, I beg you once more to forgive me. I'll do anything in my power to make amends."

"What happened between us isn't the reason I'm leaving. I lost the one thing in America I wanted most. The one person."

"The Vanderhoff girl."

"Yes. I wanted to make a home with her, but she married that rich man. It's time I explore some other country."

The general was stricken silent. Paul was tired; his wound was hurting badly. "I should go in, Uncle."

"Yes, certainly. I've kept you too long."

Uncle Joe helped him back to the hospital house. "I'm going to leave this place soon," Paul said. "I must film more of the fighting."

"I'll look for you in the field."

"I will do the same, Uncle."

"Excellent. Till then." The general put his hands on Paul's shoulders. "Please take care of yourself." He gave his nephew a clumsy but fervent embrace and walked away quickly, striding up the beach with fine German precision. Paul watched until he disappeared in the dark.

WILLIS ✦ A yawl took them ashore in choppy sea Sunday morning. The harried doctor in charge of the Cuban house welcomed them warmly. In fact, he almost wept. The hospital desperately needed their attention and their supplies. Piles of sand

and debris clogged the corners of the dingy rooms. Mosquitoes hovered. The smells were vile. Wounded Cuban soldiers were scattered throughout the house, a few resting on grimy scraps of blanket. The others had the bare wood floor.

Miss Barton marched through the house like a field general. "We have kerosene for lamps, we must light these rooms. We have screen wire, we'll cover the windows to keep out the flies. We have cots, we'll use them for the injured." At last the Red Cross unit was fulfilling its mission.

Willis got down on her knees with a soapy bucket and began to scrub floors, she and the other volunteer, Olive Shay. That night, Willis slept four hours. When she awoke, she washed walls, changed bandages, stood at the tiny iron stove in purgatorial heat, frying mush. She assisted with the amputation of a soldier's mangled foot. Seventy-seven-year-old Clara did no less than any of them.

Willis felt it was a damn shame the doctors thought they were unfit to offer the same help to the American boys. There was an exhilaration in being here, a sense of purpose and meaning Willis found missing from her life at other times.

The next day, Monday, at about five p.m., Clara came dashing in, highly excited. "Ladies, attention. Tomorrow we begin cleaning and tending the American house." Major Lagarde, chief surgeon in Siboney, had made the rounds of the Cuban house and issued the order. "Dr. Winter is preparing a written apology."

Early on Tuesday, June 28, Clara Barton and her women invaded the American house. The routine was much the same. Sweep, scrub, tack up screens, set up cots, cook, pass out drinking water.

Throughout the day they heard occasional news from officers and noncoms. The campaign against Santiago had bogged down while men and supplies were moved forward over a single rutted road that had once borne the proud name Camino Real. There was an almost lighthearted air in Siboney—much bragging about the Las Guásimas victory, as though that were the whole war.

That evening Willis decided she should familiarize herself with the names of the patients. Until now they had been merely faces.

"That one is a civilian?" she said, studying a roster.

One of the nurses said, "Yes, he's a camera operator. He photographs those motion pictures they show at variety halls."

Willis read the name in the flickering lamplight. Paul Crown.

IN THE SMALL HOURS OF Wednesday morning, Paul awoke. He called for a drink. Willis had been waiting for the moment all night, her stomach hurting from nervous excitement.

"Here you are, young man." Willis handed the tin cup to the sleepy patient. Then she pulled a stool over to his cot.

The young man braced on his elbow to drink. He drained the cup and returned it. "Thank you very much."

Willis sat down. "Young man, my name is Miss Fishburne. I understand yours is Paul Crown?"

"That's right."

"Are you by any chance related to Joseph Crown of Chicago?"

A wariness sprang into his eyes. "Yes. Do you know him?"

"Not personally. But I know you."

"What do you mean? I'm sure we've never met before."

"That's true. But I have things to say to you. Julie Vanderhoff is my niece. My first name is Willis."

He gasped. "She talked about you often." He strained to sit up.

"Listen to me," Willis said softly. "You know Julie's married. Elstree, the department store heir. Her mother, my dear sister, forced her into it. Julie detests her husband, and rightly so. He's a wastrel, and arrogant. What's more, he's a notorious philanderer. Julie wants to divorce him."

Paul was too stunned to speak.

Willis took a breath.

"Paul, Julie's miserable. It's you she loves, no one else. She told me so. I'm positive she'd leave Elstree in a moment if you asked her. As soon as you set foot in the States again, go to her. Steal her away. If you don't, both of you will regret it the rest of your lives."

"Where can I find her, Miss Fishburne?"

"She spends summers on Long Island. Southampton. Elstree has a mansion on the ocean. Belle Mer is its name."

DUTCH ✦ On Wednesday, June 29, 1898, Paul walked out of the American hospital house shortly after sunrise. On the stoop, Miss Fishburne hugged him, kissed his cheek, and once more charged him to find Julie as soon as possible.

Paul promised, and hobbled away, his taped bandages itching under his shirt, his back wound still hellishly painful. But his head was awhirl. Julie . . . did he dare believe there was a chance?

Not yet. He'd tell no one. Not Uncle Joe, and certainly not Michael. He would heed Miss Fishburne's charge and investigate the moment he was back. But he daren't expect a happy outcome, much as he longed for it. One more heartbreak would be too much.

He visited the cantina. Yes, his grip was safe. He paid the proprietor a dollar to continue to guard it, and set out to look for the canvas bag at the spot where he'd fought with Jimmy. Reaching it would require a hike of two or three hours, very hard in his weakened state.

Paul made it. The sight of the tall grass, the memory of what nearly happened to him there, sent awful shivers up and down his back. He began to search the surrounding grass. He found the canvas bag almost at once. It lay where it had fallen.

Mold covered the bag, and beetles had crawled inside. Very likely the exposed magazines were ruined, but at least he could take them back to Shadow as proof that he'd tried. He slung the bag over his shoulder and went in search of the bivouac of the 10th Cavalry.

He reached the gate and spoke to the sentry, who told him, "Ott died this morning. Yellow fever. Sorry."

Paul turned around and stumbled toward the road. Ott's eyes seared his memory. Ott's face, and his entreaties.

Ain't no place on God's earth won't disappoint you sometimes. Our country needs folks like you. Don't turn your back. Please don't.

In sorrow and confusion, Paul let the tears come.

THAT night he made his bed in the sand, against the wall of the Cuban hospital house, covered by a blanket Miss Fishburne brought to him. When he awoke in the morning, he was surprised at how deeply he'd slept. Perhaps it was to escape thoughts of Ott.

It was Thursday, the last day of June. Siboney was a ghost camp. Since Saturday nearly fifteen thousand men had been moved forward beyond Las Guásimas.

With Lieutenant Criswell's help, Paul wrote his deposition and signed it. "Daws will be sent back to Illinois for trial," Criswell said, holding the foolscap sheets. "This should guarantee he'll go to prison."

A chapter closed. Paul was grateful.

"Where are you going now?" Criswell asked.

"To load my camera, then walk up to the front."

"Better hurry. Word's out that the attack will be made tomorrow morning. Shafter wants to go against everything at once—the San Juan heights and the fortifications at the village of El Caney, farther inland."

Travel to the forward area was hard; everything was moving that way—infantry, cavalry, artillery caissons drawn by sweating horses. Paul reached General Shafter's field headquarters about one in the afternoon. He had one last magazine, four hundred feet of film, carefully loaded into the Luxograph. He prayed that the climate hadn't fogged it. There would be fighting; he must have pictures.

Before dawn, Friday, July 1, white mist formed in the low places below the fortified heights protecting Santiago. The Americans confronted the heights from the far left, south of the main road to the village of El Caney, four miles north. The village was defended by a stone fort, El Viso. Smaller blockhouses and, presumably, trenches were waiting on the San Juan heights.

At first light General Lawton's division opened its attack against the entrenchments at El Caney. The Spaniards enjoyed both superior visibility and artillery supremacy.

As Lawton was advancing, the left pressed forward along the Santiago road. A critical place in the advance was a low ford on the Aguadores River, a highly visible target for the enemy artillery. By midmorning the crossing had earned the name Bloody Ford.

Paul pushed toward the ford among black cavalrymen advancing on foot. A few were already wounded and stumbling to the rear. The roar of artillery and the crackle of rifle fire were constant.

Paul caught up with Lieutenant Pershing, the officer who'd come to his room in Tampa, just as a thunderous burst overhead scattered shrapnel on the road. "Down!" Pershing shouted, a moment late. Two of his black soldiers fell, badly hit.

"Come on, lads, keep moving," Pershing said in a firm voice.

All around him Paul saw terrified faces. He followed Pershing and his men down to Bloody Ford.

The water at the ford was brown and swirling. A pennon with a red cross identified a dressing station set up on the bank. In the center of the river, six officers sat on their horses, waving and calling encouragement to the men. Wheeler was one, Uncle Joe another. All seemed astonishingly calm.

Lieutenant Pershing jumped into the shallows at the ford. As each of his black soldiers reached the water, Pershing gave him a little pat, a supportive word. "Go on, Bob. That's it, Linc, straight across Hurry up, now, don't stop."

Paul was standing just short of the water. The whistle of a shell made him look up. The first of Pershing's men were at midstream. There a corporal lost his footing. Uncle Joe booted his horse forward and leaned out of the saddle, extending his left arm. The soldier grabbed it with both hands. The shell burst. Shrapnel ripped the water all around the men. A piece of it went into the corporal's head. He sank, still holding Uncle Joe's arm and dragging him from the saddle. Paul saw a bright red blotch erupt on his uncle's left thigh. "Get him out of there—save him," Paul shouted, laying his camera aside and jumping into the water.

Other soldiers had gone down between Paul and his uncle. They blocked his way. Somehow a corpsman from the dressing station reached Uncle Joe and lifted him over his shoulder; Paul saw the corpsman stagger up to the dressing station.

Paul got to shore and picked up his camera. He weaved through the underbrush to the tent with the red pennon.

The corpsman had laid the general on a litter. Uncle Joe's face was pale as milk. At the far side of the tent, a surgeon was working on the leg of a black soldier who was biting down on a hickory baton. The surgeon shouted at Paul, "Stay out of here unless you're bleeding."

"This officer is my uncle. I want to know how badly he's hurt."

"I'm busy. You'll have to wait."

Paul watched Pershing's black soldiers pouring across the ford. "I can't wait. I will be back."

He shouldered the tripod and waded into the bloody river.

BEYOND the Aguadores, the land opened out to another grassy plain, which ran upward to the San Juan heights and to a lower eminence on the right, Kettle Hill. Here Colonel Roosevelt led a fierce attack shortly after twelve o'clock.

All the commands had gotten horribly tangled. Paul found himself in the middle of the 6th Infantry protecting themselves as best they could behind clumps of palmettos. There was a great deal of blood on the grass, and corpses were strewn about. On the heights, nothing could be seen of the Spaniards except for an occasional conical hat poking up near some large, well-kept farm buildings. The fire from up there was steady and decimating.

At one fifteen a furious *brrrr* made Paul jump. The Gatling-gun detachment had crossed the ford at last. The Americans now had mechanized fire to counter the artillery on the heights. Officers shouted orders for an advance. Across a broad front the infantry and cavalry charged San Juan Hill at a rapid walk.

The Gatlings roared. The Spanish fire cut down the Americans climbing the hill, infantry and cavalry, black and white, tangled together without organization but advancing steadily, without pause.

Paul saw Roosevelt going up among the black men from the 10th, brandishing a revolver, hallooing and waving them on. Paul slung the tripod over his shoulder and ran uphill through the smoke, toward the spreading flames that marked the crest.

Roosevelt was among the first Americans to reach the heights. He and some black cavalry and some of his Rough Riders sheltered where they could, firing as the Spaniards readied a countercharge. Paul lay prone just to the rear of the group, embracing his tripod and camera, his right hand crushing his straw hat to his head, as if that would somehow stop a bullet.

He heard intimidating screams, watched the Spaniards rise from their trenches in an attempt to overwhelm the attackers. Roosevelt kept shouting encouragement, leaping up to fire his revolver. More and more soldiers were coming up the hill, and superior numbers, along with the devastating fire of the Gatlings, made the difference. The countercharge fell apart. The Spanish began retreating toward Santiago, a mile and a half away.

About half past four the shooting stopped. Paul was finishing his last frames, running out the magazine with the camera tilted down to look into Spanish rifle pits. The contents were gruesome. Dozens of dead soldiers lay where they had fought and fallen.

Audiences at Pflaum's would probably loathe Paul's pictures of the dead bodies, and the rest of what he'd filmed, if it came out: the final, slow climb to the summit, the Spanish flag being torn down. He'd even cranked while an infantry major came upon a wounded Spaniard and killed him. Americans would hate the scene because it disgraced one of their own. Paul hated it for a different reason. It was despicably inhuman. Then he thought of Wex and said to himself. Yes, but the pictures are the truth, and people should see.

A man in a boater came walking along the hilltop. It was Stephen Crane. Paul was too tired to do more than nod hello.

A shot rang out. Crane paid no attention. He stopped at one of the rifle pits and gazed down. "Incredible, eh, Dutch? In the *Red Badge* I only imagined it. This is ten times worse."

Paul nodded dumbly. Jotting in a notebook, Crane walked away.

THE GENERAL ✦ On Sunday morning, July 3, vessels of the Spanish squadron, destroyers and cruisers, attempted to break out of the American blockade of Santiago harbor. The American vessels gave chase, maneuvering and firing salvos. One by one, the Spanish ships were grounded or sunk. The battle was over by early afternoon.

Full of opium pills for pain, Joe Crown listened to the noisy sea battle from a cot in a field-hospital tent behind the lines. When news of the great victory reached the hospital, weak as he was, Joe joined in the cheering.

On that same Sunday, he learned later, General Shafter sent a warning to the Spanish high command in Santiago that at ten a.m. Monday he would begin shelling the town. He requested that all women, children, and foreign nationals leave Santiago before firing commenced. The exodus of civilians began before sunset. The American bombardment opened precisely at ten the following morning. During the next few days the Spaniards counterattacked, with little success. The Americans gained ground a little at a time. There were bloody engagements, and casualties on both sides. But the end of the campaign was no longer in doubt. Contemplating the increasingly hopeless situation, the Spanish commander instructed a general to commence negotiations for a surrender with honor.

The first meeting between American and Spanish officers was held July 13. Terms were quickly agreed upon, and the transfer of power was scheduled for noon on Sunday, July 17. General Shafter would enter the city then.

Joe Crown was still in the field hospital; Paul visited him every day or so. Paul had no more film and was exceedingly anxious to get out of Cuba.

By the end of the week Joe was on his feet again. The wound still hurt unmercifully, but he could hobble about with the aid of a stick of tough ceiba wood. When the victory procession assembled on Sunday, with considerable pain Joe sat his saddle in full uniform.

General Shafter led the advance into Santiago astride a huge, powerful cavalry horse, which nevertheless looked swaybacked under its mountainous burden. The long column of American officers was trailed by a band of reporters. Paul was back there, on foot.

In the broad and handsome plaza, an enormous crowd waited. But there was no cheering, no shouting, as the conquerors rode in.

There were tiny children on the cobbled streets. Children with bloated stomachs. Santiago was starving. It confirmed what Joe had learned long ago. There might be certain accomplishments in war, certain brief celebrations. But there was no real joy. None.

After the treaty ceremonies the bell in the tower of the old cathedral clanged twelve times. Joe Crown felt no thrill of pride when an American color guard smartly raised the red, white, and blue. Then a regimental band struck up "The Stars and Stripes Forever." Joe Crown stood with perfect military correctness. But he wept inside.

Ilsa, I'm tired of war. I want to come home to you. I want to heal our family. Ilsa, I love you. I have made so many mistakes.

DUTCH ✦ Paul had enjoyed visiting Uncle Joe in the field hospital. His uncle was mending well. Paul's own wound also hurt less every day. He collected his valise from the cantina in Siboney and went to the tiny office used by the correspondents to file their stories. He cabled Shadow that he was returning soon.

Doing all these things, he still had trouble keeping his mind off Julie. The war was virtually over. He'd be going home soon, to see whether his film survived, then to search for her.

No, put that in reverse order. He'd search first. The film would keep a little longer. He ran into Billy Bitzer and talked it over with him. Yes, Bitzer thought the Biograph laboratory in New York might process Paul's negatives as a courtesy, provided Bitzer set it up first. He promised to telegraph the company from Florida. Everyone assumed they'd be returning to Key West or Tampa, and Paul intended to be on the first transport carrying civilians. In Florida he'd exchange his return ticket to Chicago for a ticket to New York. London was there in case everything Miss Fishburne said proved wrong. London was his escape hole.

ON SUNDAY MORNING, AUGUST 7, Paul and his uncle walked down the Alameda, Santiago's waterfront promenade. Uncle Joe was still hobbling on the ceiba-wood stick. Ahead of them, at the dock, the transport *Miami* swayed gently on her mooring lines. Paul could hardly contain his excitement, or believe his fantastic luck. *Miami*, the first vessel to carry American troops home from Cuba, would sail on the evening tide. She wasn't going to Florida, but straight to eastern Long Island, a place called Montauk Point, where a quarantine camp was being built for troops stricken with yellow fever. Uncle Joe, working through Joe Wheeler, had gotten Paul a place on the transport.

Paul and his uncle neared the ship. The Rough Riders were already queued up at two gangways. "Could we go a little more slowly, Paul?"

"By all means. Take hold of my arm." Soon they were standing in the shadow of *Miami*'s great iron prow.

"Well, nephew, your gear's aboard?"

Paul nodded. "Last night."

Uncle Joe tucked his stick under his arm to free both hands. "We'll meet again soon. I will get a message to your aunt. She'll be overjoyed. I confess to the same feeling." They embraced. *"Auf Wiedersehen, lieber Paul."*

"Wiedersehen, Onkel."

"Chicago," Joe Crown said.

"Chicago."

For a little while anyway.

The next week or two—Long Island—would determine the rest of his life.

MIAMI docked on Long Island on Monday morning, August 15. Crowds were waving hats and small American flags. A band crashed out "Rally Round the Flag, Boys."

Paul rented an ancient buggy with a plodding old mare. It was late afternoon by the time he reached Southampton.

He tied the buggy in front of a hardware store, where a middle-aged woman was wielding a broom. "Ma'am, can you give me directions to the Elstree house?" he asked.

"Belle Mer." The woman pointed. "First Neck Lane to the shore, left on Dune Road. It's the only house. No one's there but the caretaker," she added. "You aren't from around here, are you? Bill Elstree was shot and killed a few weeks back."

He felt cold terror. "Who killed him?"

"Some woman he kept in the city."

And then relief. "And the widow? Where is she?"

"Mrs. Elstree left a week ago."

"For Chicago?"

"Why, she didn't stop around to share that information with me."

"You say the caretaker's at the house?"

"Yes."

"Thank you." Paul hurried on.

He had no trouble finding Belle Mer. When the horse stopped, the click of hedge shears could be heard. Paul followed the sound to the east face of the mansion. There he found a small, stocky man at work. "Are you the caretaker?"

"I am." The man lowered the shears, taking Paul's measure.

"My name is Paul Crown. From Chicago. I am an old friend of Mrs. Elstree. Can you tell me where to find her?"

"I can't. I don't know." After another speculative look at Paul, he went on. "Lots of sorrow in this house. I think Mrs. Elstree went away to heal herself. Sorry I can't help more."

Paul thanked him and left. His sole hope now was Mrs. Vanderhoff in Chicago.

In New York City, he found a cheap hotel. Early next day he called at the American Biograph offices on Broadway. Billy Bitzer had telegraphed, as promised. For a price, the owners developed his negatives and struck prints. Paul sat in the dark and watched the prints projected.

All the magazines were ruined, fogged, except the last. That four hundred feet was mottled and streaked. But the images were spectacular. He decided it should be called *Conquest of the San Juan Hill*. He thought Wex Rooney might admire it.

"Great stuff," said the projectionist. "Looks damn dangerous."

"Yes," Paul said, and left. He rode the overnight train to Chicago. At the Dearborn Street depot the following afternoon, he hired a cab to go directly to the Vanderhoff mansion.

When he arrived, Paul stood frowning at the house. Every window on every floor was curtained.

412

The servant who opened the front door refused to let him step in. Paul craned to see past the man. Sheets hid the furniture.

"I would like to speak with Mrs. Vanderhoff, please."

"She is in California for health reasons."

"Her daughter, then? Mrs. William Elstree—"

"We know nothing of her whereabouts. Mrs. Vanderhoff has no contact with her. Good day." He slammed the door.

Wearily Paul walked away. All right, it was settled. He would deliver the film to Shadow and, at the same time, give notice.

PAUL climbed the familiar stairs, smelling savory kitchen odors. He knocked at the kitchen door and walked in. Mary was at the stove, the colonel at the table in his undershirt, noisily sucking cabbage soup from his spoon.

"Kid!" Shadow cried, jumping up, flinging his arms wide. "It's you! Put those things down. Mary! A bowl—food!"

Paul set the canvas bag on the table. "I'd like to show you the pictures first. The weather ruined all the magazines but one. But that one is pretty good."

"If it's half as good as what you sent, they'll go wild at Pflaum's. That stuff from Tampa—the drills, the alligator—Iz was ready to kiss me when he saw the ticket lines. Come on, let's look."

In the darkened parlor, silent images of destruction and death flickered on the screen, casting silvery patterns on the stunned faces of Shadow and Mary. When the film ran out, Shadow snapped on the lights. "Kid—sensational. No other word for it."

"Thank you, Colonel. Could I have a bowl of soup now?"

"Anything you want," the colonel cried, beaming.

Afterward Paul gave his notice.

Shadow took it hard. He begged Paul not to quit, promised to raise his salary. They talked for over three hours. At the end Shadow dismissed the matter of Paul's notice by saying they'd discuss it after the première of *Conquest of the San Juan Hill*.

Paul sighed, said he really needed to visit his family tonight, and fled down the stairs.

IN THE great house at Michigan Avenue and Twentieth, all the family cried when Paul walked in with his valise.

Fritzi cried, then pretended to swoon on the floor of the front

413

parlor, so overcome was she. Carl cried, a few manly sniffles suitable for one who had become a football player for his school. Aunt Ilsa cried to overflowing.

"Your uncle will be home in a few days," Aunt Ilsa said. "He is in Tampa at this moment— Oh, my heavens, this is too much." She fanned herself with her handkerchief.

Later Aunt Ilsa saw him to his old room and drew his bath. After he'd soaked and pulled on a flannel nightshirt and settled himself, she knocked and tiptoed in.

"Oh, Paul. Dear Paul. *Willkommen.*" She threw her arms around him and hugged him fiercely. "You met my Joe. Patched things up, he said. How extraordinary. I'm so glad. What now for you?"

Paul drew a long breath. "I gave Colonel Shadow my notice this afternoon. I'm leaving for London as soon as possible."

"London? But why? America's your home now, Paul."

"*Nein, Tante Ilsa.* The home I wanted was with Julie, and she's gone, no one knows where." He took his aunt's hands in his. "You've been wondrously kind to me, Aunt Ilsa. We won't be out of touch, ever. But I must leave this country. It's time."

She searched his face for a long moment, saw he was determined. She kissed his cheek and went out. Not until she was gone did he realize something was different. She hadn't called him Pauli.

THE GENERAL ✦ Late August. He tap-tapped his way from the hot kitchen to the stifling front hall, leaning on the ceiba-wood stick. He checked the lock on the front door. He checked every door every night; Germanic habits of thoroughness didn't change easily.

He heard a footfall and discovered his daughter peeping out of the music room. Fritzi was in her nightdress, barefoot. She was seventeen now, still lean as a scarecrow. But her liveliness only increased as time passed. It even made her pretty in certain kinds of light.

"Papa, might I speak to you a moment?"

He followed her into the music room, where she faced him soberly and said, "Papa, you know I'm going to be an actress."

"Is that what you wanted? To tell me nothing's changed?"

"Yes, Papa, that's all. I don't want you to forget."

He sighed. "I can't pretend I like this very much, Fritzi. But I learned a few lessons while I was gone. I won't hinder you. I'll help

414

you financially if you need that. I'll even"—he cleared his throat— "give you my reluctant consent. If it matters."

"Oh, Papa, yes, it does! Thank you!" She jumped to his arms. They embraced warmly; then father and daughter walked up the long staircase, arms around each other, voices murmuring.

A HALF hour later he lay beside Ilsa. His ardor had taken her by surprise. Now they were resting.

The house was still, everyone in their beds. Paul had gone back to Shadow's. He'd stayed at the Crown house only two nights. Until the first showing of his film, Paul thought he should live where he worked. He'd come to supper several times, though. Relations were more or less normal again.

Around the country the war was still the topic of the moment. A giddy spirit of victory prevailed. Pflaum's Music Hall was spending a lot of money to promote *Conquest of the San Juan Hill*. There was prominent mention of Paul in the newspaper advertisements.

After the première showing, Paul would leave for England. Joe had pleaded with him to give Chicago, and his adopted country, a second chance. Paul said no. He was polite but adamant. Joe laid a great part of the blame on himself.

He lay on his back, staring up into the dark. "Ilsa."

Drowsily, "Yes?"

"I would like to make another search for Joe Junior. Hire the detective bureau once again."

"I think it's futile. Nothing mailed to us in many months."

"Still, I would like to do it." He paused. "If you'll consent."

"I consent, my dearest. There are far worse ways to spend money. Far worse things to spend it on than hope."

DUTCH ✦ September. Torrential rain falling. Cabs impossible to find. In spite of it, Pflaum's Music Hall was sold out for the première of *Conquest of the San Juan Hill*.

In the lobby, wearing white tie and tails, Iz Pflaum greeted newspaper writers and other important people. Shadow was suavely elegant in a new amber-colored frock coat and big white sombrero. Mary was with him, in her most revealing dress.

Iz Pflaum had scheduled the short film after the variety program, which was due to begin at eight o'clock. Paul was extremely nervous. He stood alone, twisting a brand-new checkered cap bought for the occasion together with a handsome new suit.

The doors to the lobby kept opening to admit patrons. He saw the Crown carriage under the marquee. Uncle Joe jumped out and helped Aunt Ilsa alight. Next came Fritzi and Carl.

In the lobby, Aunt Ilsa and Fritzi embraced Paul. Carl shook his hand. Not wanting to prolong the meeting, Uncle Joe said, "I believe we should find our seats. It's almost eight." As he stepped past Paul he squeezed his arm. "I hope it will be a huge success."

Pflaum had put them in the third row on the left aisle, directly behind Shadow and Mary. Paul had the aisle seat, with Uncle Joe to his right, then Aunt Ilsa, Fritzi, and Carl. At five past eight Pflaum's bandleader began the overture.

No one wanted to see the variety bill of jugglers and other acts. Finally, mercifully, the show ended and the screen was rolled into place behind the velvet curtain.

A hush fell. The orchestra struck up "The Stars and Stripes Forever." An arc light threw a hot white circle onto the curtain, and into the spotlight bounded Iz Pflaum.

"And now, ladies and gentlemen," he boomed from the stage apron, "prepare yourselves for the most remarkable and soul-stirring living pictures you have ever seen." The curtain began to part to reveal the screen. *"Conquest of the San Juan Hill!"*

Fanfare and drumroll from the pit. Paul sank low in his seat, fairly twitching with nerves. The screen began to glow and flicker with scratchy, jerky images of the war he remembered too well.

During the last sequence—the stark views of the Spanish dead in the trenches—the bugler in the pit blew taps. Although the dead belonged to the enemy, they had belonged to the human race as well. There were no outcries against the Spaniards, only silence.

Paul glanced from the corner of his eye. Uncle Joe sat motionless. Paul heard Aunt Ilsa and Fritzi weeping.

On the screen there was an abrupt cut to a great billowing American flag whipping in the wind. Paul had photographed it on the roof at Shadow's request, and patched it to the end. It rescued the audience from grim scenes of death and brought them to their feet in a thundering ovation. Uncle Joe was among the first to stand.

He reached for Paul's arm, a strange look on his face, then took a handkerchief from his pocket and blew his nose. He was shaken.

"It was so real. I felt I was there again. Hearing the guns, the cries of the wounded. Walking among the dead. It moved me very much." Then he said, "Come, Ilsa, children."

The aisles filled with spectators equally overcome, everyone talking at once. Shadow hugged Paul and slapped his back. "They loved it. Even that grisly stuff." He kept pounding. "Damn it, kid—Dutch—you're a genius." He was incoherent. He was crying. The base, crude, dishonest R. Sidney Shadow III was *crying*.

Uncle Joe stayed beside Paul as they slowly ascended the crowded aisle. "This isn't the low trash I thought it to be. It's honest, important work," he said. "History lives in those pictures."

Paul was euphoric over the vindication.

The sluggishly moving crowd finally brought Ilsa, Fritzi, and Carl to the doorway. Outside, Iz Pflaum was waving his hands like semaphore flags. "Dutch, hurry, we have journalists waiting to speak to you."

Paul couldn't hear clearly in the hubbub. Just to his left, the last row of the center section was empty save for one person still seated. A woman in a coat with a black fur collar, gloves, a large hat with a gossamer gray veil. While he was taking notice of her, she stood up. She lifted the veil.

"Paul." Julie held out her arms. "I made a vow to find you."

SHE had a large suite at the Palmer House. Paul spent the night. They made love hungrily, and then they talked.

She explained that she had left the Long Island mansion for a flat already rented in New York. There she had hired detectives. The firm's Chicago bureau made inquiries in the Crown neighborhood. No one had seen or heard of Paul in some time. The chief of the bureau was ready to approach Ilsa Crown when he noticed one of the advertisements for Pflaum's special showing. There was the name Paul Crown.

"I found the courage to do all that because you and Aunt Willis always said I had courage if only I could call it up. I knew you were alive somewhere. I knew I could find you if I tried hard enough, took enough time, spent enough money—heaven knows there's plenty to spend. Elstree was one of the richest men in America."

"And you've inherited all of it. I will never make a tenth as much in my entire life."

"It won't be a problem—I won't let it." She caressed his cheek, kissed his mouth. "I promised myself that if I did find you, and you had someone else, I'd go away. But not without telling you once more that I love you, I'll never love anyone else."

He took her in his arms again.

Shortly after dawn he awoke to feel her leaving their warm nest of blankets. In a dark corner of the bedroom a drawer slid in and out. She returned with something in her hand, clambered onto the bed, and knelt next to him. Her shining black hair cascaded to her waist.

"Paul dearest, I swore that if we were ever reunited, I'd ask you to do something. I hope you won't think it too strange. It's very important to me." She laid a pair of silver scissors in his hand. "Cut my hair."

LATE in the morning, at the telegraph desk downstairs, he sent a cable to Michael Radcliffe at the London *Light* in Fleet Street.

REGRET WILL NOT BE COMING TO LONDON. SITUATION CHANGED. PLAN TO STAY WITH PRESENT EMPLOYER. AM MARRYING YOUNG WOMAN I SPOKE ABOUT. WILL SEND NEW ADDRESS AND FULL DETAILS SOON. THANK YOU FOR YOUR KINDNESS. YOUR FRIEND ALWAYS. DUTCH.

Part Ten
HOMECOMING
1900–1901

DUTCH ✦ Monday, December 31, 1900; the eve of the new year. Germans called it *Sylvesterabend.*

It was the cusp of the new century as well. As the newspapers repeatedly pointed out, each year ending in zero concludes a series from one to ten. Thus 1900 was the last of a series that started with 1891. The twentieth century would begin in the first minute of the first day of January 1901—tomorrow.

For weeks every paper and periodical had been delivering visions of the future, forecasts for the next century. There were predictions of high-speed trains operating on a single magnetized rail, hemlines rising indecently, more business degrees for "new" women, German "commercial expansionism," the masses discovering the new winter sport of "skeeing." The latest edition of the papers also carried large display advertisements relating to the holiday. Elstree's was featuring an end-of-the-century china, glassware, and crockery sale.

On the last day of the old century Paul and his family and friends went to court.

Paul wore a new three-piece cutaway sack suit. Julie had taken a comb to his hair, to little avail. Paul knew he was disheveled, but it didn't matter—his wife looked smashing in her tailored dove-gray suit.

He loved her with an undiminished passion. He loved her gentility and her innate kindness to others. She was intelligent and good-humored, and, in an unassuming way, she was developing an independence her mother would have hated.

A whole troop of well-wishers had come along with Paul and Julie. Uncle Joe sat in the first row of the spectators' section, behind the railing. Beside him were Aunt Ilsa, Fritzi, and Carl.

Aunt Ilsa was no longer campaigning against spirits, wines, and beers. That issue was resolved for the present. However, she still sent money to Hull House.

Carl was home from college for the holidays. He was eighteen, with enormous shoulders that suited someone who played the murderous game of football for Princeton, in New Jersey.

Fritzi, who would soon be twenty, had taken a short leave from her acting company and rushed from Albany, Georgia. She was on tour with Mortmain's Royal Shakespeare Combination. She was supernumerary, assistant wardrobe mistress, part-time cook, and occasional performer. Her most important role was Viola in *Twelfth Night*. Uncle Joe and Aunt Ilsa had traveled all the way to Owensboro, Kentucky, to see her perform. Uncle Joe still disapproved of the profession, but proudly said his daughter was outstanding.

So here they were, together again. But there was one void. Cousin Joe. Paul wished he were there too, but he had disappeared entirely, and little was said of him. It was too sad a subject, especially for Aunt Ilsa.

Spotted about in other seats were Paul's friends and mentors. Colonel Shadow was present, smelling magnificently of bay rum and high-priced cigars. Mary Beezer had put on her best and gaudiest dress. She and the new prince of the living pictures had left the Levee and moved into a six-room suite on the top floor of Allerton's Hotel on fashionable North Michigan.

The most flamboyant woman in the cold, drafty room was Aunt Willis. Over her flared skirt she wore a short, snug red coat—a Parisian automobile coat, she called it—set off by a plumed black hat and rolled black umbrella.

Perhaps the most special visitor, at least for Paul, was Wexford Rooney. Wex was accompanied by his stout, blunt-jawed wife, Lucille, the former widow Suggsworth of Charleston, West Virginia. She'd sold her boardinghouse in order to finance her husband in a new Temple of Photography, in Lexington, Kentucky. Wex said his studio was highly successful, though how this could be in a place where horseflesh abounded and sporting gentlemen wagered on everything from the speed of two-year-olds to the accuracy of their watches, Paul couldn't imagine.

Paul and Julie were living on the sunny first floor of an apartment building on treelined Paulina Street, in the pleasant neighborhood of Ravenswood. Julie had sold Belle Mer. She never saw—nor heard from—her mother.

Paul was in this courtroom because of Julie. They'd been married for two years; now she was in her third month of carrying their child.

On a snowy night early in December they had been sitting in front of a fire in their snug Victorian parlor, holding hands and talking softly of the marvelous prospect of parenthood. On the wall, next to the display shelves that held his globe and other souvenirs, hung one special item—the left half of the stereoscope card, which Julie had framed and presented to Paul for his twenty-third birthday, in June.

"Paul."

"Mmm?"

"I don't ask for things often."

"No. The last time, as I recall, it was a simple request involving a pair of scissors."

"This would require a little more of you. Once again, it's important to me." She took a breath. "I'd like our child to have American parents. Two of them."

He had looked at the framed picture of the ship's bow and the Statue of Liberty while the impact settled on him. Now here he was in the courtroom. He rose to face the Honorable Jacob Müller of the circuit court.

Paul stood in front of the dais, curiously tight with anxiety. *From Müllerstrasse in Berlin to Judge Müller's chambers in Chicago. From Pauli to Dutch. What a long journey.*

Marriage to Julie hadn't quite ended the journey. He still needed a sign—the sign of which old Frau Flüsser in Berlin had spoken. He needed it to banish the deep and haunting questions of childhood, to put a clear mark at this journey's end. To show him where he truly belonged.

The judge looked down from the high place. "You are Mr. Crown?"

"Yes, Your Honor."

"I'm ready to take your declaration. Clerk, please."

The court clerk came forward with the Bible. "Left hand on the Bible, right hand raised." Paul obeyed.

"Paul Crown, do you declare under oath before this court that it is your bona fide intention to become a citizen of the United States of America?"

"I do."

He was further asked to declare that he renounced forever all allegiance to any foreign prince or sovereignty.

"I do, yes."

Judge Müller's pen scratched. "So sworn, so noted, so entered."

The judge laid his pen aside, removed his eyeglasses, shot up from his chair, and leaned over to shake Paul's hand.

"Congratulations, Mr. Crown. Come back in two years, we'll make it binding."

SINCE 1898 Paul's road to this courtroom had been colorful, convoluted, and, at times, highly dangerous. Shadow's appetite for "actualities" had only been whetted by the Spanish war films. In December 1899 Paul and his new assistant, Ollie Hultgren, were sent to the war zone in South Africa to film the conflict between Great Britain and the rebellious Boer farmers.

In May of 1900, when Ollie sailed back to America with the now battered camera and gear, Paul took a ship bound for France.

In Paris, he was once again reunited with his friend Michael Radcliffe. The occasion was a great fair, the Paris exposition. Two of the largest and most popular exhibits were those of armament companies showing an array of long-range cannon and rapid-fire machine guns.

Michael, as usual, held forth. "Ah, Paul, why do we deceive ourselves, proclaim that we're uplifting our brothers and our sisters with the scientific marvels of the new age? Uplift is a fiction we created to hide the truth. The human animal is a cowardly and vicious beast. And think how much worse it will be when he has his hands on quantities of rapid-fire guns, cannon that can hurl a shell twenty miles to drop on civilian populations. A dark time, the next century. The beast is already prowling. He smells blood coming down the wind. Armageddon.

"Nothing to do, I suppose, but have a drink, have a woman, try to survive for one more day."

Paul returned to America to find Bryan and Debs running for President, and Stephen Crane dead at twenty-eight of tuberculosis.

Shadow was jubilant about the South African pictures. He gave Paul a bonus and sent him off on yet another assignment.

AND so it went, the hours and days rolling into weeks and months, sweeping Paul from one side of the globe to the other, one remarkable sight or experience to the next, exactly as he'd dreamed in the little windowless room in Berlin. Unbelievably, the dream had come true.

Tomorrow, New Year's Day, 1901, he and Ollie had railway tickets to New York. A new Ellis Island had just opened, rebuilt after a disastrous fire in 1897 had destroyed the original wooden buildings. Millions of immigrants were pouring into the country. Ellis Island was a topic of the moment, and Shadow wanted an "actuality."

Tonight, however, was all his, and Julie's. Tonight there was Uncle Joe's party, to celebrate the new century and Paul's intent to become a citizen.

The party was held at the city's newest German restaurant, Zum Rothen Stern—the Red Star Inn—a replica of a Bavarian public house, offering dark wood paneling, leaded glass windows, colorful beer steins, and a long menu of German specialties. The waiters, in their short black jackets and long white aprons, were good-humored but mercilessly efficient.

The banquet Uncle Joe had arranged was huge, with steaming tureens of oxtail soup, bowls of dumplings, platters of roast pork and veal, sauerbraten with vegetables, and fresh hot loaves of bread. All of this was liberally supplemented with spirits. Not only Crown lager and Heimat, but Mumm's Champagne.

The table was U-shaped, with places assigned by little cards Aunt Ilsa had lettered. The strolling accordionist was playing "The Stars and Stripes Forever" while people clapped and stamped to the beat. The march was a favorite of Paul's, and he heard it everywhere—parlors, concert halls, saloons, street corners—as if Sousa's melody summed up America's mood of strength, optimism, growing importance in global affairs.

The accordionist came to their table and asked what they wished to hear. Carl said, "Play 'Ragtime Rose.'" Mary Beezer and Willis applauded. Though not fond of that fast-time raggedy sort of music, Uncle Joe was soon tapping his foot.

Then Shadow said, "I want a cakewalk." He tipsily rearranged chairs to create space. The cakewalk was the most popular dance in America, and he insisted on demonstrating his familiarity. "Here we go, Mary." Colonel Shadow and Mary did a cakewalk, receiving enthusiastic applause.

The party grew louder and more convivial. The guests left their seats between courses. Paul lit a cigar and watched Shadow weave around the table with a tall stein of beer to toast Uncle Joe.

Wex cornered Paul and quizzed him about his travels. Paul in turn wanted reassurance that Wex was doing well, wasn't squandering his profits on Kentucky horse racing. "Are you serious, my boy? My dear wife gives me a small betting allowance. When it's gone, there isn't any more. It doesn't pay to argue with Lucille, bless her. She tamed my demons—no, ordered them to move out."

Later Paul overheard Miss Fishburne talking spiritedly with his aunt. Miss Fishburne had been rather glum when she arrived. Julie had discovered the reason; her aunt was recovering from a failed romance with a handsome young Portuguese yacht captain.

"I can't decide what to do next, my dear Ilsa. I'm mad to study plein-air painting in Provence. Or sail to the Hebrides. Of course, I could settle down at a spa and read Count Tolstoy's *War and*

Peace to the end. I've started it nine times. Right now I'm having hellish difficulty with a book called *The Interpretation of Dreams*. It's very controversial. Written by some Viennese doctor, Sigmund Freud."

Aunt Ilsa was enraptured. Or, possibly, overwhelmed.

At a few minutes before midnight the accordionist began a familiar *Neujahrslied*. Almost at once, people were on their feet, swaying, bellowing the sentimental farewell to the old year.

Then the restaurant owner called for quiet. He rang a ship's bell with a mallet while eyeing his large gold pocket watch. On the last stroke people threw streamers, and pounded the tables, and shouted, "*Glückliches neues Jahr!* Happy New Year!" Everyone, including the Crowns and their guests, kissed and embraced and uttered sentimental good wishes.

Joe hugged each of his children, then Paul and Julie, and finally Ilsa. Over her shoulder he observed his nephew. Paul was standing with his head canted forward so that his forehead touched Julie's. He was murmuring to her, and she responded with an adoring look. Joe had never seen his nephew so happy.

ILSA ✦ It was happenstance, Ilsa's answering when the front bell rang next morning.

Joe had left about seven. He complained of a headache from all the celebration last night, but he went to the brewery anyway, to weed through the thickets of paper forever sprouting from his desk. Fritzi and Carl were still in their rooms. Julie was at the depot, saying good-bye to Paul, and the servants were on holiday.

There was a second ring of the bell. "Wait, please. I'm coming," Ilsa called.

She opened the door and saw a tramp standing there, supporting himself with a crutch under his right arm. She couldn't see him clearly because of the dazzling winter sun.

Even so, a few details registered. The man was slightly built, with curly hair that fell over his collar. A heavy beard concealed his chin and neck. He wore a patched mackinaw, and a cloth cap that cast a shadow below his nose. His right trouser leg was pinned just above the ankle; his right foot was missing.

It flashed through Ilsa's mind that Germans said the first person you encountered outside your house on New Year's Day had special significance. Seeing an old woman meant bad luck for the coming year, a young man the opposite. What did a tramp signify? She had no idea.

She raised a hand in front of her forehead to shield the sun. "I'm very sorry," she began—she'd recited the same litany often. "We don't feed anyone at the front door."

"Mama, don't you know me? Mama, it's Joe."

THE GENERAL ✦ Brauerei Crown was quiet as a church. Joe was in shirtsleeves, clearing his desk as the telephone rang. Annoyed by the interruption, he reached for the instrument. "Yes?"

"Joe, I have some news." Ilsa's low voice was a signal that something had happened. He forgot everything, rocked with fear of a tragedy. A dozen gory alternatives flashed in his head.

"Joe Junior. He is here."

"Here?"

"Here in the house, yes. I answered the door—there he was."

"I'll drive home immediately."

"Joe, don't come home. Not for a while. I will talk to him."

Vaguely hurt, he exclaimed, "It's my duty. I'm his father."

"I will talk to him. Then you can see him. I don't know why our son came home, but now that he has, I want him to stay if he will. I want to heal the old wounds. I don't want them opened again."

"But—"

"Joe." It was a definite declaration, a warning. *"I will do it."* He'd never heard such mettle in her voice.

Now he was the one who was silent. She'd changed. His whole family had changed. But so had he, he realized with a mingling of amazement, bewilderment, and not a little sadness.

"All right, Ilsa. I'll come home later."

"Thank you, my dear one."

He put the earpiece on the hook and sat staring at the black upright telephone. It was a new century, in a world that was so changed he sometimes recognized nothing but a few outer trappings. Well, shattering changes had come and gone, and the Crowns had survived. He would survive. The strength of the family was his strength. And now he had a reason more compelling than any he had known for a long time. His boy was home. With the aid of lessons painfully learned, Joe would keep him home.

DUTCH ✦ On Thursday morning, the third of January, Paul left Ollie at the hotel and walked through the crowds on New York's Sixth Avenue. He missed Julie terribly, as he always did when they were apart. But he didn't miss the three-piece suit. He was at work again, able to dress in the comfortable outfit he liked because it set him apart: a khaki shirt, matching cavalry riding pants, black boots, and a long black leather coat. An expensive black-and-brown-checkered golf cap completed the outfit of the chief operator.

At the corner of Sixth and Seventeenth, he turned into the large and handsome two-story mercantile emporium of the F. W. Woolworth Company. Somewhere he'd lost his winter gloves.

As he stepped into the store he heard piano music. It came from a song plugger on a high circular platform near the front doors. The platform was completely surrounded by racks of sheet music.

Paul found exactly the right pair of gloves—gauntlets of black leather with warm fleece linings—paid for them, and headed for the street while the plugger plaintively sang "The Blue and the Gray," the most recent hit of the famous Paul Dresser. The pianist had gathered a large crowd, including a man whose appearance, from the back, plucked some faint chord in Paul's memory. The man's brushy black hair stuck out in many directions. Paul stepped to one side for a better view of him.

The man was young, about Paul's age. He wore an expensive gray suit and silk cravat, and carried a gray overcoat. Lively blue eyes darted over the racks of sheet music. Paul recognized him.

The plugger swung into another hit of the moment, "Ragtime Rose." Half a dozen of the racks were filled with copies of the piano piece. The name of the composer, Harry Poland, was printed large in scrolled type.

The young man with black hair bounced up and down on his toes, immersed in the music. Slowly Paul walked around the platform and stood opposite him. Absolutely no mistake . . .

The young man noticed him. Paul waited, smiling. The man's mouth fell open.

Paul grinned, snatched off his golf cap, and walked swiftly back to the other man. "Herschel? Herschel Wolinski?"

"Pauli? Yes, it is I, Herschel, your friend!"

With a whoop, he tossed his overcoat onto the platform and

threw his arms around Paul, slapping his back and shouting, "Pauli, Pauli!" Annoyed listeners shushed them. The pianist was the most annoyed. Herschel said to him, "Keep on playing. It's my music."

He leaned back, gripping Paul's shoulders. "It's really you?"

"It is. Pauli, or Paul, whatever you want—I have a lot of names in America. What do I call you? Herschel or Harry?"

"Harry. Now and forever." His accent was surprisingly light.

"How long have you been here?"

"It will be four years in March. My mother passed away, and my sisters chose to remain behind in Poland. I told you I'd make it, didn't I? I never doubted. I have a new name, as you noticed, Harry Poland. It's very American, don't you think?"

"Yes. I like it, it's catchy." Still amazed, Paul picked up a copy of "Ragtime Rose." He opened it, gazed at the incomprehensible black notes. "You wrote this."

"I did."

"It's a hit. I hear it everywhere."

"I must say modestly—that's so. Sales to date are excellent. It's published, as you see, by Howley, Haviland, the firm in which the great Paul Dresser is a partner. I started there as a song plugger. Now I'm staff composer."

"Herschel, I cannot believe this."

"Nor I, really." Herschel snatched Paul's hand and waltzed him around. A prim floorwalker strode toward them.

"See here, we can't allow—"

But they were already gone, arm in arm, into Sixth Avenue. Herschel had stuck a copy of the song in Paul's coat pocket, calling over his shoulder, "I'm the composer. I get free copies."

They drank beer through the afternoon, adjourned to Charles Rector's splendid restaurant at dusk, and there dined on venison washed down with glasses of red Bordeaux. They could hardly stop talking.

"Let's leave," Paul said suddenly. "I'm thirsty for some good beer."

"So am I, old friend."

Their whereabouts soon blurred in Paul's mind. At one place they sang "Ragtime Rose" over and over. Finally they exchanged addresses, and Herschel clasped Paul's hand and promised to visit Chicago to meet Julie.

At seven in the morning, his head bursting, Paul telephoned Ollie at the hotel. "Did you hire the launch? Good. We're filming at Ellis Island before noon."

"Here they come," Paul said.

The Luxograph was set up on the esplanade at the Ellis Island immigrant depot, a much more substantial building than the one Pauli Kroner and old Valter had passed through. The new structure was solid red brick, accented with sand-colored stone.

A squat ferry named *Weehawken* was churning toward the slip, her decks thronged with newcomers from steerage. Today's arrivals were off the *Karlsruhe* of the North German Lloyd line, Bremen.

Ollie crouched over the camera with his cap reversed. The Luxograph lens pointed at the anxious faces of the immigrants at the rail. "I'm grinding, Dutch."

"Get as much as you can. It's good stuff."

The ferry's portside bumped the esplanade. Crewmen leaped off with mooring lines. At the front of the crowd, waiting for the gangway to be lowered, was an old gentleman with a fine guardsman's mustache. Paul saw that all of his possessions were in one large bundle. He looked frightened. So did many others.

The gangway was lowered. Men and women surged off the ferry, pushing, exclaiming. Someone bumped the old man; he staggered. Paul grabbed his arm to prevent a fall. He pulled the old man out of the crowd, supported him with one hand while he reached down to rescue his bundle.

The old fellow was trembling, didn't even notice the camera.

"Here, sit down. Catch your breath." Paul helped the old man sit on his bundle.

Ollie kept grinding as the immigrants streamed up the walk to the doors. The old man fanned himself with his cap. *"Vielen Dank."* Many thanks. Paul nodded to show he understood.

In a few moments, recovering, the old man stood up and shook Paul's hand. He spoke rapidly, still in German. "What a pleasure to meet you. My first American."

"I'm not really—" Something stopped him. In German he said, "Yes, welcome."

"Your German is excellent. You are a countryman?"

"Berlin. Some time ago. A long time ago."

429

"I'm Swabian." Paul had recognized the accent. "A little town I'm sure you never heard of. Schwäbisch-Gmünd."

"I know it well. My family's from Aalen, just up the road."

"Imagine that. A neighbor, clear on the other side of the ocean." The old man glanced at the doors; all the other arrivals were inside, where immigration officers could be heard shouting at them.

"I'll help you rejoin your group." Paul took the old man's paper tag from the breast pocket of his corduroy jacket. "Four-two. Follow me." Ollie was surprised to see his partner moving away with the old man holding fast to his arm, like a child.

"I've heard awful stories. How they turn back most everyone."

"No, no, it isn't true. If you're healthy and act confident, there's no problem. Is someone meeting you?"

"My brother Reinhardt."

"Good, that makes things easier."

The old man gasped when he saw the chaotic hall, packed with newcomers. Strident voices roused memories in Paul. "Keep moving." "Manifest four this way. Step lively!"

"Manifest four, that's you. Let the gentleman through, please." They fought their way forward to the proper spot. Paul patted the old man's shoulder. "Stay with your group. Good luck."

"Thanks again. I'm sorry I took you for an American."

Paul looked at him. There it was at last. The sign. "But I am." He waved the old man on.

THE next morning was warmer, with low clouds moving across the harbor. The launch tied up at the pier, and they unloaded their gear. Occasional glimmers of sun subtly changed the color of the copper-green robe of Liberty Enlightening the World.

Ollie said, "Where are we putting the camera, Dutch? Up on that balcony at the base of the statue?"

"Higher. We're going all the way up to the torch. I was told there's an iron ladder and a catwalk up there."

Ollie stopped, stricken. "It must be over three hundred feet straight up." He looked green.

"Come on, Ollie, this is a lark. You'll remember it always."

"Sure, if I live through it."

Paul showed his letter of authorization to one of the guards at the entrance. Inside, they rode an elevator up toward a stair landing. As the elevator cage rose, Ollie was bug-eyed at the superstructure dropping past them. There was a whole webwork of iron braces—the armature—supporting the skin of the statue.

The elevator stopped at the landing, where another guard inspected their papers, then stepped back to show a narrow iron ladder beyond a curving brace.

"All yours, boys. Door up above is small—you'll have to stoop some. It's windy up on the catwalk, so don't get careless."

"Oh, no," Ollie said. He looked at Paul, then tipped his head back and looked up the ladder, which seemed to grow smaller, more insubstantial, the higher it went in the statue's arm.

Ollie took a breath and stepped up onto the ladder. From the second rung, he reached down to take the camera with one hand, while Paul supported the tripod and mounted the first rung.

Up they went, a perilous step at a time. When Paul finally looked down, he wished he hadn't. The guard on the landing was already small as a doll. Paul heard the wind moaning outside.

At the top, light came through a series of round windows at the base of the torch. Ollie forced the small door open. Bending, struggling, Paul got the camera through the door, into Ollie's hands, and climbed out on the catwalk.

They were three hundred and five feet above the bay. The wind seemed formidable. Grasping the rail and looking down, Paul found the perspective of the statue strange and dizzying.

With Ollie's help he set up the camera to overlook the ship channel. "What ship is it again?" Ollie asked.

Paul said, "*Statendam.* Holland America line, from Amsterdam."

"Immigrants, right?"

"Plenty. I contacted the local office to make sure."

"When's she due?"

He snapped open his pocket watch. "Any minute now."

Paul stepped to the rail again, gazing around him at New York and the harbor traffic. He gulped when he felt the copper lady sway in the wind, and held on to the rail. He remembered old Valter when *Rheinland* steamed in past the statue. How excited he was, reading from his little guidebook . . . but no more excited than the boy Pauli.

What did it all mean, this journey of his, this search, this passage through time and distance and hundreds of experiences? The answer flowed back to the very beginning, when he was adrift in Berlin, asking himself where he belonged—where home was, if he really had one.

Yesterday he had seen the sign. His place was with Julie, here in America. Here he was loved, and here also men were free. Free to do good, and free to do evil, but free. Freer, perhaps, than in the repressive and decaying autocracies of the Old World. Hundreds of thousands were still coming from the Old World, lured by the promise of freedom symbolized by the torch whose frozen copper flame rose up behind him.

Michael Radcliffe, who dwelt in clouds of pessimism, said there was a new world threat, a new outbreak of an old sickness of nationalism, and before long millions would die of it. The increasingly willful Kaiser and his military clique were prime carriers. So were certain Americans, such as Colonel Roosevelt, now the Vice President. Paul himself was infected with it to a degree.

The land he'd chosen wasn't perfect, but neither was he. There was something more important. America had given him his love, his family, and his purpose. And the freedom to search for all three. The old warnings of the baker of Wuppertal were laid to rest.

A great whistle blasted in the ship channel. Out of the mist came the prow of the Dutch ship. "You're right," Ollie said, "I can see them all over the deck down there."

A tug small as a toy sped toward the steamship, tossing up a wake. Another followed. *Statendam*'s whistle blew again, so resoundingly, Paul thought he felt the statue vibrate.

Out of the glowing mist came the ship. Paul crouched behind the camera on the catwalk high above the harbor. He swiftly turned the bill of his cap to the rear. "I'm cranking."

He was home.

432

Of all the colorful novels John Jakes has written, *Homeland*—inspired by his own family history—is perhaps closest to his heart. Jakes has always wanted to write about the immigrant experience in America, he says, and about Chicago particularly, "that prairie melting pot in which I was born and raised." But his famil-iarity with his own European heritage was very skimpy. Virtually all he knew was that his maternal grandfather, William Carl Retz, had come to the Midwest in the 1800s from Aalen, Germany.

Then, quite by chance, Jakes made an intriguing discovery. He learned from friends traveling in Europe that a family with the last name Rätz was living in Aalen, where they owned an old hotel. Could they be related to him? The author investigated, and sure enough, they proved to be cous-ins from a long-lost branch of the family. A happy reunion followed, and it was that experience, Jakes says, that "planted the seed for this story."

John Jakes

This book comes close to home in another way. Jakes' grandfather Retz "loved good stories," and his grandson has surely inherited the story-loving genes. Jakes has written more than sixty books in various genres. Historical fiction is his favorite, and his American sagas have made him famous, from *The Kent Family Chronicles* to *California Gold* (a Condensed Books selection).

John Jakes does most of his writing at his home on Hilton Head Island, South Carolina, where he is about to begin a sequel to *Homeland,* the second book in a projected three-volume work. Readers can expect to meet members of the Crown family again, this time as they move through the period leading up to World War I.

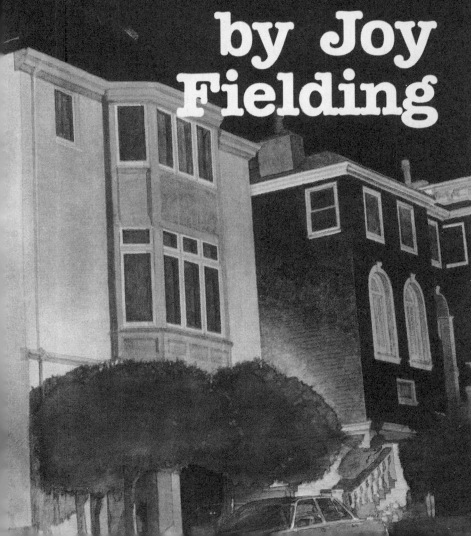

TELL ME
NO SECRETS

by Joy
Fielding

The sullen stranger waiting in the crowd—
　　there one moment and gone the next.
A shadowy figure outside her window—
　　there one moment and gone the next.
Was it her imagination?
Or is someone watching her every move?

CHAPTER 1

HE WAS waiting for her when she got to work. Or so it seemed to Jess, who spotted him immediately, standing motionless at the corner of California Avenue and Twenty-fifth Street. She felt him watching her as she left the parking garage and hurried across the street toward the administration building, his dark eyes colder than the late October wind that played with his straggly blond hair, his bare hands clenched into tight fists outside the pockets of his well-worn brown leather jacket. Did she know him?

As Jess drew closer, she saw that his full lips were twisted into an eerie half grin. It was a smile devoid of warmth, the smile of one who, as a child, enjoyed pulling the wings off butterflies, she thought, turning away and running up the steps, suddenly afraid.

Jess knew without looking that he was mounting the stairs after her. She reached the landing and pushed her shoulder against the heavy glass revolving door, the stranger stopping at the top of the steps, his face appearing and reappearing with each rotation of the glass, the sly smile never leaving his lips.

I am Death, the smile whispered. *I have come for you.*

Jess heard a loud gasp escape her lips, attracting the attention of one of the security guards. He approached cautiously. "Something wrong?" he asked.

"I hope not," Jess answered. "There's a man out there who . . ."
Who what? Who wants to come in out of the cold? Who has a creepy grin? Was that a crime in Cook County? The guard looked toward the door, Jess tracking his gaze. There was no one there.

"Looks like I'm seeing ghosts," Jess said apologetically.

"Well, it's the season for it," the guard said, waving her through the metal detector as he'd been doing routinely every morning for the past four years.

Jess liked routine. Every morning she got up at six forty-five, quickly showered, dressed in the clothes she had carefully laid out the night before, gobbled a piece of Pepperidge Farm frozen cake directly from the freezer, and was behind her desk within the hour, her case files ready. If she was prosecuting a case, there would be details to go over with her assistants, strategies to devise, questions to formulate, answers to determine. If she was preparing for trial, there would be leads to run down, witnesses to interview, police officers to talk to, timetables to coordinate. Everything according to schedule. Jess Koster didn't like surprises outside the courtroom any better than she liked them inside it.

After she had a full grasp of the day that lay ahead, she would sit back with a cup of black coffee and a jelly doughnut and study the morning paper, always starting with the obituaries. "Ashcroft, Pauline, died suddenly in her home, in her sixty-seventh year"; "Barrett, Ronald, after a lengthy illness, age 79." Jess wasn't sure when she'd begun making the obituaries part of her morning routine, and she wasn't sure why. It was an unusual habit for someone barely thirty, even for a prosecutor with the Cook County state's attorney's office in Chicago. There was never anyone she knew. Was she searching for her mother, as her ex-husband had once suggested? Or was it her own name she somehow expected to see?

The stranger with the evil grin pushed his way rudely into her mind's eye. *I am Death,* he teased. *I have come for you.*

Jess lowered the paper and glanced around the room. Three scratched walnut desks sat at random angles against dull white walls. Lawbooks filled the strictly utilitarian metal shelves. Jess shared the office with Neil Strayhorn and Barbara Cohen, her second and third chair respectively, who would be arriving within the half hour. As first chair, it was up to Jess to make all major decisions as to how her office was run. There were seven hundred and fifty state prosecutors in Cook County, over two hundred of them in this building alone, with three attorneys to every room. By eight thirty the offices would be very noisy. Jess usually relished these few moments of peace before everyone arrived.

Today was different. The young man had unnerved her. What about him was so familiar? she wondered. She hadn't seen much past the eerie grin, could never have picked him out of a lineup. He hadn't even spoken to her. So why was she obsessing on him?

Jess resumed her scanning of the obituaries: "Bederman, Marvin, 74, died in his sleep"; "Edwards, Sarah, in her ninety-first year . . ."

"You're here early." The male voice traveled to her desk from the open doorway.

"I'm always here early," Jess answered without looking up. No need to. If the scent of Aramis cologne wasn't enough to give Greg Oliver away, the swagger in his voice would. It was an office cliché that Greg Oliver's winning record in the courtroom was surpassed only by his record in the bedroom. Jess always kept her conversations with the forty-year-old prosecutor from the next office strictly professional. Her divorce from one lawyer had taught her that the last thing she ever wanted to do was get involved with another.

Greg crossed to her desk in three quick strides. He leaned forward to peer over the top of her newspaper. "You're reading the obits?"

"Greg, I'm really busy," she told him, taking quick note of his conventionally handsome face, made memorable by the liquid chocolate of his eyes. "I have to be in court at nine thirty."

He checked his watch. A Rolex. Gold. She'd heard rumors that he'd recently married money. "You've got lots of time."

"Time I need to get my thoughts in order."

"I bet your thoughts are already in order," he said, his hand brushing against a stack of carefully organized paperwork. "I bet your mind is as neat as your desk." He laughed, the motion tugging at one corner of his mouth, reminding Jess instantly of the stranger with the ominous grin. "Look at you," Greg said, misreading her response. "You're all uptight because I accidentally moved a couple of your papers. You don't like anybody touching your stuff, do you?" His fingers caressed the wood grain. The effect was almost hypnotic. A snake charmer, Jess thought, wondering momentarily whether he was the charmer or the snake.

"I think you better go. I'm delivering my closing argument this morning in the Erica Barnowski case and—"

"Erica Barnowski? The girl who says she was raped—"

"The *woman* who *was* raped," Jess corrected.

His laugh invaded the space between them. "Jess, she wasn't

wearing panties! You think any jury in the land is going to convict a guy of raping some woman he meets in a bar when she wasn't wearing panties? No panties smacks of implied consent to me."

"With a knife at her throat?" Jess shook her head, more in sadness than disgust. Greg Oliver was notoriously accurate in his assessments. If she couldn't manage to persuade her fellow prosecutors that the man on trial was guilty, how could she hope to convince a jury?

Greg walked toward the door, then turned. "I'll give you this much, Jess. If anybody can win this case, you can."

"Thanks," Jess said to the closing door. She walked to the window and stared absently out at the street eleven stories below.

There were no other high buildings in the area. At fourteen stories tall, the administration building stuck out like a sore thumb. The adjoining courthouse was a mere seven stories high. Behind them stood the county jail, where accused murderers and other alleged criminals who couldn't make bail or were being held without bond were kept until their cases came to court. Jess often thought of the area as a dark, evil place for dark, evil people.

I am Death, she heard the streets whisper. *I have come for you.*

She shook her head, glancing up at the October sky. It was a dirty gray, heavy with the threat of early snow. Despite the weather forecast, she hadn't worn boots. They leaked and had unsightly salt rings. Maybe she'd go out later and buy a new pair.

The phone rang. Barely past eight o'clock and already the phone was ringing. She picked it up. "Jess Koster," she said simply.

"Jess Koster, Maureen Peppler," the voice said with a giggle.

Jess pictured her older sister's crinkly smile and warm green eyes. "I'm glad you called." Jess had always likened Maureen to a Degas sketch of a ballet dancer, all soft and fuzzy around the edges. People said the sisters looked alike, but while they shared basic variations of the same oval face and were both tall and slender, there was nothing fuzzy around the edges about Jess. Her brown shoulder-length hair was darker than Maureen's, her eyes a more disturbing shade of green, her small-boned frame more angular—as if the artist had drawn the same sketch twice, one in pastels, the other in oil. "What's doing?" Jess asked. "How are Tyler and the twins?"

"The twins are great. Tyler's still not thrilled. He keeps asking when we're sending them back. You didn't ask about Barry."

Jess felt her jaw tighten. Maureen's husband, Barry, was a successful accountant, and the vanity license plates on his late-model Jaguar said EARND IT. Did she really need to know more? "How is he?" she asked.

"He's fine. Business is terrific. Anyway, we want you to come to dinner tomorrow, and don't tell me you already have a date."

Jess almost laughed. When was the last time she'd had a date? "No, I don't have a date," she answered.

"Good, then you'll come. I don't get to see nearly enough of you these days. Tomorrow at six. Dad's coming."

Jess smiled. "See you tomorrow." She replaced the receiver to the sound of a baby's distant cry. She pictured Maureen running toward the cribs of her six-month-old girls, seeing to their needs while making sure that the three-year-old at her feet was getting the attention he craved. A far cry from Harvard Business School, where she'd earned her M.B.A. We all make choices, Jess thought.

She sat back at her desk, trying to concentrate on the morning that lay ahead, praying she would be able to prove Greg Oliver wrong. Securing a conviction in this case would be next to impossible. She and Neil Strayhorn would have to be very convincing.

The state's attorney's office always tried jury cases in pairs. Neil, her second chair, was set to deliver the closing argument, recounting the facts of the case. This would be followed by the defense attorney's closing remarks, and then Jess would handle the rebuttal, a position that allowed ample room for creative moral indignation. "Every day in the United States, one thousand eight hundred and seventy-one women are raped," she began, rehearsing in her office. "That translates to one point three rapes of adult women every minute." She was still going over the sentences in her mind when Barbara Cohen arrived twenty minutes later.

"How's it going?" Barbara asked. At five feet eleven, with red hair that cascaded down her back in frenzied ripples, Barbara Cohen often seemed the anthropomorphic version of a carrot. No matter how bad Jess was feeling, just looking at the young woman who was her third chair always made her smile.

"Hanging in there." Jess checked her watch.

Neil Strayhorn arrived a few minutes later and went straight to his desk. Jess could see his lips moving, silently mouthing the words to his closing statement.

All around her the offices were coming to life, with computers being activated, fax machines delivering messages, phones ringing.

"Every day in the United States—" she began again.

One of the secretaries stuck her head through the doorway. "Connie DeVuono's here," she said to Jess. "She says she has to talk to you."

Jess scanned her appointment calendar. "Our meeting isn't until four. Did you tell her I have to be in court in a few minutes?"

"I told her. She says she has to see you now. She's very upset."

"That's not too surprising," Jess said, picturing the middle-aged widow who'd been brutally beaten and raped by a man who'd subsequently threatened to kill her if she testified against him, an event that was scheduled for ten days from today. "Take her to the conference room, will you, Sally? I'll be right there."

"Do you want me to talk to her?" Barbara Cohen volunteered.

"No, I'll do it," Jess said.

The conference room was a small windowless office, taken up by an old walnut table and eight mismatched chairs.

Jess saw Connie DeVuono standing just inside the doorway. She seemed to have shrunk since the last time Jess saw her, and her black coat hung on her body as if on a coatrack. Her complexion was white, the bags under her eyes a sad testament to the fact that she probably hadn't slept in weeks. Only the dark eyes themselves radiated an angry energy, hinting at the beautiful woman she had once been. "I'm sorry to be disturbing you," she began.

"It's just that we don't have a lot of time," Jess said softly, afraid the woman might shatter, like glass. "I have to be in court in about half an hour." Jess pulled out a chair for Connie to sit in. The woman collapsed like an accordion inside it. "Are you all right?"

"I can't testify," Connie said, looking away, her voice low, her hands shaking.

"What?" Jess asked, though she'd heard every word.

"I said I can't testify."

Jess lowered herself into one of the other chairs and leaned toward Connie DeVuono, cupping the woman's hands in her own. Connie's were freezing. "Connie," she began slowly, "you're our whole case. If you don't testify, the man who attacked you goes free."

"I'm sorry. I can't go through with it." She started crying.

Jess quickly drew a tissue from her jacket pocket and handed it

442

to Connie, who ignored it. Jess thought of her sister, the effortless way she seemed able to comfort her crying babies. Jess had no such talents. She could only sit by helplessly and watch.

"I know I'm letting you down," Connie DeVuono continued.

"Don't worry about us," Jess told her. "Worry about you. Think about what that monster did to you."

The woman's angry eyes bore deeply into Jess's. "Do you think I could ever forget it?"

"Then you have to make sure he isn't in a position to do it again."

"I can't testify. I just can't. I can't. I can't."

"Okay, okay, calm down. Try to stop crying." Jess leaned back in her chair. Connie, though frightened, had previously been adamant about testifying. "Has something happened?" Jess asked.

"I have to think about my son," Connie said forcefully. "He's only eight years old. His father died of cancer two years ago, as you know. If something happens to me, then he has no one."

"Nothing's going to happen to you."

"My mother is too old to look after him. What will happen to Steffan if I die? It was hard enough for Steffan to lose his father at so young an age. What could be worse than losing his mother too?"

Jess felt her eyes well up with tears. She nodded. There could be nothing worse.

"Rick Ferguson said I'd never live to testify against him," Connie said.

"He made that threat months ago and it didn't stop you. What happened, Connie? What's frightening you? Has he contacted you in any way? Because if he has, we can have his bail revoked."

"There's nothing you can do." Connie reached inside her purse, pulled out a small white box, and handed it to Jess.

Jess opened it, gingerly working her way through layers of tissues, feeling something small and hard beneath her fingers.

"The box was in front of my door when I opened it this morning," Connie said, watching as Jess pulled away the final tissue.

Jess felt her stomach lurch. The turtle that lay lifeless and exposed in her hands was missing its head and two of its feet.

"It was Steffan's," Connie said, her voice flat. "We came home a few nights ago and it wasn't in its tank. We couldn't understand how it could have gotten out. We looked everywhere."

Instantly Jess understood Connie's terror. Three months ago

443

Rick Ferguson had broken into her apartment, raped her, beaten her, then threatened her life. Now he was showing her how easy it would be to make good on his threats. He'd broken in again, as effortlessly as if he'd been handed the key. He'd killed and mutilated her child's pet. No one had seen him. No one had stopped him.

Jess rewrapped the dead turtle and placed it back in its cardboard casket. She walked to the door and quickly signaled for Sally, the secretary. "Get this over to forensics for me, will you?"

Sally took the box from Jess's hands as carefully as if she were handling a poisonous snake.

Suddenly Connie was on her feet. "You know as well as I do you'll never be able to connect this to Rick Ferguson. He'll get away with it. He'll get away with everything."

"Only if you let him." Jess returned to Connie's side, knowing she had only a few minutes left to change Connie's mind. "You can refuse to testify, ensuring that Rick Ferguson walks away scot-free, that he's never held accountable for what he did to you, for what he's *still* doing to you." She paused, giving her words time to register. "Or you can go to court and put him where he can't hurt you." She waited, watching Connie's eyes flicker with indecision. "Face it, Connie. If you don't testify against Rick Ferguson, you're only giving him permission to do it again."

Jess held her breath, sensing Connie was on the verge of capitulating, afraid to do anything that might tip the balance in the other direction. "Come on, Connie," she said, giving it one last try. "You've fought back before. After your husband died, you didn't give up—you went to night school, you got a job so that you could provide for your son. You're a fighter, Connie. Don't let Rick Ferguson take that away from you. Fight back, Connie. Fight back."

Connie said nothing, but finally she nodded.

Jess reached for Connie's hands. "You'll testify?"

Connie's voice was a whisper. "God help me."

Jess checked her watch. "Come on, I'll walk you out." She ushered Connie in silence along the corridor of the attorney's offices, through the reception area to the elevators, and down to the main floor. The halls were decorated in preparation for Halloween, large orange paper pumpkins, and witches on broomsticks taped across the walls, like in a kindergarten class, Jess thought. They proceeded to the glassed-in hallway that connected the administration building to the courthouse next door. "Where are you parked?" Jess asked.

"I took the bus—" Connie DeVuono began, then stopped abruptly, her hand lifting to her mouth.

"What? What's the matter?" Jess followed the woman's frightened gaze.

The man was standing at the opposite end of the corridor, leaning against the cold expanse of glass wall, his lean frame heavy with menace, his features partially obscured by the thick mass of long, uncombed dark blond hair that fell over the collar of his brown leather jacket. As his body swiveled slowly around to greet them, Jess watched the side of his lips twist into the same chilling grin that had greeted her arrival at work that morning.

I am Death, the grin said.

Jess shuddered. It was Rick Ferguson.

"I want you to take a taxi," Jess told Connie, guiding her through the revolving doors onto California Avenue and thrusting ten dollars into her hand. "I'll take care of Rick Ferguson."

Connie said nothing, as if she had no more strength to argue. She allowed Jess to put her in a cab. Jess tried to still the thumping in her chest as she pushed her way back inside.

He hadn't moved.

Jess strode toward him across the long corridor, her heels clicking on the granite floor. With each step the vague menace he projected—white male, early twenties, five feet ten inches tall, a hundred and seventy pounds—became more individualized. His shoulders stooped slightly; he had unkempt blond hair, deeply hooded eyes, a nose that had been broken several times, and always that same unnerving grin.

"Stay away from my client," Jess announced when she reached him. "If you show up within fifty yards of her, if you try to contact her in any way, if you leave any more gruesome little presents outside her door, I'll have your bail revoked and you in jail."

"You know," he said, as if he were in the middle of a different conversation, "it's not a great idea to get on my bad side."

Jess almost laughed. "What's that supposed to mean?"

Rick Ferguson shrugged, managing to appear almost bored. "It's just that people who annoy me have a way of . . . disappearing."

Jess found herself taking an involuntary step back. A cold shiver snaked its way through her chest to her gut. When she spoke, her voice was hollow, lacking resonance. "Are you threatening me?"

Rick Ferguson pushed his body away from the wall. His smile widened. *I am Death,* the smile said. *I have come for you.*

Then he walked away without a backward glance.

CHAPTER 2

"**E**VERY day in the United States, one thousand eight hundred and seventy-one women are raped," Jess began, her eyes tracking the two rows of jurors sitting in the majestic old courtroom. "That translates to one point three rapes of adult women every minute and a staggering six hundred and eighty-three thousand rapes each year." She took a brief pause to let the sheer volume of her statistics sink in. "Some are raped in the streets; others in their own homes. Some by the proverbial stranger in a dark alley; far more by people they know. Perhaps, like Erica Barnowski," she said, indicating the plaintiff with a nod of her head, "by someone they met in a bar. The women come in all sizes, all religious denominations, all ages and colors. The only trait they have in common is their sex, which is ironic because rape is not about sex. It is about power. It is about domination and humiliation. It is about the infliction of pain. It is an act of rage, an act of hate. It only uses sex as its weapon of choice.

"The defense would have you believe otherwise," Jess continued, switching her focus to the defendant. The defendant, Douglas Phillips—white, ordinary, respectable-looking in his dark blue suit and quiet paisley tie—made a small pout with his lips before looking toward the floor. "The defense would have you believe that what happened between Douglas Phillips and Erica Barnowski was an act of consensual sex. They have told you that on the night of May thirteenth, 1992, Douglas Phillips met Erica Barnowski in a singles bar called the Red Rooster. They have called several witnesses who testified seeing them together, drinking and laughing, and who have sworn that Erica Barnowski left the bar with Douglas Phillips of her own free will. Erica Barnowski, herself, admitted as much.

"But the defense would also have you believe that after they left the bar, what transpired was an act of runaway passion between two consenting adults. Mr. Phillips explains the victim's bruises as the unfortunate by-product of making love in a small car. He dismisses the victim's subsequent hysteria, observed by Dr. Robert Ives at Grant Hospital, as the ravings of a hysterical woman, furious at being discarded, in his sensitive phrase, 'like a piece of used Kleenex.' "

Jess now devoted her full attention to Erica Barnowski, who sat beside Neil Strayhorn at the prosecutor's table. The pale young woman was absolutely still except for her trembling bottom lip. There was little about her that was soft. The hair was too yellow, the eyes too small, the blouse too blue, too cheap. There was nothing, Jess knew, to inspire compassion in the jurors.

She took a deep breath, returning her gaze to the jury, who were now hanging on every word. "The defense has made a big deal of the fact that when Erica Barnowski went to the Red Rooster that night, she wasn't wearing any underwear. She was looking for action, the defense tells you. Oh, she may have gotten a little more than she bargained for, but, hey, she should have known better.

"Well, maybe she should have. Maybe going to a bar like the Red Rooster and leaving her panties home wasn't the smartest thing Erica Barnowski could have done. But don't think for a moment that a lack of common sense on one person's part eliminates the need for common decency on another's. Don't believe for a second that Douglas Phillips, who repairs computers for a living, has trouble understanding the difference between yes and no.

"And Erica Barnowski said no loud and clear, ladies and gentlemen. She not only *said* no, she *screamed* it. She screamed it so loud and so often that Douglas Phillips had to hold a knife to her throat to silence her."

Jess found herself directing her remarks to a juror in the second row, a woman in her fifties with auburn hair and strong, yet delicate, features. There was something about the woman's face she found intriguing. Maybe it was the intelligence that was obvious in her soft gray eyes. Or maybe it was just because Jess felt she was getting through to her and that, through her, she might be able to reach the others.

Jess chose her words carefully. "Even in today's supposedly enlightened times, the double standard looms very large. Large enough for the defense to try to convince you that the fact Erica Barnowski wasn't wearing panties that night is somehow more damning than the fact that Douglas Phillips held a knife to her throat.

"Erica Barnowski might be guilty of an error in judgment," Jess said simply in conclusion. "Douglas Phillips is guilty of rape."

She returned to her seat, gently patted Erica Barnowski's hands. The young woman thanked her with a hint of a smile. "Well done," Neil Strayhorn whispered. At the defense table Douglas Phillips and his lawyer stared resolutely ahead.

Judge Earl Harris cleared his throat, signaling he was about to deliver his instructions to the jury. Judge Harris was a handsome man in his late sixties. There was a genuine kindness to his face, a softness to his dark eyes, that underlined his deep commitment to justice. "Ladies and gentlemen of the jury," he began, "I want to thank you for the attention and respect you have shown this court-room over the past several days. Cases like this one are never easy. Emotions run very high. But your duty as jurors is to keep your emotions out of the jury room and concentrate on the facts."

Jess concentrated on the jury members. They were all leaning forward in their chairs, listening attentively. Which side's vision of the truth were they most likely to adopt as their own? she won-dered, aware that juries were notoriously difficult to read.

The woman juror with the intelligent eyes became aware of Jess's scrutiny and twisted self-consciously in her seat. There was a famil-iarity about her that Jess hadn't noticed before: the way her neck arched forward on certain key phrases, the slant of her forehead, the thinness of her eyebrows. She reminded Jess of someone, Jess realized, drawing in an audible intake of air, trying to block out the thoughts that were taking shape in her mind. A dreaded tingling was creeping in her arms and legs. She fought the urge to flee.

Calm down, she castigated herself silently, feeling her breathing constrict, her hands grow clammy, her muscles tense. Why now? she wondered, fighting the growing panic.

The woman turned to look Jess squarely in the eye. Jess held the woman's gaze for an instant, then closed her eyes with relief. What had she been thinking of? she wondered, feeling her muscles start to uncramp. The woman looked nothing at all like the woman she had fleetingly imagined her to be, Jess thought, feeling foolish.

No, nothing remotely like her mother at all.

Jess lowered her head. It had been eight years since her mother disappeared, since she had left the house to keep a doctor's ap-pointment and was never seen again. Eight years since the police gave up searching and declared her the probable victim of foul play.

In the first few years after her mother disappeared, Jess would often think she'd seen her mother's face in a crowd. She'd be grocery shopping and her mother would be pushing an overflowing cart down the next aisle; she'd be at a baseball game when she'd hear her mother's distinctive voice cheering for the Cubs. Her mother was the woman behind the newspaper at the back of the bus, the woman in the taxi going the other way.

As the years progressed, the sightings had diminished in frequency. Still, for a long while Jess had been the victim of nightmares and virulent panic attacks. They would start with a mild tingling sensation in her arms and legs and develop into virtual paralysis as waves of nausea swept over her. They would end— sometimes in minutes, sometimes after hours—with her sitting powerless, defeated, her body bathed in sweat.

Gradually, painfully, like someone learning to walk again after a stroke, Jess had regained her equilibrium, her self-esteem. She had stopped expecting her mother to come walking through the front door, stopped jumping every time the phone rang, expecting the voice on the other end to be hers. The nightmares had stopped. The panic attacks had ceased. Jess had promised herself that she would never be that vulnerable, that powerless, again.

And now the familiar tingle had returned to her arms and legs. Why now? Why today?

She knew why. Rick Ferguson.

Jess watched him push through the doors of her memory, his cruel grin surrounding her like a noose around her neck. "It's not a great idea to get on my bad side," she had heard him say. "People who annoy me have a way of . . . disappearing."

Disappearing. Like her mother.

Jess tried to refocus on what the judge was saying. But Rick Ferguson kept positioning himself in front of the prosecutor's table, his brown eyes daring her to provoke him into action.

What was it about her and men with brown eyes? Jess wondered. Rick Ferguson, Greg Oliver, her father—even her ex-husband.

The image of her ex-husband quickly relegated the others to the back of her mind. So typical of Don, she thought, to be so dominant. Eleven years her senior, Don had been her mentor, her lover, her protector, her friend. "He won't give you room to grow," her mother had cautioned when Jess first announced her intention to marry the brash bulldozer of a man who'd been her first-year tutorial instructor. "Give yourself a chance," she'd begged. "What's the rush?" But the more her mother objected, the more determined Jess became, until her mother's opposition was the strongest bond between Jess and Don. They married soon after she disappeared.

Don immediately took charge. During their four years together it was Don who picked the places they went, the furniture they bought, who they saw, what they did, even what food she ate.

Perhaps that was what she'd needed after her mother's disappearance: to be taken care of, looked after, the chance to disappear herself, inside someone else. In the beginning Jess made no objections to Don running her life. Didn't he know what was best for her? Wasn't he always there to wipe away her tears, nurse her through each crippling panic attack? How could she survive without him?

But increasingly Jess had struggled to reassert herself—picking fights, wearing colors she knew he despised, filling up on junk food, applying for a job at the state's attorney's office instead of joining Don's firm, and ultimately moving out.

Now she lived on the top floor of a three-story brownstone in an old part of the city, instead of in the glassed-in penthouse of a downtown high rise, and she ordered pizza instead of room service, and her closest friend—except her sister—was a bright yellow canary named Fred. But at least she was no longer the invalid she'd allowed herself to become during much of her marriage to Don.

"It is not only by refusing to be swayed by either sympathy for the victim or the accused," Judge Harris was concluding, "but by deciding the case strictly on facts, that you will turn this dark, dank building into a true, shining temple of justice."

Jess had heard Judge Harris deliver this speech many times, and it never failed to move her. She watched its effect on the jury. They filed out of the courtroom as if guided by a shining star.

Erica Barnowski said nothing as the courtroom emptied out. Only after the defendant had left the room did she stand up.

"I'll get in touch with you as soon as I hear anything," Jess said instead of good-bye, then watched the younger woman walk briskly down the hall toward the elevators.

"You did a great job," Jess told Neil. "I think I'll grab some of that fresh October air."

Jess opted for the stairs over the elevator, despite the seven flights. She could use the exercise. Maybe she'd take a long walk, buy those winter boots she needed. Maybe she'd just grab a hot dog from the vendor at the curb, then go back to her office to wait out the verdict and start on her next case, she decided.

Outside, the cold air hit her like a slap to the face. She hunched her shoulders and pressed forward down the steps to the street, surreptitiously peeking toward the busy corner, assuring herself that Rick Ferguson was nowhere to be seen. "A hot dog with everything on it," she shouted with relief, watching as the vendor expertly tossed a giant kosher hot dog into a bun and smothered it with ketchup, mustard, and relish. "That's great, thank you." She deposited a fistful of change into his hand, then took a large bite.

"How many times do I have to tell you those things are deadly? They're solid fat." The voice—full, cheery, masculine—came from somewhere to her right. Jess turned toward the sound.

She was tempted to rub her eyes in disbelief. "I was just thinking about you."

"Good thoughts, I hope," Don Shaw stated.

Jess stared at her ex-husband. He was such a remarkable presence, she thought, watching the rest of the street disappear into a soft blur around him. Although he was only of average height, everything about him seemed oversized: his hands, his chest, his voice, his eyes. What was he doing here? she wondered. She'd never run into him like this before. She hadn't spoken to him in months. And now she had only to think of him and he was here.

"You know I can't stand watching you eat this stuff," he was saying, grabbing the hot dog out of her hands and tossing it into a nearby trash bin. "Come on, let me buy you some real food."

"I can't believe you did that!" Jess signaled the vendor for another hot dog. "Touch this one, you'll lose your hand," she warned Don, only half in jest.

"One of these days you're going to wake up fat." He smiled, the kind of loopy grin that made it impossible not to smile back.

Jess bit into the new hot dog, thinking it wasn't as good as the first. "So how've you been?" she asked. "What's this I hear about a new girlfriend?"

"Who said anything about a girlfriend?" They started walking slowly toward Twenty-sixth Street, as if this impromptu walk had been carefully choreographed in advance. Around them swirled an indifferent chorus of police and pimps and drug dealers.

"Word gets around, Counselor," she said, surprised to find that she was genuinely curious about his new romance, perhaps even a little jealous. "What's her name? What's she like?"

"Her name is Trish," he answered easily. "She's very bright, very pretty, has very short blond hair and a very wicked laugh."

"That's a lot of verys."

Don laughed. "And you? Seeing anyone special?"

"Just Fred," she answered, gulping down the rest of her hot dog.

"You and that canary." They reached the corner. "I have a confession to make," he said, guiding her across the street.

"You're getting married?" She was surprised by the urgency in the question she hadn't meant to ask.

"No," he said lightly, but his voice betrayed him. It carried serious traces just beneath its surface, like a dangerous undertow beneath a deceptively smooth ocean. "Rick Ferguson is my client."

"What?" Jess stopped dead in the middle of the sidewalk, the hot-dog wrapper dropping from her open palm.

"I didn't just run into you today, Jess," Don told her sheepishly. "I called your office. They said you were in court."

"Since when have you been representing Rick Ferguson?"

"Since last week."

"I don't believe it. Why?"

"Why? Because he hired me. What kind of a question is that?"

"Rick Ferguson is an animal. I can't believe you'd agree to represent him."

"Jess, I'm a defense attorney. It's what I do."

Jess nodded. Her ex-husband had always been fascinated by the marginal elements of society, but the years since their divorce had magnified this attraction. Increasingly he took on the kind of seemingly hopeless cases that other lawyers shunned. And won more often than not, she realized, not relishing the thought of facing Don in court. That had happened on two occasions in the last four years. He'd won both times.

"Jess, has it occurred to you that the man might be innocent?"

"The man, as you generously refer to him, has been positively identified by the woman he attacked. He broke into her apartment and beat her almost unconscious. Then he made her undress, nice and slow, so she had lots of time to get a good look at his face before he raped her."

"Rick Ferguson has an airtight alibi for the time of the attack," Don reminded her.

Jess scoffed. "I know—he was visiting his mother."

"The woman put her house up as collateral for his bail. She's fully prepared to testify for him in court. What makes you so sure Rick Ferguson is your man?"

Jess told him about Rick Ferguson waiting for her when she arrived that morning and their altercation in the lobby.

Jess saw Don struggling to pretend she was just another attorney and not someone he still cared deeply about. "I don't understand why you waste your talent on such lowlifes," she told him gently. "Weren't you the one who told me that a lawyer's practice is a reflection of his own personality?"

He smiled. "Nice to know you were listening."

She kissed him on the cheek. "I better get back to work."

"I take it that means you won't consider dropping the charges?"

"Not a chance."

He smiled sadly, taking her hand, and walked her back to the administration building.

Watch to make sure I get inside safely, she urged silently as she raced up the concrete stairs.

But when she reached the top and turned around, he was gone.

CHAPTER 3

THE nightmare always started the same way: Jess was sitting in the reception area of a doctor's office, while somewhere beside her a phone was ringing. "It's your mother," the doctor informed her, pulling a phone out of his black doctor's bag.

"Mother, where are you?" Jess asked. "The doctor's waiting."

"Meet me in the John Hancock building in fifteen minutes. I'll explain everything when I see you."

Suddenly Jess stood before a bank of elevators, but no elevator would come. Locating the stairs, she raced down the seven flights only to find the door to the outside locked. She pushed, she pulled, she begged, she cried. The door wouldn't budge.

In the next instant she was in front of the Art Institute on Michigan Avenue. "Come inside," an auburn-haired woman called from the top step. "The tour's about to begin. Everybody's waiting."

"I really can't stay," Jess told the crowd, and hailed a cab, only to have the driver misunderstand her instructions and take her to Roosevelt Road.

He was waiting for her when she stepped out of the taxi, a faceless figure all in black, standing perfectly still by the side of the road. Immediately Jess tried to get back in the car, but the taxi had disappeared. Slowly the figure in black advanced toward her.

Death, Jess understood, bolting for the open road. "Help me!" she cried as she raced up the steps of her parents' house. She pulled open the screen door, pulling it shut after her, desperately trying to secure the latch as Death's hand reached for the door, his face coming into clear view.

Rick Ferguson.

"No!" Jess screamed, lurching forward in her bed, her heart pounding, the bedding soaked in sweat.

No wonder he'd felt so familiar, she realized, drawing her knees to her chin and sobbing, her breath slamming against her lungs. A product of her darkest imaginings, he'd stepped, quite literally, out of her dreams and into her life. The nightmares that used to haunt her after her mother's disappearance were back, and the Death figure had a name—Rick Ferguson.

"Please," she muttered. "Please stop. Please go away."

Jess stretched toward the white china lamp on the night table and flipped on the light. The room snapped into focus: soft peaches mixed with delicate grays and blues, a double bed, a dhurrie rug, a white wicker chair, a chest of drawers, a poster by Henri Matisse. She tried to will herself back to normalcy by concentrating on the pale peach curtains, the white duvet, the expanse of high ceiling.

It wasn't working. Her heart continued to race as her breath curled into a tight little ball in her throat. She pushed away the wet sheets and forced herself to her feet, teetering toward the tiny bathroom. She ran the tap and threw cold water across her face and shoulders, afraid that she would throw up.

And now the nightmare was back, along with the paralyzing, nameless dread that permeated every fiber in her body. It wasn't fair, Jess thought, leaning over the toilet bowl, gritting her teeth against the possibility of what might follow.

She could call Don, she thought. He always knew what to do. So many nights he'd held her trembling against him, his hands softly stroking the damp hair away from her forehead, assuring her that she would be all right. Yes, she could call Don. He'd help her. He'd know exactly what to do.

Jess pushed herself back to the bedroom, perched on the edge of her bed, and reached for the phone, then stopped. She knew all she had to do was phone Don, and he would leave whatever he was doing—whomever he was with—and race to her side, stay with her as long as she needed him. She knew Don still loved her, had never stopped. That was why she knew she couldn't call him.

He was involved with someone else now. Trish, she thought. Probably short for Patricia. Trish, with the *very* wicked laugh, she heard him say, recalling the proud twinkle in his eyes. Had the possibility that she might be losing Don to another woman been enough to precipitate this anxiety attack?

The attack was over, she realized with a start. Her heart was no longer racing; her breathing had returned to normal. She fell back against her pillow, luxuriating in the sense of renewed well-being. Surprisingly, she discovered she was hungry.

Jess shuffled to the kitchen and popped a frozen pizza into the microwave oven. When her pizza was ready, she gently carried it into the large combination living-and-dining area. She switched on the stereo and listened to the beautiful strains of a violin and piano concerto. Beside her, her canary, his cage covered for the night, started to sing. Jess sank into the soft swirls of her old velvet sofa, listening to the sweet sounds and eating her pizza in the dark.

"LADIES and gentlemen of the jury, have you reached your verdict?" the judge asked, and Jess felt a rush of adrenaline. It had been almost twenty-four hours since she delivered her closing argument. The jury had deliberated for almost eight hours, with no consensus, and they had resumed at nine o'clock this morning. But only an hour later they were ready.

The jury foreman said yes, they had reached their verdict, and Judge Harris instructed the defendant to please rise. Jess listened, her breathing stilled, as the jury foreman intoned solemnly, "We, the jury, find the defendant, Douglas Phillips . . . not guilty."

Jess felt a pin prick her side, sensed her body slowly losing air.

Not guilty.

"They didn't believe me," Erica Barnowski whispered.

Doug Phillips embraced his attorney, who gave Jess a discreet victory smile.

"Damn," Neil Strayhorn said. "I thought we had a chance."

"What kind of justice is this?" Erica Barnowski demanded. "The man admitted holding a knife to my throat, and they say he isn't guilty?"

Jess could only nod. She'd been part of the justice system too long to harbor any delusions about its so-called justice. Guilt was a relative concept, a matter of ghosts and shadows. Like truth, it was subject to interpretation.

"What do I do now?" Erica Barnowski was asking. "I lost my job, my boyfriend, my self-respect. What do I do now?" She fled the courtroom before Jess had time to think of a suitable response.

What could Jess have said? Don't worry, tomorrow is another day? She gathered her papers together, glancing over her shoulder as the defendant shook hands with each of the jurors in turn. The woman juror with the intelligent face and soft gray eyes was the only one who said good-bye to Jess. Jess nodded in return, curious as to what part this woman had played in the jury's final decision.

"Do you want to talk about it?" Neil asked.

Jess shook her head. There would be plenty of time later to analyze and discuss whether they could have done things differently. Right now there was nothing anyone could do. It was over.

She knew she wasn't ready to return to the office. Quite apart from having to acknowledge Greg Oliver's superior savvy, she needed time alone to come to terms with the jury's decision, time to deal with her anger and frustration. With her loss.

Jess found herself on California Avenue with no clear memory of having left the courthouse. It was unlike her not to know exactly what she was doing, she thought, feeling the cold through her tweed jacket. The weather forecasters were predicting snow. She bundled her jacket around her and, on impulse, boarded a bus headed for downtown.

"What am I doing?" she muttered, taking a seat near the driver.

She wasn't sure how long the bus had been in motion when she first realized that the woman juror with the auburn hair and soft gray eyes was sitting at the back of the bus. She was even less sure at what moment she decided to follow her. It was certainly nothing she had consciously planned. And yet, here she was, approximately half an hour later, exiting the bus several paces behind the woman.

Several blocks down Michigan Avenue the woman stopped to look into a jewelry store window, and Jess did the same. She'd never been into jewelry. The only jewelry she'd ever worn was her simple gold wedding band. Don had given up buying her trinkets during their marriage, when he found them consigned to the back of her drawer. It just wasn't her style, she'd explained. She always felt like a little girl playing dress-up in her mother's things.

Her mother, she thought, realizing that the woman juror had moved on. How could she have considered, even for an instant, that the woman looked anything like her mother? This woman was approximately five feet five inches tall and a hundred and forty pounds; her mother had been almost four inches taller and ten pounds heavier. Not to mention the differences in the color of their eyes and hair. Her mother's eyes were green, her hair brown, attractively sprinkled with gray. No, Jess thought, there was nothing similar about the two women at all.

The woman gathered the collar of her dark green coat around her chin and stuffed her gloved hands inside her pockets. Jess found herself mimicking the actions, following several paces behind.

They crossed the Chicago River, the Wrigley Building looming high on one side of the wide street, the Tribune Tower on the other. The woman continued for several more paces, then stopped abruptly, spinning around. "Why are you following me?" she demanded angrily.

"I'm sorry," Jess stammered, wondering again what she was doing. "I didn't mean to. . . ."

"I saw you on the bus, but I didn't think anything of it," the woman said, clearly flustered. "But when I saw you by the jewelry store, I knew you had to be following me. Why? What do you want?"

"I don't want anything. I . . . I'm not sure why I was following you," Jess admitted. She couldn't remember a time she'd felt more foolish.

"It wasn't you, you know," the woman began, relaxing slightly. "If that's what you wanted to know."

"I beg your pardon?"

"We thought you were wonderful," she continued. "The jury—we thought what you said about a lack of common sense not excusing a lack of common decency, we thought that was wonderful. We argued about it for a long time. Quite vehemently."

"But you didn't accept it," Jess stated.

The woman looked toward the sidewalk. "It wasn't an easy decision. We know that Mr. Phillips was wrong, but to put the man in prison for years . . . for an error in judgment, like you said . . ."

"I wasn't talking about *his* lack of judgment!" Jess heard the horror in her voice. How could they have misunderstood?

"Yes, we knew that," the woman quickly explained. "We just thought that it could apply to both sides."

Wonderful, Jess thought, catching a gulp of cold air, finding it hard to appreciate the irony of the situation, harder still to exhale. She felt light-headed, her heart starting to pound. Her legs were getting heavy.

"I really should get going," the woman said. "Are you okay?"

Jess could only nod, forcing her lips into what she hoped was a reassuring smile. The woman smiled in return, then walked briskly down the street.

She wouldn't give in to this, Jess thought angrily. She would not let these stupid panic attacks get the better of her.

Think pleasant thoughts, she told herself. Think about a holiday in Hawaii; think about your baby nieces. She suddenly realized she was supposed to be at her sister's for dinner at six o'clock.

Jess felt the bile rise in her throat. Was she going to throw up in the middle of Michigan Avenue? "Take deep breaths," Don used to tell her, so she did. Nobody noticed her suffering. Pedestrians continued to file past; one even asked her the time.

Soon her breathing started to normalize. She felt the paralysis lifting. "You're okay now," she told herself, stepping gingerly off the curb.

The car came out of nowhere. Jess felt a rush of air beside her, her body spinning like a top, and took fleeting note of the white Chrysler as it disappeared around the corner. She fell, kneeling on the side of the road, her knees and palms stinging. Only then did she hear the voices.

"Are you all right?"

"He came this close! Missed you by not more than two inches."

"I'm fine," Jess said, rising shakily to her feet. "I guess I wasn't paying attention." She'd bruised her hands and scraped her legs when she hit the pavement. And she was feeling guilty about causing a scene.

"I'll be fine," she said, limping toward the opposite corner and hailing a passing taxi, crawling inside. "I'll be fine."

CHAPTER 4

Jess pulled her red Mustang into the driveway of her sister's large white wood-frame house on Sheridan Road in Evanston at three minutes before six. "You'll be fine," she told herself, gathering up the shopping bag from the seat beside her. "Stay cool, don't let Barry draw you into any silly arguments," she continued, walking up to the glass-paneled door.

The door opened just as her hand reached for the bell.

"Jess," Barry said, his voice blowing down the treelined street like a gust of wind. "Right on time, as always."

"How are you, Barry?" Jess stepped into the large marble foyer.

"Never better," came the instant reply. Barry always said "never better." "How about you?"

"I'm fine." She took a deep breath, thrust a bottle of wine in his direction. "It's from Chile. The liquor store recommended it."

Barry examined the label skeptically. "Well, thank you. Here, let me help you off with your coat." He discarded the wine on a small antique table and started awkwardly pulling at her sleeve.

She decided against playing tug-of-war for her coat. "It's okay, Barry. I think I can manage. Is Maureen upstairs?"

"She'll be right down. She's putting the twins to bed." He hung her coat in the closet and led her toward the predominantly rose-and-white living room, accented by a black concert-grand piano and a black marble fireplace, in which a fire already roared.

"I'll go upstairs and say hello. I bought them something." Jess indicated the Marshall Field's shopping bag in her hand.

"They'll be awake again in a few hours. Give it to them then."

Jess smiled and sat in one of two white wing chairs across from Barry, who perched on the edge of the sofa as if ready to pounce. What was it about him that rubbed her the wrong way? she wondered. He wasn't stupid. He wasn't overtly unpleasant. Maybe it was his habit of always wearing a shirt and tie, even under a casual cardigan sweater, like tonight. More likely it was the thinly veiled chauvinism of his remarks, she decided, his casually dismissive ways, the fact that he could never admit he was wrong. Or maybe it was the fact that he had taken a bright young graduate of the Harvard Business School and turned her into Total Woman, someone who was so busy decorating their house and producing babies that she had no time to think about resuming her once promising career. What would their mother have thought?

"You look nice," Barry told her. "That's a lovely sweater. You should wear blue more often."

"It's green."

"Green? No. It's blue."

Were they really arguing about the color of her sweater? "Can we settle for turquoise?" she asked.

Barry shook his head. "It's blue," he pronounced.

Jess took a deep breath. "So, Barry, how's business?"

"Business is great. Terrific. Couldn't be better."

"Good."

"Not good." He laughed. "Great. Terrific. Couldn't be better."

"Couldn't be better," Jess repeated, looking toward the stairs. What was keeping her sister?

"How was your day?" Barry asked, managing to look as if he cared.

"Could have been better," Jess replied sardonically, using Barry's words, not really surprised when he failed to notice. I lost a case I was desperate to win, she continued silently to herself. I had an anxiety attack in the middle of Michigan Avenue, and I was almost killed by a hit-and-run driver.

"So, what can I get you to drink?" he asked.

"A Coke would be great."

There was a moment's silence. "We stopped buying soft drinks," he said. "We figure if we don't keep soft drinks in the house, then Tyler won't be tempted."

There was a sudden cascade of footsteps down the stairs. Jess saw an explosion of dark hair, enormous blue eyes, and small hands waving frantically in the air. In the next instant Tyler, her three-year-old nephew, was across the pink-and-white carpet and into her arms. "Did you buy me a present?" he said instead of hello.

"Don't I always?" Jess reached into the Marshall Field's bag.

"Just a minute." Barry's voice was stern. "We don't get any presents until we've said hello. Hello, Auntie Jess," he coached.

Tyler said nothing. Ignoring the boy's father, Jess pulled a model airplane out of the bag and deposited it in her nephew's hands.

"Wow!" Tyler dropped off her lap onto the floor, studying the toy plane from all angles, whirling it through the air.

"What do we say?" Barry said, trying again, his voice tight. "Don't we say, thank you, Auntie Jess?"

"It's okay, Barry," Jess told him. "He can thank me later."

Barry looked as if his collar had suddenly shrunk. "I don't appreciate your attempts to undermine my authority," he pronounced.

"To what?" Jess asked. Surely, she must have misunderstood.

"You heard me. And don't give me that innocent look. You know damn well what I'm talking about."

Tyler ran happily between his father and his aunt with his new plane, oblivious to the tension in the room. Neither Barry nor Jess moved, as if waiting for something to happen, someone to interrupt.

"Isn't the doorbell supposed to ring now or something?" Jess asked, grateful when she saw Barry's jaw relax into a close approximation of a smile. She had promised herself that tonight if there was going to be an argument—and there was always an argument when she and Barry got together—it would not be her fault.

"Oh, good," Maureen said, suddenly appearing in the doorway. "You two are getting along."

Barry was immediately at his wife's side, kissing her cheek. "Nothing to it," he assured her.

Maureen gave her husband and sister one of her luminous smiles. Despite the fact that she had to be exhausted, she looked radiant in a crisp white shirt over black wool pants. Her figure was almost back to normal, Jess noticed, wondering if Barry had talked his wife into resuming her strict exercise routine. As if looking after a big house and three small children weren't enough.

"You look wonderful," Jess told her sister truthfully.

"And you look tired," Maureen said, giving her sister a hug. "You getting enough sleep?"

Jess shrugged, recalling her recent nightmare.

"Look what Auntie Jess gave me," Tyler said from the floor, proudly brandishing his new airplane.

"Isn't that wonderful! I hope you said thank you."

"Your sister doesn't believe in thank-yous," Barry said, walking across the room to the wet bar and pouring himself a Scotch and water. "Can I get anybody anything?"

"Not for me," Maureen said.

"Are the twins asleep?" Jess asked.

"For the moment. But that never lasts very long."

"I bought them a little something."

"Thank you." Maureen took the Marshall Field's bag from Jess's hand and reached inside, then held up two white terry-cloth bibs festooned with bright red apples and berries. "Oh, look at these. Aren't they sweet, Barry?"

Jess didn't hear Barry's reply. Could this really be her sister? she was wondering. Could the woman she'd watched graduate with honors from one of the top colleges in the country be so enthralled with a couple of five-dollar bibs?

"So, what happened in court today?" Maureen asked, as if sensing Jess's discomfort. "You get a verdict?"

"The wrong one."

"You were kind of expecting that, weren't you?" Maureen took Jess's hands and led her to the sofa. "It must be tough."

"So's your sister," Barry said. "Aren't you, Jess?"

"Something wrong with that?" Jess heard the dare escape her voice.

"Not as long as it's confined to the courtroom."

Don't bite, she thought. Don't let him get to you. "I see," she said, despite her best efforts. "It's okay to be strong when I'm fighting someone else's battles, just not my own."

"There's a big difference between being strong and being tough," Barry said. "A man can afford to be both; a woman can't."

"Jess," Maureen intervened softly, "Barry's just teasing."

"No, he's not!" Jess glared at her brother-in-law. He'd gotten to her again, she realized, ashamed of herself. "I didn't start it." Jess heard the hurt child in her voice, was angry and embarrassed that they could hear it too.

"It doesn't matter who started it," Maureen said, speaking as if to two children. "What matters is that it stops before it goes any further."

"Consider it stopped." Barry's voice filled the large room.

Jess nodded, her head swimming with anger and guilt.

"So, what's next on the prosecutor's agenda?" Maureen's words were full of forced joviality.

"A few drug charges I'm hoping we can plead out," Jess told her. "I have a meeting Monday with the lawyer who's representing that man who shot his wife with a crossbow." Jess massaged the bridge of her nose, disturbed by the matter-of-factness in her tone.

"With a crossbow!" Maureen shuddered. "How barbaric."

"You must have read about it in the paper a few months back. It made all the front pages."

"Well, that explains why I missed it," Maureen stated. "I never read anything in the papers these days but the recipes."

Jess struggled to keep her dismay from registering on her face, knew she was failing. She got up.

"It's just too depressing," Maureen explained, her voice as much apology as explanation. "And there's only so much time."

"What's happened to you, Maureen?" Jess said, pacing the room. "You used to be this fabulous smart woman who knew the morning paper backward and forward. Now you only read recipes? You were on your way to a vice presidency! This man has you up to your eyeballs in dirty dishes and dirty diapers."

"You know, Jess," Barry said angrily, "I think you're jealous."

"Jealous?"

"Yes. Because your sister has a family and she's happy. And what have you got? A freezer full of frozen pizzas and a damn canary!"

"Next you'll tell me all I really need is a man."

"What you really need is a good spanking," Barry said, walking to the piano and slamming his knuckles against the keys. The sound, an unpleasant fistful of sharps and flats, swept through the house. From upstairs the twins started to cry.

Maureen's eyes filled with tears. Then, without looking at either Jess or Barry, she bolted from the room.

"Oh, no," Jess whispered. In the next instant she was on the stairs, behind her sister. "Maureen, please. Let me talk to you."

"There's nothing you can say," Maureen told her, opening the door to the lilac-and-white nursery to the right of the stairs.

The smell of talcum powder immediately invaded Jess's nostrils. She watched as Maureen ministered to her infant daughters. A million excuses fought their way to the tip of her tongue, but she

463

allowed only an apology to escape. "I'm sorry. I shouldn't have lost control like that. I don't know what happened."

"Same thing that always happens when you and Barry get together. Only worse."

Jess leaned against the doorway, listening to the babies settle down at the sound of their mother's voice. Maybe she should tell Maureen about Rick Ferguson's threat and the nightmare and anxiety attacks that threat had subsequently unleashed. "I've had a really rotten day."

"We all have rotten days. They don't give you the right to be mean and unpleasant. Here, Carrie, go spit up on your mean auntie Jessica." Maureen deposited the baby in Jess's arms.

Jess hugged the infant to her breast, feeling the softness of the baby's head against her lips, inhaling her sweet smell. If only she could go back, start all over again. There were so many things she'd do differently.

"Come to Mommy, Chloe." Maureen lifted the second baby into her arms. "Not everything has to be a confrontation," she told Jess.

"That's not what they taught us in law school."

Maureen smiled, and Jess knew all was forgiven. Maureen had never been able to stay angry for long. She'd been like that since they were children, always eager to make things right, unlike Jess, who could nurse a grudge for days.

"Do you ever think . . ." Jess began, then hesitated. She had never broached this subject with Maureen before.

"Do I ever think what?"

Jess began rocking the baby in her arms back and forth. "Do you ever think you've seen Mommy?" she asked slowly.

A look of shock passed through Maureen's face. "What?"

"You know, in a crowd. Or across the street."

"Look at me, Jess," Maureen ordered, and Jess reluctantly turned toward her sister. The two women, each cradling an infant in her arms, stared into each other's green eyes. "Our mother is dead," Maureen said.

The doorbell rang. "That's Daddy," Jess said, desperate to escape her sister's scrutiny. Jess listened as her father and Barry exchanged pleasantries in the foyer.

Maureen's eyes refused to release her. "Jess, I think you should talk to a therapist."

Jess was about to argue but thought better of it when she heard her father's footsteps on the stairs.

"Well, look at this," her father bellowed from the doorway. "All my gorgeous girls together in one room." He walked to Jess and engulfed her in his arms, kissing her cheek. "How are you, doll?"

"I'm fine, Daddy," Jess told him.

"And how's my other doll?" he asked Maureen, hugging her against him. He lifted Chloe from her mother's arms, smothering her face with kisses. "Oh, you sweet thing," he said. "I love you. Yes, I do." He smiled at his own two daughters. "I said that to a bigger girl last night," he told them, then waited for their reaction.

"What did you say?" Maureen asked.

Jess said nothing. Maureen had taken the words right out of her mouth.

JESS spent the first hour after she left her sister's house driving around Evanston trying not to think about the things her father had said at dinner. Naturally, she could think of nothing else.

"I said that to a bigger girl last night," he'd announced, sounding so pleased, so sure of himself. As if falling in love were no big deal.

"Tell us all about her," Maureen had urged at dinner, ladling out mock turtle soup as Jess struggled to banish the image of a child's decapitated turtle from her mind. "We want to hear everything."

No, Jess thought. Don't say another word.

"Her name is Sherry Hasek," her father stated proudly. "She's just a little bit of a thing. Not too tall, dark hair—almost black. We met at my life-drawing class about six months ago. She always liked to draw, never had the time. Like me."

She was divorced. Had been for almost fifteen years. She was fifty-eight, the mother of three grown sons, and she worked in an antiques store. She had been the one to first suggest coffee after class. Evidently she knew a good thing when she saw it. Art Koster was definitely a good thing.

Certainly her father deserved to find love, Jess thought on the drive home, turning right and finding herself on a street she didn't recognize. She looked for a sign, didn't see one, turned left at the next corner. Still no street sign. Didn't people in the suburbs want anyone to know where they were?

Jess had always lived in the heart of the city. When she was little

465

and her father had worked as a buyer for a chain of clothing stores, they'd lived in a duplex on Howe Street. They'd moved when she was ten, her father then the successful manager of his own store, to a house on Burling Street, only a block away. Nothing fancy, just comfortable. They'd loved it, planned on staying in it forever. And then one afternoon in August, her mother left for a doctor's appointment and never came back.

After that, everybody went their separate ways—Maureen back to Harvard, Jess back to law school and into marriage with Don, her father on increased buying trips to Europe. The once loved house sat empty. Eventually her father worked up the necessary resolve to sell it. He could no longer bear to live in it alone.

And now her father had a new woman in his life.

It shouldn't have come as such a surprise, Jess realized, turning another corner and finding herself back on Sheridan Road. How long had she been circling the dark streets of Evanston? Long enough for it to have started raining, she realized, activating the car's windshield wipers, seeing one of them stick and drag itself across the window. She could barely see to drive.

Women had always found her father attractive. True, he was only average in appearance and his hairline had receded, but there was still a twinkle in his brown eyes and a ready laugh in his voice.

For a long while after Laura Koster went missing, there had been no laughter. It had taken Art Koster years to resume the rhythm of his daily life. For a time he lost himself in his work. He drifted apart from old friends. He rarely socialized. He moved to an apartment on the waterfront, spent hours staring at Lake Michigan, seeing only Jess and Don and Maureen. Everyone coaxing everyone else. Come on, it'll be good for you. You need to get out. We need to see you. We're all we've got. Maybe it was just a question of time, Jess thought.

She didn't see the white car until it was coming right at her. Instinctively Jess swerved to the side of the road, the wheels losing their grip on the wet pavement, the car spinning to a halt as her foot frantically pumped the brake. "You moron!" she shouted. "You could have gotten us both killed!"

But the white car was long gone. She was screaming at air.

That was twice today she'd barely missed being demolished by a white car—the first a Chrysler, this one she wasn't sure. Could have been a Chrysler, she supposed, trying to get a fix on the car's basic shape. But it had sped by too quickly, and it was raining and dark. And one of her windshield wipers didn't work. And what difference did it make anyway? It was probably her fault. She wasn't concentrating on what she was doing, where she was going.

Sheridan Road eventually became Lake Shore Drive. Jess started to relax, feeling better as she approached Lincoln Park. Almost home, she thought, noting that the rain was turning to snow.

Home was on Orchard Street. The area was lined with beautiful old houses, most having undergone extensive renovations during the last decade. The houses were an eclectic bunch: some large, some tiny, some brick, others painted clapboard.

Jess parked her old red Mustang on the street, then ran through the light snow to the building's front door. She unlocked the door and stepped into the small foyer, switching on the light and relocking the door behind her. To her right was the closed door of the ground-floor apartment. She began to climb the stairs, hearing jazz emanating from the second-floor apartment as she passed by.

She rarely saw the other tenants. Both were young urban professionals, like herself—one a divorced architect, the other a systems analyst. The systems analyst was a jazz fan, and the wail of a saxophone accompanied her to her door. Once she was in her apartment, the mournful sounds gave way to the happier song of her canary.

"Hello, Fred," she called, closing the door and walking to the bird's cage. Behind her the radio, which she left on all day, was playing an old Tom Jones tune. "Sorry I'm so late, Freddy. But trust me, you're lucky you stayed home. My brother-in-law was in top form, and I got sucked in again," Jess stated. "My father is in love, and I can't seem to be happy for him. It's actually starting to snow out there, and I seem to be taking it as a personal affront. What do you think, Fred? Think your mistress is going crazy?"

The canary flitted between his perches, ignoring her.

"Exactly right," Jess said, approaching her front window and staring down onto the street from behind antique lace curtains.

A white Chrysler was parked across the street. Jess gasped, retreating from the window and pressing her back against the wall. Another white Chrysler. Had it been there when she arrived?

"Stop being silly," she said over the pounding of her heart, the canary bursting into a fresh round of song. "There must be a million white Chryslers in this city." Just because in a single day one had almost run her down, another had almost plowed into her car, and a third was now parked outside her apartment, that didn't necessarily add up to more than coincidence. She reminded herself that she wasn't even sure that the car that had almost collided with her in Evanston had been a Chrysler. Jess edged back toward the window, peering out from behind the curtains. The white Chrysler was still there, a man sitting motionless behind the wheel, shadows from the streetlights falling across his face. "Rick Ferguson?" she asked out loud.

Jess scurried out of the living room, down the hall, and into her bedroom. She threw open her closet door and rifled through her seemingly endless supply of shoes, many still in their original boxes. "Where did I put it?" she demanded. "Where did I hide that gun?"

She finally discovered the small snub-nosed revolver inside a pair of pewter pumps, the bullets painstakingly lodged inside the shoes' toes. Her hands shaking, Jess loaded six bullets into the .38-caliber Smith & Wesson that Don had insisted she take with her when she moved out on her own. She let the gun lead her back into the living room, tapping its barrel against the light switch and throwing the room into darkness. The canary abruptly stopped singing.

Jess approached the window, the gun at her side, and parted the lace curtains with a trembling hand. There was nothing there. No white car of any kind. Nothing white except the snow that was gradually peppering the grass and pavement. Had there been a white car at all?

"Your mistress is definitely going crazy," Jess told her canary. She covered the bird's cage with a dark green cloth and turned off the radio, carrying the gun back to her bedroom.

"What a night!" she said, staring at the gun in her hand. Would she have actually been able to use it? She shrugged, grateful not to have been put to the test. She began to return the weapon to the shoe box, then lifted the gun back out. Maybe it would be better to hide it somewhere more accessible. Just to make her feel better. Opening the top drawer of her night table, Jess tucked the gun into the rear corner behind an old photograph album. "Just for tonight," she said out loud.

Just for tonight.

CHAPTER 5

SCOOZI was a huge old warehouse that had been converted into a restaurant, with high ceilings, old Chicago-style windows, and loud Italian music. To the front was an always crowded bar. The main floor of the restaurant was filled with wooden tables; to either side sat a raised deck with booths and more tables. Jess estimated the room could easily accommodate over three hundred people. The restaurant was the perfect choice for celebrating Leo Pameter's forty-first birthday.

Jess hadn't seen Leo since he'd left the state's attorney's office to go into private practice. She'd been sorry to see him leave. Unlike many of the other prosecutors, Leo was soft-spoken and respectful, a calming influence on those around him. Everyone liked him, which was one of the reasons everyone would be here tonight.

Jess was the first of the party to arrive. At the bar she ordered a glass of white wine, took a long drink, and grabbed a fistful of cheese crackers in the shape of little fish, stuffing them into her mouth.

"Just look at the junk she eats," came the voice behind her.

Jess spun around, spilling a small school of fish onto the lap of her brown skirt, and jumped off the barstool to her feet. "Don! I don't believe this." His arms encircled her, drawing her into a comforting embrace. She was disappointed when he pulled away.

"Once again, it's not quite a coincidence," he explained. "Leo and I went to law school together. Remember?"

"I'd forgotten," Jess admitted.

"I knew you'd be the first one here," he said. "Thought we'd come early to keep you company."

We? The word fell, like a blunt instrument, on Jess's ears.

"Jess, this is Trish McMillan." Don pulled a pretty woman with short blond hair and a wide smile to his side. "Trish, this is Jess."

"Hi, Jess," the woman said. "It's nice to meet you."

Jess muttered something inane, conscious of the woman's deep dimples and the fact that her arm was around Don's waist. She finished her wine, tasted nothing.

"Two house wines and a refill," Don told the bartender. "My treat," he insisted when Jess began searching through her purse for her wallet. "You here alone?"

Jess shrugged. Why had he asked? She hadn't had a date in

months. She sipped her drink. "What do you do?" she asked Trish, feeling she had to say something.

"I'm a teacher at Children's Memorial Hospital."

"What do you teach?" Jess said.

"Everything," Trish answered, laughing over the rapidly increasing din of the restaurant.

Jess thought: Everything. Of course. Don had been right. Her laugh *was* wicked. Jess took another long sip of her drink.

"I teach kids in grades one through twelve who are hooked up to dialysis machines or who've had brain operations. The ones who are in the hospital for the long haul."

"Sounds very depressing."

"I try not to let it get me down." She laughed again. Her eyes sparkled. Her dimples crinkled. Jess was having a hard time not hating her. Mother Teresa with blond hair and a wicked laugh.

Jess took another sip of her drink, realized with some surprise that there was nothing left, and signaled the bartender for another.

"Heard you had a rather heated session this afternoon," Don said.

"Hal Bristol has some nerve trying to get me to go for involuntary manslaughter two weeks before trial." Jess heard the anger in her voice. She turned to Trish so suddenly the woman jumped. "Some jerk shoots his estranged wife through the heart with a crossbow, and his lawyer tries to convince me it was an accident!"

"You know that Bristol was probably just trying to get you to settle for some middle ground," Don said.

"There is no middle ground."

Don smiled sadly. "With you, there never is." He hugged Trish McMillan closer to his side.

Jess sipped on her glass of wine. "I wanted to ask you something," she announced in as businesslike a tone as she could muster. "Does Rick Ferguson drive a white Chrysler?"

Don made no effort to hide his obvious surprise. "Why?"

"Does he?"

"I think so," Don answered. "I repeat, why?"

Jess felt her glass start to shake. She brought it to her lips.

There was a sudden explosion of sound, voices raised in greetings and congratulations, hands being shaken, and in the next instant Jess found herself on one of the raised decks at the side of the room, another drink in hand, the party in full steam around her.

"I hear you really let old Bristol have it," Greg Oliver was bellowing above the din.

Jess said nothing, searching through the crowd for Don, hearing Trish's wicked laugh mocking her from the far end of the deck.

"So what's the story? Are you going to settle for murder two? Save the taxpayer the expense of a hung jury?"

"I take it you don't think I'll get a conviction," Jess stated. Did he always have to tell her what she didn't want to hear?

"For murder two, probably. Murder one? Never."

Jess shook her head. "The man murdered his wife in cold blood."

"He was half out of his mind. His wife had been having an affair. She said she was leaving him. He just snapped."

"The man was an abusive bully who couldn't stand the fact that his wife had finally worked up the courage to leave him," Jess countered. "Don't tell me this was a crime of passion."

"I think Bristol might be able to convince a jury of that, yes. I was right about the Barnowski case, remember."

Jess scanned the room, hoping to find someone she could gravitate toward. Anyone. But there was no one. It was her own fault, she realized. She didn't make friends easily. She was too serious, too intense. She frightened people, put them off.

"You're looking very delectable tonight," Greg Oliver was saying, leaning closer, his lips brushing against her hair.

Jess spun around, whisking her hair none too gently across Greg Oliver's cheek, seeing him wince. "Where's your wife, Greg?" she asked loudly. Then she turned and walked away.

She spent the next fifteen minutes in conversation with a waiter. The room was starting to sway, but she managed to look interested.

"Go easy on the drinks," Don whispered, coming up behind her.

Jess stretched her head back against his chest. "Where's Mother Teresa?" she asked.

"Who? You mean Trish?"

"Trish, yes."

"She went to the washroom. Jess, why did you ask me about Rick Ferguson's car?"

Jess told him. About her narrow escape on Michigan Avenue, her near collision in Evanston, the white car waiting outside her apartment. Don's face registered concern, then anger. "Did you get the license-plate number?"

Jess was horrified to realize she hadn't even thought of it. "It all happened so fast," she said lamely.

"There are a lot of white Chryslers in Chicago," Don told her, and she nodded. "But I'll check it out, talk to my client. I can't believe he'd do anything so stupid so close to trial."

"I hope you're right." Jess downed the remainder of her drink, took a deep breath, and tried to keep her eyes from crossing.

Jess heard Trish's laugh, saw her arm snake around Don's waist, reclaim her territory. She turned away, watching the room spin to catch up. In the next instant she was on the floor.

"REALLY, Don, I can take a cab," Jess was saying.

"Don't be silly. I'm not letting you go home alone."

"I'm sorry. I didn't mean to ruin your evening."

"You aren't, and you didn't, so just get in the car."

Jess crawled into the front seat of the black Mercedes, heard the car door shut after her. She leaned against the soft black leather, eyes closed. "I'm really sorry," she began again, then stopped. He was right. She wasn't sorry.

No sooner had they started than they stopped. She heard a car door open, then close. Now what? she thought, opening her eyes.

They were in front of her brownstone. Don came around to her side of the car, opened her door, and helped her out. She leaned against him, allowed him to guide her toward the front door. He searched through her purse for the key.

"Could you do me a favor?" she asked once they were inside.

"You want me to leave?"

"I want you to carry me up."

Don laughed, draping her left arm around his right shoulder, and they began their slow climb.

What on earth had possessed her to drink so much? Jess wondered. She wasn't a drinker, rarely had more than a single glass of wine. What was the matter with her? And why did she seem to be asking herself that question so often lately?

By the time they reached the top of the stairs, Jess felt as if she had conquered Mount Everest. Don continued propping her up as he twisted the key in the lock and pushed the door open. Jess closed her eyes against the lights as he lowered her to the couch.

The phone was ringing. It continued to ring, and then suddenly, mercifully, stopped. She opened her eyes. Where was Don?

"Hello," she heard him say from the kitchen. "I'm sorry," he continued. "I can't understand what you're saying."

Jess wobbled into the kitchen, holding her hand toward the telephone. Don handed her the phone. "It's a woman, but I can't make out a word she's saying. She has a very thick accent."

The woman's voice assaulted Jess's ears before she had time to say hello.

"I'm sorry. What? Who is this?" Jess had a terrible sinking feeling in the pit of her stomach. "Mrs. Gambala?"

"Who's Mrs. Gambala?" Don asked.

"Connie DeVuono's mother," Jess whispered, her hand across the receiver. "Mrs. Gambala, you have to calm down. I can't understand you. What? What do you mean she didn't come home?"

Jess listened in stunned silence. When she hung up, she was shaking. She turned to Don. "Connie didn't pick up her son at her mother's house after work," she said, dread audible in every word. "Connie's disappeared. I can't believe I was so stupid. I just assumed he was talking about me."

"Who? What are you talking about?"

"Rick Ferguson!"

"Rick Ferguson? What has he got to do with this?"

"Come on, Don. You know as well as I do that Rick Ferguson is responsible for Connie DeVuono's disappearance. Don't play games with me. Not now." Jess marched into her living room, pacing restlessly in front of the birdcage.

Don was right behind her. "Jess, tell me what happened."

Jess took a deep breath. "Connie DeVuono called her mother at approximately four thirty this afternoon to say she was leaving work, she'd be there in twenty minutes to pick up her son."

"Connie's mother looks after her son?"

"He goes to her house after school, waits there for Connie to pick him up when she's finished work. Connie always calls before she's leaving. Today she called. But she never showed up."

"Okay. So what we *know*," Don emphasized, "is that Connie DeVuono didn't pick her son up after work. But we don't know whether anybody saw her leave work or if she told anybody she had to stop off somewhere or if she was depressed or anxious."

"Of course she's depressed and anxious. She was raped. She was

473

beaten. The man who attacked her is out on bail. Connie De-Vuono's supposed to testify in court next week. And your client has threatened to kill her if she tries. You're darned right she's depressed and anxious. In fact, she's scared to death!" Jess heard the shrillness in her voice. Her canary started singing.

"Scared enough to just take off?"

"She wouldn't leave her son," Jess said quietly. She walked toward the window, stared out onto the street. Patches of snow lay across the grass and sidewalks, like torn doilies.

Don came up behind her, massaged the back of her neck with his strong hands. "Jess," he began, speaking in slow, measured tones, "not everyone who doesn't show up on time disappears forever."

"This isn't about my mother," she told him carefully. She maneuvered away from him, dropping lifelessly onto the sofa, burying her face in her hands. "It's all my fault," she began. "I'm the one who convinced Connie she had to testify when she didn't want to."

"Jess, you did what anybody would do."

"I did what any *prosecutor* would do! If I'd had an ounce of real compassion for that woman, I'd have told her to drop the charges and run. That animal told me right out—though I was too full of myself to really hear him—he told me that people who annoyed him had a way of disappearing. And I assumed it was me he was threatening! Only it wasn't me he was talking about. It was Connie. And now she's gone. Disappeared. Just like he threatened."

"Jess—"

"So don't you dare try to tell me that your client had nothing to do with her disappearance! Don't you dare try to convince me that Connie would leave her son, even for a day or two, because I know she wouldn't. We both know that, barring a miracle, she's already dead."

Jess rose to face him. Tears traced the length of her cheeks. "We have to find her body, Don. Because if we don't, that little boy will spend the rest of his life wondering what happened to his mother. Searching crowds for her, thinking he sees her, wondering what he did that was so awful she went away and never came home. He'll never be able to put it behind him, to grieve for her the way he needs to." She stopped, allowed Don to take her in his arms, hold her.

They stood that way for several minutes. It was Don who finally broke the stillness. "I miss her too," he said quietly, and Jess knew he was talking about her mother. Then he led her toward her bedroom. "Will you be all right if I leave you alone?"

Jess smiled weakly as Don tucked her, fully clothed, between the covers of her bed. Part of her wanted him to stay; part of her wanted him to go, the way it always was when they were together. Would she ever figure out what she wanted?

"I'll be fine," she assured him as he bent over to kiss her forehead. "Don? You're a nice man."

He laughed. "Think you'll remember that a few days from now?"

She was too tired to ask what he meant.

BARELY forty-eight hours later she was screaming, "You miserable creep! I can't believe you'd pull a stunt like this."

"Jess, calm down." Don was circling the oblong wooden table backward, trying to keep an arm's length away from her. "Can't we discuss this like the two rational attorneys-at-law we are?"

Jess folded her arms and stared at the floor. They were in a small windowless room on the second floor of the downtown police station. In the next room, which was even smaller, sat Rick Ferguson, sullen and silent. He hadn't said a word since the police brought him in for questioning that morning. When Jess tried to question him, he'd yawned, then closed his eyes, feigning indifference. He'd looked interested only when Don, his attorney, arrived, threatening to break down the door if he wasn't allowed to see his client.

"You have no right to be here," Jess told him, her voice steady. "I could report you to the attorney disciplinary committee."

"If anybody's going to report anybody," he shot back, "it'll be me. You're the one who violated the canon of ethics," he told her. "You had no right to arrest my client. You certainly had no right to try to question him without his attorney present."

"Your client is not under arrest."

"I see. He's sitting in a locked room because he likes it."

"Your client wasn't being very cooperative."

"It's not his job to cooperate. It's *your* job to make sure he's treated fairly."

"Did he treat Connie DeVuono fairly?"

"That's not the issue here, Jess," Don reminded her.

"Did you treat *me* fairly?"

There was a moment's silence.

"You used me, Don." Jess heard the combination of hurt and disbelief in her voice. "You were with me the night Connie De-Vuono disappeared. You knew I suspected Rick Ferguson, that we were planning to pick him up."

"I knew you suspected him. I had no idea you were planning to pick him up. What do you expect me to do, Jess? Allow you free rein because you used to be my wife? Am I supposed to let my feelings for you override my responsibilities to my client?"

Jess said nothing.

"Now, either charge my client or release him."

"Release him? No way I'm releasing him."

"Then you're arresting him? On what grounds? On what evidence? You have absolutely nothing to link Rick Ferguson to Connie DeVuono's disappearance."

Don was right. She had no evidence to justify holding him. "Don, I don't want to arrest him. I just want to talk to him."

"But my client doesn't want to talk to you." He paused. "Now, is my client free to leave, or isn't he?"

Defeated, Jess walked into the hall and knocked on the next door. It was opened almost immediately by a uniformed police officer. Jess and Don stepped quickly inside. Rick Ferguson, in black jeans and his brown leather jacket, sat on a wooden chair.

He rose slowly, almost casually, and stretched. "I told her I had nothing to say," he said, staring at Jess. "She didn't believe me."

"Let's go, Rick," Don advised from the doorway.

"Why is it you never believe me, huh, Jess?" Rick Ferguson held on to the final *s* of her name so that it emerged as a hiss.

"Enough, Rick." The edge to Don's voice was unmistakable.

"Almost made me miss Halloween," he said, his lips stretching into the familiar evil grin. "Trick or treat," he said.

Without a word Don steered his client out the door. Jess heard the echo of Rick Ferguson's laugh long after he'd left the room.

CHAPTER 6

"I WANT him charged with murder," Jess told her trial supervisor. Tom Olinsky peered across his desk from behind circular wire-rimmed glasses much too small for his round face. He was an enormous man, close to six feet six inches tall and at least two hundred and fifty pounds. As a result, he seemed to overpower almost everything that crossed his path. Whenever Jess set foot in this office, she felt diminished, inadequate. She compensated for these feelings by speaking louder and faster than was necessary.

"Without a body we'll be laughed right out of court," Tom said. "I know you think this guy committed murder, and you're probably right. But we just don't have any evidence."

"We know he raped and beat her."

"Which was never proved in court."

"Because he killed her before she could testify against him."

"Prove it."

Jess threw her head back, stared at the ceiling. "Rick Ferguson threatened Connie, told her she'd never live to testify."

"We have only her word. We wouldn't get past a preliminary hearing."

"What about a grand jury?"

"Even a grand jury will want some proof the woman is dead. Jess, do I have to remind you that the man has an alibi for the time Connie DeVuono disappeared?"

"I know—his alcoholic mother. He keeps her supplied with booze; she keeps him supplied with alibis. So we just let him get away with it?" Jess said. She stood up and walked toward the door so that he wouldn't see the tears in her eyes.

"What's going on, Jess?" Tom asked. "You're more involved in this case than you should be. Don't get me wrong," he continued. "One of the things that makes you so special as a prosecutor is the empathy you develop with the victims. It makes you fight that much harder. But even *you* have to have something to fight with. We need evidence. We need a body."

Jess recalled the image of Connie DeVuono, eyes ablaze. "Who will look after my son?" she'd demanded. Jess clamped down on her jaw, gritting her teeth.

She said nothing, nodding her head in acknowledgment of the facts, and left her trial supervisor's office. The Halloween decorations along the corridors had been removed and replaced by an assortment of turkeys and Pilgrims in anticipation of Thanksgiving.

Jess returned to her office only long enough to pick up her coat. After ten days of "I really can't, I'm up to my eyeballs," she had finally given in to her sister's exhortations to meet Sherry Hasek, the new woman in their father's life. Dinner at seven. Bistro 110.

Her brother-in-law and her father's new love, all in one evening—two headaches for the price of one. "Just what I need," Jess moaned out loud, relieved at finding the elevator to herself. "Just what I need to cap off the end of a perfect day."

The day's events replayed quickly in her mind. She saw herself standing in front of Judge Earl Harris, her ex-husband at her side demanding his client's right to a speedy trial.

She saw Rick Ferguson's mocking grin, heard her own weak response: "Judge, our witness isn't available for trial today. We want thirty days."

"Getting awfully close to Christmas," the judge reminded her. "Thirty days it is."

"Sure hope the old lady shows up," Rick Ferguson said. "I hate to keep dragging my butt down here for nothing."

Jess leaned back against the elevator wall, recalling her later frustration with the shop to which she'd taken her car that morning. "What do you mean, my car won't be ready by tonight? It's just a windshield wiper!" She'd never get a cab now. She'd have to take the el home, and it would be crowded and unpleasant. And she'd have to rush to make the restaurant by seven. The elevator stopped, and Jess hurried through the lobby.

It was very cold outside. Those fearless Chicago weather forecasters had predicted an unusually bitter November, and so far they'd been right. Jess still hadn't bought new winter boots.

She rode a bus to California and Eighth, took the subway to State Street, and transferred to the el, all with a minimum of fuss. If Don could only see her now, Jess thought. "Don't you know how dangerous the el is," she could hear him yell, "especially at night? What are you trying to prove?"

Just trying to get myself home, she answered silently, refusing to be intimidated by someone who wasn't there.

The platform was crowded, littered, noisy. Everyone just a little afraid of everyone else, she thought, seeing her mother's face suddenly appear in the front window of the approaching train.

The train stopped, and Jess felt herself being pushed toward its doors. In the next instant she was swept up and deposited into a cracked vinyl seat. A whistle blew. The train lurched, then started.

Jess closed her eyes, saw herself as a small child holding on to her mother's hand as they stood on a platform waiting for the el. "It's just a train, honey," her mother had said, scooping the terrified youngster into her arms as the train barreled toward them. "You don't have to be afraid."

Where was I when *you* were so afraid? Jess wondered now.

"I don't need this, Jess," her mother had shouted on the morning of her disappearance, tears streaking her beautiful face. "I don't need this from you."

Jess kept her eyes shut as the train raced through the center of the city. She was remembering the morning of the day her mother disappeared.

It had been very hot, even for August. Jess had come down to the kitchen wearing shorts and an old T-shirt. Her father was away on a buying trip. Maureen was at the library, preparing for her return to Harvard in the fall. Her mother was standing by the phone in the kitchen, dressed in a white linen suit, obviously ready to go out. "Where are you going?" Jess had asked.

Her mother's voice had emerged as if on pinpricks. "Nowhere," she'd said.

"Since when do you get so dressed up to go nowhere?"

Now the words reverberated to the rhythm of the train. *"Since when do you get so dressed up to go nowhere? Since when do you get so dressed up to go nowhere?"*

The train jerked, then twisted, and Jess felt someone fall across her knees. She opened her eyes, saw an elderly black woman struggling to regain her footing. "I'm so sorry," the woman said.

It was then that Jess saw him. "Oh, no!"

"Did I hurt you?" the old woman asked. "I'm really sorry."

"I'm fine," Jess whispered, staring past the woman at the sneering young man who stood several feet behind her.

Rick Ferguson stared back. Then he disappeared behind a wave of bodies.

Maybe she hadn't seen him at all, Jess thought, peering through the crowded car, recalling her experience with the white Chrysler. Maybe it was her imagination having cruel fun with her.

Definitely not, Jess told herself, tired of pretending things were other than the way she knew them to be. She pushed herself to her feet and worked her way to the other side of the car.

He was backed against the door, wearing the same brown leather

479

jacket, his long dirty-blond hair hanging loose, his eyes an opaque brown that contained his entire past: the broken home, the abusive father, the alcoholic mother, the soul-destroying poverty, the frequent trouble with the law, the anger, the bitterness, the contempt. And always the smile—tight-lipped, joyless, *wrong*.

"Well, well," he said. "As I live and breathe."

"Are you following me?" Jess demanded.

He laughed. "Me? Following you? Why would I be doing that?"

"You tell me."

"I don't have to tell you anything. My lawyer said so."

The train slowed in preparation for its next stop.

"What are you doing on this train?" Jess persisted.

"Takin' a ride," he said lazily.

"What stop are you getting off at?" Jess demanded.

He smiled. "I haven't decided yet."

"What have you done with Connie DeVuono?" she asked, hoping to catch him off guard.

Rick Ferguson looked up toward the ceiling. "Objection!" he taunted. "I don't think my lawyer would approve of that question."

The train lurched to a sudden stop. Jess lost her balance, falling against Rick Ferguson's chest. He grabbed her, his hands gripping her arms so hard Jess could almost feel bruises starting to form.

"Let go of me," Jess screamed. "Let go of me this instant!"

Rick Ferguson lifted his hands into the air. "Hey, I was only trying to help. You looked like you were headed for a nasty fall. And we wouldn't want anything to happen to you. Not when things are just starting to get interesting."

"What does that mean?"

He laughed. "Well, what do you know?" he said, looking past her toward the window. "This is my stop." He sneaked through the doors of the train just as they were closing.

As the train pulled away from the station, Jess watched Rick Ferguson waving good-bye from the open platform.

SHE was sitting on the bed, her black dress laid out carefully beside her, unable to move. She wasn't sure how long she'd been like this—her legs numb and her breathing labored. This is ridiculous, Jess told herself. Everyone's expecting you. You'll be late.

The panic had started as a prickling in her side as she stepped out

of the shower. She'd tried rubbing it away with her towel, but it had quickly spread to her hands and feet. She became light-headed, was forced to sit down. Soon it hurt to breathe.

Beside the bed the phone began to ring.

Jess stared at the phone, unable to reach for the receiver. "Please help me," she whispered, her body shivering from the cold, fear rising in her throat. "Please, somebody help me."

The phone rang once, twice, three times, stopped at ten. She stared into the mirror across from her bed. A small frightened child stared back. "Please help me, Mommy," the little girl wailed. "Promise me I'll be all right."

"Help me," Jess moaned, doubling over, her forehead touching her knees. "What's happening to me? What's happening to me?"

The phone began ringing again. Once . . . twice . . . three times.

"I have to answer it," she said. "I have to answer it."

Jess forced herself back upright. Four rings, five. She willed her hand toward the phone, watched it bring the receiver to her ear.

"Hello, Jess? Jess, are you there?" the voice demanded.

"Maureen?" Jess expelled the word in a desperate whisper.

"What are you doing at home? It's almost eight o'clock. We've been waiting since seven. Everybody's starving, not to mention worried half to death. What's going on? You're never late."

"I just got home," Jess lied, still unable to feel her legs.

"Well, get right over here."

"I can't. I'm not feeling well. Please tell Dad I'm really sorry."

"Don't do this, Jess. You promised."

She could hear her sister crying.

"Please don't, Maureen. I have my dress laid out and everything. I just can't make it."

There was a second's silence. "Suit yourself," her sister said. The line went dead in her hand.

Jess slammed the receiver back into its carriage, her crippling lethargy suddenly gone. She jumped to her feet. What the hell was going on? What was she doing to herself? To her family?

Didn't she hate when people were late? Wasn't she always the first to arrive? Eight o'clock! It was too late to go now. She'd been sitting on her bed for ninety minutes, unable to move. The worst attack yet. What would she do if these attacks were to paralyze her in the courtroom?

CHAPTER 7

"**C**AN I help you?"

"I'm just looking, thank you."

What had possessed her to come into this store? Jess wondered, examining a green suede flat. The last thing she needed was another pair of shoes. She checked her watch. Almost twelve thirty. She had an appointment with Hilary Waugh, the Cook County chief medical examiner, in one hour.

"If you give me some idea of the type of shoe you have in mind . . ." the salesman persisted.

"I really don't have anything in mind," Jess told the salesman, a short middle-aged man with an ill-fitting brown toupee. He bowed and moved quickly toward a woman coming in the front door.

Jess let her eyes travel down a long table covered with an astonishing variety of colorful shoes. Nothing like a new pair of shoes to make problems disappear, she thought.

Except for one problem. Rick Ferguson.

Not that he was the first felon who had threatened her. Hate, abuse, intimidation—they were all part of her job description. For the last two years she had received a Christmas card from a man she had successfully prosecuted and put away for ten years. He'd threatened to come after her as soon as he got out. The Christmas cards were his way of reminding her he hadn't forgotten.

In truth, such threats were rarely carried out.

Rick Ferguson was different.

"People who annoy me have a way of disappearing."

Disappearing. Like her mother.

"I don't need this, Jess. I don't need this from you."

Somehow Rick Ferguson had been able to reach into her most secret self, to trigger long-dormant feelings of guilt and anxiety.

Anxiety, yes, Jess acknowledged, lifting a shiny black shoe into her hand, squeezing its toe so hard she felt the leather crack. Not guilt. What did she possibly have to feel guilty about? She began banging the sharp end of the high heel into the palm of her hand.

"Hey, be careful," a voice called from somewhere beside her. A hand reached out and stopped hers. "It's a shoe, not a hammer."

Jess stared at the creased shoe and then up at the man with the light brown hair and worried brown eyes whose hand rested on her

483

arm. The tag pinned to his jacket identified him as Adam Stohn. White male, early to middle thirties, six feet tall, approximately a hundred and eighty pounds, she summed up, as if reading from a police report. "I'm so sorry," she began. "I'll pay for them."

"I'm not worried about the shoe," he said, gently lifting it from her hand and returning it to the table. "What about your hand?"

Jess felt it throbbing, saw a round purple splotch that sat like a discolored quarter in the center of her palm. "It'll be okay."

"Can I get you a drink of water?"

Jess shook her head.

"How about a candy?" He pulled a mint from his pocket.

Jess smiled. "No, thank you."

"How about a pair of shoes?"

Jess laughed out loud.

"That's better," he said.

It had been a long time since a man had made her laugh out loud. She liked the sound. She liked the feeling, and she found herself reluctant to leave. "Actually, I could use a new pair of winter boots," she said. It was a legitimate reason to stay.

"Right this way." Adam Stohn directed her toward a display of leather and vinyl boots. "Have a seat."

Jess lowered herself into a chair. She'd shopped here before, though she had no memory of Adam Stohn.

"Are you new here?" she asked.

"I started this summer."

"You like it?"

"Shoes are my life," he said, his voice a sly smile. "Now, what sort of boot can I show you?"

"I'm not sure. I hate to spend a lot of money on a leather boot that's only going to get ruined by the snow and salt. But I like some style. And I like my feet to be warm."

"The lady wants style *and* warmth. I believe that I have just what you need."

"Is that so?"

"Have I ever lied to you?"

"Probably."

He smiled. "I see we have a cynic in our midst. Allow me." He reached over to a small display of sleek and shiny black boots. "These are vinyl, fleece-lined, waterproof, absolutely no-maintenance winter boots. They are stylish, guaranteed to withstand the worst Chicago winter." He handed Jess the boot.

"And they're very expensive!" Jess exclaimed, surprised at the two-hundred-dollar price tag. "I can buy real leather for that."

"But you don't want real leather. You have to take care of it. And real leather leaks and marks. This boot," he said, tapping its side, "is indestructible. Would you like to try them on?"

"Size eight and a half," Jess said.

"Be right back."

Jess watched Adam Stohn disappear through a door at the back. She liked the casual determination of his gait, the straightness of his shoulders. Confidence without arrogance, she thought.

"You're not going to believe this," Adam Stohn said upon his return, his arms filled with two wide boxes, "but I'm out of size eight and a half. I have a size eight and a size nine."

She tried them. Predictably, the eight was too small, the nine too big. Jess shrugged, checked her watch, stood up. She couldn't afford to waste any more time.

"I can call one of our other stores," Adam Stohn offered.

"All right," Jess answered quickly. What was she doing?

He walked to the counter at the front of the store, picked up the telephone, and made several calls. "Can you believe it?" he asked upon his return. "I called three stores. No one has size eight and a half. But one store has several on order and will call me as soon as they come in. Would you like me to call you?"

"I beg your pardon?" Was he asking her out?

"When the boots come in, would you like me to call you?"

"Oh, oh sure. Yes, please. That would be great." Jess realized she was talking to cover her embarrassment. Why had she thought he might be asking her out? Because he'd offered her a candy? Because she thought he was attractive and charming?

Don't be an idiot, Jess, she scolded herself, following him to the counter. The man was a shoe salesman. Hardly a prize catch.

Don't be such a snob, a little voice admonished. At least he's not a lawyer.

"Name?" he asked, reaching for a nearby pad and pencil.

"Jess Koster."

"Phone number where you can be reached during the day?"

Jess gave him her number at work. "Maybe I better give you my home number too," she said, not believing the words coming out of her mouth.

"Sure." He copied the numbers down as she recited them. "My name is Adam Stohn." He indicated the tag on his jacket, pronouncing the Stohn as stone. "It shouldn't be more than a week."

"That's great. Hopefully, it won't snow before then."

"It wouldn't dare."

Jess smiled and waited for him to say more, but he didn't. Instead, he looked just past her to where a woman stood admiring a pair of tomato-red pumps. "Thanks again," she said on her way out, but he was already moving toward the other woman.

"I can't believe I did that," Jess was muttering as she slid into the back seat of a taxi to go to the medical examiner's office. Could she have been any more obvious? Why didn't she just wear a large sign around her neck that stated LONELY AND DEEPLY DISTURBED?

HILARY Waugh had to be close to fifty, yet she had the skin of a woman half her age. She wore her dark hair pulled back into a French braid, and her hazel eyes were framed by large black glasses. They sat in the tiny white cubbyhole that served as her office.

Jess cleared her throat. "I'm looking for a woman, mid-forties, Italian American, about five feet six inches tall, a hundred and thirty-five pounds, maybe less. Actually, here," Jess said, reaching inside her purse, "this is her picture." Jess held out a photo of Connie DeVuono, standing with her arms proudly around her son, Steffan. "Her name is Connie DeVuono. She's been missing over two weeks."

"This is the woman you called me about last week?" Hilary asked.

Jess nodded sheepishly. "I'm sorry to be such a pest. It's just that I keep thinking of her little boy."

"Looks just like his mother," Hilary remarked as Jess reclaimed the photograph, carefully returning it to her purse.

"Yes. And it's very hard on him . . . not knowing exactly what happened to her." Jess swallowed the catch in her throat.

"I'm sure it is. And I wish I could help. We have no bodies matching Connie DeVuono's description. But I'll call you if anyone even remotely resembling her turns up."

"I'm going to have Connie's dental records sent over here," Jess said. "Just so you'll have them on hand if . . ." She stopped, cleared her throat, started again. "It might speed things up a bit."

"That would be very helpful," Hilary Waugh agreed. "Assuming we find her body."

"Assuming we find her body." The words followed Jess down the corridor and into the lobby. She pushed open the door to the outside and inhaled a deep breath of fresh air.

Assuming we find her body, she thought.

"Four hundred and eleven dollars?" Jess yelled. "Are you crazy?"

The young man behind the counter remained calm. He was obviously used to such outbursts. "The bill is carefully itemized."

"I've looked at the bill. I still don't understand what could have cost over four hundred dollars!" Jess realized that her voice was becoming shrill, that the other patrons of the shop where she had taken her car to be serviced almost three weeks ago were staring at her.

"There was a lot that had to be done," the man said.

"There was a windshield wiper!"

"Both wipers, actually," the man, whose tag identified him as Robert, stated patiently. "You recall we phoned you, told you that both would have to be replaced, along with the catalytic converter and the alternator. We had to order some parts."

Jess checked the large clock on the wall: seven fifty-five, it read. "Look, I really don't have time for this. Can I give you a check?"

"Cash or charge only."

"Naturally." Jess handed over a charge card, thinking that what was even more remarkable than the number of murders every year in Chicago was the fact that there weren't more.

"Ladies and gentlemen of the jury," Jess began, making eye contact with each juror in what the press was calling the Crossbow Murder Trial, "on June second of this year, Terry Wales, the defendant, shot his wife through the heart with a steel-tipped arrow from a crossbow, in the middle of the intersection at Grand Avenue and State Street. No one here disputes that. It is a fact, pure and simple."

Jess backed away slightly from the jury box, drawing the jurors' eyes toward the defendant, Terry Wales, a small mousy-looking man of forty. It was his lawyer, Hal Bristol, a beefy man of maybe sixty, to whom all eyes were naturally drawn. Terry Wales sat beside him looking meek and overwhelmed.

"The defense will try to tell you that the cold-blooded, premeditated murder of Nina Wales was, in fact, a crime of passion. Yes, they will concede, Terry Wales did purchase the crossbow and arrow; yes, he did shoot his wife. But don't you understand? they'll say. He didn't really mean to hurt her. He only wanted to scare her. He loved her, and she was leaving him. He was beside himself with grief over the thought of losing his wife.

"They will also try to convince you that Nina Wales was not without blame in her own demise. They will tell you that she was cheating on her husband, that she ridiculed his manhood, baited him relentlessly for his failure to satisfy her voracious needs.

"Finally, the defense will tell you that Nina Wales not only threatened to leave her husband, she threatened to take him for everything he owned and to take his children away.

"And still he loved her, they will tell you. Still he pleaded with her to stay. And still she refused.

"I ask you," Jess said simply, her eyes traveling across the double rows of jurors, "what's a man supposed to do? What other choice did Terry Wales have but to kill her?"

Jess paused, giving her words time to sink in, taking in the room at a glance. She saw Judge Harris, Neil Strayhorn, the rows of spectators, the reporters scribbling notes, the television news artists sketching hurried portraits. She saw Rick Ferguson.

He was sitting in the second row from the back, on the center aisle, his eyes staring straight ahead, his odious Cheshire cat grin firmly in place. Quickly Jess looked away, her heart pounding.

What was he doing here? What was he trying to prove? That he could intimidate her? That he could harass her at will?

Don't lose it, Jess told herself. Concentrate. Deal with Terry Wales now, and with Rick Ferguson later.

Jess turned back to the jury, saw that they were anxiously waiting for her to continue. "Take a good look at the defendant," she instructed. "He looks pretty harmless, doesn't he? But don't be fooled by appearances. The fact is that Terry Wales has a black belt in karate; the fact is that we have hospital records that show a history of broken bones and bruises inflicted on Nina Wales by her husband. The fact is that Terry Wales was a wife beater.

"Ladies and gentlemen of the jury, is it reasonable to expect us to believe that Terry Wales shot his wife in a fit of passion even though they hadn't seen each other in days? Even though Terry Wales purchased the murder weapon the day before he shot his wife?" Jess forced her eyes back to the spectators. Rick Ferguson smiled back.

"The prosecution will prove," Jess stated firmly, turning back to the jury, "that Terry Wales threatened, on more than one occasion, to kill his wife if she ever tried to leave him. We will prove that after Nina Wales worked up the courage to take her children and run, that Terry Wales purchased a crossbow and that he used that crossbow to shoot Nina Wales through the heart. This was no crime of passion. This was cold, calculated, premeditated murder. Murder in the first degree. Thank you."

"Mr. Bristol," Judge Harris was saying as Jess returned to the prosecutor's table.

Hal Bristol was speaking even before he got to his feet, his voice booming across the courtroom. "Ladies and gentlemen of the jury, Terry Wales is not an educated man. He's a salesman, like some of you. He sells household appliances. He's very good at it. He's not a rich man. But he *is* a proud man. Like you, he's had to tighten his belt in these recessionary times. Not so many people out there buying high-ticket items like appliances. Commissions are scarce. We're living in uneasy times."

Jess sat back in her chair. So this was to be the defense's approach. The killer as someone we could all identify with. The killer we could understand because his reflection mirrored our own.

Jess let her eyes drift toward the rear of the courtroom. Rick Ferguson, seemingly mesmerized by what the defense was saying, was nodding his head. Damn him, Jess thought.

"It is our contention that Terry Wales never meant to kill his wife," Hal Bristol was saying, "that his only intention was to frighten her, bring her back to her senses. During the course of this trial, I'd like you to put yourself in Terry Wales's shoes. We all have our breaking point, ladies and gentlemen. Terry Wales reached his." Hal Bristol paused dramatically before concluding. "What would it take to reach yours?"

"Is the prosecution ready to proceed?" Judge Harris asked.

"The prosecution requests a ten-minute recess," Jess said.

"We will recess for ten minutes," Judge Harris agreed.

"What's up, Jess?" Neil Strayhorn asked, caught off guard.

But Jess was already on her way to the back of the courtroom. If she expected Rick Ferguson to jump to his feet when she approached, he didn't. He didn't even look her way. "There's an easy way to do this," she began, "and a hard way. The easy way is that you walk out of here now, of your own volition," she continued, unprompted.

"And the hard way?" he asked, eyes on the empty judge's chair.

"I'll call the bailiff and have you thrown out."

Rick Ferguson stood up. "I just wanted to see what I might have been up against if that old lady hadn't disappeared the way she did," he said. "Tell me, Counselor, you as good in bed as you are in court?"

"Bailiff," Jess called loudly.

"Hey, the easy way." He turned and walked from the room.

Jess was still shaking when the judge called the court to order.

AN ARMED sheriff's deputy escorted Jess to the parking garage across from the administration building that night.

She had spent the two hours after court was dismissed conferring with Neil and her third chair, Barbara Cohen, and trying to reach her ex-husband, but his office said he'd been out all afternoon and they weren't sure what time he'd be back.

"I'm on level three," Jess told the deputy. Armed deputies always escorted prosecutors to their cars after dark.

"Finally got your car back," the young man said, his hand near his holster as he led Jess to the multistory garage. Jess told him the sad saga of her red Mustang as they waited for the elevator.

When they stepped out at the third level, she motioned to where she'd parked.

They turned the corner.

"What the hell happened here?" the guard exclaimed, pulling his gun from the holster and spinning around.

"There's nobody here," Jess said, surprisingly calm, staring at her car. "He's long gone."

"Don't tell me this is your car," the guard stated, though Jess was sure he already knew the answer. "What sicko would do this?"

Jess stared at her Mustang, which only this morning had been freshly washed and as good as new. Now it stood covered with mud, its tires slashed, its new windshield wipers broken and twisted. Jess felt her eyes sting, and she turned away.

The guard was already on his walkie-talkie, radioing for help. Jess sank down onto the cement floor, dissolving into peals of helpless laughter. She could laugh or she could cry, she decided.

She'd save the crying for later.

CHAPTER 8

"WALTER, you left the front door unlocked again!" Jess knocked on the door to the second-floor apartment of the brownstone, wondering if she could be heard over the music.

The door opened, and her short, roundish downstairs neighbor stood before her, sipping a glass of red wine. "Oh, did I forget to lock it again? I was bringing in the groceries and kept making trips to the car. It was easier to leave the door unlocked. Bad day, huh?"

"Just keep it locked," Jess said, heading up to her apartment.

The phone rang as soon as she opened her door, and she hurried to answer it. "Hello." Her voice was a shout.

"Ouch! Somebody's not happy."

"Don, is that you?"

"My office said you've been trying to reach me. Something wrong?"

"Nothing that seeing Rick Ferguson in the electric chair wouldn't cure. Your client shows up in my courtroom today, and several hours later my car, which I've just spent over four hundred dollars repairing, turns up trashed."

"Jess, I'm so sorry."

"Just tell your client that if he ever sets foot in my courtroom again, I'll have him arrested."

"I've already warned him to stay away from you."

"Just keep him away from my courtroom."

"You won't see him there again." After a long pause he said, "Look, it's almost nine o'clock. Knowing you, you haven't eaten. I can be there in twenty minutes. We'll go out, grab a steak."

"Don, I don't have much of an appetite. Another time?"

"Anytime. Get some sleep."

491

They hung up without saying good-bye.

Almost immediately Jess felt her stomach growl. "Great. Perfect timing." Jess decided against calling Don back. She was too aggravated to go out. Besides, she had pizzas right in her own freezer.

She popped two into the microwave, then grabbed a Coke from the fridge, thinking of her brother-in-law's no-soft-drinks rule. "I think you're jealous," Barry had said. "Because your sister has a husband and a family, and she's happy. And what have you got? A freezer full of frozen pizzas and a damn canary!" Was he right? Was she jealous of her sister's happiness?

For the first time in years Maureen hadn't invited her over for Thanksgiving dinner. She'd said something about having dinner with Barry's parents, but probably she was just fed up. They were all fed up. Even her father stopped suggesting times to meet his new love. He appreciated how busy Jess was, he'd told her.

What was she doing to her father? Was she jealous of his happiness too? Or did she believe her father's interest in another woman was somehow a betrayal of her mother, even after all these years? The microwave oven beeped, and Jess snapped back to reality. She lifted the steaming pizzas onto a plate, then carried the plate and the Coke into the living room and sat down on the sofa.

"And how was your day, Freddy?" she asked her canary. "Better than mine, I hope." She took a bite.

The phone rang.

Jess quickly swallowed the piece of pizza. "Hello."

"Is this Jess Koster?" The man's voice was vaguely familiar.

"Who's calling?" Jess asked, her body poised, on alert.

"Adam Stohn. From Shoe-Inn. The boots you ordered came in late this afternoon. I tried to call you at work. They said you were in court. You didn't tell me you were a lawyer."

Jess felt her heart start to race. "I didn't get a message."

"I didn't leave one."

Silence.

"So my boots are in," she said after what felt like an eternity. "Thanks for letting me know."

"You can pick them up at any time. Or I could drop them by."

"What?"

"Save you the trip down. You could just give me a check."

"When?"

"Now if that's convenient."

"Now?"

When had she turned into such a sparkling conversationalist?

"They're calling for snow tomorrow," Adam said. "Actually, I haven't had dinner yet. How about you? Feel like splitting a pizza?"

She put her plate aside. "That sounds great."

"Name the place."

Jess named a small Italian restaurant on Armitage Avenue, within easy walking distance.

"Fifteen minutes?"

"See you there."

"YOU'RE early," he said, sliding into the red vinyl booth at the back of the restaurant. He wore blue jeans and a black bomber jacket over a gray turtleneck.

"I'm always early. Bad habit," she told him, studying his face, thinking him better-looking than she remembered. Was he having similar thoughts about her? She wished now that she'd changed into something more interesting than a plain black sweater and pants. Probably a touch more makeup wouldn't have hurt either. All she'd done was splash some cold water on her face, applied a little lipstick, and dashed out of the house.

"Hello, signorina," the middle-aged proprietress greeted Jess, laying two menus on the table. "Nice to see you again."

"Nice to see you," Jess agreed, smiling at the dark-haired, moon-faced woman. "Carla makes the best pizzas in the world."

"In the De Paul area anyway," Carla qualified. "Can I bring you a carafe of Chianti while you look over the menu?"

"Sounds good," Adam said.

"I already know what I want," Jess said eagerly. "I'll have the special pizza. It's my all-time favorite thing to eat."

"In that case, make it a large," Adam said quickly. "We'll share." Carla retrieved the menus and headed for the kitchen.

"I take it you come here often," Adam said.

"I just live down the street. And I'm not much of a cook," Jess added. "My mother hated to cook, so she never taught us how. Maybe she figured if my sister and I didn't know how, we'd never get trapped into doing it."

"Interesting theory."

"Not that it worked. My sister has lately turned into Julia Child."

"And you don't approve?"

"I'd rather not talk about my sister."

Carla returned with the carafe and two wineglasses. "I was reading about the crossbow killer in the paper tonight," Carla said, pouring some dark red wine into each glass. "They mentioned your name and everything. Very impressive."

Jess smiled. "Winning would be impressive."

Carla made a dismissive gesture with her hands. "No question. You win." She made her way to the front of the restaurant.

"So I'm having dinner with a celebrity," Adam stated, lifting his glass to hers in a toast. "To your imminent victory."

"I'll drink to that." They did. "So what about you? How long have you been selling shoes?"

"At Shoe-Inn, since the summer."

"And before that?"

"Odd jobs. This and that. Itinerant salesman. You know."

"My father was a salesman."

"Oh?"

"Then he owned his own store. Now he's retired."

"And driving your mother crazy?"

Jess took a long sip of her drink. "My mother's dead."

"Oh, I'm sorry," Adam said. "When did she die?"

"Eight years ago. I'm sorry—would you mind if we talked about something else? Tell me more about you. Are you from Chicago?"

"Springfield."

"Why'd you leave?"

"Time for a change." He shrugged. "And you? Chicago born and bred?"

She nodded.

"You went to law school here?"

"Northwestern."

"From which you graduated in the top third?" he guessed.

"I stood fourth."

He smiled. "And from there you turned down all offers of lucrative private practice to become an overworked, underpaid prosecutor in the state's attorney's office."

"I didn't want to find myself in some big firm, where the only litigation I'd ever see was a war of memos crossing my desk."

494

"So what's it like there?"

She laughed. "I love it. At least I do now. In the beginning, it was pretty dry. They started me out in traffic court. That's not wildly exciting, but you have to pay your dues, I guess. I was there for about a year; then I went into the first municipal division, which prosecutes misdemeanors—the stuff that's serious to the victims, but not to anybody else. Does that sound callous?"

"I'd imagine you'd have to develop a pretty hard shell working in the state's attorney's office."

The image of a headless turtle popped itself into Jess's line of vision. "I stayed there for another year," she said, speaking quickly. "Then I went to felony review. That's a lot more interesting. It involves real investigative work, getting out there and talking to the victims and the witnesses. You work pretty closely with the police."

"So then you went on to the trial section?"

Jess looked surprised. "How'd you know that?"

"What else is left?" he asked simply.

The pizza arrived, steaming and hot, a variety of vegetables and sausages spread across its face. "Looks fabulous," Adam remarked, smiling as Jess immediately lifted a piece into her hands and stuffed the end into her mouth.

Adam laughed. "You look just like a little kid."

"Sorry. I should have warned you. I'm a total slob when I eat."

"It's a pleasure to watch you." Adam lifted a piece of pizza into his large hands and carried it to his mouth.

"It's wonderful, isn't it?"

"Wonderful," he agreed, his eyes never leaving hers. "So tell me more about Jess Koster."

"I've said more than enough. Don't all the books advise women to let men do the talking? You know, find out what his interests are? Fake interest in same?" She paused, her pizza in midair. "Or is that what you're doing with me?"

"You don't think you're interesting?"

"Just because I find the law fascinating doesn't mean everybody else will."

"What is it about the law that fascinates you?"

Jess lowered her pizza to her plate, giving serious thought to his question. "I guess that it's so complicated. I mean, most people like to think of the criminal justice system as a fight between right and

495

wrong, the whole truth and nothing but. But it isn't like that at all. Both sides subvert the truth, try to use it to their own advantage. The sad truth is that truth is almost irrelevant in a court of law. . . . Did that sound as hopelessly pompous as I think it did?"

"It sounded charming."

"Charming? I sounded charming?" Jess laughed. "Charming is rarely a word I hear used to describe me."

"What words do you hear?"

"Oh . . . intense, serious, intense, dedicated. A lot of intense."

"Which is probably what makes you such a good prosecutor."

"Who said I was any good?"

"Asked she who stood fourth in her graduating class."

Jess smiled self-consciously. "I'm not sure one thing has anything to do with the other. You can study the law backward and forward, but you have to have a *feeling* for what the law is. It's a little like love, I guess." She looked away. "A matter of ghosts and shadows."

"Interesting analogy," Adam said. "I take it you're divorced."

Jess reached for her wineglass. "Interesting assumption."

"Two interesting people," Adam told her, once again clicking his glass against hers. "How long were you married?"

"Four years."

"And how long have you been divorced?"

"Four years. And you?"

"Married six years, divorced three."

"Any children?"

He took the time to finish his wine and then shook his head.

"Are you sure?" Jess asked, and laughed. "That was a very pregnant pause."

"No children," he said. "And you?"

"No. Too much of a child myself, I guess."

"I doubt that. You look as if you have a very old soul."

Jess disguised her sudden discomfort with nervous laughter. "I guess I need more sleep."

"You don't need a thing. You're very beautiful," he said, suddenly focusing all his attention on his pizza.

Jess did the same. For several awkward seconds nobody spoke.

"So what did your husband do?" Adam asked, shifting gears.

Jess smiled. "He's a lawyer. What about your ex-wife?"

"She's an interior decorator in Springfield. Last I heard, she'd remarried." He took a deep breath, as if he'd exhausted himself on the subject. "Anyway, enough about past lives."

"That was quick. You don't like talking about yourself, do you?"

"No more than you do."

Jess was incredulous. "What do you mean? I've been talking about myself since I got here."

"You've been talking about the law. Whenever the questions get more personal, you clam up."

"I'll make you a deal," Jess said, surprised to find herself so transparent. "I won't tell you my secrets if you don't tell me yours."

Adam smiled, his brown eyes impenetrable. "Tell me no secrets; I'll tell you no lies."

They resumed eating, finishing the pizza in silence.

"Why did you call me tonight?" Jess asked, pushing away her empty plate.

"I wanted to see you," he answered, signaling for the check. "Why did you accept?"

"I guess I wanted to see you too." Jess laughed. "And I hear it's going to snow tomorrow. I could use a new pair of winter boots."

"I have just the thing in the back seat of my car. Can I offer you a ride home?"

Jess hesitated, wondered what she was afraid of.

"So you like the pizza?" Carla inquired of Adam.

"Without doubt, the best pizza in the De Paul area."

Jess thought of offering to split the cost, then thought better. Next time, she decided, dinner would be on her.

If there was a next time.

CHAPTER 9

"So, ALL in all, how would you say it went today?" Jess looked across her desk at Neil Strayhorn and Barbara Cohen.

"Pretty well," Neil said. "We made some important points."

"Such as?" Jess nodded toward Barbara Cohen.

"Ellie Lupino, Nina's best friend, testified that she'd heard Terry Wales threaten to kill his wife if she tried to leave him," Barbara answered. "She swore that Nina Wales wasn't having an affair."

"She swore, *to the best of her knowledge*," Jess clarified. "She also admitted that she heard Nina Wales publicly disparage her husband's performance in bed, that she threatened to take him for everything he had."

"So?" Barbara asked.

"So that goes to the heart of the defense's case. If they can convince the jury that Nina Wales provoked her husband into an uncontrollable fury— The only thing those jurors are going to be asking themselves is whether, under similar circumstances, they might be capable of the same thing."

"So what are you saying?" Barbara asked.

"I'm saying that we better know everything Terry Wales is going to say to that jury before he does, and not only be ready to call him on it but to tear him to shreds. I'm saying that it's not going to be easy to win this case. I'm saying it's late and you guys better get out of here."

Barbara and Neil headed for the door. Jess glanced menacingly at the phone. So what if a week had passed and Adam hadn't called? Had she really expected him to? Their evening together had ended on a very businesslike note—he'd handed over the boots, she'd handed over a check. He'd deposited her in front of her brownstone without so much as a peck on the cheek. No "Can I see you again?" No "I'll call you." So why had she been expecting more?

She'd ended up having Thanksgiving with the systems analyst from downstairs and eight of his friends, pretending she wasn't listening through the ceiling for her phone to ring.

Jess lowered her head into her hands, thinking of her car, vandalized beyond all recognition. She hadn't immediately noticed the gutted upholstery or the brake pedal ripped from the floor. It was days before she learned the extent of the damage. A total write-off.

They hadn't found any prints, nothing to link Rick Ferguson to the murder of her car. Nobody had seen him in the parking garage that day. Nobody ever saw him anywhere. People disappeared; property was destroyed; Rick Ferguson went on smiling.

Jess phoned the office of the medical examiner. "Good, you're still there," she said when she heard Hilary Waugh's voice.

"Just getting ready to leave," the woman told her. Jess understood that what she was really saying was, It's late—let's make this quick.

"I take it no one's come in resembling Connie DeVuono," Jess began, as if Connie DeVuono might still be alive, as if she had somehow wandered into Hilary Waugh's office of her own accord.

"No one."

"You got the dental records I sent over?"

"I got them. They're here, ready and waiting."

"That should speed things up."

"Yes, it should. I really have to get going now, Jess. I'm not feeling so hot. I think I might be coming down with something."

"Welcome to the club," Jess said, and replaced the receiver.

The door to her office opened. Greg Oliver stood on the other side. The pungently sweet odor of Aramis raced toward her desk.

Just what she needed, Jess thought with a sigh.

"So how's the famous crossbow avenger," he stated rather than asked. "I heard they offered to make a deal."

"Murder two, ten years in prison? Some deal."

Greg Oliver's sly grin curved toward a genuine smile. "Come on, I'll drive you home."

"No, thank you."

"Don't be silly, Jess. Your car is dead and buried; you're never going to find a cab at this hour."

After her last excursion she refused to take the el.

"All right," Jess agreed. "But right home."

"Whatever you say. Wherever the lady wants to go."

GREG Oliver's black Porsche pulled to a halt outside Jess's brownstone. The loud rock music, which had accompanied them on the drive, mercifully making conversation all but impossible, came to an abrupt stop. "So this is where you live."

"This is it." Jess reached for the door handle, eager to escape the smell of his cologne. "Thanks, Greg. I really appreciate the ride."

"Aren't you going to invite me in?"

"No," Jess said simply. She opened the door and boosted herself out of the car's low frame.

"You did that very well," Greg said, getting out of the car.

"Greg," Jess began, walking quickly ahead of him toward her front door, "I'm not inviting you up."

"You can't mean that," he persisted. "Come on, Jess. All I want is one drink. We're colleagues, and I like to think we could be friends."

"One drink," Jess told him, too tired to argue further.

He followed her up the stairs, like a dog at her heels. "Trust you to live on the top floor," he said as they reached her apartment. She unlocked the door. Greg Oliver was inside before she was.

"You leave the radio on all day?" he asked, his dark brown eyes quickly assessing, then dismissing, the contents of her living room.

"For the bird." Jess threw her purse on the sofa and walked to the kitchen. Greg Oliver approached the birdcage, peered through the bars.

Jess located a few beers toward the back of the fridge and uncapped one, returning with it to the living room. Greg Oliver had already made himself at home on her sofa, his coat thrown across the dining-room table, his tie loosened, his shoes off. "Don't get comfortable," Jess warned, handing him the beer.

"Don't get cranky," he countered, patting the seat beside him. "Come on, sit down."

Jess took off her coat, but left her boots on, and took stock of the situation. She'd allowed a man she could barely tolerate, a man obviously on the make, to drive her home. That man was currently sitting on her living-room sofa, drinking a beer she'd handed him herself. How had she managed to put herself in this position?

"Listen, Greg," she told him, "just so we set the record straight: I have no intention of going to bed with you."

"Who said anything about going to bed with me?" Greg Oliver managed to look both surprised and offended.

"Just so we understand each other."

"We do," he said, though his eyes said otherwise.

"Good, because I want you to know that I have a loaded gun in the end table beside my bed, and if you so much as lay a hand on me, I'll blow your head off." She smiled sweetly, watching Greg Oliver's mouth drop.

He sat for several seconds in stunned silence. "No wonder you haven't had a date in fifty years."

"Drink up and go home, Greg. Your wife is waiting."

"Why the hell did you invite me up here?" His voice radiated righteous indignation. "You're what the boys in the schoolyard used to call a real tease," he said, stuffing his feet inside his Gucci loafers and reaching for his coat. He thrust the beer bottle in her direction, the cold liquid splashing across her blouse. "Thanks for the hospitality," he said, and slammed the door shut after him.

"That was cute," Jess said, watching her canary flit from perch to perch. "Real cute." She rubbed her forehead, wondering at what point exactly she had started losing control of her life. She, who made lists for everything from important appointments to when it was time to wash her hair, and then crossed each item off as it was accomplished. When had she lost control of her life?

She walked back to the sofa. The heavy scent of Greg's cologne still clung to the spot where he'd been sitting. Jess went to the window, opening it slightly to allow a breath of fresh night air inside. The antique lace curtains swelled in gentle surprise.

There was a knock at her door.

"Go home, Greg," she called sharply.

"Do I have to go home if my name is Adam?"

"Adam?" Jess said. She opened the door.

"I see you're wearing your new boots," he said. "Were you expecting me?"

"How did you get in?" Jess asked, angry and more than a little embarrassed by how glad she was to see him.

"The door was open downstairs. Maybe Greg didn't close it on his way out." He leaned against the doorway. "I thought we could grab a bite to eat, maybe take in a movie."

"And if I'm too tired?"

"Then tell me to go home, Adam."

Jess stared at Adam Stohn, his brown hair falling carelessly across his forehead, his posture maddeningly self-assured, his face as unreadable as a suspect in a police lineup. "I'll get my coat," she said.

They went to a revival of *Casablanca*. They sat near the back and, at Jess's insistence, on an aisle. They said little on the short drive to the movie and only a few words as they walked to the restaurant afterward. They never touched.

The restaurant was small, dark, and noisy. They sat at a tiny table for two near the back and gave their orders to the waiter.

Jess grabbed a warm roll from the bread basket, tore it in half, stuffed it into her mouth.

"You have a good appetite," he commented. "You must have a high metabolic rate."

"I find that frequent hysteria helps keep the pounds off," Jess told him, wondering why they were so ill at ease with each other.

"I prefer 'high energy' to 'hysteria,'" he said.

"You think they're the same thing?"

"Two sides of the same equation."

Jess thought it over. "All I know is that ever since I was a little girl, people have been telling me to relax."

"Which only reinforced this negative image you have of yourself as a hysterical person." He looked her square in the face. Jess was startled by the intensity of his gaze. "When people tell you to relax, it usually means *they're* the ones having problems with your high energy, not you. But they've made *you* feel guilty. Neat, huh?"

"One of your interesting theories."

"I'm an interesting guy, remember?" He bit on a bread stick.

"So what are you doing selling shoes? It can't be very intellectually stimulating doing what you do all day."

"On the contrary, I like selling shoes. I meet all sorts of bright, interesting people. They give me all the intellectual stimulation I require."

"You're obviously very smart. Where did you go to college?"

He smiled. "Loyola University."

"You graduated from Loyola, and now you're selling shoes?"

"Is that a crime in Cook County?"

Jess felt her cheeks flush. "I'm sorry. I sound presumptuous."

"You sound like a prosecutor."

"Ouch."

"Tell me about the crossbow killer," he said, suddenly changing topics. "I've been following your exploits in the paper this week."

"And what do you think?"

"I think you're going to win."

She laughed, strangely grateful for his vote of confidence.

"Are you going to ask for the death penalty?"

The waiter appeared with two glasses of red burgundy.

"If I get the chance," Jess said simply.

"No sympathy for the criminal underclass at all?"

"None whatsoever."

"Let me guess—your parents were lifelong Republicans."

"Actually, my father is a registered Democrat," Jess told him.

Adam brought his glass of wine to his nose and inhaled, though he didn't drink. "That's right, you told me your mother passed away. How did she die?" he asked.

"Cancer," Jess said quickly, gulping at her wine.

Adam looked surprised, then dismayed. "You're lying. Why?"

The glass in Jess's hand started to shake, several drops of red wine spilling over onto the white tablecloth. "Who says I'm lying?"

"It's written all over your face. If you'd been hooked up to a lie detector, the needle would have been all over the page. Why won't you tell me what happened to your mother?"

"I thought we had a deal. No secrets, no lies. Remember?"

"Is there something secret about the way your mother died?"

"Just that it's a long story. I'd rather not get into it."

The waiter approached with their dinners. "Looks good," Jess said, surveying the prime cut of rare roast beef.

They ate for several minutes in silence.

"What was your wife like?" Jess asked, digging into her baked potato.

"Always on a diet."

"Was she overweight?"

"I didn't think so. Of course, what I thought didn't count for much."

"Doesn't sound like you're on very friendly terms."

"One of the main reasons we got divorced."

"I'm friends with my ex-husband," Jess offered.

Adam looked skeptical. "Is this the famous Greg? As in 'Go home, Greg'?"

Jess laughed. "No. Greg Oliver is a fellow prosecutor. He gave me a ride home."

"You don't drive?"

"My car had a slight accident."

A hint of worry fell across Adam's eyes. "What kind of accident?"

Jess shook her head. "I'd rather not talk about it."

"We're rapidly running out of things to talk about," he said.

"What do you mean?"

"Well, you don't want to talk about your car or your mother or your sister. Let's see. The ex-husband was relatively safe. Maybe we should stick with him. What's his name?"

"Don. Don Shaw."

"And he's a lawyer, and you're friends. So why the divorce?"

"It's complicated."

"And you'd rather not talk about it?"

"Why did *you* get divorced?" Jess asked in return.

"Equally complicated."

"What's her name?"

"Susan."

"And she's remarried and a decorator, and she lives in Springfield."

"And we're starting to cover familiar territory." He paused. "Is this it? We get no further than surfaces?"

"You have something against surfaces? I thought that's why you liked selling shoes."

"Surfaces it is. So tell me, what's your favorite color?"

Jess looked around the dark room for clues. "I'm not sure. Gray, I guess."

"Gray?" He looked stunned. "Nobody's favorite color is gray!"

"Oh? Well, it's mine. And yours?"

"Red."

"I'm not surprised. Red's a strong color. Forceful. Dynamic. Outgoing."

"And you think that describes my personality?"

"Doesn't it?"

"Do you think gray describes yours?"

"This is getting more complicated than my divorce," Jess said, and they both laughed.

"What else do you like?"

"I like my job," she told him. "I like jigsaw puzzles. I like to take long walks. And I like to buy shoes."

"For which I am eternally grateful," he conceded, laughter in his eyes. "And you like movies."

"And I like movies."

"And you like an aisle seat. Why?"

"Why?" Jess repeated, trying to hide her sudden discomfort. "Why does anybody like an aisle seat? More room, I guess."

"The needle just went off the page again," Adam said.

"What?"

"The lie detector. You failed."

"Why would I lie about liking an aisle seat?"

"You didn't lie about liking an aisle seat; you lied about *why* you like it. And I don't know why you'd lie. You tell me."

"If I tell you," Jess said, "you'll think I'm a total wacko."

"I already think you're a total wacko," Adam said. "I mean, come on, Jess, anybody whose favorite color is gray . . ."

"I was afraid I'd be sick," Jess said. "Don't ask me why."

"Have you ever thrown up when you didn't have an aisle seat?" he asked logically.

"No," she admitted. "Can we talk about something else?" She lowered her head guiltily, another topic eliminated.

"How long have you had this phobia?" he asked, ignoring her plea.

"Who said I have a phobia? Define phobia."

"An irrational fear. A fear that has no basis in reality."

Jess listened, absorbing his words like a sponge. "Okay, I have a phobia."

"Other people are afraid of heights or snakes; you're afraid of throwing up in a theater if you don't have an aisle seat."

"I know it's ridiculous."

"It isn't ridiculous at all. It's just not the whole story."

"Still think I'm holding out on you?" Jess asked, hearing the quiver in her voice.

"What are you afraid of, Jess?"

Jess pushed away her plate, fighting the urge to flee. After a long pause she said quietly, "I get these panic attacks. I used to get them a lot a number of years ago. Eventually they went away. A little while ago they started coming back."

"Any reason?"

"Could be any number of things," Jess said, wondering whether her half-truth would send the needle of the invisible lie detector into orbit. "My heart starts to pound. I get short of breath. I can't move. I feel sick to my stomach. I try to fight it. . . ."

"Why fight it? Does it do any good?"

Jess conceded that it didn't. "What am I *supposed* to do?"

"Why not just go with the attacks? Instead of holding your breath or counting to ten, whatever it is you do, just go with the panic, give in to the feeling. What's the worst that can happen?"

"I'll be sick."

"So you'll be sick. That's not what you're afraid of."

"It isn't?"

"No."

Jess looked around impatiently. "You're right. Actually what I'm afraid of is not getting any work done tonight if I stay out much longer." She checked her watch for emphasis, half rose in her seat.

"I think what you're afraid of is death," Adam said.

Jess froze. "What?"

"I think what you're afraid of is death," he repeated as she lowered herself back into her seat. "I imagine you receive your fair share of threats from people you've put away. You probably get hate mail, obscene phone calls, standard stuff. You deal with death every day. It's only natural for you to be afraid."

Jess said nothing, wondering how he knew about all this "standard stuff."

"I really should get going," she said finally. "I have a lot to do to get ready for tomorrow."

"I'll take you home," he said. But all Jess could hear was, "I think what you're afraid of is death."

CHAPTER 10

THE following Saturday, Jess enrolled in a self-defense course. The week leading up to it had been a strange one. Tuesday saw the wrap-up of the prosecution's case against Terry Wales. A succession of witnesses—police officers, medical authorities, psychologists, eyewitnesses, friends and relatives of the deceased—had all testified. They had proved beyond a reasonable doubt that Terry Wales had murdered his wife. The only question was one of degree. Would Terry Wales be able to convince the jury that it had all been a tragic mistake?

He'd certainly made a successful start. He had taken the stand Wednesday morning in his own defense and answered his lawyer's careful questions slowly and thoughtfully. He loved his wife, he'd said, his pale blue eyes focused on the jurors. He'd only meant to scare her when he fired that arrow into the busy intersection. He'd had no idea his aim would prove so deadly. If he'd wanted to kill her, he would have used a gun. He was an expert shot with a gun, whereas he hadn't fired a bow and arrow since he was a kid at camp.

Terry Wales finished the day in tears, his voice hoarse, his skin mottled and pale. His lawyer had had to help him from the stand.

Jess appeared in court on Thursday morning, ready for her cross-examination of Terry Wales, only to find Judge Harris recessing the case till Monday. The defendant wasn't feeling well, and the defense had requested a postponement. Jess spent most of the day talking to police detectives, encouraging them to use the delay to ferret out additional evidence that might benefit the prosecution's case.

Friday saw the arrival of her annual Christmas card from the federal penitentiary. WISHING YOU ALL THE BEST FOR THE HOLIDAY SEASON, it read in letters of bright gold. "Thinking of you," it said at the bottom, followed by the simple signature "Jack."

Jack had murdered his girlfriend, and Jess had sent him to prison for it. Jack swore he'd come visit her when he got out. *Thinking of you.*

Jess had spent the rest of Friday researching self-defense classes, eventually finding one not too far from where she lived. Two hours on three consecutive Saturday afternoons, the woman on the telephone informed her. She'd be there, Jess told her, recalling what Adam had said. Was it really death she was afraid of? she wondered, unwittingly conjuring up her mother's face.

Thinking of you. Thinking of you.

And then it was Saturday—cloudless, sunny, and cold.

"Please to give me your coat, then please to put this on, and please to go inside," the young Asian woman behind the reception counter instructed. Jess exchanged her long winter coat for a short dark blue cotton robe and sash. The woman waved her toward green, flowered curtains to her right. Jess stepped through.

The room she stepped into was bare except for a number of dark green mats stacked in one corner. Jess caught her reflection in the wall of mirrors that ran along one side of the room.

Several other women were already there, standing in a loose circle, all wearing blue robes. One was tall and big-boned, dark hair framing her olive complexion. There were two black women who could have been mother and daughter, and a short, plump woman whose eyes warily scanned the room.

"Hi," said the large woman. "I'm Vasiliki. That's a Greek name. Call me Vas; it's easier."

"Jess Koster," Jess said, stepping forward to shake hands.

Vas introduced the others—Maryellen and her teenage daughter, Ayisha, and Caterina Santas.

Just then the curtains parted, and a young man with a dark pompadour and a healthy strut approached the women. He was short, and the muscles of his well-sculpted arms could be discerned beneath his blue robe.

"Good afternoon," he said. "I'm Dominic, your instructor. How many of you think you could fend off an attacker?" he asked, hands on his hips, chin thrust forward.

The women hung back, said nothing.

"Well, the experience of Wen-Do is realizing that you may be weaker than your potential attackers, but you are not all-weak and your attackers are not all-powerful.

"You have to learn to trust your instincts. Even if you're not sure what you're afraid of, the best thing you can do is remove yourself from the situation. Running away is what works best most often for women," Dominic concluded simply. "Okay, line up."

The women shuffled warily into a straight line.

"Give yourself plenty of room. We're gonna be moving around a lot here in a few minutes. Roll your shoulders back. That's right. Swing your arms. Get nice and relaxed."

Jess swung her arms and rotated her shoulders.

"Okay, now pay close attention. The first line of defense is called kiyi. Kiyi is a great yell, a roar from the diaphragm. Its purpose is to wipe out the picture the attacker has of you as being vulnerable. It also helps ensure that you don't freeze up with fear. *Hohh!*" he shouted. The women jumped back in alarm. "Also, it has the element of surprise. Surprise can be a very useful weapon." He smiled. "Now you try it. Let's hear it!" Dominic encouraged. *"Hohh!"*

"Hohh!" Jess ventured meekly, feeling totally ridiculous. Similar sad sounds echoed throughout the room.

"Not 'hohh.' *Hohh!*" Dominic emphasized. "We want to scare our attacker, not encourage him. Now, let me hear you get angry." He approached Maryellen. "Come on, Mama. There's a man attacking your daughter."

"Hohh!" screamed Maryellen. *"Hohh! Hohh!"* She smiled.

"Feels good to assert yourself, doesn't it?" Dominic asked, and the woman nodded. "What about the rest of you?"

"Hohh!" the voices began, then louder, *"Hohh! Hohh!"*

Jess tried to join in, but when she opened her mouth, no sound emerged. What was the matter with her?

Think anger, she told herself. Think about your car. Think about Terry Wales. Think about Erica Barnowski. Think about Greg Oliver. Think about Connie DeVuono. Think about Rick Ferguson.

Think about your mother.

"Hohh!" Jess screamed into the suddenly silent room. *"Hohh!"*

"Perfection," Dominic enthused. "I knew you had it in you. Now, if kiyi doesn't frighten off a potential attacker, you've got to learn to use whatever weapons are at hand, starting with your hands, your feet, elbows, shoulders, fingernails. The eyes, ears, and nose are among the targets." Dominic made his fist into a hook, his fingers like talons. "Eagle claws through the attacker's eyes," he said, demonstrating. "Zipper punch to the nose, using those bony knuckles. Hammer fist down on the nose." Again he illustrated. The women watched with something approaching awe.

"I'm gonna show you how to do all that later," he told them. "Believe me, it's not hard. The important thing is not to expect to match your force against your attacker's. Instead, what you've got to do is learn to use the attacker's force against him."

"I don't understand," Jess said, surprised she had spoken.

"Okay, let me explain. If someone pulls you toward him, instead of resisting and pulling back, use that attacker's force to be pulled into his body, and then strike when you get there. Now come here. I'm going to use you to illustrate what I mean."

Jess stepped reluctantly forward.

"I'm going to pull you toward me, and I want you to resist." Dominic suddenly lunged forward, his hand clamping down on Jess's wrist, pulling her toward him.

Her adrenaline immediately in overdrive, Jess pulled back, trying to steady her feet. She was no pushover, she decided, feeling the tugging at her arm. In the next instant she was flat on her back on the floor.

"What happened?" she panted.

Dominic helped her to her feet. "Now let's try it the other way. Don't fight me. Let my force pull you close to me. Then use that momentum to push me away."

Again Dominic's hand encircled her wrist. But this time she allowed herself to be pulled toward him. Only when she felt their bodies connect did she suddenly use the full force of her weight to push into him, sending him to the floor.

"Way to go, Jess!" Vas cheered.

"That's it, girl, you did it," chimed in Maryellen.

Dominic slowly rose to his feet. "I think you understand now," he said, dusting himself off.

Jess smiled. "*Hohh!*" she said.

"Hoнн, нонн, ноннǃ" Jess whispered to herself, emerging from the subway. She felt stronger than she had in weeks, maybe months. Empowered. Good about herself. "Hohh!" She laughed, walking toward Michigan Avenue.

Who said she had to wait for Adam to phone her? This was the '90s, after all. Women didn't sit around waiting for guys to call. They picked up the phone and did the dialing themselves. Besides, it was Saturday, she had no plans for the evening, and Adam would probably be delighted to see her take the initiative. "Hohh!" she said again, almost singing, approaching the window of Shoe-Inn and peering inside.

"Is Adam Stohn here today?" she asked the salesman in the ill-fitting toupee as she stepped through the front door.

"He's with a customer." He directed Jess to the rear of the store.

Adam was standing beside a young woman, his hands full of shoes. Jess approached quietly, not wanting to disturb him in the middle of a sale.

"So you don't like any of these shoes. Well, let me see. Can I interest you in a glass of water instead?" Adam was saying.

The young woman laughed, her long blond hair falling across her carefully rouged cheek as she shook her head.

"How about a candy?" Adam reached into his jacket pocket for a red-and-white-striped mint.

Jess felt tears sting her eyes and quickly backed away. Why did she think that just because she was feeling good, Adam would be interested? He was interested in his commission. Why had she thought she was any different from the hundreds of other women whose feet he fondled? And why was she so disappointed?

"Hohh!" she said, standing alone in front of the store. But her heart wasn't in it, and the word fell to the sidewalk to be trampled on by a parade of passing feet.

"Well, hi, stranger," Don was saying, his voice an oasis, even over the phone. "This is a pleasant surprise. You've barely said two words to me since our little disagreement at the police station."

"That's why I'm calling," Jess began, closing the door of the phone booth. "I'm downtown, and I thought maybe if you weren't doing anything tonight . . ." Her voice trailed off, leaving only silence. "You're busy," she said quickly.

"I'm sorry, Jess," Don said. "Any other time, you know I'd jump at the chance, but . . ."

"But it's Saturday night and Mother Teresa is waiting."

Another silence. "Actually Trish is out of town this weekend," Don said easily. "So I accepted an offer to have dinner over at John McMaster's." John McMaster was one of Don's partners.

Jess found it suddenly hard to catch her breath. Why had she called? Did she really expect her ex-husband to be waiting by the phone every time she felt depressed? Jess felt she was choking. She pulled at the folding door, but it refused to open.

Don was saying, "Why don't I drop over tomorrow morning with some bagels, and you can make me coffee and tell me who died."

Jess struggled with the door, numbness teasing at her fingers. She couldn't breathe. She had to get out.

"Jess? Jess, are you there? That was a joke. Don't you read the obituaries anymore?"

"I really have to go now, Don." Jess pounded against the door with her fist.

"How does ten a.m. sound?"

"Fine. Sounds great."

Jess dropped the phone, pushing and pulling at the door of the phone booth. "Let me out of here!" she screamed.

Suddenly the door opened. A gray-haired old lady, not more than five feet tall, stood there. "These things can be tricky," she said with an indulgent smile before shuffling on down the street.

Jess shot out of the phone booth, sweat streaming down her face. "How could I do that?" she whispered. "I forgot everything I learned today. How am I going to defend myself against anybody when I can't even get out of a phone booth?"

It was several minutes before the numbness left her hands and she was able to hail a cab to take her home.

After some Stouffer's macaroni and cheese Jess covered the birdcage for the night. She put on a pink-and-white flannelette nightgown, then laid out her clothes for the following day. It was barely nine o'clock, she realized with surprise as she crawled into bed.

IN HER dream she was facing a jury wearing only her flannelette nightgown and tatty pink slippers.

"We love your pajamas," one of the female jurors told her, reaching across the jury box to stroke the soft arm of Jess's nightgown. But the woman's hand was an eagle's claw, and it ripped through the material, drawing blood.

"Let me take care of that," Don offered, vaulting over the defense table and reaching for her bleeding arm.

Jess allowed him to draw her close, then suddenly pushed her full weight against him, throwing him to the floor.

Judge Harris banged his gavel. "Order in the court," he demanded in Adam Stohn's voice. Then, "Jess, are you there? Jess?"

Jess sat up in bed, not fully awake, foolishly grateful to find herself in her bedroom and not in court. "Jess," the voice from her dream continued. "Jess, are you there?"

The banging continued. Only not a gavel, but someone knocking on the door to her apartment, Jess realized, coming fully awake and reaching across to the night table. She reached inside the top drawer for her gun.

"Who's there?" she called as she walked to the door.

"It's Adam," came the response from the other side.

"What are you doing here?" Jess asked without opening the door.

"I wanted to see you. It was an impulse thing."

"How did you get in the house?"

"The front door was open. Look, I really hate yelling through the door this way. Are you going to let me in?"

She opened the door and motioned him inside with her gun.

"Good Lord, is that thing real?"

Jess nodded, thinking he looked wonderful, wondering if she looked as ridiculous as she felt in her pink-and-white flannelette nightgown, fuzzy pink slippers, and Smith & Wesson revolver. "I'm wary of late-night visitors," she told him.

"Late? Jess, it's ten thirty." He stared nervously at the gun. "Think you could put that away now?" He took off his jacket, threw it on the sofa, and stood before her in a white sweater and pressed black jeans, a bottle of red wine in his hands. "Tell you what," he continued, "you get rid of the gun; I'll open the wine."

Jess nodded again, not sure what else to do. She went to her bedroom and put the gun back in its drawer. By the time she returned to the living room, Adam had opened the wine and poured them each a glass. They sat down on the sofa, their knees touching briefly before Jess pulled away, tucking her legs beneath her.

They clicked glasses. "It's nice to see you," Adam said.

Jess became aware of a slight trace of alcohol already on his breath and wondered where he'd been before he arrived on her doorstep. Out with the customer she'd seen him with this afternoon? Had their date ended early, leaving him with nothing but time and a bottle of wine on his hands?

Now she was less charmed by his spontaneity than she was angered by his presumptuousness. Did he really think he could ignore her all week, then show up unannounced anytime he felt like it?

"What are you doing here?" Jess asked, surprising them both with the suddenness of her question.

Adam took a long sip of his drink. "I wanted to see you."

"When did you decide that? At two o'clock? Four? Ten?"

Adam fidgeted on the sofa, took another long sip of his drink. "What is this, Jess? An interrogation?"

"Why didn't you phone first?"

"I already told you. It was an impulse."

"Are you married?" Jess asked.

"No," Adam proclaimed loudly. "Of course I'm not married." He finished the wine remaining in his glass in one gulp.

"Then why don't you ever call? Why do you just show up on my doorstep at all hours of the night?"

"Jess, for goodness' sake, it's ten thirty!" He poured himself more wine, drank it down in two gulps. "I'm not married, Jess. Honest."

There was a long pause. Jess stared into her lap, her anger spent, more relieved than she cared to acknowledge.

"I just don't like to plan things too far in advance." He finished the wine, stared into the bottom of his empty glass.

Jess laughed. "I plan everything."

Adam leaned back against the sofa, shaking his shoes from his feet, lifting his legs off the floor, and casually stretching them across Jess's lap. Her body tensed, then relaxed, welcoming the contact. "I think I may have had too much to drink," he said.

"I think you're right." There was another pause. "Maybe you should go," she said, fighting the urge to cradle him in her arms.

"Ten minutes' sleep is all I need," he said, his eyes closing.

"Adam, I'm going to call for a taxi." Jess tried lifting his legs, but they were like deadweights. After a few minutes she managed to lift his legs just high enough so that she could slide out from under.

Face it, Jess, she told herself, covering him with his jacket. Adam Stohn isn't going anywhere. At least not tonight.

She studied his face, all traces of turmoil hidden by the peaceful mask of sleep. What secrets was he hiding? she wondered, brushing some hair away from his eyes, her fingers tingling at the contact. How many lies had he told her?

Jess tiptoed away from the sofa, wondering whether she was doing the right thing in letting him stay. "Trust your instincts," Jess heard her Wen-Do instructor repeat as she crawled back into bed. *"Trust your instincts."*

But just in case her instincts were wrong, she removed the gun from the night table and tucked it underneath her mattress.

She awoke the next morning to find him staring at her from her bedroom door.

"Do you always lay out your clothes so neatly?" he was asking.

"How long have you been standing there?" she asked, ignoring his question, sitting up in bed, slipping her robe on.

"Not long. A few minutes, maybe."

Jess looked toward her clock. "Nine thirty!" she gasped.

"Shouldn't drink so much," he said, smiling sheepishly.

"I can't believe I slept till nine thirty. I have so much to do."

"First things first," he said. "Breakfast is ready."

"You made breakfast?"

"It wasn't easy. You weren't lying when you said you don't cook. I had to run out and buy some eggs and vegetables—"

"How'd you get back in?"

"I borrowed your key," he said simply.

"You went into my purse?"

"I put the key back." He approached her bed, held out his hand. "Come on, I've been slaving over a hot stove all morning." He pulled her through the hallway to the dining area.

The table was set, orange juice already poured into glasses.

Jess felt herself relax. If he was some psychotic sociopath who was going to kill her, he'd obviously decided to do it after breakfast. "What's on the menu?" she asked, her stomach rumbling.

"The best western omelet in the De Paul area," he answered, sliding one of two perfectly shaped omelets onto her plate, the other onto his, garnishing each with a sprig of parsley.

"It looks wonderful. I can't believe you did all this."

"It was the least I could do after the way I behaved last night."

"You didn't do anything last night."

"Precisely. I finally get to spend the night with a beautiful woman, and what do I do? I pass out on her sofa."

Jess ran a self-conscious hand through her tangled hair.

"No, don't do that," he said. "You look lovely."

They ate for several minutes in silence.

"I took the cover off the birdcage," Adam said, "and I brought in your morning paper. It's on the sofa."

Jess looked from the birdcage to the sofa. "Thanks." She paused. "Anything else you did that I should know about?"

He leaned across the table and kissed her. "Not yet."

Jess didn't move as Adam leaned forward to kiss her again. Her lips were tingling; her heart was pounding. She felt like a teenager. His arms wrapped around her, pulled her against him.

"I shouldn't be doing this," she said as his kisses became deeper, as hers responded in kind. "I have so much work to do to be ready for tomorrow."

"You'll do it," he assured her, burying his lips in her hair.

Suddenly a buzzer sounded. It beeped once, then again.

"What's that?" Adam asked between kisses.

"The intercom," Jess answered. "Someone's downstairs."

"They'll go away."

The buzzer sounded again. Who was it? Jess wondered. Now, of all times. Ten o'clock on a Sunday morning!

"Oh, no!" Jess said, pulling out of Adam's embrace. "It's my ex-husband. I forgot. He said he'd drop by this morning." Jess went quickly to the intercom by the door and spoke into it. "Don?"

"Your bagels have arrived." His voice filled the apartment.

"This should be interesting," Adam said, flopping down on the living-room sofa, obviously enjoying the situation.

"Oh, brother," Jess whispered, hearing Don's footsteps, opening the door before he could knock. "Hi, Don."

He was wearing a heavy parka over dark green corduroy pants, and carrying a large bag of bagels.

"It's freezing out there," he remarked. "What kept you? Don't tell me you were still asleep." He took two steps inside the apartment, then froze at the sight of Adam on the sofa. "Sorry," he said,

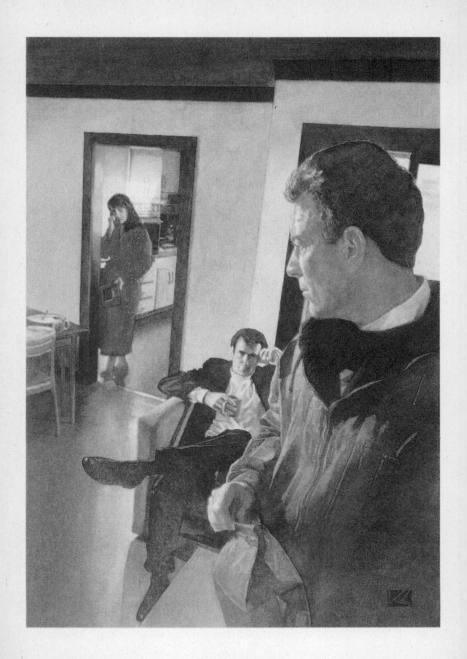

confusion evident in his face as he extended his hand. "I'm Don Shaw, an old friend."

"Adam Stohn," Adam replied, shaking Don's hand. "A new one."

There was silence. No one seemed to breathe.

"There's coffee," Jess finally offered.

Don looked toward the dining-room table. "Looks like you've already eaten."

"Jess forgot to tell me you were dropping by," Adam explained, smiling. "I'd be glad to whip up another omelet."

"Let me hang up your coat." Jess held out her arms.

"No. I think I'll get going. I just wanted to get these bagels to you." Don headed for the door.

The phone rang.

"Don, wait a minute. Please," Jess urged.

Don waited while Jess went to answer the phone. When she came back, she was pale and shaking, her cheeks streaked with tears. Both men moved instantly toward her. "That was the medical examiner's office," she said quietly. "They found Connie DeVuono."

"Where? When?" Don asked.

"In Skokie Lagoons. An ice fisherman stumbled across her body late yesterday afternoon and called the police." A cry caught in Jess's throat. "She'd been strangled with a piece of wire rope, so tight she was almost decapitated."

"I'm so sorry, Jess," Don told her, drawing her into his arms.

Jess cried softly against his shoulder. "I have to go see Connie's mother. I have to tell her."

"The police can do that."

"No," Jess said quickly, seeing Adam tiptoe toward the door, his jacket over his arm. "I have to do it. Don, what can I say to her? What can I say to her little boy?"

"You'll think of just the right words, Jess."

Jess said nothing as Adam opened the door and threw her a delicate kiss good-bye. The door closed softly after him.

"Go get dressed," Don said. "I'll drive you over." If he was aware of Adam's departure, he said nothing.

"No, Don, you don't have to do that."

"Jess, you don't have a car, and there's no way I'm letting you go through this alone. Now, please, don't argue with me on this one."

Jess stroked her ex-husband's cheek. "Thank you," she said.

CHAPTER 11

"**A**RE you all right?" he was asking.

"No." Jess was still crying. She couldn't stop. Even in the shower her tears hadn't abated. She'd cried as she slid into the front seat of Don's Mercedes, cried as they spoke of Connie DeVuono's death to Mrs. Gambala and Steffan, quietly promising Mrs. Gambala to tell her everything as soon as the autopsy report came in.

"Are you going to issue a warrant for Rick Ferguson's arrest?" Don had asked as they were returning to his car.

There was nothing Jess wanted to do more, but she had to know exactly what, if any, evidence there was to link Rick Ferguson to Connie's death. "Not yet. Are you going to call him?"

"What reason would I have for calling him if you're not going to arrest him?" he'd asked in exaggerated innocence.

"Thank you," Jess had told him, then started crying again.

Now Don reached across the front seat and took her hand in his. "What are you thinking about?"

"I always thought it would be better to know," Jess confided, "no matter how awful, to know the truth, for there to be a resolution. Now I'm not so sure. At least before today there was hope. Even if it was false hope, maybe that's better than no hope at all."

"You're talking about your mother," Don said quietly.

"All these years I thought that if only I'd known one way or the other what happened to her, then I could get on with my life. Emotionally, I'm still stuck back on the day my mother disappeared."

"And you think that if you'd known what happened to her, you would have been better off?"

"I don't know. At least I would have been able to deal with it once and for all. I would have been able to grieve, to go on." Jess wiped at her tears and looked out the window, noticing for the first time that they were traveling east on I-94. "Where are we going?"

"Union Pier."

"Union Pier?" Jess immediately conjured up the image of the small lakeshore community approximately seventy miles outside Chicago, where Don maintained a weekend retreat. "Don, I can't. I have to get ready for court tomorrow."

"You haven't seen the place in a long time," he reminded her.

"Come on, I'll have you back by five o'clock. Besides, we both know you're as prepared for tomorrow as anyone could possibly be."

They continued in silence, Jess watching the scenery. A few drops of rain started falling and turned gradually to snow. Buildings gave way to open fields. They took the Union Pier exit, continued east to Lake Michigan. ELSINOR DUDE RANCH, a large wooden sign announced over an arched wrought-iron gate. HORSE TRAILS AND LESSONS. INQUIRE INSIDE.

UNION PIER GUN CLUB, another sign stated as they continued east, the snow becoming heavier, more insistent. Jess sat up, her senses alert. "Since when did they have a gun club out here?"

"Since forever," Don reminded her. "Why?"

"Do they have an archery range?"

"I wouldn't think so. Why the sudden interest in archery?" He broke off abruptly. "The crossbow killer?"

"Terry Wales swore on the stand that he hadn't shot a bow and arrow since he was a kid in camp. What if I can prove he did?"

"Then I'd say you have a clear shot at murder one."

"Can I use your phone?"

Don lifted the car phone off its receiver, handed it to Jess. She quickly dialed Neil Strayhorn at home.

"Neil, I want you to find out about all the archery clubs within a two-hour drive of Chicago," she said without preliminaries.

"Jess?" Neil's voice filled the car over the speakerphone.

"I want to know if Terry Wales is a member of any of them, if he's even been near an archery range in the last thirty years. Detective Mansfield can probably be of help. Tell him we need the information by tomorrow morning. I'll call you later." She hung up.

"You're a hard taskmaster," Don told her, turning left onto an unpaved, bumpy one-lane road.

"I had a good teacher," Jess reminded him.

Summer cottages lined the secluded route. The car bounced toward Don's pinewood cottage, the snow swirling around them.

"It's really starting to snow," Jess said as the car came to a stop.

"Race you to the door," Don said, and Jess was off and running.

"I'D FORGOTTEN how beautiful it is here." Jess stood by the large window that made up the back wall of the cottage and stared through the snow at the small garden she herself had planted many

519

years ago. The bluff stood just beyond, a series of steps carved right into its steep side, leading down to the lake. Large spruce trees separated Don's property from his neighbors on either side, guarding his privacy. Behind her a fire roared in the brick fireplace. Don sat next to the remains of their picnic lunch on the white shag rug between the fireplace and one of two old chesterfields.

"We miss you," Don said quietly. "The garden and I. Do you remember when you planted those shrubs?"

"Of course. It was just after we got married. We argued about what bushes would grow the fastest, be the prettiest."

"We didn't argue. We *discussed*. And then we compromised."

"We did it your way," Jess said, and laughed. "This was a nice idea, coming here. Thank you for thinking of it." She returned to the white shag rug, lowered herself to the floor.

"We had a lot of nice times here," he said nostalgically.

"Yes, we did," she said. "I think I liked May the best, when everything was just starting to bud and I knew I had the whole summer to look forward to."

"And I always liked winter best because I knew that no matter how cold it got outside, I could come up here and build a fire and make a picnic lunch and be warm and happy."

"Do you bring Trish here often?" she asked, staring out the window at the steady downfall of snow.

"Not often."

"Are you in love with her?" Jess asked.

"I'm not sure," Don said. "What about you?"

"I'm definitely not in love with her."

Don smiled. "You know what I mean. You gave me quite a surprise this morning."

"It wasn't the way it looked," Jess said quickly. "Adam had a little too much to drink and passed out on my couch."

"Charming."

"He's really a very nice man."

"I'm sure he is, or you wouldn't be interested in him."

"I'm not sure I am. Interested in him." Jess wondered if she was protesting too much.

"How long have you known him?"

"Not long. Maybe a month," she said.

"What does he do?"

Jess could hear the strain in Don's voice from trying to sound casual, and was touched by it. "He's a salesman."

"A salesman?" He didn't bother to hide his surprise. "What does he sell?"

"Shoes." Jess cleared her throat. "Don't be a snob, Don," she said quickly. "There's nothing wrong with selling shoes. Adam likes what he does."

"So much so that he has to drink himself into a stupor?"

"Objection. Calls for a conclusion."

Don stood up and walked to the window. "It doesn't look like we're going to be able to get out of here this afternoon. The snow's not letting up at all. If anything, it looks like it's getting worse."

"But I have to get back." Jess was on her feet behind him.

"I'll get you back. Just not this afternoon. We may have to wait until after dinner." He walked toward the large open pine kitchen to his left and opened the freezer. "I'll defrost a couple of steaks, open up a bottle of wine, and call the highway patrol, find out how bad weather conditions are on the roads. If worst comes to worst and we can't get out of here tonight, I'll have you back in time for court in the morning. Even if I have to carry you back on snow-shoes. Okay? Does that set your mind at rest?"

"Not really," she told him.

"That's my girl," he said.

JESS spent the rest of the afternoon on the phone.

The medical examiner had nothing new to report. The autopsy on Connie DeVuono hadn't been completed; it would be a few days until they could interpret all their findings.

Neil Strayhorn had contacted Detective Mansfield. They had managed to find the names of two archery clubs in the Chicago area and another four within a hundred-mile radius of the city. The police were already on their way to question the management. Luckily, all the clubs were open on Sundays, although two had closed early because of the storm and couldn't be reached until Monday morning. Neil would call her as soon as they had any news.

Jess went over in her mind the list of questions she had prepared for Terry Wales. Don was right, she acknowledged, watching him prepare dinner. She was as ready as she was ever going to be. The only thing that she had to do now was show up in court on time.

"The radio just said they expect the snow to stop by midnight," Don told her. "I say we get a good night's sleep here and head back around six. That way we're in the city by seven thirty at the latest, and you still have plenty of time to get ready for court."

"But what if the snow doesn't stop by midnight? What if we can't leave here in the morning?"

"Then Neil will ask for a continuance," Don said simply.

"And if we leave now?"

"Then we'll probably spend the night in a snowbank."

Jess stared out the back window at a blizzard in full rage. She had to acknowledge the insanity of trying to go anywhere in weather like this. "How soon till dinner?" she asked.

"THAT was Detective Mansfield," Jess said, pushing the phone off the shag rug. "None of the four archery clubs they were able to contact has any record of Terry Wales being a member."

"That still leaves a couple of places, doesn't it?"

"Two. But we can't reach them till morning."

"Then there's nothing to do but get a good night's sleep tonight." Don, sitting beside Jess on the floor, reached over to twist the long wire cord of the telephone around his fingers, returning the phone to a small pine table between the two couches.

Jess followed the motion of his hands, mesmerized by the slow, circular movement. When she spoke, her voice was equally slow. "Did I tell you that the coroner said the wire was twisted around Connie's neck so tightly she was almost decapitated?"

"Try not to think about that now, Jess," Don said, wrapping his arms around her.

"It's my fault," she told him. "If I hadn't convinced Connie that she had to testify, she'd still be alive."

"Jess, that's ridiculous. You can't blame yourself."

Tears spilled down her cheeks. Don quickly brushed them aside, first with his fingers, then his lips.

"It's all right, baby," he was saying. "Everything will be okay. You'll see. Everything will be all right."

His lips felt gentle, soothing against her skin as he traced the line of her tears from her cheeks to the sides of her mouth, then followed the tears as they ran between her lips, his mouth softly covering her own.

Jess closed her eyes, picturing Adam as he'd reached across her dining-room table to kiss her, felt herself respond, knowing she was responding to the wrong man, but unable to stop herself.

"I love you, Jess," she heard Adam say, but when she opened her eyes, it was Don she saw.

THE dream began as it always did, in the waiting room of the doctor's office, the doctor handing her the phone, telling her her mother was on the line.

"I'm starring in a movie," her mother told her. "I want you to come see me."

The theater was dark, the movie about to start. Jess located an aisle seat, sat down, waited. "I found a lump in my breast," her mother was saying as Jess looked toward the screen.

"It's my fault," Jess whispered to Judge Harris, who was sitting beside her. "If I'd gone to the doctor with her that afternoon like I promised, she wouldn't have disappeared."

Jess sat up with a start, her breath coming in gasps.

It took her a moment to assess where she was. "Oh, no," she whispered, seeing Don sleeping peacefully beside her on the rug. She threw off the blanket he had covered them with and gathered her clothes around her, wondering how she could have allowed what had happened between her and Don.

"I love you," she could still hear him say.

I love you too, she wanted to tell him now, but she couldn't, because she didn't, not in the same way he loved her. She'd used him, used the love he'd always felt for her. For what? So that she could feel better for a few minutes? Feel less alone?

Her hands shaking, she slipped into her clothes, straining to breathe, as if a giant boa constrictor had wrapped itself around her and was slowly tightening its coils. She staggered to her feet and fell back onto the chesterfield behind her, bringing her knees to her chest. "No," she gasped, fighting to keep from throwing up.

And suddenly she saw Adam's face and heard his voice. "Don't fight it," he was telling her. "Just let yourself go."

The same advice, Jess realized, as her self-defense instructor had given her. When faced with an attacker, don't fight him, go with him. Strike when you get there.

Jess stopped fighting, letting the panic fill her body. She closed her eyes against the dizziness that enveloped her. She felt sure that at any second she would lose consciousness.

But she didn't lose consciousness. She didn't die.

She wasn't even going to throw up, she realized with growing amazement, feeling a gradual loosening at her chest, the giant snake slowly losing interest and slithering away. A few minutes later her breathing returned to normal. She was all right. She hadn't died. Nothing had happened to her at all.

"It's over," she whispered, feeling suddenly confident and happy, wanting to wake Don, tell him the news.

Except it wasn't Don she wanted to tell.

Jess pushed herself to her feet, walked to the window, and stared out through the darkness at the bluff beyond.

"Jess?" Don's voice was full of sleep.

"It's stopped snowing," she told him.

"You're dressed." He propped himself up on one elbow.

"I was cold."

"I would have warmed you."

"I know," she told him, an unmistakable note of melancholy creeping into her voice. "Don . . ."

"You don't have to say anything, Jess." He slipped his watch over his wrist, snapped it shut. "I know you don't have the same feelings for me that I have for you." He tried to smile, almost succeeded. "If you want, we'll just pretend that last night never happened."

"The last thing I ever wanted to do was hurt you again."

"You haven't, Jess. I'm a big boy. I can deal with last night if you can." He paused. "Do you want me to make you a cup of coffee?"

"How about I make you one back at my apartment?"

"Are you saying you want to leave now?"

"Would you mind very much?"

"Would it matter?"

Jess knelt on the rug beside her ex-husband and gently stroked his cheek. "I *do* love you," she said.

"I know that," he told her, placing his hand over hers. "I'm just waiting for *you* to figure it out."

THE drive home was slow and treacherous. It was almost seven o'clock before they arrived in the city. A couple of times they'd slid on a hidden patch of ice, but Don had continued resolutely on.

She was on the phone the instant she arrived back in her apartment. "Anything?" she asked Neil instead of saying hello.

"Jess, it's seven o'clock in the morning," he reminded her. "The clubs don't even open till ten."

Jess replaced the receiver, watched Don as he tidied up the remains of the breakfast Adam had prepared for her yesterday. "You don't have to do that," she said.

"Yes, I do. There isn't a clean dish in the place. Now get out of here. *I'll* make the coffee; *you* take a shower."

Jess walked into the living room. "Hello, Fred," she said, bringing her nose up against the narrow bars of his cage. "How are you doing, fella? I'm sorry I didn't come home last night to cover you up. Did you miss me?"

The bird hopped from perch to perch, oblivious to her concern.

Jess headed down the hall toward her bedroom. The room was as she'd left it, the bed unmade. Jess hated unmade beds, the way she hated anything left unfinished. She quickly set about making it, fluffing the pillows and tucking in the corners. Then she selected her gray suit and pink blouse for today's appearance in court, laying them neatly across the white wicker chair.

She had just pulled a fresh pink lace bra and underpants from her dresser drawer when she noticed a rip in the panties. "Great. How did that happen?" she asked, examining the uneven tear.

She tossed them into the wastebasket, retrieved another pair, her eyes quickly fixing on the jagged tear. With growing panic Jess examined all her underwear. All had been slashed in the same way. "Don!" she cried, unable to say anything else. "Don!"

He was instantly at her side. "What is it? What's the matter?"

She handed him her torn underwear. "All my panties are ripped," she said. "Look. It's like they've been slashed with a knife."

"Jess, that's crazy. They must have gotten torn in the washing machine."

"I wash them by hand," Jess snapped, losing patience. "Rick Ferguson did this. He's been here. He's been in my things."

"Jess, I can understand your being upset, but don't you think you're flying a little fast and loose with the assumptions here?"

"Who else *would* it be? It has to be Rick Ferguson. Who else could get in here as easily as if he had a key—" She broke off abruptly.

Adam had borrowed her key while she'd been asleep, she thought. Had he had another key made? Had he used it to get back into her apartment when she was away?

She pushed the thought aside.

"It had to be Rick Ferguson," Jess continued. "He broke into Connie's apartment without any problem. Now he's broken into mine."

"Jess, we don't know that there *was* a break-in here," he said.

"What does that mean?" Jess asked, anger swelling her throat.

"Who is this Adam Stohn anyway, Jess?"

"What?" Had he been able to read her most secret thoughts? Tell me no secrets, I'll tell you no lies, she thought.

"Adam Stohn," Don repeated. "The man who passed out on your sofa Saturday night. He could easily have gone through your things while you were sleeping, maybe had a little fun with one of your kitchen knives."

"That's ridiculous," Jess protested.

"He's the wild card here, Jess. Just who is this shoe salesman? Who introduced you?"

"No one," Jess admitted. "But I certainly don't need a lecture on dating by my ex-husband."

"I'm not trying to lecture you; I'm trying to protect you!"

"That's not your job!" she reminded him. "Your job is defending men like Rick Ferguson. Remember?"

Don slumped down on the bed. "This is getting us nowhere. Now the first thing we're going to do is call the police."

"Don, I don't have time to deal with the police now."

"You can tell them what happened, over the phone. They can come over later and dust for prints."

"That won't do any good."

"No, I don't think it will. But you have to report the incident anyway, you know that. Get it on the record. Including your suspicions about Rick Ferguson."

"Which you don't share."

"Which I *do* share. I'm not a complete idiot, even where you're concerned. But suspicions are one thing, assumptions are another. The second thing I want you to do," he continued, "is pack a suitcase. You're moving into my apartment until this whole thing gets straightened out."

"Don, I can't move into your apartment."

"Why not?"

"Because this is where I live. Because all my things are here. Because of Fred. Because . . . I just can't."

"Okay, then, at the very least, I want that lock replaced," he told her. "I want a dead bolt and a chain installed."

"Fine."

"I'll have my secretary come over with the locksmith. Lastly," he continued, "I'm hiring a detective to keep tabs on Rick Ferguson."

"What? Hiring a detective to spy on your own client?"

"I almost hired one after your car was destroyed. I should have. Anyway, if he's innocent, he has nothing to worry about."

"But won't it be expensive, hiring a detective?"

"Jess, I love you. I'm not going to take a chance on anything happening to you. Consider it my Christmas present."

"Thank you," she said.

"I'll tell you one thing," he told her solemnly. "If it *is* Rick Ferguson who's been harassing you, then, client or no client, I'll shoot the animal myself."

CHAPTER 12

"Could you state your full name for the jury, please?"

"Terrence Matthew Wales."

Jess rose from her seat behind the prosecutor's table and approached the witness stand, eyes fastened on the defendant. Terry Wales stared back steadily, even respectfully, creating the impression of a man who had tried all his life to do the right thing.

"You live at Twenty-four twenty-seven Kinzie in Chicago?"

"Yes."

"Isn't it true that the police were called to your house on the nights of August third, 1984"—Jess knew the dates by heart—"September seventh, 1984, November twenty-second, 1984, and January fourth, 1985?"

"I don't remember the exact dates."

"It's all on file, Mr. Wales. Do you dispute any of it?"

He shook his head, then answered, "No."

"On each of those occasions your wife showed obvious signs of having been beaten. Once she even had to be hospitalized."

"I've already testified that our fights often got out of hand, that I'm not proud of my part in them."

Jess walked to the prosecutor's table and picked up a police report. "This report states that on the night of January fourth, 1985, the night your wife was hospitalized, Nina Wales had bruises to over forty percent of her body and was bleeding internally, that her nose and two ribs were broken, and that both eyes were blackened. Isn't it true that your wife had recently given birth to your second child, a little girl?"

"Rebecca, yes."

"How old was she on the night of January fourth, 1985?"

Terry Wales hesitated.

"Surely you remember your daughter's birthday, Mr. Wales."

"She was born on December second."

"Just four weeks before the fight that put your wife in the hospital? That would mean that those three other attacks—"

"Objection!" Hal Bristol was on his feet.

"Those other *incidents*," Jess corrected, "all occurred while your wife was pregnant. Is that correct?"

Terry Wales dropped his head. "Yes," he whispered.

Jess retrieved another police report from Neil Strayhorn's out-stretched hand, then returned to the witness stand. "Jumping ahead a few years, if we could, to the night of February twenty-fifth, 1988, you put your wife in the hospital again, didn't you?"

"My wife had gone out and left the kids alone. When she came back home, it was obvious to me she'd been drinking. Something inside me just snapped."

"No, Mr. Wales, it was something in your wife that got snapped. Specifically her right wrist."

"Ms. Koster," Judge Harris warned, "can we please skip the sarcasm and get on with it?"

"I'm sorry, Your Honor," Jess said, smoothing her skirt, suddenly reminded of the new underwear Don's secretary had brought over just prior to the start of court. "Would you say you have a quick temper, Mr. Wales?"

"These last few years have been difficult ones in the retail business. There was less money coming in. On occasion I was unable to control my temper. Nina was constantly complaining that I wasn't making enough money—even before the recession hit."

"I see. How exactly did your drop in income affect the household, Mr. Wales?"

"Well, the same way everybody else has been affected, I guess," Terry Wales answered carefully. "We had to cut down on entertaining, eating out, buying clothes. Stuff like that."

"You were the sole supporter of your family, isn't that right?"

"Nina wanted to stay home with the children."

"So the only money your wife had was the money that you gave her. How much did you give her every week, Mr. Wales?"

"I'm not sure. Enough for groceries and other essentials."

"Fifty dollars? A hundred? Two hundred?"

"Closer to a hundred."

"A hundred dollars a week for a family of four. Your wife must have been a very careful shopper."

"We had no choice. There was simply no money to spare."

"You belong to the Eden Rock Golf Club, do you not, Mr. Wales?"

A slight pause. "Yes."

"How much are the yearly dues?"

"I think they're just slightly over a thousand dollars."

"Eleven hundred dollars, to be exact. Did you give that up?"

"No."

"And the Elmwood Gun Club. You're a member there as well?"

"Yes. Look, I know it was selfish, but I worked hard; I needed some sort of outlet. . . ."

"Do you belong to any other clubs, Mr. Wales?"

Jess watched for a look of hesitation in Terry Wales's eyes, but there was none. "No," he said clearly.

Jess nodded, looking toward the rear of the courtroom. Where was Barbara? They must have heard from the police by now.

"Let's go to the night of January twentieth, 1992," Jess stated, "the last time police were called to your house to investigate a domestic dispute. You testified that was the night your wife first told you she had a lover."

"That's right."

"So you beat her to a bloody pulp, and the neighbors called the police," Jess summarized, feeling Hal Bristol object even before the word was out of his mouth. "Your wife *did* end up in the hospital that night, didn't she?" Jess said, rephrasing her question.

"Yes."

"You testified that after that, your wife told you that she'd consulted a lawyer and was moving out."

"That's correct."

"You testified that you begged her to change her mind," Jess stated, watching the rear door of the courtroom open and Barbara Cohen walk through. Even from a distance Jess could see the glint in her assistant's eye. "Your Honor, may I have a minute?"

Judge Harris nodded, and Jess strode to the prosecutor's table.

"What've we got?" she asked, quickly scanning the report.

"I'd say it's just what we need," Barbara Cohen answered.

Jess bit down on her lower lip to keep from laughing out loud. She spun around, then held back. Move in slowly, she told herself. Then move in for the kill. "So you were distraught, and you decided to do something to make your wife come to her senses?" she asked.

"Yes."

"So you went out and you purchased a crossbow, a weapon you hadn't shot since you were a kid in camp, is that right?"

"Yes."

"What camp was that?"

Terry Wales looked toward his lawyer, but Hal Bristol's subtle nod directed him to answer. "Camp New Moon, I believe."

"And they taught you how to shoot a bow and arrow?"

"It was one of the activities offered."

"And you won several medals, did you not?"

"Yes. But that was almost thirty years ago."

Jess smiled. "And until you fatally shot your wife through the heart on June second of this year, it had been almost thirty years since you'd shot a bow and arrow?"

"Twenty-five or thirty," Terry Wales qualified.

Jess checked the folder in her hand. "Mr. Wales, have you ever heard of the Aurora County Bowmen?"

"I'm sorry, the what?" he asked, a flush blotching his cheeks.

"The Aurora County Bowmen," Jess repeated. "It's an archery club about forty-five miles southwest of Chicago. Do you know it?"

"No."

"According to the brochure I have, it's a nonprofit organization providing facilities where archers can pursue their sport. 'No matter what area of archery your interest lies in,'" Jess read, "'be it hunting or target shooting, longbow or *crossbow.*'"

Hal Bristol was on his feet. "Objection, Your Honor. My client has already stated he has no knowledge of this club."

"Interesting," Jess said immediately, "since club records show Terry Wales has been a member there for the past eight years." Jess held up a faxed copy of the club membership. "Do you remember the club now, Mr. Wales?" Jess asked pointedly.

"I joined the club eight years ago and hardly ever used it," Terry Wales explained. "Frankly, I'd forgotten all about it."

"Oh, but they didn't forget you, Mr. Wales. We have a signed affidavit from a Mr. Glen Hallam, who's in charge of the equipment at Aurora County Bowmen. The police showed him your picture this morning, and he remembers you very well. Says you're a regular there and quite a shot, Mr. Wales. Bull's-eye nearly every time."

A collective gasp emanated from the jury box. Hal Bristol looked toward his lap. Terry Wales said nothing.

Bull's-eye, Jess thought.

"I UNDERSTAND you pulled off quite a coup today," Greg Oliver greeted Jess as she walked past his office at the end of the day.

"She was brilliant!" Neil Strayhorn exclaimed, a step behind Jess, Barbara Cohen at his side.

"My favorite moment," Barbara Cohen was saying as they settled in behind their desks, "was when you asked him if he'd ever heard of the Aurora County Bowmen. He didn't move."

Jess laughed. That had been her favorite moment too.

"Well, well, the ice maiden cracks." Greg ambled toward Jess's desk. "I've got a present for you."

Jess looked Greg Oliver coolly in the eye and waited.

"No guesses?"

"Look, Greg, I'm going home. It's been a very long day."

He dropped a set of keys onto her desk. "The keys to Madame's apartment."

Jess reached for the new set of keys, the stale scent of Greg's cologne bouncing off the shiny metal. "How did you get these?"

"Some woman delivered them this afternoon. Kind of cute actually, except that her thighs were in two different time zones." He sauntered back to the door, then disappeared down the hall.

"Where's my crossbow?" Barbara Cohen asked.

"They're never around when you need them." Jess glanced over the list of witnesses who would be testifying the next day, feeling her eyes cross with fatigue. "That's it. I'm gonna call it a day, gang."

"Come on, I'll drive you home," Neil volunteered.

"Don't be silly, Neil. It's out of your way."

"When are you going to buy a new car?" Barbara asked.

"As soon as I get Rick Ferguson behind bars," she said.

THE phone was ringing when she got to her apartment. "Just a minute," she called out, fiddling with her new key in the lock.

The phone continued to ring, the key refusing to connect properly. Maybe Greg Oliver gave her the wrong set of keys. Maybe if she just calmed down and stopped trying so hard . . .

The key turned in the lock. The door opened. The phone stopped ringing.

"At least you're inside," Jess said. With a wave at her canary she set her briefcase down, then pulled off her boots and tossed her coat across the sofa. "So, Fred, I was positively amazing in court today."

She stopped.

"This is pathetic," she said out loud. "I'm talking to a canary." She went into the kitchen, looked toward the phone. She should call Don, she thought, thank him for everything he'd done for her today.

The buzzer sounded. Someone was at the door downstairs. Jess approached the intercom cautiously, wondering who was there, not sure whether she wanted to find out.

"Who is it?" she asked.

"Adam," came the simple response.

She buzzed him up. Seconds later he was outside her door.

"I tried to phone," he said as soon as he saw her. "No one answered. Are you going to invite me in?"

"He's the wild card here, Jess," she heard Don say.

"You must have been very close by," Jess said.

"I was around the corner. Waiting for you."

Her mind raced back to when she'd first met Adam Stohn. The vandalization of her car and the torn underwear had both taken place since their first meeting. Adam Stohn knew where she worked. He knew where she lived. He'd even spent the night on her sofa.

All right, so he'd had the opportunity to do these things, Jess acknowledged silently, losing herself momentarily in the soft stillness of his brown eyes. But what possible motive could he have for wanting to terrorize her? He doesn't want to kill you, she thought. She stepped back and let Adam inside her apartment.

"I was curious about what happened yesterday," he told her, taking off his jacket and throwing it over her coat.

Jess told him about breaking the news of Connie DeVuono's death to her mother and son, and about today's triumph in court. She left out that she'd spent the night with her ex-husband.

"He's still in love with you, you know," Adam said.

"Who?" Jess asked, knowing full well whom he meant.

"The bagel man," Adam said. He walked slowly toward her. "How do you feel about him?"

"I told you, we're friends." Jess ached to sit down, was afraid to.

"I think there's more to it than that. I called you last night, Jess," he told her, very close now. "I called you till quite late. I think it was three in the morning when I finally gave up and went to sleep."

"I wasn't aware I had to answer to you."

Adam took two steps back, hands in the air. "You're right. I guess I just want to know where I stand. If you're still involved with your ex-husband, just say the word and I'm out of here."

"I'm not involved," Jess said quickly.

"And the bagel man?"

"He's involved with someone else."

"Unless you change your mind."

"I won't."

They stared at each other without speaking. In the next second they were in each other's arms, his hands in her hair, her lips on his.

He's the wild card here, Jess, she heard Don say again. How could she have let last night happen?

"I can't do this," she said quickly, pulling out of the embrace.

"Can't do what?" His voice sounded hoarse.

"I'm just not ready for this yet," she told him, searching the room for disapproving eyes. "I don't even know where you live."

"You want to know? I live on Sheffield," he said quickly. "A one-bedroom apartment. A five-minute walk from Wrigley Field."

And suddenly they were laughing. Jess felt the tension of the last few days dissolve. She laughed for the sheer joy of it. She laughed so hard, tears spilled from her eyes. Adam quickly kissed the tears away.

"No," she said, pulling out of his reach. "I need time to think."

"How much time?"

"I could think over dinner," she heard herself say. "How about I make us something here?"

"I didn't think you cooked."

"Follow me," she said, laughing, picking up the bag of bagels on her way to the kitchen.

"So you were an only child," Jess said as they sat on the floor in front of the sofa finishing their dinner of bagels and water.

"A very spoiled only child," he elaborated.

"My sister says that children aren't apples—they don't spoil."

"She sounds like a very good mother."

"I think she is."

"You sound surprised."

"It's just not what I expected from her, that's all," Jess said, wondering how the conversation always reverted back to herself, away from him. "You and your wife never wanted children?"

"We wanted them," he said. "It just never worked out."

Jess understood from the way his voice dropped that it was a topic he didn't wish to pursue. She lifted the glass of water to her lips.

"What was your mother like?" he asked suddenly.

"What?" Jess's hand started to shake, the water spilling from the glass onto the floor. She scrambled to her feet. "Oh, my."

His hand was immediately on her arm, gently pulling her back down. "Relax, Jess, it's only water." He used his napkin to wipe up the spill. "Why won't you talk about her?"

"Why should I?"

"Because you're afraid to," he said evenly.

"Another one of my phobias?" Jess asked sarcastically.

"You tell me."

"Anybody ever tell you you'd make a good lawyer?"

"What happened to your mother, Jess?"

Jess closed her eyes, saw her mother standing before her in the kitchen of their home, tears falling down her cheeks. *"I don't need this, Jess,"* she was saying. *"I don't need this from you."* Jess quickly opened her eyes. "She disappeared," she said finally.

"Disappeared?"

"She'd found a small lump in her breast, and she was pretty scared. The doctor said he'd see her that afternoon. But she never showed up for her appointment. Nobody ever saw her again."

"Then it's possible she's alive?"

"No, it's not possible," Jess snapped. "She wasn't the kind of woman who would just walk out on her family because she couldn't face reality. No matter how scared she was. No matter how angry."

"Angry? What was she angry about, Jess?"

"She wasn't angry. I didn't mean angry."

"She was angry at you, wasn't she?"

Jess looked toward the window. Her mother's tear-streaked face stared back. *"I don't need this, Jess. I don't need this from you."*

"I came downstairs and found her all dressed up," Jess began. "I asked where she was going, and at first she wouldn't tell me. But it came out that she'd found a lump in her breast and she was going to the doctor that afternoon. She asked if I'd go with her. I said sure. But then we got into an argument. She thought I was being headstrong. I thought she was being overprotective. I told her to stay out of my life. She told me not to bother taking her to the doctor, and I slammed out of the house. When I got back, she'd already left."

"And you blame yourself for what happened." It was more statement than question.

Jess pushed herself to her feet, walked to the bird's cage with exaggerated strides. "Hi, Fred, how're you doing?"

"Fred's doing great," Adam told her, coming up behind her. "I'm not so sure about his owner. That's a big load of guilt you've been carrying around all these years."

"Hey, whatever happened to our pact?" Jess asked, swiping at her tears, refusing to look at him, concentrating all her attention on the small yellow bird. "No secrets, no lies—remember?" She made awkward chirping noises against the side of the cage.

"Do you ever let him out?" Adam asked.

"You're not supposed to let canaries out of their cages," Jess said loudly, hoping to still the shaking in her body with the sound of her voice.

"So you never have to worry he'll fly away," Adam said softly.

The implication was too blatant to ignore. Jess spun around angrily. "Just when did you give up psychiatry for selling shoes?" she demanded bitterly. "Who the hell are you, Adam Stohn?"

They stood facing one another, Jess shaking, Adam absolutely still.

"Do you want me to go?" he asked.

No, she thought. "Yes," she said.

He walked slowly to the door.

"Adam," she called, and he stopped, his hand on the doorknob. "I think it's probably a good idea if you don't come back."

For an instant she thought he might turn around, take her into his arms, confess all. But he didn't, and in the next instant he was gone and she was alone in a room full of ghosts and shadows.

CHAPTER 13

BY THE end of the week the medical examiner's report on Connie DeVuono was in, and the jury in the Terry Wales murder trial was out.

Connie DeVuono had been raped, then beaten, and strangled with a piece of thin magnetic wire. Forensics had determined that the wire was identical to wire found in the factory that employed Rick Ferguson. A warrant had just been issued for his arrest.

"How long do you think the jury will be out?" Barbara Cohen was asking when the phone rang on Jess's desk. "It's already been over twenty-four hours."

Jess shrugged, as anxious as her assistant but reluctant to admit it. She reached over and picked up the phone. "Jess Koster."

"He's disappeared," Don said instead of hello.

Jess felt her stomach lurch. She didn't have to ask who Don was talking about. "When?"

"Probably sometime in the night. My guy had been watching the house, and when he didn't see Ferguson leave for work this morning, he got suspicious. It looks like Ferguson picked up on the tail, figured the police were about to arrest him, and escaped."

"The irony is that the police *were* about to arrest him," Jess admitted. "We issued a warrant this morning."

Don's tone became instantly businesslike, no longer the concerned ex-husband. "What've you got?" he asked.

"The wire used to kill Connie DeVuono was the same kind of wire found in the warehouse that employs Rick Ferguson."

"What else?"

"What else do I need?"

"More than just a flimsy piece of wire!"

"Strong enough to kill Connie DeVuono," Jess told him. "Strong enough to convict your client."

There was a slight pause. "Okay, Jess, I don't want to get into all this now. We can talk about the case as soon as the police bring him in. In the meantime I've asked my guy to keep an eye on you."

"What? Don, I don't want a baby-sitter."

"*I* want," Don insisted. "Indulge me, Jess. It won't kill you."

"Any ideas where your client went?"

"None."

"I better go," Jess told him, already thinking ahead to what she would tell the police. "I'll call you later." She hung up.

The phone rang again on Jess's desk.

"Looks like it's going to be one of those days," Barbara said.

Jess answered the phone. "Jess Koster."

"Jess, it's Maureen. Is it a bad time?"

Jess felt her shoulders slump. "Well, it's not the best, but I can spare a few minutes. So how've you been?"

"Fine," Maureen said. "Anyway, I know how busy you are, but I didn't want you to think I was ignoring you." Her voice threatened to dissolve into tears.

"How's Dad?" Jess asked, realizing she hadn't spoken to her father in weeks, feeling the familiar pattern of guilt.

"He's really happy, Jess."

"I'm glad."

"Sherry's very good for him. She makes him laugh, keeps him on his toes. They're coming for dinner next Friday night at six o'clock. We're going to decorate the Christmas tree." She paused. "Would you like to join us?"

Jess closed her eyes. How long could she go on hurting the people who meant the most to her? "Sounds great," she said.

"Yeah, it *will* be great. We've missed you. Tyler hasn't stopped playing with that airplane you bought him. And you won't believe how much the twins have grown."

Jess laughed. "Really, Maureen, it hasn't been that long."

"Almost two months," Maureen reminded her, catching Jess off guard. Had two months really elapsed since she'd seen her family?

"I better go now," Jess told her.

"Oh, sure. You must be swamped. See you next week."

"Something wrong?" Barbara asked as Jess replaced the receiver.

Jess shook her head, pretended to be studying a file on her desk. Two months, she thought, since her last visit to her sister's house.

Since she'd hugged her nephew and nieces. Since she'd seen her father. How could she have let that happen? And why couldn't she stop obsessing about her mother? Damn Adam Stohn. He was responsible. He'd gotten her to open up, to talk about her mother. He'd unleashed all the sadness and the guilt she'd been suppressing for so long.

The ringing of a telephone interrupted her reverie. Jess watched as Neil picked up the phone on his desk. "Neil Strayhorn," he pronounced clearly, his eyes locked on Jess. "They are? Now?"

Jess took a deep breath. She didn't have to ask. The jury was in.

"LADIES and gentlemen of the jury, have you reached a verdict?"

Jess felt the familiar surge of adrenaline race through her body, though she was holding her breath. She both loved and hated this moment. Loved it for its drama, its suspense. Hated it for the same reasons. Hated it because she hated to lose. Hated it because, in the end, it was really just one lawyer's truth against another's. No such thing as the whole truth.

The foreman cleared his throat. "We, the jury, find the defendant, Terry Wales, guilty of murder in the first degree."

The courtroom erupted. Reporters ran from the room; friends and relatives of the deceased hugged one another tearfully. Jess embraced her partners, caught the look of resignation in Hal Bristol's eyes, the sneer on the defendant's lips as he was led away.

Outside the courtroom, the reporters thronged around her. "Were you surprised at the verdict? Did you expect to win?" they asked as cameras clicked and strobes exploded.

"We have great faith in this country's jury system," Jess told the reporters. "We never doubted the outcome for a minute."

"How does it feel to win this case?" a woman shouted from the back of the throng.

Jess knew she should remind the reporters that what was important here wasn't winning but the truth, that justice had been served. She smiled widely. "It feels great," she said.

"HEY, was that your picture I saw in the paper this morning?" Vasiliki asked.

"That was me," Jess acknowledged shyly, her head still thumping from too many beers at Jean's Restaurant the night before.

She'd called her father right after she got back to her office, but he wasn't home; phoned her sister, but she was busy with the babies. She'd called Don, heard him mumble his apologies about not being able to celebrate with her. Trish, Jess thought.

Then she'd done something she'd never done before. She'd gone into the washroom, closed her eyes, and just stood there. "I won," she'd said softly, allowing the ghost of her mother to pull her into a proud embrace.

The celebration at Jean's lasted until the early hours of the morning. Her trial supervisor, Tom Olinsky, had driven her home, making sure she got inside safely. Jess never saw the man Don had hired to watch her, but she knew he was there, and was grateful in spite of herself.

She'd fallen into a deep sleep, hadn't even heard her alarm clock go off, and was almost late for her self-defense class.

The women worked on eagle claws and zipper punches and hammer fists until they were fluid motions. They learned flips, how to use their shoulders to carry the weight of an attacker. At the end of almost two hours they were breathing hard and fighting harder.

"Okay, let's see you put this together," Dominic told them. "You," he said, pointing at Jess, "come with me."

Jess took several tentative steps toward Dominic. Suddenly he reached out and grabbed her, pulling her toward him. *"Hohh!"* she screamed loudly, hearing the word fill the room. She allowed herself to be pulled forward, fell against him, then pushed her full weight into him, quickly using her feet to trip him and her shoulder to upend him before falling with him to the ground.

She'd done it, she thought triumphantly. She threw her head back and laughed out loud.

Suddenly she felt a tapping at her forehead, turned to see Dominic smiling at her, the index and middle fingers of his right hand pressed against her temple, like the barrel of a gun. His thumb snapped down, then up, as if pulling an imaginary trigger. "Bang," he said calmly. "You're dead."

JESS was still mad as she walked along Willow Street. Here she'd been roaring away, feeling invincible, and all it took was a couple of fingers to rip her illusions to shreds.

Next week, Dominic had assured them, next week he'd show

them how to disarm a knife-wielding or gun-toting attacker. Great, Jess thought, crossing the road. Something to look forward to.

She saw him as soon as she turned the corner onto Orchard Street. He was coming down her front steps, the collar of his bomber jacket turned up against the cold. She stopped, not sure whether to run as fast as she could in the other direction.

She didn't run. She just stood there waiting on the sidewalk until he turned and saw her, stood there while he walked toward her, stood there as he reached for her, drew her into his arms.

"We need to talk," Adam said.

"I GREW up in Springfield," he was saying, leaning across the small table of the Italian restaurant they had gone to their first evening together. "My family is quite well-off. My father is a psychiatrist," he said, and laughed softly. "You weren't so far off the mark when you asked me when I'd given up psychiatry for selling shoes. And my mother is an art consultant. I grew up with the best of everything. I learned to expect the best of everything. I thought I was entitled to the best of everything."

He stopped. Jess watched his hands fold and unfold on the table. "Things always came pretty easily for me: school, grades, girls. Everything I wanted, I more or less got. And for a long time I wanted a girl named Susan Cunningham. She was pretty and popular and as spoiled as I was. I set my sights on her, and I married her. Needless to say, it was not a marriage made in heaven. We didn't have a thing in common except we both liked looking in the mirror.

"The only thing we did right was Beth."

"Beth?"

Adam quickly looked away. "Our daughter."

"Go on," Jess directed softly, holding her breath.

"She was the sweetest little thing you ever saw. Here," he said, shaking hands fumbling for the wallet in his pocket, removing a small color photograph of a blond, smiling little girl in a white dress.

"She's lovely," Jess agreed, trying to still his hand with her own.

"She's dead," Adam said, returning the picture to his wallet.

"What? How?"

Adam looked across the table at Jess, but his eyes were unfocused, and when he spoke again, his voice was strained, distant. "She was five years old. My marriage was pretty much over. My father could see what was going on and he suggested counseling, and we tried it for a while, but our hearts weren't really in it. Susan's parents could see what was going on too, but instead of therapy, they bought us a cruise to the Bahamas, a few weeks alone together to sort through our differences. They offered to take care of Beth. We said okay, why not?

"Beth didn't want us to go. I guess she was afraid that if we left, one of us might not come back—I don't know." He stared toward the door, saying nothing for several seconds. "Anyway, she started having tantrums, stomachaches, that sort of thing. The morning we were leaving, she complained about a stiff neck. We didn't pay too much attention. We just figured it was her way of trying to get us to stay home. Susan's parents assured us that they'd take good care of her. So we left on our cruise.

"That night she developed a slight fever. Susan's parents called the doctor, who told them to give Beth a couple of Children's Tylenol and bring her to his office in the morning if she wasn't any better. By the middle of the night her fever had spiked to almost a hundred and five and she was delirious. My father-in-law took her to the hospital, but it was too late. She was dead before morning.

"Meningitis," Adam said, answering the question in Jess's eyes.

"How awful."

"They called us on the ship, arranged for us to get home—but of course, there was no home. The only thing that had been keeping us together was gone.

"I thought of suing the doctor, but we had no case. Instead, I sued for divorce. And then I ran. Gave up everything. I came to the big city and got a job selling shoes, and the rest is history."

He looked from Jess to the door and back to Jess. "I met a lot of women, but I stayed clear of any involvements. I sold lots of shoes. And then you walked into the store, and you were banging the heel of that shoe into the palm of your hand. And I looked into your eyes, and I thought, This person is as wounded inside as I am."

Jess felt tears fill her eyes and looked briefly away.

"I wasn't going to call you," he continued, his voice drawing her eyes back to his. "The last thing I was looking for was to get involved in somebody else's problems. But when those boots came in, I knew I had to see you again. I kept telling myself it would be a one-shot deal. But I kept finding myself at your door.

"And all this past week I've been thinking about you and that even though you told me not to come back, I had to see you, and I haven't sold a single pair of shoes. . . ."

Jess found herself laughing and crying at the same time. "You didn't sell shoes back in Springfield, did you?" she asked.

He shook his head.

"I have this awful feeling—you're a lawyer, aren't you?"

He nodded guiltily. "I wanted to tell you, but I kept thinking that since I wasn't going to call you again, what difference did it make?"

"What kind of law did you practice?" She started laughing even before she heard his answer.

"Criminal," came the expected response.

"Of course," Jess said, thinking she should have run when she had the chance.

"I really never intended to lie to you," he reiterated. "I just never thought it would get this far."

"How far is it?" Jess asked.

"Far enough for me to know I don't want to lose you. Far enough for me to think I'm falling in love," he said softly.

"Tell me about your daughter," Jess said, reaching across the table and taking his hand in hers.

"I remember when she was four years old, and she was all excited because it was her birthday the next day. She'd invited a bunch of kids over for a party," Adam began, his voice shaking. "We went to bed, I'm sound asleep, and all of a sudden I felt this gentle tap on my arm, and there was Beth standing there looking at me. And I said, 'What is it, sweetie?' And she said in this very excited little voice, 'It's my birthday.' And I said, 'Yes, it is, but go back to bed now, honey; it's three o'clock in the morning.' And she said, 'Oh, I thought it was time to get up.' And there she was—she'd put on her new party dress all by herself, and her shoes and her white frilly socks, and I remember thinking how wonderful it was to be that excited about something. And I walked her back to her room, and she got back into her pajamas, and I tucked her into bed, and she fell right off to sleep."

"I love that story," Jess told him.

Adam smiled, tears forming in the corners of his eyes.

"You sound like you were a good daddy."

"I like to think I was."

He signaled for Carla, who was hovering nearby. "We'll have the special pizza and two glasses of Chianti, please."

Carla nodded her approval, then hurried off.

"Do you ever think about going back to the law?" Jess asked.

"Yes, I think about it."

"Would you do it?"

"I don't know. Maybe if an inspiring case came along, I might be persuaded. Who knows?"

Carla brought their drinks to the table. Jess immediately lifted her glass in the air, clicking it against Adam's.

"To sweet memories," she said.

"To sweet memories," he agreed.

As soon as they got to her apartment, Jess knew something was wrong. She stood frozen outside her door, waiting, listening.

"What's the matter?" Adam asked.

"Can you hear that?" she asked.

"I hear your radio. Don't you usually leave it on for the bird?"

"Not that loud." Jess twisted her key in the lock, gently pushing open the door. "It's freezing in here!" she exclaimed, seeing her antique ivory lace curtains billowing into the air.

"Did you leave the window open?"

"No," Jess said, hurrying toward the window and bringing it quickly shut. The curtains collapsed around her.

"Let's get out of here and call the police," Adam was saying. "Whoever broke in might still be here."

Jess took two steps toward him, then stopped dead. "Oh, no! Fred!" Her hand pointed toward the birdcage. "He's gone," she shouted. "Somebody let him out." Tears filled her eyes. "Why would anyone do that? Who would want to hurt a poor little bird?" Jess moaned into Adam's arms, the unwanted image of a boy's mutilated pet turtle appearing before her eyes.

They called the police from Walter Fraser's apartment downstairs, waited there while the police looked through her apartment.

"They won't find anyone," Jess said as Walter fixed her a cup of tea and insisted that she drink it. "He's long gone."

"You sound like you know who it is," Adam commented.

"I do." Jess nodded, telling them briefly about Rick Ferguson. "Did you see anyone suspicious, Walter?" Jess asked.

"Just your friend here," Walter remarked, winking at Adam. "He was pacing around outside. Waiting for you, I guess."

Jess looked toward Adam.

"What about the music?" Adam asked quickly. "Do you know what time the volume went up?"

"Well, I was out most of the afternoon," Walter said, "and when I came home, the music was already blaring."

The police asked the same questions, received the same answers. They found no one in Jess's apartment. Nothing in the other rooms appeared to have been touched.

"We can send someone over to dust for prints," the male officer offered.

"Don't bother. He didn't leave any." Jess told them there was already a warrant out for Rick Ferguson's arrest.

"Would you like an officer to watch the house tonight?" the young female officer asked.

"I'll stay with her," Adam said, his voice brooking no arguments.

The young woman followed her partner out the door.

AFTER the police left, Jess and Adam had returned to her apartment, collapsing on top of the bed. There'd been no attempt at romance. They'd simply lain there in each other's arms, Jess occasionally closing her eyes, opening them to find Adam watching her.

"I'm hungry," she said now, sitting up, rubbing at the sleep in her eyes. "How about I pop a few frozen pizzas in the microwave?"

"Sounds wonderful."

She shuffled toward the kitchen. Adam was right behind her as she pulled out the pizzas.

"Just one for me," he said.

Jess placed three small pizzas on a plate, carried the plate to the microwave oven, pulled open its door.

Immediately she felt a giant wave of revulsion sweep through her body. She brought her hand to her mouth in silent horror.

The small canary lay stiff on its side, its yellow feathers charred and blackened, its eyes glassy in death.

"Oh, my God," Jess sobbed, falling backward, her body caving forward, nausea causing her head to spin and her legs to wobble.

"What is it?" Adam asked, rushing to catch her before she fell.

Jess opened her mouth to speak, but no words came.

SHE WOKE UP THE NEXT MORNING to see Adam sitting at the foot of her bed, extending a mug of black coffee toward her. "How do you feel?" he asked.

"Like someone's knocked the stuffing right out of me."

"Someone did," he reminded her.

Jess took the mug from his hand, downed a long sip of coffee. She vaguely remembered Adam getting her into her nightgown, tucking her into bed.

"Oh, Adam," she moaned. "My poor Fred. And the thought of cleaning up . . ."

"It's all taken care of," Adam said simply.

Jess stared at him with gratitude, her sniffling the only sound in the still apartment. "I'm a real treat," she said finally, swiping at her tears with the back of her hand. "Stick with me."

"I intend to," Adam said, kissing Jess gently on the lips. "I'll see what I can rustle up for breakfast. Think you could eat anything?"

"I'm ashamed to say, yes."

He smiled. "Go take your shower. You'll feel a lot better." He kissed the tip of her nose, then left the room.

Jess had never realized before how quiet her apartment was without her canary. His song had always been there, she thought as she started the shower and slipped out of her clothes. Such a gentle sound, she remembered, closing the bathroom door, stepping under hot spray. So soothing, so constant, so life-affirming.

Now silenced.

"Damn you, Rick Ferguson," she whispered.

He was getting closer, cleverly orchestrating his every move to achieve the maximum effect, Jess realized. Exactly what he'd done with Connie DeVuono. The effortless, unseen break-ins, the mounting campaign of terror, the sadistic slaying of innocent pets. Jess recalled the smile that had sent shivers through her body the first time she'd seen him. The smile had said it all.

"*Hohh!*" Jess cried, taking several breaths. Then she reached for the soap, rubbing it harshly across her body, suddenly reminded of the shower scene from Alfred Hitchcock's *Psycho*.

In her mind she watched a hapless Janet Leigh begin her innocent ablutions, saw the bathroom door creak slowly open, the strange shadowy figure approach, the large butcher knife rise into the air as the shower curtains were pulled open.

545

"What's the matter with you?" Jess exclaimed, impatiently rinsing the soap off. "Are you trying to do Rick Ferguson's job for him?"

And then she heard the bathroom door open and saw Rick Ferguson walk through.

Jess tried to force a scream from her mouth, to make any kind of sound at all. *Hohh!* she thought wildly, but no sound emerged. Jess twisted the shower taps to OFF. Suddenly he was striding toward the tub, his arms extended. Where was Adam? Jess wondered, fumbling for whatever weapons were at hand, seizing on the soap. How had he gotten inside? What had he done to Adam?

Hands grabbed the shower curtain, pushed it aside. Jess lunged forward. *"Hohh!"* she cried loudly, hurling the soap at her attacker's head. He flinched, fell backward against the sink, his hands raised to protect his face.

"For heaven's sake, Jess," she heard him yell. "Are you nuts? Are you trying to kill me?"

Jess stared at the man cowering in front of her. "Don?" she asked meekly. "You scared the life out of me."

"*I* scared *you?*" Don demanded. "I almost had a heart attack."

"Jess, are you all right?" Adam called, racing to the door.

Jess wrapped herself in a bath towel. "It's okay, Adam," she reassured him.

He looked at Don, a smile playing at the corners of his mouth. "We have to stop meeting like this," he told Don before returning to the kitchen.

Don turned to Jess. "Adam told me to wait back here until you were finished with your shower. I called your name a couple of times, and I thought I heard you say something. I assumed you said to come in. So I did. Next thing I know, I'm getting beaned with a bar of soap."

"I thought you were Rick Ferguson."

"Rick Ferguson?"

"My imagination's in overdrive these days," she told him, walking into her bedroom, pulling on her housecoat and using the towel to dry her hair. "You still haven't told me what you're doing here."

"I was worried about you," he said. "The guy I hired to watch you said there was some excitement here with the police last night. What happened?"

Jess told him about returning home, meeting Adam outside,

finding her window open, the bird missing. About waking up in the night hungry, finding her dead canary inside the microwave oven.

"I'm so sorry, Jess," Don said sadly. "There are a lot of sick people out there."

Jess wiped away a few stray tears. "One in particular."

"I have something to tell you," Don stated, "that should put your mind at rest. Rick Ferguson turned himself in this morning."

"What?" Jess ran to her closet for some clothes.

"He claims he had no idea the police were looking for him. He'd been with a woman he'd met. . . ."

"Sure he was. He just doesn't happen to remember her name."

"I don't think he asked."

Jess pulled on some jeans and a heavy blue sweater. "How long have you known about this?"

"Since this morning," Don said evenly. "Rick Ferguson called, telling me he'd been home, found out the police were looking for him, and that he was headed for the station to turn himself in. I'm on my way down there now."

"Good. I'm going with you."

"What about Chef Boyardee?"

Jess looked toward the kitchen. "Breakfast will have to wait till I get back."

"You're going to leave the man alone in your apartment?" Don's voice was incredulous. "Jess, the last time he was here, you woke up to find all your panties slashed to ribbons."

"Don, don't be ridiculous."

"Was it just a coincidence that he turned up here last night, Jess?" Don asked impatiently. "Hasn't it even occurred to you that it might have been Adam who broke into your apartment? That it might have been Adam who killed your canary?"

"It doesn't make sense, Don. Why would Adam be doing these things? What motive could he possibly have?"

"I have no idea. I only know that ever since you met this guy, a lot of strange and dangerous things have been happening to you."

"But Adam has no reason to hurt me."

The look on Don's face changed from concern to sadness. "Are you falling in love with him, Jess?" he asked.

Jess released a deep sigh. "I don't know."

"Jess, he's a shoe salesman! What are you doing with this guy?"

547

"He isn't a shoe salesman," Jess said quietly. "He's a lawyer. . . . It's a very long, very complicated story."

"Only lies are complicated," Don told her. "The truth is usually very simple."

Jess looked away, refusing to consider the possibility he might be right. "We should get over to the station," she said. "I'm going to have your client arrested for the murder of Connie DeVuono."

"Jess, wait a minute. You don't have a case."

"Stop telling me I don't have a case. I have motive. I have opportunity. I have the murder weapon. What more do I need?"

"Some fingerprints on the murder weapon would be nice. A few witnesses who might have seen my client and the victim together around the time she disappeared. A bridge between the dead body and Rick Ferguson, Jess, something to connect the two."

"I'll connect them."

"I wish you luck."

CHAPTER 14

J ESS was arguing with her trial supervisor right up to the moment of Rick Ferguson's preliminary hearing the following Friday.

"I still think it was a mistake not to take this before the grand jury," Jess told Tom Olinsky. She paid scant attention to the Christmas and Hanukkah decorations that covered the walls as she walked beside him through the administration building to the courthouse. The hearing was being held in one of the smaller courtrooms on the second floor.

"And I told you that we don't have a strong enough case to take before the grand jury. Your ex-husband has already hit us with a motion *in limine*."

"Damn him," Jess muttered, still smarting over Don's move to limit the state's introduction of evidence. "A grand jury would have rubber-stamped the indictment. We'd have a trial date set by now." Jess also wouldn't have had to face her ex-husband in court so early, she admitted to herself, since the defense wasn't present at grand jury proceedings.

Jess hadn't seen Don all week, hadn't even spoken to him since he'd filed his motion.

She hadn't seen Adam all week either. He was in Springfield, visiting his parents for the first time in almost three years. He'd be back in Chicago on Sunday. Meanwhile he called every night at ten o'clock to wish her a good night's sleep. And to tell her he loved her.

Jess hadn't yet spoken of her feelings. She wasn't sure quite what they were. She was afraid to let herself go enough to find out.

"Go with it," she heard distant voices murmur. *"Go with it." "Trust your instincts."*

Maybe after she'd succeeded in getting Rick Ferguson bound over for trial, she could let go of the nagging doubts about Adam that Don had planted in her brain.

INSIDE the courtroom, the spectator section was filling up, mostly lawyers and their clients awaiting their turn before the judge. Tom Olinsky sat down beside Neil at the prosecutor's table. Jess looked around. Don and Rick Ferguson had yet to arrive.

The court clerk loudly cleared his throat before calling the court to order and introducing Judge Caroline McMahon, a pale woman with short dark hair, in her early forties.

Don pushed through the courtroom doors with appropriate dramatic flourish just as the clerk was saying Rick Ferguson's name.

"Here, Your Honor," Don said loudly, leading his client to the defense table.

"Is the defense ready?" Caroline McMahon asked.

"Yes, Your Honor."

"And the state?"

"The state is ready, Your Honor," Jess answered.

"I'm going to reserve judgment on your motion, Mr. Shaw," Caroline McMahon announced immediately, "until I see where the prosecution's case is going. Ms. Koster, you may proceed."

"Thank you, Your Honor," Jess stated, walking toward the witness stand. "The state calls Detective George Farquharson."

Detective Farquharson—tall and fair-skinned and balding—marched to the stand and was duly sworn in.

"On the afternoon of December fifth," Jess began, "did you have occasion to investigate the death of Connie DeVuono?"

"I did."

"Can you tell us about it?"

"My partner and I drove out to Skokie Lagoons in response to a telephone call from a Mr. Henry Sullivan, who'd been ice fishing and come across Mrs. DeVuono's body. It was obvious as soon as we saw the body, she'd been murdered."

"How was it obvious?"

"The piece of wire was still wrapped around her neck."

"Thank you, Detective."

Don rose briefly. "Did you find any evidence at the scene, Detective, other than the wire around Mrs. DeVuono's neck?"

"No."

"So there was nothing at the scene linking my client to the deceased?"

"No, sir."

"Thank you." Don returned to his seat.

"You may step down, Detective," Judge McMahon told him.

"The state calls Dr. Hilary Waugh."

Hilary Waugh, the chief medical examiner for Cook County, wore a royal-blue pantsuit and a simple strand of pearls, her dark hair in its French braid.

"Dr. Waugh," Jess said as the woman settled into the witness stand, "what were the results of the postmortem on Connie DeVuono?"

"We found that Connie DeVuono died of asphyxiation as the result of being strangled with a piece of magnetic wire. The wire also severed her jugular, but that was after death. Her left wrist had been broken as well as several ribs, and her jaw had been dislocated. There was also evidence of trauma from sexual assault."

"How long had Mrs. DeVuono been dead before she was found?"

"Approximately six weeks. We identified her through her dental records."

"Thank you."

"Were there any traces of blood or saliva that weren't Connie DeVuono's?" Don asked, quickly jumping to his feet.

"We found no traces. Mrs. DeVuono was in a state of advanced decomposition."

"Thank you, Doctor."

"The state calls Dr. Rudy Wang," Jess said, immediately following Hilary Waugh's exit from the stand.

An expert in forensics, Dr. Wang was short, gray-haired, and, despite his Asian-sounding name, of Polish extraction. He wore a brown pin-striped suit and a worried expression.

"Dr. Wang, did you examine the wire that was used to strangle Connie DeVuono?" Jess asked, approaching the witness stand.

"Yes, I did."

"Could you describe it, please?"

"It was a magnetic wire, steel gray, eighteen inches long and approximately a quarter of an inch around. Very strong."

"You also examined a similar piece of wire taken from the Ace Magnetic Wire Factory, where the defendant works, did you not?"

"I did. They were identical."

"Thank you, Dr. Wang."

Don was on his feet and in front of the witness before Jess had returned to her table. "Dr. Wang, were there any fingerprints on the wire that was found around Connie DeVuono's neck?"

"No."

"How common would you say this type of wire is?"

Rudy Wang shrugged. "Pretty common, I guess."

"You could buy it in any hardware store?"

"You might be able to find it in a hardware store, yes."

"Thank you." Don smiled at Jess before returning to his seat.

"The state calls Mrs. Rosaria Gambala," Jess said loudly, anger gripping her hands, twisting them into tight fists.

Mrs. Gambala, in a long-sleeved black sweater over a long black skirt, ambled slowly toward the front of the courtroom. She steadied herself against the witness stand as she was sworn in, her dark eyes nervously scanning the room. A muffled cry escaped her lips when she saw the defendant.

"Are you okay, Mrs. Gambala?" Jess asked. "Do you need a glass of water?"

"I'm okay," the woman said, her voice surprisingly strong.

"Can you state your relation to the deceased?" Jess asked.

"I'm her mother," the older woman answered.

"When did you report your daughter missing, Mrs. Gambala?"

"On October twenty-ninth, 1992, when she didn't pick up Steffan after work."

"Steffan being her son?"

"Yes. My grandson comes to my house after school, till Connie is finished working. She always calls before she leaves work."

"And on the afternoon of October twenty-ninth your daughter called, but then never showed up—is that right?"

"I called the police. They say I have to wait twenty-four hours. I call you. You no home."

"Why did you call me, Mrs. Gambala?"

"Because you were her lawyer. You were supposed to help her. You knew her life was in danger. You knew about the threats he made." She pointed an accusatory finger at Rick Ferguson.

"Objection!" Don called out. "Hearsay."

"This is a preliminary hearing," Jess reminded her ex-husband. "Hearsay is admissible."

"I'm going to allow it," the judge ruled. "Proceed, Ms. Koster."

"Rick Ferguson made threats against your daughter's life?"

"Yes. She was so afraid of him. He say he's going to kill her."

"Objection," Don called again. "Your Honor, can we approach the bench?"

The two lawyers moved directly toward the judge.

"Your Honor, I believe now would be a good time to rule on my motion to limit the evidence introduced in this case on the grounds that almost all the evidence against my client is hearsay and highly prejudicial," Don said, taking the initiative. "There is no direct evidence that my client ever threatened Connie DeVuono."

"The state will call two more witnesses who will testify that Connie was scared of the defendant, that he threatened to kill her if she testified against him in court," Jess said.

"Your Honor, such hearsay evidence is not only prejudicial, but irrelevant."

"Irrelevant?" Jess asked. "It goes to motive, Your Honor. Connie DeVuono had accused Rick Ferguson of raping and beating her. I will call several police officers to testify that Connie DeVuono positively identified Rick Ferguson as the man who beat and raped her."

"Hearsay, Your Honor," Don stated flatly. "And since Connie DeVuono didn't say anything to the police about Rick Ferguson until three days after she was attacked, her statement is not an exception to the hearsay rule. The only person who can identify my client as her assailant, who can testify that he threatened her life, is dead. Since it was never proved in a court of law that my client had anything to do with the attack on Mrs. DeVuono, I must ask that you disallow the introduction of such highly inflammatory and prejudicial evidence against my client."

"Your Honor," Jess stated quickly, "the state contends that this evidence, while admittedly hearsay, is definitely probative. It goes to the heart of the state's case against Mr. Ferguson."

"What is going on?" Mrs. Gambala cried from the witness stand.

Caroline McMahon looked sympathetically toward the older woman. "You may step down, Mrs. Gambala," she told her softly.

"You don't need to ask me any more questions?" Mrs. Gambala asked as Jess helped her down.

"Not at the moment," Jess said quietly.

"I'm prepared to rule on your motion, Mr. Shaw," the judge said. Don and Jess drew closer to the bench.

"I'm inclined to side with the defense on this one, Ms. Koster."

"But Your Honor . . ."

"The prejudicial effect of the evidence clearly outweighs its probative value, and I will prohibit the state from introducing this evidence at trial."

"But without this evidence, Your Honor, our hands are tied. The state can't prove motive. We simply don't have a case."

"I'm inclined to agree," the judge stated. "Are you prepared to bring a motion to dismiss?"

Jess looked from the judge to her ex-husband. To his credit, he refrained from visibly gloating.

The next minute all charges against Rick Ferguson were dismissed.

"How could you?" Jess demanded angrily of her ex-husband in the empty corridor outside the courtroom. "How could you let that killer walk free?"

"You didn't have a case, Jess."

"You know he killed her. You know he's guilty."

"Since when did that count for anything in a court of law?" Don demanded, then immediately softened. "Look, Jess, I know how badly you want Rick Ferguson behind bars. Frankly, I'd feel better about him behind bars too, at least until we figure out who's been terrorizing you. But I'm not at all convinced it's Rick Ferguson we have to worry about, and I can't abandon my obligation to my client because I happen to be in love with you." His eyes searched hers for understanding. Stubbornly Jess refused to comply. "Look, let's call a truce," he offered. "Let me take you out for dinner."

"That wouldn't be a very good idea under the circumstances."

"Come on, Jess. You can't take these things personally."

"Well, I do. Sorry if that disappoints you."

"You never disappoint me."

Jess felt the crest of her anger ebbing. "I can't tonight, Don. I've already made plans," she said.

"Adam?"

"My sister," she said. "And my brother-in-law. And my father. And his new love. A fitting end to a perfect day. I'll talk to you soon." She spun around on her heels, found herself face to face with Rick Ferguson.

"I was hoping we could go out and celebrate," he said to Don, speaking over Jess's head.

"I'm afraid I can't make it," Don said coldly.

"Oh, too bad," Rick said, his smile belying his words. "I'm feeling so good, I just wanted to spread some of that good feeling around."

"Go home, Rick," Don said. He grabbed Rick by the elbow and guided him toward the elevators, one opening as they neared. But just as they were about to step inside, Rick Ferguson scrambled free of his lawyer's grasp and darted back to Jess.

"Want to know how good I feel, Counselor?" he asked, staring directly into Jess's eyes and speaking so quietly only she could hear. "I feel just like the cat who swallowed the canary."

"You s.o.b.," she whispered.

"You bet," Rick Ferguson said, seconds before Don wrestled him away.

CHAPTER 15

Jess drove her rental car to Evanston, pulling into her sister's driveway at five minutes to six o'clock. Her father's blue Buick was already in the driveway. "Great," she whispered, wishing she'd had time for at least one drink before she had to meet the new recruit. "Now just stay calm. Smile. Look happy."

The front door opened, and Barry appeared, motioning for her to come inside with a giant sweep of his hands. She stepped out of her car, hesitating when she saw her father appear in the doorway behind his son-in-law.

"Come on, Jess," Barry called out. "Get in here. It's freezing."

As if to underline his point, the wind blew a gust of cold air in from the lake, shaking a paper wreath that was hung in the doorway.

"Tyler made it in nursery school," Barry said proudly as Jess came up the front steps. "Where'd you get the car?"

"I rented it this afternoon," Jess explained, stepping inside and allowing her father to take her in his arms. "Hi, Daddy."

"Hi, sweetheart. Let me look at you." He pushed her an arm's length away, careful not to let go, then drew her back into his embrace. "You look wonderful."

"I'm sorry I've been so busy lately," Jess apologized. She hung her coat in the closet.

"I understand, sweetie," her father told her, and Jess could see from the compassion that shaped his soft brown eyes that he did.

"I'm sorry I forgot to bring anything for anyone," Jess apologized again, seeing Maureen appear in the foyer holding one of the twins, Tyler wrapped around her legs.

"I'm so glad you could make it," Maureen said.

Art Koster put his arm around Jess and they all went into the living room. The first thing Jess noticed was the enormous Scotch pine Christmas tree in front of the grand piano. The next thing she saw was the Madonna figure sitting next to it on the rose-colored sofa, holding the other twin.

"Sherry," her father said, leading Jess to the sofa, "this is my younger daughter, Jess. Jess, this is Sherry Hasek."

"Hello, Jess," the woman said, handing the baby to Jess's father as she stood to shake Jess's hand. She was as slim as her father had described and even shorter than Jess had imagined. Her black hair looked surprisingly natural and was pulled back with a jeweled clasp at the nape of her neck. Her handshake was firm, though her hands were ice-cold.

She's as nervous as I am, Jess thought. "I'm sorry it's taken so long for me to meet you," Jess told her sincerely.

"These things happen," Sherry Hasek said.

"What can I get you to drink?" Barry asked.

"I'll have some white wine," Jess said, lifting the baby from Maureen's arms, thinking her sister was right—the twins really had grown in the last two months.

"They're really something, aren't they?" Barry said proudly, pouring a glass of white wine. "I'll take Chloe," he said, exchanging the glass for his daughter.

Jess tried to concentrate on Sherry Hasek's oval face. Her eyes were dark and wide apart. Not at all like her mother, Jess thought, recalling the blue-green eyes, the nose in perfect proportion to the mouth, the high and prominent cheekbones. It was a face that made those around her feel secure.

Her mother had always been that way, Jess realized, so comfortable with herself that she had effortlessly been able to make those around her feel comfortable too. She rarely lost her temper, almost never yelled. She treated everyone with respect, Jess thought now, seeing her mother's face streaked with tears, even when those around her were undeserving of that respect.

"I don't need this, Jess. I don't need this from you."

"Earth to Jess," she heard Barry say. "Come in, Jess. Come in."

Jess felt the glass of wine slipping through her fingers, and squeezed it tightly before it could fall to the floor, feeling the fragile glass crack, her hand becoming sticky and wet. She looked down to see her blood mingling with the wine, her ear suddenly open to the sounds of horror and concern that were filling the room.

"Mommy!" Tyler cried.

"Oh, Jess, your hand!"

"How did you do that?" Barry rushed a napkin under her hand before she could drip blood on the carpet.

"I'm all right," Jess heard herself say.

"That's quite a grip you've got there," her father was saying, gently opening his daughter's fist to examine her injured hand.

"I'll get some antiseptic for that," Maureen said. She deposited both babies into Jolly Jumpers near the doorway.

"I'm really sorry," Jess said.

"Why?" Sherry asked. "Did you do it on purpose?"

Jess smiled gratefully. "It hurts like hell."

Maureen returned. "Here, let me rub some of this on." She rubbed the soothing salve into Jess's palm. "And I brought some gauze."

"I don't need gauze. The cuts aren't that deep."

Jess let her father lead her to the sofa, where he carefully positioned her between himself and his new love.

"Did they ever find out who trashed your car?" Maureen asked.

Jess shook her head, feeling Rick Ferguson's eerie presence in the room. She shooed it away with the sound of her voice. "So I understand you're quite an artist," she said to the woman sitting beside her.

Sherry laughed. "I just play around really, although I've always had a very deep love of art," she explained, looking at Jess's father for approval.

"Is that art or Art?" he asked playfully.

Again Sherry laughed. "Both, I guess."

"Do you prefer oils or pastels?" Jess asked, anxious to get away from the subject of love.

"I'm better with pastels. Your father prefers oils."

Jess winced. Her mother would never have presumed to speak for her father. She wondered what her mother would make of this pleasant little family scene: Maureen standing beside Barry, his arm draped across her shoulder, her arms around her son; Jess snuggled on the sofa between her father and the woman he wanted to marry; the twins bouncing in their Jolly Jumpers, keeping a guarded eye out for their mother. That's right, Jess thought, keep an eye on your mother. Watch out that she doesn't disappear.

"Earth to Jess," she heard again. "Earth to Jess. Come in, Jess."

"Sorry," Jess said quickly, catching the look of annoyance in Barry's eyes. "Were you saying something?"

"Sherry asked you if you liked to paint."

"Oh. Sorry. I didn't hear you."

"That much was obvious," Barry said as Jess caught the worried look that suddenly clouded Maureen's eyes.

"It's not important," Sherry immediately qualified.

"Actually I don't know whether I like painting or not," Jess said. "I haven't done it since I was a child."

"Remember the time you drew all over the living-room walls with crayons," Maureen said, "and Mom got so mad because they'd just been freshly painted. It was the loudest I ever heard Mom yell."

"She didn't yell."

"She did that day. You could hear her for blocks."

"She never yelled," Jess insisted.

"I remember lots of times she yelled," Maureen said.

Jess shrugged, trying to disguise her anger. "Never at me."

"Always at you."

Jess stood up, walked to the Christmas tree, her hand throbbing. "When are we going to decorate this thing?"

"We thought right after dinner," Barry said.

"You never knew when to let go of things," Maureen continued, as if there had been no interruption. "You always had to have the last word." She laughed. "I remember Mom saying that it was so nice living with someone who knew everything."

Everyone laughed. Smile, Jess thought. Be nice. Don't fight. Stay calm. "Speaking of dinner . . ."

"Ready whenever you are," Maureen said.

Jess found herself staring at the woman who was poised to take her mother's place. "Ready or not," she said.

"THIS roast is delicious," Sherry Hasek was saying. "It's so rare these days that I eat red meat. I've forgotten what a treat it is."

"I've tried to wean Maureen away from red meat," Barry said, "but she says she was raised on mother's milk and good old-fashioned Chicago roast beef, so what are you going to do?"

"Enjoy it," Art Koster said. "I was reading an article in the doctor's office the other day," he began. "And—"

"Did you say you'd been to the doctor?" Jess interrupted. "What's wrong, Dad? Haven't you been feeling well?"

"I'm fine," her father stated. "It was just my annual checkup."

"*Where are you going?*" Jess asked her mother.

"*Nowhere,*" she answered.

"*Since when do you get so dressed up to go nowhere?*"

"Earth to Jess," Barry was saying again. "Come in, Jess."

"The first time was cute, Barry," Jess said more sharply than she'd intended. "Now it's merely tiresome."

"So is your behavior. I'm just trying to figure out whether you're preoccupied or whether you're being deliberately rude."

"Why on earth would I be deliberately rude?" Jess demanded.

"You tell me. I don't profess to have any understanding into what you're all about."

"I'd say we understand each other pretty well, Barry," Jess told him, her patience evaporated. "We hate each other's guts."

Barry looked stunned. "I don't hate you, Jess."

"I can't believe you'd say such a thing, Jess!" Maureen was crying. "You haven't given him a chance from the day we got married."

"That's not true," Jess countered. "I liked him fine until he turned you into Donna Reed."

"Donna Reed!" Maureen gasped.

"How could you let him do it?" Jess demanded, deciding that

now that she was in it, she might as well go all the way. "How could you give up everything and let him turn you into Superwife?"

"Why don't I take the twins upstairs?" Sherry offered, deftly lifting the girls from their Jolly Jumpers and carrying them, one under each arm. Tyler followed them.

"Children, why don't we stop this now before we say things we'll regret," Art Koster said, then sighed.

"Just what is it exactly that you think I've given up?" Maureen demanded. "My job? I can always get another job. My education? I'll always have that. Can't you get it through that thick head of yours that I am doing exactly what I want to do? That it was *my* decision, not Barry's, to stay home and be with my children while they were young. What is so wrong with that?"

"What's wrong with it?" Jess heard herself say. "Don't you realize that your whole life is a repudiation of everything our mother taught us?"

"What?" Maureen looked as if she had been struck by lightning.

"Jess," her father said, "what on earth are you talking about?"

"Our mother raised us to be independent women," Jess argued. "The last thing she would have wanted was for Maureen to be trapped in a marriage where she wasn't permitted room to grow."

Maureen's eyes glowed with red-hot fury. "How dare you criticize me. How dare you presume to know anything about my marriage. How dare you drag our mother into it. *You* were the one, *not me*," she continued, "who was always fighting with Mother over these exact issues. *You* were the one, *not me*, who insisted you were going to get married while you were still in school, even though Mother pleaded with you to wait until you were finished. *You* were the one who fought with her all the time, who made her cry, who made her miserable. So stop trying to assuage your own guilt by telling everyone else how to live their lives!"

"What do you mean, my own guilt?" Jess asked, almost breathless in her anger. "What are you talking about?"

"I'm talking about the fight you had with Mommy the day she disappeared!" Maureen shot back. "I called home from the library that morning, I guess just after you stormed out of the house, and she was crying. I asked her what was wrong, and she admitted that the two of you had been going at it again pretty good. I asked her if she wanted me to come home, and she said no, she'd be fine. And that was the last time I spoke to her." Maureen's features dissolved into a flood of frustrated tears.

Jess, who had risen to her feet during the confrontation, sank back into her seat. She looked around, saw not her sister's dining room, but the kitchen of her mother's house on Burling Street, saw not her sister's tear-streaked face, but her mother's.

"You're all dressed up," Jess observed, coming into the kitchen and noting her mother's white linen suit. "Where are you going?"

"Nowhere."

"Since when do you get so dressed up to go nowhere?"

"I just felt like putting on something pretty," her mother said, then added casually, "and I have a doctor's appointment later on this afternoon. What are your plans?"

"What kind of doctor's appointment?"

"I'd rather not say until I know for sure whether I have anything to worry about."

"You're worried already. I can see it in your face. What is it?"

"I found a little lump in my left breast."

"Oh, God."

"Don't worry. It's probably nothing. Most lumps are."

"Are you scared?"

Laura Koster didn't answer for several seconds. Only her eyes moved. "Yes, I'm scared."

"Would you like me to come to the doctor's with you?"

"Yes," her mother said immediately. "Yes, I would."

And then the conversation had somehow veered off track, Jess recalled now, seeing her mother at the kitchen counter making a fresh pot of coffee.

"My appointment's not till four o'clock," her mother said. "Will that ruin your plans?"

"No. I'll call Don. Tell him our plans will have to wait."

"That would be wonderful," her mother said, and Jess understood immediately that her mother wasn't referring to simply the plans they'd made for the afternoon.

"What is it you have against Don, Mother?" she asked.

"I have absolutely nothing against him."

"Then why are you so against my marrying him?"

"I'm not saying you shouldn't marry him, Jess," her mother told her. "I think Don is a lovely man. The problem is that he's eleven years older than you are. He's already done all the things you've yet to try. And he's already figured out what he wants from his life. He won't give you room to grow."

"How can you say that?"

"Honey, all I'm saying is wait a few years. You're only in first-year law school. Wait till after you pass the bar exam. Wait till you've had a chance to find out who you are and what you want."

"I know who I am. I know what I want. I want Don. And I'm going to marry him whether you like it or not."

Her mother sighed. "Okay, let's just drop it."

"No, I don't want to. You think you can raise these issues and then drop it just because you don't feel like discussing it anymore?"

"I'm sorry, honey. I shouldn't have said anything. I guess I'm a little nervous today." Tears filled her mother's eyes.

"Please don't cry," Jess begged, looking to the ceiling. "Why do you always have to make me feel so guilty?"

"I'm not trying to make you feel guilty."

"You have to stop trying to live my life."

"That's the last thing I want, Jess," her mother said, tears falling the length of her cheek. "I want *you* to live your life."

"Then stay out of it. Please," Jess added, trying to soften the harshness of her words, knowing it was too late.

Her mother shook her head, dislodging more tears. "I don't need this, Jess," she said. "I don't need this from you."

And then what? Jess wondered now. More careless words. More angry protestations. Pride speaking for both of them.

"You don't have to take me to the doctor's. I can get there on my own."

"Have it your way." Storming out of the house. The last time she saw her mother alive.

Jess jumped to her feet, raced toward the foyer, stumbling into the Jolly Jumpers, almost knocking them over.

"I'm sorry, Jess," Maureen was crying after her. "Please don't go. I didn't mean to say those things."

"Why not?" Jess asked, stopping abruptly, turning toward her sister. "They're all true. If I'd taken her to the doctor's like I promised, she would never have disappeared."

"You can't know that."

The phone rang.

"I'll get it," Barry said, crossing into the living room.

"Why don't we go back and sit down?" Maureen offered. "We never really talked about what happened, about how we felt. I think we have a lot to talk about. Don't you?"

"I want to," Jess told her, her voice like a small child's. "But not tonight. I just want to go home and crawl into bed."

Barry appeared in the hallway. "It's your ex-husband, Jess. He says it's very important."

"Don?" Jess vaguely recalled having told her ex-husband she was having dinner at her sister's.

"We'll be in the dining room," Maureen said, allowing Jess her privacy as she walked, trancelike, toward the phone.

"Has something happened?" she asked. "Did Rick Ferguson confess?"

"Rick Ferguson is on his way to Los Angeles. I put him on the plane myself. It's not Rick Ferguson I'm concerned about."

"What are you concerned about?" Jess asked.

"Are you seeing Adam tonight?"

"No. He's out of town. Why?"

"Jess, I had my office do some checking. They called the state bar. They've never heard of any lawyer named Adam Stohn. And if he lied to you about who he is and what he does, then there's a good chance he's lying about being out of town. Now do me a favor and stay over at your sister's, at least for tonight."

"I can't do that," Jess whispered, thinking of everything that had happened tonight, the things that had been said.

"Why not?"

"I just can't. Please, Don, don't ask me to explain."

"Then I'm coming over."

"No! Please. I'm a big girl. I have to take care of myself," Jess told him, feeling numb from head to toe. "Adam isn't going to hurt me," she mumbled, speaking away from the receiver.

"Did you say something?"

"I said not to worry," Jess told him. "I'll call you tomorrow." She hung up and tried to make sense of what Don had told her. No record of a lawyer named Adam Stohn? But why would he have lied? And did that make everything else he'd told her a lie as well?

Jess stared at the bare Christmas tree waiting patiently for adornment, heard the quiet voices emanating from the dining room. "I think we have a lot to talk about," her sister had said. She was right. And it was time to let go of the suffocating guilt that had coated her for the past eight years like a second skin.

Grabbing her purse and coat, Jess silently opened the front door. In the next instant she was speeding south in her rented car, tears streaming down her cheeks, wanting only to crawl into her bed, pull the covers up over her head, and disappear until morning.

CHAPTER 16

SHE was still crying when she arrived home.

She pushed her key into the lock, feeling the front door of her brownstone give way, locking it again securely behind her. There were no trumpets or saxophones to accompany her up the stairs, no light creeping out from underneath Walter Fraser's door. Probably away for the weekend, she thought. Maybe she'd call Don when she got inside her apartment, suggest a few days in Union Pier. Forget about Adam Stohn. Or whoever he really was.

She unlocked the door to her apartment and stepped over the threshold, allowing the silence and the darkness to draw her in. No need anymore to leave the radio or the lights on all day. No more sweet melodies to welcome her home. She double-locked her door.

The streetlights filtered in through the lace curtains, casting an eerie glow on the empty birdcage. She hadn't had the courage to put it away. Poor Fred, she thought, giving in to fresh tears.

"Poor me," she whispered, slouching toward her bedroom.

He came at her from behind.

She didn't see him, didn't even hear him until he was almost upon her. Then the wire was around her throat and she was being rudely yanked backward into oblivion. Her hands automatically dropped her purse and flew to her neck as she frantically sought to dig her fingers in between the wire and her flesh. She heard herself gagging, gasping for air. The wire was cutting off her supply of oxygen, slicing into the flesh at her throat. With everything in her she fought to pull herself away from her attacker.

And then, somewhere inside the panic, she remembered: *"Go with it. Strike when you get there."*

She stopped fighting, although it went against every instinct she had. Instead, she allowed her body to cave in against her assailant's chest as he pulled her toward him. Her neck throbbed in pain. For a terrifying instant she thought she was blacking out. She found the idea surprisingly seductive.

But then suddenly she was fighting back, using her assailant's weight against him, allowing the force of her body to knock him to the ground. She fell with him, knocking against the side of the birdcage, sending it crashing to the floor. Her assailant yelled as she quickly used her feet to kick at his legs, her nails to scratch at his arms, her elbows to jab at his ribs.

She felt the wire around her throat loosen just enough for her to break free. She scrambled to her feet, gasping for breath.

Then she heard him moan, turned, saw his dazed, muscular form sprawled across the floor, the tight jeans, the dark T-shirt, the long hair across the side of his face hiding all but his twisted grin.

I am Death, the grin said even now. *I have come for you.*

Rick Ferguson.

A small cry escaped her throat. Had she actually thought he'd quietly board a plane to California and disappear from her life?

A million images flooded her brain as she saw him struggle to regain his footing—eagle claws, zipper punches, hammer fists. Then she remembered: Forget the heroics. Getting away comes first.

But Rick Ferguson was already on his feet, lumbering toward her, blocking her way to the front door. Scream, her inner voice commanded. *"Hohh!"* she cried, watching him flinch, momentarily startled by the sound. *"Hohh!"* she yelled again, even louder, wondering if she could get to the gun in the end table beside her bed, her eyes scanning the dark room for whatever weapon was at hand.

If anything, her outburst seemed to bring him new life. Rick Ferguson's evil grin turned into an outright laugh. "I like a good fight," he said.

"Stay away from me," Jess warned.

"Connie just kind of crumpled up and died. No fun at all. Not like you," he told her. "Killing you is gonna be a pure pleasure."

"Likewise, I'm sure," Jess said, scooping the birdcage into her hands, hurling it at Rick Ferguson's head, watching it connect, seeing a thick line of blood race down his cheek from the gash in his forehead. She turned on her heels and ran from the room.

Her bedroom had never seemed so far away. She tore through the hall, hearing him only steps behind her. She had to get her gun.

She threw herself at the small table, pulling open the top drawer, her desperate fingers searching for her gun. It wasn't there.

The mattress! she thought, falling to her knees, reaching under the mattress. It wasn't there. It wasn't there!

"Looking for this?" Rick Ferguson stood in the doorway, dangling the revolver from the end of his fingers.

Jess rose slowly to her feet as he aimed the gun directly at her head. Her heart was pounding wildly; her ears were ringing; tears were falling. If only she could get her thoughts together . . .

"Nice of you to invite me to your bedroom," he said, moving slowly toward her. "Of course, I already know where you keep your panties."

"Get the hell out of here," Jess yelled, seeing the blood from her neck smeared across the white of her duvet.

He laughed. "You sure are a feisty little thing, aren't you? Telling a man with a loaded gun to get the hell out. That's real cute."

Jess looked toward the window. Maybe if she could just distract him long enough to get to the window. Then what? Jump? Scream? A scream could only travel so far against a loaded gun. She almost laughed—tomorrow was the day she was supposed to learn how to disarm a would-be assailant. Tomorrow—not much chance of that.

Her forehead was wet with perspiration, the sweat dripping into her eyes, mingling with her tears. She thought she heard voices from outside, but they were distorted, like a record being played on the wrong speed. Too slow. Everything too slow. So this was how Connie must have felt, Jess thought. This was what death felt like.

"I thought Don put you on a plane to California," she heard herself say.

"Yeah. Generous of him. But I decided it could wait. I knew how bad you wanted to see me. Take off your clothes."

He said it so casually the words didn't quite register. "What?"

"Take off your clothes," he repeated. "The fun's about to start." Jess shook her head. "No."

"Then I'll have to shoot you." He shrugged, as if this were the only logical alternative.

Jess's heart was beating so furiously it threatened to burst out of her chest. How could he be so calm? she thought. "You'll shoot me anyway," she said.

"Well, no. Actually, I was planning on using my hands to finish you off. But I'll shoot you if I have to." His smile grew, his eyes roaming across her body. "In the shoulder. Or maybe the knee. Maybe in the soft part of your inner thigh. Yeah, I kind of like that. Just enough to make you a little more cooperative."

She could barely stand for the shaking in her legs. If she could just keep him talking, she thought. Isn't that what they always did in the movies? They talked, and then someone came along just in the nick of time to rescue them. She pushed words out of her mouth. "You shoot, and it'll alert the neighbors."

"Think so? Didn't look like there was anybody home when I got here. Now take off your clothes, or I'm liable to get bored."

"How did you get in here?" Jess asked.

"The lock hasn't been made that can keep me out." He laughed again, then cocked the trigger of the gun. "Now you've got thirty seconds to get those clothes off and lie down on the bed."

Jess said nothing, her throat suddenly too dry to form words. So this is how it ends, she thought.

What would it be like? she wondered. Would there be a white light, a long tunnel, a feeling of peace, as was often reported by those who claimed to have died and come back? Or would she simply cease to be? She thought of her mother. Would she finally get to see her again, to find out what fate she had met? Had her mother experienced this same kind of terror before she died?

And what would this do to her father, her sister?

Jess took a deep breath and removed her coat. She pulled off her sweater and dropped it to the floor. Her skin started to throb.

"Very nice," he said. "Now the rest."

Jess watched the scene unfold, as if from a great distance. Maybe she was already dead. Or maybe she still had time to save herself, she thought, feeling a renewed surge of adrenaline. *"Use whatever weapons are at hand,"* she heard Dominic instruct. But what?

How about her shoes? she wondered. Rick Ferguson jabbed the gun into the air. "I have to take my shoes off—" she stammered. "I can't get my pants off if I don't take my shoes off first."

"Okay," he said, relaxing. "Just hurry up about it."

She bent over, slowly removing her left shoe and tossing it aside, thinking she was out of her mind, he would kill her for sure. Then moving to her right foot, knowing she had only seconds left, lifting the black flat off her foot, gripping it tightly, she hurled it with all her strength toward the gun in his hand.

She missed completely. "Oh, no," she moaned.

But the sudden action caught him by surprise, and he jumped back in alarm. What now? Jump from the window? Try to disarm him?

It was too late. Already he'd recovered his equilibrium. Already the gun was pointed at her heart. "I think I'm going to enjoy killing you even more than I enjoyed roasting that canary," he said.

There was no time left. He was going to shoot her. Render her defenseless long enough to rape her. Then finish her off with his hands. Without even knowing what she was doing, Jess was leaping across her bed to the window, screaming at the top of her lungs.

The shot exploded into the air around her, and she knew she was as good as dead. It was so loud, she thought, louder than she had ever imagined it could be, like a burst of thunder at her ear. The room assumed an eerie glow, as if the contents had been hit by lightning. Her body felt light, suspended in midair.

And suddenly she was spinning around and Rick Ferguson was coming at her, his face white with fury, his smile gone. And then he was falling, tumbling toward her, and Jess realized that she was all right—that it was Rick Ferguson who was plunging to the floor.

Darkness swirled around her as her eyes absorbed the gaping hole in his back, the blood soaking his T-shirt, spilling onto the rug.

And then she saw him in the doorway, the gun dangling from his hand. "Don!" she gasped.

"I told you if that bastard ever tried to hurt you, I'd kill him myself," he said. The gun slipped from his fingers to the floor.

Jess rushed into his arms. Immediately they encircled her, pulling her tight against him. He felt so good. He felt so safe.

"You're safe now," he said, kissing her over and over again.

"I was so scared. I thought he was going to kill me."

"I'm just glad I got here in time." Don hugged her tighter.

"I can't believe you did," Jess said. Her eyes drifted back to the body on the floor. "Are you sure he's dead?"

"He's dead, Jess." Don smiled indulgently. "I can shoot him again if you'd like."

Jess laughed, surprised at the sound. She'd been attacked with a wire rope, almost raped, almost murdered, and she was laughing. Her eyes traveled the length of Rick Ferguson's body, and she understood how easily that body could have been hers.

It was uncanny how well Don knew her, Jess thought, how he

always knew when she needed him, whatever her protestations to the contrary. She'd told him on the phone that she was all right. And still he'd come, saving her from a gruesome death.

As if watching a television rerun, Jess saw herself locking the downstairs door, racing upstairs, entering her apartment, locking the door after her, feeling the sudden tug of wire around her throat.

Her mind's eye narrowed in on the locked door of her apartment, as if she were adjusting a kaleidoscope. What's wrong with this picture? a little voice asked, snapping her sharply back into the present. The door to her apartment had been locked, she realized, as was the outside door. How had Don gotten inside?

Jess pulled away from him. "How did you get in the house?"

"The door wasn't locked," he said.

"Yes, it was," she insisted. "I locked it after I came in."

"Well, it was open when I got here," he told her.

"And my apartment?" she asked. "I double-locked the door."

"Jess, what is this?"

"A simple question. How did you get inside my apartment?"

There was a moment's silence, then, "I used my keys."

"Your keys? What do you mean? What keys?"

He swallowed. "I had a second set made when you had your locks changed. I was worried something like this might happen."

Jess looked down, saw Rick Ferguson dead at her feet, her gun still inside his open hand. Don had saved her life. Why was she suddenly so angry with him?

She felt an annoying tickle at her throat, then felt it creeping stealthily toward her chest, leaving everything it touched numb. Was she going to have an anxiety attack now? she wondered incredulously. Now, when it was all over?

Then she heard Adam's voice. "Go with it," he said. Adam, she thought, whom Don distrusted. What did Adam have to do with any of this? "I don't understand," she said.

"Don't worry about anything now, Jess. All that matters is that you're safe. Rick Ferguson is dead. He can't hurt you anymore."

"But it wasn't Rick Ferguson you were worried about," Jess persisted, remembering his phone call to her sister's, trying to make sense of what had happened. "It was Adam you claimed was dangerous. You said you'd had him investigated; you said the state bar had never heard of him."

"Jess, what's this got to do with anything?"

"But Adam was never a threat to me. It was Rick Ferguson all along. So why would Adam lie?" Once again the kaleidoscope shifted, its contents scrambling to present yet another picture. "Unless he didn't lie. Unless it was you who lied to me," she said, scarcely believing her own ears. Was she really saying these things? "You didn't call the state bar, did you? And if you did, then you found out that Adam Stohn is exactly who he says he is. Isn't he?"

There was silence. "He isn't right for you, Jess," Don said finally. "Isn't that for me to decide?"

"Not when it's the wrong decision. Not when it affects me, when it affects us, our future together," he told her. "You need me to take care of you, Jess. You always have. Tonight proved that."

Jess looked to the body on the floor, then to her ex-husband. "Why did you come here tonight? How did you know to have a gun . . . unless— You set this whole thing up," she said, the sudden realization of what she was saying slicing through her as painfully as a wire rope. "You did, didn't you? You set this whole thing up!"

"Jess—"

"You coached him, told him what to say, what buttons to push. Right from the beginning."

"I used him to bring us back together. Was that so wrong?"

"He almost killed me!"

"I would never have let that happen."

Jess shook her head in disbelief. "You orchestrated everything. The way he was waiting for me when I got to work that first morning, like he'd stepped right out of my nightmares—nightmares you knew all about. It wasn't a coincidence that he used the word disappear. You told him about what happened to my mother, didn't you? You knew exactly the effect it would have on me."

"I love you, Jess. All I've ever wanted is for us to be together."

"Tell me. Tell me everything," Jess said.

He took a deep breath. "What do you want to know?"

"Did you know Rick Ferguson killed Connie DeVuono?"

"I suspected."

"And you offered to get him off if he'd do you a favor in return."

"I suggested we might be able to help each other out."

"But why? Why now?"

Don shook his head. "It was something I'd been thinking about for a long time, a way to prove to you how much you needed me. And suddenly there he was—opportunity knocking, as it were. And the idea sort of came together in my mind. And then along came Adam Stohn, and I knew I couldn't afford to wait."

"What exactly did you tell Rick Ferguson to do?"

"I told him to frighten you. I left the details up to him."

"He killed Fred!"

"A canary. I'll buy you a hundred canaries."

Jess felt the tickle spreading. "And tonight?" she asked. "What was he supposed to do tonight?"

"I told him that, considering your tenacity, you'd never rest until you saw him convicted of murder. I knew he couldn't resist coming after you, and I wanted to make sure I controlled the time and place, so I simply encouraged him to finish the job quickly."

"You sent him here to kill me."

"I sent him here to be killed!" Don laughed. "Hell, I even gave him a key. I used him to get what we both wanted."

"What we *both* wanted?"

"Be honest, Jess. Wasn't the death penalty what you were after? The state wasn't going to do it. I did it for them. For you. For us."

"But you called me at my sister's, urged me to spend the night."

Again Don laughed. "Knowing you'd do just the opposite. Knowing your pride would send you scurrying home."

Jess raised her hands to her head to stop the sudden spinning. None of this was real, she thought. This was Don, the man who'd always been there for her—her teacher, her husband, her friend. The man who'd nursed her through years of crippling anxiety attacks. And now he was telling her that he'd been behind Rick Ferguson's campaign of terror, that he'd come here tonight to commit murder. All in the name of love. What else was he capable of?

Jess's mind raced backward through the last eight years. Her anxiety attacks had begun just after her mother's disappearance, had lasted throughout her marriage, abated only after her divorce.

"He won't give you room to grow," she heard her mother say.

Her beautiful mother, she thought, slowly approaching Rick Ferguson's body and kneeling over it.

"I love you, Jess," Don was saying. "No one could ever love you the way I have. I could never let anyone come between us."

The kaleidoscope in Jess's mind refocused, the last of the pieces falling into place, arranging themselves with startling clarity. Suddenly she knew exactly what else he was capable of.

Jess found herself staring at her ex-husband. "It was you all along," she said. "You killed my mother." Slowly she rose to her feet. "Tell me," she said, her voice barely audible.

"You won't understand," he told her.

"Make me understand," she said, forcing her voice into a gentle caress. "Please, Don, I want so much to understand."

"She was trying to keep us apart," Don said, as if this was all the explanation necessary. "And she would have succeeded. You didn't know that. But I did. It was a risk I couldn't take."

"Because you loved me so much," Jess said.

"Because I loved you more than anything in the world," he qualified. "I didn't want to have to kill her, Jess. I kept hoping she'd come around. But I came to understand that she never would."

"So you decided to kill her."

"I knew it had to be done," he began, "but I was waiting for the right moment, the right opportunity." He shrugged, as if everything that had happened had been beyond his control. "And then one morning you called and told me about the fight the two of you had had. I could hear the guilt in your voice. I knew that you were already regretting the fight, that if the lump in her breast proved to be malignant, you'd agree to postpone the wedding. I recognized that if I didn't move quickly, it would be too late.

"So I drove to your house, told your mother you'd told me what happened, and said I didn't want to be the source of any more problems between you, that I'd talk you into postponing our wedding." He smiled. "She was so relieved."

"So you offered to drive her to the doctor's."

"I *insisted* on it," Don elaborated. "I said it was such a lovely day, why didn't we go for a nice drive first. She thought that was a lovely idea." His smile grew wider. "We drove to Union Pier. I had everything worked out. Once she got in the car, it was easy, really. I said that I wanted her opinion on some renovations I'd been thinking about for the cottage. She was happy to help, even flattered, I think. We walked around the house; she told me what she thought would look nice. Then we went out back, stood looking at the bluffs.

"She never saw it coming, Jess. One clean shot to the back of the head. And it was all over."

Jess swayed, almost lost her balance, but managed to hang on.

"She was a dying woman, Jess. In all likelihood, she'd have been dead of cancer within five years. Instead, she died on a beautiful sunny day, not worrying about her daughter for the first time in months. I know this must be hard for you to understand, Jess, but she was happy. Can't you see? She died happy."

Jess opened her mouth to speak, but it was several seconds before any sounds emerged. "What did you do . . . afterward?"

"I gave her a proper burial," he said. "Out by the bluffs. You were looking at her grave a few weeks ago."

Jess pictured herself standing by the back window of Don's cottage, staring through the swirling snow toward the bluffs beyond.

"I thought of telling you the truth then," he continued, "to put your mind at rest, to let you know that your fight with your mother had nothing to do with her death, that it was a foregone conclusion from the moment she tried to interfere with our plans. But I knew the timing wasn't right."

Jess recalled the feel of Don's arms around her, the false comfort he'd provided. That he'd always provided.

"And the gun?" Jess asked. "What did you do with the gun?"

Again Don smiled, a smile more terrifying than Rick Ferguson's had ever been. "I gave it to you as a present after you left me."

Jess stared down at the revolver in Rick Ferguson's outstretched hand, the gun Don had insisted she take to protect herself after their divorce, the same one he had used to end her mother's life.

"I liked the irony of it," Don was saying, as if he were commenting on a point of law, not confessing to her mother's murder. When had his obsessiveness crossed the boundary into madness? How had she failed to recognize it for so long?

"And now what?" she asked.

"And now we'll call the police and tell them what happened. That Rick was waiting for you inside your apartment, that he tried to kill you, that I got here just in time. And then you'll come home with me. Back where you belong."

Nausea swept across Jess's body like a giant wave, sending her crashing to her knees. She reached out instinctively for something to grab onto, something to keep her from going under. Her fingers found a branch, grabbed hold, tightened their grip. The gun, she understood, curling her fingers around its handle, straightening her shoulders as she fought her way free of the deadly current. In one quick and fluid motion Jess brought the gun up, pointed it directly at her ex-husband's heart, and pulled the trigger.

Don stared at her in surprise as the bullet ripped through his chest. Then he crumpled forward and fell to the floor.

Jess rose slowly to her feet and walked to his side. "Bull's-eye," she said calmly.

She wasn't sure how long she stood there staring down at her ex-husband. She wasn't sure when she became aware of other sounds, of traffic outside her window, of her phone ringing.

She looked over at the clock. Ten o'clock. It would be Adam, calling to check on how she was, to find out how her day had gone, to wish her a good night's sleep.

She almost laughed. She wouldn't get any sleep tonight. That much was sure. She'd have to deal with the police, contact her family. Tell them about Rick Ferguson, about Don, the truth about what had happened here tonight, about what had happened eight years ago. The whole truth. Would they believe any of it?

Did she?

Jess walked to the phone and picked up the receiver. "Adam?" she asked.

"I love you," he answered.

"Could you come home?" Her voice was soft but in control, surprisingly anxiety-free. "I think I'm going to need a good lawyer."

Joy Fielding didn't know what she was getting into when she decided to write a thriller about a Chicago-based prosecutor. For one thing, the author lives in Toronto, and so her research had to be done long-distance. Moreover, Chicago has such a complicated legal system, she says, "that I had to take a crash course in the law."

How did she do that?

Fortunately, she was able to find a Chicago defense attorney willing to spend hours on the telephone lecturing at her. "Then he would quiz me," Fielding says, laughing. "Like I was back in school! It was quite intimidating."

But this author isn't one to be easily intimidated. And, indeed, after mastering the fine points of legal procedure, she went off to Chicago, met with judges, and even managed to sit in on a murder trial.

Was this extraordinary effort at factual accuracy necessary?

Joy Fielding

Fielding, who is lively, funny, and fast talking—much like Jess Koster in the story—has a ready answer. "My husband's a lawyer," she says. "I wanted him to read the book and *not* say, 'This is ridiculous!' "

An unlikely reaction, all things considered. But now Joy Fielding is facing another challenge: that of writing her next novel while trying to raise two adolescent daughters, ages fourteen and seventeen. And what is that like?

She laughs again and says, "Talk about anxiety!" Then, like the proud mother she is, Fielding adds that both girls are interested in acting *and* writing, that both are talented, and that she is wholeheartedly encouraging them to pursue creative careers. Like mother, like daughter?

The original editions of the books in this volume are published and copyrighted as follows:

The Cat Who Went into the Closet
Published by G. P. Putnam's Sons
distributed by BeJo Sales Inc. at $24.95
© 1993 by Lilian Jackson Braun

Homeland
Published by Doubleday Canada Ltd. at $29.95
© 1993 by John Jakes

Tell Me No Secrets
Published by Stoddart Publishing Co. Limited at $24.95
© 1993 by Joy Fielding

ILLUSTRATORS
Richard Williams: *The Cat Who Went into the Closet*
Joseph Cellini: *Homeland*
Kazuhiko Sano: *Tell Me No Secrets*

189 227 9403